HUBERT'S ARTHUR

VALANCOURT CLASSICS

FREDERICK ROLFE, BARON CORVO

HUBERT'S ARTHUR

BEING CERTAIN CURIOUS DOCUMENTS FOUND
AMONG THE LITERARY REMAINS OF MR. N. C.,
HERE PRODUCED

by

PROSPERO AND CALIBAN

Edited with an introduction and notes by

Kristin Mahoney

Kansas City:
VALANCOURT BOOKS
2009

Hubert's Arthur by Frederick Rolfe (Baron Corvo)
First published in 1935 by Cassell and Company, Ltd., London
First Valancourt Books edition, 2009

Introduction and notes © 2009 by Kristin Mahoney
Special features of this edition © 2009 by Valancourt Books

Library of Congress Cataloging-in-Publication Data

Rolfe, Frederick, 1860-1913.
Hubert's Arthur : being certain curious documents found among
the literary remains of Mr. N.C., here produced by Prospero
and Caliban / Frederick Rolfe, Baron Corvo ; edited with an
introduction and notes by Kristin Mahoney. – 1st Valancourt
Books ed.
p. cm.
ISBN 1-934555-20-7 (alk. paper)
1. Arthur I, Duke of Brittany, 1187-1203–Fiction. 2. Burgh, Hubert
de, d. 1243–Fiction. I. Mahoney, Kristin Mary. II. Title.
PR5236.R27H83 2009
823'.8–dc22

2009001774

Design and typography by James D. Jenkins
Published by Valancourt Books
Kansas City, Missouri
http://www.valancourtbooks.com

CONTENTS

INTRODUCTION

In his "experiment in biography," *The Quest for Corvo* (1934), A.J.A. Symons, an avid book collector and self-proclaimed epicurean, reconstructed the literary career of an impossibly strange author of impossibly strange books, Frederick William Serafino Austin Lewis Mary Rolfe, otherwise known as "Baron Corvo." According to the text, Symons began his "quest" in 1925 during a conversation with another collector, Christopher Millard, about "books that miss their just reward of praise and influence."[1] Millard lent Symons *Hadrian the Seventh* (1904), a novel in which Rolfe's alter-ego becomes pope, and allowed him to read Rolfe's letters to Charles Masson Fox, which entreat the recipient to come to Venice to enjoy the sexual favors of Venetian adolescent boys. Symons was fascinated, but his "curiosity was still unslaked."[2] He set about searching for the unpublished manuscripts and surviving acquaintances of Rolfe, piecing together the story of the author's unfortunate life. When he found the manuscript of Rolfe's semi-autobiographical *The Desire and Pursuit of the Whole*, he encountered a description of another missing manuscript, a "history-as-it-wasn't-but-as-it-very-well-might-have-been," a work that was, in the author's mind, "almost as far above the ordinary as he wished it to be." An alternative narrative of medieval succession written from the perspective of Hubert de Burgh, the story, according to Rolfe, "[bristled] with personal knowledge of men famous and infamous, with statesmanlike policy, heraldry, archæology, love, wit, sorrow, humour, courage, suffering, every high and noble human interest and activity, all illumined by the insight and pathos and power of his own personality."[3] Symons

---

[1] A.J.A. Symons, *The Quest for Corvo: An Experiment in Biography* (New York: Macmillan, 1934), 1. This scenario was apparently created for dramatic effect. Symons had been working for a time on a bibliography of Nineties writers that was to include material on Rolfe, so it was not in fact Millard who first introduced him to Rolfe's work.

[2] Symons, *Quest*, 14.

[3] Frederick Rolfe, *The Desire and Pursuit of the Whole*, edited by Andrew Eburne

pined for the work, spending a year hunting for it in "every hole or corner which [his] imagination could suggest," but he began to doubt that he "should ever find the lost manuscripts of the unlucky, gifted man who had occupied [his] mind for so long."[1]

In the final pages of the *Quest*, Symons reveals that he did finally uncover this "pearl," a work entitled *Hubert's Arthur*.[2] Symons lays the foundation for what will become the most prominent Corvine myth, the image of the stubborn but proud author, homeless and starving to death aboard a tiny boat in Venice while nevertheless dutifully and fastidiously working on an obscure masterpiece. As Symons notes, on the first page of the manuscript, Rolfe requests leniency from his readers, for the novel "was done by day and night in a small fishing boat on the Venetian lagoon with the natural interruption of storms, bad weather, and occasional overwhelming weariness."[3] Nevertheless, the manuscript is, according to Symons, "written in unfaltering and faultless script on the finest hand-made paper." Symons pronounces the work a "queer masterpiece" and wonders at the lack of insight on the part of editors who did not take their chance with it.[4]

This novel was a favorite for Rolfe. He referred to *Hubert's Arthur* as his "*magnum opus*," and he gushed repeatedly in his letters to his collaborator, C.H.C. Pirie-Gordon, about its prospects for success.[5] He acknowledged that *Hubert's Arthur* was "an awful piece of work," but he insisted that the novel would "be unlike any book ever written" and that "it [would] pay."[6] He exclaimed to Pirie-Gordon that *Hubert's Arthur* was "SUCH a book!!!! A book to *revel* over."[7] Yet this work, for which Rolfe had such high hopes, which in his mind promised to solve his financial woes and make his name in the literary marketplace, was rejected by publishers again and again.[8] John Buchan, who read *Hubert's Arthur* for one

---

(New York: G. Braziller, 1994), 124.

[1] Symons, *Quest*, 269.

[2] *Id.*, 282.

[3] Quoted in Symons, *Quest*, 282.

[4] *Id.*, 282.

[5] Frederick Rolfe, *Letters to C.H.C. Pirie-Gordon* (London: Vane, 1959), 104.

[6] *Id.*, 50

[7] *Id.*, 90

[8] *Hubert's Arthur* was rejected by Longmans, Ralph Shirley, Smith Elder, and

of the publishers that rejected the novel, told Rolfe, "[T]he more I look at it the more I admire it, and the more convinced I am that no publisher in Britain could make a success of it."[1] In an attempt to account for the novel's fate, Symons speculates, "Perhaps it was too long, or too strange, or too full of heraldry or incident, or too arch, or too well written; for it is all these things."[2]

Hubert's Arthur finally appeared posthumously in an edition of 1,500 copies in 1935, edited by Symons himself. Reviews were conflicted, reflecting a mix of intrigue and distaste, and the novel did not sell very well. The excessive violence, anti-Semitism, and homoerotic content in the novel could certainly account for this response. Graham Greene, for example, lamented "the homosexual and the sadistic elements in the lushness and tenderness of his epithets" for the boy martyr, Little St. Hugh of Lincoln. Noting the "really devilish mind which gives the formula for a throat-cutting with the same relish as in his book on the Borgias he had translated a recipe for cooking a goose alive," Greene remarked that Rolfe offers support for T. S. Eliot's assertion that the awakening of one's spirituality endows one with the capacity for real Good as well as the capacity for true Evil.[3] A review in the *Times Literary Supplement* made note of Rolfe's "sadistic pleasure in torments and butchery, his spite against the clergy, his hatred of the Jews," as well as the fact that the novel's hero is a "beautiful young tiger-cub" of the sort that tends to populate Corvine works.[4] The book was perhaps too dark, too violent, too anti-Semitic, and too homoerotic to receive proper appreciation in the early twentieth-century literary marketplace. But now, at a moment when critics are increasingly attentive to the role representations of Jewishness played in the making of modernism, to the role of violence and fascism in avant-gardism, and to the reproduction and contestation of conventional masculinity in the works of the early

---

Constable. See Miriam Benkowitz, *Frederick Rolfe: Baron Corvo* (London: Hamish Hamilton, 1977), 231, 280, 282.

[1] Symons, *Quest*, 282.

[2] *Id.*

[3] Graham Greene, "A Spoiled Priest," *The Spectator* CLV (Dec. 6, 1935): 956.

[4] "King Arthur the Conqueror: Baron Corvo's Might-Have-Been History," *Times Literary Supplement* (Nov. 23, 1935): 766.

twentieth-century avant-garde, Rolfe's works should be of more interest than ever before.[1]

The persisting critical blindness to Rolfe's works may arise from the fact he seems to resist categorization within any single movement or period. Rolfe represents to some a final flowering of the 1890s and to others a missing link in our understanding of the emergence of a modernist aesthetic. A 1924 reviewer seemed to feel that he might have been properly appreciated had he only come a bit later in the literary chronology, arguing that his "linguistic coinages are sumptuous and would have offended no one had he written in an age of greater linguistic fluidity," while R. C. Churchill suggests that he rather came too late, "the last Pre-Raphaelite," refusing to relinquish an obsolete aesthetic.[2] In an early review, Shane Leslie noted that his "*floruit* can be placed between the Victorian and Georgian era, which may account for the complete disregard and disdain he has received from critics."[3]

---

[1] For discussion of Jewishness and modernism, see, for example, the recent special issue of *Modern Fiction Studies* devoted to the topic of "Modernism's Jews/ Jewish Modernisms" (Summer 2005); Maren Tova Linett, *Modernism, Feminism, and Jewishness* (New York, Cambridge University Press, 2007); Neil R. Davison, *James Joyce, Ulysses, and the Construction of Jewish Identity* (New York: Cambridge University Press, 1996); Anthony Julius, *T.S. Eliot, Anti-Semitism, and Literary Form* (New York: Cambridge University Press, 1995); or Bryan Cheyette, *Constructions of the Jew in English Literature and Society* (New York: Cambridge University Press, 1993).

For discussion of the role of violence or fascism in avant-gardism and modernism, see, for example, Charles Ferrall, *Modernist Writing and Reactionary Politics* (New York: Cambridge University Press, 2001); Edward Comentale, *Modernism, Cultural Production, and the British Avant-Garde* (New York: Cambridge University Press, 2004); Mark Antliff, "Fascism, Modernism, and Modernity," *The Art Bulletin* (March 2002): 148-169; or Andrew Hewitt, *Fascist Modernism: Aesthetics, Politics, and the Avant-Garde* (Stanford: Stanford University Press, 1993).

For discussion of the relationship between modernism and masculinity, see, for example, Gerald Izenberg, *Modernism and Masculinity* (Chicago: University of Chicago Press, 2000); Terry Smith, *In Visible Touch: Modernism and Masculinity* (Chicago: University of Chicago Press, 1998); or Michael Kane, *Modern Men: Mapping Masculinity in English and German Literature, 1880-1930* (New York: Continuum, 1999).

[2] "Baron Corvo: *In His Own Image*," *Times Literary Supplement* (Dec. 18, 1924): 865; R.C. Churchill, "Reporting Progress in the Quest for Corvo," *Birmingham Post Saturday Magazine* (Aug. 21, 1971): 11.

[3] Shane Leslie's essay "Frederick Baron Corvo" first appeared in the *London*

Rolfe is, according to Leslie, too in-between, neither Victorian nor Modern, a sentiment echoed in Symons's remark that the Corvine style resembles "the styles of Mr. Max Beerbohm and Mr. James Joyce if they could be fused into a fluent solution."[1] He is neither here nor there, to be owned by no one.

Frederick Rolfe, 1860-1913

This sense of Rolfe as an outsider, which registers so clearly in criticism and scholarship pertaining to his works, similarly pervades biographical treatments of his persona. Rolfe's hardships and eccentricities have played an integral role in the limited amount of appreciation he has received. The image of Rolfe nibbled by crabs and terrorized by rats aboard his boat as he dutifully works to complete *Hubert's Arthur* has been reproduced and romanticized in criticism and biographies. Starving in Venice while wearing a tattered yet fine suit and penning pornographic letters in an attempt to secure financial assistance, or scribbling furious, paranoid tirades against the Catholic church or any other imagined enemy, he is admittedly a fascinating figure, and the oppositional stance he occupied throughout his life does in many ways serve to illuminate his aesthetic choices.

Though Rolfe referred to himself as a "Baron," he was in fact of firmly middle-class origins, and he spent most of his adult life living in poverty. He chose to envision himself as aristocratic, regardless of the fact that his father was a piano manufacturer whose business fell on hard times while Rolfe was a child. Rolfe was raised as an Anglican, but he converted to Catholicism when he was in his twenties. Having a tendency to go to extremes, he could not simply be a Catholic, but decided he must also be

---

Mercury in September 1923. This essay is often hailed as one of the first important works of criticism on Rolfe. The essay was reprinted and enlarged as the introduction to Rolfe's *In His Own Image* (London: Bodley Head, 1924).
[1] Symons made this remark during a speech at the second Corvine banquet in 1929. See *A True Recital of the Procedure of the Second Banquet Held by the Corvine Society: December 12th, 1929, at the Ambassadors Club*, 23. The proceedings of the Corvine banquets of 1929 were privately printed and are available in the University of Notre Dame's Special Collections.

a priest. However, due to a lack of "vocation," he was dismissed from two seminaries, St. Mary's in Oscott and the Scots College in Rome. This final dismissal, which he referred to as his "life's great disappointment," left him bitter, angry, and in Italy, where he took up with the circle of the Duchess Sforza-Cesarini.[1] The Duchess, Rolfe claimed, endowed him with the title "Baron Corvo" and played the part of his patron for a short while. Upon returning to Britain, however, his hardships and his persecution were renewed. He became embroiled in a feud with a priest, whom he accused of swindling him, and he came under attack in a series of libelous articles written against him in the Aberdeen press. These events enlarged his sense of persecution, alienation, and paranoia. He moved frequently, often leaving cities and towns due to some sort of economic disgrace, and along the way, he generated countless schemes for making money. He tried his hand at painting, and he wrote for a socialist newspaper. He experimented with photographic technology, attempting color photography and submarine photography, and took photographs of naked boys that appeared in *The Studio*.

In the 1890s, Rolfe published some of his most well-known works, his Toto stories, in which a young Venetian boy explains Catholic myths and Italian folklore to an adoring older man. The heady, homoerotic atmosphere of these stories, populated with what a review in *The Bookman* referred to as "beautiful fauns and wood and water spirits, the embodiments of grace," meshed seamlessly with the aesthetic of *The Yellow Book*, where they first appeared, and the stories were well received.[2] Following on the success of these stories, John Lane, the publisher of *The Yellow Book*, made the grievous mistake of promising Corvo that he would "make [him] not only an artistic success, but a commercial success as well," and Rolfe continued to hound him to fulfill this promise for five years.[3] He proposed countless "valuable schemes" to the publisher, including a travelling commission to Persia and

---

[1] Frederick Rolfe, "About Doing Little Lavishly," in *In His Own Image* (London: Bodley Head, 1901), 145.

[2] *The Bookman* XX 117 (June, 1901): 93-94.

[3] Frederick Rolfe, *Without Prejudice: One Hundred Letters from Frederick William Rolfe, Baron Corvo to John Lane* (London: Allen Lane, 1963), 54.

an anthropological trip to the remains of the Greek colonies of Italy.[1] Lane rejected the majority of Corvo's propositions. Like many Nineties authors, Corvo worked with both John Lane and Grant Richards, who ran a similar periodical called *The Butterfly*. Richards published one of Corvo's "Toto" stories in *The Butterfly* as well as Corvo's voluminous study of the Borgia family, *Chronicles of the House of Borgia* (1901). Corvo lived on a pound a week from Richards while composing the Borgia book, and, though he was hungry and frequently ill, he maintained a belief that this work would be a tremendous commercial success and create what he referred to as a "Borgia boom."[2] Rather than acknowledging that his work was, as one reader put it, "exceptionally well devised to escape popularity," Rolfe insisted that his lack of success arose from the fact that those responsible for placing and marketing his books were "entirely uninfected" with the proper "commercial principles."[3] His petulant and abusive correspondence with Lane and Richards casts the blame for his own commercial failure on their inability to successfully employ advertisement, and he believed that each had been waiting for the other to take the trouble and expense of making his name. Though his paranoid fancies might have been unfounded, he did emerge from his dealings with the two publishers destitute and basically unknown.

Rolfe was quite prolific during this period, writing two semi-autobiographical and two historical novels as well as poems, short stories, and reviews. *Nicholas Crabbe, or, The One and the Many* exposes the inadequacies and injustices of the turn-of-the-century publishing industry, holding thinly-veiled caricatures of Lane and Richards responsible for the failures of Nicholas Crabbe, Rolfe's alter-ego. In *Hadrian the Seventh*, another Corvine avatar, George Rose, finds success and vindication for past wrongs when

---

[1] *Id.*, 47.

[2] Frederick Rolfe, *Letters to Grant Richards* (Saint Ives: Guido Morris, 1952), 10.

[3] The Unicorn Press referred to Rolfe's *Don Renato* as "exceptionally well devised to escape popularity." In a letter to Leonard Moore, Rolfe wrote, "It's no good for an agent to tell me that I've got to write what the Public likes. I know instantly that he's entirely uninfected with commercial principles, and (therefore) no earthly good to me. My agent will be the one who, by judicious paragraphing and advertisement, will make the Public want what I write." See Frederick Rolfe, *Letters to Leonard Moore* (London: Vane, 1960), 54, 62.

the Catholic Church comes to its senses and elects him pope. *Don Renato* and *Don Tarquinio* (1905), set in the Renaissance and written in the "Macaronick" style, a combination of Latin and English, rival *Hubert's Arthur* in terms of difficulty and peculiarity. Only *Hadrian* and *Don Tarquinio* found publishers in Rolfe's lifetime,[1] and he finally returned to Italy in 1908, unknown, somewhat poor, but continually optimistic about his impending fame.

Rolfe lived out his final years in Venice, travelling around the lagoons in a pupparin, often homeless, often engaged in battle with the city's expatriate community. Rolfe adored Venice, but the final years he spent there were incredibly trying. He was evicted from the Belle Vue hotel in 1909, and wandered the streets, dying, as he put it, *"as slowly and as publicly and as annoyingly to all . . . professing and non-practising friends of [his] as possible."*[2] He sabotaged attempts to assist him on the part of the expatriates. For example, a doctor, Ernest van Someren, offered him a room and fed him for eight months while he worked on the semi-autobiographical *The Desire and Pursuit of the Whole*. However, when Mrs. Van Someren asked to read the manuscript, she found her family and friends libeled and satirized in its pages. Evicted from this situation, he slept aboard his pupparin. He fell ill frequently and was hospitalized for pneumonia. He experienced a brief respite from hardship in his final days after finding another benefactor, but his years of privation and homelessness in Venice had taken their toll on his body. He died in 1913 at the age of fifty-three.

Collaboration, the "Divine Friend," and the Composition of Hubert's Arthur

Corvo spent most of his life in search of the "divine friend," his "Other Half," who would, among other things, assist him in the composition of literary works.[3] He tested and rejected many

---

[1] *Don Renato* was accepted for publication by Francis Griffiths of Maiden Lane. The text was ready for the printer by December 1907. According to A.J.A. Symons, "an edition of 500, or perhaps 1,000 copies had actually been struck off the press" before the printer went bankrupt, and the novel was not issued during Corvo's lifetime. See Symons, *Second Banquet*, 21.

[2] Rolfe, *Pirie-Gordon*, 101.

[3] Corvo dedicated *In His Own Image* to *"Divo Amico Desideratissimo,"* and *Nicholas*

potential divine collaborators, including Robert Hugh Benson
and Sholto Douglas, but his most prolific and successful partner-
ship was with his "Caliban," Charles Harry Clinton Pirie-Gordon.
Harry Pirie-Gordon initially sought out Corvo at Jesus College
in order to tell him of his admiration for *Hadrian the Seventh*. He
arrived at midnight, "gigantically attired in a coat-dress with
high (but huge) vermillion heels," expressed his admiration for
the novel, and the two became fast friends.[1] Pirie-Gordon, who
came from a relatively wealthy family, adored strange clothes and
heraldry and shared Rolfe's love of the medieval past. Together
they founded the Order of Sanctissima Sophia, a secret society
for the purpose of enlarging the world's learning. Rolfe visited
extensively with Pirie-Gordon's family at their home, Gwernvale.
The two sunbathed naked by the side of the river and played at
"composing savouries." In one round, they agreed "about putting
a mushroom baked in milk upon a roundel of fried bread and
surmounting it with a small square of cold grouse; Rolfe then
suggested the addition of five drops of lemon-juice but gracefully accepted Sir Harry's amendment of 'half a mulberry' on the
ground that the lemon juice would be too sharp."[2] During this
pleasant time amidst these idyllic surroundings, they began to
collaborate on two novels, *The Weird of the Wanderer* and *Hubert's
Arthur*.

   The relationship between Rolfe and Pirie-Gordon began
to sour almost immediately after Rolfe departed for Venice in
1908. He wrote frequently to Pirie-Gordon to reprimand him for
neglecting their work and to accuse him of countless other slights.
As his financial situation declined, he became increasingly suspicious, believing that Pirie-Gordon was conspiring against him
with another former friend, Benson. In retaliation, Rolfe painted
a very unflattering portrait of Pirie-Gordon in *The Desire and Pursuit of the Whole*, the semi-autobiographical text that Rolfe wrote
while living in Venice:

Crabbe details his search for this friend. *The Desire and Pursuit of the Whole* imagines
him eventually finding this divine friend.

[1] Rolfe, *Desire*, 43.

[2] Benkovitz, *Rolfe*, 191.

> In private life, he affected flappy white scarlet waistcoats and
> very blood evening dress of white bound with violet moire,
> or rowing shorts only, during warm weather: but of his stars,
> garters, jewelled decorations, and unmarried frock-coated
> pyjamas, there was no end. Insignia of sovereign orders being
> not in his way, he designed his own; and had them made at the
> expense of an opulent maiden-aunt. In fact, you may take it
> that his life was mainly occupied in conferring upon himself
> the right to wear strange clothes and making opportunities to
> wear other people's.[1]

Rolfe made sure to clarify that the works upon which they had
collaborated were in fact mostly written by "Prospero": "Caliban
wrote one-tenth of each, to console his parents; and during the rest
of the time, he was either sprawling in the yellow-drawing room
having his bare feet tickled by his papa or gadding about England
peacocking in his costume at pageants."[2] Because Pirie-Gordon
refused to play his proper role in the collaboration, *Hubert's Arthur*
was, in Rolfe's mind, now completely and entirely his.

Rolfe and Pirie-Gordon's other novel, *The Weird of the Wanderer*,
was accepted by the publishing house of William Rider and Son
in 1910 and went into print in 1912 under Corvo's direction as the
work of "Prospero and Caliban." Corvo's willingness to abnegate
responsibility for *The Weird of the Wanderer* points toward the ide-
alist impulse in his approach to creative production. To cooperate
with a divine friend in the creation of a literary work and then to
remove all clues to one's own individual identity from that work
is a mode of self-effacement that flies in the face of the cult of original genius. However, as Jonah Siegel's recent work on attribution
suggests, we are often too quick to celebrate collaboration as a
radical form of production that rejects modern notions of individuality and harkens back to a mythical cooperative past: "It is more
accurate to say that collaboration itself is how working together
is described within an already individualistic concept of creativ-
ity; the term identifies two individuals working together, rather
than the loss of, or indifference to, individuality."[3] It would be

---

[1] Rolfe, *Desire*, 43.

[2] *Id.*, 45.

[3] Jonah Siegel, "Leonardo, Pater, and the Challenge of Attribution," *Raritan: A*

similarly hasty to conclude that Corvo was altogether successful in eschewing individualism. The utopian title page of *The Weird of the Wanderer* masks a bitter, economically motivated, and highly individualist battle that waged over the details of the novel's publication. The source of the quarrel was a suggestion from a friend of Pirie-Gordon's that certain "violent and horrifying passages" be edited from *Hubert's Arthur*. Corvo erupted in a rage, writing to Caliban, "Fancy ME appearing as author of *Hubert's Arthur* after your Quaker has been rooting and snouting in my lovely Catholic Garden! Oh what a feeble person you are to have let yourself be blown about by people who have other interests, instead of sticking loyally to your spontaneously-chosen partner who had made such sacrifices for you."[1] Pirie-Gordon responded with an agreement for Corvo's signature, authorizing Pirie-Gordon to revise their works, publish them anonymously, and retain fifty percent of the profit. This suggestion sent Corvo into an absolute fury:

> The Agreement which you ought to give me, as between Enemies, should contain a clear statement as to how much of the *Weird*, and of *Hubert's Arthur* is your work, and how much mine. . . . I refuse you the right to alter the names and contents of those books in any way, or to publish them under the name of 'C.H.C. P.-G. and Another' or anonymously, now. . . . And I will not even consider question of sale, or of publication excepting on royalty. . . . I will treat you all most generously if you accept this offer. If not, I will fight you as fiercely as I can. . . . I will be quite open with you. I will circularize all the publishers concerning the *Weird* and *Hubert's Arthur* so that they never shall be published and I will come straight back to Crickhowell Workhouse and die there or give your father the pleasure of committing me to gaol. I have your threats. Now you have mine.[2]

While the fact remains that Rolfe finally chose to publish *The Weird of the Wanderer* under their pseudonyms, his decision to keep his name off the text arose primarily from the desire to

---

[1] Frederick Rolfe, *Letters to R.M. Dawkins* (London: Vane, 1962), 48.
[2] Rolfe, *Pirie-Gordon*, 109.

shield potential profits from solicitors to whom he owed money. Additionally, the pseudonyms themselves speak to an unequal and less-than-ideal type of literary relation, one in which a savage who does not know his own meaning gabbles like something brutish until a learned scholar endows his purposes with words that make them known.

Rolfe sent taunting letters and postcards to Pirie-Gordon for the next few years. When the Pirie-Gordons finally sent the belongings he had left at Gwernvale to Rolfe's mother, his mother forwarded a manuscript of *Hubert's Arthur* to Venice. Rolfe furiously revised the novel. He did actually complete much of the work while living on his boat, losing pages to the oil from lamps and to the wind and waves. He was often "eaten alive" by crabs, and the threat of rats made it impossible to sleep: "I must keep continually awake; for the moment I cease moving, I am invaded by swarms of swimming rats, who in the winter are so voracious that they attack even man who is motionless. I have tried it. And have been bitten. Oh . . . you can't think how awful fearless ferocious they are."[1] He nevertheless continued revising until the work was completed. The final result diverged widely from the initial plan devised by Pirie-Gordon and Rolfe at Gwernvale. While Pirie-Gordon's influence can be seen in the extensive use of heraldic devices and the chapters relating to the Crusades, the work may be understood as primarily Corvine.[2]

History and Hubert's Arthur: *Contexts and Sources*

Though Rolfe insisted that his works could be wildly popular if simply marketed correctly, his incredibly difficult historical novels do at times seem purposefully devised to escape fame.

---

[1] This passage is taken from a 1913 letter to Rev. Justus Stephen Serjeant in the Bodleian Library. Quoted in Benkovitz, *Rolfe*, 277. See also Robert Scoble's *Justus Stephen Serjeant* (Portsmouth, UK: Callum James, 2007) for more information on the date of the letter's composition.

[2] According to Pirie-Gordon, "Caliban might, perhaps, be given credit for the five chapters in *Hubert's Arthur* dealing with events in Palestine and the journey thither. These have been adorned with some of Hadrian's verbal enrichments, but remain substantially as Caliban wrote them." See Rolfe, *Pirie-Gordon*, 16.

Hubert's Arthur in particular is so excessive in its historical detail
and obsolete language that the novel truly necessitates annota-
tion in order to be comprehensible. As Vincent O'Sullivan noted,
"every impediment in the way of spelling, punctuation, esoteric
words, that he can roll in the way of the reader, he rolls."[1] The
novel is overrun with vocabulary that has not been used since the
sixteenth century. Rolfe employs archaic spellings, obscure mon-
ikers, lengthy titles, and saints' days rather than dates, forcing the
reader to decode and deduce, to grapple with rather than receive
each sentence. He goes to great lengths in *Hubert's Arthur* to dizzy
the reader with minutiae, noting that Arthur's hose were "knitted
by Stamyn Segille" and alluding to competing theories about the
manner in which the black beetle was first introduced to England. Each of Rolfe's notes pulls the reader down another avenue
of history, another potential morass of arcane knowledge, Latin,
and biblical allusions. Other notes work to reinforce the sense of
an impenetrable and unknowable past, insisting that the "editor"
not does quite know or understand to what Hubert alludes in a
particular passage.

Rolfe was committed to composing historical texts that,
like his favorite novels by Sir Walter Scott, "had the glamour of
verisimilitude."[2] If a text was concerned with the past, it should,
in Rolfe's mind, seem truly *of* the past, completely and utterly historically other, as if it was, as many of his texts pretend to be, a
medieval manuscript found hidden away in a tower. Rolfe insisted
that it was this sense of true historical otherness that the public
truly desired. While writing his Borgia book, for example, he told
Richards that any editing of the book, which was "crammed with
items to make you think," would render the book less historically
accurate and therefore less marketable. In a letter to Richards, he
stated, "I perceive that we are in imminent danger of watering
that book down to mediocrity, and then, its commercial failure is
ensured."[3] When Richards insisted upon alterations, such as the
removal of an appendix that dealt with charges of homosexual-

---

[1] Vincent O'Sullivan, *Opinions* (London: Unicorn, 1959), 168.
[2] Frederick Rolfe, *Don Renato: An Ideal Content* (London: Chatto & Windus, 1963),
21.
[3] Rolfe, *Richards*, 18.

ity made against the Borgias by historians of the Renaissance, Corvo capitulated but considered the text "gelded" and threatened to remove his name from the book.[1] He stormed at Richards for having him "rewrite the Borgia Book because 'it was full of lewdness and contained a graphick account of a bishop raping a boy.'"[2] He asserted that the deleted material "was, and is, of vital importance to the success of your book among your beloved 'library Publick', who can be disagreeable when a book known to be inaccurate is placed before them."[3] When Richards published the edited version of the book in Corvo's name, Corvo retaliated in a column in the *Saturday Review of Books and Art* of *The New York Times* entitled "The Borgias: Curious Facts from Behind the Scenes, Showing How a Book was Published under an Author's Name without Authority." Corvo expressed no surprise when the work was in fact a commercial failure, for, according to his notion of the consumer's appetite for accurate historical material, the revised text was completely undesirable.

Hubert's Arthur, however, disorients and dizzies the modern reader even further than, for example, the Borgia book by straining after the "glamour of verisimilitude" while engaging in "what-might-have-been-history." Preoccupied with the highly contentious succession following the death of Richard the Lionheart, the novel asks what might have happened had the mistakes of John's reign been rectified and the reign of Henry III avoided altogether. The novel begins with historical facts, with Richard's death and the chaos that ensued as Arthur, Duke of Brittany, the son of John's older brother, Geoffrey, contested John's right to the throne. Richard did in fact name John as heir before he died, but the legality of the succession was in question. Alan Lloyd notes, during this period in English history, "the establishing of precedence between two or more candidates of the same blood could lead to confusion."[4] The contest between the claims of a younger

---

[1] *Id.*, 19.

[2] *Id.*, 38.

[3] *Id.*, 38.

[4] Lloyd cites "the author of a twelfth-century treatise on English law" who "confessed himself uncertain whether a younger brother, or the son of a deceased older brother had the better claim" and finally "opted for the nephew,"

brother and the son of the deceased older brother would not be easily resolved. During the struggle over the succession, Arthur laid siege to the castle where John's mother, Eleanor of Aquitane, was hiding. John marched quickly to her rescue, covering eighty miles in forty-eight hours, and in turn captured Arthur. Fearful of continued opposition on the part of Arthur's supporters, John decided he had to eliminate his nephew. He had him removed to Rouen under the guard of the chief justiciar, Hubert de Burgh.

It has never been settled what happened to Arthur next. According to Roger of Wendover, "Shortly afterwards the said Arthur suddenly disappeared."[1] Some accounts say John killed Arthur in a drunken rage. Ralph of Coggeshall asserts that John ordered Hubert de Burgh to blind and castrate Arthur, but Hubert de Burgh spared Arthur and lied about the completion of his orders in the hopes of deflating the opposition. According to some accounts, John then took matters into his own hands, killing Arthur on his own. A poem by Philip's chaplain, Guillaume le Breton, sets the murder on the Seine. John and Arthur rowed out on a boat alone, John ran his sword through his nephew, and then tossed the body into the river.

Rolfe chooses to hinge his what-might-have-been history on a slight alteration to Guillaume le Breton's narrative. In *Hubert's Arthur*, Arthur escapes John's clutches by diving into the river and swims back to dance insolently on John's dinner table, slapping him in the face with river-weeds and kicking bread into his lap. John retaliates to this taunt by selling Arthur to the Jews to be crucified. After escaping this attempted crucifixion, Arthur visits the Pope, who encourages Arthur to make a name for himself before seeking the throne again. Arthur then heads off on a crusade and returns to kill John's heir, Henry III, in hand to hand combat. At this point, John has been reduced to a sniveling wreck, and Arthur takes the throne, defeats a baronial uprising, and settles tensions between the Church and England.

According to the mythology of English democracy, John's

---

as well as an authority on Norman customs who "had no doubt that that in such circumstances the uncle rather than his nephew was the closest heir" (*The Maligned Monarch* [New York: Doubleday: 1972], 80).

[1] Roger of Wendover, *Flowers of History* (London: Bohn, 1849), 205.

injustices and Henry's inadequacies served as a fertile soil for the growth of modern political institutions. In 1215, in order to protect themselves from John's abuses, the barons demanded that John sign the Magna Carta, which placed limitations on monarchical power. While previous kings had granted charters of liberties, the Magna Carta is often seen as a first step towards the establishment of English constitutional liberty. In a sense, the charter might be dismissed as nothing more than a guarantee of feudal rights rather than an expression of democratic principles. However, the precedent set by this document facilitated further agitation for reform during the reign of Henry III. In 1258, a group of barons led by Simon de Montfort drafted what may be understood as England's first constitution, the Provisions of Oxford, which provided for a council of fifteen nobles who would advise the king. When Henry annulled these reforms, the barons took arms against the king and compelled him to reaffirm the Provisions. While Simon de Montfort was eventually defeated by Henry's son, Edward, the democratic momentum built up during Henry's reign continued during his son's rule, and Simon de Montfort's initial forays into parliamentary government are frequently celebrated as the foundation of England's modern institutions of democracy.

Rolfe allows the signing of the Magna Carta to occur in his own what-might-have-been history, but he nips democracy in the bud by replacing Henry III, "ambitious yet unsure of himself," with a confident and noble King Arthur who defeats Simon de Montfort. Rolfe redirects history away from the progress toward parliamentary democracy made during this period and leads England in a far different direction.[1] Arthur renegotiates England's relationship to the Church, the troublesome reign of Henry III is avoided altogether, and the rumblings of democracy that began during John's are silenced and forgotten. Through Arthur, Rolfe makes for England a new future, monarchical and Catholic. Rolfe was working on a response to Edward Carpenter's *Towards Democracy*, entitled *Towards Aristocracy*, while in Venice.[2] Though

---

[1] Alan Harding, *England in the Thirteenth Century* (New York: Cambridge University Press, 1993), 279.

[2] In *The Desire and Pursuit of the Whole*, Crabbe describes the experience of reading Carpenter's *Towards Democracy*: "The splendid language of the poem

the manuscript has never been found, *Hubert's Arthur* could be understood as a fictional equivalent to the missing work.

Though *Hubert's Arthur* departs radically from historical fact, the novel also mimics, paraphrases, and sometimes lifts entire passages almost word-for-word from its historical sources. One of Rolfe's most deeply mined sources of material is Joseph Jacobs's *The Jews of Angevin England* (1893). Joseph Jacobs played an integral role in the development of the study of Jewish history in the late-nineteenth century. In the 1880s, he wrote a series of articles for *The Times* on the persecution of the Jews in Russia. He served as president of the Jewish Historical Society of England and revised and edited the *Jewish Encyclopedia*. His *Jews of Angevin England* attends to the role Jews played in medieval English history, particularly during the twelfth century, and foregrounds the persecution of the Jews and the sources of anti-Semitism in English usury laws. The text is composed primarily of extracts from the Pipe Rolls with commentary and appendices by Jacobs. A footnote in *Hubert's Arthur* acknowledges Rolfe's indebtedness to Jacobs: "The learned Mr. Joseph Jacobs's treatise, called *The Jews of Angevin England*, contains very many indeed of the facts narrated here, and onward, though there they are naturally criticized from the Israelite point-of-view, as here (not unnaturally) from the opposite."[1] Rolfe reproduces many of the extracts printed in *The Jews of Angevin England* nearly verbatim in *Hubert's Arthur*, but he inverts Jacobs's intentions by reinforcing, rather than critically historicizing, medieval anti-Semitism.

Hubert's Arthur dwells as much on blood libel and boy martyrs as it does on reversing the march towards democracy. In *The Jews of Angevin England* Jacobs calls into question the validity of the various "blood accusations" leveled against the Jews in medieval Europe. He traces the origin of the myth to the story of the martyrdom of William of Norwich, who was purportedly bought by the Jews before Easter and tortured "with all the tortures wherewith our Lord was tortured."[2] Jacobs draws attention

pleased him: its doctrine set him in revolt." *Towards Aristocracy* was to serve as a "counter-blast" to this text. See Rolfe, *Desire*, 238.

[1] See note on p. 446 in this edition of *Hubert's Arthur*.

[2] Joseph Jacobs, *The Jews of Angevin England* (London: D. Nutt, 1893), 19.

to the "improbability or rather the absurdities of the narrative" as
well as to the fact that the popularity of the boy martyrs "brought
custom to the monasteries that were lucky enough to possess the
shrine of one."[1] Rolfe, however, disregards Jacobs's skepticism and
places the blood accusation at the center of his novel. Arthur's
brush with crucifixion lends him an aura of holiness as well as
scars on his palms, and these markers work together to reinforce
his right to the throne. The novel's final chapters are devoted to a
litany of the Jews' offenses, "The Gallimaufry of the Giwen," and
the crucifixion of another young boy, Little Saint Hugh of Lincoln.[2] Arthur must find it in himself to forgive the Jews for their
offenses against both himself and Hugh. He toys with the idea
of a holocaust but expires with words of forgiveness on his lips.
He does, however, require that all Jews in England wear a yellow
cross on their cloaks "at all times, and in all places, now, and evermore." The text's anti-Semitism is remarkable in that it relies so
much upon the work of a Jewish historian who labored to place
the persecution of the Jews at the turn of the century into historical context. Rolfe perverts and ridicules the political intention of a
source that played an integral role in the composition of his novel.

Rolfe's dealings with his other sources are somewhat less
outrageous and a bit more comical. The novel is incredibly inter-
textual, a collage of medieval manuscripts and canonical literature. He toys with the reader by reproducing well-known scenes
from Shakespeare's *King John* and Chaucer's "The Prioress's Tale,"
implying that his precursors cribbed their tales from Hubert de
Burgh's manuscript. Notes to lines lifted from *King John* acknowledge the similarity between the two texts but imply that the theft
was on Shakespeare's part: "All of this is simply Shakespeare,
more or less. We have no grounds for asserting that Shakespeare
could never have seen any of Hubert de Burgh's manuscript,
nor are we competent to discuss the point." Rolfe posits his own
bizarre and unknown novel as the source material plundered by
his illustrious predecessors, situating his decidedly minor novel

---

[1] *Id.*, 21.

[2] Here Rolfe draws heavily from Chaucer's "The Prioress's Tale," which ends with
an invocation to Little Saint Hugh. His account of Hugh's murder closely resembles
Chaucer's account of the murder of a young boy "in Asie in the great citee."

at the center of literary history. The novel's narrator, Hubert de
Burgh, sets himself up in opposition to one of the more prominent
medieval historians, Matthew Paris, arguing that the monk was
not qualified to record history from his position on the sidelines.
A seaman, warrior, and statesman such as Hubert de Burgh, a
true participant in the pageant of history, can far better speak the
truth than a "small crawling monk . . . who knows not anything
at all saving from hearsay and keyhole-peeping." Hubert then
proceeds to reproduce the words of Matthew Paris and countless
other medieval chroniclers, such as Roger of Wendover, Giraldus Cambrensis, and Richard of Devizes. Again Rolfe turns the
tables on those from whom he has thieved, implying that they did
the stealing: "[T]hroughout the whole of these documents, one
is continually being rendered liable to the suspect scores of subsequent writers, including even such extremely prosaic scribes as
the compilers of the Pipe Rolls, of a certain unmistakable conversation with the writer of this history; or vice versa of course."
Prospero and Caliban leave the decision about where these words
originated up to the "affable reader."

The novel relies just as firmly, however, on modern source
material, as it may also be understood as a sequel to Maurice
Hewlett's *The Life and Death of Richard Yea-and-Nay* (1900). The
interplay between the two novels seems strange, as Hewlett
wrote semi-popular historical romances in a decidedly un-
experimental style. Hewlett, at least, seemed to be aware of the
disparity between the two authors' aesthetics, for having read
Hubert's Arthur for a publisher to whom Rolfe had submitted the
manuscript, he "implored him to make a more usual use of his
gifts."[1] Nevertheless, *Hubert's Arthur* is continually in conversation with *Richard Yea-and-Nay*, referring frequently to Hewlett's
own what-might-have-been inventions as if they were historical
facts and drawing one of *Hubert's Arthur*'s central characters, Fulk
the Flame, from the pages of Hewlett's novel. Hewlett invented
Richard's bastard, Fulk, as well as the union from which he came,
an affair between the king and the fictional Jehane de Saint-Pol.
Hewlett's what-might-have-been history of the lovers and their

---

[1] Symons, *Quest*, 282.

offspring could be understood as an attempt to redraw the sexuality of an improperly gendered monarch who left no legitimate heirs. It is surprising that Rolfe would rely to such a great extent on a source so staunchly heterosexual while writing a homoerotic novel. However, Rolfe often expressed admiration for Hewlett's "delicious stories," and in *The Desire and Pursuit of the Whole*, he devotes some time to discussing Hewlett's reliance on the "literary eccentricity" of "the girl in boy's guise." He draws out the gender fluidity in Hewlett's relatively conventional popular novels, and Rolfe's citation again works to rewrite the intention of the source.

The Reception of Rolfe's Works

The rich and bizarre intertextuality of *Hubert's Arthur* seems to demand a particular type of reader, well-versed in medieval history and Latin as well as in modern popular fiction, dedicated, and certainly not easily offended. What needs to be stressed, however, is the humor of Rolfe's works and the extent to which they can be incredibly enjoyable to read. As G. P. Jones notes, "Rolfe's linguistic ingenuity and stylistic versatility are also a major source of comedy in his writing. The common image of Frederick Rolfe as a humourless paranoiac is largely belied by his works, particularly his historical works, but it is precisely his wit and playfulness that have been consistently undervalued by commentators." According to Jones, the dense and difficult historical novels promise the most pleasure to the reader, as "Rolfe patently enjoys himself and lets himself go [in the historical texts] in ways that he cannot permit himself in the more defensive autobiographical fiction."[1] The question then remains why works this unique, this bizarre, and this enjoyable have for the most part remained outside of the purview of literary history.

The strange position that Rolfe's writing occupies in relation to the literary canon may in part be explained by his reception in the early twentieth century. The cultish reception that his works

---

[1] G.P. Jones, "Frederick Rolfe's Historical Gallimaufry," *Papers on Language and Literature* XIV (Winter 1978): 99.

tend to receive, the association of his works with an outsider-
ish mode of epicureanism, has its origins in the banquets of the
Corvine Society. In his biography of his brother, A.J.A. Symons,
Julian Symons refers to the Corvine Society as "the most fantastic
of all pieces of Corviana."[1] The banquets of the Corvine Society,
held in 1929, created a space where decadent men could engage
in decadent behaviors in a manner that reflected their fine tastes
and their esoteric knowledge. The banquets resembled the lavish
Renaissance banquets described by Corvo in his historical fiction.
Attendees feasted on caviar and cantaloupe, "*epigrammes d'agneau
en aspic,*" and "*côte de volaille Palermo.*" They drank "Corvo Gran
Spumante," Montrachet, and Courvoisier from 1811, and they
drank a great deal. The proceedings note that "as the evening proceeded, larger and larger libations were poured more and more
freely," and the company became "dissipated."[2] In Corvo's novels,
relations between men are privileged, and women are relegated
to the periphery. Consequently, at the banquets held in his honor,
women are absent altogether. The matter of Corvo's distaste for
women is handled with a strange delicacy and related to his admiration for cats: "It was said that he adored and admired cats, while
he loathed and vilipended dogs. . . . His attitude to the human
race was the reverse of his feline feelings." Because Rolfe hated
women, "it has been decided by the Grand Master of the Society
that no member of the devout female sex should be permitted to
commit access by her presence to any meeting of this society."[3] Sir
Shane Leslie, who spoke "as or for" the Grand Master of the Corvine Society, encouraged the members to be tight-lipped about
the proceedings when they returned home to their wives:

> Many of you will return after this banquet to meet the ques-
> tionnaire of feminine curiosity and the impatient queries of a
> sex ungallantly designated by the Baron as the vacuous and

---

[1] Julian Symons, *A.J.A Symons: His Life and Speculations* (London: Eyre and
Spottiswoode, 1950), 122.

[2] *A True Recital of the Procedure of the First Banquet Held by the Corvine Society: June
27th, 1929, at the Ambassador Club*, 19; *Second Banquet*, 26. For additional discussion
of the Corvine Banquets, see Robert Scoble, "The Corvine Banquets of 1929,"
The Book Collector 56.1 (Spring 2007): 67-74.

[3] *First Banquet*, 4.

vaccine. To them you need only reply in the mystical humour
that Outis is our Master Secretary's name, and in that recondite symbolism practiced by Jules Verne that the name of the
Grand Master is Nemo.[1]

In the absence of feminine inspection and regulation, celebrating
an author of aberrant sexuality, the members of the Corvine Society were invited to revel in their own aberrations. At the first banquet, Symons announced that "it is a condition of membership
that on election, each candidate must place in the Grand Master's
hands written evidence of at least two indiscretions of his early
years." Symons noted with pleasure that "it is a testimony to the
harmonious composition of our body that the brethren have com-
plied with a willingness that could almost be called alacrity."[2]

At the Ambassador Club, while consuming the finest foods
and cocktails, upper-class and upper-middle-class men could celebrate their immunity to Philistine morality and denigrate Philistine taste. The speeches given at the banquets of the Corvine
Society emphasized that Corvo's works were fine, editions of
them were rare, and exposure to or ownership of these texts was
a privilege as well as a marker of distinction. At the first banquet,
Leslie stated proudly that Corvo's crown came from "the Happy
Few" and that "the readers of Rolfe, and the cravers of Corvo" are
a "discreet and discriminating" "literary elite."[3] They and only
they knew about or cared for "the ripest fruit of the Nineties,"
and his "omission from the *Dictionary of National Biography,* that
splendid Baedecker to the Valhalla of British mediocrity," only
proved that he was too fine of a thing for the masses to enjoy.[4]
These events were integral in the production of the identity of the
Corvine connoisseur, the elite, dandyish fan of an author Julian
Symons referred to as "one of the strangest artificial orchids of
the Nineties."[5]

The emphasis on rarity or scarcity at these meetings deter-

---

[1] *Second Banquet,* 2.
[2] *First Banquet,* 11.
[3] *Id.,* 6-7.
[4] *Id.,* 4.
[5] Julian Symons, *A.J.A. Symons,* 117.

mined the tone of future Corvine scholarship, which for the remainder of the twentieth century treated his works as collectible
curios. Symons published *The Quest for Corvo* five years after the
banquets were held, and this experimental biography is in essence
a distillation of the homosocial epicureanism that the banquets
fostered. The text exposed its readers to a literary underworld inhabited by eccentric book collectors, such as Christopher Millard,
the secretary of Robert Ross who assisted in a bibliography of the
writings of Oscar Wilde and was later imprisoned for homosexu-
ality. As Symons notes, "What had been folly at Oxford became
criminal misdemeanour in later life, and he felt the lash of the
law."[1] Millard is cast as a poor epicurean whose "simplicity was of
the sort that is only satisfied with good things."[2] Millard's knowledge of Corvo begins the quest, and Maundy Gregory's wealth
and his skills as a book collector/adventurer end it. Gregory was
a fabulously wealthy dandy who claimed to have worked as a spy
for British intelligence and who was later convicted of selling
knighthoods. This "resplendent personage" with "an expensive
flower in his button-hole, an air of constant good-living, an affable smile, a glittering watch-chain, good clothes and . . . beautiful boots" reinforces the sense of secretive glamour and elite
mystery that has surrounded Symons's entire investigation.[3] At
champagne lunches and over feasts at the Ambassador Club, Symons and Gregory indulged in luxuries and discussed the details
of the sale of Corvo's notorious Venice letters. These men, with
their taste for the rare and the fine, marked themselves as members of a secret society through their knowledge of and desire for
Corvo's writings. In *The Quest for Corvo*, Symons assembled a cast
of dandyish and alluring admirers of Corvo who served as models
for future collectors.

The most significant outburst of Corvine scholarship occurred
in the 1960s with the issue of *New Quests for Corvo* (1961). This collection of essays, while seemingly calling for a re-examination of
Corvo or rallying for his place in the canon, also expresses a certain satisfaction with the lack of notice his works have received.

---

[1] Symons, *Quest*, 2.
[2] Id.
[3] Id., 269.

Almost all of the contributors testify that they were first initiated into the world of Corviana when they read Symons's *Quest for Corvo*, and the imprint of Symons's experiment in biography is evident throughout the collection. In "The Anatomy of Corvinism," Rabbi Bertram Korn indicates that the "anatomy of Corvinism" has not altered very much since the days of the Corvine Society. Reinforcing the sense of secrecy and elitism surrounding the consumption of Corvo's works, Korn asks, "What is it about Corvo that compels us to become his enthusiasts? Not that we number so many in our ranks!" According to Korn, "the number of actual Corvinists . . . is still extremely limited, perhaps to less than two hundred readers and collectors. . . . Rolfe-Corvo will never achieve major status in any history of literature. His books are, at the best, for the delectation of those who like the unusual taste, who share some of the author's tendency towards the bizarre and the peculiar."[1] Korn's enthusiastic discussion of the "Happy Few" who admire Corvo echoes the tone of elitist epicureanism found in the speeches delivered at the Corvine banquets. In "A Corvo Collection," Donald Weeks, who later wrote a biography of Corvo, tells the story of his collection of Corviana, which was inspired by his contact with *The Quest for Corvo*. The essay is a reproduction of *The Quest* in miniature, a tale of longing for and finally acquiring rare goods, a catalogue of the fine things obtained by a refined consumer. Additional essays, such as "The Rolfe-Benson Manuscript" by George Sims, similarly reproduce the sense of a literary underground of book collectors and dealers in rarities engaged in a determined quest to uncover the literary remains of Corvo. *New Quests for Corvo* indicates that these literary remains will be only partially uncovered, that they will be recovered but remain the property of an elite and secret society of epicurean insiders.

Rolfe's works have continued to be reissued in limited editions, and they have from time to time received critical attention in discussions of aestheticism and decadence by, for example, Regenia Gagnier, as well as in histories of gay literature by, for

---

[1] Rabbi Bertram Korn, "The Anatomy of Corvinism," in *New Quests for Corvo*, edited by Cecil Woolf and Brocard Sewell (London: Icon Books, 1965), 65-66.

example, Gregory Woods.[1] However, Rolfe's novels have, for the most part, remained the property of a Happy Few. New editions of *Hadrian the Seventh* and *The Desire and the Pursuit of the Whole* appeared recently, but Rolfe's historical novels have been severely overlooked, and *Hubert's Arthur* has been especially neglected.[2] Our sense of literary history could truly benefit by allowing Rolfe's works to receive attention from a somewhat larger circle. *Hubert's Arthur*, in particular, could offer tremendous insight into the politics of decadence and the interplay between avant-gardism and anti-Semitism in the early twentieth century. It is a dense and difficult novel, but it is also a unique and bizarre testament to the persistence of late-Victorian decadence into the twentieth century as well as a wonderful example of alternative or outsider strands of modernism. There is much to be gained from engaging with Rolfe and with this peculiar, often aggravating, and bewildering work.

KRISTIN MAHONEY

May 4, 2008

KRISTIN MAHONEY is an assistant professor in the English Department at Western Washington University. Her article, "Haunted Collections: Vernon Lee and Ethical Consumption," recently appeared in *Criticism: A Quarterly for Literature and the Arts*. She is currently working on a study of the afterlife of aestheticism in the twentieth century entitled *Old Guard/Avant-Garde: The Politics of Post-Victorian Aestheticism*.

---

[1] See Regenia Gagnier's chapter on "Rolfe, Wilde, and New Women at the Fin de Siècle" in *The Insatiability of Human Wants* (Chicago: University of Chicago Press, 2000); and Gregory Woods, *A History of Gay Literature* (New Haven: Yale University Press, 1998).

[2] New York Review Books Classics published an edition of *Hadrian the Seventh* in 2001. George Braziller published *The Desire and Pursuit of the Whole* in 1994.

Note on the Text

This edition aims to place one of Rolfe's most difficult works in context in the hopes that the novel will garner more critical and scholarly attention in the future. I have attempted to flesh out some of the historical and literary references in the text without overwhelming the novel with endless annotations, which might serve to make a difficult text unreadable. Foreign terms are translated (except for heraldic descriptions) and historical events elucidated. A list of the major figures in the text, historical and fictional, may be found at the beginning of this edition. Minor figures are discussed in brief annotations.

The text of this edition is that of the first published edition of 1935, which was edited by A.J.A. Symons. Symons notes in his introduction to the novel:

> Shortly before his death [Rolfe] entrusted a copy of the manuscript, written entirely in his beautiful script, to an American friend, Mr. Morgan Akin Jones, in whose hands it remained until 1928, when I recovered it. Another MS., in two volumes, is referred to in Rolfe's correspondence, and may exist somewhere in the world. The earliest draft, much of it in Mr. Pirie-Gordon's hand, is in the possession of Dr. G.C. Williamson. The MS. from which this text is taken now belongs to Mr. Hugh Walpole.[1]

The Walpole manuscript is now in the Bodleian Library. However, Robert Scoble's recent work on Rolfe has cast some doubt on Symons's assertions about the manuscripts of *Hubert's Arthur*. In *Justus Stephen Serjeant*, Scoble establishes that Rolfe's final manuscript was sent by the British Consul to Reverend Serjeant, a man Rolfe had befriended in Venice, after Rolfe's death. Symons acquired the manuscript from Serjeant in 1929. It is unclear which of the manuscripts referred to here is the one that had been in the hands of Serjeant. As Scoble indicates, Serjeant wished to keep his name separate from Rolfe's, asking Symons to refer to him

---

[1] Frederick Rolfe, *Hubert's Arthur* (London: Cassell, 1935), 3.

only by pseudonym in *The Quest for Corvo*.[1] Presumably Serjeant requested that his name also not be used in the introduction to *Hubert's Arthur*. The Martyr Worthy collection at Columbia University contains another manuscript of *Hubert's Arthur*.

Symons chose to preserve Rolfe's strange spelling and punctuation, and I have done the same. I have also made silent corrections to obvious typographical errors.

Acknowledgments

I am grateful to Robert Scoble and Teresa Huffman Traver for all of their assistance as I prepared this edition. I would also like to thank Kathryn Vulic, who provided translations of Latin passages. Kaveh Askari provided helpful support and advice.

---

[1] See Robert Scoble, *Justus Stephen Serjeant* (Portsmouth, UK: Callum James, 2007).

MAJOR CHARACTERS

Aloys: Louis VIII (1187-1226), king of France from 1223. When the barons rebelled against John, they offered the throne to Louis in return for his aid.

Lady Alys: Alix of Thouars (1201-1221), daughter of Constance of Brittany and Guy of Thouars, thus half-sister of Arthur. She married Peter of Dreux in 1213, but Rolfe chooses to marry her to the fictional Fulk the Flame.

Eleanor of Aquitaine (c. 1122-1204): Queen consort of Henry II, mother of Richard and John. She supported her sons in insurrections against their father. When Richard died, she worked hard to secure John as king, defending Anjou and Aquitaine against Arthur. Arthur was holding Eleanor in a siege at Mirebeau when he was captured by King John.

John Brienne (c. 1170-1237): King Philip arranged for John to marry Mary of Montferrat, thus making him king of Jerusalem, in 1210. Rolfe chooses to avert this marriage and marries her instead to Duke Arthur of Brittany.

Duke Arthur of Brittany (1187-1203?): Grandson of Henry II, son of Geoffrey Plantagenet, the fourth of Henry's sons. After Richard's death, he contested John's right to the throne. He was captured by John during the battle over the succession. Though his true fate is unknown, it is said that John either ordered him to be murdered or killed Arthur himself. Rolfe rewrites history, allowing Arthur to survive John's murder attempt and go on to take the throne.

Constance of Brittany (1161-1201): Wife of Geoffrey Plantagenet, mother of Arthur.

Hubert de Burgh (c.1175-1243): Justiciar for John and Henry III of England. Played a large role in restoring royal authority during baronial uprisings that occurred during both John and Henry's reigns. He was one of the most prominent figures in the government after William Marshal's death in 1219. Hubert de Burgh fell out of favor with Henry late in his career and was imprisoned on charges of treason. He later reconciled with the king. Rolfe represents Hubert de Burgh as disloyal to John. He also extricates Hubert de Burgh from his relationship to Henry III, positioning him as Arthur's most important advisor.

Fulk the Flame: The fictional bastard son of Richard and Jehane de Saint-Pol, drawn from Maurice Hewlett's historical novel, *The Life and Death of Richard Yea-and-Nay* (1900).

Pope Innocent III (c. 1160-1216): Pope during the reign of John. Imposed an interdict on England and excommunicated John when John refused to accept Stephen Langton as archbishop of Canterbury.

Pope Innocent IV: Pope from 1243 to 1254. Pope Innocent IV's reign was marked by tremendous conflict with the Holy Roman Emperor Frederick II.

Jezebel: Isabella of Angoulême (1187-1246), wife of John of England, mother of Henry III. Married John at a very young age after he had annulled his first marriage to Isabella of Gloucester.

Stephen Langton (died 1228): Appointed as archbishop of Canterbury, which led to a conflict between King John and the Pope. Langton supported the baronial uprising against John.

Lady Mariolanthe: Mary of Montferrat (1192-1212), daughter of Isabella I of Jerusalem and Conrad of Montferrat. She married John of Brienne in an arranged marriage in 1210.

Adam Marsh: Adam de Marisco (c. 1200-1259), Fransciscan friar and scholar. He was a spiritual advisor to Simon de Montfort. The king also sent him abroad on diplomatic missions. He was highly critical of the careerism and selfishness of the clergy and worked to purge the church of such abuses. Rolfe chooses to make Marsh an advisor to Arthur, disentangling the friar from his associations with both Simon de Montfort and Henry III.

William Marshal: (c.1146-1219) Lord Marshal and regent of England. William Marshal was one of John's closest advisors, and he was loyal to the king during the baronial uprising.

Old Man of the Mountain: Leader of the Hashashin sect in Syria. He figures prominently in Hewlett's *Richard Yea-and-Nay*.

Pandulph (died 1226): Papal legate sent to secure John's acceptance of Langton as archbishop of Canterbury. Suspended Langton for refusing to excommunicate the barons when they rebelled. Langton convinced the pope to recall Pandulph during Henry III's reign.

Philip II of France (1165-1223): King of France. Initially supported Arthur's claim to the throne but accepted John as king once John bound himself as a vassal to Philip. Philip later dispossessed John of these lands and engaged in war with him. He defeated the allied forces of John, Emperor Otto, and Earl Ferdinand of Flanders at the Battle of Bouvines in 1214.

Richard I: Richard the Lionheart (1157-1199), son of Henry II, was king of England from 1189-1199. He spent very little time in England, choosing to spend his time in battles abroad, such as the Third Crusade.

John Softsword: John Lackland (1167-1216), son of Henry II, was king of England from 1199 to 1216. Much of his notoriety rests on his loss of Normandy and most of England's French possessions to Philip. Following a baronial uprising, he was forced to sign the Magna Carta in 1215.

Queen Ysabel of Jerusalem: Isabella I of Jerusalem (1172-1205), queen of Jerusalam, mother of Mary of Montferrat.

Hubert's Arthur

NOTE.

It is not proposed to discuss either the authenticity of these documents, or the question as to senile delusion with its amazingly circumstantial particularity: to attempt to do so would (perhaps) be poaching on the preserves of the professional critic; and, in any case, it is our most singular anxiety to avoid incurring any taint (however faint) of Modernism.[1] But we do feel compelled, in fairness, to offer a brief explanation of the way by which Hubert de Burgh's MSS. (if such, indeed, they be) came into our hands.

One of us happens to be the literary heir and executor (so to speak) of a certain well-known but grossly misunderstood and over-rated writer, whom (for the present purpose) we will call Mr. N. C.[2] It appears (from that gentleman's remains) that, in the year 1901, he applied to the Constable of The Tower of London for leave to study that fortress, in freedom, for literary purposes. The Constable's courteous answer was, that such leave could only be accorded if N. C. would consent to be closely attended by a warder specially designated as his escort. It appears, further, that our acquaintance soon came to an agreeable (and inexpensive) understanding with his attendant, who made him practically free of the place, and permitted him to moon and meditate therein to his heart's content. It does not appear, however, that he used his privileges for the production of any patent or important work on The Tower of London: though,

---

[1] John Tytell has suggested that by "Modernism," Rolfe means "the development of democracy, the merger of the individual with the group, [and] the rise of the lower classes." See Tytell's essay, "Frederick Rolfe and His Age: A Study in Literary Eccentricity," *Studies in the Twentieth Century* XI (Fall 1972): 69-89. However, Rolfe may also be referring to the early twentieth-century Modernist movement within the Catholic Church. The latter seems the most likely. In 1907, Pope Pius X issued an encyclical that condemned Modernist Heresy. While the term "Modernism" was used to describe many types of secularism and heresy at the turn of the century, it was often used to describe historicist approaches to church dogma and rationalist reading of the Bible. If Rolfe is using the term "Modernism" in this sense, Prospero and Caliban would be expressing their wish to avoid the skeptical attitude exhibited by Modernist Bible critics.

[2] Nicholas Crabbe, the protagonist in Rolfe's novels *Nicholas Crabbe, The Desire and Pursuit of the Whole,* and *The Weird of the Wanderer.* Crabbe is often understood to be a thinly veiled self-portrait of Rolfe.

from the copious notes, plans, diaries, etc., which he left with us when he departed hence, we are inclined to think that he did intend to exert his extraordinary faculty in this direction at one time or another. Nor can we find, among his papers, any record of his discovery (if it was a discovery) and (shall we say) theft of Hubert de Burgh's MSS.: unless the entry in a diary of iiii Sept. 1901, ΕΥΡΗΚΑ ΔΟΞΑ ϹΟΙ Ο ΔΙΟϹ ΘΩΜΑϹ ΒΕΚΕΤ ("I have found it. Blessed be Saint Thomas Beket") can be made to bear such an interpretation. All which we can say, categorically and for certain, is, that the MSS. came into our hands among Mr. Crabbe's literary remains, and that we have done them in English to the best of our ability, adding a few notes elucidatory of obscurer passages, such apparently having been Mr. N. C.'s idea in leaving the documents to us. But there is no definite evidence before us shewing how they came into his possession, although investigation proves that that part of The Tower called "Traitor's Gate" (formerly known as "Saint Thomas Beket's Tower")[1] does contain such a window-cill with such a piscina as is described in the text, which cill was (till recently) concealed behind a somewhat excessive Tudor wainscot. But, whether the hollowed slab of Purbeck marble is still moveable, and whether it conceals an empty recess in the thickness of the wall, we are altogether unable to declare positively, for reasons which (perhaps) may be readily understood.

PROSPERO and CALIBAN.

VENICE,
Day of the Dead,[2] 1911.

---

[1] Traitor's Gate, the famous entrance to the Tower of London, lies beneath St. Thomas's Tower.

[2] In Italy, the Day of the Dead is celebrated on November 2.

THE FIRST TOME, CALLED FAITH

THE SECOND TOME, CALLED HOPE

THE THIRD TOME, CALLED CHARITY

THE FIRST TOME, CALLED FAITH

HUBERT'S ARTHUR

BECAUSE the day was very fair and the sun warm for the time of year, after my dinner I went to take the air, at ten of the glass,[1] on the roof of the new watergate called Saint Thomas Beket his tower. There is a parcel of silly people, who believe the superstitious nonsense written by Mr. Matthew (formerly of Paris)[2] averring that this tower is unsafe because it fell twice during its building;[3] and they avoid it. But I sit here in the sun, day by day, for the confusion of such fatwits as well as for other reasons. The place is quiet, and apt for meditation, being high above the ant-heap of fortress and city. Here, an old man's eyes may follow the silvery river, as far as London Bridge, on the one hand; and, on the other, lose themselves far away over Lamehythe Marsh among the clean white pinnacles of the abbey and hall and palace of Westminster.

I had many matters for my meditation. There was a great crown-wearing this day in King William Redhair his hall at Westminster. And my lord the king was to do more awful and more

---

[1] The word "glass" was used to refer to the amount of time taken for the sand in an hour-glass to run out. "Ten of the glass" would mean "ten of the hour."

[2] Matthew Paris was a monk at St. Albans. After the death of St. Albans' historiographer, Roger of Wendover, Matthew took over and reworked Roger's chronicle of the history of England, *Flores Historiarum*, which ends in the year 1235. Matthew Paris's history continues until 1259, but after his death this work was extended up to the year 1326. This compilation of writing by many hands was also referred to as the *Flores Historiarum* and, until the nineteenth century, was attributed to "Matthew of Westminster." This attribution began with an edition published in 1567 by Archbishop Matthew Parker. While Hubert de Burgh states that he wishes to correct Matthew Paris's account of history, the majority of the events discussed in this novel occurred before Matthew Paris took over as historiographer. Therefore, Rolfe is drawing primarily from accounts written by Roger of Wendover and then revised or embellished by Matthew Paris. At times, he also reproduces passages from the later, extended work attributed to Matthew of Westminster.

[3] It is recorded in the *Flores Historiarum* that the new walls built around the Tower fell in 1240 and then fell again, exactly one year later, in 1241.

difficult justice than ever before during his whole long reign. I had
wished to stand in my place by his throne, where I always have
stood in all his grave affairs. But his sweet grace, mindful of a very
old earl's infirmities, bade me to take care of my health, for his
sake and the kingdom's, sitting at home at my ease. Nevertheless, I
thought of naught but the king's affairs throughout this sunny day.
And, in the middle of the afternoon, Fulk the Flame, *vert, a heart
between eight lyonceux or*, came to me, hot from the crown-wearing.
His fiery face was ashen-grey, and his manner quiet as cold cinders.
"Hubert, the king is dead:" says he.

After we had prayed for that most kingly soul, Fulk told me the
whole matter from the beginning. It was so splendid and so gracious a history, that we could not be mournful, but glad. None but
a fool would mourn, when his sweetheart departs in the blissful
company of archangels: or a traitor, when his liege lord ascends
to hold dominion among celestial dominations.

We went down together to supper in the great hall. There,
was mighty silence. Every man satisfied his body's needs; and
went away in peace. None stayed to dally with the pleasures of
the table. Fulk helped me, when I also sought my privy chamber.
There, awhile, we sat, thinking our own thoughts. At twilight, I
was moved to speak to that earl as follows: "I and you, lord earl," I
said, "have served our lord the king faithfully these five-and-fifty
years: there is but one more service left for us to do, before we
follow him whither he has gone this day with England's newest
saint."

"For my part," says Fulk, flame-like as ever, "I know of no duty
undone which need delay us."

"Consider, first," says I, "that abbot Milo . . ."[1]
Fulk snorted.

"Consider, secondly, then," says I, "a certain paunchy monk
well known to both of us, by name Mr. Matthew (formerly of
Paris) a scavenger of other men's deeds, upon whom I have had
my eye these many years. There he has been, squatting in his

---

[1] Abbot Milo plays a key role in Maurice Hewlett's *The Life and Death of Richard
Yea-and-Nay* (1900). He was the abbot of the Monastery of Saint Mary du Pin
and a fixture at Richard's court. He is supposed to have written an account of
Richard's life, but the manuscript has never been found.

convent, first at Saint Alban's, then at Westminster, with a pen
in the tips of his fingers, and an ink-horn in his girdle, and skins
of new vellum before him, reading the writings of us (his betters), squinting out at the great world (and at us who dare and do
therein) through the little black peep-hole of his writing-room,
twisting his ears of an obsequious ass to catch gossip and tittle-
tattle and hearsay floating in the air like fluffy seeds of dandeli-
ons; and, whatsoever he may see thus or hear thus, that same he
(twittering) straightway sets down upon his vellum. For, as a dog
sweats through his tongue, such being the nature of that beast,
so Mr. Matthew by nature has the writing-flux. But, while the
function of the dog goes unnoted and nameless, the function of
the monk is called (forsooth) by him the Chronicle and History of
England."

"Such indeed is his trade:" says Fulk the Flame.

"Consider, thirdly," I continued, "whether the said Mr. Matthew, even though he be adept at writing a fair hand and also
able to embellish his margins with ridiculous distorted images of
us (his betters) of whom he writes (monkishly malignant those
images are)[1], is at all likely to know and to understand the truth
about the matters of which he dares to write."[2]

"School of God," cries Fulk, in a fume, "no man knows the
truth of any matters, saving those with which he himself has had
to do."

"Therefore," I concluded, "seeing that this Mr. Matthew (late
of Paris) writes the history of England without having been concerned in the making of it, and seeing that no man can write the

---

[1] Matthew Paris's manuscripts contain many illustrations, including
representations of monarchs and key historical events, illustrations of saints'
lives, and maps of Britain and the Holy Land.

[2] Matthew was very critical of some of the king's policies, and his prejudices
against the figures in his chronicle come across quite clearly. However, as
Clarence Ellis notes, Matthew Paris takes great pains to "impress his readers with
the integrity and valour" of Hubert de Burgh. Most of the passages in his history
that treat the deeds of Hubert de Burgh in detail are not found in Wendover's
account and are embellishments added by Paris. Consequently, Ellis argues that
Matthew Paris probably had friendly contact with Hubert de Burgh and that the
accounts of his deeds were given to the monk by Hubert himself. See Clarence
Ellis, *Hubert de Burgh: A Study in Constancy* (London: Phoenix House, 1952), 31.

truth of things in which he has not been concerned, it follows that the histories of England and of our dear lord the king stand in a very fair way of being written falsely."

"I concede the consequence:" says Fulk the Flame.

"Who, then," I asked, "can best write the history of our lord the king? Is it this quivering lump of monk, who writes admiringly of that wild woman who took to preaching in defiance of Messire Saint Paul Apostle[1]—who calls the king of the Franks the king of all earthly kings both because of his heavenly inunction[2] and his power and pre-eminence in war[3]—who also has dared to draw a picture of me in his *Chronicle*, where I look like a baby-girl with a curl in a nightcap, wide-eyed and eager to whine for the teat, clapping my hands at the cross, and (moreover) bare-legged, having but four toes altogether, and kneeling on nothing?[4] Is it this small crawling monk, who knows not anything certainly, who knows not anything at all saving from hearsay and keyhole-peeping. O manners. Or (I said), is it the seaman, the warrior, the statesman, who (for five-and-fifty years) has been with the king or acting for the king, at home and abroad, in war and in peace: who has been chamberlain to two kings and a half, namely, King Richard Lionheart and Earl John Softsword[5] of Mortain and King Arthur Left-hand: who has been five times embassador, namely, to Portingall once, to the magnates twice, and twice to the Franks: who has been Steward of four Honours, namely, Wallingford, Peverel, Rayleigh, Hagenet, and Keeper of Causton Park: who has been Constable of twenty castles, namely, Windsor, Dover, Dunster, Launceston, Wallingford, Lafford, Orford, Canterbury, Rochester, Hereford, Norwich, Montgomery, Bristol, Odiham, Arundel, Knaresborough, Chinon in Touraine, and the three

---

[1] Hubert refers to St. Paul's injunction, "I do not permit a woman to teach." The medieval women mystics, Elizabeth of Schönau and Hildegard of Bingen, are spoken of favorably in the *Flores Historiarum*.

[2] Anointing (*OED OL*).

[3] It cannot be denied that the *Chronicle of England* does fawn thus precisely.—P. and C. [Rolfe's note.]

[4] This comical caricature of Hubert de Burgh is quite accurately described. Any earl might well be splenetic about it.—P. and C. [Rolfe's note.]

[5] "Mollensis." [Rolfe's note.] John of England was referred to as "John Softsword," because he opted for peace rather than war with France in 1200.

castles of Grosmont, Scenefrith, and Candidachester, with Monmouth, a quadrilateral: who, also, has been Shire-reeve[1] of eleven
shires, namely, Dorset, Hereford, Somerset, Cornwall, Berkshire,
Lincolnshire, Kent, Surrey, Suffolk, Norfolk, and Westmoreland:
who, moreover, has been Lord of the Honour and Soke and Forest
of Knaresborough, and Lord of the Manor of Eye: who, furthermore, has been lord of the Manors and Castles of Cardigan and
Carmarthen, Justiciar[2] of England, Justiciar of Ireland, Warden of
the Marches,[3] Warden of the V Ports,[4] Warden of the Exchange
and Mint of London and its Chamberlain also, Warden and Admiral and Regent of All England, and, even now, I am Earl of Essex
and of Gloucester, Earl-palatine of Kent, Knight-Founder and
Brother of the King of the Most Valiant Order of Messire Saint
George of England, and Constable of the Tower of London for
my life?[5] Which, then, I ask, of these two men, can best write the
history of our lord the king's regal majesty, I who speak, or that
splotch of monk?"

"No man alive or dead has been more in the heart of the king's
affairs than Hubert de Burgh:" says Fulk, very generously.

"And, many times in my long life," says I, "have I praised The
Lord our God, for that he deigned to let me be taught the art
of writing well, in Latin far more fluent than the Latin of that
absurd Mr. Matthew (late of Paris), by the Gilbertines of Sempringham,[6] when I was a boy. And now I thank Him again with
my whole heart. Moreover, I here vow to the Said Lord God, and
to Madame His Maiden Mother, and to Messire Saint George of
England our protector, and to Messire Saint Hubert my patron,
and to my angel-guardian, and to Messire the new saint acclaimed
this very day at Westminster" (says I), "that, while my old fingers

---

[1] Sheriff (*OED* OL).

[2] The chief political and judicial officer under the Norman and Plantagenet kings
(*OED* OL).

[3] The part of England that borders on Wales.

[4] The Cinque Ports were a group of coastal towns on the eastern end of the
English Channel where ships were maintained for the military needs of the
king.

[5] Hubert de Burgh does not much overstate his magnificent and unique record.—
P. and C. [Rolfe's note.]

[6] An order of monks founded by St. Gilbert.

still can govern a pen, I will begin instantly to write the true history of my dear sweetheart, lord and brother, the king, namely,
the Lord Arthur Plantagenet[1] called Lefthand, King of England,
King of Hierusalem, Lord of Ireland, Duke of Armorica,[2] Duke of
the Normans, etcetera, nor shall any worldly power impede me.
And thus I vow and swear."

Fulk looked very kindly at me: for we three have ever been the
faithfullest of lovers; and he said: "Are you then young enough
and able enough for so great a work, dear Hubert?"

"Far be it from me," I answered, "to affirm that I am still a
sucking-child, or to deny that I have passed my climacteric.[3] But
I hope that I am neither too senile nor too stupid to do justice for
my lord the king, contradicting the horrible lies of that scribbling
monk. And this I take to be my duty. But yours, Fulk, is to see
to it that Arthur's heir has his grandsire's crown and canopy and
throne and regal dignity. For these are the services which I and
you must accomplish, before we go hence to attend our lord the
king, where he is."

Fulk, then, agreed with my words, as usual; and went about
his business. I, to mine.

Now the manner of the histories which I will write shall be
on this wise. Seeing that the acts of our lord the king are known
to four persons, namely, to his regal self, to Queen Mariol his
consort, and to us his faithful lieges and lovers (who always have
been of his company, either together or singly), namely, Fulk fil-
Richard and Hubert de Burgh, *lozengy, vair and gules*, therefore, I
will write of the said acts, as they were told to me by my lord the
king, or by the queen, or by Earl Fulk, or as I myself had to do
with them.

And, because monks are what they are, namely, black, small,

---

[1] The Plantagenet, or Angevin, kings are descended from Geoffrey, Count of
Anjou, and Matilda, the daughter of Henry I. The term is most frequently used
to refer to Henry II's offspring.

[2] Armorica was a name for the northwestern part of Gaul, now Brittany.

[3] According to ancient Greek philosophy and astrology, climacterics, or critical
moments in a person's life, were reached every seven years, and the sixty-third
year, the "grand climacteric," was thought to be particularly critical. Hubert de
Burgh seems to be referring here to the passing of his grand climacteric.

silly, selfish, slippery, it will be necessary to place my writings in security, until the time when they shall be finished and the truth of them clear to all men who choose to read them. Therefore, I say, I will store my skins of vellum, as I shall write on them, in a hiding-place which I myself made after the masons had ceased from working on this tower. Of which hiding-place, I have a little word to say.

Now I have determined to make my privy-chamber in the south-eastern turret of this barbican on the river, where I can attend to my affairs and watch the traffic on Thames, and have access to the rampart when I wish to take the air in solitude. For solitude, above the heads of other men busy with their own matters, greatly pleases me. The tower, also, is commodious enough: having an oratory below where the health of the soul may be cherished, and a solar above, where the health of the body may be nourished in quiet light and warmth. The window-cills, I must say, of the said oratory are single slabs of marble from Purbeck, hollowed in the middle to hold holy water. And I, Hubert, secretly have caused one of these cills to slide out of its sockets: nor does any other man know of it, not even Fulk the Flame, for I did it in an idle moment, as a pastime, not intending to make any use of it. For, in the night when the slab was first in place, I (being sleepless) was moved to amuse myself by picking out the wet cement from the crevices with my dagger, so that the slab became loosened and fit to be drawn out at will. And, when I saw that the masons did not note what I had done, I went again and again secretly, watching the unfixed slab, until all the rest of the building was completed. For, it occurred to me that I might cut a little hollow in the thickness of the wall beneath the window-cill, wherein I might hoard certain treasure, if so be that malignant stars should at some time bring evil upon me and the kingdom. And I made it my nocturnal habit, thenceforward, to ply mallet and chisel, when I could not sleep (for, at my age, many nights are wakeful); and, so, now, I have a cubical recess, two-and-a-half spans deep and broad and long, ready for my purposes under the mobile window-cill.

Here, then, night by night, I will place the histories which I will write, day by day, in my privy-chamber, until I shall have finished them all; and, when Fulk the Flame has read them, we will consult my son Boniface the Primate, *azure, a pall epingled and a crozier, all proper,* as to the manner in which they, my said histories, shall be placed in the Chronicle of England, instead of the fables of that Mr. Matthew (late of Paris). But, not until this has been well and thoroughly done, may Fulk and Hubert make up their own accounts, preparing their souls to follow their lord and brother the king's in the due and usual order.

THE FIRST TOME, CALLED FAITH[1]

---

[1] The three books of *Hubert's Arthur* are entitled Faith, Hope, and Charity. Faith, hope, and charity are the three key Christian virtues.

I

THE BOOK CALLED THE MANIFESTATION OF ARTHUR

1. *About this Book and the Writing of Histories*

This book, like all other books, has far greater interest for him who has written it than for any of you who shall read it. Wherefore I will write it in a manner which is pleasing to myself, beginning at the beginning, telling everything which I know, and coming to a tidy end. If that is not pleasing to you too, God help you.

The writing of history resembles a going from place to place: as a knight questing, who leaves his tower and the precincts which he knows, journeying elsewhere, at first rides over the open heath, where foes may not hide, nor anything impede his view. Soon, he comes to the forest, where mighty trees on all sides block his passage; and, through them, he must go warily, marking them well in passing, so that they may guide him when he returns to tell the tale of his travels. The writing of history also resembles a swimming in strange waters. There are sedges,[1] which the swimmer must touch and thrust aside. There are boulders, which he must note and avoid without bruising his belly or scraping his shins. There are weeds, which twine (like temptations) round his legs; and, if he wrestles with them, they drag him down to a death by drowning: but, if he gently floats, refusing to come to grips, then they let him slide freely into the clear deep stream, where the current carries him strongly swimming whither he wills to go.

I am like the swimmer swimming in strange waters: I am like the knight riding through the forest. I must mark my trees, and pass on: I must slip smoothly through my intanglements. Please you, be silent. Let me alone. I know the way. And I will go as speedily as possible. I start from the place where I was at my sixteenth year.

---

[1] Coarse rush-like grasses that grow in wet places (*OED* OL).

II. *About Hubert de Burgh, a youth*

The Gilbertines blundered egregiously, as priests are wont to do when they not seldom blunder. They would not let me have my will (which was for the life of a quiet clergyman), because I was rather large and robust, and I pulled a thin female orphan (name forgotten) of the community out of the mill-race. I never have been able to understand why a big boy, who did not let a spare girl drown, should be debarred from serving the Saviour of men. So, once every day since that time, I have cursed those monks out of a full heart: because none of the many deeds which I did thereafter have afforded me perdurable pleasure. And also I cursed them, because there were no priests of my family then, nor have there been any until I myself made them, namely, my son Boniface the Primate happily reigning, *azure, a pall epingled and a crozier, all proper,* and my grandson Bishop Hubert of Llandaff, *gules, seven lozenges conjoined three three and one, vair,* who ascended to the superiors[1] but two years ago. But, if we were not priests, we were nobles, being of the legitimate line of Lady Herleva whose Great Bastard was The Conqueror.[2] She married Sir Herluin de Burgh, the seventh in descent from Charlemagne himself; and, of these nuptials, I am of the third generation, as may be seen in the genealogy. Here, also, will be seen that my father, John de Burgh, *lozengy, vair and gules,* was a younger son; and he, not being able to abide his elder brother, Aldhelm de Burgh, *masculy, vair and gules,* came to live modestly on his Lincolnshire manor, where I was born and bred till I went of my own free will to the monks of Sempringham, being thirteen years old and lusty for my age. And it fell out that, when that parcel of purblind pastors mistook exuberant youth and vigorous wits for marks of an unclerical character, they being doltish and unable to deal with aught save caterpillars or sycophants,[3] I, Hubert, was thrust out into a very fair

---

[1] *"ad superos euolauit."* [Rolfe's note.]
[2] According to a now suspect genealogy, Hubert de Burgh traced his descent from Robert Mortain, the legitimate half-brother of William the Conqueror.
[3] *"erucis exceptis aut assentatoribus."* [Rolfe's note.]

way of becoming an aggrieved and cantankerous nobody,[1] while my cousin William fil-Aldhelm was lording it in Ireland.[2] That was not to be borne. And, having been rejected by the clergy, I instantly turned aside, giving myself violently and whole-heartedly to the affairs of the laity. Let the flat foot of blame, if any blame there be, fall upon the beetles[3] who merit it.

III. *About Hubert de Burgh, a youth, and King Richard Lionheart*

That year, being the year 1194 of Man's Redemption, King Richard Lionheart chanced to come to Nottingham; and I forced my way into The Presence, demanding some place in that king's service. The Lionheart roared, being gay, when I burst upon him bawling my petition, and holding out at arms' length the two large billmen who guarded his tent, one struggling in my right hand, the other in my left; and I wrang their noses in my clenched knuckles so very bitterly, that they blasphemed, kicking nothing, and being unable to use their arms lest their heads should be more awfully jarred. For I was very strong, and determined not to take any more disappointments meekly. King Richard granted my prayer;[4] and I followed him through his war with the king of the Franks, receiving belt and spurs and accolade of knighthood three years later, on account of a little deed which I did naked in the water when we burned the corn-ships of traitors at Saint Valery-on-Somme.[5] King Richard Lionheart also made me his privy chamberlain; and he gave me custody of all his secrets, specially one secret: so that I never left him till he had ascended to

---

[1] Hubert's disappointment at his dismissal recalls Rolfe's response to his "life's great disappointment," the moment when he was dismissed from a seminary due to a lack of vocation.
[2] William Fitz-Aldhelm and Hubert's brother, William de Burgh, were often confused in genealogies, and this confusion resulted in the mistakes concerning Hubert's ancestry. Hubert's older brother, "William the Conqueror," was the conqueror of large territories in Ireland in the late twelfth century.
[3] "*blattis*." [Rolfe's note.]
[4] According to Roger of Wendover, Hubert de Burgh served King Richard from his boyhood.
[5] When Richard found out that ships were coming from England to Saint Valori with supplies for his enemies, he burned the ships and had the sailors hanged.

the superiors from his camp at Chaluz. Enough about Hubert de Burgh, for the present.

Here, I come to a forest so full of trees, that I must cut at a few to make me a path. I begin with John Softsword, Earl of Mortain, *gules, two lyons or, with a difference, all defaced.*

IIII. *About damned Traitors*

When King Richard Lionheart, wounded by the Assassin at Chaluz,[1] was in the very article of ascension to the superiors, all we in his tent fell into enormous confusion: for the question suddenly arose, Who should have his crowns, canopies, dignities, and royal seats. This had already been settled once; and I was ware of it, as also were many of my betters there present: but, to my shame, I did not instantly proclaim the truth, first, because I was stunned by the weight of the great secret (weighing exactly twenty-thousand gold ounces) which King Richard with his last breaths had confided to me just before the ladies came, secondly, because greater men than I were beginning to make themselves nuisances. For which heinous sin I still do penance.

Earl William Marechal of Pembroke, *paly vert and or, a lyon gules,* took Walter then the Primate[2] by his pall, leading him into a

---

[1] Rolfe chooses to follow Maurice Hewlett's fictional account of Richard's death. In *The Life and Death of Richard Yea-and-Nay*, Richard dies at the hands of Syrian Assassins sent by the Old Man of the Mountain. The Old Man of the Mountain was the leader of the Hashshashin, or the Assassins, a medieval secret society and militant sub-sect of Ismaili Muslims, and he was said to have collaborated with Richard in plotting the assassination of Conrad of Montferrat, the king of Jerusalem. In Hewlett's novel, the Old Man of the Mountain marries Richard's one true love, Jehane de Saint-Pol, a character invented by Hewlett. When Richard contacts Jehane again in hopes of reuniting, the Old Man orders his Assassins to kill the king.

[2] William Marshal, first earl of Pembroke, did support John's claim to the crown. He played an integral role in the events that occurred during John's reign, but he has in large part been neglected in this narrative. According to *The History of William Marshal*, Hubert Walter, the Archbishop of Canterbury, initially supported Arthur and then relented to William Marshal's insistence that John should be the next king, but he insisted Marshal would come to regret this decision. The conversation here is drawn almost word for word from *The History of William Marshal*, which was written shortly after Marshal's death.

corner of the tent for private conversation; and, when these huge magnates came near me (panting to myself with amazement), then, I listened eagerly: for I was so astounded, that my mind was in a fog, and it is not my habit to act unless I see my duty and my advantage clearly. "My lord," says the earl, shouting to let his voice be heard above the din, "now we must hasten to elect someone whom we may make king." "I think and believe," says the archbishop, "that (according to right) we ought to elect Duke Arthur." "To my mind," says the earl, wantonly lying in his hairy throat,[1] "that would be bad: for Arthur is counselled by traitors, and he is haughty and proud; and, if we set him over us, he will seek evil against us: for he loves not the people of England. He shall not come there by my advice. But let us rather look upon Earl John: for my conscience and my knowledge point him out to me as the next heir to lands which were his father's and his brother's." "William," says the archbishop, rubbing his warty dewlap,[2] "is this really your desire?" "It is, my lord," says the swart earl,[3] blustering, seeing that he could have his way with this clergyman; "and I say that it is sound reason: for unquestionably a son has a nearer claim to his father's lands than a grandson. So it is but right that John should have the crown." The heavy archbishop polished his dewlap a little more: it bristled with short hairs, like hoar-frost, because of the warts which impeded his razor.[4] And he let his righteous judgment be overborne by the prepotent sophistry of the earl. "So be it, then," says he: "but, mark my words, William, for of nothing which you ever did in your life have you such cause to repent as you will have of what you do this day." "I thank you," says the earl: "nevertheless I am content that thus it should be."

v. *About Hubert de Burgh and John Softsword, both traitors, one stupid, the other damned*

I know that I ought instantly to have afflicted that primate and that earl with daggers well-driven in the soft hole under

---

[1] *"in pilosis eius faucibus mentiens."* [Rolfe's note.]

[2] *"uerrucosa pendula palearia."* [Rolfe's note.]

[3] *"comes adustus."* [Rolfe's note.]

[4] *"uerrucarum causa quae nonaculam impediuerunt suam."* [Rolfe's note.]

their back-hair: but, because of the hurly-burly at the moment all around me, and because they were the greatest magnates of the kingdom, I was unable to think righteously just then. For the codfish-faced Queen-Mother Alianora was barking[1] about one son over the corpse of the other; and the Queen-Widow Berengere and Lady Helvise of the Franks were being carried out in their relative swoons; and Lady Johanna was going away with her boy in her hand, escorted by William Barres, *lozengy, or and gules*, and by Eustace Saint Pol her brother, *gules, three palets vair, a chief or, and a label of five points azure*, with their trains all very truculent;[2] and the Earl of Mortain was prancing everywhere, whispering, persuading, promising. And to me, standing aghast in my station, he came; and he said, "As you were King Richard's chamberlain, be now King John's." Thus, in one moment, dalliance with sin confirmed me in the same; and I, a stupid traitor (for I will not conceal my crime), became John's man. But there was one thing which I had sufficient grace to determine; and it was that I must keep King Richard's dying secret as a sacred trust, never divulging it save to the proper person when benignant stars should give occasion.

Now, we all knew John; and most of us loved him as men love a wild ass.[3] By that nickname, indeed, we knew him. While the Lionheart was absent, on his crusade, or in the archduke's dungeon, this Wild Ass had capered as ruler of the English as well as of the Normans and the Angevins. And now it seemed that he was to claim our allegiance as his regal right. This is how he stood. The archbishop of Canterbury, and the earl of Pembroke, and Geoffrey fil-Peter the Justiciar, were his chief friends. He also had the Queen-Mother Alianora, a very sturdy hag[4] of nine-and-seventy years. As for his power: he had his own, and the levies of his forenamed friends; and, beside these, he took over his dead

---

[1] "*latrubat*." [Rolfe's note.]

[2] Rolfe reproduces Hewlett's account of the scene at Richard's deathbed. According to Hewlett's account, as Richard dies, he is confronted by the three women in his life, his wife, Berengere, his lover, Jehane, and Alois, the French princess to whom Richard had been betrothed.

[3] "*Onagrum*." [Rolfe's note.]

[4] "*robustissima anus odiosa et peruicacissima*." [Rolfe's note.]

brother's household with the mercenary cotterels commanded
by Mercadet. As for his business: that was, to capture instantly
the caps and the crowns of Anjou-Touraine, Maine, Acquitaine,
Poictou, Normandy, England.[1] But, a man without money cannot
do anything. Wherefore, Softsword sent his friends (with their
levies) to secure him in England, and the Queen-Mother (with
the cotterels under Mercadet) to secure him in Poictou, while he
himself went to snaffle[2] King Richard's little hoard at Chinon.[3]

VI. *About Duke Arthur and his Three Wrongs*

Thus, were three singular wrongs done. Queen Alianora dug
her claws into Anjou by the way:[4] but Hugh IX le Brun, Earl of the
March, *barruly, argent and azure*, prisoned her till she surrendered
certain estates. In England, the magnates, finding themselves to
be masterless men, were amusing themselves with miscellaneous
brigandage,[5] so that the shire-reeves strove hardly to get their
allegiance for Softsword: but, at length, assembling at Northampton, they agreed to follow William Marechal's example. And even
magnates, who had been friendly to Duke Arthur, now swore to
John: such as Ralf Blondeville IIII Earl-palatine of Chester, *azure,
three gerbs or*, and his sister's husband Earl David of Huntingdon,
paly, or and sable, a bend gules (who was brother of King William
the Lyon), and Roger Lacy the Constable of Chester, *quarterly, or
and gules, a bend sable, with a difference*, and Earl Richard Clare of
Hertford, *or, three chevronels gules*, and Earl Waleran of Warwick,
chequey, or and azure, a chevron ermine, and Sir William Mowbray
of Axholme, *gules, a lyon argent*, all damned traitors also. Thus,

---

[1] The "Angevin empire," which included England, Anjou, Maine, Aquitaine,
Poictou, and Normandy, is a modern term used to describe a set of states ruled
by the Plantagenets during the twelfth and early thirteenth centuries. Henry II
had divided the territories between Richard and Geoffrey, neglecting John. The
name "John Lackland" refers to the manner in which Henry divided the Angevin
empire. The early years of John's reign involved enormous conflict over the
Angevin empire, and one of the most discussed of John's failures was his loss of
portions of this empire to Philip of France.

[2] Steal (*OED* OL).

[3] The repository of the Angevin treasury was in Chinon.

[4] "*cum unguibus fodit in uia.*" [Rolfe's note.]

[5] Pillaging (*OED* OL).

then, was Duke Arthur, *ermine, for Armorica*, wronged of his rights in France, and in England. The third wrong was done to him by Softsword in person, who (at the same time) wronged also Earl Hottho of Brunswick and York, the King of the Romans.[1] For King Richard Lionheart's last will and testament had devised, to the said Hottho two-thirds of his regal treasure and all his baubles, the German being a very needy earl and king: but the remaining third was devised to Duke Arthur, rightful heir of our king, lord of the castles of the kingdom.[2] And Softsword stole the whole of the said treasure from the treasury at Chinon.

There was also the little matter of the wrong done by the Wild Ass to Almighty God, by perjury. For, before the said treasure was surrendered to him, he swore to observe all good laws and customs, not intending to keep his oath, being a proper Wild Ass just come to the pride of his strength, obscenely prancing here and there, braying with hideous hollow laughter out of every hole of his body,[3] rolling and wallowing in filthy offal when feasible, snatching, tossing, tearing. And having (by overweening fraud) obtained the sinews of war, he flippantly galloped to Rouen.

VII. *About Softsword his cacophonies, culpabilities, coronations*

At Fontevrand, he shocked Great Saint Hugh of Avalon, Lincoln's holy bishop, *azure, a Blessed Virgin and The Child throned and crowned and sceptred or*, by his unpleasant beastly behaviour at the offertory. For he offered his gold wedge neither shyly nor solemnly, as one about to receive crowns, but ribaldly, giggling stridently, teasing the saint, till that one rejected offering and offerer.[4] And the Wild Ass sacked cities, Le Mans for one, merely out of levity as he passed them by. Even when Walter the Primate gave him the cap and sword of the Dukes of the Normans at

---

[1] Otto of Brunswick, one of two rival kings of the Holy Roman Empire. Otto's rival was Philip, Duke of Swabia.

[2] *"rite regnis regni castellorum rector et hacres."* [Rolfe's note.]

[3] *"per cuncta caua corporis."* [Rolfe's note.]

[4] John supposedly baited Bishop Hugh during mass, shaking coins in his palm and making irreverent statements about the grudging manner in which he donated his gold to the church. Bishop Hugh then refused to touch John's coins.

Rouen with the ducal banner, he jested so violently that the lance of the banner lapsed to the ground.[1] Still on the trot,[2] while we trailed behind, he crossed the Narrow Sea to Shoreham, hastening Westminsterward for the crown of England. And there was a queer coronation, with only seventeen bishops and ten earls: but Softsword's half-brother, Archbishop Geoffrey of York, bastard of King Henry fil-Empress by Lady Rosamund Clifford, was absent, for reasons known unto himself.[3] And Walter the Primate stammered words put into his mouth, but assuredly displeasing to his mind, when he said, "We, therefore, after asking for the Guidance of The Holy Spirit, have elected the illustrious Earl John of Mortain, as well on the ground of his merit as of his relation to King Richard Lionheart." Of which merit, the Wild Ass instantly gave signal example, wickedly refusing to consecrate his crowning by eating The Body of The Lord: whereat there was no little horror and dissatisfaction.[4] So much for the middle of Earl John's ill-gotten dominions. Remain the questions of the north, and of the south.

VIII. *About Softsword and the King of the Scots*

The Scots King, William the Lyon, *or, a lyon gules,* for Scotland, demanded Northumbria.[5] Softsword played with him, as a whelp with a rat, offering a discussion at Nottingham: this, to get the Scot into his clutches without war, for the question of the Frankish dominions was worrying John dreadfully.[6] William the

---

[1] John is said to have behaved irreverently at the Cathedral of Rouen as well, turning to make a joke to one of his companions when the Archbishop presented him with a lance bearing a banner of the Dukes of Normandy and allowing the lance to fall to the ground.

[2] *"adhuc tolutarius."* [Rolfe's note.]

[3] Archbishop Geoffrey of York, Henry II's illegitimate son, quarreled frequently with both John and Richard.

[4] The biographer of Saint Hugh insists that John never received communion after he reached the age of discretion.

[5] William the Lion, the king of Scotland, demanded Northumberland and Cumberland in return for declaring allegiance to John. John refused, and William threatened to invade. He was deterred, according to Roger of Hoveden, by a divine admonition.

[6] *"foede Johannem excerebat."* [Rolfe's note.]

Lyon raised an army, threatening war after forty days. Softsword secured himself, by setting over the Northumbrian castles that stout knight Sir William Stutville, *quarterly, argent and sable, a pale and saltire ermine and ermines counterchanged*. And then he pranced on a pilgrimage at Bury, where he made measly offering of thirteen pennies and a silken cloth borrowed from the sacristan and never repaid: but he pilgrimized also to the shrine of Messire Saint Thomas Beket at Canterbury, the glory of all England. In this way, he both scorned the Scot, and estimated the value of two shrines with intent to plunder them. Which done, he galloped from Shoreham to Dieppe, and thence to Rouen, where he made friends with his half-brother Archbishop Geoffrey of York, a termagant,[1] for certainly abominable reasons.

VIIII. *About Softsword and the King of the Franks*

I have much to say about Philip the August, *azure, semé of lys or*, *for France*. He was a clammy-souled pig; and I have King Richard Lionheart's word for it. He had fearful worries of his own; and these be they. Alleging his regal displeasure, he had dismissed his queen on the morning after the day when he had married her. She was Lady Ingebiorg of Denmark, daughter of King Knud VI. The Frankish clergymen instantly discovered that the marriage was consanguineous; and they nulled it. Lady Ingebiorg appealed to our Lord Pope Celestine. He favoured her suit: but died at once.[2] King Philip, to make the breach impassable, married Lady Agnes, daughter of Duke Berthold of Meran, *azure, an eagle displayed, or*. But he reckoned without the new Pope, Lord Innocent of Tusculum, *gules, an eagle chequey argent and sable gorged and ungled of the first and crowned or*, a man of God and a prince of Kings and such. For His Paternity maintained the judgment of Pope Celestine; and was menacing King Philip with an awful censure. Also, France was in difficulty about his alliances. On the one side, he might

---

[1] A violent or quarrelsome person (*OED* OL).

[2] Philip asked for an annulment on the grounds that the marriage had not been consummated. Ingeborg, however, insisted that it had and that she was the rightful Queen of France. After Celestine's death, Pope Innocent III took up Ingeborg's cause against Philip.

join himself to Softsword, if that earl would do homage to him for the Angevin fiefs.[1] On the other side, he might join himself to one of the two Germans, who (by chance) were claiming the Empire. These were, Duke Hottho of Brunswick and York and King of the Romans, *gules, two lyons or,* and Duke Philip of Suabia, *argent, three lyons gules, with a difference.* But Pope Innocent, Who was about to damn King Philip for misconduct to Lady Ingebiorg, was also about to favour Duke Hottho for the Empire: but the Germans themselves were supporting Duke Philip of Suabia. And it must be said that the latter was a manly and wealthy duke, while the former was a needy niddering.[2] Still, if Hottho (who already enjoyed pontifical favour) could also get that legacy of King Richard Lionheart from Softsword, he would become either a worthy ally or an important enemy, as the case might be. The Frankish king's predicament, then, was this: he was at cross-purposes with the Pope, and (consequently) with the Pope's man Hottho; and his magnates would not let him ally with Softsword. But an alliance with the other claimant to the Empire seemed to afford fine chances of gaining (by force of arms) both the Pope's favour and the fiefs of the Angevins. And, there being yet a third difficulty which worried him, he decided to risk alliance with Duke Philip of Suabia.

For there was the third great and frightful difficulty of Duke Arthur Plantagenet, of whom I am hastening to manifest the whole nude truth. But there is yet a great mass of brushwood (so to speak) to be cleared away before I can chop down Earl John.

x. *About the Wild Ass his Wiles*

Now mark the wiliness of Softsword. Acquitaine was the Queen-Mother's inheritance. She was to leave it to John by will. And he could only hold it when he had done homage for it to the king of the Franks. But he wished to hold it by right. His wile, therefore, was to defer the said homage, while he wove such a cobweb of wiles as would render such homage not due. See what

---

[1] By paying homage to Philip for the Angevin fiefs, John acknowledged Philip as overlord of the French lands. John bound himself as a vassal to the French king.

[2] "*inops erat et ignauus.*" [Rolfe's note.]

a web he wove. He made his wretched old mother do homage for
Acquitaine to King Philip at Tours. So, the fief became hers. Then,
he secretly granted the same fief to her, and took her homage for
it. So, when Queen Alianora should die (and her age was nine-
and-seventy years), John's overlord would be dead, leaving no
heir but John, which John could then claim to hold Acquitaine of
himself alone, he being both heir and the heir's overlord. In this
knotty way, he devised to debar the king of the Franks from his
feudal right.

XI. About the Allies of Softsword, and of King Philip the August

Thus, then, the combatants stood. On the one side, was the
king of the Franks, allied with Duke Philip of Suabia. On the other
side, was Earl John of Mortain, usurping England and Normandy
and the Angevin fiefs, allied with Duke Hottho of Brunswick and
York and king of the Romans (who was hoping, by this alliance,
to snaffle that legacy), and also with the said Hottho's supporter,
Pope Innocent (Who was to learn better by and by). Moreover,
Softsword allied also with Earl Baldwin of Flanders, *or, a lyon sable
within a bordure gules*, and with Earl Reinald Dampmartin of Boulogne, *or, three torteaux gules*, both having axes of their own to
grind, but no grindstones.[1]

XII. About Hubert de Burgh his deeds at this time

While Softsword was setting snares for the king of the Franks,
he sent me away to confine my one-and-twenty years with the
bond of matrimony. Knowing how I had served his brother faithfully, he also was minded to employ me in secrets: yet, such was
his suspicious nature, that he never trusted anyone to serve him
out of love or loyalty or even for gain, but he always took hostages, even from earls whom he employed, and on the most insignificant occasions. So, saying that he was minded to entrust very
high matters to me, he bade me to wive and to beget sons without
delay, that I might have hostages ready to offer when such should

---

[1] *"quippe qui cotium et ipsi et secures ipsorum egerent."* [Rolfe's note.]

become necessary. I, therefore, espoused Lady Beatrix,[1] daughter of Earl Warenne of Wirmegay, *argent, a verm saltant sable*. Well it was that I did so: for, beside that she was a fair meek damsel, very loving and docile, the twelve days which I spent with her gave me space wherein I began to become displeased with my disloyal and sinful estate. And, with my mind thus annoyed,[2] I returned to Softsword where he was in Normandy, quite ready to jump at any chance of contentment. For the burthen of King Richard Lionheart's secret weighed grievously upon me.

John instantly gave me a petty mission. Not that he had no better men about him: but I suppose that he chose me while I was young and flexible (though I could not yet give him sons as warranty of my fidelity), to try me whether I was able and might be trusted to deal with great matters in the future.

The affair was no less than a conference touching the claims of Softsword. That Wild Ass led his power from Rouen to encamp in King Richard's castle of Boutevant. King Philip came in force from Paris to Le Goulet, also on River Seine; and the meeting-place of their ambassadors was fixed at a point equidistant between the two. At first, the English and the Franks did little beside surveying each other, visiting opposite camps, exchanging civil speeches, as cats do before they spit and scratch. And so it came about that I first saw my rightful lord and king, in the circumstances which I will now narrate.

XIII. *About Duke Arthur of Armorica, now manifested*

Let it be understood that Duke Arthur was the son of Duchess Constance of Armorica, *ermine*, by her husband Geoffrey Plantagenet called Longcheek,[3] son of King Henry II fil-Empress, and brother of King Richard Lionheart and of Earl John of Mortain.

---

[1] Hubert de Burgh's marriage to Beatrice de Warenne lasted five years and, according to Clarence Ellis, produced his only son, John de Burgh. Many earlier works, however, such as the *Shakespeareana Genealogica* (1869) by George Russell French, claim that Hubert had another son named Hubert.

[2] "*distenta*." [Rolfe's note.]

[3] "*Longuejoue*." Query? Is this a twelfth-century pun upon "*L'Anjou*"? [Rolfe's note.]

I mention the fact, that my lord the king may be better known, when it is seen of what rare stuff he was made.

His mother was the most stormy[1] of all women: she beat down her opponents by sheer force of will and profusion of language.[2] His father had the sagacity of Duke Odysseys and the beauty and the bravery of Duke Akhilleys. From such stock, Arthur sprang to mortal birth, in the Sign of the Maid, under the planet Mercury, with the Sun at zenith, on the fifth day of September, in the year 1187 of Man's Redemption. What could so glorious a sprout[3] be, but sage, clean, lovely, lithe, courageous, and indomitable?

When he was three years old (his father having ascended to the superiors before his birth), King Richard Lionheart played the good uncle to him (of the wicked uncle, I shall write anon), confirming the regal imp in his duchy of Armorica, acknowledging him as his own well-beloved nephew and heir, and (moreover) he betrothed him to Lady Albina, a baby, daughter of King Tancred of Sicily, *azure, semé of lys or, a label gules*, obtaining also her dowry of twenty-thousand ounces of pure gold, which he hid and made a secret of it. The girl besottedly broke troth at the age of reason, before she ever set eyes on Duke Arthur, marrying Earl Walter Brienne of Lecce, who wore the ugliest coat which I have ever seen, namely, *quarterly per saltire, or, a cross-patty gules, argent, an eagle displayed sable, an escallop for difference*: but the dowry remained where King Richard had hidden it for his nephew and heir's use and comfort. By God, that was a good uncle. So, the boy grew in favour with God and man, confidently expecting his rights: for which, indeed, at the very moment when King Richard was so improvisedly ascending to the superiors, he was qualifying himself, being then not twelve years old. For the people of Touraine hold the singular and sapient belief that it is best to be ruled by a belted knight who is also a clergyman. Hence, while King Richard was in his agony at Chaluz, Duke Arthur was at Tours, receiving the sacred tonsure and taking his seat as a canon of the

---

[1] *"Omnium mulierum saeuissima erat mater eius."* [Rolfe's note.]
[2] Rolfe seems to be drawing on Shakespeare's representation of Constance as aggressive and vociferous in *King John*.
[3] *"surculus."* [Rolfe's note.]

cathedral-church of Messire Saint Martin.[1] And here I record that this sacrosanctity of his person, this mark of The Lord's service, which Duke Arthur took on himself at this time, was perdurable, was indelible, as we were to know who were his loving servants.

XIIII. *About Duke Arthur his Condition*

Now his mother (though noisy[2]) was quite faithful and friendly to her son. And of her some words must be said.

When Geoffrey Longcheek died before the birth of Arthur his son, Ralf Blondeville IIII, Earl-palatine of Chester, Earl of Richmond and Lincoln, Lord of Bolingbroke and of Saint Semer in Normandy, induced the widowed Duchess Constance to marry him: for he fondly imagined that he could displace her son (when born), and rule his duchy. She felt, at the moment, that she really needed a man; and Ralf was as good as another: but she did not complete her marriage, so that she might free herself upon occasion. When that occasion came, she egged on her vassals to expel him: but he carried her with him, and kept her in durance[3] for a year and a half. And, having borne her son, and certified herself that he was likely to live and be strong, she bartered part of her duchy with Ralf for her freedom.[4] Which done, she talked (as she could talk) to King Richard Lionheart, who annulled her marriage with Chester, and confirmed all Armorica to Arthur, as has been shewn. If King Richard had lived, he would have seen all the other provisions of his will fulfilled. But the Assassin of the Old Man of the Mountain slew him; and Duke Arthur was left without protectors of his childhood, other than his said mother and Sir William Roches, *azure, a rock or, in a river argent*, his seneschal[5] of Anjou and Maine. Duchess Constance instantly married

---

[1] St. Martin of Tours was an ex-soldier who became bishop.
[2] "*turbulenta.*" [Rolfe's note.]
[3] Imprisonment.
[4] King Henry II had arranged for Constance to marry Ranulph de Blondeville, but the marriage did not go well. At one point, Ranulph imprisoned Constance, and the marriage was dissolved soon after.
[5] An official in the household of a noble who administered justice and controlled domestic arrangements (*OED* OL).

Viscount Guy de Thouars, *or, semé of lys azure, a canton gules;* and these three were the only friends on earth of the orphan.

It is not necessary to enumerate his enemies. I simply say that they were all those damned traitors who deliberately supported Earl John of Mortain, his wicked uncle and rival.

King Philip the August was far too flabby[1] to be an open friend or an open foe. That fat cold pig of a Frank considered nothing but his own advantage. If Earl John would do homage for the Angevin fiefs, King Philip would take his part: if not, King Philip would worry Earl John for Duke Arthur. I imagine that the Frank preferred Softsword for a foe and Arthur for a friend, it being easier to manage a child than a man. So, twelve days after King Richard Lionheart had ascended to the superiors, Duchess Constance with Thouars and Roches led her power of Armoricans to Angers, and proclaimed Duke Arthur lord of Anjou and Maine and Touraine. This, for a beginning. Next, she flung herself and her little son and his cause into the gladly-opened arms of King Philip the August. The eagerness, with which he firmly clutched the suppliants, these histories will shew. O times.

xv. *About Fulk the Flame*

The Frankish king had also another of the Lionheart's kin in charge. Lady Johanna returned to Syria, leaving Fulk the Flame (at that time Lord of Cuigny) with his wardens, the Queen-Widow Berengere, *England, Navarre in pretence,* and William Barres, and Eustace Saint-Pol.[2] These, seeing how King Richard's brother was for comporting himself abominably, escorted King Richard's said son to the court of King Philip, that he might get knightly breeding against the time when he could fend for himself. For the

---

[1] *"marcidus."* [Rolfe's note.]

[2] William des Barres plays a key role in Hewlett's *Richard Yea-and-Nay*, plotting against King Richard until Richard saves his life. Eustace Saint-Pol is another one of Hewlett's invented figures. In *Richard Yea-and-Nay*, he is the brother of Jehane, Richard's lover. At the end of the novel, Richard asks Jehane to leave Fulk behind to be brought up by Saint-Pol and Des Barres as a "good knight." See Maurice Hewlett, *The Life and Death of Richard Yea-and-Nay* (New York: Macmillan, 1900), 405.

Lionheart's will was that Fulk should be Bastard of Anjou, holding that fief of Duke Arthur, whose senior he was by a month,
having been born in the Sign of the Lyon (as was most meet) with
the Sun for his magnanimous Planet, on the fifth day of August in
the year 1187 of Man's Redemption.

XVI. About Hubert de Burgh and the Manifestation of Duke Arthur

So, by God's Grace, it chanced that I walked in King Philip's
camp at Le Goulet; and the courteous Frankish knight, who
accompanied me, said the word which drew me back at length into
the path of rectitude. He was that William Barres, warden of Fulk
the Flame, an impetuous fool, but commendable in this affair. We
were passing through the quarters of the hostages, where companies of noble imps diverted themselves as usual, impishly. Of
these, I marked three. They seemed to be more worthy than the
rest, and almost equal in age. The first was an earnest blunderer:
he emulated two who were peerless. Dark-haired he was, florid,
short-winded, very anxious to excel, but harassed by a fat long
body with short thin legs and a natural inconstancy. I knew him
for Aloys of France, King Philip's son, from his surcoat of blue
powdered with golden lilies. The second, I knew from his likeness
to the Lionheart his sire, though I had seen him but once before
and only for a moment. Red as fire was his hair, blazing green
were his eyes, his skin (like cream) was all aflame with freckles,
and fervent honesty sat radiant on his brow. He answered to the
nickname of Le Flamme. His surcoat was as green as grass, with
a blazon of lyons and a heart of gold. Thus I saw Sir Fulk, the Lord
of Cuigny. The third made me think of a cold flash of lightning.
His hair was quite the palest of yellow, shining like silver. He wore
an ermine cloak and cap with a badge of broom. His grave bright
eyes were long, straightforward, untroubled, unseeking, austere,
and of the very darkest brown. His skin was white and warm as
honeycomb. He was a huge boy, tall, of handsome countenance,[1]
as the Chronicle of Lanercost says truly; and his gait proclaimed

---

[1] "*vultu decorus, corpore procerus.*" [Rolfe's note.] This is in fact a direct quotation
from *The Chronicle of Lanercost*, which states that Arthur was "handsome of face
and tall of body."

him a king. Slow it was, swift it was, but always unhesitating, following his nose of delicate fastidious disdain: it was airy, it was supple, vivid, serene, always reserving force even when freely spending it: it was shy, it was brave, it was most sensible and quite fearless, it was subtile and sinuous, its youth and its innocence were very formidable: it was the proud gait of the stainless pure secure in himself, wholly perfect in himself, severe with himself as with all, strong in disgust of ill, utterly careless save to keep high, clean, cold, armed, intact, apart, glistening with candid candour both of heart and of aspect,[1] like a flower, like a maid, like a star. As I gazed upon his awful young whiteness, I had much ado to keep from trembling, so black and loathsome did appear the sin in which I lived. And, to conceal my misease, I asked my guide who this might be.

"Arthur Plantagenet, heir of the Lionheart, your duke, and your king:" says Barres.

This was the word which sufficed to show me my way. I did not even wait to think of anything more: but I simply went down on my knees, there, where I stood, looking earnestly toward my lord the king, until he noticed me and in his regal majesty came near me. To whom I said: "Lord King, deign to hear a traitor renounce treason, purging himself, promising as christian and belted knight to be your true man henceforward."

---

[1] "*candida candescens candore et cordis et oris.*" [Rolfe's note.]

II

THE BOOK CALLED THE BARGAINS AND BRAWLS OF REGAL ROBBERS

1. *About the Rebuff which Duke Arthur deigned to Hubert de Burgh*

Some sins resemble a bog. Your fine young man lightheartedly strolls in his life's fair meadow. Suddenly, he finds himself off the path and up to his middle in slime. To struggle to win through to the other side, is to court instant engulfment. To remain inactive, is to be engulfed more slowly. The only safe method is to retire, with as little ado as possible (excepting in the way of silent prayer, which ought to be extremely vigorous). Even when he regains foothold on the brink, his condition is nauseous and lamentable: for his garments reek with defilement, and foetid also is the very flesh of him. Long, indeed, is the time of his cleansing. And Hubert de Burgh was in such a predicament, when he was moved to purge his treason.

Duke Arthur treated me very kingly: but he by no means soothed me. I, on my side, boiled with contrition. He, on his side, cold as frost, severe with the awful rigour of a boy, let me know the foulness of my sin, the long pain of due penance. "Rise, Sir Stranger," says he, sharply; "and be secret: for We wish to hear more of this matter in a place which is not full of eyes and ears." Up I jumped, feeling as though my sire had cuffed me; and I stood by Barres, tingling, while Duke Arthur looked me through and through during a whole minute. Then he turned his back on me; and said a word to Sir Fulk the Flame, who instantly challenged the Frankish imp there to a bout of fisticuffs. And, when young Aloys (nothing loath to be seen engaging with one whom he evidently regarded as a paladin[1]) began to fight, the said Sir Fulk gave him such a welting that, anon, he was leaning breathlessly

---

[1] A chivalrous or heroic knight (*OED* OL).

and cheerfully against a tent-pole, letting a very bloody nose drip
away from his surcoat: for he lacked not pluck, then, but force and
agility and tenacity. But Duke Arthur, content to lose his company, dismissed Barres on an errand one way, and Sir Fulk on
an errand the other way, and himself conducted me to the tent
which was his in the quarter of the Armoricans.

He sat him up on his chair of state, lord of his presence and no
land beside,[1] observing me standing in silence before him, until
his messengers returned. I am a very old man: but I remember,
even now, that I was quite abashed, blinded, by the clean unwinking terrible glare of those childish eyes. Sir Fulk came, and Barres,
bringing Duchess Constance and Thouars and Roches and Saint-
Pol. Duke Arthur put his mother on his own seat; and stood
beside her, with the Lord of Cuigny also on the dais at his right
hand. The four knights ranged themselves below, two on a side.
I knew that I was to be tried before the king in privy council. "Sir
Stranger," says Duke Arthur, "be pleased to rehearse, before these
present, the words which you have lately spoken." I, in a mood to
humour a solemn youngster, said my little piece again. Duchess
Constance battered her knees, and would have spluttered much
loud talk. I came to the step of the dais, kneeling, expecting Duke
Arthur to put out his hands for my homage. And I began to glow
with gladness in my mind: for I was deciding to disclose King
Richard Lionheart's secret, and to earn thereby no small credit,
when once I should have been taken into favour. As for Softsword
and the matter of my embassage to King Philip, I was not thinking of them at all. But the inflexible child moved not. "Sir Traitor,"
says he, simply, "be pleased to let Us know who you are and how
came you hither." I confess that my stomach began to move: but
I kept my patience while I answered him. I was known by his
knights; and they nodded assent to my words, from time to time.
Duke Arthur required them each in turn to deliver an opinion,
when I had made an end of speaking. Says Barres: "It is known
how King Richard esteemed this knight; and it seems that the earl
of Mortain makes much of him, in sending him as ambassador
to King Philip." Says Saint-Pol: "A knight, who slips into treason

---

[1] "*sui dominator sed nullae dicionis dominus.*" [Rolfe's note.]

as easily as a cockroach into an ale-cask,[1] ought to prove himself
a true man by certain ideals." Says Thouars: "It would be a fine
thing to make King Philip ware of how slight a hold Softsword has
upon his lieges: for, so, the Frank would be drawn more closely
to our side." Says Roches: "I would use Sir Hubert de Burgh for
persuading Earl John of Mortain: for surely it is better to come to
an agreement with the English than with the Franks." Says Duchess Constance, gushing out words no longer to be restrained:
"O Lord God, my boy, my Arthur, my fair son, my life, my joy,
my food, my all-the-world, my widow-comfort, and my sorrow's
cure, break not thy mother's heart, but seize and use whatever
weapon may come first to hand."[2] Duke Arthur quieted her with a
cold gesture; and there was silence in the tent, while he pondered
these opinions. Strange and terrible it was, to see one of his tender
years so self-contained, so grave, so competent. I remember that
Sir Fulk put his arm round his cousin's neck; and I was ware that,
whatever Duke Arthur's mind might be, Sir Fulk's would follow
it. This was the first time when I saw the tremendous force of the
alliance of these two imps, the one as severe as frost, the other
as perfervid[3] as flame, both acting as one. Says Duke Arthur, at
length: "Go, Sir Traitor, in peace; and purge your treason, acting
discreetly for Us in the train of Our well-beloved uncle, the Earl
of Mortain. This done, We shall be willing to hear more of you."
Sir Fulk nodded: Duchess Constance swallowed her own breath
hardly: the knights, who knew their master, made no sign at all.
But I was thoroughly angry, that my good intention should be
thus cruelly rebuffed; and I rose from my knees speechless with
indignation that a prim little whippersnapper[4] (so, Heaven pardon
me, I thought of the Regal Majesty) should slap my face in this
manner. And I retired, as proudly as possible, followed by Barres
to whom I did not say one word, making my way in silence to the
place appointed for my meeting with the Frankish ambassador.

---

[1] *"tanquam blatta cereuisiae in uas."* [Rolfe's note.]
[2] *"Ho Dompnedez, ho puer mi, Arthure mi, ho gnate mi formose ho zoe mea, ho laetitia,
ho mihi cibe, ho uiduae consolator mihi, ho aegrae medicina mihi,"* etc. [Rolfe's note.]
[3] Ardent or impassioned (*OED* OL).
[4] *"catulaster priscus et morosior."* [Rolfe's note.]

II. *About Hubert de Burgh the Salutary Slapping of his Face*

While I went, my fury cooled; and I formed a saner judgment.
It seemed to me that Duke Arthur's sentence was not quite unreasonable. It was cruel: but then the sin of treason is an awful one,
incalculably damning to the honour of a knight. I had expected
to be welcomed with open arms, because my contrition was true
and my intention genuine. But, whereas my dear lord King Richard (being a man) could read his man as easily as a clergyman
reads a book, my lord Duke Arthur was but a child, and I myself
was young enough to be fool enough to look in him for that facility of judgment which age and experience alone can give. Rather
should I have been thankful that he was prudent beyond his years.
And, as for the smarting weals, wherewith his distrust had seared
me, it behoved me to endure them manfully. What was I, after all,
but a traitor, self-confessed, smirched in my honour? What right
had I even to dream of being taken into favour, till I had done
deeds deserving favour? Thus, then, I admonished myself, arriving at certain decisions. I became thankful that I had been denied
an opportunity of delivering myself of King Richard Lionheart's
secret. That, I would reserve, for the salving of my wounded
pride: for I was malignant enough to hug the thought that Duke
Arthur had deprived himself of a great benefit in rejecting me;
and I decided to hold the said secret against the time when he
should look more favourably upon me. Also, I decided to remain
in Softsword's service, as I had been bidden, and to work secretly
therein on every safe occasion for the comfort and solace and prerogatives of Duke Arthur. In brief, I decided to do my duty, to
render implicit obedience to my liege lord, conscientiously, but
not enthusiastically. Just that. No more. The fervour of my heart
was frozen; and I shut up my bowels of compassion. O manners.

III. *About Hubert de Burgh and the Ambassador of the King of the Franks*

The Frankish ambassador was an excessive and garrulous
knight, chiefly eyebrows, moustaches, and shoulders. It seemed

good to me to encourage him to say his piece first, in order that I
might criticize it afterward, obtaining for my lords (the right one
and the wrong) whatever might be obtainable and fit to be mentioned to them. He came prepared to propose terms. He said that
Duke Arthur was a bone of contention. But for that imp, England
and France might couch side by side like lambs or lions, I forget
which. Still, there he was. And France was in honour bound to
see that he had his rights. What rights? Who could lie so foully
in a hairy throat as to deny to Arthur the duchy of Armorica?[1]
Did anyone covet that bleak domain of sounding sea and rugged
rock and devil-frequented dolmens[2] and ridiculous rustics whose
speech was something between the barking of bitches, the booming of bitterns, and the yells of the eternally-damned?[3] Ho, but
no, by the Back of God which He demonstrated to that holy
bishop Messire Saint Moses on Sinai.[4] Let it be freely admitted
that Arthur was Duke of Armorica. What, then, should we say of
Acquitaine and Poictou and Maine and Touraine and Normandy
and England? Let us be honest men and say this. King Philip the
August, that singularly pious christian prince, urgently yearned
to obey one of the sacred evangels where it was written that
we ought to love our neighbours. Was there a caitiff[5] anywhere
wicked enough to impede so admirable affection? Ho, but no, for
example. But rather let us strive to find for King Philip a neighbour worthy of his love. England? Anyone, who nourished a predilection for a people whose tails hung down behind,[6] might have
England. It was too far away for King Philip to consider. Acquitaine? Was a duchy held by Queen Alianora, that stark female,[7]
who had done homage for it to King Philip; and it did not come
into the question. Remained, then, only Anjou, Maine, Touraine

---

[1] Arthur was declared Duke of Brittany at the age of seven.

[2] Dolmens, also referred to as cromlechs, are prehistoric structures consisting of
a large stone supported by two smaller, upright stones (OED OL).

[3] The people of Armorica, or Brittany, spoke Breton, a Celtic language.

[4] "And again he said: Thou canst not see my face: for man shall not see me and
live. . . . [T]hou shalt see my back parts: but my face thou canst not see" (Exod.
33:20-23).

[5] A wretched, miserable person (OED OL).

[6] "quorum a tergis dependebant caudae." [Rolfe's note.]

[7] "Ducatus ista femina Alianora improba Regina habitus." [Rolfe's note.]

and Normandy. Supposing that Duke Arthur had them, as the Lionheart's nephew and heir: was not King Philip the warden of that white child[1] and his overlord also? And what more commodious than that the warden should administer the ward's domains? That, in effect, would be as though they were King Philip's, if so be that the said mere child would do homage for them. Also, let us suppose that Duke Arthur should elect to ascend to the superiors during his minority: would not his said fiefs revert to his overlord? But, after all, what was a mere white child? What use, as an ally to his neighbour, as a liegeman to his lord? A mighty prince like Philip the August, a Mars in war, a perfect Titus in generosity,[2] preferred (for his neighbour and ally) a prince as powerful and as pious as himself. Where, then, could such an one be found? Ho, where, for example? Now let us speak of Duke Arthur's uncle, that renowned amiable polished paladin whose virtue and whose valour had gotten him the crown of England. Let us speak of King Philip and King John. Ought not joyful tears to spout[3] from the eyes of all contemplating that pair of prodigious potentates sitting side by side on thrones, billing and cooing each to other like doves in the Sacred Scriptures? Was it not the bounden duty of every christian knight to conspire for so blissful an alliance. Ho, but yes, ten thousand times. Then, let all men forthwith labour to remove stumbling-blocks besetting the road which led to so laudable a consummation. King Philip would recognize King John in the fief of Acquitaine on the death of the present tenant: he would confer the fief of Touraine now, and also the fief of Normandy, excepting that absurd little parcel of land called the Volquessin which everyone knew to be Frankish by prescription. Could any prince be more generous than Philip? Could any other prince be more affable and apt to affairs than John? Then, thus, we conclude the whole matter; and Duke Arthur could be compensated by investiture with those unimportant fiefs called Anjou and Maine. Thus, also, Christendom might be enabled to sit down

---

[1] *"istius candidi pulli custos."* [Rolfe's note.]
[2] The emperor Titus was known for his generosity. He once complained that he had lost a day because he had allowed twenty-four hours to pass without giving a gift.
[3] *"emicare."* [Rolfe's note.]

comfortably to a spectacle of lovely peace among peoples, exquisite comity among princes, unblemished honour among knights.
Amen. Selah.[1] Hallelujah.

Having heard this rhodomontade[2] to the very end, and having
satisfied myself as to the essential turpitude of the Frankish
plans, and having perceived that Duke Arthur was not menaced
by any immediate danger, I responded, saying, that I would lay
the matter before my master, and take his mind thereupon. The
Frankish ambassador returned to Le Goulet: I, to Boutevant.

Softsword gnashed his clay-coloured teeth[3] when he heard my
news. "Nails of God,"[4] says he, "I will have all which my father
and my brother had, and France as well." And he made his intention known. O manners.

IIII. *About two Spiders and one Fly*

King Philip retorted on John with open war, advancing from
Evreux and capturing Conches the castle of the lords of Tosny. He
also took, and began to dismantle, the castle of Ballon in Maine.

This gave William Roches food for thought, he being seneschal
of Duke Arthur's castles, of which Ballon was one. If the Frank
would deal thus arbitrarily with Ballon, what hope had Duke
Arthur of justice in other matters? So Roches sent secret letters to
Softsword, praying him to make terms favourable to his nephew.

Sweetly, demurely, Softsword responded, like the wolf in
Red-ridinghood's grandmother's bed.[5] His heart grieved that the
Lionheart's heir should place himself at the mercy of false Franks,
when a loving uncle yearned to do him right, taking up his cause
against all comers, and investing him with inheritances which he
now held merely nominally. And Roches, that dull-witted drivel-
ling doodle,[6] foolishly deceived by these blandishments, instantly

---

[1] "Selah" is a Hebrew word often found at the end of a verse in the Psalter. The
term is used to indicate a pause or a break.

[2] A brag or a boast (*OED* OL).

[3] "*frendebat Mollensis dentibus eius luteis.*" [Rolfe's note.]

[4] "*Unguezdez.*" [Rolfe's note.]

[5] "*tamquam lupum in auiae lecto puellae purpureae paenulatae.*" [Rolfe's note.]

[6] "*stolidus et bardus blennus.*" [Rolfe's note.]

came in with Duke Arthur, accompanied by Duchess Constance and Thouars, surrendering the fly to quite the worst of spiders, with the city of Le Mans as a sop for winning favour. For which fatuity, Roches is severely to be blamed: for he acted against Duke Arthur's will, and against the advice of Barres and Saint-Pol whom he left behind (with Sir Fulk fil-Richard) in the camp of the Franks. O times.

But Softsword, elated by the easy success of his wile, acted imprudently. When Duke Arthur rode in, about dusk, his uncle greeted him with strident yells of laughter barely concealing threats. Nor was ducal accommodation prepared. And, at supper, John bellowed, boosing,[1] as though to nerve himself for the commission of crime. But, if this was his intent, he over-reached himself: for he became so tipsy that he fell under the table in a torpor, foaming greenly at the mouth. Duke Arthur, then, seeing his mother's terror and horror, bade Roches to conduct the party back to the Frankish camp, saying (in the words of the adage), *Better the devil you know than the devil you don't.*

v. *About our lord Pope Innocent*

One way of knowing what a man will do, is to find out the secret which he nourishes in the recesses of his mind, and to use it precisely as one uses an ordinary thumb-screw. I knew King Philip's: and I knew Softsword's: had I been older and wiser, I should have looked further afield.

Our lord Pope Innocent, in Whose holy hand were all princes and peoples then, also had a ruling passion: for He desired nothing in the world so much as to deliver the Holy Land from the bonds of Saracen[2] infidels. Had I been ware of this, I should have known what to expect. I should have known that the said Lord Innocent would come between Philip and John, to prevent them

---

[1] Drinking or boozing. John did have a reputation as a drunkard. In the *Flores Historiarum*, John is described as a lush who devoted all the hours of the night to drinking and then slept late into the day.

[2] The term "Saracens" was used by Greeks and Romans to refer to the nomadic people of the Syro-Arabian desert. However, during the crusades, the term "Saracen" simply meant Muslim and became synonymous with "infidels."

from wasting (in war among themselves) the powers which He would prefer to use in a crusade. As it was, however, I was much astonished when the lord cardinal Peter of Capua suddenly appeared with power to place a truce between the two. What I thought then, I am quite sure of now, namely, that our lord the Pope was ignorant of Duke Arthur's merits and of the justice of his claims. This, no doubt, was due, as much to King Richard's soft-footed panther-like way of making his dispositions, as to the superb maidenly reticence of Duke Arthur. For my dear lord the king never shrieked his wrongs to the celestial constellations. He took ill-fortune, as he took good-fortune, in silence, setting his teeth in toleration till the gods of his stars became benignant. Many misfortunes he bore alone, when a word would have set lovers flying to his succour: yet he never said the word. Afterward, when Pope Innocent knew my lord the king, he did him justice. But, at this time, the end in view was not the defence of the oppressed but the reconciliation of enemies. O times. Cardinal Peter, therefore, made this treaty between the Wild Ass and the Frankish king. Philip agreed to recognize John as heir to all King Richard's domains. John agreed to do homage to Philip for these, and to pay him a feudal relief of twenty-thousand marks. As for Duke Arthur, he was to do homage to his uncle for his own duchy of Armorica and for the palatine earldom of Richmond in England. Thus, thieves (as usual) were to be comforted at the cost of the honest. O lepers. Why did the oppressors of the fatherless and the widow so eagerly cease from ravening each against other? Because their own embarrassments made such meekness desirable. Softsword's captain of cotterels, Mercadet, had just contrived to get himself assassinated;[1] and a leader, whom mercenaries will follow (and obey) is not to be found in every corner. King Philip, too, was glad to please the Pope in this matter: for he hoped, in return, to be treated leniently in regard to his matrimonial entanglements. O manners.

---

[1] Mercadier, the captain of a band of Brabançon mercenaries, was in the service of both Richard and John. He was slain by a rival mercenary captain while escorting Eleanor of Aquitaine as she returned from Spain.

VI. *About our lord Pope Innocent His pontifical Methods with Rascals*

But ill deeds never prosper for long. Our lord Pope Innocent, having won one step, promptly proceeded to the next, threatening to lay an Interdict[1] on France, unless King Philip would dismiss Lady Agnes and cohabit with Lady Ingebiorg his lawful wife. From which the fat Frank might have learned that even his new ally, Softsword, could not prevent his ground from being cut away under his very feet. The same Softsword projected himself back to England, in search of those twenty-thousand marks which he was vowed to pay to Philip. It was not his custom to touch his own treasure (that is to say King Richard's, which he was stealing from Duke Arthur and the German Hottho) while any sheep remained for him to shear. And, also he had to settle the affair of William the Lyon. So, coming to Westminster, he imposed a new tax of three shillings on each hide of land in England; and he tried to entice the Scots king southward to York. He brought Archbishop Geoffrey with him in brotherly friendship; and fancied that all would go well. But all went quite ill. William the Lyon would not come to be eaten. Every Cistercian monk in the kingdom got up at once and coughed horribly[2] at the new tax: for they affirmed, and rightly, that not any king but only the General Chapter of their Order had the right to demand their dues. The Wild Ass kicked out, and snorted a sentence of outlawry, forgetting that he was banishing the realm's best graziers and woolmen. But the Primate Walter was ware of it; and he tickled Softsword's palm with a present of a thousand marks just to let him see reason. The monks, however, had taken fright; and were conspiring for their own protection. Moreover, a comic consequence ensued, to the stupor of everybody and the deep delight of many.[3] For Archbishop Geoffrey, who came back so sweetly with Softsword, detested Archbishop Walter; and, seeing that Primate supporting

---

[1] An interdict debars a country (or an individual) from ecclesiastical functions and privileges.

[2] "*surgebant et modo horribili tussiebant.*" [Rolfe's note.]

[3] "*cum omnium stupore plerorumque alta delectatione.*" [Rolfe's note.]

the new tax, he promptly skipped[1] to his northern archbishopric, fortifying himself in York Castle, whence he launched horrible censures and maledictions on all laymen who demanded taxes from clergymen. Him, however, Softsword fraternally paralyzed, by confiscating his temporalities.[2]

VII. *About Softsword his Matrimonial Excesses*

One diseased heifer will infect a herd. The king of the Franks played fast and loose with the sacrament of matrimony. What more natural, then, that his new friend should also demonstrate bestiality? Lady Havis fil-Robert, the Countess Gloucester, had been a good wife to Earl John since she came to him just marriageable, bringing him her rich earldom to add to his poor morsel of Mortain: for, at that time he had not the slightest chance of cutting a figure, excepting by marriage with an heiress. And she was said to be the mother of his sole legitimate heir the fatuous Henry Lackland. True, strict old Primate Baldwin (then reigning) opposed the nuptials on the ground of consanguinity in the fourth degree: but our lord Pope Celestine had granted a dispensation. And now, after some years, the Wild Ass went to wrong that wise woman (whose worth, above rubies, I, Hubert, have the very best reasons for knowing):[3] for he put her away, his tender conscience preferring a Primate's principles to a Pope's; and, more, he took Henry Lackland, for whom she had a singular affection, as a hostage to prevent her from becoming a nuisance.

This done, the dastard again pranced southward, seeking a new mate. The Queen-Mother Alianora also shot her bleared old eyes here and there, looking for dainty desirable partners for her darling. And what of the king of Portugal's sister? I myself was named ambassador to make that marriage.[4] But Softsword

---

[1] *"adsaltabat."* [Rolfe's note.]
[2] Material possessions owned by clergymen (*OED* OL).
[3] Hubert de Burgh married John's ex-wife, Isabella of Gloucester (Avisa) in 1217. She died soon after the wedding.
[4] John sent Hubert to persuade the king of Portugal to allow him to marry his daughter, but he married Isabella of Angoulême while Hubert was still on the way to Portugal.

pleased himself. Lady Jezebel[1] was daughter of Earl Adhemar of
Angoulesme, and betrothed to young Hugh le Brun of Lusignan, son of Earl Hugh of The March, that great crusader whose
brothers Guy and Amaury reigned as kings in Cyprus one after
the other. Also, she was a passionate precocious bold wicked
little hussy of twelve years,[2] when Softsword's bloodshot glance
lit on her. The earldom of Angoulesme could be changed into a
kingdom on one sole and simple condition, brays the Wild Ass
in her father's elongated ear. Dazzled by this idea, Earl Adhemar
instantly sent for a jeweller to make a crown of his old coronet;
and, meanwhile, he stole his own daughter from the Lusignans
who were breeding her for their young Hugh, and paid her to
John as the price of what he never got.[3] Bordeaux's archbishop
wedded the precious pair; and Softsword bore away the prize
which rendered his damnation sure. If, hitherto, Earl John had
ramped through England and France like an animal, hereafter he
raged like a hag-ridden devil. Young as she was, tender as she was,
tiny as she was, Lady Jezebel drove Earl John. Bishops and even
abbots strewed themselves unicorporeally before her, like reeds
in a roaring hurricane. Primate Walter cowered: but he crowned
her as queen-consort in the abbey of Westminster Hall. Both John
and Jezebel were mad with lust and utterly shameless. He infected
her with his frenzy. She, a mere slip of a girl, avidly responded,
a willing pupil, wallowing in new-gotten freedom, whetting his
appetite, leading him on. They heeded not what men thought of
them. She desired to be shewn: Softsword was proud to shew her.
Thus they went a-crown-wearing throughout all the kingdom, in
insolent scorn of decorum, defiant of sober opinion.[4] O manners.

---

[1] Isabella of Angoulême was not well liked, and she was referred to as malignant,
wicked, and, most often, as "Jezebel."

[2] "*et erat scortiuncula libidinosissima et praecoquis et dura et prava.*" [Rolfe's note.]

[3] John strengthened the French opposition to his claim when he divorced his wife
and married Isabella, who was twenty years his junior. Isabella had been betrothed
to Hugh de Lusignan, one of John's continental vassals. The Lusignans became
John's sworn enemies and called on Philip of France to help them avenge this
insult to their family. Philip used this affront as further ammunition against John.

[4] As Rolfe's representation of John and Isabella's marriage indicates, the union
was seen as suspect, disruptive, and decadent, serving as a fleshly distraction from
the king's political responsibilities.

VIII. *About the Progresses of Jezebel and her John*

First, they invaded Lincoln, setting at naught the tradition which prohibits kings from entering that city. They were not kings: but they pretended so to be; and, as such, in this case, I damn them. Three archbishops and thirteen bishops and twenty magnates bustled there to amuse them. O manners. Rumour was made to trumpet the Wild Ass's affability. He donated a new chalice (stolen from somewhere else) to the new minster which they were building. Great Saint Hugh of Avalon ascended to the superiors from the Old Temple by Holborn Bars in London: they brought his sacred relics to his episcopal tomb at Lincoln. Softsword put his own shoulder to that coffin, from the south gate to the new minster; and was not mercifully blasted, a much more horrible end being prepared for him. Walter the Primate, by way of being astute, took advantage of Softsword's mood to smoothen the matter of the Cistercians. He brought the whole parcel of their abbots to Lincoln, to say their pieces to Softsword. All went admirably. The Wild Ass conceded their liberties; and, more, he founded a new abbey for them at Beaulieu.[1] Encouraged by these delicious reports, not Scotland only but Wales also fell into line. William the Lyon, and Grwffydd Aprhys both came, under safeconducts, and did homage with certain wry grimaces: but the Scot got nothing of Northumbria.[2] The mood of the fickle Wild Ass changed; and he took to the road again with Lady Jezebel, sweeping through all the midlands, and up once more to the north, in the bitter wintry weather, burning with the heat of their passions. And, when a second time they came to Lincoln, Softsword must needs interfere with the canons electing their new bishop, the successor of Great Saint Hugh, so that the chapter sat

---

[1] The Cistercian abbots complained that the foresters were harming their cattle and pushing them out of the royal forests. John asked for their forgiveness and promised to build them an abbey for the good of his own soul, the souls of his parents, and the security of his kingdom.

[2] The Welsh and Scottish kings met with John at Lincoln, and William the Lion did homage to John but renewed his demand for Northumberland, Cumberland, and Westmoreland. John asked for more time to deliberate.

awfully still and refused to elect anybody. The pair pranced on,
across Humber to York, to be seen of Archbishop Geoffrey. Again
the half-brothers came to an agreement; and the elder (a born
fighter, wasted on an archbishopric) was left free to quarrel as
fiercely as he pleased, but only with his own clergymen: while
Softsword ramped onward, through Beverley and Scarborough
and Durham and Hexham and Bamborough and Newcastle, and
thence along the Roman's Road by Choller Ford on Tyne to Carlisle, where no Plantagenet had been seen for fifty years. And, so,
southward, for a great crown-wearing at Canterbury.

VIIII. *About Hubert de Burgh his Machinations*

What of England, while the usurper flaunted himself (a grown
man) with that beef-mouthed female child,[1] younger in years than
his own son, but old as himself in appetite, and perfectly insa-
tiable? This much, for certain. The people of England mistook the
Wild Ass which their eyes could see, for their King whom they
couldn't. And that was what Softsword intended. O poxy fox.

More, I know not: for I had to do my business daily while we
rushed from place to place, ordering the household, having an
eye to the camps of the hostages and of the mercenaries: no easy
matter, seeing that we travelled with a train equal in number to
the population of a city. And, beside, I never lost a single opportunity of snatching at things likely to serve the cause of Duke
Arthur. That I did my ostensible business beautifully, there can be
no doubt. Else, why did Softsword make me Shire-reeve of Dorset
and Somerset, Constable of the great castles of Dover and Windsor, and Warden of the V Ports, when it seemed that I merited
reward and needed a little vacation? These promotions suited me
well. I was ware, now, that I could not do anything by myself for
my lord the king: but I was ware, also, that by accumulating such
wealth and such power as accompanies possession of castles and
dignities, then, indeed, I might do some excessively notable purging of my treason. These things I pondered, while I lived a little
space with Lady Beatrix my wife in Dover Castle, going up and

---

[1] *"cum ista feminuncula cuius os carnis color bubulae habebat."* [Rolfe's note.]

down that coast to oversee my V Ports, and to take their gover-
nance firmly into my own hand. For, this was the lock on the gate
of England. And I was slowly but surely clutching the key of it.

x. About Softsword and a Nest of Hornets

The Wild Ass was about to engage in fresh plans: for he was not
unaware of the nest of hornets wherein he had planted his hoof.

The magnates of England and France were black in the
face with fury, because of the insults which Softsword habitually heaped upon their order. Especially the Lusignans burned
to avenge the wrong done to young Hugh le Brun. They were
arming to overrun Acquitaine. The haggish Queen-Mother
Alianora hardly could hold them in check. Softsword, therefore,
came southward to prepare pains for them. He issued writs to
his military tenants, ordaining instant assemblage at Portsmouth
for a foreign war. Had he approved himself in England, I suppose that a very mighty army would have followed him gladly.
But the case was otherwise. His frenetic progresses to and fro,
with so enormous a company, wasted and impoverished England.
Farmers sickened at farming their land solely for his locusts to
devour. And, as farmers could not pay their rents to their respective magnates, the said magnates refused to spend their hoards
and treasures on the fool whose fury spoiled them of those rents.
Moreover, there was one of Softsword's peculiar habits which
made him particularly unpopular. He had a nasty custom of confiscating the persons of heiresses, widows, orphans, minors, and
wards, wherever he found them; and these he sold, like cattle, to
anyone willing to pay him his price for pleasing pieces of flesh
or the seizin[1] of rich estates. For avarice was not the least of his
infamies. The English magnates, therefore, agreeing among
themselves at Leicester, sent Softsword a message, saying, that
Great Saint Hugh had pronounced no magnate liable for service
over-sea: wherefore they would not obey his writs of summons,
excepting as a favour, and not even as a favour unless he would
keep the oath which he swore to them[2] before the Primate Walter

---

[1] Possession (*OED* OL).
[2] "*nisi ille redderit eis iura sua.*" [Rolfe's note.]

at his coronation. By which artful threat, they of course intended to extort some new concessions for themselves. Now each magnate naturally had a power of his own tenants: but these powers were not used to acting united together; and no single magnate had a power anything like as great as the power which Softsword possessed in his mercenaries. Knowing this, he led his mercenary cotterels against one magnate at a time, compelling each in turn either to surrender his castle and begin life over again as a hermit or a mendicant, or to give hostages for his good behaviour. Nor was the Wild (but wily) Ass content with ordinary hostages: he would take nothing lower than a son, generally the heir, as he did from Earl William III d'Aubigny of Arundel, *gules, a lyon or*, for that one's castle of Belvoir.[1] Seeing themselves thus hideously lashed, the magnates scurried to heel at Portsmouth, all with their tails flapping most dejectedly low between their legs, and only to have insults piled upon their injuries. For Softsword had altered his mind; and, instead of accepting the service which they feverishly offered, he commuted it for a two-mark scutage,[2] and he also made them pay fines for this enforced commutation, nor did he release the hostages. In this way, he vastly increased his treasure, crushed the opposition of the magnates, and secured himself against rebellions.[3] Indeed he was a proper devil. But, at the same time, he was obliged to hire many more mercenaries: for the hostages became like a veritable monkish boarding-school, unmanageable in numbers, so that not a week passed without the escape of nine or nineteen. We lived in the midst of incessant alarums.

XI. *About Softsword his Expedition against the Lusignans in Poictou*

Softsword sent on in advance William Marechal and Roger Lacy with two hundred cotterels, to see to the security of Nor-

---

[1] After marrying Isabella, John took one hundred and fifty hostages from the noble families in order to exact good behavior from the nobility.

[2] A tax paid in lieu of military service (*OED OL*).

[3] The barons' privileges were becoming increasingly curtailed due to administrative changes that took place during Henry II's reign. At Leicester, the barons made their grievances known in hopes of reversing this trend, but John responded firmly, and the barons capitulated.

mandy. Hubert de Burgh he made Shire-reeve of Hereford, Warden of the Welsh March, and Constable of the Three Castles of Grosmont and Scenefrith and Candidachester with Monmouth, giving me a hundred picked cotterels to serve me in training my tenants. There was no end to the cunning of this beast. What could be more masterly than these his dispositions? But God made all his deeds to work together for his own damnation, specially this delicious quadrilateral of fortresses over which he set me: though, at the time, I was minded to curse him cordially, being unaware that he was preventing me from plucking my fruit before it was fully ripe. To pass the time, and to prevent myself from being spied upon by his men, I began by buying those hundred cotterels body and soul, paying them their own price, and attaching them to myself, all secretly.

Earl John set out for Normandy with Lady Jezebel, she brazen as a Scots wench who has gotten her man, and unashamed at carrying horrid war against her own kin. Normandy being quiet, they visited King Philip in amity at Les Andelys. That Frank's part was to cultivate this alliance; and he vacated his palace in Paris that his guests might lie regally. At Chinon, they encountered the Queen-Widow Berengere, penniless, accomplishing her fate in a convent, because Softsword was defrauding her of King Richard Lionheart's provision. It was not a time when the Wild Ass could afford to win ill-repute in France: so he consoled her with meaningless words and purely flocculent[1] promises[2] of a jointure worth a thousand marks annually, payable in halves from the English treasury at London and from the Norman treasury at Caen.[3] Then, he thought well to begin his war. Now the Lusignans had incited the Poictevin magnates to open rebellion. And Softsword planned to deal with them in a new and very wily manner. He offered to impeach them of treason, challenging each one to clear himself in turn by ordeal of battle. At the same time, he was privately buying expert and invincible and unscrupulous duellists, as his champions, for settling the little business pleasantly. But

---

[1] Resembling tufts of wool (*OED* OL).
[2] "*cum fidibus puriter floccis.*" [Rolfe's note.]
[3] John refused to pay Berengaria's pension after Richard's death. Pope Innocent finally threatened John with an interdict if he continued to refuse to pay.

the Poictevins perceived the snare; and refused it, coughing and sneering in a highly exasperating manner. So Softsword left them to his aged mother, to deal with them as best she could, till he had invented more diabolical plans. But he retired with his girl to Argentau in Normandy.

XII. *About Duke Arthur his Attraction for King Philip the August*

Duchess Constance brought forth Thouars his baby, whom she called Lady Alys; and incontinently ascended to the superiors. Thouars sent his said baby to the nuns of the hermitage at Brest for her breeding. And, because Duke Arthur was now an orphan indeed, whose step-father (Thouars) was a fussy lightminded knight, far too prone to consider his little comforts[1] before his little conscience—whose seneschal (Roches) also was perhaps the most shatterpated hoddy-doddy[2] between Thames and Loire, it was no more than natural that my lord the king should now be drawn into closer connection with King Philip. Moreover, that flabby Frank's private affairs took a turn just at this time; and certain important consequences ensued.

Lady Agnes of Meran, bored to death on account of her pseudo-matrimonial state of sin, sat up and got leave from our Lord the Pope to be properly buried at Pontigny; and she instantly died and was buried. Thus, a way was paved whereby King Philip might pass to reconciliation with Pope Innocent. The king made as though he would take back Lady Ingebiorg, his lawful wife. The Pope, willing not to make so holy a deed uneasy, offered to legitimate the Frank's bastards by Lady Agnes, as a favour. Philip, though the Interdict on his kingdom was highly inconvenient, showed himself rather artful than precipitately pious and penitent: but he let it be known that he was not disinclined to behave obediently. So, our lord the Pope, to encourage his admirable affections, raised the Interdict from France. Then, indeed, that fat Frank's hands were freed; and he was ware that he might do extremely well for himself by an alliance with Pope Innocent,

---

[1] *"uitae solatiunculos."* [Rolfe's note.]

[2] *"fungus et bucco erat super omnes homines inter Tamesim,"* etc. [Rolfe's note.] A "shatterpated hoddy-doddy" is a shatter-brained simpleton (*OED* OL).

and with the pontifical ally King Hottho of the Germans, who now was Elect-emperor of the Romans. Such an alliance, also, permitted him to indulge a more than friendly interest in Duke Arthur, and to dispense entirely with Earl John of Mortain. But he did nothing rashly; and waited an opportunity. One soon came.

XIII. *About the King of the Franks his new Motions in Despite of Softsword*

Softsword's spies warned him of matters in train against his peace. He instantly summoned me to his ear, desiring my best counsel, and giving me writs of nomination to another parcel of great offices as handsel[1] of greater rewards in store. In this way, I accumulated yet more power for my lord the king, as Shire-reeve of Cornwall and Buckinghamshire, Constable of the castles of Dunster and Wallingford and Launceston, and Steward of the Honour of Wallingford.

My little plan being to entice the Earl of Mortain to get himself into serious trouble, my rede[2] to him (on this occasion) was that he should not sit still to be smacked, but that he should make a motion of that particular kind which should force a declaration from his foes. He, therefore, seized the castle of Driencourt in Normandy belonging to Sir Ralf of Lusignan; and summoned the tenants of The March to do him service, in despite of their allegiance to Earl Hugh of Lusignan. Those two magnates of course retorted promptly, lodging appeals with the king of the Franks, the lord-paramount of the lot of them. King Philip the August threw off his mask with a loud bang.[3] He required three frightful things of the Wild Ass as his vassal, namely, that he should surrender Normandy and Anjou and Poictou to Duke Arthur, appear in person at Paris to respond to certain charges, and submit himself to the judgment of the Frankish magnates his peers. This was all as it should be: but it set Hubert de Burgh thinking. And I concluded that a knight, who also is king of the English, has his hands full enough, and that it is better by far that such a king should

---

[1] A gift given as a pledge of what is to follow (*OED* OL).

[2] Advice (*OED* OL).

[3] "*strepitantissime.*" [Rolfe's note.]

hold no fiefs of France as a knight, rather than risk so awful an indignity from a king of the Franks desiring to show himself hairy.[1] To which counsel, I constantly adhere. When King Philip's insolent summons came, Earl John exploded with vociferous yellings and went mad. He was larking in the camp of the hostages at the time; and he instantly had the two nearest hanged on tentpoles then and there, to terrify the others by their convulsive jumpings, for he had them hanged slowly, and to let the Frankish herald and pursuivants[2] see how he defied his liege. They were little whimpering Lancashire boys of eleven years: I forget their names. And, when their thin legs stopped jerking, I found it desirable to make the Wild Ass dead drunk without delay, there being no other means of preventing him from offering regrettable violence to the said herald. But, in the morning, being unwell and all of a quiver, he replied most meanly to the summons, protesting that dukes of the Normans owed no service to the king of the Franks: but he did not omit to send me with Bishop Eustace of Ely, *gules, three open crowns two and one or,* to obtain a safe-conduct for him, being so worried that he contemplated crouching at the Frank's fat feet. Not that Earl John was a perfect coward: but he was without sense of honour or dignity, seeing no shame in whining or crawling when such currishness and caterpillarism[3] would serve his purpose. And he was ware that Poictou, though turbulent, was held for him by the Queen-Mother Alianora. King Philip, stern and pitiless because temporarily strong, said that Softsword's ancestors had been dukes of the Normans (and, as such, vassals of France) long before they became kings of the English. Did an overlord lose his rights because his vassal by chance obtained extra dignities? Ho no, by our Lady her lily. Moreover, he would only give a safeconduct for John's journey to Paris. As for his return, that would depend upon the judgment of his peers. Thus was Softsword slurred. Let me be quite plain. Philip was determined to have either John's person or his property, and both if possible: I wish to say that Philip's notion was to annihilate

---

[1] *"suam hirsutiam demonstrare."* [Rolfe's note.]

[2] Junior heraldic officers attendant on heralds or noblemen (*OED OL*).

[3] *"caninismus atque uermismus."* [Rolfe's note.] The term "caterpillar" was used figuratively to refer to a greedy person who fed upon society.

John, by law-process, by murder, or what-not, so that he might
have merely the child Arthur between him and the Angevin fiefs.
That John should be abolished, was (no doubt) extremely desirable. That Duke Arthur should be put quite at the Frank's mercy,
was not to be thought of for a moment. I, therefore, having got
him into a most devilish pickle, found it convenient not to act any
more against Softsword in this particular case. O times. Philip's
refusal of safeconduct, to go and to return, gave Softsword more
than an inkling of mischief intended. He, therefore, held aloof,
while the court of Frankish magnates in Paris festively adjudged
him contumacious[1] and absent and his fiefs forfeit to his overlord,
on account of his breach of feudal duty. But he cared nothing at
all. He lay at Rouen, oblivious of loss and of dishonour, triumph-
ing in the toils of Lady Jezebel as one bewitched, proud (indeed)
of her ever-increasing witchery, scorning all beside.

XIIII. *About the Knighting of Duke Arthur by the King of the Franks*

Philip proceeded, in awful and sinful pomp, through the
duchy of Normandy, with his power, capturing Softsword's
cities one after the other. All the Norman magnates joined the
said Frank, excepting Sir Hugh Gournay, *sable*, whom he had to
wash out of his castle by cutting the cisterns of it. In honour of
this exploit, King Philip knighted Duke Arthur there, giving him
solemn investiture of Armorica, and also of Anjou and Maine and
Touraine and Poictou when God should permit him to conquer
those domains. Furthermore, he betrothed my lord the king to
his daughter Lady Mary, *France*, she being four years old. Thus
free was the Frank with fiefs which he owned but did not hold. As
for newly-conquered Normandy, he intended to take that and to
keep it for himself.

And Softsword dawdled at Rouen with Lady Jezebel all this
time. But, when King Philip besieged Radeport on River Andelle,
only ten miles away from him, then, on the eighth day, John
jumped up and was done with his dalliance, chasing the Frank
and Duke Arthur back to Paris.

---

[1] Obstinately rebellious (*OED* OL).

III

THE BOOK CALLED THE WICKED UNCLE

1. *About Duke Arthur his malignant Misfortune at Mirabel*

King Philip and Duke Arthur lay at Paris, recollecting their powers. Earl John lay at Le Mans in Maine, a Wild Ass stiffening himself to be mischievous. The Queen-Mother Alianora, unable to hold Poictou any longer, haggishly[1] fortified herself at Mirabel, waiting for relief. Now Arthur yet had done no deed of arms.[2]

The king of the Franks led the bulk of his power to besiege Arques, taking with him Sir Fulk fil-Richard and his wardens: but to Duke Arthur he gave two hundred mounted men-at-arms, instructing him to ride southward to join the Lusignans in Poictou, waging war there upon Softsword. The boy obeyed: but first he ridded himself of Roches, bidding that fatuous beetle-brained old seneschal[3] to betake himself with a warning to the Wicked uncle then trespassing in his earldom of Poictou. This, Roches did, making matters worse. But Duke Arthur launched his power against Mirabel, to deal righteously with Softsword's most dangerous partizan. The Queen-Mother Alianora, despite her eighty years, had a fit of Angevin[4] anger at her grandson's approach: even her abbots avoided her, she being very particular in her maledictions. And, having taken into her castle four respectable burgesses of Mirabel with their entire families, she chose a son from each, whom she sent (with secret news of her plight) to Earl John, bidding them to return with him and his power on

---

[1] *"aniculariter."* [Rolfe's note.]

[2] *"Arthurus enim uirtutem suam in armis nondum demonstrauerat."* [Rolfe's note.]

[3] *"fatuum seneschallum mentis inopem sicut blattam."* [Rolfe's note.]

[4] The Angevin, or Plantagenet, family had a reputation for being short-tempered and passionate.

the fourteenth day, on pain of seeing all their relations dangling by their necks like a fringe from her battlements. One fulfilled his task: three met death by the way. Duke Arthur made short work of her town; and even captured her castle: so that his cankered grandam became closely besieged in the keep. But, being a novice at war, the objurgations of his captive sounded so sweetly in his ears, that he needs must linger in her vicinity; and, instead of making dispositions to protect his rear, sending out scouts to warn him of inimical approaches, and providing an open road for retreat should such become necessary, he took his whole force into the castle, and sat down to the investment of the keep. Then, the Wild Ass erupted.

Softsword had an overwhelming power of Flemish mercenaries, under Sir William Braose lord of Brecon, *barry of six, vair, ermine and gules and argent*. This magnate was one of the greatest in England: his noble wife was Lady Maud of The Haye: his daughter married Sir Walter Lacy, *quarterly, or and gules, a bend sinister sable, with a difference*: his sister's son was Earl of Derby, *vair, or and gules*. Softsword trusted him implicitly; and he marched this power the hundred miles from Le Mans to Mirabel in a night and a day, trapping his mother's besiegers like sparrows in a net.[1] Duke Arthur was pinned between two powers. Here, was his haggish grandmother, screeching like a hoarse old owl, in the keep. There, was his wicked uncle, whooping with hideous hollow laughter, outside the castle-walls. Braose summoned him to surrender. There were no means of sending to King Philip for reinforcements. Ensued an abominable scene with the prisoners. Conceive that inveterate warrior Geoffrey of Lusignan, brother of King Guy, fettered by the violator of Lusignan honour. Conceive his nephew, young Hugh le Brun, dragged in chains to inspect his perjured betrothed Lady Jezebel, lolling in Softsword's lap. Conceive my lord the king delivered by Braose to the mercies of his wicked uncle. All the way from Le Mans to Mirabel, Roches had been making himself a nuisance, demanding pledges from Softsword for Duke Arthur's security.

---

[1] When Arthur laid siege to the castle where Eleanor was hiding, John marched quickly to her rescue, covering eighty miles in forty-eight hours, and in turn captured Arthur.

He had done the same at Boutevant. Pledges had been given, and belied. Yet the unteachable old zany did it again. The Wild Ass willingly gave him all the pledges in the world, not weighing words, not demurring from anything: for words could not bind John. When, then, Roches saw his duke a prisoner, and how the wicked uncle seemed inclined to treat him, he pattered piteous petitions for the fulfilment of these pledges. If the matter had not been very grave, I should have laughed when I saw Softsword denying him: for he looked more like a just-sheared sheep, bleating its first baa-a-ah, than any knight ought at any time to look. For he stamped once or twice with his fore-foot, and butted at nothing in particular; and then he trotted off to seek a pasture with King Philip, preternaturally solemn, and with his mind absolutely blank. I have never known why Softsword did not slay him then, to prevent him from making mischief. Considering John's condition, such slaughter of a Frankish knight (who was no tenant of his) would of course have been extremely irregular; and, for that precise reason, I expected it. But, as Softsword habitually cultivated motley in his crimes, I can only surmise that his omission to kill Roches, or at least to fork his tongue, was due to absence of mind in the excitement of the moment. For Softsword was elated beyond measure at the success of his scoop. A long train of country-carts containing chained captives trailed away from Mirabel. Some prisoners were interned in Norman castles: others, in castles in England. Of the last, twenty-two knights were slowly starved to death in the regal castle of Corfe, where Softsword (on his return) spent several hours each day in inspecting their agonies.[1] He took a great fancy to this castle, and enlarged it, and delighted in living there; and he made it his treasury and his chief dungeon on account of its strength. He held very few of his prisoners to ransom: for he valued the spectacle of brave knights in lingering torments even more than riches. He was not a good man, ever.

But he sent Duke Arthur to the castle of Falaise, in charge of Hubert de Burgh.

---

[1] The twenty-two knights starved to death by John in the castle at Corfe were loyal to Eleanor, Arthur's sister, who was also imprisoned at Corfe.

11. *About Hubert de Burgh and his prisoner Duke Arthur*

When King Philip the August had heard the news from Roches, he savagely raided Touraine and burned Tours: but Earl John came up and ate his garrison. The Frank returned to Paris, much pained. Softsword capered through Anjou and Maine.

Despite his success at Mirabel, all was not going quite nicely with the Wild Ass. He was losing allies. King Hottho of the Romans was howling for payment of the Lionheart's legacy; and John's bath of lust and crime (in which he wallowed like a black duck in a stable cesspool) blinded him to the important law that a villain must not be villainous to villains who support him in his villainies. Beside the disagreeableness of Hottho, Earl Baldwin of Flanders, *or, a lyon sable, within a bordure gules,* ran away to become Emperor of Romania and to avoid his creditors: while Earl Reinald Dampmartin of Boulogne, *or, three torteaux gules,* sickened so awfully at the outrageous flaunting of Lady Jezebel that he defied John and joined himself to King Philip. Furthermore, old Roches was convening (at Angers) the bishops and magnates of Armorica; and these, with one voice, screamed for the release of their Duke Arthur.

My lord the king was the easiest prisoner whom I have ever held. He lived as regularly as a clergyman, preferring privacy and silence, not hiding or secluding himself, but moving among us all in the castle of Falaise as though we were walls or not there. A prince imprisoned usually intrigues with friends without, or buys new friends within, or bribes the constable who keeps him close to take a nap. I kept ceaseless but unnotable watch upon Duke Arthur; and I know that neither word nor sign from him went out, not even to Sir Fulk the Flame, and no sign or word came in, not even from Sir Fulk fil-Richard the Flame. My heart bled for the stern stony loneliness of that white child. Not that I let him see how I pitied and loved and adored him. Not that I gave him any inkling of how hot I was to serve and worship him. He never looked at me: he very rarely spoke to me. I seemed to be merely a piece of the wall which imprisoned him, within which he was content to live, serenely, tranquilly, healthily, exercising himself all day in a weird and wonderful manner neither English nor Frankish, making himself as wiry and as lithe and as agile as a kitten or a bird, whose motions are so swift and unexpected that man's eye fails to follow them. And, at night, he slept like a child: for he was but a child, careless, fearless, not even concerned or aware of the peril of his plight. As for Hubert de Burgh, my fault, my fault, my very great fault, it must be written that I continued in the sin of anger, because of my lord the king's indifference to me. I confirmed my secret vow that, while no harm should come to the Regal Majesty, I being his warden, yet, I would not aid him, as I yearned to aid him, until he should treat me less severely. For, be it known, that, at this time, I was able to aid him most signally, having my ten castles with their garrisons beside my five counties wherewith to enforce him. God, be merciful to Hubert de Burgh, a sinner.

III. *About Softsword his Coming to Gloat and his Staying to Incite to Crime*

Earl John of Mortain came one day to visit his captive. Duke Arthur amazed me more than ever. He treated Earl John as a loving nephew treats a loving uncle, whom he sees but seldom, on account of some regrettable family feud, in which neither of them are at all interested. He made no plaint about the wrongs which he was tolerating so superbly. His manner was easy and princely. Indeed, it was said afterward that John might have been the prisoner and Arthur the lord of the castle. For Softsword slank uncomfortably here and there, like a wild ass in a courtyard, lashing his tail, twitching his ears, whispering in corners with Lady Jezebel. That slut did not leave him for a moment. She never left him. There was not one motion of hers, or of his, which did not signify desire to cling and to be clung to. There was not one moment when they ceased from eating each other with eyes and hands. And Duke Arthur played the courteous modest host to these incontinent devils his guests.

Softsword, on arriving, screwed a word out of himself to mutter to me. "By God's Teeth, Hubert," says he, "I am nigh ashamed to say what good respect I have of you."[1,2]

It was not a saying which needed a response. Later, when his train was collecting for departure, he muttered in my ear again. Duke Arthur stood not very far away, wrapped in his ermine cloak, viewing the horses of the knights with a slightly eager air. Says Softsword to me, snarling horribly, but earnest: "Good Hubert, Hubert, Hubert, cast an eye on yon young boy. I tell you this, my friend, that little fellow is a serpent which obstructs my way; and wheresoever this foot of mine shall tread, he lies before me. Do you understand me, you, who are his keeper?"[3] "I understand," says I, "and I'll so keep him that he will not lack a faithful keeper."[4] "Enough:" says Softsword: "now, I shall have peace, although I am not yet laid in my grave: for they say, Hubert, that only in the grave there's peace."[5] And so he went, leaving my brain buzzing with his incoherent and indelible sayings. Always we had to trace his beastly meanings through a maze of words.

When the gate was shut, young Bobo Kemp, my page, son of one of my best tenants at Candidachester and a faithful-minded clean-eyed lad, said to me that Lady Jezebel—he called her the queen, and was smacked[6] for it—had spoken previously to Earl John when he joined her in the litter, desiring sudden evils for someone, and urging her man to do violences. "Crush the root, or cut it out," says

---

[1,2,3,4,5] All this, of course, is simply Shakespeare, more or less. We have no grounds for asserting that Shakespeare could never have seen any of Hubert de Burgh's manuscript, nor are we competent to discuss the point. But, whether Shakespeare owes anything to Hubert de Burgh or not, we humbly venture to think that our version fairly represents the sense of the Latin here appended.—P. and C. [Rolfe's note.] Here Rolfe reproduces almost verbatim lines from Shakespeare's *King John*. For example, in *King John*, John praises Hubert by stating, "By heaven, Hubert, I am almost ashamed/To say what good respect I have of thee." For further discussion of the circumstances surrounding Arthur's imprisonment and murder and Rolfe's use of sources such as Shakespeare's *King John*, see the introduction to this edition.

[2] *"Denzdez Huberte dicit me paene pudet dictu quanti te faciam."* [Rolfe's note.]

[3] *"ho probissime Huberte oculum Huberte adjce pusioni iste Huberte. tibi ego hoc dico amice instar anguis in uia mihi obstat paruulus iste ubicumque hic pes meus ingrediatur ibi est et ille. Intelligisne tu qui es custos eius?"* [Rolfe's note.]

[4] *"capio inquam et illum ita custodiam ut fidus custos illi non desit."* [Rolfe's note.]

[5] *"satis dixisti respondebat Mollensis ita mihi pax erit quamquam adhuc non sepulto dicunt enim Huberte pacem non nisi in sepulchro extitere."* [Rolfe's note.]

[6] *"alapasque tolerabat."* [Rolfe's note.]

she, "that the branch may wither, nor bear fruit to set our teeth on edge." And, "Stamp out the light, at least," says she, "so that he may not see to strike us." Awful words. When I had dismissed my page, I sat and sweated all by my lone during four hours; and my hair kept on slowly standing straight up and sitting down again, all that time. After which, I cursed with all my might, until I vomited. For those horrible sayings of the jade, coming along with Softsword's mysterious snarlings, assured me that a certain unspeakable danger was menacing Duke Arthur. Strong reasons make strong actions. So I ate a pudding; and I set myself to guard him much more closely. For, notwithstanding his accursed frigidity to me, I had my own knightly honour to care for.

IIII. *About one of the Wickednesses of the Wicked Uncle*

On the eighth day, verifying my foreboding, came Querdelours and Piedechien, cotterels of Softsword, with a secret warrant for me to permit the cauterization of Duke Arthur's eyeballs. O manners.

I decided that nothing of that kind should be done: but I knew that it behoved me to be very wily about not doing it. What ruled all my plans was, that I wished Duke Arthur of his own free will to take me into his comity. Not for a king's ransom would I force him: not for the Pope's own eye would I see him harmed; and I was certain that his terrifying innocence and helpless youth alone would suffice to tame any sort of ruthless ruffian who might be sent to wrong him. It was plain, then, that (if I intended to remain of Softsword's company, for the benefit of Duke Arthur, till my lord the king should deign to condescend to me), I ought not to resist these cotterels openly, but rather (by some stratagem) cause them to evade their job. And the finest stratagem which I could think of was to confront them with the splendour of their intended victim. Therefore, with no fuss, I accompanied them to the torture-chamber to prepare their tools for the work which was not to be done. There was difficulty about finding a fork of convenient size: for men are more frequently blinded than boys; and a fork whose prongs are far enough apart to sear neatly (being red-hot) the eyeballs of a man, would be too wide for a boy's, and, indeed, would inflict very unsightly wounds where scars are neither desirable nor necessary. But the prongs of an ordinary fork were reduced to a suitable width by heat and a hammer; and having packed a brazier with glowing charcoal round and about the said prongs, I concealed the two cotterels behind the arras of my own chamber, ready (as they thought) to do their deed, but really (as I knew) to see their victim and, on sight, to convert themselves. To which chamber, I caused Duke Arthur to be summoned.

He came in, all unaware of the work toward; and "Good morrow, Hubert," says he, coldly, but not unkindly. "Good morrow, little prince,"[1] says I, looking upon him stonily.

He waited, having nothing to say to such an one as me, but giving me free leave to speak to him. I also waited, that the cotterels might mark well that delicate brave imp whom they were due to mutilate: but I did not wait too long, lest my stomach should master my wits and spoil my stratagem. But I presented to my lord the king the warrant of his wicked uncle, that he might read it. And, at length, slowly says he: "You must with hot iron burn out both mine eyes?"[2] I answered not a word: but continued to look stonily. His steady voice went on. Says he: "My uncle practises this harm to me because he is afraid of me. It is not my fault that I am Geoffrey Longcheek's son. And I am set, whether I will or no, between that borrowed majesty of England which John Softsword holds and Philip the August. O dreadful discord of incensed kings. But, while I have my breath, I may not shunt one jot or tittle of my right: for I am I, however I was begot. Let, then, my uncle harm me, if he will. If Heaven be pleased that you should harm me, Hubert, be it so. Yet, I believe indeed that iron itself, red from the fire, would quench its flaming indignation in my innocence rather than sear my sight."[3] He paused. He

---

[1] *"salue tu dominule."* [Rolfe's note.]

[2] Cf. note to previous chapter. *"et exurendi sunt gemini oculi mei tandem et tarde dize ille."* [Rolfe's note.] Here again Rolfe follows Shakespeare very closely.

[3] *"hoc damno me affligit patruus quia timet me. non meum delictum est me ab Gioffredo de Longa Gena pullulari. nolens uolens inter Angliae regalitatem a Johanne Mollense tam false usurpatam et Philippum Augustum positus sum. o dira regum iratorum discordia. sed dum spiro iuris mei nihil nullo modo amittam ego enim ipsissimus ego semper ero quocumque modo genitus. noceat itaque patruus si nocere uult. si dis placet Huberte te mihi nocere fiat. ferrum ipsum tamen et a fornice rubrum credo equidem potius quam aciem meam crematurum flammeam eius sacuitiam in tantae aqua innocenti . . . extinctu. . . ."* [Rolfe's note.]

stood firmly, and quite still, disdaining to plead or to complain, the bravest loveliest male on earth, facing a frightful fate more dauntlessly than any other knight whom I have ever seen or even known. For it is very hard not to resist an ill. Even now, old as I am, I see those glittering young eyes which no fear could dim. I knew that enough had been seen, and said, to tame hearts however pitiless. I called the cotterels to disclose themselves.

They came from the arras, shambling, full of shame, grievously displeased, bringing the brazier and the fork. Piedechien, with downcast eyes, kneeled to blow the charcoal. Querdelours came nearer, with a cord to bind the boy's hands and legs: but he also eyed the ground very compunctiously.[1] Both thought me a perfect devil. As for me, I stood like a rock. Never have I known my lord the king to be afraid. Even then, slight and boyish as he was, he did not flinch. But the cotterels, and their cord, and the thought of the outrage of their touch on his sacred person, nauseated him; and he spoke out boldly in defence of his sacrosanctity. "How now," says he unblenching, "what need to be so boisterous rough? I will not struggle. I will stand stone-still. For Heaven's sake, Hubert, let them not bind me. Drive them away; and I will be as quiet as a lamb: I will not stir, nor wince, nor say a word, nor look upon the iron angrily. Thrust these men away; and I'll forgive whatever torment you shall put me to."[2]

Piedechien rose from his knees, breathing hard, and eyeing his fellow. Querdelours snatched the fork from the flame, and waved it in the air to cool it. The moment had come when I might safely dismiss them. "Go, stand without. Leave me alone with him:" says I. "I am best pleased to be from such a deed:" says Querdelours, going. "God blind my bloody soul if I should harm the child:" says Piedechien, going. And they went out, leaving me with their instruments before my lord the king.

We gazed at each other during several moments. Duke Arthur was trying to find out what I meant to do. I was trying to compel his mind to know what I wished to be to him, so that he might be gracious and use me as I would be used. The charcoal died in the

---

[1] Remorsefully (*OED* OL).

[2] We do not think it possible to better Shakespeare, here, and onward.—P. and C. [Rolfe's note.]

brazier. The iron grew cold. "Lord king," says I, at length, "I will not harm your eyes for all the treasure which your uncle owns. Yet, danger threatens you, and me. Earl John must think that what he wished to do has failed by reason of some magic charm, the relic of some saint, which keeps you whole from injury. Have you there such a matter?" "I carry The True Cross in this jewel on my breast, to keep me pure," says he, panting lightly, and smiling as he smiles who has run a race and won. "Enough," says I, kneeling before that body of sweet life, and breathing to his breathless excellence a vow, a holy vow: "I'll fill these dogged spies with false reports," says I; "and you, fair king, sleep doubtless and secure that Hubert for the wealth of all the world will not offend you. For, here, I swear never to taste pleasure, nor to be infected with delight, nor conversant with ease or idleness, till I have set a glory to my name, avenging all your wrongs, winning for you the maiden virtue of your rightful crowns." Duke Arthur said no word: but his frost-cold glance softened as it swept me; and, from that day, he began to treat me less austerely. O times.

v. About Softsword deceived by a Tale of a Cock and a Bull

It was in my mind to instruct those cotterels, as well for their own security as for the accomplishment of my design: for, while John held Arthur's lands, it was more desirable to frighten him than to enrage him, he being most ingenious when in a fury. And my lord the king was his captive, unable to oppose him with an equal power at that moment. But, as with all of us in the castle of Falaise, and indeed with all men not possessed of devils as well as hag-ridden, Softsword's cotterels needed no persuasion to make them friendly and not hostile. The knightly bravery, the delicate unerring dignity, the radiant candour, of the regal boy, pleaded his cause far better than the words which he did not (and I could not) speak. Querdelours and Piedechien gossiped with my cotterels in the bailey, while they waited for me, letting it be known what atrocity they had come to do and would not do: so that indignation against the uncle, and compassionate reverence for the nephew, inspired the hearts of all. This made my next step easy; and, having replenished their gullets and bellies and burses,

I returned the two cotterels to Rouen, primed with a story, of the type of that about the cock and the bull,[1] of how all assistance had been given them, and how everyone in the castle of Falaise excelled in affability, adoring the uncle, detesting the nephew, and how (when they thrust the red-hot fork against Duke Arthur's eyes) he had laughed, mocking them, and had actually dashed forward his head, so that the prongs sank sputtering into the face of him plain for all to see, and yet how his eyes remained whole, nor had he taken any injury whatever, this being due to a certain relic which he wore, and also to the sacrosanctity of his person, he being a clergyman and a canon, which property of him had frozen the red-hot iron on sight nine several times, refusing to harm him, and, indeed, their humble opinion was that no harm could possibly be done to him. Whereupon they wept bitterly, confessing themselves at a loss, and requesting further instructions. When he heard his cotterels' tale, Softsword shivered shockingly for forty minutes while Lady Jezebel cuffed him, whispering: after which, he said: "Since he is immune against fire, he shall be tried with water." O manners. And this saying being reported to me, I directed my vigilance accordingly, preparing for Softsword's next attempt, for it was not likely that he would be turned aside by a single failure.

VI. *About a second Wickedness of the Wicked Uncle*

Sir Robert Vipont, *or, six annulets gules*, came to Falaise with John's mandate for escorting Duke Arthur to Rouen, where a nephew might have better comfort from his loving uncle.[2] The regal imp at once elected to go. I had to obey. Nothing could be more distinct than the boy's noncurance:[3] he was every inch an Englishman and a prince of Englishmen, and a great deal more even than that. And he was admirably able to take care of himself.

---

[1] A long, rambling, and misleading story (*OED* OL).
[2] According to the *Flores Historiarum*, at this moment, Arthur disappeared. All of France suspected that John had murdered Arthur, and, from this point on, John was looked on with suspicion by all men.
[3] Indifference. The word "noncurance" is rarely used, and one of the *OED*'s two examples of usage is drawn from Rolfe's *Hadrian the Seventh* (*OED* OL).

And he coveted periculous[1] adventures. So I gave him a little train of three pages and four cotterels, all of faithful minds and lucky stars, and all hardy, expert, and very handsome, for he could never bear ugliness near him: and I covertly warned each of these that the length and quality of their lives depended absolutely on the length and quality of his. Also, I made occasion to ride to Rouen with a rosemary pudding for him three days later, and again in Passion Week on a pretext of consulting the Wild Ass about the new locks for my dungeons, but really to see that my lord the king was being properly treated. And I found no cause for complaint.

A regal ship lay by the quays at Rouen, for Softsword's pleasure, in case his fits should precipitate him back to England. On this ship, the *Mated Leopard*, there was a gromet or ship-boy named Gaubert: he came from Mantes, and was a freak of nature, being monstrous large and long in form, but his bones were small and fine, and he could hold in his breast as much breath as three men and a boy can hold in theirs without bursting. Having been born in a riverside town, he was an adept swimmer; and, for this pursuit, the great heat and the straight slippery smoothness of his body, and the length of his legs, and his powerful shoulders, eminently fitted him.[2] With which prodigy, Duke Arthur was pleased to strike up a sort of fellowship, seeing his extraordinary fish-like ability: for my lord the king always admired bodily skill, and cultivated the same in his proper person, specially when he was with Sir Fulk the Flame, who brought all kinds of slippery postures out of Syria.[3] And I was glad that Duke Arthur should deign to amuse himself thus with the ship-boy: nor could I see that Lady Jezebel was very offensive to him: but he was not an imp of that species which it is possible to offend, excepting (of course) in the way of slaughter. Which did not seem just then to be the game. But, soon

---

[1] Perilous (*OED* OL).

[2] A young Frenchman named Gaubert of Mantes distinguished himself during the battle between Philip and John at Rouen by swimming through the water with an ax in his hand and hewing through a stockade. He also swam through the water with vessels coated in pitch and filled with burning charcoal and threw these against the palisade. See Kate Norgate's *England Under the Angevin Kings* (London: Macmillan 1887), 412-415.

[3] Fulk the Flame was supposedly raised in Syria by his mother, Jehane, and her husband, the Old Man of the Mountain.

after my second departure, Softsword got to work in earnest. On Monday in Holy Week, quite oblivious of his prayers, he openly went to Le Moulineau, as it were to divert himself with hunting. If I had been there, I should have suspected some hideous ruse, seeing that he left Lady Jezebel behind him. For, such was his bestial infatuation that he had not yet been able to leave her. Moreover, that oaf, Henry Lackland, his son, was not of an age to be given charge of so awful a female, to say nothing of the castle and the city. But no one dreamed of evil. And the rest I will tell as my lord the king told it to me afterward.

"The Earl of Mortain," says the Regal Majesty, "came back from Le Moulineau secretly on Maundy Thursday[1] at midnight, I being in my bed; and he sent me a word by Quixapres to come down to the watergate, where he had a boat ready, for a pleasant jaunt down the river in the clear of the Easter moon. And I, nothing loath, and soothed by so gentle a message, wrapped my cloak about me, and descended eagerly, wishing very much to be on friendly terms with my father's own brother: for I had confessed my sins and received my rites that day, fulfilling the precept; and, it being Eastertime, I was forgiving my enemies and anxious to be at peace with all men." O Holy Innocent! "The Earl of Mortain," says the Regal Majesty, "was alone in the boat, governing the oars, wearing only a belted tunic and hosen. He smiled, when I came, signing me to become seated in front of him while he rowed. The night was clear, fresh, fair, and immense in silence. I crouched myself low in the poop, comfortably covered with the ermine of my cloak. Mortain rowed tranquilly down stream, away from the sleeping city. Sometimes we passed a word to each other, always speaking gently of gentle matters. One would have thought that my uncle loved me." O Sacred Simplicity! "After a while," says the Regal Majesty, "I began to note the whites of his eyes glittering in the moonlight; and they did not quite amuse me. The Earl of Mortain never looked truly clean. Also, I noted that his right thumb touched the knife-hilt in his belt whenas that his hands came back with the oars at the end of each stroke; and the nail (black as usual), of the said thumb hitched itself to the said hilt, loosening the said knife in its sheath.

---

[1] The Thursday before Easter that commemorates the Last Supper.

Moreover, the moon at the moment being behind me, owing to the meandering of the stream, I noted a large stone, attached to a coil of new rope, lying in the prow behind my uncle. When I saw this, it seemed due to change my posture quite covertly; and I gathered my legs under me, standing on my toes but squatting on my hams, not disturbing the folds of my cloak in the least, but ready to spring up if there should be need. And, with my hands, I unlatched the clasp of my cloak openly, folding it more closely in front of my breast. And it seems that I did very well: for, just when I was ready, Mortain suddenly shipped his right oar with a curse, shrieked, snatching his knife to drive into my face not a yard away from his."[1] Hup,[2] Bug! "But," says the Regal Majesty, "I instantly sprang out of my cloak, swinging my left arm round, as fiercely as I could; and my hardened hand-edge chopped him a frightful clout on his side-nose, where the wen was, squashing it,[3] so that he tumbled backward, sprawling in great pain, spouting his dirty blood." Ha, Saint George! "But I," says the Regal Majesty, "had had about enough of that boat. And I went out of it, diving deep over the left oar as silently as Gaubert of Mantes, emerging at a long distance, in the shade of a bush which had met my eye as I met the river; and I took order not to betray my whereabouts by splashes, or even by a ripple on the stream, lest that loving uncle of mine should try to have another dab at me.[4] But he reranged himself; and rowed hastily back to the castle." Hoo, Rat! "I," says the Regal Majesty, "swam by the same way, not knowing precisely what I should do. But, when I approached the quays, Mortain having disappeared in the castle, I thought that I might do worse than gain the *Mated Leopard* which lay alongside, where Gaubert would succour me. For, though I had been thanking the angels of my stars for sending me on this adventure naked as I left my bed, nevertheless I was numb

---

[1] This anecdote is drawn from a poem composed by Philip's chaplain, Guillaume le Breton. According to the poem, John and Arthur ventured out alone together on the Seine, and John ran a sword through Arthur's body. A similar account of Arthur's murder also appears in the annals of Margam, a Cistercian abbey in Glamorganshire.

[2] A call to a horse to quicken his pace or turn to the left or the right (*OED* OL).

[3] "*ego indurata manus acie colaphum ei foedum ducebam in nasus latere ubi erat ganglium id contundens.*" [Rolfe's note.]

[4] At this moment, Rolfe's narrative turns in the direction of speculative fiction.

with the night-cold water; and I needed clothes of some kind before going further. So Gaubert warmed me with beer and his hot body, and let me sleep in the ship, all the shipmen having gone ashore for their customary diversion. It would have been wiser if I had used my escape for coming forthwith to you, Hubert, letting my uncle think me drowned, until you could send him your defiance and lead a power against him. But my mind, then, was for worrying him horribly, playing some ghastly jape upon him, he being much more delectable in his fevers[1] than at other times. So, I sent Gaubert up to the castle, there to linger in the bailey as he was wont to do when waiting for me, and to bring me such current rumours as he could collect. And he returned with news that I had drowned myself, through pettishness, at the very moment when that loving uncle of mine was about to give me most singular tokens of affection; and the witness of it was my ermine cloak drenched with water, which was all that my said loving uncle had been able to save. And the Earl of Mortain was praying feverishly in the chapel." O manners. "Then," says the Regal Majesty, "I made Gaubert give me his Sunday clothes; and he invested[2] me, because I was unused to go in so very short a skirt: but I drew the hood of the tunic over my head, lest a defect of black hair and rosy face should betray me. I made him give me, also, a large bundle of river-weeds, trailing and slimy, wrapped in a pitched cloth to keep them dripping-wet; and, with these, I, in my turn, went up to the castle, disguised in ship-boy's semblance,[3] at about eight of the dial. Their business of the morning was occupying everybody; and no one saw me slip into the hall and on to the dais, the tables being already set for dinner. I concealed myself under the high table, in the shades of the napery, waiting there in silence, till the place was filled with hungry people and the servers were bringing in the meats. Then, I stripped off my ship-boy's garments, and hanged the watery weeds about me, so that the green slime dripped down. And, when the business of eating was well begun, I, with one great spring, vaulted quite softly on to the table in face of Mortain. There, I awfully danced, silently, solemnly, waving my weeds, spattering the company with

---

[1] "delectabilior in mentis tumoribus suis." [Rolfe's note.]
[2] Cloaked (OED OL).
[3] "sub seruuli simulacro nautici permutatus." [Rolfe's note.]

the wetness of them. From time to time, I slashed a clammy trail across the well-swelled nose of my loving uncle. He was having a furtive fit,[1] and foaming at the mouth. Lady Jezebel sat back stiffly, screaming like a skinny little red pig being snout-ringed. Henry Lackland (about to gulch a gobbet) prayed aloud, eyeing his sop and saying *In thy conception thou wast immaculate* and so on.[2] The bishops were for going away suddenly. The knights blessed their breasts without stint. The hostages each made a little round o of their silly mouths. And, all the while, I undulated along the tables, capering among the trenchers, kicking bread into laps which became greasy with gravy, and letting myself be thoroughly seen. And, when the whole company was worried almost to swooning, I called my pages and cotterels, and retired silent to my turret, there to prepare for what might next occur. I knew that Mortain would not make a new attempt on my life immediately: because he dared not do that openly, I being favoured by all and singular of his men; and I hoped to prevent private violence, by using a little circumspection. As for the administration of a powdered diamond,[3] I felt no misease on that score: because I neither ate nor drank, saving with all the household in the hall—where my seat was at Mortain's right hand; and I ate only from his portion and drank only from his cup, giving him (as he firmly persuaded himself) a token of timid friendliness. This, I did, to keep him quiet." O young Solomon![4] "Also," says the Regal Majesty, "for the time I forsook my custom of going alone; and I kept my pages and my cotterels about my person both by night and day, till I could send the gromet[5] to you, Hubert, with news of my adventure."

Those are the very words of my lord the king, which, when (long after) he had taken me into favour, he deigned of his sweet grace to give me. I humbly advised Duke Arthur to watch for

---

[1] "*furtim morbam comitiale tolerabat.*" [Rolfe's note.]

[2] "*immaculata in conceptione tua fuisti etcetera.*" [Rolfe's note.] The Litany of the Immaculate Conception.

[3] "*adamantum pulueratorum.*" [Rolfe's note.] Stories of poisoning by powdered diamond abound in the Renaissance. Catherine de Medici, for example, supposedly used a mixture of diamond and arsenic, referred to as the "powder of succession," to murder her opponents.

[4] Solomon was known for his wisdom.

[5] A ship's boy (*OED* OL).

another opportunity of escaping to me at Falaise, when I instantly would defy John, and join my whole power to the king of the Franks, then preparing a new war for Softsword. O times. O manners. But Duke Arthur said that that fat cold pig, King Philip, tired him, and he would not incur a debt to him. Nothing remained, but to go on as we were, taking precautions, and offering earnest prayers that Earl John might be summoned to heaven as soon as possible, where there were Those competent to deal faithfully with him. For, though a good christian may not pray for his enemy's death, it is very christian indeed to ask for heavenly joys (which, be it remarked, are supreme joys) on behalf of a knight who uses one despitefully.

VII. *About Hubert de Burgh his Artifices in Despite of Softsword*

King Philip the August wriggled in a bog of excessive ignorance concerning Duke Arthur. So also did Roches and the Armoricans, and indeed all men outside the castle of Rouen, excepting Hubert de Burgh: for Softsword dared not disown his prematurely published lie; and he ruled his affairs very straitly. Mobs applied to me for news. Sir Fulk fil-Richard raved at me. But, by command of my lord the king, I sucked my thumb and displayed my stoniest face.[1]

Some things, I did, at my own discretion, and without the slightest compunction. I omitted to persuade anyone to join the Wild Ass; and I secretly caused a many to take service with King Philip. For I did not want to incur suspicion, by increasing my own garrisons unduly; and, when a man came to me, if he was a better man than my worst, then I kept him in place of the other, whom I sent to the Frank, till my own power contained only select men, pre-eminent in fidelity and good luck and cunning and strength. And I took care that Gaubert of Mantes should be wary with his

---

[1] According to Ralph, Abbot of Coggleshall, a thirteenth-century chronicler, Hubert defied John's orders to blind and castrate Arthur. However, in order to convince the Bretons that theirs was a lost cause, he spread the rumor that the orders had been carried out and the young duke had died. The Bretons became further incensed at the news, and Hubert then attempted to convince them that Arthur lived. Hubert was unable to produce Arthur, probably because he had already been murdered by John.

tongue; for, having richly rewarded him, I neatly split it into a forked and silent member: which stratagem caused the *Mated Leopard* to cut her anchors off the very same night, and to sail up Seine to join King Philip at Paris, the shipmen believing me to be one of Softsword's ordinary tormentors. O indiscriminates.

VIII. *About Philip the August his new Worrying of Softsword*

The king of the Franks, ready for war, sent an embassage to the Wild Ass, summoning him to account for Duke Arthur. The Frank was so seriously concerned about this matter, that he offered four hostages for production of my lord the king's person. One of the hostages naturally was Sir Fulk fil-Richard all aflame to lay down his life for his amy.[1] John, drowned in dalliance with Lady Jezebel, refused to give any answer at all. Philip, therefore, determined to find out whether Duke Arthur was alive or dead, led out his power, with the powers of Roches and the Armoricans; and made short work of a parcel of Softsword's constables with their castles, namely, Sir Robert of Seez, *azure, three towers argent*, Sir Hugh Gournay again, Sir Guerin Glapion seneschal of Normandy, *azure, three fesselets or, within a bordure gules*, Sir Robert fil-Walter, *or, a fesse between two chevronels gules*, Sir Saer Quincy earl of Winchester, *or, a fesse gules, a label of eleven points azure*. But Sir Robert Turnham, *vert, three covert-cups or*, kept intact his allegiance and his castle. Made bold by these five victories, the Frank came down Seine toward Rouen, for the siege of Saucy Castle, that lovely fortress of the Lionheart's, which Sir Roger Lacy was defending. And John's new captain of mercenaries, Wolf by name, who learned his trade from Mercadet, almost burst his belly with indignation, when Softsword, lolling at ease, said: "Let alone: I will regain all in a few days." But Philip gained ground and men every day. Barres joined him wholeheartedly, with Sir Fulk fil-Richard and all his power. And that ship-boy, Gaubert of Mantes, did a fine deed in Softsword's despite, quite as I should have wished. For he swam in the river by night, leading (in his teeth) the tow-rope of a fire-ship, mooring it at the island-outwork of Saucy Castle in

---

[1] A friend (*OED* OL).

Seine, so that John's garrison, stunk out by the fumes, perished of suffocation and displeasure; and the Franks took the fort, as well as the other outwork called Little Andeley. Moreover, the castle of Radeport fell to Philip after a mere fifteen days of siege, before the tremendous trench for isolating Saucy Castle was completed. Now Saucy Castle was the key of Normandy.

VIIII. *About Softsword beginning to be Fussy*

The Wild Ass became dreadfully worried. He gravely doubted the fidelity of his mercenaries and remaining knights, none of whom he ever paid; and he was ware that he would certainly lose the duchy of Normandy, unless he could scratch up some money immediately. Of course he would not use his own treasure; and England was the only place where he could get gold. He, therefore, swooped suddenly from Rouen through Barfleur to Portsmouth, carrying Duke Arthur with him. And, from England he fussily set to work to extract both money and men. Nothing could equal the volubility with which he cursed the magnates who had jibbed[1] at service oversea. He assigned all his losses to their defection, saying that, if they would not work, they should pay; and he laid a tax of a seventh on moveables,[2] to be paid by all in the kingdom, from the highest to the lowest, not exempting clergymen. Walter the Primate and Geoffrey the Justiciar were appointed tax-collectors: their dirty job was to diminish the treasure-chests of magnates, to shake the bags of avaricious abbots,[3] to thrust sticky paws into old women's stockings, and to draw gold out of stones, if possible. But Softsword himself dealt with the king's Giwen.

x. *About Hubert de Burgh his Opinions concerning the Giwen*

The Giwen[4] are the curse of the kingdom of England, because

---

[1] Balked at.

[2] Property capable of being removed or displaced, as opposed to fixed property, such as land or a house (*OED* OL).

[3] "*auarorum saccos sollicitare abbatum.*" [Rolfe's note.]

[4] For a discussion of Rolfe's anti-Semitism and his use of medieval source material in his representation of the Jews in *Hubert's Arthur*, see the introduction to this edition.

they know not how to be faithful and honest when they are treated fairly and generously. They have quicker wits than other men: which is all very well; and I do not vituperate them for that. But they are also more crafty, more avaricious, and quite devoid of scruples; and they gibe at the bare notion of keeping faith, excepting among themselves, if then. In brief, they are beasts of prey by nature, and spoilers by open profession. They allege that they spring from the seed of Messire Saint Abraham, a Patriarch of Hierusalem in ancient times, to whom the earth was promised by Divine Providence in a vision. I do not dream of denying this, since we have the fact recorded in the Sacred Scriptures. But they say, also, that we Christians, who hold any part of the said earth, are simply usurpers of their said divinely-promised rights, whom their laws oblige and encourage them to harass and embarrass and dispossess by any and every means. This doctrine, I utterly spit upon and abhor from: because it is capable of being stretched out so as to include (with approval) such crimes as cheating and fraud and even murder.

We Englishmen do not like being despoiled by shrewd unscrupulous very-undesirable aliens; and it is our custom to treat the Giwen (who thrust their company upon us) as dangerous animals, kept encaged and enchained, but allowed to live and to thrive under suitable restrictions: it being a sin for us to take human life, excepting in a good cause, for we by no means believe it lawful for a Christian to slay (with impunity, according to his pleasure), any Giwe who behaves as he ought.[1]

We Christians are forbidden (by our religion) to commit the sin of usury: but, with the Giwe, it is far otherwise. His religion (which we respect, and damn), permits and approves of usury; and he does a thriving trade by outwitting and nefariously oppressing us.[2] O manners. Not that I blame clergymen, not that

---

[1] "nam licere cuilibet Christiano quempiam pro libito suo benemerentem Giuudeum ita impune occidere nequaquam credimus." [Rolfe's note.]

[2] According to medieval English law, Christians could not recover more than the original loan amount, while Jews could collect interest. Because almost every part of national life in medieval England involved the taking of some kind of religious oath, Jews were barred from careers in agriculture, trade, and public or municipal office. Moneylending was essentially the only career open to them.

I blame magnates, who borrow money from Giwen: for, thereby,
many important abbeys and castles are builded; and clergymen
and magnates are strong enough (as a rule) to protect themselves
from knavery. But the Giwen are wont to inveigle poor needy
knights and burgesses to their ruin; and thus they have thrust
themselves under the displeasure of the major part of our nation.

Hence, because the devout fervour of the English (irritated
beyond toleration, by the crimes of the slippery Giwen), used to
revolt against them, and to beat them badly[1] (perhaps sometimes
rather more than justice strictly demanded), then, the kings of
the English deigned to take the said Giwen under their regal protection entirely, as tributaries, dividing them from the rest of the
nation, making them a nation apart, giving them separate laws
whereby (and separate sites whereon) they might live and nourish in perfect security.[2] Yet they are not content: but, ever and
again, they burst out in scorn of us Christians, committing hideous crimes and outrages against us and our holy religion. For,
in their canonical books it is written (as it is written in the Sacred
Scriptures[3]) that, without bloodshed, there can be no remission.
But they, swayed by the devil,[4] perfidiously distort this saying, so
as to mean that they may never return to their dear fatherland
unless they shed Christian blood. O generation of vipers. Hence,
it was laid down by them in antique times, that, every year, they
must sacrifice a Christian, in some part of the world, to The Most
High God, in scorn and contempt of Christ, so that they might
revenge their sufferings on Him, inasmuch as it was because of
His Death that they had been shut out from their fatherland and
were in exile in foreign countries. Wherefore, the princes and
rabbis of the Giwen, who dwell in Spain, assemble at Narbonne,
where their regal seed is and they are held in highest esteem; and
they cast lots for all the countries which the Giwen inhabit; and

---

[1] *"et eos concidere."* [Rolfe's note.]

[2] It was in the king's best interest to protect the Jews, because all wealth acquired
through usury passed into the king's treasury at the usurer's death.

[3] Cf. *Epist. to Hebrews ix. 22.*—P. and C. [Rolfe's note.] "And almost all things,
according to the law, are cleansed with blood: and without shedding of blood
there is no remission."

[4] *"suadente diabolo."* [Rolfe's note.]

the metropolis of that country, upon which the lot falls, has to carry out the same method with the other towns and cities; and the place, whose lot is drawn, has to fulfil the duty imposed by the said decree.[1] And this means to say that, at the time of their Passover, which is the Paschal Season, they must take a Christian, spotless and virginal, whom they must afflict as their forefathers afflicted the Human Person of The Lord our God, with mocking and scourging and crowning with thorn and crucifixion and with such other torment as their demons may suggest to them.[2]

In the year 1144 of Redemption, when King Stephen Bowman was reigning,[3] thus did the Giwen of Norwich with Messire Sweet Saint William the Martyr, who (as everyone well knows) is illustrated with wondrous and unspeakable miracles even at this very day.[4] I myself have seen the close-clustered ruddy flowers which sprang from his boyish body (dripping with blood) in the wood where they hid it on Mousehold Heath. I myself have offered at his shrine a candle of my own weight in virgin wax, the work of the mother-bee, to gratify the natural love for candles of him who was born on Candlemas Day. And my lord the king has frequently done the same. What more true? When King Henry fil-Empress was reigning in England, the Giwen became boundless in audac-

---

[1] "unde ab ipsis antiquitus decretum est omni anno eos in Christi obprobrium et contumeliam Christianum ubicumque terrarum Deo litare Altissimo ut sic suas in Illum ulciscantur iniurias Cuius Mortis causa ipsi et a sua exclusi sunt patria et exulant in aliena. qua de re principes et rabite Giuudeorum qui Hispaniam inhabitant apud Narbonam ubi semen regium et eorum maxime uiget gloria pariter conueniunt atque uniuersarum regionum quas Giuudei inhabitant sortes ponunt. quam uero sors designauerit regionem eius metropolis urbium ceterarum et oppidorum sortes applicabit atque illud decretale explebit negotium cuius sors exierit." [Rolfe's note.]

[2] As I discuss in the introduction, most of the material on the Jews in this novel has been lifted almost verbatim from Joseph Jacobs's The Jews of Angevin England (London: D. Nutt, 1893). Jacobs devotes much attention to the history of "blood accusations," accusations of human sacrifice, against the Jews during the Middle Ages. During the twelfth and thirteenth centuries, Jews were repeatedly accused of kidnapping and crucifying young boys, who were then venerated by Christians as boy martyrs. For more on anti-Semitism and blood accusation, see the introduction to this edition.

[3] "regnante Stephana Sagittario rege." [Rolfe's note.]

[4] William of Norwich died in 1144. This was the first case of blood accusation in medieval Europe.

ity. In the year 1165 of Redemption, it is said that they crucified Messire Saint Harold of Gloucester.[1] In the year 1181 of Redemption, it is said that they crucified both Messire Saint Robert a boy of Bury Saint Edmund's, and Messire Saint Herebert a boy of Huntingdon. In the year 1182 of Redemption, it would seem that the lot fell upon France: for we hear how they crucified Messire Saint Richard, a boy of Pontoise, whose sacred body was first enshrined in the church of the Holy Innocents at Paris, until King Henry fil-Empress translated it with awful pomp to Rouen, leaving the head only to the Franks. And I well remember hearing how (in the year 1192 of Redemption), when King Richard Lionheart was reigning in England, the Giwen did the same atrocious sacrilege and homicide on the virginal body of Messire Saint Yvo, a boy of Winchester, who came from Armorica to get a living as a mime in that regal city.[2]

Now there are several individuals still at large—whether they be puzzolent[3] pestiferous turpilucricupidous[4] knaves, like Softsword, or merely sentimental fools, like that maggotty-witted[5] Roches, it is not for me to say—who fondly affirm that these things are either fables invented by clergymen in despite of the Giwen, or (if not fables) they are only rather-questionable indiscretions committed by the Giwen in the sheer madness of revenge and despair, to which we Christians have goaded them by our unprovoked unmerited atrocities. And, in this, I say, out loud, and at once, that these knaves or fools lie foully in their hairy throats. No Christian ought to make such allegations of Christians, nor Englishmen of men of England. In any case, I fearlessly affirm that we Christians ought not to be called upon to respond to an accusation of this sort, before the Giwen are purged from the murder of one of us, of which they are known to have been

---

[1] Most sources, including Jacobs, actually date Saint Harold's martyrdom as 1168.

[2] Most of the aforementioned boy martyrs are discussed in Jacobs's *The Jews of Angevin England*.

[3] Smelly (*OED* OL).

[4] A "Macaronick" term defined by Rolfe in the glossary of his *Don Renato* as "covetous of base or dishonest gain." Rolfe used "Macaronick" language, a combination of Latin and English, in many of his historical novels.

[5] "*mentis uermiculatae.*" [Rolfe's note.]

accused ere now, and they are not purged.[1] I speak of the Martyrdom of Messire Sweet Saint William. Nevertheless, I will make a certain answer. In the first place, let us consider that it is only a fool who kills the goose which lays him golden eggs; and I say that clergymen are not such fools as to damage the Giwen, from whom the Cistercians alone could and did borrow the money for building no fewer than nine of their northern abbeys, namely, Rievalle, Revesby, Ruford, Rupe, Newminster, Kirkested, Kirkestall, Parcolude, Betlesden. In the second place, concerning the alleged cruelties wherewith we Christians goaded the Giwen as far as homicidal mania, I simply demand, What cruelties? Let us take things in the proper order. All the people of England are under the protection of the kings of the English: but the Giwen have a special and particular protection. The question is this: Do they languish thereunder, or do they flourish? And here is the answer. The Giwen were the first men in this kingdom to be rich enough to build their houses of stone: all the rest of the nation, excepting the few who had castles, were obliged to dwell in walls of wood or wattle or mud. The Giwen came to us as mendicants and guests, piteously whimpering for hospitality. It was granted to them, full measure, pressed down, and running over the pottle, so that less fortunate Christians actually envied them. And, from the stronghold of their incalculable riches entirely gained nefariously under our own kings' protection, they spoil the widow and the fatherless, rob the orphan, oppress the poor, and mock our holy religion. Is it surprizing, then, that Christian patience occasionally gives way to passionate outbreaks of carnage, as at York?[2] Let us next consider the difference between the king's protection of Christians and of Giwen. Both are liable to affliction under a bad king. But, whereas the king is the only tyrant whom

---

[1] *"nos Christiani respondisse non debuissemus ad huiusmodi accusationem nisi primo Giuudei de Christiani nostri nece purgarentur unde et ipsi pridem accusati et non purgati dinoscuntur."* [Rolfe's note.]

[2] Anti-Semitic riots took place in York in 1190, resulting in a massacre of the Jewish people living in the city. Joseph Jacobs argues that the riots were a result of the prevalence of the crusading spirit during this period, growing anger about the boy-martyrs, as well as a desire on the part of York's upper classes to get rid of their debts through violent means.

the Giwen have to fear, excepting when they (by their ungrateful malpractices) wilfully and wantonly incur the ire of the mobile vulgar, Christians suffer as much from a tyrannous king, and, also, from that tyrannous king's tyrannous Giwen.

Of what, precisely, do the querulous cantankerous[1] Giwen complain? They complain, forsooth, that they may not hold offices of state in England. That is true. England is a Christian kingdom. The Giwens are invaders of it, generously tolerated, but not wanted. As Christians, we enforce Christian laws. The officer of a Christian king swears fidelity in The Name of Father, Son, and Holy Ghost. Which oath, the Giwen will not swear; and, so, they debar themselves from office. Are we excessively unreasonable herein? Are the Giwen more easy and less strict in this respect? I think not. Hear me spue my scorn upon such presumptuous chicanery. When a Christian (diabolically swayed) lusts to become a Giwe, is he admitted to their conjuration without test? Ho no, indeed. What of those two Cistercian monks, demoniacs of our own times, who, worn out by the sweet light burthen of Christ His easy yoke, fled to the synagogue of Satan, home of damnation, asylum of depraved and pestiferous rites. To cut short the wretched story, upon which I dilate merely to express my detestation, the said monks were forced to renounce the sacred laver of their baptism, and to submit to a physical diminution, before the Giwen would receive them.[2]

Now let us consider the singular privileges and advantages enjoyed by the Giwen under the king's protection. They are quite

---

[1] "importuni." [Rolfe's note.]

[2] Cf. Giraldi Cambrensis Opera, R.S. iiii. 139.—P. and C. [Rolfe's note.] This story is also drawn from Jacobs's Jews of Angevin England: "A certain monk of the same order, or rather a certain demoniac in our own times, being as it were tired of the Catholic faith and worn out with the sweet and light burden of Christ's yoke, and scorning, at the instigation of the devil, any longer to walk in the way of salvation. . . . as if phrenetic and mad, and truly turned to insanity, fleeing to the synagogue of Satan . . . caused himself to be circumcised with the Jewish rite, and as a most vile apostate joined himself, to his damnation to the enemies of the cross of Christ. Also on the northern borders of England, in a house of the same order called Geroudon, a certain brother, likewise in our own days, by a similar error, or rather madness, presuming to set at naught the part of Christ and reconciling himself with Satan, . . . fled with ruinous and ruin-bearing ways to Judaism, the home of damnation and the asylum of this depraved reprobation" (283-285).

free (as no other man is free) to accumulate wealth; and the king jealously guards it for them against all interference. No one may meddle with any Giwe, for good or evil, excepting at the king's own bidding. In the year 1194 of Redemption, King Richard Lionheart made and confirmed an Ordinance for the Giwerie, stablishing a special exchequer called Giuudeorum Saccarium at Westminster, where they might keep their parchments which they call Starrs and have their lawsuits tried before two justiciars of their own.[1] They have jurisdiction among themselves, according to rabbinic law, excepting for the major felonies; and their rabbis advise the regal exchequer on points of rabbinic law. In the chief cities of the kingdom, they have their Chests kept for them by the king's officers. And, above all, they are exempted altogether from all tolls and taxes and fines of justice. Is it wonderful that they suck up the gold of England as a sponge sucks up water? Could anyone fail to accumulate riches, when he is helped thus to take, and exempted from giving? But what do the Giwen give, in return for these tremendous and unheard-of favours? One thing only, namely, the tallages, reliefs, fines, and amercements, which (be it noted) the king levies on all his dependants alike, Christians as well as Giwen. The Giwen have suffered hideously from bad kings. Ho yes. But so also have we Christians, and far more hideously: for we have suffered both from bad kings and from those bad kings' bad and protected Giwen as well.

God knows how hard it is for a man to make good laws for men. I know a great deal about it myself, having made a many laws, good and bad, in my time. But I am unable to imagine fairer or more righteous or more desirable laws, than those which the kings of the English have made for their Giwen, to the detriment and at the expense of their Christians.

And, as for the gross ingratitude which the Giwen (with their whoopings and their whinings) show in return for our ridiculous generosity, I cannot conceive of anything more deservedly reprehensible as being quite contrary to decorum or good manners.

---

[1] Before the Ordinance of the Jews was established in 1194, the king made informal use of the Jews as tax collectors. With the passing of this ordinance, the position of the Jews was formally recognized and a special branch of the Treasury was created to control British usury.

And I repeat: The Giwen are the curse of the kingdom of England. That is my opinion of the Giwen. I have spoken. Let it stand.

XI. *About a third Wickedness of the Wicked Uncle*

Softsword himself, as I have said, dealt with the king's Giwen. But he did more than to take the proper dues from them this time, he being undoubtedly swayed by the devil and inspired by the diabolical prepotence of Legion.[1] For, he sent to all the cities where the Giwen had their Chests; and he took note of the parchments stored therein: from which he informed himself of the cities which contained the richest Giweries, and of the Giweries which kenneled the richest Giwen. And, from the last, he demanded Dona, gifts of bullion, most flagitiously.[2]

When the said rich Giwen demurred, he squeezed them till they exuded gold, ill-gotten (it is true) and now ill-taken. Of the chief of them, one Ysaak of the Bristol Giwerie, he required no less than ten thousand marks. The Giwe, being reluctant to pay, was accommodated in a dungeon of the castle, where he sustained cold, hunger, stenches, and attacks of toads,[3] for quite a long time: but persevered in his recalcitrant behaviour. John, then, took to tearing a tooth out of the back of his jaw, one every day after mass, seven in all; and the tearing was not done tenderly.[4] On the eighth day, Ysaak was found to have lost his face, only a festering swelling representing it, nor was any mouth seen whereby the tongs might enter. The tormentor, therefore, began to slit what he took to be a cheek: but the first snap of his scissors caused so much and so profound displeasure, that the Giwe cheerfully submitted to Softsword's indefensible illegalities. Seeing, then, how the Giwen might be parted from their wealth, and, knowing exactly how much each Giwe had in hoard from which he might be parted, Softsword decided to go further in this direction. But he wished to be affable, if they would let him: for some bishop had told him

---

[1] The "prepotence of Legion" means the overwhelming influence of the demons in Hell.

[2] Villainously (*OED* OL).

[3] *"algorem inediam fetores et buffonum incursiones sustinuit."* [Rolfe's note.]

[4] This anecdote is drawn from Roger of Wendover.

that the wise grazier shears his sheep without flaying them, and
that bargains are more pleasant than pillage and more profitable
than plunder. The said Ysaak of Bristol having been healed, he,
with two other Giwen named Yomtob of Lincoln and Beleasez
of Oxford,[1] who were among the most eminent Giwen in the
kingdom, were brought to the Wild Ass in his castle of Corfe: for
he had a most horrible plan in his mind, and dispensed with his
trumpets on this occasion. "Sir Giwe," says he to Ysaak, "I desire,
making you amends for your teeth, to sell you a male lamb without blemish for your passover: for I hear that your nation has not
been able to find a sacrifice worth your buying, or one which ye
could buy with security, these nine years." The Giwen began to
tremble at these frightful words: for they suspected snares. But
Softsword was excessively affable, and gave clear tokens that he
was in earnest. Therefore, they proceeded cautelously,[2] neither
denying him, nor incriminating themselves, being anxious to
propitiate him, as well as to satisfy their own religion and their
own cupidity. Mortain then bade the Giwen to observe Duke
Arthur, now a gigantic flower of boyhood,[3] who (by chance) was
strolling in the outer bailey: but, all the while, he spoke of the
lamb which he had for sale, saying that it was an orphan, merely
an encumbrance to its present owner on account of its rarity, he
preferring a commoner sort of sheep of which he had already as
many flocks as he could manage. The Giwen timidly inquired the
price of this lamb. To whom Softsword answered that the price
must be a high one, seeing that the said lamb was perfect even
in the most minute particulars, and to be sold for sacrifice and
nothing else. And he bade them to say what sum they were willing to offer. Then Beleasez of Oxford was very bold: for he saw
all which was intended, the dastardly cupidity of John desiring
to be ridded of his nephew, and the glory to accrue to the Bristol

---

[1] Here (presumably) we get the thirteenth-century Jewish original of the modern
catholic cognomen "Bellasis."—P. and C. [Rolfe's note.] Edward Bellasis (1800-
1873) was part of the Tractarian movement and a convert to Catholicism. His
son, Edward Bellasis (1852-1922), held the office of Lancaster Herald of Arms in
Ordinary and appears as "Lancaster" in Rolfe's *Hadrian the Seventh*.

[2] Cautiously (*OED* OL).

[3] "*florem pueritiae gigantem.*" [Rolfe's note.]

Giwerie by so magnificent a victim; and he spoke up like a man, giving a famous answer. "Our forefathers," says he, "paid thirty silver marks for a Lamb a long while ago; and we, more generous than they, will pay thirty-thousand silver marks for this lamb."

See reincarnate Judas: see now a second Herod.[1] Sixteen days later, Earl John pouched the price of blood; and my lord the king, his pages and his cotterels having been pushed into the castle-oven and baked, was delivered by night, gagged and bound, to the myrmidons[2] of the Giwen, who conveyed him secretly to Bristol, and sent word of the impending sacrifice to all their synagogues in the kingdom. For, considering the highness of their victim and the splendour of his every perfection, they expected no less than the redemption of their whole race on account of so magnificent a sacrifice. All this, I had from Beleasez of Oxford himself, when (much later) he was engaged in dying.[3]

xii. *About Hubert de Burgh his Loss of Duke Arthur*

It being undesirable to excite Softsword's suspicion, by coming too often from my castle of Falaise to Rouen, I was not instantly ware of these horrible doings. Duke Arthur treated the attempt at drowning him so very lightheartedly, refusing to escape to me, or to let me avenge him, saying: "It is Our will to have a game with Our uncle, as cat with rat, or as prince with fool." And I knew better than to disobey my liege lord. Boys will be boys. A spice of peril adds zest to any adventure. And it was exhilarating to see my lord the king dallying so deftly with his dangerous circumstances. But, when I next thought well to ride to Rouen, and found Softsword and his nephew and their trains gone secretly and suddenly to England, then, a horrid gelidity[4] glided up my back into my short hair. Instantly, I decided that my English castles ought to be inspected without delay. Every hour of breath increased my foreboding of evil. I determined to do what I was to

---

[1] *"Ecce Iudas alter Herodes ecce secundus."* [Rolfe's note.]
[2] In the *Iliad*, the Myrmidons are a warlike people from Thessaly. The term is now used to refer to hired ruffians or mercenaries.
[3] *"occupato morte impeditoque."* [Rolfe's note.]
[4] Extreme cold or frigidity (*OED* OL).

do very thoroughly, even (if necessary) to act against Softsword before I had duly defied him, he being inaccessible by my defiance just then, having left no address to which I might send it. O manners. I, accordingly, ate a pudding and regarrisoned Falaise with the best tenants of that vicinity, leaving a score of my picked veterans to stiffen them; and I placed the castle in a state of siege. This done, I took my power (a formidable power) under a flag of truce to the Frankish camp, where I conferred with young Sir Fulk fil-Richard, the lord of Cuigny, he being Duke Arthur's amy and next of kin-male; and to him I unfolded the news of Softsword's attempts to blind and to drown. He had known nothing; and he blazed with Angevin anger at being apart from his amy's adventures. But, when I added that, now, Softsword had carried my lord the king secretly and suddenly to England, then, "School of God,[1] Hubert," says Fulk the Flame, "I am coming with you instantly to pursue him." Which was what I had come to make him say: being ware that Duke Arthur would be better for having two lovers on his track than one; and two heads are always better than one, even when they are the heads of a boy of fifteen and a man of twenty-five as we were then, I, and Fulk the Flame. Remained only the question of the said Fulk his wardens: but he was of a regal nature, true son of his father, and few crossed the Lionheart's will without falling split in two jagged halves on the spot or quite near by. So, Barres and his power agreed to stay with King Philip who was attending to Saucy Castle; and we did not admit that clammy Frank to our confidence, for good reasons. But Saint-Pol accompanied Sir Fulk, escaping by a ruse which I need not describe now; and the two joined me on the next night, without any further fuss or fiddling.

XIII. *About the Quest of Duke Arthur*

We nosed about Normandy till we found Softsword's trail; and followed it step by step. At Barfleur, I had to split my power, owing to lack of sufficient shipping. The greater part I left to find the speediest way to my castles on the March of Wales, giving

---

[1] *"Ludedez."* [Rolfe's note.]

them the passwords admitting them to the garrisons thereof.
But I, with Sir Fulk and Saint-Pol and twenty men-at-arms, took
ship at once for Portsmouth. Here, I made a redivision: for I had
invented an excuse for showing myself to Softsword: but I did not
wish him to see my noble companions. They, with ten men-at-
arms went one way to the priory of Twynham: I, with the other
ten, to the castle of Corfe, all instructed to collect gossip. I made
the Wild Ass caper excitedly, telling him that a leper had been
prophesying about him at Falaise, having seen our lord the Pope
in a vision snatching his crown and pelting him with pears.[1] He
was dreadfully worried at this, being a superstitious beast; and
would know whether the leper was dead. And, when I denied it,
he bade me to go back instantly and see to it: which appeared to
comfort him, for (at my turning to go) he picked up the thread
of his knavery, inquiring why I had not brought him news of his
beloved nephew at Rouen. I said that Rouen lay off my road and
the prophecy was of most serious importance. But I knew, in that
moment, that Duke Arthur was neither here nor there. And so I
pretended to return to Normandy.

As I rode to Twynham to collect my companions, I listened to
the babble which my men-at-arms had netted at Corfe, namely,
of the coming and going of Giwen from parts unknown, of their
coming again with an immense treasure guarded by Earl John's
own cotterels, and of their going again most hilariously at midnight with a covered litter guarded by a power of Giwen. When
Sir Fulk and Saint-Pol heard this also, it was agreed that we certainly ought to investigate Giweries. But I was for going first to
my March, where I could assemble a power sufficient to overcome
any opposition; and so, we went thither through Bristol, where I
did a fine stroke of business for myself and we also fell hot on the
trail. For, first, when we entered the city, it occurred to me to go
to the Templary[2] for hospitality. And, when I saw the strength of
the fortress and the good knights housing there, I thought that I

---

[1] "*et piris in cum iacentem.*" [Rolfe's note.]

[2] The estate belonging to the Knights Templar, a medieval military and religious
order that protected pilgrims to the Holy Land. The Knights Templar would
frequently oversee the financial matters of the pilgrims, acting almost like a bank
by holding their money while they went on pilgrimage.

should do as well to give a great part of my private treasure into their charge, as a provision for the future. Which I presently did, the Master being agreeable. And, from time to time thereafter, I increased the hoard which the Templars kept for me, as occasion served, to my great benefit: for, when, at a later time, I defied John, losing temporarily much means of wealth thereby, the Templars simply spat censures at him when he would have confiscated my money and jewels in their charge. And, secondly, when we came to Bristol, we perceived quite an unusual number of the extraordinary noses of Giwen pervading that city. The Templars also had noted it, but ignored the cause of it, though they were gravely scandalized by the audacious demeanour of those depraved ones. But I, having my suspicions, began to make enquiries, as did also my companions. And, because every Giwe (whom we accosted) gave a different answer, tired of such tergiversation,[1] we made our dispositions; and setting all law at defiance, we penetrated deep into the Giwerie by night, which, by God's Mercy, we did in the very nick of time.

XIIII. *About Duke Arthur his most glorious Martyrdom*

The night was dark, moonless, and starless. We armed ourselves from head to foot. Fulk flamed with a torch by my side; and I led the way. The gate of the Giwerie was guarded by two, who fled inward at my approach. We saw many lights within the gate. We heard multitudinous murmuring. I felt myself directly inspired by The Lord God. I gave the word to draw long-swords, and to slay without mercy. So, we rode in at full gallop, using our weapons like scythes. The Giwen ran like rabbits to an inner gateway. Fulk followed me; and, flinging off my horse, I entered also. The crime was in the very article of perpetration.

There were about thirty Giwen in the small courtyard, twenty ancients with torches, ten young and lusty otherwise occupied. Their backs were toward me; and they were engaged on the ground before them. There, lay a huge cross of oaken timber. On the cross, was the Regal Majesty of my lord the king, naked as born, bleeding from weals, crowned with thorn.

---

[1] Equivocation (*OED* OL).

His left knee was bent, and his left foot nailed flat to the cross. His right leg was pulled long and straight, and tied to the wood with cordage. A great filthy Giwe was riding straddled on his belly, pressing his shoulders down to the transom. His left arm was pulled long and straight, and tied to that transom with cordage. Every part of him, which was not nailed or corded, writhed and struggled most awfully. His well-toothed head darted, and bit, and cursed, with the anger of all the Angevins and the passions of all the Plantagenets.

Two stout young Giwen were gripping the finger and thumb of his right hand, lying on their bestial backs with their hooves in his armpit, stretching and straining his right arm out at full length on the transom. Another Giwe, much younger, kneeled near by, pointing a nail into the palm of the open hand. A fourth Giwe had swung up his heavy hammer. It came down. The nail shuddered, screeching, through regal flesh, and hid its shamed point in the wood.

All this, I saw in the flash of an eye.

Then, I got to work with both hands and my long-sword, sweeping round and round irresistibly.

xv. *About Duke Arthur his Deliverance*

Their heads sprang off the executioners, butchers; and bounced away into the corners. I sliced the standing Giwen into halves by twos and threes, and those who foolishly jumped up to oppose me. Fountains of blood spouted everywhere, extinguishing fallen torches. Out of the darkness, my lord the king cursed yet more scathingly, choking and bubbling, cursing my clumsiness. I roared to Fulk for his torch. I saw no more Giwen left alive: but the place was very much littered by their pieces; and my lord the king was hidden under a heap. I lifted away each lump with care, until he was uncovered. He was dyed crimson from hair to heel, spitting, regally infuriated. I cut the cords which bound his right leg and his left arm; and he began to move them, while I took the thorn-crown from his head. Fulk suddenly shouted: "Ware, Giwe." And he swang his long-sword at a whole Giwe who moved, the one with the hammer. "No:" says I to Fulk, striking up his blade. And, to the Giwe, "Out nails:" says I. He drew them, with the pincers from his girdle. My lord the king ground his teeth with anguish, when the nail came out of his foot. When the nail came out of his hand, he swooned away. I took the torch from Fulk; and let him slash the Giwe into little pieces, a bit at a time, so that he might have his share of the glory. Then, I went to take up my lord the king: but all his lovely regal back was torn to strips from nape to heel; and I, perforce, carried his hallowed adorable young body face-downward in my mailed arms. So, we three gushed[1] out of the shambles. My men-at-arms and Saint-Pol had hewed a path through the great crowd of Giwen outside, strewing them in swathes at the edges of the way. While some pillaged the Giwe-rie, we washed my lord the king at a cistern, and bandaged his wounds with our pennons;[2] and cleaned ourselves; and, having taken a litter, we brought the regal and sacred majesty away.

XVI. *About Hubert de Burgh his Concealment of Duke Arthur*

I am flabbergasted now when I remember the number of manœuvres which came into my mind at that time; and I render humble thanks to The Lord God for disposing me to serve my lord the king really well.

All night we rode by muddy River Avon, through the gorge, past the old sea-wall; and, at daybreak, we seized a ship and crossed River Severn, going up River Wye as far as my castle of Monmouth. But I was not hiding Duke Arthur there, or (indeed) anywhere whence a word concerning him might go to Softsword. I saw that that place was ordered securely; and I took oaths of secrecy from all and singular: for Softsword was to think of me as being in Normandy. We went on to Candidachester, and did the same. Then, I asked Sir Fulk fil-Richard whether he would stay with Duke Arthur and be useful, or part from his amy for the time and be more useful. He, true loyal son of the Lionheart his father and of the mate of the Lionheart his mother, snarled at me for asking such an unnecessary question. So I gave him fifty sturdy men-at-arms out of my veteran-garrison, and I sent him

---

[1] *"emicuimus."* [Rolfe's note.]

[2] A long, narrow flag attached to a lance or a helmet (*OED* OL).

with Saint-Pol into Wales, up Uskvale and beyond Dinas where the black man was,[1] there to encamp, and to set the savage Welsh quarrelling among themselves in a small but annoying manner. But I took Duke Arthur, with certain stores and no more than six of my most faithful cotterels, and my page Bobo Kemp (who knew the place, for he it was who told me of it, having himself discovered it); and we also oozed[2] over the March into Wales, very secretly indeed, avoiding Abergavenny, and creeping up Uskvale to the caves of Llangattwg.[3]

XVII. About the admirable Caves of Llangattwg

These caves are a most happy work of The Lord God Himself, and entirely admirable. After passing Llangattwg, one ascends, from the bank of River Usk, through the steep slope of a forest, until a narrow ledge is at length attained, where a precipice towers upward to the stars, confronting the view like a mightily battlemented rampart. Behind and below, is the river in the vale. Before and above, is the rocky wall, wherein is the adit[4] to the caves well-hidden among bushes. There are, indeed, four entrances: but three are so fearfully concealed that they cannot be found, excepting with the greatest difficulty; and thus they are valuable as a means of escape when the main entrance is forced by a foe. On entering by the ordinary way, a narrow passage soon leads to the right. A little further on, this is joined by a wide passage which leads to the left. By continuing along the narrow passage, open air is reached again at the second entrance. But the wide passage, at some distance is joined by a second narrow passage,

---

[1] *"ubi erat niger."* We do not quite know what this means. Crusaders, of course, frequently brought back nigger slaves, who (naturally) excited the rustics of this country, and, when not slaughtered as demoniacal, have been known to attain local celebrity as hermits (cf. Saint Gattwg). But we can find no appropriate tradition in the vicinity of the ruined castle of Dinas. A similar bald and unconvincing detail, however, frequently corroborates the narrative of the *Mabinogion*, q.v. [Rolfe's note.] The *Mabinogion* is a medieval Welsh manuscript that includes stories of characters of African descent.

[2] *"manauimus."* [Rolfe's note.]

[3] This cave system is about eighty miles long.

[4] An entrance (*OED* OL).

which leads to a great hall as large as an abbey's, with a sort of
chapterhouse attached to it. Here, we stabled our frightful horses,
near a spring of sweet water. At the end of this vast hall, two more
narrow passages lead to the third and fourth adits of the caves.
Very small they are: but we instantly blocked them with rocks
wedged from inwards and having a natural aspect outwards. But
the wide tunnel still continues to the right for a long way; and, at
length, it turns round upon itself in a smallish loop. And, in the
farthest curve of this loop, there is a smallish pit,[1] at the bottom
of which is another narrow passage leading to a cave as large as
three large chambers, dry and miraculously fresh, having a spring
of sweet water in a corner, all a veritable labyrinth high up above
the wicked world in the heart of a mighty mountain. Here, I concealed Duke Arthur, with Bobo the page at the threshold, and a
couple of cotterels in the passage by the pit, out of sight and hearing. But I placed the other four in the passages above, to guard the
same for their lives.

XVIII. *About Duke Arthur his Plight*

Duke Arthur was in a piteous plight. His head and his brow
were lacerated by the shameless thorns: the whole back of him
was cut and wealed by sacrilegious scourges: his right hand and
his left foot gaped open, pierced by nefandous[2] nails, so that my
little finger probed them. Of the wound in his regal youthful
heart, I am to speak presently. His healthy age soon dismissed the
fever of his wounds; and they began to cicatrize[3] themselves. He
was, however, much weakened by the ordeal of his martyrdom,
and whiter than ever, so white that I could see him in the dark
cave with no torch-light. But he lay all day and all night, on his
breast, quite straight, quite still, hiding his face in his left arm,
uttering no single sound. The only word which he had spoken,
since the crime in the Bristol Giwerie, was the word *Defiled*. Many
years after, when I asked him of this mystery, he said that it was
not his poignant torments, or the drenching with lewd blood,

---

[1] *"puteus supparuus."* [Rolfe's note.]

[2] Horrible (*OED* OL).

[3] To skin over or heal (*OED* OL).

which offended him, but the touch of infamous depraved perfidi-
ous hands, pawing and mauling[1] every inch of his flesh, had been
as a spear-thrust in his heart nine-times-nine-times repeated,
outraging his personal sacrosanctity, violating his regal dignity,
defiling the sacred enclosure of his self-respect. O never-sullied
soul. When I saw my lord the king thus languishing, nor making
any effort to recollect his strength, I tried very humbly to comfort
him, speaking more like a loving elder brother to a younger, than
a traitor to the majesty of his liege lord. But he gave no sign of
hearing me. I told him that Fulk the Flame was not far away, not
out of call. I prayed him to declare his sovereign will and pleasure, swearing that it should be fulfilled instantly and at any cost.
But he gave me no word. I felt that my heart would burst right
out of the cage of my bones, when I saw him so crushed down by
sorrow and displeasure, when I remembered one by one the fearful wrongs which he had encountered so cheerfully and endured
so majestically. And, at last, to keep myself from suffocating, I
went out from his presence suddenly; and, having eaten a pudding, I did a most audacious and most sagacious deed.

XVIIII. *About Lady Maud of The Haye her Motherliness*

I took a single cotterel; and rode straight over the Black Mountains, in a night to Braose his castle of The Haye, the same knight
who had captured my lord the king for Softsword at Mirabel.
There, I said my piece to Lady Maud of Saint-Valery,[2] wife of that
magnate, the tale of the blinding and drowning and the sacrilegious crucifixion of Duke Arthur, his beautiful boyhood, his regal
majesty, his most piteous plight. That good lady, faithful wife,
noble mother of a splendid progeny, knew in a minute what to do.
She took me up and trounced me finely with her terrible tongue.
Never had I felt so bethumped since they horsed me at Sempringham:[3] nor had I a word to give back to her. Indeed, so drubbed did
I feel that (for a long time after) I sat delicately, and never by any

---

[1] *"palpans et attrectans."* [Rolfe's note.]

[2] Maude de Braose, wife of William de Braose, accused King John of murdering
Duke Arthur. Rolfe draws here on her reputation for outspokenness.

[3] *"ex eo tempore quo in equuleo porrigebar."* [Rolfe's note.]

chance suddenly. But, when she had finished, she summoned a power of ten; and rode back with me to the cave. How she swore, panting as she climbed up the steep clift where the forest was, and when she squeezed her maternal form through the dark and narrow passages from the pit to the regal chamber, I have not the skill to narrate. But, at length, we had silence when I admitted her to the presence of my lord the king. He was lying as he lay when I left him, his face hidden on his unwounded hand. Lady Maud signed to me to retire with the page to the threshold. But she went forward, and kneeled by the couch of bracken; and, "Lord King," says she, "saving Your Regal Majesty's grace and favour, come and tell a mother what ails thee, Darling."[1]

He turned, and looked. Tears welled in his eyes. But her kind arms held him. He was only a boy.

As for me, I fairly bolted, scut up and quite blind, out of the pit and along the passages far away to the hall where the horses were; and there I howled. In time, Bobo the page interrupted my exercises, summoning me to attend the Lady Maud. She was to govern affairs now: I, to act as her lieutenant. "Our lord the king," says she, and I never heard a herald proclaim a proclamation more proclamatorily, "deigns to accept my castle of The Haye," says she, "where he will be healed of his wounds, and not be starved by reason of the smoky flavour of his puddings, nor kept away from the sweet sunlight, nor be given damned damp blankets[2] to his bed, the poor lamb," says she, flinging the last at my head in a hurried parcel. "Let the Lord of Cuigny be warned to come to his amy instanter:" says she. "Saint-Pol may accompany his ward: but he must be content to serve among my knights:" says she. "As for my lord Braose of Brecon, he stands for his rightful lord and king from this moment; and his wife will see to it, or her name is not Maud of The Haye:" says she. "And all the rest of you, fly," says she, "fly like nighthawks back to Falaise: so that, when the barbaric Welsh beg to be fussy,[3] Softsword will be able to find his Warden of the Welsh March:" says she. "Begone to Falaise, Sir

---

[1] *"Domine Rex, inquit, ut Tua Regali Maiestate gratiam et fauorem donare digneris et quod Tibi dolet dic ad matrem, mi Mellitule."* [Rolfe's note.]

[2] *"lodices humentes."* [Rolfe's note.]

[3] *"satagebunt."* [Rolfe's note.]

Hubert; and know that you returned thither three weeks ago:"
says she. "Above all, remember this," says she: "until you have
defied Softsword, you may not lift an open finger against him for
our lord the king (my sweet bird): nor may you defy till the king
gives you the word, which he will give when he has his health and
knows his right mind (my pretty dear):" says she, pouring out her
hard words like the marbles which patter out of the wallet of a
tripped-up school-boy.

IIII

THE BOOK CALLED THE WICKED UNCLE WORRIED

I. *About Softsword discomfited by the King of the Franks*

King Philip was taking Normandy very seriously: but I had such a power at Falaise as enabled me to inspect his actions with security. Softsword got a council at Oxford to vote him a two-marks scutage, no more, and he wanted ever so much more. He yelled frenetic appeals in the iron faces of the magnates. All was vain. And he had to give up the notion of relieving Saucy Castle. Had he been man enough to wrench himself from that eel his suc-cuba,[1] instead of faring sumptuously every day and staying in bed till dinner-time, when Philip the August first began to comfort himself haughtily, who knows but what he might have stemmed the Frankish flood.[2] But he dillydallied: while King Philip trenched round three sides of that great fortress, and held the river-front with his fleet, so that none might go or come. And, there being no hope of reinforcement, Sir Roger Lacy surrendered, with forty knights and one-hundred-and-twenty men-at-arms. Thus, John lost the key of Normandy, and a power which he could ill afford to lose. He sent Walter the Primate and the bishops of Ely and Nor-wich, *azure, three mitres or*, with Marechal and Earl Robert fil-Per-nell of Leicester, *gules, a cinquefoil ermine*, to sue for peace, intend-ing (of course) to take some foul advantage. But that clammy pig of a Frank coughed hideously and scouted the bare notion. Why should Philip make peace, when he had Maine and Anjou and nearly all Normandy in one hand, and was about to grab Poictou

---

[1] A female demon that has sexual intercourse with men while they sleep (*OED OL*).

[2] Roger of Wendover similarly argued that John lost Normandy because he was "finding all kinds of delights in his queen," indulging in pleasures with her while his castles fell to Philip.

with the other? And he sarcastically retorted an enquiry as to the whereabouts of Duke Arthur. O horror. Softsword had no answer to give to that: for he firmly believed his nephew to be in heaven; and it was altogether out of the question that he should describe the road by which he had sent him thitherward. So he sulked in sullen silence. And, seeing Normandy as good as lost, and, desiring to save Touraine and Poictou, he sent me order to evacuate Falaise, and named me Constable of the castle of Chinon. I will give the tale of Softsword's power. I held Chinon; and Sir Gerald d'Athys, *argent, three fesslets sable, a bend gules*, held the castle of Loches, both in Touraine. In Poictou, John had the castles of Niort and Rochelle with Sir Robert Turnham and Sir Savary Malaleone, *gules, a lyon or*, and the castle of Thouars under Viscount Amaury, brother of Guy. Further south, the Earl of Angoulesme was friendly to the Wild Ass, on account of Lady Jezebel his daughter; and many Gascon magnates also were friendly, because their port of Bordeaux sent much wine to the English. But Sir Guy de Thouars favoured neither Philip nor John, having made himself a snug little nest in Armorica, which duchy he ruled as regent for his baby, Lady Alys—he being one of that very great multitude who knew not that her half-brother Duke Arthur still had life in this naughty world. King Philip, then, gobbled up[1] the remainder of Normandy, eating Falaise and Bayeux and Coutances and Cherbourg and Barfleur and Caen and Avranches like a pudding, by mouthfuls, one after the other. And, the more he ate, the more his appetite increased. He allied with Duke Henry of Louvain, *gules, a fess argent*, and with Earl Reinald Dampmartin of Boulogne. And then he cast a lickerish[2] eye on England.

II. *About Softsword discomfited by the Magnates*

The English magnates became frightfully excited, not relishing the notion of another Conquest. In this, they played for Softsword; and he took good care to goad them on with panics and alarums. He writted[3] his military tenants. He offered two shil-

---

[1] *"obsorbit."* [Rolfe's note.]
[2] Greedy (*OED* OL).
[3] Served them with a summons (*OED* OL).

lings (instead of one) to men-at-arms, in a council at Northampton. He dashed to Porchester to collect an enormous army. But the magnates remained quite firm in refusing to serve oversea. Walter the Primate and Marechal went to speak for them to Softsword, saying that they were willing enough to fight in defence of England, but they fancied that an offensive expedition against that Frank (now flushed with triumph) was far too risky. "Go you at least to serve me in Poictou:" says John in a fume to Marechal. "Nay: for I have done homage to King Philip for my Poictevin domains, and I may not bear arms against my liege:" says Marechal. "Then give me your son William, your heir, as hostage for your good conduct in England while I war in Poictou:" snarls Softsword. Mark, o most affable reader, that William Marechal was the magnate who first forced John into the regal seat of Duke Arthur in contempt of all right and justice. Mark the reward of the wicked, o most affable reader. O manners.

The Wild Ass pranced to Portsmouth for the shipping of stores and munitions of war, by no means relinquishing his plan. And, what a condition he was in there, surrounded by a talkative and ever-increasing muster of magnates, utterly useless to him since they would not go to the only place where he could use them, and tantalizing him by their stupid readiness to serve him in the place where he could not use them. Is it any wonder that he performed the solemnity called Tearing the Hair?[1] In the end, he tried a compromise. Many magnates resembled the muster which Messire Saint David King and Confessor, that celebrated warrior of Hierusalem, collected in antique times:[2] for they were either lepers, or in debt or distress or discontentment; and these were ready to take the risks of a war in France. Their condition could not be worse, here: there, it might become very much better. So, Softsword proposed that magnates, who would not serve oversea, should pay for those magnates who would. Grunts and groans and tooth-gnashings greeted this great idea. Many magnates objected to being summoned to Portsmouth at great expense, and to being dismissed not only without compensation but with this new tax to tap their trea-

---

[1] Tearing the hair is a sign of grief. See Ezra 9:3.

[2] After leaving Saul's court, David led a band of outlaws, debtors, and fugitives in the Judaean desert.

suries. Thus was the Wild Ass hobbled, unable to go forth, unwilling to go back. O leper. Meanwhile, I arranged to lose Chinon, and Athys lost Loches, we becoming King Philip's prisoners. This was convenient: for it gave me a little leisure with my dear wife among the merry Franks, whose circumstances I made occasion to examine, covertly but carefully, for divers eminent reasons.

III. *About Softsword beginning to be Discomfited by Clergymen*

Walter was the Primate weak enough to let William Marechal foist John into the regal seat of Duke Arthur, in contempt of all right and justice and also of his own judgment. And, when Walter the Primate finished his life at the archiepiscopal manor of Teynham in Kent, the grateful Softsword, on hearing of it, said: "Now, I am beginning to be King of the English;"[1] and he pranced to Canterbury to steal the archbishop's treasure, wherewith he might buy a new army. O manners. And, at Canterbury, comical events occurred. A mob of monks,[2] and a bunch of bishops, and one wild ass,[3] simultaneously (but separately) discovered that they alone enjoyed the right of electing the new archbishop. Softsword put forward Bishop John Grey of Norwich; and the other bishops mentioned (with mild and ghibelline[4] stolidity) that that was the very clergyman whom they themselves had just been about to elect. But the Canterbury monks had stolen a march upon the rival electors, by convening a midnight chapter and electing their superior Mr. Reinald, whom they promptly packed off to Rome for our lord the Pope His confirmation. They did their deed in secret; and they bade their Mr. Reinald to conceal his dignity by the way, lest Softsword should catch him before Pope Innocent had sealed him securely in the primacy. For most clergymen nourished a holy horror of Softsword. And amazing events sprang from this beginning, as I shall narrate anon.[5]

---

[1] "*nunc primum Anglorum sum rex.*" [Rolfe's note.] This anecdote is drawn from Matthew Paris.

[2] "*Monachorum multitudo.*" [Rolfe's note.]

[3] "*Episcoporum circulus atque onagrus unus.*" [Rolfe's note.]

[4] The Ghibellines were an aristocratic political party that opposed the Pope.

[5] John's disagreement with the Pope over who should be the next bishop of

IIII. *About Softsword his Spasms in France*

Viscount Amaury squealed for help from John, alleging that he merited it, because he had tried to bring his brother Guy with Armorica to Softsword's side, and because he could not hold his castle of Thouars without it. But King Philip, to teach the said Sir Guy that Is is better than Might-be, carefully demolished his castle of Brissac-on-Loire; and so prevented him from behaving ill-advisedly. But Softsword got magnates enough out of England to form a respectable power; and led them from Portsmouth to Yarmouth in Wight, where he took ship for Poictou. Seven days later, he landed at Rochelle. Aquitaine welcomed him. And a fortnight's siege of Bourg-on-Gironde smashed up Philip's partizans in their headquarters. If John, wild and asinine, had not been addicted to spasms of periodic crime and carnality, I do not deny that he might have been a notorious war-lord. The king of the Franks crumpled up, like vellum in a torch-flame, before him when he took the field; and, indeed, fat Philip could do nothing more than to garrison Chinon, and Poictiers, and Mirabel, for defending that Frankish frontier wherein he hastened to seclude himself. But Softsword raged on. He sacked Angers, plundering even the churches. He raided Anjou and Armorica. And he entrenched himself at Thouars. But, there, Philip found him a nuisance; and was compelled to offer him battle. Everybody expected a cataclysm, when those two great powers should collide. They did not collide. Philip the August had the frigid flutters. And John suddenly slid back with a slap into the clutch of his slut. The knights of both powers gazed vacantly into what they could see of one another's faces, till many of their minds actually

---

Canterbury was one of the important events to occur during his reign. The king wished for his close friend, Bishop John Gray, to occupy the position, but the monks of Canterbury secretly elected their subprior, Reginald. Faced with this disagreement, Pope Innocent encouraged the monks to abandon their candidate and elect Stephen Langton, who shared the Pope's views on church reform. John was furious, and he expelled the monks of Canterbury from England. When John refused to receive Langton into England and allow the monks of Canterbury to return, Pope Innocent placed England and Wales under an interdict.

became unhinged. So, both potentates jumped at the proposal of a two-years' truce, whereby each kept the allegiance of his own tenants. But Softsword also consented to lose all rights north of River Loire, he being in a hurry to enjoy ease with (or without) dignity. He spent weeks in pleasure at the seaside by Rochelle: whence, sailing to Wareham, he went on to Bere Regis.

v. *About Braose his convenient Behaviour*

I cannot remember exactly all that Braose did at this time: nor is such remembrance necessary. I know that Duke Arthur gradually became less shocked and more comfortable at the castle of The Haye; and I also know that Braose behaved conveniently without defying Softsword. He, this Braose, was a ruddy auburn-haired crisp-headed rather-clownish magnate, with a profound habit of silence owing (no doubt) to the overpowering loquacity of his good Lady Maud; and I believe that he knew as much as I knew, and did as I was doing, by specific command of Duke Arthur.[1] But, not being as skilful a Janus[2] as Hubert de Burgh, he was not able to be perfectly happy and careless in Softsword's vicinity. So, he took from the Wild Ass certain feofs in Munster, for which he was to pay five-thousand marks in ten yearly instalments, five-hundred marks each year; and he went to Ireland, ostensibly to set the said feofs in order, but really to evade impertinences from Softsword's messengers visiting him at The Haye: which visitations would certainly have incommoded Duke Arthur. Wherefore, I assert that Braose behaved conveniently.

vi. *About Softsword discomfited by Clergymen and by the Immeasurable Clergyman*

Softsword found himself at grips with a far lustier antagonist than that mere Philip the August.

---

[1] William de Braose was in fact suspected of involvement in Arthur's death. He was treated quite well during the early part of John's reign, but he fell out of favor with the king after Arthur's disappearance.

[2] Roman deity, the gatekeeper of heaven, with two faces facing in opposite directions.

As soon as Mr. Reinald (late of Canterbury) had crossed the
Narrow Sea, he clean forgot his brother-monks' injunctions. Not
every day is a small superior bunted up to a primacy; and the
chops of Mr. Reinald watered copiously at the savour of brank-
new[1] archiepiscopality. Accordingly, he happed himself up in
highly-conspicuous archbishopskins and trumpeters, and proudly
pervaded the road to Rome all a-quiver with awful and sinful
pomp and peacockism. When, thus, he reached the Apostle's
Threshold, "And who may Your Blessedness be?" says some curial
quidnunc.[2] "We, Reinald," says Mr. R., "are the successor of Messires Saints Augustine, Alphege, Dunstan, Anselm, and Thomas
Beket,[3] primate of all England, pope of an opposite orb;[4] and, if it
please you, We have come for Our pall." So they kindly took him
in to see about him.[5]

Hot on his heels, comes that small bishop of Norwich. "And
who may Your Blessedness be?" says our lord the Pope. "Bishop of
Norwich by Your Paternity's favour: but the King of the English
would have me now to be Archbishop of Canterbury, also by Your
Paternity's favour; and, if it please You, I have come for my pall:"
says Lord John Grey. So he also was kindly taken in, that they
might see about him too.

"It appears to Us," says the Lord Pope Innocent to His cardinals, and He was a man of whipcord and tempered steel, with
the eye of a squinting lambkin,[6] and very affable to lepers (for
so King Arthur told me)—"it appears to Us," says the said Lord
Pope, "that these English rustics will have to learn a little lesson."
And, "Shame on you, Mr. Reinald," says He, "for thinking that
a primate is a thing to be made out of midnight whispers." And,
"Shame on you, John Bīp.,"[7] says He, "for thinking that a primate
is a thing to be made by a king (and not so very much of a king

---

[1] Brand new.

[2] A person who is constantly asking, "What now?"; an inquisitive person. (*OED*
OL).

[3] Augustine, Alphege, Dunstan, Anselm, and Thomas Becket were all archbishops
of Canterbury.

[4] "*alterioris papa orbis.*" [Rolfe's note.]

[5] "*eum acceperunt comiter ut et ei prouiderent.*" [Rolfe's note.]

[6] "*paetuli agniculi.*" [Rolfe's note.]

[7] "*Epe.*" [Rolfe's note.]

either), or by a bunch of bashful obsequious bishops.[1] Palls are
not for the likes of either of you two clergymen, nor primacies,"
says He: "so get you both back to your pews again, and let Us have
here those shocking monks of Canterbury, who shall learn of Us
how a primate of all England ought to be elected." So Bǐp. John
Grey returned to Norwich to pursue a mischievous career: but
Mr. Reinald went into business as a pirate among the Portuguese,
where (I believe) he did extremely well. And sixteen monks were
sent, as the Pope ordained, with proxies to act for the chapter of
Canterbury. In Rome, they stood; and trembled.

"Cast your eyes over Christendom," says our lord the Pope
to them, "and see you which clergyman, engendered of putrified
blood in the fury of lust,[2] you will choose for your archbishop."
And they rolled their obedient eyes round, and round, and round,
over Christendom, like lepers in their fits of prophesying. "May it
please Your Paternity," they say, dreadfully worried and shaking
like palsied hares on their forms, "we, as it seems, are so dazzled
by the splendour of the Apostolic Presence that we cannot see,
excepting with the eyes of Your Paternity." "Very good indeed,"
says our lord the Pope: "then see ye here this lord, the Lord Stephen Langthon, a fine one of Our cardinals, well known to Us personally as a most learned and worthy clergyman." The mouths of
the Canterbury monks began to bubble. "Speak your minds (such
as they are) freely:" says our lord the Pope. And the sixteen Canterbury monks intoned in magniloquent unison, "We elect the said
Lord Stephen for our archbishop." "And We, in token of Our singular affection, do most lovingly impart our Apostolic Benediction
to you all, and to your holy house:" says Pope Innocent the Great.
And He instantly proclaimed and confirmed the said election.

VII. *About Softsword minded to make a Meal of Clergymen*

When the shocking news of the Primate Langthon came to

---

[1] "*uerecundorum et episcopalium assentatorum.*" [Rolfe's note.]

[2] "*conceptum de sanguine per ardorem libidinis putrefacto.*" (This elegant and far from
weak expression seems to have been characteristic of Innocent the Third's idea
and style: for it actually does occur in a not dissimilar context in that pontiff's
treatise *De Contemptu Mundi.*—P. and C. [Rolfe's note.]

England, several people capered very excitedly;[1] and the Wild Ass
was the chief of them. He also vociferated a quantity of sudden
language,[2] applying weird and exquisite names to the Pope and
Cardinal Stephen. The Lord Innocent remained serene; and
Himself consecrated Canterbury's new archbishop, as a token
that the matter was settled. Softsword retorted by sending Sir
Fulk Cantelupe, *gules, three lys or,* and a notary called Reinald of
Cornhill to confiscate the lands both of the Canterbury convent
and archbishopric; and he forbade appeal to Rome. The Canterbury monks scampered headlong in a mob to the convent of
Saint-Bertin at Saint-Omer. The Cardinal-Primate took up his
abode at Pontigny, where (like his glorious predecessor Messire Saint Thomas Beket of Acre) he archiepiscopized in exile.
In this way, Softsword began seriously to make a meal of clergymen. Not content with a quarrel which would have daunted
his betters, the Wild Ass made no attempt to fortify himself by
agreeing with those others whose necks he was already biting.
On the contrary: he comported himself even more disagreeably
than ever to the English, laying yet another tax of twelvepence
in the mark on rents and moveables, compelling clergymen as
well as laymen to pay it. Of course his pugnacious half-brother,
Archbishop Geoffrey of York, withstood him to the face, launch-
ing ex-communications on tax-collectors who buzzed[3] in the ears
of his clergymen. And, of course, having set this blight to work,
he scurried to Rome, leaving his archiepiscopal estates for Softsword to confiscate, as usual.

VIII. *About Hubert de Burgh his News of Duke Arthur*

John sent me news of his difficulties, where I was in France.
Most of his magnates, and all of his clergymen but two, were bris-
tling their backs, and looking obliquely, and expatiating in an insolent manner. One would have thought (from his letters) that he
was a very ill-used sovereign. Moreover, he was shocked to say that

---

[1] *"motus incitatissimos dederunt."* [Rolfe's note.]
[2] *"Et sermones nociferabatur copiosos repentesque."* [Rolfe's note.]
[3] *"bomba facientes."* [Rolfe's note.]

there was a certain humming going on in the Welsh hive,[1] foreboding mischief; and he desired me to pay my ransom to Philip like an honest knight, and to quit France for the guarding of my March of Wales. This I gladly did: for I also had news of Duke Arthur.

My lord the king desired to depart from The Haye. Not that he had outstayed his welcome. Not that the Braose displeased him. He always deemed them friends in need. Lady Maud, he said, was one of the very best.[2] That hard pleasant dictatorial garrulous virago, rich in love, had mothered the motherless, fathered the fatherless, healed the sick, comforted the outraged soul, accompanied the lonely heart, most faithfully served the king. Her big sons also had done their part, specially young Bishop Giles Braose of Hereford, who, being a clergyman, understood, and treated intelligently, the fancy which had worried the heart of the regal canon of Saint-Martin's of Tours. But Duke Arthur wished to relieve these loyal lieges of the danger of his presence: for, now that the excitement of the Welsh barbarians was accomplished, there was other work to be done. Beside, it was far from unlikely that the Wild Ass, hearing rumour of movements, might gallop thitherward; and, if he found The Haye closed against him, undesirable suspicion would infect his beastly mind. And, lastly, Duke Arthur was for moving, because a great and notable change of life had come to him, and to Sir Fulk the Flame.

---

[1] The Welsh had historically caused many problems for English kings. During his reign, John frequently stirred conflict between the Welsh princes in order to prevent the emergence of a single powerful leader. Soon after John took the throne, a warrior prince, Llywelyn ap Iorwerth, had come into power in Wales, taking over most of the region. John was forced to confront this new and powerful ruler and decide whether to attempt to conquer him or transform him into an ally.

[2] "*quaedam esse egregiam inter optimis.*" [Rolfe's note.]

V

THE BOOK CALLED THE AWAKENING OF ARTHUR

I. *About Duke Arthur and his Amy their admirable Aspect at Adolescence*

When I left Duke Arthur, he was a very large boy in his full ripe bloom, sprightly and lithe as his panthers of England, clean as a wild white primrose of Messire Saint George in body and soul. When I left the Lord of Cuigny, he was a red-hot enormous boy, portentously supple and strong as befitted the cub of the Lionheart. When I saw the pair again, they were altered. They had just passed the line which divides boyhood from youth. They had entered a new world and strange, wherein they stepped with a certain curious reticence, or hesitation, which had no relation whatever to timidity. The change in them was most significant. Sir Fulk the Flame was more fiery, more forceful, more nimble than ever, very much larger, much more terrific: because his knowledge had grown with his sinuous body and his sinewy limbs. But the burthen of new youth weighed heavily on Duke Arthur; and his splendid form burned with the fever of sudden strong increase of power. In height, he towered above men. He was very long of his legs, and rather gaunt of his frame, whereon his youth-hood was building up the virile muscles day by day. His clean eyes gleamed brightly: but fatigue veiled them till the whole work should be completed; and the hectic flush on his still-smooth cheeks gave token of the fresh fire flaring up within. From which portents I augured that I must deal as with men.

II. *About Hubert de Burgh his Account rendered to Duke Arthur*

Thus, then, I saw my lord the king and his cousin, when I made occasion to go secretly from my castle of Candidachester

to The Haye. Duke Arthur sat in his state to receive me; and he
gave me memorable words. I know what I owe to Lady Maud. My
grief is that my duty to my king prevented me from ever paying
her her just due: for, though she was wont to scold me horribly
to my face, I never paid a better trumpeter to praise my deeds
behind my back. And these were the words of Duke Arthur. Says
he: "We give you welcome, Hubert, with a powerless hand, but
with a heart full of unfeigned love."[1] That is what he said; and set
my heart on fire. But he refused to accept my faith: for, said he,
the time had not yet come when I might defy his uncle, with the
certainty of skinning that usurper bare of all his usurpations; and
nothing less was to be considered even for an instant. "We will
have all, or nothing:" said Duke Arthur, in the words of Messire
Saint Julius Cæsar, Emperor of the Romans and Martyr.[2] And he
required me instantly to propose plans. I told him all about Softsword, the unbridled slavery of that beast to little Lady Jezebel,
his convulsive scrimmages with magnates,[3] his infuriate tyranny
in the kingdom, his disgraceful eviction of Philip the August, his
uproarious ferocity to clergymen and lepers, and his obstreperous
caperings in face of our lord the Pope. I described the enormous
army of cotterels whereby he maintained himself, a strident ass in
the pelt of the panthers of England.[4] I mentioned those magnates
who were certain to keep faith with him. I gave the tale of my
military tenants on whose service I could count, the tale of my
veteran mercenaries, the tale of the picked garrison of my ten
castles, with the tale of those magnates whom I could persuade to
defy John with me, and the tale of their several powers. You perceive, o most affable reader, how that my lord the king, in all his
tribulations, was ever faithful to his own regal majesty, inspiring
us also, his lieges and lovers, with the same most splendid faith.
And here, in the tome which I shall call The Tome of Faith, I will
mark the point where the seeds of the strong flower of Hope were

---

[1] "*te Huberte salutamus manu impotente sed simplicis amoris animo et apert repleto
dixit Arthurus Dux.*" [Rolfe's note.]

[2] "*Aut Cæsar aut nihil,*" meaning "Cæsar or nothing," was the motto of Julius
Cæsar.

[3] "*de rixis eius spasticis cum magnatis.*" [Rolfe's note.]

[4] "*asinum stridentem pantherarum pell. Anglicarum tectum gerete.*" [Rolfe's note.]

planted, when I rendered my account to Duke Arthur at the castle of The Haye.

My lord the king, having heard me, required me to provide a place where he might lie securely while he pondered my hope-inspiring news; and his will was to quit The Haye within the week. I offered my four neighbouring castles on the March, saying as follows, Grosmont and Scenefrith and Candidachester were situate in lonely places: but Monmouth was on the highway of River Wye (and on that account to be avoided). Grosmont was an old castle, not very strong, and needing to be rebuilded (as I did rebuild it later): but it was well placed, with a distant view on all sides of an approaching enemy. Scenefrith, on the contrary, was inconspicuous and hard to find, hidden in the vale of River Monnow, a brank-new tower in a squarish curtain-wall with bastions, surrounded by a labyrinthine reticulation of vast moats, thoroughly palisaded. And Candidachester also was quite new, placed even higher than Grosmont, and much more commodious, being (in fact) entirely my own work and the very apple of my eye. I also offered certain excellent advice, which Duke Arthur deigned to accept. And these are the things which were done in consequence.

III. *About Duke Arthur going from The Haye and coming to the Manor of Turberville*

I rode away without concealment on the next day. What suspicion could attack the Warden of the March when he went from one of his castles to another? Why should I not visit Braose at The Haye, he being lord of Brecon and also of Radnor and Abergavenny and Chepstow, and, like me, he also had in charge to see the king's peace kept on the Welsh March. But Braose understood the real business in hand as well as I did; and he looked down his nose most admirably.

I rode through the valley called Golden, by the Llanthony priory where the Augustinians were beginning to be jolly again[1] despite their black garb; and they made much good cheer for me during half-a-day, which was all the time I could spare from affairs

---

[1] *"hilaritatem integrabant."* [Rolfe's note.]

of state. Thence, by the Patricio hermitage, I came into Uskvale to
the manor of the Turbervilles right in face of Llangattwg, those
knights being very friendly to me because I did a little service
to Mr. Roger their uncle, a monk of Christchurch, who actually
had been the friend of glorious Messire Saint Thomas Beket of
Acre. It was but a trifling affair. An ambitious and overweening
young secular clergyman complacently desired to buy a house for
the treatment of lepers in a mode of his own, that being (in his
opinion) his shortest cut to bishopskins; and he tried to extort the
money for his scheme out of poor old Mr. Roger by bullying him.
I only trumpeted slightly; and the bully retired much shocked and
(some say) with his mind unhinged, leaving the lepers untended
and Mr. Roger in the cloistered obscurity which was his right: but
the Turbervilles were very pleased with me, and asked nothing
better than an opportunity to serve me. So, finding myself able
to use them, I gave them certain explicit instructions, and rode
onward again to my high little castle of Grosmont, where I sat
down to wait for the maturing of my plan.

Two nights after my departure, Lady Maud opened the secret
postern in the dungeon of her castle of The Haye, at midnight;
and let out Duke Arthur and Sir Fulk the Flame, with Saint-Pol
and two entirely faithful cotterels whom I had left for the purpose, namely, Aimar of Ilsley and Reimbert the Ram. This party
went a mile underground by the secret passage to the watch-
tower at Mouse; and there they emerged into open country. They
were all disguised as travelling tumblers, with bare legs and feet
strapped in leathern skins, and very short petticoats of homespun
wool, with good long knives hidden in them. The cotterels had
rustic bows and arrows: but the knights carried ashen jumping
poles useful for other purposes than jumping. And they plunged
straight into the forest, making their way over the Black Mountains from north to south, avoiding lepers and every haunt of
men. Duke Arthur spoke (long afterward) of the delights of this
journey: he always had a quaint taste for divesting himself of
majesty and wandering in the wilds half-naked. Day by day, they
walked among mighty trees, near nothing alive save the birds or
beasts of the forest: they killed their meat to eat with the puddings in their wallets, and they drank sweet water from springs.

Night by night, they slept on the odorous carpets spread beneath the pines. And, after a week in the wilderness, where there is no law, they came to the crest of the last spur of the mountains, which is the rock of Hwylaprhys towering above the Turberville manor of Tirwronowvwyl, so called from the bald Welshman whom the first Turberville dispossessed. There was a secret path down the escarpment of this rock of Hwyl, which a very agile and cool-headed climber need not fear. This, they descended, coming by night to the manor, where they were admitted secretly, their arrival being expected. They rested here during one day, to wash and refresh their bodies, and to do on new disguises. The place was almost as secure for them as a castle, there being no approach from the north, excepting by the fore-named precipice, which three men-at-arms could hold, and not a single leper (who might spy and betray) anywhere in the vicinity. The manor-house itself was strongly fortified. It lay under the precipice, at the apex of a triangle which had a bastion at each corner of its base connected by an impassable palisade. And, below the palisade, was a wide deep moat fed by perennial springs from the mountains. And, below the moat, were earthworks descending steeply to the valley of River Usk. It was safer for Duke Arthur to rest here than in the neighbouring tower of Crwghwyl by Llangattwg, for a tower on a highway, with a village attached to it, is far more liable to visitations than a small fortified manor in the open country. Beside, I had the faith of the three brothers Turberville, namely, Sir Hugh the priest, *argent, a lyon gules,* and Sir Thomas, *ermine, a lyon gules,* and Sir Geoffrey, *sable, three lyons or,* who were my military tenants formerly, and most affable, providing plain liveries of their own for disguising the party, and sending them on the next day, with ten of their own cotterels similarly garbed and all well-mounted, and letters saying (what we all well-know) that the Welsh barbarians required watching. This was the subterfuge whereby Duke Arthur was brought to me safely in my castle of Grosmont.

IIII. *About Duke Arthur occupying the Castles of Grosmont and Scenefrith and Candidachester*

Once within my walls, my lord the king resumed his regal

majesty. He lived in a tower apart, with Sir Fulk the Flame. They spent much time in eating puddings and planning adventures, high up on their battlements. For recreation, they fought and wrestled and did the most astounding tricks of twisting with their bodies. This, at first. My lord the king was by far the best fighter: such, too, was his skill with a common long-bow, that he could (in a twinkling) shoot his arrow between the two legs of a wren: such was his firmness, such his inerrancy, with a common long-sword, that with one slash he could cut a haw[1] from the eye of a gnat without hurting the animals, as far as my observation went; and, moreover, when it pleased him, he could stretch his long legs so shockingly that he seemed to be as tall as the tallest tree in a forest. But Sir Fulk the Flame, had, then, more facility in feats, as is only natural when we remember that he had spent the first thirteen of his sixteen years in Syria, among men who are all very nearly related to serpents or apes or birds or cats. They say that he had this peculiarity (but I cannot vouch for it, as I never observed it), that his breath lasted nine days and nine nights under water: but I firmly say that I have seen him cheerful and strong after going nine days and nine nights without sleeping or eating or drinking. Very subtile was Fulk the Flame.[2] And he had this other peculiarity, that, so fierce was the blazing heat of his nature that water never chilled him, no matter how long he was immersed, and, when it rained hardest, whatever he carried remained dry for a handbreadth above and a handbreadth below his hand: so that, when my lord the king was coldest, his amy was to him as the glow of a fire. The two practised themselves at hanging by a finger, a hand, an arm, a foot, a leg, as agreed, till one or other dropped from sheer exhaustion. They walked up walls, by toes and fingers, carrying one another pick-a-back and otherwise. They leapfrogged over each other,[3] standing erect or bending, going forward and backward with or without reversing. They leaped over everything and everybody, high and low, on sight and incessantly, leaping also back again immediately.

---

[1] "Haw" is a term used to refer to the "third eyelid," or triangular cartilage, in the inner corner of the eye of a horse, dog, etc. (*OED* OL).

[2] "*Subtilissimus erat Fulkus le Flamme.*" [Rolfe's note.]

[3] "*diuaricatus alter alterius cruribus terga transiliunt.*" [Rolfe's note.]

They dived, or flung each other, into my moat, and carried one another swimming. And, falling, they never concussed the earth, crashing, spouting blood, spitting teeth or tongue-tips, or breaking bones, as we do: but they lighted lightly, either on their toes and skipped elsewhere, or on their rumps and bounded up again like corks or bladders. O portentous imps. In brief, from morning to night, we others walked warily in that small castle, for fear of being bunted out of it by collision with a couple of indefatigable and sweaty youngsters who bounced and flew and darted and sprang without warning everywhere, dazing the sight, jerking the body, abashing the mind in a manner perfectly indescribable. But, when, one day, they took to racing round the top of the curtain wall, with flying leaps from battlement to battlement, in full view of the townsfolk across the moat, and also in full view of any chance enemy who might be riding the country for miles around, then, indeed, I up and spoke my mind loudly. Duke Arthur feverishly demanded a less conspicuous asylum; and we rode the same night to Scenefrith in the marshes. Here, they did as they pleased, though the tower was less commodious; and I placed a watch far up all the ravines, which led to it, to give smoke warning of anyone approaching. The low-lying tower, however, and the enclosure of the mountains, soon put us all in low spirits; and we were forced to go onward again, this time to Candidachester, my large new castle of white walls, very high up in a bright and breezy world of blue and white sky, where enormous clean green billows of earth rolled toward on all sides, from vast distances, crested with heathery moorlands of purple, and furred with copses in the dingles.[1] Here, the two might have hardened and suppled themselves to their hearts' content. There was the great gatehouse, with its pair of huge round-towers, and the mighty curtain connecting it with four smaller towers, all enclosing the middle ward. And the moat surrounding it was thirty-six yards wide and twelve yards deep, a dew-pool (they call it),[2] most wonderful there on the top of a mountain, always full and fresh, fed neither by springs nor by streams, but mysteriously, by elves or by angels of the Lord God,[3]

---

[1] Copses are thickets of small trees; dingles are deep dells or hollows (*OED OL*).

[2] "*roris lacuna (ut dicitur).*" [Rolfe's note.]

[3] "*arcane, per numina siluestria, uel per angelos Domini Dei.*" [Rolfe's note.]

and no man knows when or how. There was also the little barbacan[1] at the south, on a crescent-shaped moat, formidably revetted
and counterscarped.[2] And, at the north, was the great barbacan,
also moated, and fortified with an extern gatehouse and four
towers on a massive curtain-wall. And this castle was (as I say)
the apple of my eye, though nothing like as large or important or
magnificent as my castle of Dover, for example: for I had had it
all rebuilded, on an antique Roman castle, after a plan of my very
own.

v. About Planta Genista rooted at Candidachester

But, ample and commodious as Candidachester was, suitable
also as seemed the opportunity, my lord the king was not long to
disport himself there. The monstrous burthen of his fast-grow-
ing youth came even more heavily upon him from the very day
when he first entered my fortress; and a great lassitude of limb
and a great heaviness of mind began to weigh him down. As with
Duke Arthur, so with Sir Fulk fil-Richard. They moved little and
slowly: they ate and slept portentously; and their preference was
for a grassy breezy nook in a secluded meadow beyond the wall,
so that I set guards constantly to attend them unseen. One thing I
did, at this time, which made Duke Arthur love me a little more.
For, four of my knights came from Anjou, having paid their ransoms in order to attend to their affairs in England; and, by my
bidding, they brought me a growing bush of Planta Genista[2] as
big as a boy, rooted in a barrel of Angevin earth: for I have a liking
for that honest cheerful very-splendid herb; and, knowing it to
be hardy, I was minded to set it in my favourite castle to give
me pleasure. And, when they brought this yellow broom, I made
an oblation of it as homage to my lord the king, it being clearly
due to him as the badge of his regal race. And he returned sweet

---

[1] A barbacan, or barbican, is an outer fortification for a city or castle (*OED* OL).
[2] A revetment is the retaining-wall that supports the face of an earthen rampart
or the side of a ditch. A counter-scarp is the outer wall or slope of the ditch that
supports a covered way (*OED* OL).
[2] *"Planta genista"* is the common broom plant, which the Plantagenet kings used
as an emblem and from which they took their name.

thanks; and, with his own hands, he set it in the earth of Candi-dachester, barrel and all, where it flourishes in golden glory to this day. And the two imps bore a broom-sprig in their caps there-after, as long as they were in the neighbourhood. And, that same day, came secretly to me most shocking tidings from the castle of The Haye. O times.

VI. *About Pope Innocent severe with Softsword*

Our lord the Pope set out to be frightfully firm with Soft-sword. It is the most ticklish job in the world to eat clergymen, and impossible to assimilate them without tolerating untimely borborygms,[1] cataclysmal eructations,[2] very bilious paroxysms. If then. Pope Innocent sent shocking letters to Lord William Saint-Mère-Eglise, *argent, on a cross azure, an M crowned or* (who had been a foundling,[3] as his cognomen shows, before he was Bishop of London), and to Bishops Eustace of Ely and Mauger of Worcester, instructing them to threaten the Wild Ass with a horrible interdict on England, because of his boorish wild and asinine behaviour to clergymen, of whom the Cardinal-Primate was chief and living in exile. Also, the said Pope Innocent sent shocking letters to all the other bishops, inciting them to render to Cæsar (meaning Softsword) not a tittle more than his dues, and the rest elsewhere, without being tepid about it or caring one jot for persecution. Also, His Paternity sent shocking letters to all the magnates (never was there such a writer of letters as little Pope Innocent the Great), bidding them to show true and faith-ful lealty to John by opposing him till he quitted his present path of a Rehoboam[4] who used scorpions for scourges, having a little finger thicker than his father's loins. And, moreover, our lord the Pope commanded three bishops to go and insist that Softsword

---

[1] Rumbling in the bowels (*OED* OL).

[2] Belches (*OED* OL).

[3] *"puer expositus fuerat."* [Rolfe's note.]

[4] Rehoboam was a king of Judah (922 B.C.-915 B.C.). Taxes had been high under Solomon, and the people asked for taxes to be lowered when Rehoboam became king. He responded, "My father beat you with whips, but I will beat you with scorpions." See 1 Kings 12:1-14.

should make honourable amend to the factious Archbishop Geoffrey of York: which three bishops were Ely, and Worcester, and
young Bishop Giles Braose of Hereford. The Wild Ass pranced
a bit, at their trumpetings; and began to shuffle his feet and his
intentions. "Tell the Pope," says he, "that I will obey His mandate,
saving my prerogative and my heirs." The three bishops shared
this message with the Cardinal-Primate at Pontigny on their
road to Rome. "Go no further, my beloved suffragans,"[1] says that
indomitable rigid clergyman: "for, for my part, I will not consent
to the beast's submission on any conditions whatever." And he
sent this ultimatum, with the bishops and their message, to our
lord the Pope, Who loudly applauded him, and remitted a bull to
the said bishops ordaining the affliction of England with a shocking interdict, on such and such a day, unless Softsword should
have eaten a dirt-pudding before it. So, Softsword brayed more
stridently than ever; and sought for someone on whom he might
vent his fury. O manners.

VII. *About Softsword assaulting Braose of The Haye*

His choice of a victim fell upon The Haye: because young
Bishop Giles Braose was acting very particularly for the Pope: but
that was not the reason given. Softsword affirmed that Sir William Braose was cheating him, having paid no more than seven-
hundred out of the five-thousand marks agreed for his feofs in
Munster. Now the five-thousand marks were not yet due; and
the feofs were poor ones; and Braose asked either for a remission
of part of the price, or for time in which to squeeze his tenants
more thoroughly. This was so just, that the Wild Ass perforce
consented: but he took the Braose castles of Brecon and Radnor as
security; and, further, he demanded the person of William junior,
Braose's heir, as a hostage. "No child of mine shall be entrusted to
the murderer of Duke Arthur:" roars Lady Maud, with appalling
audacity, to Softsword's pursuivant.[2] And she gathered her chick-

---

[1] Assistant bishops (*OED* OL).
[2] A royal or state messenger (*OED* OL).

ens beneath her wings in her nest of The Haye, preparing her castle for siege. O maternity.

VIII. *About Hubert de Burgh his Reason for keeping Duke Arthur in Ignorance*

I carefully and most artfully prevented the shocking news of Braose from reaching my lord the king: for I was ware how hardly the onrush of new youth was afflicting him. The proverb says, *Change not your horses while crossing a stream*; and I was well determined that no new troubles should worry Duke Arthur, till his strength was able to support and to wield and to brandish the burthen of youth. For this is the most awful period in the life of a youngster; and many a one is ruined, or rendered a niddering,[1] by being forced or permitted to use his untried weapons before he has learned how to hold them. I myself had the felicity of coming late to my own youth among the monks of Sempringham. Thereafter, I had the necessary tranquil months, alone, at my father's manor, in which to settle firmly in my new shape: so that I know quite well what I am saying. And I have done the same with my own four sons and two grandsons in their turn, namely, I have helped and even incited them to use and to test and to risk themselves in absolute freedom, during their boyhood: but, during the first fierce months of youth, I have kept away from them every single distraction which might perchance impede them in learning their lesson. For the lesson is no less than the lesson of birth and of death. And herein are mysteries. Every man is born alone; and every man must die alone. Twice he is born; and twice he dies. The first birth and the last death do not matter: because a man is unconscious of the pangs of his birth, these being borne for him by the mother of him; and he learns how to bear the pangs of his death, by the exercises in which (during life) he engages. But, when a man has lived his first merry careless fifteen or sixteen years, suddenly he comes to the point when he must watch the death of his own boyhood and assist at the birth of his own youth. At first, he is frightened; and he shuns the gaze even of

---

[1] A coward (*OED* OL).

his lovers. Then, he sets his teeth, and sits still to observe the fearsome thing. His youth is born, with mind-rending body-tearing pangs; and he becomes more terrified than ever at the awful event which has happened to him. He secludes himself, palpitating. Then, he braces up every scrap of courage which he can find in every cranny and crevice of himself, and nerves himself to carry the weight of his new self as artfully and as graciously and as unashamedly as possible; and, lo, the bogey (faced) is not so very terrifying or unusual after all. Nevertheless, the shock of the death of boyhood, and the horror of the birth of youth, is that which marks a man indelibly, as it is borne well or ill. Hence, it behoves knights to behave most gently and most perspicaciously and most firmly in a matter of this sort. Therefore, I kept Duke Arthur in total ignorance of the misfortunes of the Braose. I did this quite deliberately. I had to sin mortally, this-way, or another way. I chose this way, with my eyes quite wide open; and I am content to be responsible; and you, o most affable reader, may think of me just what you please.[1]

ix. *About the Interdict on England*

The three bishops announced the date when the interdict would be inflicted upon England. The Wild Ass rent the firmament with his rageful braying. "Teeth of God,"[2] he swore, "if this be done, I will pack off every singular clergyman to Rome, with his eyes torn out and hanging on his ugly face by their natural strings." O manners. The day came. The three bishops boggled no longer. They proudly placed the interdict on England; and fled forthwith to safer shores, without even their trumpeters. London, Ely, Worcester, Bath, Hereford, fled to France. Bishop Herbert le Poer of Salisbury, and Bishop Gilbert Glanville of Rochester, went with permission to Scotland. I do not excuse any of these. Bishop Philip of Durham and Bishop Geoffrey of Coventry migrated to The Lord. Only two bishops remained with Softsword, namely, Bĩp. John Grey of Norwich and Peter Roches of Winchester, both

---

[1] *"et iudicas me, o lector affabilissime, perinde ut quod tibi libet."* [Rolfe's note.]
[2] *"Dendez."* [Rolfe's note.]

bad ones. Awful indeed was the plight of England, deprived of
the service of respectable clergymen: though I cannot deny that
the Cistercians did a manly thing. For, when all other clergymen
ceased from massing,[1] or dispensing christian rites and closed
their churches, the said Cistercians did the same, dutifully obeying the decree of our lord the Pope: but, seeing soon how evil it
was for men to lose their rites, those monks set themselves out to
be harmless as doves and also wily as serpents, all for good; and
they were ware that (after all) they were not bound to observe
interdicts proclaimed by bishops, but only the decrees of the Cistercian abbot of abbots decreed in general chapter. They, therefore, not wishing to create unnecessary fusses, kept their churches
closed as the interdict ordained; but they forthwith set up altars
on village-greens and in marketplaces, whereon they sacrificed
suitably, with candles lighted and ringing of bells, whereby many
excellent christians and lepers were much comforted. But, when
news of this came to our lord the Pope, He hastened to emit anathemas: it being His holy intention to afflict Softsword by raising
England in indignation against him; and this could not be done
while the English remained not incommoded. So, He gave a mandate to the Cistercian abbot of abbots, who, in turn, commanded
his monks to light no candles and to ring no bells and to say no
masses for the solace and enjoyment of the people of England.
And, this being duly obeyed, there ensued a great deal of secret
sobbing, which very shortly turned into hearty cursing of Softsword, whose sinfulness had brought us into such discomfiture.
But, as long as we did nothing but curse, the Wild Ass was not
seriously inconvenienced: for he was by no means a pious person;
and the loss of his rites did not afflict him individually. He frisked,
bellowing, on the road of revenge, thinking to worry the Pope
by insulting clergymen, putting them on pittances, and harass-
ing them with taxes on their wives and housekeepers.[2] Nor was
this all. Highwaymen murdered a clergyman on my March. O
manners. When I sent them to the King's court for the capital sentence, Softsword himself intervened to enlarge them: "Let them

---

[1] "*sacrificio intermittebant.*" [Rolfe's note.]

[2] "*eos uectigalibus distinens pro uxoribus suis et focarus.*" [Rolfe's note.]

go free, for they have only slain one of my enemies," says he. O
manners. And, on this becoming known, unruly and masterless
men everywhere engaged in the piking of priests as a pastime.
So, disorder increased. Everyone with a grievance endeavoured
to mend it by force, secure of escape from justice when might was
right amid the chaos which religion had failed to illuminate. O
times.

x. *About Braose in rebellion and flight*

Sir William Braose caught the common fever so badly that his
mind became unhinged. He exploded in open rebellion, giving
no one any warning, and sacked the city of Leominster, as a token
of his opinion of Softsword and to defray his own expenses. Then,
he fled to Ireland with his wife and family, refuging with the
Lacys his relations: for he had sense enough to see that it was all
over with him in England. Softsword swooped on to the March
to grab the leavings of Braose. And, lest his wicked uncle should
catch him again, I returned Duke Arthur with Sir Fulk fil-Richard
and Bobo Kemp the page and four choice cotterels to the caves in
the heights of Llangattwg. As I have said, I did not let him hear
a word of the ruin of Braose: for a chivalrous youth very often
ruins himself in such a case. And Arthur was the only hope of all
England.

xi. *About the Portentous Event at the Caves of Llangattwg*

Let it be understood how we were. I guarded the frontier-
line of the March with my quadrilateral of fortresses, Grosmont,
Scenefrith, Candidachester, and Monmouth; and none of the bar-
barous Welsh could pass by me into England. But the Braose castles of Abergavenny, Tretower, Brecon, Radnor, and The Haye,
being inside the said March, had been used to break the shock
of Welsh onsets before they reached me. Now that Braose was
a fugitive rebel, the case was different. All Uskvale was creeping with ferments unchecked; and the Welsh barbarians surged
along, from Brecon, right down past the castle of Dinas (where
the black man was), as far as undefended Abergavenny; and, every

now and then, the wave of revolt dashed itself to pieces against my white walls of Candidachester. It was at this time when Soft-sword, for no known reason but a wild and asinine one, named me Shire-reeve of Lincoln and Constable of the castle and city of Lafford. And then a portentous event occurred at the caves of Llangattwg. The summer sun was blazing in the sign of the lion. Duke Arthur, now full-flushed with new virility, found himself very susceptible to the deathly chill of the caves. It was, therefore, his habit to wake and come out at dawn, to spread and comfort himself in the rays of the sun rising over the Black Mountains on the opposite side of the valley. And it happened that a troop of the little black Welshmen, creeping down Uskvale on some mischie-vous errand, had lost their way in the night of the forest below the caves. At grey dawn, they were crawling, on their hairy bel-lies, upward, through the bracken. Above them, was the ledge whereon was the cave-door. They believed that, by ascending to some crag above the low-lying mists in the valley, they might see their way more clearly. So, they clambered up, black in the grey-ness; and, just when their heads peered on to the ledge, the sun rose over the distant mountains behind them, flooding the preci-pice of rock before them with golden glory. At that very instant of time, out of the obscure mysterious opening of the cave on the ledge, appeared my lord the king, straight from his bed, burn-ing-white of flesh, radiant with vigorous youth, regal, gigantic. He came out into the sunlight, opening his breast, spreading his arms to the warm fresh air, tossing the smooth swathes of his yellow-silver locks from his star-like eyes. Thus, he stood in the glory, concluding his young dreams, awakening with the world to a new day. At his feet, was the line of Welsh heads, observing him with stupefaction: but he was not ware of them. All this, I had from Sir Fulk the Flame.

The little black savages glared, open-mouthed, at the appari-tion of such resplendent magnificence; and, anon, Duke Arthur lowered his eyes, and saw them. Very still he was, and very fixed of gaze: so that they hanged there lolling out their tongues which dripped with the juices of amazement. Sir Fulk, also, awakening and missing his bed-fellow, had come to the door of the cave. He paused in the darkness, looking, and listening. And this is what

he saw and heard. The little black Welshmen fed their eyes on
the huge white king's young splendour, gazing at them silent and
still as crucified, while they held themselves hanging near his
feet. And, at length, the chief of them recovered the use of his
voice, wherewith (in the Welsh tongue) he whimpered, "Lord,
who art thou?" Now the Welsh language is the same as the language of Armorica (I know not why;)[1] and my lord the king easily
made thoughtless answer, saying: "I am Arthur." At which the
little black savages were so strangely and dreadfully worried,
that their crooked fingers straightened; and most of them slid
violently backward down the slope. There, they babbled shrilly
and excitedly among themselves for a while. Sir Fulk came out
of the cave: but Duke Arthur, standing stark and still, gave him
a sign to remain behind. And, anon, the Welshmen climbed up
again, with an idea: and, says their chief in his little whimpering
whining voice, "Art thou," says he, "Arthur our king who comes
again." "I am King Arthur:" says my lord the king.[2]

XII. *About Duke Arthur his Conquest of the Welsh*

The Welshmen climbed up on to the ledge; and laid themselves
out for my lord the king to tread on. By his side, in silence, their
standard-bearer raised their banner of the dragon, redder than
whatever is reddest. The rising sun sucked out the night-mists
from the valley below as they stood up there, the boy stark-naked
and the splendid dragon exalted high above that sea of clouds,[3]

---

[1]   Both Breton and Welsh are Celtic languages.
[2]   The roots of the Arthurian legend lie in early Welsh tradition. Both Breton and
Welsh bards prophesied a second coming of King Arthur.
[3]   *"puerus plane nudus dracoque splendescens supra mare nebulosam alte sublati."* It is
interesting to read this with Lord Tennyson's verse, "The shining dragon and the
naked boy."—P. and C. [Rolfe's note.] Rolfe is referring to the account of the birth
of Arthur in Tennyson's *Idylls of the King*:
  Then from the castle gateway by the chasm
  Descending through the dismal night—a night
  In which the bounds of heaven and earth were lost—
  Beheld, so high upon the dreary deeps
  It seemed in heaven, a ship, the shape thereof
  A dragon winged, and all from stern to stern
  Bright with a shining people on the decks,

with the savages prone at his feet, thinking that they were about to die since Arthur had really come again. For the Welshmen have a tradition of a great king of theirs named Arthur in antique times, slain by treachery in battle, whose tomb is known to none; and they faithfully expect that he will heal him of his grievous wounds, and come again, naked as born, but clothed with the effulgent youth of godhood, to take vengeance of his enemies. And, when Duke Arthur did not strike these Welshmen dead, they looked more earnestly, half-blinded though they were by his transcendent splendour, recognizing him, and thinking, If we die not we are not his foes. But he, wonderfully quick to understand that he had them in his fist to bind them to himself, opened to them the solace of his majestic smile, saying: "Pax uobiscum."[1] And, when they had finished gasping, they took satisfaction of his glorious scars, and did homage in the usual manner, singing *Te Deum*.[2] Duke Arthur made his Welshmen ware of as much as was necessary for them to know; and dismissed them to spread news of his coming among their nation very secretly. He bade them to arm secretly in bands, and to retire from the March, never coming nearer to England than the castle of Dinas (where the black man was), and to take orders only from knights who should show his token, namely, a sprig of bloom having two flowers or pods and three leaves. But he sent their chief with two bald youths, bearing his said token, instantly to me at Candidachester, desiring a con-

---

And gone as soon as seen. And then the two
Dropt to the cove, and watched the great sea fall,
Wave after wave, each mightier than the last,
Till last, a ninth one, gathering half the deep
And full of voices, slowly rose and plunged
Roaring, and all the wave was in a flame:
And down the wave and in the flame was borne
A naked babe, and rode to Merlin's feet,
Who stoopt and caught the babe, and cried "The King!
Here is an heir for Uther!" And the fringe
Of that great breaker, sweeping up the strand,
Lashed at the wizard as he spake the word,
And all at once all round him rose in fire,
So that the child and he were clothed in fire.

[1] Peace be with you.
[2] An early Christian hymn of praise.

ference with me in his cave as soon as might be. Hearing which
news, I said to myself that nothing could possibly be nicer.

XIII. *About Duke Arthur his Dispositions for the Achievement of his Rights*

Duke Arthur no longer wore the hectic weary air of misease.
In these few weeks, he had become master of himself, governor
of his resolute mind, lord of his great lithe form. He was ware of
all which he willed to do and would do: I was to be purveyor of
the knowledge wherewith he would devise his schemes, and his
steward for carrying these into effect. Just that. O king. He had
settled the affair of the Welshmen in his mind before I came to
the cave. Believing what they believed of him, they asked nothing better in their wildest ecstasies than to be kinged by him.
He, knowing that a king (who fights his people) fights himself,
was minded to treat these savages precisely as they wished to be
treated. And his scheme was to employ them to tickle his wicked
uncle to exasperation, with innumerable nasty little insurrections in the March of Wales, whereby Softsword's attention could
(at a fitting time) be more or less diverted from England and the
Angevin dominions. Also, he had settled the affair of himself. He,
with Sir Fulk the Flame, would fare forthwith to Rome, there to
lay his cause before our lord Pope Innocent, Whose sacred task it
was (he being the Father of princes and kings, specially oppressed
orphans) to see that rightful heirs were not diminished of their
rights. And, for this purpose, Duke Arthur required me to supply
him with the means of travelling to Rome, and of making a suitable appearance there.

VI

THE BOOK CALLED THE HONEST GOOD UNCLE

1. About Hubert de Burgh his Custody of the Secret of King Richard Lionheart

"Now I thank God," says I, "for making me rather slow to act and tenacious as a crab[1] in holding that into which I once have snapped my claws. And many times, lord king," says I, "have I been on the point of delivering myself of a secret which I hold in your regard: but, though I confess that I have kept it so long out of pique at your regal coldness to me, intending to use it some day for compelling your clemency, now, indeed, I rejoice that I have held it closely until this time, when I see that disclosure will produce great aids for the Lionheart's regal heir at the moment when he best can use them, and I myself may free my mind without incurring the dishonour of thereby gaining favour." For, such was the formidable force of the candid chastity, the luminous innocence, of that regal majesty, that I was ashamed because I ever had thought to coerce him, by keeping King Richard's secret to use it for my own aggrandizement when Duke Arthur (in some dire strait) should have no hope save in me. But, now, he was lord of the wild Welsh, as well as of Hubert de Burgh; and, my tongue being loosed, I spake plain. "Free your mind, Hubert:" says my lord the king, very grave. So, I kneeled before him as he sat in the sun at the mouth of the cave; and a juniper bush cast a grateful shadow over me. And I began to tell what King Richard Lion-

---

[1] Rolfe's alter ego, Nicholas Crabbe, frequently compares himself to a crab. For example, in *The Desire and Pursuit of the Whole*, Crabbe is described as "a man cased, cap-à-pie, like a crustacean, in hard armour of proof . . . [with] no means of exhibiting his feelings, excepting with his crookedly-curving ferociously-snapping claws and (perhaps) with his bleak rigid glaring eyes" (17). Here, as is frequently the case, Rolfe seems to be linking himself to his narrator.

heart said to me, before he ascended to the superiors, from his tent at the siege of Chaluz, in the year of Redemption 1199.

II. *About King Richard Lionheart his Taking of Gold from King Tancred of Sicily, for Duke Arthur fil-Geoffrey his Heir*

"Before the ladies came," says I to Duke Arthur, "the King had the tent cleared; and he pulled my ear to his mouth; and thus he said a secret."

" 'King Tancred gave me gold,' says he, 'and a golden table, and a golden bed, and likewise a brace of mutes; and I accepted them, because he was unbelievably my debtor.[1] He would very willingly have given me also the length of a dagger in my nape: but I refused it, he being my kinsman by marriage.[2] But, Hubert, I was obliged to give half of my gold to that clammy-souled pig King Philip the August.'

"Now I knew all this; and I marvelled that a dying king should worry himself with the telling of well-known tales. But he went on.

" 'King Tancred,' says he, 'wished to become still more allied to me by marriage, then: so we made a match between Duke Arthur of Armorica, my nephew and heir, and Lady Albina of Sicily, daughter and heiress of the said King Tancred. Seeing, however, that these imps were not nubile, being of extremely tender years, we merely betrothed them by proxy:[3] but I insisted on taking Lady Albina's dowry into my own charge, then, and there. King Tancred coughed: he haggled: but he paid it, the dowry of the Lady Albina, the price of my nephew and heir. And what did I, King Richard, do with it?'

" 'You gave half to the King of the Franks, and you expended the rest:' says I to calm him: for he had just told me what he did with the gold of King Tancred.

---

[1] William II, King Tancred of Sicily's predecessor, had left a large legacy to Henry II. However, Henry died before William, so Tancred had decided that this part of the will was null and void. Tancred was also withholding the dower due to Richard's sister, Joan, on the death of her husband, William II.

[2] Tancred was an illegitimate cousin of William II.

[3] At the time Tancred promised to marry one of his daughters to Arthur, Arthur was only four.

" 'No,' says he.

" 'Then you expended all of it:' says I.

" 'Tears of Heaven, but you are a fool, Hubert—nay, perhaps not a fool, but only very young and English:' says King Richard.

"Now I, being rather proud of having attained knighthood for valour before the age of twenty years (that being the age of me then) stood stiff, waiting for my lord's next word. He laughed gently, so as not to hurt himself: for the Lionheart was no lover of pain.

" 'I buried it all,' says he, 'all,' says he; 'and so I was an honest good uncle for the first and last time in my life:' says he. 'And I have great hopes of my merciful salvation, inasmuch as I refrained myself from robbing that fatherless boy:' says he.

"All this, King Richard said clearly and firmly into my very ear, speaking just over a whisper: for, though Death was quite near him, his heart and his tongue were as yet unstiffened. And, after he had named his one chance of salvation, saving Christ His Cross and Passion, he was quiet for a space, looking very high and reverent, and a solemn light gleamed in his eyes. I think that he prayed God, then; and I dare to say that, if (out there in the Holy Land) he would not permit himself to gaze upon Hierusalem the earthly (as we know) because of a just and proud humility,[1] now, indeed, he was very nigh upon the blissful vision of Hierusalem the heavenly, which would seem to be a far more proper city than the one in Syria. Thus much, I opined from the Lionheart's aspect; and, so, I comforted myself until he deigned to speak again.

" 'Mark me, Hubert,' suddenly says he: 'I took Duke Arthur's price in gold from that sly fox Tancred, who was nothing but a three-tongued Sicilian notwithstanding his pretence of Norman blood; and I stored it all on shipboard, aided by my brace of mutes: sewn up, it was, twenty-thousand ounces of pure gold[2] in four-and-

---

[1] Richard put a shield up to cover his eyes so as not to see Jerusalem, the city that he could not rescue from the "infidels."

[2] The relative value of this sum computed in modern currency may be obtained in the following manner. *Pipe Roll I, Rich. I*, 106, gives the contemporary value of an ounce of gold as fifteen silver shillings. Mr. Joseph Jacobs's *Jews in Angevin England*, p. 320, learnedly proves that thirty is (roughly) the multiplying number for reducing a twelfth-century sum of money to its modern equivalent.

twenty goatskins, which we hid very artfully on my ship Chastel Orgoilous under a regal bed of rugs. And I, being honest in this matter, had grave doubts of the virtue of my allies, specially that cold but august pig Philip. But, though well-hidden from these, the filthy lucre was not quite safe from me: for it kept me wakeful at night, and devils to the number of nineteen score came tempting me: but I prayed like five bishops and four abbots, till they scampered away, spitting. All this I did while I lay at Messina.

" 'When I departed,' says the Lionheart, 'I went to King Tancred; and I asked him (before cold Philip and his magnates) whether or no he would play me fair and pay that dowry. Whereat he was gravely bemused; and everyone looked down their noses[1] while thrusting their tongues into their cheeks; and they esteemed King Tancred a very cunning man and more sticky-fingered than a Giwe. But I went out in my rage at his supposed niggardliness, and flung myself down to my ships; and my friends commiserated the poor Gryphons[2] of Sicily in that they had so mean a king as Tancred, saying that I showed a proper pride, and a christian spirit withal, in that I did not pluck his palace of mosaic-work down about his ears. Thus, then, I contrived that none should suspect me of having Duke Arthur's gold. But I sacked the city of Messina and burned the port, as a token of my opinion concerning King Tancred.'

III. *About King Richard his Intention concerning the Gold of Duke Arthur*

" 'I sailed for nineteen hours, or thereabouts,' says the Lionheart, 'being swept along by the powerful streams of the sea, past many cities of the Gryphons which I left unsacked, though they were inhabited by christians who had damned themselves by practising most efficacious necromancy. But I had enough to do with the devils on shipboard, and would not increase their number by

---

Therefore, twenty thousand ounces of gold = three hundred thousand silver shillings X thirty = nine million silver shillings ÷ twenty = four hundred and fifty thousand pounds sterling (£450,000 stg.) which, though not a Civil List, is quite a comfortable sum for a trip on the continent.—P. and C. [Rolfe's note.]

[1] *"praeter nasos despectantes suos."* [Rolfe's note.]

[2] Greeks.

going ashore. But, when we had evaded infected regions, and all the wind had blown itself away, and the streams of the sea were lost in the depths, then, I began to talk (as it were carelessly) of an exceedingly beautiful person dwelling in the city called Siracusa[1] (which we were approaching) of whom I was fain to have speech. And I bade my shipmen to prepare a shallop,[2] and to moor it below the hindmost part of my ship, in case I should be minded to pursue my private diversions ashore. For I had deliberated that I would bury the gold, or drown it, in some known but secret place, against the time when I might return from my crusade, and carry the dowry home to my nephew and heir Duke Arthur. Which intention I established on account of weariness, first, because the King of the Franks my ally was a very pretty thief in posse, second, because of perpetual visitations of devils, spitfires, nineteen-score they were in number, tempting me. And, the gold was not mine: it being Duke Arthur's right, the price of his regal alliance and forfeit to him when the Sicilian should play him false. This being so, my intention was to bury it, or to drown it, with its attendant temptations, out of my reach, I being an honest good uncle.'

IIII. *About King Richard his Landing at Siracusa with the Gold of Duke Arthur*

" 'I chose Siracusa for disposal of Duke Arthur's gold, because both the sea-coast and the inland were suitable. The one offered me precipices descending sheer into deep water: the other afforded me certain highly-commodious pits. At first, I thought to sink the gold in the sea, cutting a mark on the near cliff, whereby its retrievement by ingenious divers might be facilitated when necessary. But, after matured consideration, I chose the pits inland, on account of their preeminent virtues. For a minstrel once sang to me of these pits, which (he said) were simply creeping with the ghosts of a sect of antique enchanters, who perished miserably there after they had been excommunicated by one Messire Dionysios, he being doubtless the bishop of that city at the time:[3] which

---

[1] A city on the coast of Sicily.
[2] Dinghy (*OED* OL).
[3] Richard is referring to the *Latomie dei Cappuccini* (the Lathomy of the Monks)

pits were shunned by all right-thinking men, for this reason. But it was not for me to be afraid of the ghosts of mere wizards: I have not been afraid of very many things in my life, and had just then tolerated very successfully nightly suspicions of the King of the Franks and the allurements of innumerable nameless hobgoblins.[1] Further, I spoke freely among my shipmen, while they were eating their puddings, of the Siracusan young person, Lady Scylle by name, very famous for beauty, but rumoured to be a fairy by nature and of unreasonable antiquity.[2] And, while I occupied their attention, my brace of mutes (who were Saracens of Sicily, and very sturdy, and lithe, and brown of complexion), stowed the goatskins under a mat in the shallop unseen by anyone. I, then, took advantage of the dead calm, and departed, saying that I was for composing a chant-regal in honour of Lady Scylle if I found her worth my while: nor would I go attended by my company, but only by my mutes, they being unable to commit indiscretions of speech because King Tancred had cut off half their tongues at puberty in the Sicilian manner. And we three sped over the sluggish sea: for my mutes rowed swiftly through the dark and thunderous night; and we came into a cove on the north of Siracusa (which city is by no means as large as its name), where was a landing-place known to my mutes. Here, with much labour, we carried the goatskins up the rock, which is formed like honeycomb but cutting sharp to tread upon. And now, Hubert,' says King Richard, 'you shall mark particularly what I say.'

v. About King Richard Lionheart his Hiding of the Gold as a Treasure for Duke Arthur

" 'There is a hill, called Arcady,' says the Lionheart, 'full of pits exceeding deep, and having polished sides internally, wherein a

---

in Syracuse, ancient stone quarries outside the city. One of the caves in the area is called the Ear of Dionysios, because the tyrant king Dionysios supposedly used it as a prison. The strange acoustics of this tunnel rendered even the softest whisper from below audible to the king.

[1] "innumerabilium nullo uocabulo insignum laruarum blandimenta." [Rolfe's note.]
[2] According to Ovid, Scylla was a nymph who was transformed by a potion from Circe into a monster with six heads who would terrorize passing sailors.

man falling shall in no wise escape even if unsmashed, the walls
being as smooth as wax and harder than iron and overhanging
like the machicolation[1] of a tower. And they are many ells deep,
a score and much more; and, in their depths, they are very large
and wide, with the smooth unclimbable walls on all sides overhanging most horribly at the very narrow summit; and, in the
midst of the depths, are pinnacles unexpectedly springing out
of the rocky floor, and caves and arches, ghastly in gloom, and
creeping with ghosts of excommunicated lepers, scorbutics,[2] prac-
tisants of necromancy. But, Hubert, there should be there more
ghosts now than there were then.' King Richard laughed: but he
took care not to shake his shoulder; and he sipped of barley-water[3]
for his dreadful thirst. The tent-door became crowded with anxious faces: an agitated leech wagged his foolish hand, clucking
tat-tet-tit-tot-tut with his silly tongue on his besotted palate like
a snubbed and deeply-chagrined fowl, because he might not use
his craft to cut the king up any more. Says the Lionheart: 'Out of
hearing, you, there'; and the congregation tumbled backward one
over another, like spillikins[4] blown by a breath. When the place
was still, save for the buzzing of flies and the yelps of some distant
leper, the king went on, in my ear, 'We had a rope, and three good
dags,'[5] says he, 'but naught else, lest any should have suspected
our purpose. And I chose a certain pit, into which I lowered first
my brace of mutes and then the four-and-twenty goatskins. And,
having fastened my end of the rope securely to a crag, fortifying
it also with The Cross against all ghouls, dwarves, hobgoblins,
and other pigwidgeons[6] of evil origin,[7] I myself descended thereby

---

[1] An opening through which combustibles, such as molten lead and stones, could
be dropped on attackers (*OED* OL).

[2] People affected with scurvy (*OED* OL).

[3] A drink made from pearl barley, used as a soothing medicine.

[4] Spillikins are small rods used in a game that involves trying to pull off each rod
by means of a hook without disturbing the rest.

[5] "Dag" was a term for handgun. However, Samuel Johnson incorrectly defined
dag as dagger in his *Dictionary of the English Language*, and this is the manner in
which Rolfe seems to be using the term in this text (*OED* OL).

[6] Fairies or elves.

[7] "*omnes contra umbras pumiliones laruas et alios mali originis lemures.*" [Rolfe's
note.]

into the pit. There was a grove of orange-trees below: for no wind blows at that depth; and the said tender vegetables bloom and fruit richly in the peaceful warmth of the pit. But my brace of mutes, gesticulating, warned me against burying Duke Arthur's treasure near these trees, where Gryphon husbandmen would be likely to find it when digging their orchards. So, we made for a mount, which heaped itself against the walls of the pit. It was difficult to see clearly in that darkness: but we were ware of a shallow cave which gaped upon the summit of the mount. Earth, not rock, was the floor of the cave, which we digged with our dags: but my mutes scooped out the loosened soil with their hands, as do dogs in the burrows of coneys.[1] Very violently we worked: so violently, indeed, that once I lost my footing, and rolled down the little mount into some dry bushes and stunted trees which grew below. At that moment, too, there came a peal of thunder; and the heavens were lighted with a fearful glare: yet, we toiled at our task, undismayed by the storm which raged above, till all the goatskins were securely interred. The rain beat fiercely upon us, and even into the cave, benignly washing away our foot-prints and every token of burial: which portent assured me that The Lord God approved my method of ridding my soul of the burthen of Duke Arthur's treasure. And, believing that what had to be done had been well done, we made free to depart, secretly, as we came.'

vi. *About the Interlopers who would have sneaked the Treasure of Duke Arthur*

" 'But, as I eased my back (weary with bending double to dig with a dag),' says the Lionheart, 'by chance I cast a glance up to the narrow mouth of the pit. And a fierce flash of lightning showed me there a peeping head, greasy, goggle-eyed, and apparently religious,[2] peering down upon my completed achievement. Now I had not wrung so regal a treasure out of King Tancred, nor had I tolerated an obsession of devils (spitfires) nineteen-

---

[1] Rabbits (*OED* OL).

[2] *"unctum, oculos eminentem habentem et specie religiosum."* [Rolfe's note.]

score during nineteen days, nor had I saved the said treasure from myself as well as from that clammy-souled piglet King Philip the August, in order that it might rejoice the fat heart of any singular abbot of monks. So, I instantly devised stratagems and counter-plots. We three, then, came out of the pit very gracefully, climbing our rope; and we made a show of going (with satisfaction) on our way. But we covertly crept back, and concealed ourselves in the bushes which fringed the verge of the pit. The storm ceased. The sky brightened in the clear of the full moon,[1] whereby we were ware of a procession, indubitably monkish and carrying spades, which furtively sneaked along on the far edge of the Lathomy, such being the name given to these pits by the Gryphons. And they let down ladders, one at a time, hooking them together as I believe: by which means they descended, eighteen in number, with their holy habits bunched into their belts behind, like the pert but stumpy tails of hens. Bald, they were, and undeniably benedictine; and the moonlight gleamed upon their baldness (as of bladders) as they bobbed about bustling below. And, last, went down a person of quality, no less than their abbot, a prelate of abominable obesity. For the space of an hour, they scuffled (sniff-ing) over the lathomy-bottom, seeking traces, till they happed upon the broken bush broken by my falling, and then the little cave, which they at once began to excavate. Now, while they were merely searching, they appeared so purely comical that my fury dozed under my gorget.[2] But, when the consecrated culprits clustered like blow-flies upon Duke Arthur's treasure to steal it from him, oppressing the orphan, then I bethought me of the temptations of my devils, perceiving that (while those had been rebuffed by prayer) certain other pious motions would have to be used with these monks. I, therefore, fixed my rope, and began to descend again; and my mutes, chuckling silently but most hor-rifically, followed me. And when we three reached the bottom, I pulled the rope after me with a mighty jerk, having a specific use for it, and being minded to return by the monks' long ladders. And we ran through the orange-grove of the lathomy, keeping in

---

[1] *"nitescebat caelum in plenilunj claritatem."* [Rolfe's note.]
[2] A piece of armor that covers the throat (*OED* OL).

the shadow of the trees, as quickly as though we were having our
necks bitten by the ghosts of those enchanters who had perished
miserably there (it was said) after they had been censured by the
bishop.'

VII. About King Richard Lionheart his faithful Dealings with the Robbers of Duke Arthur his Treasure

" 'When we barged into these sanctified runnions,'[1] says King
Richard, 'the abbot (who took us for giants) would have fled
incontinent: but, perceiving (from our method) that we were
men with a purpose, he harked on his monks to resist us. Eighteen of them there were, beside that blessed man, all armed with
spades. But they were not very sprightly in their movements; and,
before one of my mutes fell with his skull split in half, we had
slain five of them with our dags. The rest, however, came jumping on, whooping, and intoning litanies;[2] and I yearned for my
long-sword or my battle-axe or anything like a christian weapon:
but all such gear had been left on shipboard as being unsuited
for a suitor of the supposititious Lady Scylle. And, indeed, but for
the spades which we snatched from the slain, I and my remaining mute would have been dead men: but, armed with the said
spades, we dealt faithfully (albeit clumsily) with the clamouring
herd of monks; and, having killed the last of them, we used their
abbot as a beast of burthen to carry his dead monks to the ladder-
foot, whence my mute drew them up on my rope, till eighteen
religious corpses, and one dead mute, and one live one, awaited
me at the mouth of the pit. The abbot, then goaded and thumped
by me, obliterated all traces of the conflict, and of the place of
Duke Arthur's treasure, before I spinged[3] him in front of me up
the ladder. Goaded and thumped also by me, he tottered, carrying his dead monks one by one to another lathomy in that vicinity, wherein (at my urging) he tossed them, not without snuffling
and groaning, he being extremely obese. And seeing that he still

---

[1] *"nebulones sacratos."* [Rolfe's note.] Samuel Johnson defines "runnion" as "a
paltry scurvy wretch."

[2] *"Inuadebant nos reliqui uociferationes tollentes et litanias intonantes."* [Rolfe's note.]

[3] From the Italian "spingere," to push or to press.

lived after his task was done, I interrogated him; and he told me
that the pit, wherein Duke Arthur's treasure lay, was called the
Lathomy of the Monks because it belonged to his abbey. But, as
he finished speaking, the holy man heaved his fat upon me, with
intent to hurl me into the second lathomy after his deceased ones.
But I expected a gambol[1] of this sort from him, having seen how
naughtily his eyes gleamed in the clear of the moon; and I evaded
him in good time, so that (stumbling over himself) he hustled
my remaining mute over the pit's edge, and dashed his bones to
splinters down below. He, however, remained, to be treated (as
efficaciously as time would permit) by me.'

VIII. *About King Richard Lionheart his Method of Murdering
Murderous Abbots*

" 'Let me impart to you, Hubert,' says King Richard, 'knowledge of the right method by which murderous abbots ought to be
murdered, specially when they are abominably fat. Do, with such
an abbot, as you do with a duck when you prepare that filthy fowl
for eating. Catch your abbot, and make him kneel upright. Go
behind him; and take his ribs and arms between your thighs and
knees, riding him close clutched so. Take his face by the dewlap
(or goitre), tightly; and turn it upward, so that his last glance may
be toward heaven; and let him say such prayers as he can remember. Then, wriggle your dag (a blunt one, if possible), as far down
his gullet as it will go, but gently, as though you love him,[2] and so
cut his throat very delicately and thoroughly from the inside. He
will not say a word, nor even cough at you. This done, cast your
dag aside, so that it may stick in the earth to clean itself. But you
stand up, with your hands clasped below your abbot's middle, letting him droop limply a little forward to disgorge his life-blood in
an unchecked stream. When it slackens, heave him up and shake
him, to encourage the flow: but scatter not the gouts of blood
abroad, nor on his garments, nor on his person. When it ceases,
lay the corpse neatly in a dry situation; and tie up his jaw till it is

---

[1] *"lusum."* [Rolfe's note.] A caper or frisk or quick movement (*OED* OL).
[2] *"mansuete tamquam eum ames."* [Rolfe's note.]

stiff; and, if you have been careful over the business, there will be no sign, not even a bloodstain, by which the manner of his demise may be discerned: excepting the puddle of blood (large, or small, according to the capacity of your abbot), which you shall take order to conceal with loose earth and turves well-stamped down.'

VIIII. *About King Richard Lionheart his Conclusion of the Adventure*

" 'All these deeds having been duly done,' says King Richard, 'I drew up the ladders from the Lathomy of the Monks, and let them down again into the other lathomy where Duke Arthur's treasure was not. There, also, I laid the carcase of the abbot, reverently disposing it on the pile of dead monks. And I recovered the corpses of my mutes, for it is not meet that unbelieving infidels should sepulture with good christians, even though the former are faithful and loyal and the latter are far otherwise. Leaving, then, the holy persons where they were, I broke the ladders and cast their fragments into the sea, bearing my brace of dead mutes to my shallop, having tied great stones to their knees; and I sank them in the deep sea. So, I returned alone to my ship, Chastel Orgoilous, very weary; and I slept long into the next day, by reason of my delvings and other doings during the night-time. And I commanded prayers to be said and masses to be offered on shipboard, for two loyal men and nineteen others departed this life. But my company understood that I had been making expensive presents to the suppositious Lady Scylle, and exhibited no surprize at my bodily lassitude. And so I hid Duke Arthur's treasure.'

x. *About the Honest Good Uncle his Charge to Hubert de Burgh concerning Duke Arthur his Treasure*

" 'Now, I do command and enjoin you, Hubert,' says King Richard, 'to mark me well. There is,' says he, 'a treasure of twenty-thousand ounces of pure gold, contained in four-and-twenty goat-skins, concealed in Sicily, by the city of Siracusa, in a pit called The Lathomy of the Monks, in a shallow cave at the top of a little mount, the said Lathomy being a pit among pits in a rock, but it is the pit which is next to the sea. And there it is (to the best of my knowledge and belief) hidden in a place credibly reported to be haunted, and, therefore, as sacrosanct a place as can be imagined. And this regal treasure is for the sole use and comfort of Duke Arthur fil-Geoffrey Plantagenet of Armorica, nephew and sole heir of me. Take heed, therefore, Hubert,' says King Richard, 'that he shall have it in his need; and fear no ghosts, you, excepting the ghost of me horribly and awfully avenging unfaithfulness.'

"And, having said thus, King Richard Lionheart raised himself, and sipped his barley-water, till he heard the noisy arrival of Earl John of Mortain. And, anon, he heartened himself to finish his business in this world; and, before dawn, he sent me to summon the ladies of whom he desired to take leave, namely, Lady Johanna, Lady Berengere, Lady Heloise."

So, I made an end of revealing the Lionheart's secret.

Duke Arthur remained immoveable, pondering my words: nor did he relieve me from his intense gaze—that gaze which was so grim, being so guileless and so greatly young. Anon, he gave me his hallowed hand to kiss, that wounded hand wounded like The Lord's, ornate with the candour of the splendid scar; and he said: "Well done, thou good and faithful servant: because thou hast been faithful over a few things, We will place thee over many things."[1]

XI. *About Duke Arthur his Method of achieving his Treasure, his Rights, Crowns, Canopies, etcetera*

"It seems good to Us, and Our will and pleasure is," says Duke Arthur, next, to me, "that these things following shall be done. We have nothing to hope from Philip the August. We cannot yet wage successful war on the Earl of Mortain. We, therefore, are for Rome, there to demand a mandate from Pope Innocent, Who (as We believe) will not deny Us Our regal rights. And, from Rome, We proceed to Sicily, there to take Our treasure from the place where Our honest good uncle formerly hid it. For We shall need

---

[1] "*euge serue bone et fidelis quia super pauca fuisti fidelio super multa te constituamus.*" [Rolfe's note.]

an army, wherewith to enforce the Pope's mandate; and such an army We shall not deny Ourself when We have taken seizin of Our said Treasure. We, therefore, do command you, Hubert, to act in the manner following. You shall make due and secret provision for Our ensuing progress to Rome. You shall remain in England, as Warden of all Our affairs; and your duty is to prepare for Our coming again. Keep the wild Welsh loyal to Us, if possible, using the token of Our broom-sprig, constantly inciting them to carry on small irritating wars, with such of the Earl of Mortain's power as shall come into the March, and with all magnates who cannot show Our said token. Avoid pitched battles: but let the usurper have no peace. You yourself must take, and keep, all offices which the said usurper may dare to confer on you, filling your castles with trusty garrisons trained and ready to take Our part when We shall give the signal for open war. Collect and stablish a firm party of knights and magnates, whose displeasure with Our wicked uncle may incline them to support us. For this business, you will need the basilisk's[1] wisdom, the lion's daring, the unicorn's strength, the crab's tenacity, which qualities We perceive in you, and We commend them. You will need, also, Our perfect confidence, with which We hereby full willingly enrich you. And, at a proper time, We will take you for Our man."

I ate my pudding that day with unusual satisfaction; and set myself to work to merit these great favours: for I was ware that King Richard had a successor after his own heart, one who (through bodily torments the most hideous and soul-sickness the most heart-rending) never lost faith in himself or his God or his right, never swerved in his hope and intention, was more patient in affliction than Messire Saint Job the furunculous[2] patriarch, and was prompt and alert to seize his opportunity at the moment when Divine Providence dangled it before him. And, beside all this, I loved the lonely valorous boy, worshipped his luminous

---

[1] The basilisk is a mythical reptile, supposedly hatched by a serpent from a cock's egg, that can kill with a glance. Serpents and dragons are often associated with wisdom.

[2] A furuncle is a boil or a tumor. One of the many afflictions that Job bore patiently was terrible boils. See Job 2:7.

innocence, pitied his sad life, revered his regal majesty. O my
king.

This, then, was the company which I sent with my lord the
king to Rome. Sir Fulk the Flame would not be separated from
him; and Bobo Kemp (his page) had been proved suitable. To
these, I added Sir Geoffrey Turberville, and Sir Hugh Turberville the chaplain, who had been a knight and also a pirate before
he was a priest, and was very capable and well-informed. I gave
them the guise of pilgrims, and conducted them to my castle of
Monmouth: where, by great good luck, Sir Eustace the Monk
(that worthy useful pirate)[1] was waiting to see me about a certain inadvertent sacrilege at Caldey and certain trading-rights in
the Narrow Sea. He (being always ready to earn an honest penny
from a friend) took the company on ship-board, having sworn
to me, on Sir Hugh's thigh-bone of Messire Saint Gattwg,[2] that
he would bring them in security to Gaunt in Flanders, whence
they could take the road through Cologne and by River Rhine to
Rome. O times.

---

[1] The pirate and renegade monk, Eustace, was rumored to have consorted with
demonologists and necromancers and to have acquired knowledge of the black
arts. He was very active in King John's service, but he joined Louis's forces and
fought against Hubert de Burgh at sea in 1217 during Henry III's reign. Eustace
was defeated and beheaded.

[2] Saint Cadoc, a sixth-century Welsh saint.

VII

THE BOOK CALLED THE CAPERING OF THE WILD ASS

1. *About the Excommunication of Softsword*

Softsword found himself, on my March, in the situation of
an ass who has placed his clumsy hoof in a wasps' nest. Stung
at every point, and unable to retaliate, he turned (swelled and
tingling) to other affairs. It was time. England had become ware
that men cannot live without clergymen. And John was not all
fool: for even a wild ass, who chews thistles for choice, spits out
chance morsels of moss which he has failed to masticate. So John
sent Abbot Hugh of Beaulieu, his pet Cistercian, to Rome, saying
that he would reinstate the Canterbury monks, hand their temporalities to the Pope, and receive Cardinal Stephen as primate,
but not as friend, which is to say that he would not peacefully kiss
him. Our lord the Pope, knowing that half a loaf is better than no
bread, empowered the bishops of London and Ely and Worcester to take over the said temporalities, and to raise the interdict
from England when John should have performed his part of the
bargain. The Wild Ass again began to caper. He issued safe-conducts for the three bishops, and for Langthon as cardinal but
not as primate. The bishops came to England: the primate naturally came not. John kept the bishops waiting for two months;
and showed that he was not going to keep his word. The bishops
went back and told Pope Innocent, Who returned them to ful-
minate a threat of excommunication and (in due time) to pronounce the censure. But they had been so dreadfully worried by
the cacophonous braying of the Wild Ass, which made their very
mitres[1] twinkle on their heads, that they dillydallied till John felt
strong enough to be affable. He invited them to come to England

---

[1] Headdresses worn by bishops (*OED* OL).

to talk it over. They came. Softsword accepted the Pope's terms at Canterbury. The Cardinal-Primate then came also, under safe-conduct, to ratify the deed of submission. All was going beauti-fully. John advanced from Chilham to meet him, and sent on in front Geoffrey fil-Peter the Justiciar and Bishop Peter Roches of Winchester to demand new concessions which nulled the essence of his submission. The Cardinal-Primate and the three bishops said that they would not have any nonsense; and fled to France. There, they made no more fuss, but published the excommunica-tion against Softsword. So, the line was drawn tighter; and John was to be made as miserable as England.

II. *About a green Bay-tree*

Our lord the Pope, occupied with His Own affairs and with those of the Roman Emperor Hottho whom He was crowning, decided to let the Wild Ass test his situation for a season. That beast rather seemed to like it. Certainly he flourished like all great sinners. O manners. One Welsh headman, Llywelyn Api-owerth, played traitor, submitting gratuitously to John, who gave him his bastard in marriage.[1] Scotland dropped into Softsword's mouth, like a bad egg: for King William the Lyon, at Roxburgh, made terms, on John's sole promise to demolish that Tweed-mouth fortress which Bishop Philip of Durham placed as coun-terwork against the Scots castle of Berwick. King William agreed to give John fifteen-thousand marks in four half-yearly instal-ments—that is half the price of Duke Arthur, showing that a Scot is twice as avaricious as a Giwe. He also gave his daughters to Softsword, that he might marry them at his own price to English-men, namely, Lady Margaret to his oaf of an heir Henry Lackland (whom she refused, in order to marry me, as I in the proper place will narrate),[2] and Lady Ysabel to Earl Roger Bigod II of Norfolk.

---

[1] Llywelyn ap Iorwerth married John's illegitmate daughter, Joan.

[2] Under the Treaty of Norham, William agreed to abandon his claims on Northumberland, Cumberland, and Westmoreland and to pay John 15,000 marks. John promised to arrange marriages for William's daughters. Margaret was much older than Henry, and her marriage to Hubert seems to have been set up in order to free Henry from this obligation.

Further, the Scot ceded Northumbria to his son Sandy;[1] and gave that shock-headed lusty lanky leggy imp of thirteen to John to wed to whom he pleased without disparagement. Lastly, the Lyon of Scotland swore allegiance to Henry Lackland (that snivelling lout[2]) as well as to Softsword. Which done, the Wild Ass (triumphantly bellowing) brought young Sandy to London, and thence to Woodstock, where he called for a new and general homage from everybody, even from the Welsh. O scab.

III. About Softsword and divers Archdeacons

Softsword turned to usurp the Pope's privilege, by filling vacant sees: but no one wanted to be happed up in bishopskins by him, excepting a parcel of ambitious archdeacons. Now we all know, that, in those old times, most good white men invariably refused bishoprics. We know, also, that very few archdeacons (those diocesan Judases who keep the bag) can enter the kingdom of heaven, owing to the surpassing scandal of their lives and manners. From those days, indeed, to these, it has been the care of all succeeding bishops to live down the reputation of their predecessors. And, moreover, we know that archdeacons could not take the oath (in all its exiguous particulars) which a clergyman must take before he can be bishoped: some failed in one unspeakable particular, some in a scandalous other, all had indulged themselves before or after ordination, and most were habitual malpractisants, so that none could compurge[3] themselves completely; and, this being a matter of common knowledge, it was customary not to offer a bishopric with its necessary oath to all archdeacons. What shame! O phy! But Earl John named four archdeacons, Sir Nicholas Laigle bishop of Chichester, Sir Walter Grey bishop of Coventry, Sir Henry of Stafford bishop of Exeter, Sir Hugh of Wells bishop of Lincoln. The last, he sent for consecration to Archbishop Walter de Coutances at Rouen. But, as luck would have it, Sir Hugh of Wells happened to be a good archdeacon (thus proving the infamy of the rest, for the exception proves the

---

[1] Alexander II.
[2] *"muculento iste trunco."* [Rolfe's note.]
[3] Compurgation is the act of clearing one's self of charges (*OED* OL).

rule); and, when he found the said Archbishop Walter just dead, he (not to be balked of his bishopskins) rushed on to the next, at Melun, where the exiled Primate Langthon himself invested him with episcopacy. Conceive the Wild Ass his fury, at so signal a recognition of the cardinal as archbishop. But, when he had finished foaming, he exiled also Bishop Hugh, and refrained from trying to transform any more archdeacons into bishops.

IIII. *About Softsword his Excommunication when the English became ware of it*

At Christmas, news of Softsword's excommunication trickled from France into England: but the magnates (a dull lot, as a whole), saw no reason for avoiding the gaiety at Windsor Castle. And the Wild Ass wilily curried favour with the proletary, by abolishing direct taxation: which anyone could do who had snaffled and was enjoying all the clergymen's revenues.[1] On Midlent Sunday, he knighted that Scots imp Sandy at the Clerkenwell Priory, and packed this new vassal off to do homage to his father for Northumbria at Melrose. And he made another approach to the Primate Langthon, offering a safe-conduct fortified with the warranties of magnates: but, being addressed (as before) merely as cardinal and not as archbishop, the said Primate sat tighter than ever. Softsword, therefore, capered elsewhere, engaging in other activities. O manners.

v. *About the horrible end of Braose*

The rebellion of Braose rankled in Softsword's mind. He extorted yet more gold from Giwen and improverished clergymen; and swooped from Milford Haven to Crook in Waterford, intending to subjugate Ireland, and to punish the Lacys for harbouring Braose. His friend, there, was Sir John Courcy. So terrific was the show which he made, so ear-splitting his uproars, that

---

[1] Because John was appropriating church funds, he did not have to impose new taxes to fund the raising of armies, etc. This saved the barons from excessive taxation. Consequently, the excommunication could be understood as beneficial to both John and the barons.

the Irish, under King Cathal Oconchdebhair of Connaught and
King Donnchadh Obrien of Munster, gushed into Dublin to pay
him homage. He ordained for them English laws and money: he
gave them that ghibelline Bīp. John Grey of Norwich for their Justiciar, whom Earl Marechal of Pembroke was to advise in military
matters. As for the Lacys, they skipped away, firing their castles,
and came at last safely to France. And Braose escaped to Wales
again, where he lay (a fugitive) hidden from us all among the wild
Welsh. Then came the horrible end, of which I had no knowledge
till all was over: for I was enjoying a month's vacation, with my
wife, in the ship of one of my pirates, dawdling in the vicinity of
my V Ports.

Softsword captured Lady Maud of The Haye, and her daughter who married the son of Roger Mortimer, and her son William
with his wife and two young sons who were trapped for him in
Scotland by Sir Duncan of Galloway the skinny earl of Carrick,
no Scot ever being able to refrain from replaying the part of Judas
Iskarioth. John had every scrap of the Braose possessions in his
hands: but he played with his victims, promising amnesty and
reinstatement if those ruined ones would pay him forty-thousand
marks. He sent Lady Maud to borrow that great sum from his
usurious Giwen of Bristol. Who would lend a single mark to penniless folk under the ban of the tyrant? Lady Maud could give
no security: the Giwen, jocosely jeering, refused her. Back to the
Wild Ass came that haughty dame, hopeless, broken-hearted.
He brayed hideously; and he dropped her with her progeny in
a dungeon of his castle of Corfe, where he watched their agony,
starving them slowly to death. When Lady Maud had let her two
young grandsons eat off both her breasts,[1] Softsword began to
feed the company with haddock-tails, two apiece each day, giving
them no drop of water, so that they died salted, twitching with
pure displeasure of melancholy. Happier by far was Sir William,
who died alone in a gutter at Corbeil by Paris. To give the devil
his due (and he sorely needs it), I will say that these diabolical
atrocities sat uneasily on such fragments of conscience as John

---

[1] According to some accounts, when the bodies were discovered, it seemed that
the mother had in fact gnawed at her sons' flesh. It is presumed that Lady Maud
was punished by John for speaking out against his murder of Arthur.

possessed: for, before he was smashed and pulverized by me into that awful jelly which his destiny decreed, he had the grace to found a monastery for the good of the souls of Braose. May The Lord God pardon him, if such be possible.

VI. *About Softsword and the Cistercians*

Softsword returned to London Tower, discontented with the sums of money exuded by the clergymen, specially discontented with the Cistercians' contribution; and he summoned all abbots, abbesses, priors, wardens of foreign abbeys in England whose revenues went abroad, with the Templars, and the Hospitallers,[1] to meet him in synod at Saint Bridget's church by the Fleet river. There, he made himself as offensive as a leper. It must be known that the English Cistercians stank anew in his nostrils, because the Frankish Cistercians were warring violently against some mad and libidinous heretics of the Albigeois,[2] whose leader was John's brother-in-law and ally, Earl Raymond VI of Toulouse. Mark the relation. Softsword was in the bad books of the Pope, himself excommunicated, his usurped kingdom interdicted. The Pope was supporting the French Cistercians. So, being wild and asinine, the Wild Ass bit the necks of the English Cistercians,[3] demanding marks, of Dunstable twenty, of Margam twenty-seven-thousand, of Waverley thirty-thousand. He also forbade any Cistercian to leave the kingdom, even to attend the general chapter of their order: nor might any Cistercian come into the kingdom as a guest from oversea. Waverley Abbey, rather than obey him, dissolved itself, sobbing; and its monks scuttled into foreign burrows. And all English ports (excepting my V Ports) were watched, to prevent entrance of the Pope's expected maledictions.

None came. Pope Innocent was satisfied that time would prove how intolerable were interdict and excommunication.

---

[1] The Knights Hospitaller, like the Knights Templar, were a religious and military order. The Knights Hospitaller cared for sick pilgrims in the Holy Land.
[2] Albigensians, a Cathar sect in southern France. Catharism, based on a dualist theology, was considered heretical by the Catholic Church.
[3] *"ceruices promordit."* [Rolfe's note.]

VII. *About our Lord the Pope his Distractions*

The paternal hands of Pope Innocent were sufficiently occupied by a snarling Cæsar, that Hottho whom He had taken up out of a German dung-hill to set above princes, cherishing and crowning him as emperor. The snake bit the bosom which warmed him. Maledictions and censures of the most awfully scorching kind immediately blasted him; and he was howling his discontent to all Germany.[1] Beside this emperor devoid of probity,[2] there were the armed heretics of the Albigeois, against whom Pope Innocent had to defend Christendom by force of arms. And His Paternity was far too wise to bite off more than He could chew. Therefore, for the moment, He left our Wild Ass to welter in his own stench.

VIII. *About Softsword his Anxieties*

Softsword began to be anxious, and not without cause. All said and done, he had but five English magnates entirely loyal to him, namely, his bastard brother Earl William Longsword of Salisbury, Earl Aubrey de Vere II of Oxford, Geoffrey fil-Peter the Justiciar, Bishop Peter Roches of Winchester, and that Bĩp. John Grey of Norwich. He had the sense to see the fatuity of falling-out with clergymen and with magnates both simultaneously. So, he ordered all voluntary exiles to return within three months on pain of forfeiture: for, being a Wild Ass, he knew not how to apologize, and needs must continue to hector. O manners. To make him still more uneasy, I used the Welsh. That Llewelyn Apiowerth, who had done homage and gotten John's bastard Lady Johanna to wife for it, nourished an old grudge against Englishmen, builders of castles in Wales. So, I quietly set him to spue his spleen on Earl Ralf Blondeville IIII of Chester, whom I had never really pardoned for his liberties with Duke Arthur's mother, whatever other

---

[1] "*et stomachose ululabat coram Germania omni.*" [Rolfe's note.] Otto was excommunicated for attempting to unite Italy to the empire. Innocent opposed this policy.

[2] "*improbum.*" [Rolfe's note.]

people may have done. This Welshman, then, demolished the tower of Dyganwy on River Conway. Earl Ralf rebuilded it, and also the castle at the holy well of Flint. The Welshman retorted raids into the Englishman's feofs; and North Wales blazed with a neat little war. Softsword intervened, prancing from the south to kick Llewelyn, allying with Gwenwynwyn of Powys and Maelgwyn and Rhys Aprhys: but Llewelyn retired, unkicked, with his substance, to the Mount of Ereri. The Wild Ass capered after him to Bangor; and captured Bishop Robert of Shrewsbury in his own cathedral, with whom he had much indecorous sport, though not as much as he desired, the bishop being afflicted with carbuncles and unable to dance cheerfully when tossed from the blanket on to John's table. But a new fortress, erected at Aberconway, hemmed Llewelyn in, who had to send his wife to the Wild Ass to ask for terms. These were granted. The Welshman paid a paralyzing fine in cattle, and gave up stolen lands. Softsword also added the sons of several Welsh magnates to his camp of hostages: but, though victorious, he went away unhappy and insecure; and so my end in annoying him was gained.

VIIII. *About Softsword his two horrid Ideas*

John formed the reprehensible idea of trying to frighten the Pope, and, if that failed, to set the Pope and the Cardinal-Primate at loggerheads. So, he sent an envoy to Rome, charged with a certain message. In reply, the Pope sent envoys to England, Brother Durand of the Templars and a little chip of a subdeacon[1] named Mr. Pandulph, charged to converse with Softsword. No one can say that Pope Innocent was not apostolically long-suffering. The Wild Ass found himself aggrieved at the outset, wounded on his rawest and most secret sore. Pretending to be a king, he expected a cardinal at least for these conversations; and, lo, a mere subdeacon armed with plenary power, to snub him. He pranced to Northampton (ominous city for a prince at strife with his primate);[2] and there he yawped himself hoarse, kicking out at all and

---

[1] *"quemdam assulunculum e subdiaconis."* [Rolfe's note.]
[2] At the council of Northampton in 1164, Thomas Becket was tried for refusing to recognize the jurisdiction of the king's courts.

sundry with his restive heels. Then, he cooled down; and said several things suddenly, one after the other. First, he would receive the Primate Langthon properly: but he would not pay arrears of archiepiscopal revenues which he had stolen during the archbishop's exile. The fact was that he could not refund the said arrears: for he had already expended them in lustful or frantic extravaganzas; and he was penniless, excepting for his secret treasure at Corfe, which avarice forbade him to touch. Secondly, he would frighten Mr. Pandulph; and he brayed deafening menaces at that one, saying that he would make him dance on air, and so forth. In Mr. Pandulph, however, Softsword met his match. That little person had the spirit of a lady-badger. He cared not a penny for his life: all his care was for his job; and he withstood the Earl of Mortain to the face, in this way, for example. There chanced to be in ward just then, a certain low clergyman, named Sir Rumbald of Rothersthorpe, under sentence of death by hanging, after condemnation by the Justiciar for coining and uttering base money. Him, Mr. Pandulph tempestuously set at liberty, mentioning that the Earl of Mortain was not allowed to molest clergymen, who ought to be judged by clergymen and not by mere laymen. Now for my part, had I been the Earl of Mortain, quite bad, entirely vile, and already excommunicate, I would have hanged two clergymen (one small) instead of the reverend coiner only, just to show that I resisted aggression. For one may as well be hanged for a sheep as for a lamb. But our Wild Ass was not a consistent criminal; and the crack of a whip soon brings such a mongrel cur to heel. Then, the Pope's envoys scornfully returned to Rome, breaking off the conversation; and Softsword was so fearful that he sent envoys of his own with them, to converse very humbly indeed, hoping that the Lord Innocent would be persuaded thus. For Softsword was now ware of the appalling necessity of making his peace with some one, preferably with the Holy Roman Church of whose potentiality he was chewing bitter and astringent examples. For there was no longer any mystery about his excommunication: that was known by high and low. It was not nice for him. Moreover, as deposition follows unrepented excommunication, people were beginning to avoid John, preparing to defy him and to affy with[1] someone more worthy not yet named. O times. Let me not be misunderstood about the Earl of Mortain. I say that he was not a consistent criminal: I do not say that he was not an unmitigated one. But he had no tenacity, even of knavery. True, it was not difficult to turn him away from his wickedness: he was only a poor timid niddering. True, also, that, when turned from one wickedness, he instantly slid into another as easily as a black-beetle[2] into a basin of beer. He had exhaustive experience of all the highways and byeways of crime and of sin; and he tried them all in turn. But he never specialized; and remained a mere general practitioner, undistinguished excepting by the scope of his exertions. So, when Mr. Pandulph lashed him for persecuting English clergymen, and, when no one would converse with his envoys in Rome (where performance is regarded rather than promise), then, Softsword's second idea entered his wicked simple mind. Revenge on clergymen might be obtained by making the chief of all clergymen unhappy. The lord Pope Innocent might be very handsomely annoyed by a confederation of all the pontifical enemies. That was John's second idea. He himself was one pontifical enemy: the Roman Emperor Hottho was another; and both these noblemen were wincing under the apostolic flail of excommunication, and very much in the position of lepers. Softsword, therefore, employed that Earl Reinald Dampmartin of Boulogne to treat with Hottho. The choice of this Norman knight caused complications: for Normandy (lost by Softsword) was in the hands

---

[1] To bind in trust with.

[2] "*blatta.*" We question whether the writer is guilty of anachronism in mentioning blackbeetles in the thirteenth (and greatest) century. It is held by many respectable historians (such as Cæsar, Little Arthur, Lingard, Lord Acton, for example) that the Roman conquest of our island took place some years before Hubert de Burgh's era; and we see no imperative reason for doubting that our Roman conquerors brought us their insects, as well as their civilization and language, and their proverb about youth which falls in love *tamquam blatta in pelvim*. We note the theory that blackbeetles first invaded Hampshire when Gilbert White wrote his *Natural History of Selborne*: but we fearlessly leave the task of reconciling it with ours, as stated above, in the hands of specialists.—P. and C. [Rolfe's note.] Rolfe is referring to Gilbert White (1720-1793), the naturalist who wrote *The Natural History and Antiquities of Selborne* (1789). The Latin quote is drawn from Decimus Laberius (105 B.C.-43 B.C.). ("*Amore cecidi tamquam blatta in pelvim,*" which means "I fell into love like a cockroach into a saucepan.")

of Philip the August, who, hearing of Earl Reinald's mission, and
wishing to be friendly to the Pope, escheated the feof of Boulogne
and banned the earl from the duchy. The bandit fled to England;
and did homage to John, who was glad of him, for he was a useful
rascal; and he contrived to attach, to Softsword's confederation,
five sovereigns who were discontented with our lord the Pope,
namely, Earl Ferrand and old Countess Margaret of Flanders, Earl
Theobald of Bar, *argent, two barbels adossed proper*, with the Dukes
of Brabant and Limburg, all drunkards, or desiring divorcements,
or in their dotage.[1] O manners.

x. *About a Pretty Sort of Ally, and two Rather Pretty Sorts of Envoys who procured the Pretty Sort of Ally, and the Very Pretty Sort of Associate of the said two Rather Pretty Sorts of Envoys who procured the said Pretty Sort of Ally for Softsword*

Another enemy of Pope Innocent was Earl Raymond of Toulouse, friend, and (naturally) ally of John, and the heresiarch[2] of
southern France.[3] He led the filthy and bellicose heretics of the
Albigeois; and, while pretending himself as the champion of true
Christianity, he was allied (in his ferocious war against christians) with no less a person than the infidel Soldan[4] miscreants. O
most sweet and pretty and instructive combination. And, to this
infidel black man, Softsword sent secret envoys, inviting him to
join the league against the Pope. O manners. These envoys were
Sir Thomas of Erdington and Sir Thomas of London, both clergymen, but of what sort they were, I will not say. It can be seen
that they bore not their sire's cognomens; and I conjecture that
they were casual bastards bred miscellaneously. Not that I blame
them for that: for a man does not generate or breed himself, as
a rule, and therefore has no responsibility in these matters. But

---

[1] John allied with Otto IV of Germany and Count Ferrand of Flanders, and they
fought together against Philip in the Battle of Bouvines in 1214.
[2] Founder of a heresy (*OED* OL).
[3] Raymond VI of Toulouse was excommunicated twice. He was suspected of
involvement in the assassination of a papal legate with whom he had a dispute.
He was also known to tolerate heretics.
[4] Sultan.

I do vituperate these clergymen, and that without qualification, in that they consented to act for arranging an alliance between a christian (such as John was) and an infidel (such as the Soldan of Maughreb[1] was) in despite of Christianity and Christ His Vicar.

And, also, I have just one other little tiny mite of a thing to say, as it were in parenthesis. And it is this. The said clergyman, Sir Thomas of London, did his nefarious truckling with infidels so successfully, that Softsword (on his return from partibus infidelium) named him overseer of the estates of Saint Alban's Abbey, by way of premium. Mark that. And now mark this. I cannot help fancying that I have heard somewhere that that Mr. Matthew (late of Paris, now of Westminster) was, till not so very long ago, a monk of Saint Alban's Abbey. And I ask you, o most affable reader, whether it may not be somewhat pertinent to inquire how we ought to esteem, and what opinion we are justified in forming of, a pretentious scribbler of a so-called *Chronicle of England* who has been used to consort and associate with an atrocious renegade such as the said Sir Thomas of London. What indeed? O scab. O Mr. Matthew.

xi. *About Softsword his Numbering of the People*

The Wild Ass also added one of the seven sins of Messire Saint David of Hierusalem, King and Confessor, to his already wearisome category: I mean the sin of numbering the people.[2] For he issued writs for two enquiries: first, into the services owed to the king by his tenants-in-chief, namely about seven thousand knights, and, second, as to the numerous benefices in the gift of exiled bishops, the revenues of which he itched to handle. O manners. Meanwhile, he galloped through Lincoln and York to Northumbria, resting at Carlisle, and returning through Hexham and Durham and York, so as to refresh the memories of silly people as to his importance and ubiquity. And then very unpleasant things began to happen to him.

---

[1] Area of northwestern Africa that includes present-day Morocco and Tunisia.
[2] David imposed a census on the Israelites. This is understood as a sin because Satan tempted David to conduct the census. It also shows pride on David's part in his power as king and the size of his army.

XII. *About Sir Simon de Montfort his disagreeable*
Motions against Softsword

Sir Simon de Montfort, *gules, a lyon argent*, was Earl of Montfort
and Leicester, and Steward of England, elegant in shape, strenuous in religion and military matters.[1] He brushed his moustache
up to his eyes to give himself a warlike aspect, his fists were more
often covered with mail than not, but he chose to confine his hair
with a string of gilded beads. As a rule, he behaved decorously. Of
his son's depravity, I shall write in a proper place:[2] but a historian
must not be biased like that Mr. Matthew (late of Paris), or visit
the sins of the children upon the fathers in defiance of the Sacred
Scriptures. Earl Simon, then, was a true son of Mars: fighting
was his passionate pastime: nothing could keep him from war,
excepting religion; and, when occasion came for combining the
two, he asked nothing better of fortune. So, when our lord the
Pope apostolically ordained a crusade against the filthy and ferocious fanatics of the Albigeois,[3] Earl Simon was first in the fray
and pre-eminent among Christian commanders. And the admi-
rably-disagreeable smack in the face which it was appointed unto
him to administer to Softsword was this. He, in the very nick
of time, utterly routed at Navas de Tolosa that bestially infidel
Sultan of Maughreb, who was allied with John's great ally the
degenerate heretic Earl Raymond of Toulouse: which victory Earl
Simon replenished by a second, at Muret in Haute Garonne, over
Raymond himself. And our Wild Ass reared horribly, when thus
diminished of two of his precious confederates. O manners.

---

[1] *"forma elegans fide et armis strenuus."* [Rolfe's note.]

[2] His son led a baronial opposition to Henry III and is often referred to as one
of the fathers of early modern parliamentary democracy. In a text that opposes
democracy, Simon de Montfort, 6th Earl of Leicester (1208-1265) would certainly
represent villainy.

[3] The Albigensian crusades began in 1209, but the Cathar sect persisted long after.
Arthur, in fact, encounters members of this sect in *Hubert's Arthur*, Book XIII,
Chapter VII.

xiii. *About Hubert de Burgh his secret Machinations against Softsword*

To worry John awfully, I sent the token of the broom-sprig through Wales with an exciting message; and the wild Welsh promptly alleged a pontifical call to arms against an excommunicate usurper. The inner March blazed with war: the savage chiefs postponed their private feuds: Llewelyn and Gwenwynwyn and Maelgwyn joined their powers, and recovered all recently-ceded lands and all English castles in their country excepting Dyganwy and Rhyddlan. The Wild Ass, incensed and infuriated at so many wasps buzzing about his hairy ears simultaneously, vowed the extermination of the Welsh race. The news of his mishaps had met him at Nottingham, just when he and Lady Jezebel were in the article of eating their puddings; and such was his deep displeasure that he incontinently sent to his camp of hostages for the first twenty boys at hand, whom he caused to be strung up in couples on the gallows before his tent, that he might glut his rage with their screams and chokings, their elongating throats, the writhing of their little bodies, the capricious jerking of their untried limbs, the blackening horror of their twitching faces as they died in contortions by hanging.[1] But, before he had absorbed that same pudding, his affair went from bad to worse. Two couriers rode in with letters, one from the King of the Scots, the other from John's bastard Lady Johanna the wife of Prince Llewylyn; and they both warned him that he was environed by traitors ready to defy and desert him in the moment when he should dare to venture on his proposed campaign. I need not say who actually wrote these two letters:[2] but we all know that they worried him so dreadfully that he disbanded his feudal levies without more ado. This was a very great advance in the way of making matters easier for Duke

---

[1] While some of the accounts of John's cruelty are exaggerated in both this text and its source materials, this story of the hanging of twenty-eight hostages, the sons of the rebellious Welsh chiefs, seems to have been authenticated. See Sidney Painter, *The Reign of King John*, (Baltimore: Johns Hopkins University Press, 1950), 237.

[2] This anecdote concerning the letters about a baronial conspiracy against the king is drawn from Roger of Wendover's *Flores Historiarum*.

Arthur's cause. With the exception of a few miscellaneous magnates and their powers, John had no one whom he could trust now, save his army of mercenary cotterels. True, that army was an enormous one and extremely capable and dangerous. But, mercenaries have been known to desert an unlucky leader, specially when the said leader is a bad paymaster. And I hoped, in time, not only to detach the lieges from Softsword but also to dam up all the sources of his revenues, so that no one would serve him at all, either for love or for money. The task was tiresome, and tedious. O times.

XIIII. *About the Side-blows taken by Softsword from our lord the Pope*

The Wild Ass went on losing allies. The excommunicated Emperor Hottho was fast dwindling in importance: he, though under censure, had (so far) obtained the services of malefactors. But Pope Innocent left not a stone unturned in His holy endeavours to save the soul of that miserable emperor. His Paternity did more than excommunicate Hottho. Being firmly set in His apostolic intention of forcing to repentance the besotted wretch who would not be led thereto, our lord the Pope deprived him of both his imperial crowns, deposed him from the throne of the empire, and set up the little King Frederick II of Sicily as Roman Emperor in his stead. Worse followed. That cold pig Philip the August sent his defiance to Hottho, and hastened to recognize Frederick. And all this was most nasty for John.

xv. *About Softsword his new and abominable Ebulliences*

John, in his johannine[1] manner, rushed to London,[2] snatching castles on the way, exacting fresh hostages from magnates whom he suspected. The Scots Earl David of Huntingdon had to give up his son and his fortress at Fotheringham. Earl William Marechal of Pembroke had to contribute his heir, though Softsword

---

[1] Having the character of John. This term is typically used to refer to John the Baptist, but here presumably it is just meant to indicate that John is acting in a very John-like manner.

[2] *"Johannes johannizanit et Londinum uersum se iniecit."* [Rolfe's note.]

already had his second son Richard. Sir Eustace de Vesci bolted to
Scotland: Sir Robert fil-Walter (of Dunmow and Baynard's Castle
by the Black Friars) fled to France: both incurred outlawry and
confiscation of their feofs. So outrageously wild and asinine was
the Wild Ass, that even an archdeacon was inspired to testify,
namely, Archdeacon Geoffrey of Norwich, who wondered (very
loudly indeed) what would become of misguided persons daring
to remain in the service of an excommunicated earl. Softsword
at once let him taste the inconveniences accruing to archdeacons
who did not so dare: for he had him happed up in a leaden cope,[1]
hammered closely to his body, so that he presently died, fixed
standing in his tracks and starved, being unable even to lift up his
hands that he might nibble the nails thereof for fodder in extre-
mis.[2] O manners. There was, also, another spiritual person whom
John treated as barbariously, but more foolishly. He was a poor
scorbutic hermit, Peter of Pomfret by name; and he prophesied
(quite incidentally) that Softsword's reign would end on the ensuing festival of The Lord's Ascension. The Wild Ass accordingly
took him and shut him up at Corfe: whereby all the world was
most idiotically given to know that the utterances of insignificant
and scorbutic hermits are of the gravest importance; and all the
nation stood on tiptoe, watching for the verification of the prophecy.[3] But that happened later; and, meanwhile, I must narrate
events in order. Elated with the fore-mentioned barbarities, Softsword plunged into a new persecution of Cistercians to pass the
time; and incurred yet another shocking rebuff. Those monks,
taught by experience, and well ware of Softsword's uncomfortable situation, coughed so loudly and severely at him, and made
such terrifying gestures, that they actually scared him into the
opposite extreme of frenzy. For he took to remitting forest-penal-

---

[1] A leaden coffin.

[2] This story of Geoffrey being enclosed in a leaden coffin, drawn from Roger of
Wendover, is often used as evidence of John's cruelty. There is some disagreement
about the veracity of the story. See Sidney Painter, "Norwich's Three Geoffreys,"
Speculum 28.4 (Oct. 1953).

[3] The hermit Peter of Pontrefact, also known as Peter the Wise. Hubert de
Burgh's assertions about the manner in which his imprisonment lent his prophecy
validity reproduce the argument made by Roger of Wendover in his account of
these events.

ties, so as to curry favour with disaffected poachers and villains; and he permitted intercourse with foreign nations, so as to curry favour with merchants and mariners and other masters of men. And, also, he warned justiciars to do their justice justly.

XVI. *About the Curse of Softsword his Spasm of Affability*

What caused the Wild Ass to bound head over heels in a hurry, making the wildest and most asinine efforts to render himself agreeable, was the shock which he sustained from the severe Cistercians. For they made him ware of the inevitable fate of princes who (swayed by the devil) dare to defy the Father of princes and kings. King Philip the August, beaten to his knees on account of matrimonial behaviour, had been forced into obsequious submission. King Peter II of Aragon, an unimportant little potentate but persistently insubordinate, had been deprived of his kingdom. John's own ally, Earl Raymond of Toulouse, had lost his earldom. And the excommunicate Emperor Hottho had been diminished of every scrap of empire excepting his private petty duchy of Brunswick. It was these shocking examples which caused John to perpend;[1] and the result was a crisis of nerves, in which he again packed his pet Cistercian Abbot Hugh of Beaulieu off to Rome, to try once more to come to terms with Pope Innocent. But, by this time, the Cardinal-Primate was feeling very bored with exile; and he contrived to head John's envoy off, while he himself with his suffragans[2] of London and Ely got first to Rome and the Pope's pontifical ear. Into which, they poured such a tale as would colour the plain tale of John's abbot: they told the true tale of the appalling condition of England: they pressed the Pope, moreover, to deal as strongly and straitly and strictly and stringently as possible with the Earl of Mortain, and at once, without any more pious affectionate apostolic dillydallying. And, such was the force of their facts, that our lord the Pope fulminated a threat of instant deposition.[3]

---

[1] To ponder (*OED* OL).
[2] Assistant bishops (*OED* OL).
[3] Pope Innocent did issue an order to depose John from the throne, and he sent documents announcing this order to France. However, when English ambassadors arrived to say that John would accept the pope's terms, Innocent recalled the order.

xvii. *About Softsword his reverse Spasm of Demoniality*

Archbishop Geoffrey died in exile. John, finding so rich a benefice as York in his hand and himself scorned and scourged by
menaces from Rome, changed his mood (in a flash) from that of a
penitent petitioner to that of a desperate demon. Threats always
secured his resistance: only deeds daunted and defeated him. His
league of malcontents was now useless for the greater emprizes:[1]
but he still deemed it strong enough to smash the King of the
Franks; and he hoped to grieve the Pope gravely by upsetting
Philip the August. So, from Bamborough, Softsword sent nine-
thousand marks to Hottho's military chest, as a bribe for stiffening
the back of that pottering Duke of Brunswick. And I pronounce
this act purely comical: for, be it noted that these two noblemen,
John and Hottho, were both pretenders to thrones, both excommunicate, and that John had never yet paid the legacy bequeathed
to Hottho by King Richard Lionheart's will. The Dutchman, however being in dire straits, had the grace to be thankful for small
and tardy mercies; and he agreed to worry Philip the August on
his side, acting on behalf of Softsword on this occasion. Furthermore, Earl William of Holland joined the precious league, doing
homage to Softsword, and promising twenty-five knights and five
hundred footmen to prevent a Frankish invasion of England. John
became as busy as a bee. He summoned levies in mass from all
England, on pain of proclamation as culverts[2] and nidderings with
forfeiture of property; and he used his multitudinous mercenaries
to force recruits to his army. More men were driven to join him
than he could maintain. A few days later, every highway throughout the country was creeping with rejected conscripts scampering back to their homes. Chickens and female virtue suffered
more than usual; and such was due to the very wild assishness[3] of
Softsword. He, however, set his main army on Barham Downs by
Canterbury, with detachments at Ipswich and Feversham and my

---

[1] Enterprises (*OED* OL).
[2] Villains (*OED* OL).
[3] "*onagrismus.*" [Rolfe's note.]

V Ports ready to oppose a Frankish landing: but he was galloping
everywhere, overseeing his preparations. O times.

XVIII. *About the War against the Franks its Beginning*

The King of the Franks, in a parliament of his magnates at
Soissons, ordained that all Franks should muster in three weeks,
for the invasion of England, to redress the wrongs of the Church,
to stablish Philip's fatuous son Aloys as king of the English in vassalage to France, and to find out (by means of appropriate beatings) what John had actually done with Duke Arthur. So well was
our secret kept. The Franks showed much zeal in this affair: many
Angevins and Normans became much exercised about the feudal
oath which they had sworn to Softsword, whether performance
of the same would injure or benefit them; and very many, like
the shifty Sir Savary Malaleone, defied him and deserted to King
Philip. Thus, then, the great war began. And, first, the English
fleet naturally captured and burned the Frankish ships at Fecamp
and in Seinemouth, and also burned Dieppe after sacking that
city as an example. So, the two armies were left face to face, with
the said English fleet and the salt narrow sea between them, all
quite as usual on such occasions.

XVIIII. *About the War against the Franks its Interruption*
by our Lord the Pope

But Pope Innocent took occasion to say a word (a bitter biting
word) by the mouth of little Mr. Pandulph, who bobbed up,
armed with the plenitude of apostolic authority, to pronounce the
decree of deposition on the spot, and to bless Philip the August
coming to do the work of it, unless John made full submission and
amends then and there. Once more, the Wild Ass winced (when
lashed across the snout)—winced with sudden terror. All his old
timidities overwhelmed him. He remembered that his army was
untrustworthy, that many English magnates were communing
with the king of the Franks, and so on. But, above all, the craven
remembered the prophecy about Ascension Day. Of course he
collapsed in a bog of abject humiliation, refusing (after offering)

battle. O scab. He invited Mr. Pandulph to cross the narrow sea. That nuncio[1] did him that politeness; and the Wild Ass crawled meekly to meet his master at Dover. There, he sealed Letters Patent submitting to Pope Innocent's every demand, not abating a single word; and he fortified his own seal with the seals of such magnates as Earl Longsword of Salisbury, Earl Warenne of Surrey, Earl Ferrers of Derby, Earl Dampmartin of Boulogne. England and Ireland, he surrendered to the Pope, in amends for offending God and His Church, and to earn remission of the penalties of sin for himself and his heirs through all time. He vowed himself, also, to hold the kingdom of England and the lordship of Ireland, as feofs, from Messire Saint Peter Prince of Apostles His Chair, to do homage for them, and to pay a yearly rent for them, seven-hundred marks for England, three-hundred for Ireland.[2] And the charter of this vow was duly sealed by him, by Archbishop Henry of Dublin, by that ghibelline Bīp. John Grey of Norwich, and by eleven magnates as witnesses.

xx. *About Softsword his intempestive Elation at escaping Deposition*

What did the Earl of Mortain gain by grovelling about the buskins of a small archdeacon. I will tell it briefly, but truly.

Decent persons of every degree were mortified at heart, their pride of race was humiliated, they detested the usurper more than ever. But he pranced on his bestial and asinine way with reinvigorated cheerfulness. The dreaded Festival of Ascension passed. Softsword had a banquet in his tent at the Templary by Ewell. Four days later, the anniversary of his coronation also passed, and still he wore the crown of all the English. Whereat he sent to Corfe for the scorbutic hermit Peter of Pomfret, whom he gaily hanged with the son of that one hanging from his father's feet, a naked skinny little brat of six years contorted hoopwise holding his ankles in his hands. Softsword said that this was for the encouragement of similarly-minded prophets. But we English said that he really had ceased from reigning before Ascension Day, in

---

[1] Papal ambassador (*OED* OL).
[2] John essentially surrendered his kingdom to the Pope and placed himself under the Pope's protection.

accordance with the prophecy, having given the crown which he
wore (and was not his to give) to our lord the Pope most cravenly.
But he gained in this way. He had a spasm of lavishing butter and
honey in lordly dishes on the clergymen, trusting in them, having
failed with the magnates. He sent Mr. Pandulph away with twelve-
thousand marks of tribute and safe-conducts for every exiled clergyman: for he hoped (with the support of these) to divert himself
with the slaughter of many knights who had coughed at him. He
was the Pope's vassal. That clammy-necked pig Philip the August
had never fallen so low. But vassalage of this disgraceful kind was
not without its advantages: for Mr. Pandulph was solemnly warning the King of the Franks against lifting even a finger against
the Pope's vassal Softsword. Philip, of course, was much pained.
He had an army bursting with desire for war. John being now
forbidden fruit for him, he let his power loose to have a smack at
least at that forbidden fruit's ally, Earl Ferrand of Flanders. But
the Earls of Salisbury and Boulogne and Holland destroyed the
Frank's auxiliary fleet of supplies at Damme by Scheldtmouth;
and left Philip capering with impotent anger. O times.

XXI. *About Softsword delivered from the Ban of Excommunication*

Softsword, feeling firm with the Pope at (or on) his back,
wished to take a thorough revenge on King Philip: his idea being
to invade France from the English country of Poictou in the
south, while Duke Hottho and the other leaguers attacked from
the north. But this freakish fancy was thwarted by a jerk: for the
English magnates not only refused to do their feudal service for
the Wild Ass oversea, but refused to fight for him at all as long
as he remained under the ban of excommunication. So, he sat
still for a while, gnashing his teeth, hanging occasional hostages,
and biting his nails to the quick, he being a dirty-mannered earl.
The Cardinal-Primate Stephen also sat quite still in his exile at
Pontigny, till he knew for certain that the bailiffs and stewards
of all exiled clergymen really had been restored to possession of
their estates. Then, in awful solemnity, he landed at Dover, with
the bishops of London, Ely, Hereford, Lincoln, and their several
powers and trumpeters. At London, he got word to join Earl John

at Portsmouth. A regal escort attended him thither from Guildford. And the Wild Ass himself pranced as far as the hill outside
Porchester to meet him. Magnates laughed much at a subterfuge
of Softsword's. Being still excommunicate, he was ware that no
archbishop would kiss him in peace; and, being unwilling to take
a public snub, he flung himself at the Cardinal-Primate's feet,
saying, "Welcome, Father," and blowing an unreturnable kiss
from his raw-ended fingers. O manners. Ensued the highest of
jinks at Winchester, the Wild Ass on his knees outside the cathe-
dral-door saying his coronation-oath all over again and swearing
fealty to his liege-lord Pope Innocent, the fiftieth psalm called
Miserere[1] brayed by monks over his head, absolution under the
usual discipline pronounced by Stephen the Primate very much
in a hurry, with the Kiss of Peace, and permission to enter the
church for mass and *Te Deum*: thereafter, banquets for everyone
capable of eating and drinking, whereat many lepers (spiritual as
well as temporal) exceeded sobriety and decorum from pure joy,
so many indeed that I will not name them for reasons of charity.
So, John was given another chance of beginning again, free from
trammels.

---

[1] Psalm 51 (or 50 according to Greek numbering), which begins, "Have mercy on
me, O God."

VIII

THE BOOK CALLED THE CHAMPION OF THE OPPRESSED

1. *About the Refuge of the Afflicted*

"To whom shall I fly for refuge in mine affliction save to Thee, o Lord my God:" sang Messire Saint David of Hierusalem, King and Confessor, *gules, a lyon or.* And, to whom shall the afflicted here on earth fly save to clergymen, the ministers of God, says the unimportant scribe of this history. For laymen, kings and magnates and knights and suchlike, are occupied with their own affairs, namely, the snatching of others' domains or treasures or goods or persons for the benefit of the snatchers. There are, indeed, but two kinds of men, and one beside, which are the Snatchers and the Snatched-from, and the third kind includes clergymen, who (by right) have nothing here on earth, but all the powers of heaven and hell on their tongues' tips and at their fingers' ends. Hence, clergymen (if they only knew it and really believed it) might be vastly more powerful than laymen burthened and embarrassed by things of this world: for they are infinitely-much better endowed than laymen, in that they know what ought to be, and can teach (and even enforce) the same by means of their spiritual weapons. For which cause, I say that clergymen are the divinely-appointed refuge of the afflicted; and I fearlessly affirm that a man who is wronged ought to appeal to clergymen to get justice done against his wronger, and that clergymen (having no worldly interests, and the plenitude of heavenly power) ought to show themselves freely as the hope of the wronged, the refuge of the afflicted, the champion of the oppressed. Indeed I know no other. And I believe that Divine Providence has intended no other also. In which belief, I reared my own well-beloved son Boniface the Primate, and my beloved grandson the bishop of Llandaff, in token of my adherence to the same.

II. *About the Manner of These Histories*

There is a pair of doves (the most vain stupid lickerish litigious hypocritical of birds they are) which have builded them a nest on the top of this tower of Saint Thomas, where, all the morning, they have been sitting, saying to each other in the English tongue for me to hear, "Look-at-the-fool, look-at-the-fool, look-at-the-fool, look-at-the-fool." O manners. Whether an angel has instructed them to blaspheme the Constable of the Tower in so gross a fashion, I do not pretend to say. Brutes have been thus instructed before now, in defect of more celestial messengers. Consider the jackass of Messire Saint Balaam, Prophet and Confessor.[1] But, however this may be, I am not disposed to deny the foolishness of so very old a man as Hubert de Burgh, in attempting to write such tremendous histories as these all by himself. And, to say sooth (for I will not conceal it, even from myself), I am tired of Earl John of Mortain; and the recording of his wild and asinine anfractuosities[2] annoys me gravely: while the difficulty, of writing the whole truth about my lord the king without describing in full the events which surrounded him, worries me most dreadfully. Therefore, for the moment, I will avoid the woods and come forth into the plain, and pluck a very few blossoms to soothe the eye of your mind, o most affable reader, and I invite your affection to receive them.[3] Here, then, I interrupt my narration of the deed with which I myself had to do; and I will set down the tale of Sir Fulk the Flame concerning the gests[4] of Duke Arthur oversea.

---

[1] As Balaam rides to curse Israel, the ass he rides sees an angel and refuses to proceed and then is given the ability to speak and complain against Balaam's treatment as he tries to force the ass to continue. See Deut. 23:3-6.

[2] Winding, sinuous ways (*OED* OL).

[3] "*ergo declinans parumper siluam in planiciem prodeo flosculos perpaucos excerpo quibus mentis tuae demulceatur oculus lector affabilissime et ad suscipiendum inuitetur affectus.*" [Rolfe's note.]

[4] Exploits (*OED* OL).

III. *About Duke Arthur his Coming to Rome*

Says Earl Fulk: my lord the king and his company came to Rome in the guise of pilgrims, namely, Sir Fulk the lord of Cuigny, and Sir Geoffrey Turberville my knight, and Sir Hugh Turberville my priest, and Bobo Kemp the page, but no trumpeters. They were clad in leathern garments, without insignia of rank displayed, well-worn with the toil and peril of the journey of which I have nothing to say. And, having entered the city by the north gate called Of Flaminius, they put up at the English Hospice which King Alfred builded (a smallish old place in the Borough, near the Giwerie), like ordinary pilgrims. They, however, made no secret of their names or conditions; and Duke Arthur was served by his company in accordance with his state, to the great joy of the hospiciers, harmless clergymen who admired at his white immensity. But, on one point, my lord the king kept his counsel as obscure as the deep sea. On the road, he and Sir Fulk had conversed much with Sir Hugh the priest, who (knowing clergymen as well as he knew knights and pirates, that is inside and out), advised that they should go poor and needy to the Pope, mentioning nothing of King Richard Lionheart and the treasure: for, says he, "If Pope Innocent will do justice to the oppressed, then the said treasure will make it easy for Him to do: but, if not, then the same treasure will enable our lord the king to do himself justice somehow: but, to go (with a treasure) asking for justice, is to invite all the justiciar's clerks to itch till they scratch themselves and everyone else to bleeding." So, Duke Arthur came to Rome, saying nothing of the treasure hidden in Sicily, nor even going first to assure himself of it, such was his perfect confidence in God and me and his honest good uncle.

IIII. *About Duke Arthur in Rome*

Says Earl Fulk: for some days, my lord the king inspected the city and the heterogeneous mob which congregated there, tipping lepers, visiting sacred shrines and praying for his kingdoms. Abbots of indescribable sanctity were as thick in the streets as

bugs in the beds. Incalculable personages passed by on white donkeys. Clergymen of all colours slank sniffing[1] along by the walls
of every alley. Knights of every nation roared along all the roads.
Duke Arthur watched this world for several days without uttering a sound; and, afterward, he began to pay attention to certain
who wished to be polite to him, having heard that a sovereign lay
at the English Hospice garbed humbly for secret reasons: for they
imagined that, through this one, they might perchance find an
establishment for their sons, or at least take part in some shocking adventure. And the chief of them were Sir Lando Conti of
Montelongo, *gules, an eagle chequey sable and or crowned orientally
of the last, a mountain in base for difference* (who was own brother to
Pope Innocent), and his young son Lothario, and Sir Julio Cesarini, *or, a bear in base chained to a crowned column in pale, in chief an
eagle, all proper*, with his young son of the same name, and young
Sir Valerio Poplicola of Holy Cross, *argent and gules party per pale,
a cross potent counterchanged*, who was the Pope's ward and had a
fair and holy sister, all magnates of prime grade and optimates of
Rome. To whom Duke Arthur showed a serene and vivid countenance: but he would not accept favours from them. He said that
he had a matter to treat of with our lord the Pope, and he preferred to do business in the usual way, without availing himself of
the protection or intrigue which these new friends might extend
to him. Such was his Plantagenet pride.

v. *About Duke Arthur his Appeal to the Champion of the Oppressed*

Says Earl Fulk: during nineteen days, Duke Arthur and Sir
Fulk fil-Richard stood in the pontifical court at the palace of Lateran, where our lord Pope Innocent daily sat enthroned, hearing appeals from all Christendom, dispensing justice with both
hands. They made a humble but neat appearance and naturally
denied themselves trumpets, in accordance with Duke Arthur's
mind which agreed with the advice of Sir Hugh the priest: but
two such singular and enormous boys (as they were) would have
attracted prompt attention, but for the almost impenetrable

---

[1] *"furtiue reptabant nasorum pituitas retrahentes."* [Rolfe's note.]

crowd of clergymen and other petitioners who swarmed (bleating) between them and the Pope His footstool. And, on the nineteenth day, being very fatigued by this sweaty work, but having
only contrived to come within hearing distance of the Pope,
Duke Arthur said that he would now make a beginning. And, in
the very next lull of chatter, he lifted up his strong young voice,
and cried: "Deign an act of justice, o Most Blessed Father, to me
Duke Arthur of Armorica, the only rightful heir of King Richard
Lionheart: for Earl John of Mortain, my wicked uncle, nefariously
has my inheritances."

Everybody hummed like a hive; and Pope Innocent (very small
and sharp) stiffened to listen: though, says Fulk, it is not certain
that His Blessedness perceived His petitioner, for He squinted so
very obliquely that it was impossible to say out of which of His
two eyes He really was looking. But, on the instant, an uproarious
bishop with a case of his own began to bellow a tale, of enormities
committed by banausic[1] Venetians on him bringing back columns
of jasper which he had stolen in Romania for his basilica. And he
was so vociferously concerned with his wrongs, that he diverted
the Pope's attention: seeing which, Duke Arthur blazed with
Angevin anger, and shouted: "Damn me this bully of a bishop, o
Most Blessed Father, who shoves me aside and does me wrong."[2]

Now I must say that, herein, my lord the king committed
grave error, being first and last and all the time nothing but a very
keen straightforward boy, ignorant of courtly wiles, frightfully
intolerant of delay or opposition. He was not ware that (to Pope
Innocent) there was nothing in the world so important as a clergyman. Had he been properly instructed, he would have named
himself in his appeal with some such words as "Canon Arthur
Plantagenet of Tours" instead of "Duke Arthur of Armorica." But,
as it was, the Pope rebuked him, saying: "Don't be pert, you tall
and very pale youngster:[3] but run away and play, and cool your
blood, and come again on a more fitting occasion."

---

[1] "Banausos" is a term that was used to refer to the manual laboring classes in
ancient Greece.
[2] "damna, Beatissime Pater, istum Thrasonem episcopalem." [Rolfe's note.]
[3] "ne procax sis, adolescens procere et perpallide." [Rolfe's note.]

VI. *About the Champion of the Oppressed His very rash Impetuosity*

Says Earl Fulk: my lord the king and Sir Fulk fil-Richard tram-
pled their way out of the court; and, when they had eaten their
puddings, they slept heavily all the afternoon, to prepare themselves for what was to come: for Duke Arthur said: "That is only
the beginning of a series of tiresome tactics." Before next dawn,
they waited at the door of the Lateran Court; and, at the time of
its opening, they fought like rats or eels (in the Syrian mode) with
all sorts of bishops and others, until they stood in the very front
of the mob of petitioners. And, when our lord the Pope became
enthroned among the cardinals, Duke Arthur instantly cried his
plaint again, using the same words. And Pope Innocent sat like
a small hen flattened on a monstrous egg, motionless and puffy,
with an eye like a spark,[1] for twenty minutes by the glass. And no
one dared to think of aught save His twinkling eye. Then says He:
"Let these words be written down." So, a scribe, sitting at the feet
of His Blessedness, wrote them down from Duke Arthur's dicta-
tion. And His said Blessedness took the slip of parchment, and He
read the words written thereon; and, after, He laid the said slip
on His most blessed knees, saying: "Go away, and play, you tall
and very pale youngster, while We ponder this matter; and come
you again on a fitting occasion." Duke Arthur instantly exploded
with more words. He was not ware of how much knowledge of
his case the Pope really possessed; and he expected to be asked
for some token or testimony of his truth. But the Lord Innocent
struck him dumb with a nimble gesture, and repeated: "Go away,
and play, o you tall and very pale youngster, while We ponder this
matter; and come you again on a fitting occasion." So, my lord
the king and Sir Fulk the Flame gnashed their teeth and forced
their way out through the crowd, wriggling their sinewy bodies
in the Syrian mode so very horribly that several bishops began
at once to exorcise them; and they felt that the Champion of the
Oppressed was excessively prudent, not liable to err through rash
precipitancy, and no more to be blamed than a blank wall against

---

[1] "*sedebat Innocens Pontifex Maximus gallinulae similis ouo enormi complanatae immotae et sufflatae oculo scintillanti.*" [Rolfe's note.]

which one has inadvertently butted, walls being walls, and good walls not to be moved but by their proper motions.

VII. *About Duke Arthur his Diversions in the Interim*

Says Earl Fulk: every day for nineteen days, they went to the court of the Lateran; and my lord the king solemnly intoned his petition; and Pope Innocent (with equal solemnity) responded, saying: "Do not fidget:[1] We have you in Our thoughts, and We wish you well, you tall and very pale youngster; and, at a fitting time, We shall deign to declare Our pleasure," and nothing more. Hearing which, the regal imps devoted themselves to such diversions as were offered to them.

It was at this time, when they were hunting boars and buffaloes in the vicinity of a castle called Of the Heron belonging to Poplicola of Holy Cross,[2] that they gave the Roman magnates a taste of their extraordinary quality, specially their lizard-like agility and the frightful force and hardness of their hand-edges.[3] For the said Sir Valerio, of fourteen years, a worshipper of my lord the king, had a twin-sister, Lady Danae, both wards of the Pope; and she was fair and holy, and as boyish as her brother,[4] hunting with him and his guests. And, when an impious buffalo gored her horse, and would have gored her also as she lay on the ground with her breath bashed out of her breast for the moment, then Duke Arthur and Sir Fulk fil-Richard leaped at him, bare-handed and on foot, darting about him on all sides, and over him and under him, with a velocity which rendered them almost invisible, and chopping his hot nose with the hardened edges of their hands[5]

---

[1] "*ne satagas.*" [Rolfe's note.]

[2] We suggest that this was Arden.—P. and C. [Rolfe's note.]

[3] "*ei terrifici roboris duritieique manuum suarum acierum.*" [Rolfe's note.]

[4] Cross-dressing and gender ambiguity were favorite themes of Rolfe's. In *The Desire and Pursuit of the Whole*, the protagonist falls in love with a young girl who spends most of the novel in disguise as a young boy. In the same text, Rolfe praises Maurice Hewlett's use of this theme in his writing.

[5] "*aciebus manuum induratis.*" (Query whether Japan got ju-jitsu from the Syrian Assassins of Musse?—P. and C.) [Rolfe's note.] The Assassins, or Hashashin, assassinated crusaders using a fighting style called Janna. Presumably, Fulk has picked up these fighting practices through his contact with the Assassins.

so grievously and so efficaciously, that he genuflected and sobbed until he swooned from sheer chagrin, and was cut up easily by the huntsmen. Which very much gratified the girl and her brother, astonishing the Romans, who (says Earl Fulk) have not the smallest notion of the knacks which may be done with one's naked body in the Syrian mode. And, of the subsequent service rendered to my lord the king by these two Roman imps, Sir Valerio and Lady Danae, I shall write anon.

VIII. *About Duke Arthur and the noble Eavesdropper*

Says Earl Fulk: daily attendance at the Lateran Court, and majestic displeasure when the Pope gave him no news, drove Duke Arthur up the stair of indignation degree by degree: but he changed neither his frosty outward demeanour, nor the stinging intonation of his form of words, though the Pope deigned the same response every day, and though the mob of bishops and abbots became bored by his indomitable pertinacity. But it so happened that, just when Duke Arthur's stomach became intolerably molested by the Pope's monotonous but prudent procrastination, and he was advising with Sir Fulk the Flame about a more salutary and expeditious way of getting what he wanted, a word was said which piled fuel on his fiery thoughts.

Sir Lando of Montelongo (the Pope's brother) found himself moved (I suppose by God, Who moves in mysterious ways), to visit Duke Arthur at the English Hospice, inviting him and his amy to ride on the road called Of Appius, which road is less infested by lepers than the others, it being lined by sepulchres of pagans and reputed to be haunted by their phantasms;[1] and he brought two barbs[2] of Arabia that the regal imps might try their mettle. And, as they rode, the said Sir Lando led my lord the king apart from their trumpets, and enquired privately how he was progressing with his case. Duke Arthur responded glumly, saying that it was standing still. Then says Sir Lando: "My lord duke, it is on my conscience to make you ware, for the sake of the love

---

[1] The Appian Way is lined with tombs.
[2] A breed of horse known for its speed and endurance.

which this son Lothario and page of mine does bear for you, of certain matters which (by chance) I heard in the hall of my most blessed brother and Father where I supped yesterday. For, when I came to the palace of Lateran, my said most blessed brother and Father was in the article of finishing a conversation with His cardinals, on the subject (I judge) of the wrongs suffered by Your Celsitude.[1] And I heard His conclusion of the matter, which was as follows, 'Here,' says His Blessedness, 'is a youngster, poor, impotent, friendless, whose gratitude to a champion might produce profit. There, is an oldster, wealthy, powerful, well-supported, who dares to think that he can do quite nicely without Us. To that oldster, We (in Our loving-kindness) lately offered pardon on certain conditions, We being then unaware of the existence of this youngster. Now We cannot treat with this youngster, either one way or another, until We have the decision of that oldster: but, if that oldster continues contumelious,[2] We become free to transfer Our benignance to this youngster. The notion is praiseworthy, and merits Our apostolic consideration. Meanwhile, We intend Ourself to examine this tall and very pale youngster as closely as possible, both to keep his youthful rashness out of mischief, and for Our Own satisfaction: a blessing be upon you all.'"

Fulk says that, while Sir Lando was telling the tale of his eavesdropping, his young son and page Lothario Conti went from red through purple to black in the face with contemptuous disgust. Fulk says also that Duke Arthur showed much more favour to the imp from that moment; and that he frigidly thanked Sir Lando for his news, refusing any truck thereafter with a merely foolish gabbler, a betrayer of a brother's private speech; and, further, that Duke Arthur piously prepared himself to hear news at his morrow's visit to Lateran.

VIIII. *About the Oppressed exposing his Oppressions to the official Champion of the Oppressed*

Says Earl Fulk: on the next day, my lord the king amazed all men and offended the spleen of many by his inflexible and vivid

---

[1] Highness (*OED* OL).
[2] Insolent (*OED* OL).

serenity of mien during his terrible narration of his wrongs. And the Pope was extremely polite: so that all stood astounded when the regal youngster (unabashed) recited his piece,[1] adding no word of adulation, simply saying, "Deign justice to me, Duke Arthur of Armorica, the only rightful heir of King Richard Lionheart, o Most Blessed Father: for Earl John of Mortain, my wicked uncle, nefariously has my inheritances."

Then, Pope Innocent caused the court to be cleared of all other petitioners; and abominably babbled all the banished bishops:[2] but Sir Fulk the Flame attended my lord the king approaching the pontifical canopy; and cardinals, sitting on both sides of it in a semicircle, laid aside their lovely mitres to listen at ease. Says the official champion of the oppressed, in a voice which trickled rapidly and tasted smoothly and keenly like pickled apples,[3] "Tell Us the whole of your tale, o tall and very pale youngster." So, Duke Arthur began to speak. And he told of his lineage, of his father whom he never saw,[4] of his mother and her various ravishers, of his step-father who (believing him dead) held his duchy of Armorica for his infant half-sister.[5] And he told all about the miscellaneous daughters of kings, to whom miscellaneous kings (consulting their own convenience) had betrothed him from time to time, generally without his knowledge, particularly without his consent:[6] which betrothals he hereby renounced and defied, to prevent the princesses (who had married elsewhere) from pursuing life in bigamous conditions. And he told all about his honest good uncle, King Richard Lionheart, who named him as his sole heir, and confirmed him in his duchy of Armorica: but he said not a syllable about the hidden treasure. And he told all about his doings with King Philip the August, of whom he expressed an unfavourable opinion. Fulk says that, while Duke Arthur nar-

---

[1] *"Ubellum recitabat proprium."* [Rolfe's note.]

[2] *"et abominabiliter deblaterabant episcopi omnes pulsi."* [Rolfe's note.]

[3] *"malos aceto conditos."* [Rolfe's note.]

[4] Arthur's father, Geoffrey II, Duke of Brittany, died before Arthur was born.

[5] Guy of Thouars ruled as regent in Brittany for his daughter, Arthur's half-sister, Alix.

[6] Arthur had been betrothed to the daughter of Tancred of Sicily as well as to Philip's daughter, Mary of France.

rated these matters, the cardinals (turn by turn) nodded their holy heads at intervals, corroborating statements of facts within their several knowledge: but Pope Innocent was nodding His most blessed head nearly all the time, like a poplar leaf at a zephyr, so many were the matters the truth of which He knew: for the extent of that great pontiff's information was absolutely illimitable. By which sustaining noddings Duke Arthur was much cheered, though bored. Then, he began to tell all about his wicked uncle. Fulk says that, as Duke Arthur enumerated each atrocity which he had tolerated from that earl, the Pope and the cardinals beat upon their holy hams[1] in horror; and, at each such beating, Duke Arthur artfully proceeded (with rising gaiety) to the next and more leprous atrocity, augmenting the agitation of his audience. He told how the Earl of Mortain would have blinded him, of the ruse whereby that plan was nulled, naming me; and our lord the Pope said, "A blessing be upon Sir Hubert de Burgh." He told how the Earl of Mortain would have stabbed him and drowned him in Seine, of the way in which he thwarted that plan with his hardened hand-edge on the wen and with his under-water-swimming, of the ghastly gibe which he subsequently played by dancing wet and weedy and stark-naked on John's table. And he quietly chopped at a cardinal's protruded toe near by, in token of his manual ability: who screamed with pain, but the Pope and the other cardinals giggled. By this time, says Fulk, my lord the king had gotten all their holy heartstrings in his fingers. He was twanging them to laughter. Then, suddenly, he struck them so that they moaned awfully, and were dumb. For he told of the sale of him to the Giwen of Bristol, of his scourging, of his crowning with thorn, of his crucifixion. He kicked off his left shoe, baring his flexible young foot: he ungloved his right hand and held it high: he displayed the beautiful glistening scars of his passion. And Pope Innocent and all the cardinals made haste to win merit by kissing the same for a memorial, speechlessly beckoning him to continue his story. He continued briefly, says Fulk, speaking concisely as a king enumerating his power. He told all about Hubert de Burgh, how I rescued him from the Giwen, how I was

---

[1] *"poplites siloppabant sanctes."* [Rolfe's note.]

collecting castles and veterans for his use and comfort. And there, rigid as a palm-bearing laurel-crowned martyr with rayed hair, he made an end.

"Poor brave child,"[1] says the Pope, speaking from a loving human heart. And then, remembering that He was the chief of all clergymen, He needs must try to improve the occasion[2] with a platitude. "Through great tribulation," says the Pope, "we must approach our kingdom——" Duke Arthur quickly took His Blessedness up on that word. "As for me," he said, looking down his nose, "it is not denied that I have tolerated my share of tribulation; and now, therefore, I am here, expecting my kingdom." It is a mistake to hamstring (or even to upset) a clergyman who, with upturned eyes, is reciting his pious phrases. And, says Fulk, our lord the Pope jumped,[3] when Duke Arthur thus touched the root of the matter with his vocal needle. And when all the clergymen had talked together till their throats were parched, the official Champion of the Oppressed dismissed the Oppressed for the day. O manners.

x. *About the Champion of the Oppressed His Prudent fabian[4] policy*

Says Earl Fulk: day by day thereafter, my lord the king with Sir Fulk the Flame appeared at the Lateran court. And the Pope was affable to both of them, questioning them kindly but rigorously and very knowingly, at all sorts of odd moments, intervals in His daily business. And they were ware that His Blessedness was really marking them. Once, in a paroxysm of Plantagenet petulance, Duke Arthur burst out with roars for a settlement of his case: whom Pope Innocent paternally chided, saying, "Possess your soul in patience, o tall and very pale youngster." But He did not send him away. Indeed, from that moment, He became more affectionate than affable, so that the oppressed believed

---

[1] "*o animose adolescentule.*" [Rolfe's note.]
[2] "*non poterat nisi offici agere magistrum.*" [Rolfe's note.]
[3] "*saliebat Dominus noster Pontifex.*" [Rolfe's note.]
[4] In the manner of Q. Fabius Maximus, who is known as the "Delayer," because he avoided battle with Hannibal in the Second Punic War and instead sought to weaken the other side by cutting off supplies and engaging in skirmishes.

that he actually had excited his champion. So Fulk believed also. And at last, having picked all the meat off both their brains, and having showed (by His interrogations) which points of the case were really salient, our lord the Pope bade Duke Arthur to come on a certain night of leisure, and to tell his whole tale over again in presence of a full college, with whom His Blessedness was to advise Himself concerning His apostolic judgment of the affair.

This was done, with unspeakably awful pomp and solemnity. And, after they had heard and seen Duke Arthur, who, on this occasion, exposed to veneration his back parts also, the elders consulted together; and they advised Pope Innocent that the case was as valid as it could possibly be.

And, at the very moment, four shabby bishops broke in upon the assembly, eager about their perquisites as usual; and they brought letters from that little Mr. Pandulph in England, announcing our Wild Ass his uncontrollable and delirious desire to become a small doormat.[1] Confusion followed. Head knocked head, in attempting to study the said letters. Dismissal was once more the lot of Duke Arthur.

XI. *About the Champion His championing of the Oppressed*

Says Earl Fulk: four days later, Pope Innocent sent for my lord the king; and (looking very peculiarly) said some such care-fully-prepared words as these: "Well-beloved son, the time has now arrived, when we must converse together. Rash youthful impetuosity is (as a rule) very apt to lead into grave irremedi-able error: but surely, oh, surely, he only can be called the wise man who looks before he leaps. Though We Ourself are the most unworthy of all sinners, engendered (indeed) in sweat and putri-fied blood, We believe and hope that no one (swayed by the devil) can justly accuse Us of reckless or undue precipitancy in Our apostolic affairs. We should think not, indeed. This thoughtful sobriety on Our part has (it appears) received signal justification in the letters which those four shabby haggard bishops brought to Us (as you will remember) during your last visit. With which preamble, We will begin abruptly to pronounce Our apostolic

---

[1] *"tegeticula."* [Rolfe's note.]

judgment in the matter of your appeal. We dismiss it. Preserve your soul in patience. Let reason govern your gait and gesture. Be not unmindful of decorum and good manners. Where were you bred? Keep silence; and listen attentively, while We strive to give you understanding. Consider, first, then, that Our duty is to act rather for the good of the many than for the good of the one, for the happiness of the greatest number than for that of a mere unit however well-deserving, for England rather than for Arthur. Consider, second, what dire things England has suffered from Us (in christian love) through the recalcitrancy of that shocking uncle of yours. Consider, third, that that said shocking uncle of yours actually has England in his hand, and sits beneath its canopy with its crown upon his head. Consider, fourth, that your same said shocking uncle kicks now no longer against apostolic pricks— he becomes Our man, and will hold England of Us as a feof at a merely nominal fee. What else, then, We enquire, can Our clear duty be but to uphold your uncle as aforesaid in the lovely virtuous actions which he is going to do for so-long-unhappy England. So much for the multitude. Now, We will treat of the individual. We embrace you with the arms of pity. We deplore your disappointment. We lament your lot. Precluded (for reasons already stated) from helping you in the way which you suggest, We should be most happy to extend to you Our countenance and comfort in any other matter. And now, well-beloved son, you will save Us a good deal of trouble, if you will make a manly effort to look at the matter in this light; and We lovingly permit you to make Us some new proposition." O manners.

My lord the king stood stark still, tingling with the high contempt of the straight for the crooked; and his indignation was like lambent[1] flame. He spoke, in the very low strong voice which marks the first trickle of the flood of devouring fury; and he said: "I have erred, in that I took Your Blessedness to be my Father."

"No error:" says the Pope, huffily[2]: "for, by virtue of Our apostolic office, We are indeed the Father of princes, kings, widows, orphans, and so on and so forth."

---

[1] Softly radiant (*OED* OL).
[2] "*stomachose.*" [Rolfe's note.]

Duke Arthur made a very nasty disagreeable little noise in his nose: whereat Pope Innocent froze into an image of appalling austerity all of a sudden. And, says He, "Be you well aware, o tall and very pale youngster, that it is extremely unbecoming for a son to think of dictating to his father. Go away, therefore, and say your prayers, and cultivate a calm and equal mind, wherewith to appear before Us on the eighth day, when We will attempt to find some feasible way of showing you favour. A blessing be upon you, et cetera." O manners.

Fulk says that Duke Arthur returned to his lodging without saying a word; and his white face was so terrible, that mothers snatched their babies and rushed indoors, as he passed through the streets at the head of his little train. And, when he entered the hospice, he bade Fulk to deny him to any of his Roman friends who might be moved to visit him: for he was not of the temper which can tolerate condolences. And a new trouble was prepared for him. For Sir Geoffrey Turberville sickened of a Roman ague and died on the fifth day; and he was interred in the church of Messire Saint George of England which the Romans call Of the Golden Sail:[1] on whose sepulchre, Duke Arthur ordained that his coat-armour should be decently incised, with an epitaph in the English tongue. And, on the seventh night, Sir Hugh the priest concluded his grief for his said brother, and demanded audience of my lord the king for the performance of his duty as chancellor and bursar. And he had to say that, when all debts were defrayed, no more than nineteen marks remained in the common burse which he kept for the company; and furthermore, that two horses of the five had been stolen by a certain Roman magnate called Colonna, lately banned, and escaping from the city to the mountains to start in business as a highwayman. And Duke Arthur, having heard the priest, said that he would make known his pleasure after he had returned from the Lateran on the morrow.

Pope Innocent, then, greeted my lord the king very solicitously; and hoped that he had come to a sensible way of thinking. "Most Blessed Father," says the oppressed orphan, "my sensibility functions, as ever, most keenly and unchangeably." At which

---

[1] San Giorgio al Velabro.

answer, the Pope became angry, and deprecatory, and obsequious, in turn, and slightly vulgar all the time, according to Sir Fulk
fil-Richard. And, "Phy, boy," said His Blessedness, "who are you
to speak thus arrogantly? Do you splenetically imagine for one
moment that We shall depose a rich and known oldster in favour
of a poor and unknown youngster who has not yet even done a
knightly deed, for to suffer martyrdom is no more than a christian duty. But now, see here. We wish to do justice: We intend to
do kindness, if possible. What you ask of Us is out of the question,
at this time. But, if We esteem your shocking uncle at his just
price, We expect that he will certainly relapse into the dung, offal,
and other faecal matter of his pustulential crimes after a short
interval, such being the nature of that beast. And, then, We will
ponder your case again. That, We promise. Meanwhile, accept
this burse containing five-hundred marks as a token of Our singular favour. Run away, and become notable. Do some knightly
deeds, for instance. And, anon, come to Us again. A blessing be,
et cetera." O manners.

XII. *About Sir Fulk the Flame his Opinions and Duke Arthur*
his Resolutions

Says Earl Fulk, and these are his own words: "I picked up the
burse which Duke Arthur let drop as it touched him; and I contrived to get him away without bloodshed. My nose had bled many
times before and since; and what is a sprained wrist when one has
another unsprained. I also set myself to talk as much as possible,
for very good reasons. And I said that of course no sane prince
would even dream of quarrelling with the Pope, which to do
would be to rank oneself with the Johns and Hotthos and toss-pot-
tery[1] working out its own damnation. I said that, for my own part,
I was quite delighted at the turn which fortune had given to her
wheel: because we were now both free to divert ourselves, hunting in Sicily for hidden treasure, wherewith to indulge in secret
and engaging adventures. I said that I myself earnestly desired

---

[1] A "toss-pot" is one who tosses off his pot of drink, a drunkard, or a fool (*OED*
OL).

to visit my mother in Syria, but not without my amy, where the
Old Man of the Mountain[1] could (if caught in an affable mood)
cause us to be taught new warlike tricks of bodily strength. I said
that Syria was a place where many pleasant deeds might be done:
that I had a natural aversion from people who squinted and could
not look me straight in the face, specially clergymen, but, for all
that, everyone knew that Pope Innocent showed more favour to
crusaders than to any other kind of layman; and the Old Man
of the Mountain, too, detested the infidel Saracens like poison.
By which gabblings I made Duke Arthur gay: for, when I paused
for breath, he said: 'O Flame,' says he, 'first, we will go to Sicily
to get my three-times and four-times blessed treasure; and, next,
we will go to Syria, mingling with crusaders, and doing deeds of
divers kind but chiefly those deeds which are most sanguinary.'"
Which (Sir Hugh himself affirmed), was a very proper way, for a
brave and grossly betrayed prince, to satiate dissatisfaction, and
to regain his lost confidence in vain princes and other children of
men from whom he had gotten no hope. O times.

---

[1] *"Senex de Monte."* [Rolfe's note.]

VIIII

THE BOOK CALLED THE PROOF OF HONESTY

1. *About Duke Arthur his Departure from Rome and the Train which attended him then*

Earl Fulk told me all which I have written in this ninth book. Pope Innocent evidently intended that my lord the king should find his outward way smooth and not uneasy: for his three Roman friends came and sat on his doorstep at once, buzzing about their uncontrollable appetite for accompanying him as squires in such adventures as he might be undertaking. They were Julius Cesarini son of the magnate of that name, and Lothario Conti the Pope's nephew, and the lord Valerio Poplicola of Holy Cross the Pope's ward. Also, Pope Innocent sent four pages, detached from the train of the legate, three for Duke Arthur and one for Sir Fulk fil-Richard, each having a burse of fifty marks at his girdle for his expenses: they answered to the names of Matthew, Mark, Luke, and John: they were hale, lively, well-instructed, and considered fortunate as a rule; and they relinquished their burses to Sir Hugh's charge without a murmur. This, then was the company, Duke Arthur and his amy Sir Fulk fil-Richard, and Sir Hugh the priest to shrive souls and bless the meat and drink, and Bobo Kemp the English page, with the three Roman squires and the four Roman pages, eleven persons in all. They could not go southward to Siracusa in Sicily by way of the kingdom, for that realm was infested by lepers, bandits, and specially by a certain German called the Marquess Markwald[1] who was a great enemy to Pope Innocent and to all friends of the said Blessedness: which Mark-

---

[1] Henry VI, the Holy Roman Emperor, had granted domains in Italy to his German followers, and the pope demanded that these domains be returned to the Church. Markwald von Anweiler, Duke of Ravenna, who possessed some of this land, tried to elude this demand and was excommunicated by the pope.

wald (naturally addicted to atrocity) had, by means of bands of murderers and ravishers made in Germany and got from there, obtained dominion over all southern Italy, and was keeping prisoner the young King and Elect-emperor Frederick at the castle of Ziza in Sicily. O nomenclature. Nor was it desirable for them to go openly by sea, because they were but a handful of youngsters and one grown man, and all those southern seas simply creep with swarms of unregulated pirates who are chiefly infidels or habitual cutthroats. Therefore, Duke Arthur made no provision for his proper trumpets, but he put himself and his company into humble apparel, ordaining a comportment and demeanour to match it, and making known that sobbing was strictly prohibited. He also took oaths from all of implicit obedience to his will on pain of instant death; and he equipped his train with such weapons (the best to be had in Rome) as might be worn secretly and prove throughly[1] trustworthy in emergencies. And they left Rome quietly by the Gate of Saint Paul; and came to Ostia, a seaport, where Duke Arthur bought a fishing-boat and a pair of fishers: but he named Sir Hugh captain of the boat, because that priest was versed in maritime matters, having been a pirate in his youth. And, by reason of their humble aspect, they escaped the attention of lepers and of all sorts of undesirable aliens, for such make no war on mere fishers; and, having passed the fiery island, a terrible thing to see, they came into a strait called Pharos, and, in due time, they anchored in sight of Siracusa. O youth.

11. *About the Fisher called Nicholas the Fish*

One of the fishers, bought by Duke Arthur at Ostia, was a strange bald youth, a Sicilian by birth, called Nicholas, nicknamed The Fish, whom his mother's curse had doomed to an amphibious life. His flesh was of a chalky whiteness on land, and green in water: he was utterly hairless in every part; and his hands and feet were webbed up two joints of toes and fingers like the pads of an otter, whereby he used himself most artfully in the sea. Duke Arthur chose him, remembering the utility of that

---

[1] An archaic form of "thoroughly."

ship-boy Gaubert of Mantes: but Sir Hugh was extremely shy of
him at first, being a clergyman and having relinquished extravaganzas. And, indeed, the said Nicholas the Fish was much sought
after by all the stricter clergymen of Sicily, who would eagerly
have burned him as being not human but a sea-devil or at least a
marine monster. But mariners loved him: for, not being permitted to live on land, he had become very useful at sea, diving for
things lost overboard, cleaning ship's bottoms and anchors which
had fouled. Perceiving him, then, to have a singular and valuable
faculty, to be not only quite harmless but very valuable and willing to live like a christian if permitted, Duke Arthur caused him
to be thoroughly baptized, and ordained for him the treatment of
a man and not of a beast. I ought to say that he was in all respects
as well-formed and better than most other men, excepting that he
had a certain little orifice with a flap over it beneath the lope of
each ear, resembling the gills of a fish, whereby he let bubbles of
air out of him whenas he was under water. But the pages feared
him greatly, in the beginning, because of his baldness and colour;
and they recited such exorcisms as they remembered when his
business took him near them: whereat he hilariously plunged
himself into the sea, tremendously asperging them purposely to
displease them with wetted coats, but he was able to dive silently
without the least disturbance of the water when he pleased. Such,
was Nicholas the Fish.[1]

III. *About Sir Fulk the Flame his Enquiry for the Lathomy
of the Monks*

The other fisher, also a Sicilian, by name Hasdrubale, not
being in any way monstrous, was able to have life ashore at his

---

[1] From R. M. Ballantyne's *Under the Waves, or, Diving in Deep Waters* (1876): "In
the time of Frederick of Sicily there lived a man named Nicolo Pesce,—Nicholas
the Fish. This man's powers seem to have been decidedly superhuman. He was
evidently an amphibious animal. He appears to have acted the part of ocean-
postman in these old times, for it is related of him that he used to carry letters
for the king far and wide about the Mediterranean." Rolfe may have come across
Ballantyne's *Under the Waves* while conducting research related to his experiments
in underwater photography. However, Nicholas is also discussed in *The Chronicle
of Salimbene.*

pleasure; and he knew the Sicilian tongue, which is different
from the Roman tongue. He, therefore, accompanied Sir Fulk fil-
Richard when they went to sell their daily catch of fish in the fish-
market of Siracusa at a broad place on the sea-wall close to the
spring called Arethusa. There, they sold their fish; and enquired
for the convent by the Lathomy, affirming that the image of
Messire Saint Paul Apostle (there resident) had appeared to save
them from peril in a storm at sea. And having obtained news,
they went out of the city by the Watergate, and came to the convent, where they prayed as devoutly as any onlooker could desire.
Afterward, they had speech with the guest-master, who fed them
on bread-puddings (or what Fulk took for bread-puddings) and
olives, because they spoke him fair; and he showed them a place
called The Lathomy of the Monks, giving the reason for its name.
Fulk was grateful for this courtesy; and so he tolerated both the
said guest-master who was of an unclean habit of body with a
neglected nose, and the said olives which were quite black.

Here is the tale told by the guest-master. Once upon a time,
there used to be a certain very holy orange-tree growing in the
Lathomy. It had sprung from the crozier of Messire Saint Paul
Apostle, who passed Siracusa in a ship when on his way to preach
the Quaresima[1] in Rome: for, by reason of haste, he could not
stay to make visitation either of the convent or the city. But, lest
he should be deemed unmindful of the abbot's dignity and the
known piety of the monks, he blessed his blessed crozier,[2] and
cast it into the sea from his ship. And the obsequious sea, piously
receiving it, miraculously bore it with immense heaving to the
very feet of the abbot, who (by chance) was taking the air on the
summit of the cliff: which done, the said sea bowed and retired
to its proper place: nor has it ever again had occasion to heave
itself to so awful an altitude. The abbot, expert in sanctity, at once
perceived the whole virtue and significance of the crozier thus
strangely laid before him; and he caused it to be set in the earth of
the sheltered Lathomy for a perpetual memorial. Instantly it shot
out roots. In due season it blossomed and flourished fruitfully,

[1] Lent.
[2] Staff (*OED* OL).

whereupon the abbot instructed his monks how to distil a sovereign medicament, an alexipharmack[1] against all skin-diseases, of which but few flasks remained on sale at a price within the means of magnates only. And, on this apostolic endowment, the convent had bourgeoned during many years, maintaining nineteen discreet lepers, defying inroads of pirates and heathens and also temptations of demons. But, at length, some thirteen years ago, Sathanas[2] in person began to beset the place, he being jealous and much annoyed by the potency of so signal a relic; and he diabolically uprooted the holy orange-tree by night, which (in its agony) shrieked aloud with the unmistakeable voice of the apostle. The abbot and the monks were aroused, saving six who (with the prior) happened to be carrying an appeal to Rome; and they instantly performed a procession to the site of the holy tree. There, in the Lathomy, they were permitted to experience martyrdom: their corpses (diffusing a brilliant light and an odour inexpressibly exquisite), being found next day, much marked by the bufferings of the fiend and torn by his great paws. But the corpse of the abbot was not so marked, his known sanctity having no doubt won him the privilege of demising his soul from a body intact: but the holy tree was shattered and blasted by the violence of Sathanic onset. That was the tale of the guest-master.

IIII. *About Duke Arthur his Visitation of the Lathomy of the Monks*

Sir Fulk and the fisher Hasdrubale came back to the boat with no fuss; and at once put out to sea. The pages engaged in fishing for the sake of appearances; and Duke Arthur considered the news and laid his plans.

When the night was dark, Sir Hugh plied the boat round to the cliffs of honey-comb rock, cruel to the feet and hands of climbers; and some of the company went ashore. All night long, Duke Arthur and his amy and the squires searched the Lathomy of the Monks: but they found no trace of a cave such as King Richard Lionheart had described to me. And, at dawn, they decided that

---

[1] Antidote (*OED* OL).
[2] Satan.

the monks must have found the treasure after all, and (perhaps) used it for building the chapel of their beatified Barabbases[1] which stood in the middle of the Lathomy; and it seemed, also, that they must have quarried the wall of the said Lathomy, so as to erase the cave where they had found the treasure. My lord the king and his companions returned to the boat, very much displeased, and, in fact, feeling as though their minds were becoming unhinged; and they dozed moodily all day, rejecting their puddings, while the others kept up a semblance of fishing as they rode at anchor a couple of miles from shore.

Now it is my opinion that the sea possesses a certain divine quality: not only does it cleanse and cool the body and limbs of a swimmer, but it reinvigorates after fatigue, and (moreover) it clears away mildews or mists which may be affecting the mind.[2] And this opinion is strengthened in the following manner.

When the sun was hot, there being but little shade in the boat, Duke Arthur and Sir Fulk the Flame betook themselves to the water as well for coolth as for learning some of the admirable tricks of Nicholas the Fish. Which diversion, while it amused the company, was a source of profit to the swimmers: for Duke Arthur came up out of the sea refreshed and cheerful, having cleaned his mind and memory, and leaving his disappointment behind him in the water. And he took Sir Fulk and Sir Hugh apart, reminding them that (according to my narration) his honest good uncle had not left the dead monks untidily littering the lathomy where he homicided them and hid the treasure, but had chucked them into another lathomy near by, for the sake of security. From which, Duke Arthur judged that the pit where the carcases were found enjoyed the name of Lathomy of the Monks, transferred to

---

[1] At Passover, the people of Jerusalem were allowed to choose one prisoner to be released. According to the gospels, the crowd chose to release the prisoner, Barabbas, over Christ. Barabbas was traditionally thought to be a robber and a murderer, but more recently his crime is thought to have been insurrection or revolt. Rolfe seems to be operating under the assumption that Barabbas was a common criminal and implying that the beatified men to whom the chapel is dedicated are no better.

[2] Rolfe adored swimming, and he wrote often about watching boys swim as well as about engaging in the activity himself. See, for example, his "Ballade of Boys Bathing" (1890).

it from the other lathomy which (no doubt) contained the treasure. And, with hopeful hearts, the two regal imps and the priest made ready against the night for renewing their quest. During the evening, several winds got up and made the sea angry. The pages were left in the boat with the two fishers: the others landed with difficulty owing to the boisterous waves. Once more the horrid cliff had to be climbed; and then the search began. There was a very great lathomy nearest of several others to the Lathomy of the Monks, whereinto Duke Arthur and Sir Fulk descended by ropes through a huge geranium-bush on the lip of the pit; and Sir Hugh their priest dutifully lay upon the very verge, armed with a flasket of holy water, and ready to come spiritually to their aid, in case anyone of the nature of a donkey-footed hobgoblin called Empusa[1] (which is said to be indigenous in that island) should arise with a matter against them.

v. *About the Proof of Honesty*

Sir Fulk first found the cave: for Duke Arthur looked too high, being of so regal and haughty a spirit. And, having signalled their success to those above, the two boys entered; and began to dig. The earth was hard, compacted also with stones. My lord the king first touched a goatskin plump and heavy with gold. Ensued mighty and manly toil. Duke Arthur extracted the four-and-twenty goatskins from their bed. Sir Fulk attached them one by one to the ropes. The three squires hauled them up out of the lathomy. None dared to make a sound, lest ghosts or chimeras should be roused from below or monks and lepers from the neighbourhood above. Last, ascended the finders of the treasure; and, the boat having been beckoned inshore, the precious goatskins were lowered from the cliff, and stowed in place of ballast, not without ill-fortune, for (by reason of the roughness of the weather), two goatskins were dropped in the sea. Duke Arthur was for leaving them there by way of an instalment of tithe, he being only anxious to get his company safely on board, and to sail away in quest of immediate adventures. But Nicholas the Fish

---

[1] A female spectre (*OED* OL).

reverently offered an exposition of his proper ability and spunk, diving fearlessly and often into the night-dark raging sea, until he found the goatskins, and, with immense exertion retrieved them, raising them to the surface of the waves. Then, came the dangerous job of lifting them over the gunwale of the boat, which only escaped a swamping because Sir Hugh caused all the squires and pages to lie over the far side. And Messire Saint George, who has charge of the sea as well as of England and Genoa[1] where the velvet comes from,[2] caused a wind to blow off the shore, very favourable for departure. Thus was the honesty of King Richard Lionheart fully manifested.

VI. *About Duke Arthur his Voyage to Syria*

Duke Arthur sailed to Junch, where he sold a catch of fish to certain Franks recently come there to hold the place for the Prince of Akhaia.[3] There, also, he replenished his water-barrel, and obtained news of things in general. He sailed by Candia, an island fortress of the Venetians; and came to Linton in Cyprus, getting food and water according to necessity, and protected (as ever) by his sordid aspect and that of his company, from the greater thieves, and by a hardy truculent carriage from the lesser thieves. For, in these eastern cities, Fulk affirms that all men are thieves pure and simple, excepting in Candia and Venice where they are liars as well, even Templars and bishops partaking of this nature, mendacity being studied as a fine art in those islands.[4] O manners. Last, they came to Acre,[5] storm-tossed, and not a little tired of the sea, but blooming with gaiety and robustitude.

Duke Arthur and his train lay at the hospice of the English knights whom King Richard Lionheart instituted in honour of

---

[1] Saint George is the patron saint of England and Genoa.
[2] Genoa was one of the first cities to produce fine velvets.
[3] The Principality of Achaea, one of the vassal states of the Roman empire.
[4] *"cum in istis insutes ars liberalis et elegantior uideatur mendacitas."* [Rolfe's note.]
[5] Acre was the primary port for the crusaders in Palestine. It had been taken by Saladin, the sultan of Egypt and Syria, in 1187 and then recaptured by Richard the Lionheart in 1191.

Messire Saint Thomas Beket,[1] by whose powerful intercession the conquest of Acre was accomplished. And my lord the king ordered suitable habiliments and appurtenances for himself and his company; and caused to be displayed the banner and shield of his duchy of Armorica: for, now that he had ceased from being a mariner on the sea, where regal birth avails not to fortify afflicted stomachs, it was convenient that he should show his true colour: for, indeed, he was the richest prince in all that kingdom of Hierusalem. He also rewarded the Sicilian fishers with praise and pay, requiring them to trim the boat, and to keep it ready against such time when he should use it again; and he placed Bobo Kemp over them (that youngster having manifested a faculty for pious and marine matters, though he was so very red-headed), as his lieutenant, to the delight of all four. And, having had the bulky goatskins enclosed in new valises,[2] and securely bestowed, he and his train slept irrefrainably in large beds for a night and a day and another night, whenafter they were bathed and rubbed and polished in the Syrian manner and frequented by bald barbers and tailors.[3]

---

[1] The Order of St. Thomas of Acre (or Acon), a Christian military order that was founded in 1191 to tend to knights who fell in battle and to bury dead soldiers.

[2] "uidulis nouis." [Rolfe's note.]

[3] "baldis barbitonsoribus sartoribusque frequentabantur." [Rolfe's note.]

X

THE BOOK CALLED THE EASTERN QUEEN AND THE BLOODY WARRIOR

1. *About Duke Arthur rebuffed by King Amaury*

My lord the king sent Sir Fulk fil-Richard, and Julius Cesarini as his squire, with a message to King Amaury[1] at his summer-house, saying that the Duke of Armorica, Etcetera, newly-landed in the kingdom of Hierusalem, was about to visit him to pay cousinly and sovereign respects and to salute Queen Ysabel, she being a cousin by blood of the said Duke, (but of whose generation I am perfectly unable to say).

What my lord the king himself actually shouted in the ear-hole of King Amaury was a demand for permission to go away at once and act frightfully against the Saracens. But that prince put him off, saying that the war-season was over for that year, the Franks being (since Hattin[2]) averse from fighting during the warm weather; and he calmly asked, also, for an account of Duke Arthur's education in the arts of war as practised in Syria. At which rather-apposite[3] rebuke, Duke Arthur blushed from shame, perceiving that youthful impetuosity was gaining rebuffs from an expert though lethargic warrior. In which condition, he returned to his lodging, with an unusual vermillion face above his ermine mantle of Armorica; and (speechless) he closeted himself with Sir Fulk, barring out the priest

---

[1] Amalric II (1145-1205) became king of Jerusalem when he married Isabella of Jerusalem in 1197.

[2] During the Battle of Hattin, which took place in 1187, the crusaders were cut off from water sources by Saladin's forces. They had been marching all day in summer heat, and during the night Saladin's forces set fire to the dry brush, sending smoke into their camp. These factors contributed to the defeat of the crusaders. Amalric had been captured during this battle.

[3] Appropriate (*OED* OL).

who anxiously would have known what was toward. And being alone with his amy, he (raging) stripped off all his nice new clothes, and stamped, stark, gnashing his teeth. Ensued a row regal.[1] Fulk enquired how rude (precisely) King Amaury had seen fit to be. "He called me a whelp and a puppy:"[2] says Duke Arthur. "Perchance he meant no more than stripling:" says Fulk, for (having been born in those parts) he knew something of Syrian manners; and, beside, his knowledge of the niceties of Latin (which he got from Lady Johanna) was almost as extensive as mine even at that early age. "I know well what he meant," says Duke Arthur, not to be comforted by sophistry; "and he does not speak unjustly: for I am a whelp, and not a man, and I know nothing, and I have not done a deed, and I am a scorn and a laughingstock to knights." Fulk said kind words. But my lord the king continued raving. He would not be soothed; and, by God's Throat, he was simply athirst for blood, anyone's blood. "Ha," says Fulk, ware of Plantagenet passion, and himself beginning to flame, "then, why not buck up, if you can, and try to sup mine?" The two got swords and fell upon each other. Fulk, who had no real cause for fury, fought warily, though very hard pressed for his life; and his usual coolness mastered Duke Arthur's tantrums which were dangerous: for he at last disarmed him with a great twist, for the love and honour which he bore for him. But, hearing the clash of steel, Sir Hugh had the door broken down, and burst upon the scene roaring maledictions, he having been a pirate in his youth and having singular eloquence as a priest; and he sternly took both imps to task on account of their respective sins, of Angevin anger, and of attempted homicide flavoured (as regarded Sir Fulk) with sacrilege against the sacrocanct person of majesty and martyr. O noble priest. And, when they wept, he caused them to kiss peacefully, and sent them to bed without puddings for their souls' health.

11. *About Duke Arthur his Emprize which he planned with*
Sir Fulk the Flame

When all traces of the hurlyburly had been removed, and

---

[1] *"insequitur pertubatio regalis."* [Rolfe's note.]
[2] *"catulaster."* [Rolfe's note.]

Duke Arthur was once more ducally clothed and in his right mind, he asked for a revision of his penance and his amy's: they would fast, he said, but he would give three marks to the hospice for lepers, if he and Fulk might take the air in the evening for the sake of coolness, as he had great emprizes in his mind ripe for discussion. And, Sir Hugh having consented to this commutation, my lord the king walked lovingly with Sir Fulk the Flame, upon the moonlit rampart, from the tower of Saint Michael's Gate beside the sea. He took this road by advice of the knights of Saint Thomas, to avoid the lepers and scorbutic persons who mewed[1] beyond the other gates by privilege: for the great gate of Saint Michael of Acre is open all night in peace-time to those who have the pass-word. And Sir Hugh (that scitulous[2] priest) with the squires and pages attended them, and, from time to time, were admitted to their holy conversation.

This was the emprize which they planned then.

They would do something, something admirable, something enormous, at once, and all by their lone selves; and King Amaury might go on toward inevitable damnation, such being obviously his destiny. And, in the doing of it, they would dress meanly and walk humbly: nor would my lord the king wear insignia as Duke of Armorica, at least until after he should have quitted himself of the stain of inexperience: thus, he being very young and excessively Plantagenet, he was pleased to describe his condition. Sir Fulk approved: because he burned to use the knighthood which King Richard Lionheart conferred upon him at his birth and baptism. And the three Roman squires approved: because they hoped to do deeds worthy of winning knighthoods for themselves from Duke Arthur. And Sir Hugh approved: because these youngsters (he told me) were planning to keep out of mischief by following what clergymen think is the road of humility. But I told him of two pagan doctors; and one, who had cold feet, put his carpet on his floor instead of on the table, whereat the other, who had a hot head, stamped on the said carpet, saying, "I trample pride:" to whom the other answered, "With greater pride." I had this instructive story

---

[1] *"ut leprosos et scorbuticos uitaret qui querebantur."* [Rolfe's note.]
[2] Scitulous is a Macaronick term, defined in the glossary of *Don Renato* as "neat, adroit."

from the monks of Sempringham: but Sir Hugh was greatly grieved about it, and indeed excited, such being the nature of clergymen, when a layman sticks ever so small a pin into one of their silly bladders. Sir Fulk then spoke of visiting his noble and most noble mother. Even as a boy, Sir Fulk was most artful. He spoke of the joy of riding away by night, quietly, even disdainfully, saying nothing, and just going straight up to the Old Man of the Mountain, in whose court (indeed) he had been bred. For Lady Johanna married the said Old Man, solely for King Richard's safety but against his regal will, as we all know; and Sir Fulk venerated his mother, though his father's dying wish bound him to live his life in Christendom. And, the Old Man, being known to be the wisest and most powerful prince in Syria and very favourable to Lady Johanna, a word of his might be obtained through her, as to the weakest point where Saracens might be honourably attacked by so small and inexpert a power as Duke Arthur's. For the said Old Man detested Saracens also. Thus was settled the manner and scope of the emprize.

III. *About Duke Arthur: a parenthesis*

Sir Hugh remonstrated with my lord the king, warning him that he would sin by being too severe with himself in this matter: but he retired with humble reverences and tingling ears, when Duke Arthur bade him to go and try to remember that Pope Innocent had uttered a taunt very similar to King Amaury's. And there is nothing to be gained by disguising the fact that Duke Arthur was very young for his age. Most boys of his years either had made songs, or begotten sons, or won some sort of name for some sort of act or acts of knighthood. But he was virginal (because, as he naively said to me, he feared to diminish his force by letting virtue go out of him;) and his knightly shield (apart from his ducal shield of the ermine of Armorica and apart from his regal shield of the three panthers of England,[1]) was as blank as a sward of snow. And

---

[1] What actually are the arms of England? King Stephen Bowman's bade of the Archer, we know: King Henry fil-Empress's two lyons, we have heard of: King Richard Lionheart's *gules, three* (animals) *or,* we see with our own eyes wherever the King of the English is. But, whether these latter beasts are lyons (as is supposed by the mobile vulgar) or leopards (as heraldic amateurs feverishly pretend) or

I say that he was excusable: nay, more than excusable, much more to be praised than to be blamed. He had had a long boyhood, and came late to puberty. During that boyhood, he was accumulating, he was conserving, that superhuman forcefulness which made him the superman notable above all men:[1] for he emerged triumphant from shames, from torments, from lack of human love, which would have killed men; and he was a tender white boy. O my lord, my king. Moreover his hands were tied. Potentates, who should have fathered the fatherless orphan, contemned him. O manners. And, his revenues having been snaffled by consecrated and anointed robbers,[2] he could not even buy himself a footing. Who can do anything by himself? Who can live and do, without friends, or without money for purchasing friends or slaves? I say that no one can do anything without money: for bees flock to flowers and friends where money is; and out of nothing nothing is made; and so the lack of money is the chain which chains the pauper to his poverty and is the root of all misfortune. I say that. Hear it. Howl. I say it. What more? Only this. When Duke Arthur became master of a suitable and sufficient treasure, he became master of himself, he became master of innumerable friends (I speak not of Sir Fulk fil-Richard, nor of Lady Mariol, nor of one other); and he did not long delay an exposition of the regally majestic metal of which he himself was made. But this it is now my duty to display, for the confusion of that shocking Mr. Matthew, late of Paris.

IIII. *About Sir Arthur fil-Geoffrey and the Apparition of the Eastern Queen*

On the morning after the moonlit conference, my lord the king

---

panthers (as here casually stated), is a question upon which an expert's opinion, such as (say) Herald Bellasis of Lancaster, is a plain necessity. Pending that, and finding the panther a much more beautiful fierce brave awful beast than that coward the lyon and that snarly little sneak the leopard, we gratefully cherish Hubert de Burgh's panther.—P. and C. [Rolfe's note.] Rolfe refers here to Edward Bellasis (1852-1922), the Lancaster Herald of Arms, an office which would involve the conservation and protection of heraldic records.

[1] *"cum illam plus quam uidetur natura humana ferre posse quia fit ille suprauir super omnes homines notabilis."* [Rolfe's note.]

[2] *"consecratis latronibus. et unctis."* [Rolfe's note.]

proclaimed himself before his company as Sir Arthur fil-Geoffrey, a plain knight in search of adventures; and was for dashing out of doors at once, to buy suitable accoutrements. But Sir Hugh the priest suddenly fell sick of a fever; and, being alarmed, for that priest had made himself indispensable, they conveyed him to the Hospitallers, the most skilful and fortunate[1] physicians known, so that he might have the best comfort possible in his malady. These declared the fever to be a mere simple disease apt to seize newcomers, specially those exhausted by the pain and privation of long voyages; and they promised to produce him in health and fit for riding on the fifteenth day, his life being still strong in him. So, for fourteen days, Sir Arthur Lefthand and Sir Fulk the Flame quietly made their preparations: but, lest the common or damnable busybody (which infests Syria as well as Christendom) should intervene annoyingly, they spent some hours each day in hawking in the direction of Kayphas[2] toward the south. And, one day, when they were returning from this pastime, attended by the squires and pages with the falconers, they perceived a very splendid company of spectabilities coming from the city and riding southward. And, in the midst, was the most lovely maid out of heaven, in an open litter of silver tissue carried by eighteen disdainful dromedaries. She, indeed, did not escape the notice of my lord the king. He looked after her, as at a wonderful apparition, when she passed him by; and then rode silently for a long time. Eyes had been joined to eyes: indissoluble ligations[3] had been woven of their rays.[4]

At the city-gate, Sir Arthur fil-Geoffrey addressed his chief falconer, (a Pullan,[5] by the name of George and afflicted with a goitre[6] for the benefit of which he cherished a detoothed serpent, which lived wrapped about his neck in place of a kerchief,

---

[1] *"felices."* [Rolfe's note.]
[2] Christian crusaders referred to the city of Haifa as Caiphas. The city had been captured by the crusaders in 1100.
[3] Bindings (*OED OL*).
[4] *"iuncta lumina luminibus quorum radiorum plexa ligamina indissolubitis."* [Rolfe's note.]
[5] See Book XVIIII, Chapter XXVIIII of *Hubert's Arthur*. According to Rolfe, a pullan is a "[christian] of mixed or native birth."
[6] *"bronchocheta afflictum."* [Rolfe's note.]

to soothe the said boiling goitre with its cold and clammy writhing); and of him, my lord the king demanded an account of the
splendid company. The Pullan said that it was the train of Lady
Mariolanthe, daughter of Queen Ysabel, who rode often to Kayphas, where she was used to lodge with Lady Eglantine, wife of
Lord Rohart of that city; and, with Lady Mariol, were Lord Raoul
of Tibery, *sable, a plume in bar or*, who was seneschal of the kingdom of Hierusalem, and young Sir Robert Montgisart, *or, a mound
vert, a label for difference sable*, and the three daughters of the Lord
of Blanchegard, *vert six towers three two one argent*, namely Lady
Raimonde and Lady Aschive and Lady Orable who waited on the
Supernity of Lady Mariolanthe, and Sir Bertrand de Margat, *azure,
three basilisks or, a chief of the second three basilisks of the first*, rode
with them, who (so it was said) enjoyed the favour of Lady Raimonde. Sir Arthur fil-Geoffrey shut the falconer's mouth with his
hand-edge, at this: for he had a fastidy about hearing the scandals
of the court. And both used silence a great deal thenceforward, Sir
Arthur because he was thinking thoughts never thought by him
before, and the falconer because he had bitten his beastly tongue
badly. But I may add that the scandal was not really flagitious: for
Sir Bertrand married Lady Raimonde within the month, having
had a vision.

v. *About Sir Arthur fil-Geoffrey fallen in Love*[1]

Sir Fulk the Flame did not notice for three days; and then
noticed, and remembered that he ought to have noticed it before
(never yet a lover though he was), namely, that Sir Arthur took
no interest in any business nor in any pastime, nor even in his
puddings. At first, he deemed his amy infected with fever, like Sir
Hugh, specially in the matter of pudding, the neglect of which is
by no means characteristic of the Plantagenet. But, on the fourth
day, when Sir Arthur rode alone, (secretly, as he thought, for Fulk
was far too fond to lose sight of him), along the road to Kayphas,
with Fulk and the squires a little behind him on the land side,
lest lepers or suchlike should annoy him, then, his amy remem-

---

[1] *"Adamatore."* [Rolfe's note.]

bered other symptoms hitherto unnoticed, such as the setting aside of hawking which he had deemed due to the indisposition and obviously swollen face of the falconer, and the rejection of honest food. And, on the fourth night, Sir Arthur came and sat on Sir Fulk's bed, enquiring whether (by chance) that one had noticed the daughter of Queen Ysabel, the colour of her, of her eyes, her proper shape, and what-not; and, in fact, he was for discussing a plan for having speech of her, which seemed to present difficulties, seeing that he had divested himself for the time of his ducality and trumpeters. But Sir Fulk, who happened to be very desirous of sleep, up and says he, "Hi," says he, "since you are not Duke of Armorica and my liege-lord just now, but only my fellow-knight, let me say that you comport yourself like a mooncalf,[1] or like a staggering cockerel[2] of six months, all for love; and if you will not let me have my natural rest, I will take it." And forthwith he put Sir Arthur out of door, much displeased, and barred it, and composed himself to sleep. But the plight of his amy kept him wakeful; and it seemed to him (being quite a novice) that matrimony is the remedy for love. He considered also that this lover was thrice a duke and twice an earl and once (perhaps) a king, beside being very fresh and strong and of an aspect whose splendour and magnificence have never been matched out of heaven, such, indeed, as would be well worth the most serious attention of anyone, even of a queen's daughter. And, in his headstrong fiery way, Sir Fulk deemed it his duty to labour for bringing the two together. This, I say, was most proper. Sir Arthur's love-sickness and modesty made him place impediments in his own path. But Sir Fulk, his loyal amy, albeit not yet expert in love, though very apt for it and clear-headed withal, took up the task of clearing these obstacles away. So, in the morning, when Sir Arthur by chance remembered a duty and went to comfort his sick priest, Sir Fulk took horse to Kayphas, and waited on Lady Eglantine, to whom he announced the coming of Duke Arthur of Armorica in the evening to salute Lady Mariolanthe his cousin. Now Sir Fulk and Lady Eglantine had met before, in their babyhood: for he and

---

[1] A sentimental person who spends all day dreaming (*OED* OL).
[2] "*ceu uitulus plenilunio affectus ceu gallinulus titubans.*" [Rolfe's note.]

his most noble mother Lady Johanna Saint-Pol had lodged with Lady Eglantine's grandmother, Lady Douce of Neplier who was a Porcelet of Provence, *azure, on a chief ermine a porcelet gules, a mullet for difference*, when the Old Man of the Mountain sent mother and son to console King Richard Lionheart the husband and father in agony; and they had been stormbound at La Liche during nine days. So, as babies and as boy and girl, they were well-acquainted; and now Sir Fulk was a knight-errant, and Lady Eglantine had been married for her feof by Lord Rohart, a very cruel man, pitted with smallpox,[1] cold as well as hideous, no refuser of shameful commissions, and happily absent. I think that she was glad to converse with young Fulk, and that she let him see her gladness, for she was quite young. However, their converse was all of the love which Duke Arthur had conceived for Lady Mariol. Lady Eglantine arranged a meeting, in secret: for the Great Seneschal had charge to keep the girl straitly, she being like to be the queen's heritrix[2] of the kingdom, Queen Ysabel's son being humpty-backed, knock-kneed,[3] feeble in mind as in body; and there was question in the council as to who should wed Lady Mariolanthe, for not to every man does a ring bring a crown; and, such was the condition of the kingdom, that he who would wed Lady Mariol would need to have a great name, and a great sword to keep it unstained withal, beside a great heart to keep her, she being a regal Plantagenet on the distaff side, and also of the blood of the infamous Marquess Conrad, whom the Old Man of the Mountain subverted and slew because he would have slain King Richard Lionheart.[4] Also, Lady Mariol had had her breeding in Syria. When, at dinner-time, Sir Arthur heard what his amy had done for him since dawn, his only word was grieving that he had forsworn the wearing of ermine

---

[1] *"uariolis maculato."* [Rolfe's note.]

[2] Heiress (*OED* OL).

[3] *"gibber erat atque uarus."* [Rolfe's note.]

[4] Conrad of Montferrat was murdered by Assassins soon after being elected King of Jerusalem, and Richard is often thought to have bribed the Old Man of the Mountain to commit the murder. Maurice Hewlett puts a different spin on this event. In *Richard Yea-and-Nay*, Conrad conspires to murder Richard with the Old Man of the Mountain. Jehane intervenes and agrees to marry the Old Man of the Mountain if he will spare Richard's life. The Old Man of the Mountain then has Conrad murdered in order to guard Richard against further danger.

which became him most of all his raiment; and, repudiating all
idea of nutriment, he retired to inspect the contents of his valises.
From which portent, Sir Fulk justly augured that the malady was
grave and that its remedy had not been sought prematurely. Of
the wooing of my lord the king, Earl Fulk has nothing to tell me:
for he neither saw nor heard it, being entertained the while by
Lady Eglantine's conversation: she also taught him to troubadize
on the one-stringed luth, a Syrian fancy, very plaintive in sound,
when the wooing was much protracted. But my lord the king,
from time to time, has told me portions of what occurred then;
and the Regal Majesty of Queen Mariol once repeated to me the
very words, which transmuted love-sick Sir Arthur fil-Geoffrey
into a warrior (bloody for Saracens and some others) whereby he
became a man, and a duke mantled in ermine, and a husband, and
a king, as I will now narrate.

vi. *About a certain Opinion uttered by a certain fairly-sagacious*
Friar Minor

Brother Francis Salimbene of the Friars Minor,[1] who under-
stands many things hidden from me, I being no more than a man
among men, understanding men, war, ships, and (perchance)
wiles and statecraft and some fortresses, once said to Sir Fulk the
Flame that, if King Arthur Lefthand had not been a Plantagenet,
and a warrior, and a sovereign prince as well, he would have been
an artificer or poet. Which God mercifully forbade. For, said that
sagacious friar, the Lord Arthur saw things as all men see them,
yea, and more also: he saw a thing (for example) as it looked, and
as it was: he saw the said thing and the elements of which it was
composed: but he saw, also, the particular disposition of the said
elements which made the thing appear as it did appear. Wherein
he differed from ordinary men, for example, Hubert de Burgh,
Fulk the Flame, or my son the Primate Boniface. This quality,
said Brother Francis, is the reason why some men are artificers
or poets, because they have this faculty of extra-sight. But, to

---

[1] Salimbene di Adam was a thirteenth-century Franciscan friar and historian. Rolfe
draws some of the anecdotes in *Hubert's Arthur* from Salimbene's *Chronicle*.

equalize matters, they are deficient in some sense (generally the sense of hearing or the sense of modesty), or in some quality or virtue (generally the quality of charity or the virtue of continence carnally). My lord the king, however, lacked nothing, but one thing. Ah me. And he did such violence to himself in achieving it, that he died of it. O my lord, my king. But he did achieve it, as he achieved all else which he set himself to achieve, before he ascended to the superiors, as I shall narrate in proper course. Nevertheless, even as he was, he was far—far—above all other men: for which cause we served him, and feared him, and loved him. And I do not regard those wild Welsh as fools who alleged that he was their King Arthur of old, who slept entranced for a time, kneeling in vigil before the Sangraal[1] in some enchanted shrine of coral and nacre[2] beneath the deep sea, until he had word to come forth (white as a wave and as irresistible) to wash the kingdom of England from the wild ass, the cloven-hoofed swine, the lepers, the scabs, the nidderings, who ramped therein, and to restore His Holy City to the Most High God. I have tried to explain this matter: but I do not understand it myself.

VII. *About Sir Arthur fil-Geoffrey his Wooing of Lady Mariolanthe of Hierusalem: a great chapter*

Lady Eglantine admitted my lord the king to the garden of the convent where they lay, the tower of Kayphas being incommodious. This convent was very holy: the garden of it surrounded a shrine of Madame Saint Mary of Mount Carmel, which was so venerated by Greeks and Giwen and Saracens as well as Christians, that, even in war-time, no man laid hands on it or even entered therein.[3] And there was no garden like it in all the world, at that time: but there is now, for the queen's privy garden at Windsor is its daughter and image. In this convent, then, and in

---

[1] The Holy Grail.

[2] Mother-of-pearl (*OED* OL).

[3] Elijah lived in a grotto on Mount Carmel. He challenged a group of prophets to a contest to decide whose deity controlled the kingdom of Israel. The contest took place at an altar on Mount Carmel. The site is considered sacred by many faiths. The Carmelite order founded a monastery dedicated to Mary on the site where Elijah's cave was alleged to have been.

the guest-house thereof, was Lady Mariolanthe bestowed: for Lady Eglantine, being a Châtelaine[1] of Kayphas, was protector of the said convent.

Sir Arthur fil-Geoffrey entered the garden, which lay in terraces overlooking the sea, fringed with feathery palms and solemn pines and the smooth greyish green of cactus flaming with strange waxen scarlet flowers. Aloes, there were with sharp brown spikes, each spike patterned in two shades of green in the shape of the next. And the said terraces were starred with white oleanders from Baffo, and with red oleanders from Kishon (that antique city), and with monstrous bushes of azalea, offering tables of heavenly flowers to the eye, some as red as glowing fire, some as yellow and bright as light, some like the hues of a sea-shell, rosy, pearly, iridescent, or the faint-flushed ivory flesh of a healthy mind. And the terraces were bordered by wide beds thick with wall-flowers, solid masses of wall-flowers of a wonderful kind, having an odour delicious, fresh, clean, warm, alive, wholesome, exquisite, solid masses of wall-flowers, of every singular warm live tint from black through lovely brown and brownish red and ruddy-red and reddish-yellow and yellowish pink and pinkish white to the dazzling white of mother-of-pearl. And all the paths of the garden were white with tiny broken shells. And, on the middle terrace was a fair paradise, with a little fountain gently plashing into a deep cool basin wherein swam lazily great golden carp of incalculable antiquity. And, on the rocks round the basin, were stone-crop and moss and our Lady's hair. And the whole of the little paradise was carpeted (not with grass, but) with a dense and ordered growth of fragrant thyme, beyond which were the low and solid thickets of wonderful wall-flowers. All this, Sir Arthur Lefthand noticed, as he slowly paced the path which led to paradise, waiting for Lady Mariol. She came, in the evening light, among the wall-flowers, leaving her trumpets at the gate.

My lord the king himself deigned of his sweet grace to tell me how my lady the queen seemed when she first appeared to him. We were walking in what was then the queen's new garden in the castle of Windsor. For it is my duty to say, o most affable

---

[1] A female castellan; the mistress of a castle (*OED* OL).

reader, that, as soon as King Arthur stablished himself in his kingdom, the queen sent four busses to Syria to be laden with roots of
the flowers and shrubs which flourished in that paradise at Kayphas, wherewith she caused to be made that grove at Windsor
which all the world admires. Here, then, we were walking when
King Arthur told me how Queen Mariol seemed when he went
a-wooing. He said that she seemed like a flower. And, even as
he said it, his eyes moved to dwell upon the queen who walked
with her ladies among the wonderful azaleas, fire and light and
flesh by name: for he was always her fervent constant lover. He
said that she seemed like a flower. "Lord King," says I, "the simile
is a sweet one, but by no means new: for every lover, since Messire Saint Adam Patriarch and Confessor, has said the name of
his lass. And I myself have said it more than once on my own
account." "Amend it for me, Hubert," says the King, forgiving my
cavillation,[1] but now silenced, by reason of that regal and maiden-
like reserve, which (throughout his long life) prevented him from
ever letting even me see more than a morsel of his heart at one
time. "Amend it for me, if you can, Hubert:" then says he. "Lord
King," says I, "Your Regal Majesty has deigned to describe the
paradise at Kayphas wherein you wooed; and my lady queen
shows me here, in this new garden, what like the Kayphas paradise was. Consider," says I, "the queen, now walking over there
among her wonderful eastern wallflowers; and, methinks, an apt
simile is not far to seek. For the black of the wallflowers is her
eyes, and the lovely brown and brownish-red of them her hair,
and the ruddy-red her lips, and all the other healthy-coloured tints
her beautiful flesh, and the pearly white her teeth, and the dainty
pure and strong aroma of them her virtue and her fame." Says
the king: "Hubert, you speak like a lover." "Lord King," says I,
"I speak for you who bade me to find a just simile. And I simply
say that the queen, whom you brought to us out of the east, is
comparable to her wonderful wallflowers." "Let them be called
by her name, the Eastern Queen:[2] the king wills it:" says my lord
the king, gravely gleeful. And he began to speak of other matters,

---

[1] Quibbling (*OED* OL).
[2] There is a salmon-red variety of wallflower referred to as the Eastern Queen.

which are of no concern here, seeing that I am set to narrate but the story of Sir Arthur Lefthand's wooing.

Daily, then, they met and walked and loved in the Kayphas paradise; and, on the fourteenth day of Sir Hugh's fever, Sir Arthur had finished revealing himself and his plans, and Lady Mariolanthe her forebodings: he, how he was to fare northward to visit Lady Johanna, through whom he would taste the mind of the Old Man of the Mountain as to the achievement of some notable knightly deed upon Saracens or other caitiffs,[1] whereby he might win the renown of a person of consequence: she, how she was liable to become heritrix of the kingdom, and to be married (for its sole sake) to the stoutest warrior who should be at hand, quite regardless of her will, as had been the lot of Queen Ysabel her mother, treated as a brood-mare to raise heirs for a crumbling crown.[2] Ardently they desired each other, the lovely healthy girl, the strong gigantic boy a year and four months her senior. But how could he in honour take her: for, says he, "That I am nephew and heir of the Lionheart, head of the body Plantagenet, is but an accident and due to no work of mine, for otherwise I am without name or fame, never of all God's enemies and mine having slain or taken vengeance of one: but thou art of a race of warriors." Then, Lady Mariol made superb response, such response as one would expect from a maiden born in the Sign of the Bull and under the planet Venus, having Sol but one day from the centre of her sign.[3] "Oh, go," says she, "go to the Old Man of the Mountain, and learn how to do a great deed. Then, do it; and, having done it, do a greater, coming to save me lest I be put to some beefy beery braggart of the Franks for the sake of this kingdom. Ah, win your ermine: nor dare to speak to me again till you can come clothed in ermine greatly won." And she turned and fled from him, weeping, and fearful for him, despite the high brave words which she had said to him. This, Queen Mariol herself told me, even now unknowing her own magnificence.

---

[1] "nebulones." [Rolfe's note.]
[2] Isabella of Jerusalem was married four times, and each of her marriages served a political purpose.
[3] This would indicate the fourth or the sixth of May.—P. and C. [Rolfe's note.]

VIII. *About Sir Arthur fil-Geoffrey his Journey to the Confines*
of Christendom

Says Earl Fulk as follows. Sir Arthur and his company set out
by sea for Tortosa, using his fishing boat, and going humbly and
without fuss, for the sake of the security of his treasure. The
first night they lay off Scandalion, which was Lord Raymond's,
coming on the morrow to Tyre, where was a colony and a county
of the Republic of Saint Mark,[1] though the city of Tyre belonged to
the kingdom of Hierusalem. They harboured here for the second
night; and passed to Saiete, of which city the Earl of Leicester's
brother Guy was baily and warden, on behalf of young Sir Balian
Garnier, his stepson and its lord. Thence, they came to Daruth
which young Sir John of Ibelin ruled: he who was afterward Baily
of the Kingdom, *or, a cross patty gules*. He indeed was a half-brother
of Queen Ysabel, being the son of her mother's second marriage
with Sir Balian who begot him. He entertained Sir Arthur and
his company very courteously for the night, and sped them on
to Giblet, which Sir Guy de Lembriac held from the Republic
of Saint George.[2] Thence, they came to Tripoli in the day-time,
passing Boutroun the lordship of Sir Plivian the Pisan at noon.
And, in Tripoli, they spent the night, and came to Tortosa on the
morrow with a fair wind. Tortosa was a fortress of the Templars,
and Brother Philip de Plaissiez was their grandmaster: but my
lord the king did not, at that time, think as well of the Templars as
Sir Hubert de Burgh thought, for he had not such tokens of their
sterling honesty and good faith and lack of commercial enter-
prize as I had. Wherefore he did not seize this opportunity of
relieving himself of the anxious charge of his treasure, depositing
it with the Templars (those most stolidly honest and least usurious of bankers): but he sailed in haste from Tortosa to the port
below Margat, where a castle of Saint John[3] was, to whose warden
he had a letter-commendatory from the Hospitaller of Acre. And

---

[1] Venice.
[2] Genoa.
[3] The Knights Hospitaller are also known as the Order of Saint John, and Margat
was one of their major fortresses.

the said warden was a noble gentlemen of Auvergne, by name Brother Guerin, *gules, a tower argent*; and he was at that time Marshal of the Hospital, and, later, its grandmaster; and he had for brothers Brother Peter (a knight of the Temple and anon grandmaster of that Order), and Lord Bernard (bishop of Puy), and Lord Eustace (archbishop of Nikosia in Cyprus), and Lord Fulk (bishop of Limasol in the same island), a family of very unworthy clergymen who were also doughty warriors. This Marshal of the Hospital at Margat entertained Sir Arthur and his company very handsomely for four days, because a stream in spate[1] was rendering impossible their further progress. And, being a clergyman as well as a knight of Saint John, he felt it his solemn duty to enquire of Sir Hugh the priest whether it was not perhaps slightly foolhardy for christians to risk themselves dealing with the Old Man of the Mountain, a potentate whose reputation in Christendom hovered between sanctity and demoniality not touching any mean: for he is the chief of the actual lieges of Muhammed called the Prophet, and these are the Grand Order of the Kadria, while the infidel Turks and Saracens are but a sect detached from the parent tree, a branch cut off and rotting, as the filthy fanatics of the Albigeois are detached from us christians.[2] At this Fulk flamed, saying that he had the privilege of knowing the Old Man of the Mountain personally; and he let the Marshal of the Hospital know who he was, and how his mother was the queen of the said Old Man dwelling in Musse, and he also affirmed that he had been taught the secret sign of the first initiation of the Assassins, on account of the honour in which the Old Man held Lady Johanna, which sign warranted a safe-conduct to go and to return at least and perhaps much more. The Marshal said a few words about young blood, finding it hard to believe that a company of such humble aspect possessed any actual importance, though he did not change his courteous demeanour, nor abate his hospitality, but remained quite cheerful. And, when the spate had spent itself, my lord the king left his boat with the fishers and Bobo Kemp in the herborough of Margat, and deposited his treasure with the Marshal of

---

[1] A body of water that is "in spate" is flooded (*OED* OL).
[2] In fact, the Assassins were seen by orthodox Muslims as heretics.

the Hospital; and he crossed with his company the confines of Christendom, after two hours journey from the sea.

VIIII. *About Sir Arthur fil-Geoffrey admitted to the Kingdom of the Assassins*

They came to a ravine, at the bottom of which was the torrent whose swelling had delayed the company; and Sir Fulk fil-Richard desired all to disarm themselves, lest inadvertent injury should be inflicted on an Assassin appearing somewhat unexpectedly. And they went, disarmed, along the different road, till about sunset: when it was seen that a party, clad in white but very naked, awaited them at the head of the said ravine. Sir Fulk said that this was an outpost of the Assassins, but not the first, it being the custom for the others to remain ambushed while strangers entered their kingdom. One advanced, making a sign unseen of all save Sir Fulk. He told Sir Arthur of it; and said that he was about to give the countersign: which he did; and (says my lord the king) if it was not given with the left annular,[1] it was unseen by christian eyes save perhaps the giver's. The Assassin then said, in the Syriac tongue, which Sir Fulk understood because he had been there before, "My august sovereign the holy one commands me to bring this company to the Inner Mountain." Sir Fulk said that, henceforth for a period, there were no wills save the will of the Old Man of the Mountain; and he made the canonical response to the Assassin, saying, "Hearkening and Obedience." So, they encamped where they were for the night, very handsomely served by the Assassins, in pavillions of silk on silken carpets; and, in the morning, after Sir Hugh had sung the mass before the company the chief Assassin present made a seen sign. Whereupon, Sir Fulk bound a veil of white silk over Sir Arthur's eyes, saying that it was only the Old Man's way and portended nothing ill; and in like manner did the Assassins with the others. But, when one came to veil Sir Fulk's eyes, the Flame flared, saying something in a certain tone. At which the Assassin responded, saying something else; and desisted from his purpose, perceiving that Sir Fulk really

---

[1] Ring finger (*OED* OL).

was of the first initiation. And, all being veiled, they proceeded
on their journey, the Assassins courteously leading them; and Sir
Fulk (walking with his amy) said that he remembered perfectly
how the land lay. They halted at dinner-time, and were unveiled
to eat in a grove; and the Assassins provided excellent puddings
for the christians: but they themselves ate not nor drank, nor
(indeed) did Sir Fulk, though he was very hungry, for he desired
to make a good impression on the Assassins. Wherefore, he sat
on his hams after their manner, rolling his eyes round the site of
his navel and concealing his thumbs for luck.[1] Afterward, they
went on again, veiled as before, but now they went in silence:
for, among the Assassins (performing some special duty) no one
has any power of speech (excepting at the will of the Old Man);
they give or answer pass-words, or say such words as have been
given them to say: but, otherwise, they are as inarticulate as tur-
nips. After three hours, they came to a ravine where was a fourth
gate; and, here, Sir Fulk's eyes also were veiled: for, within that
gate, was the second initiation, which he had not then undergone.
They entered the gate; and passed along an echoing gallery for
some time, until they emerged again into the open. And their
escort, which was of the second initiation, retired; and Assassins of the third initiation led them onward. And, anon, they
were made to ascend so many hundred of stairs, that Sir Arthur
at length broke silence, saying spiritedly, "In my flesh I shall see
God."[2] Whereat the company laughed, but said no word, nor did
the Assassins. And, coming to the top, they were much whirled
round and round, very genteelly, till they staggered with giddi-
ness and were like to fall: but the Assassins carried them into a
chamber fitted with vast cushions, whereon they rested; and,
their veils having been removed, delicate puddings and bever-
ages were placed before them. Sir Arthur complained about the
veiling; and would have been haughty. But Sir Fulk persuaded
him to respect the customs of the place, saying that the Old Man
undoubtedly was not ill-disposed toward them, for he plainly
was ware of their coming, having means of knowing everything,

---

[1] "*quamobrem in poplitibus sedebat circum umbilicus situm oculos reuoluens pollicibus in fortunam secundam celatis.*" [Rolfe's note.]

[2] "*in carne mea uidebo Deum.*" [Rolfe's note.] Job 19:26.

and, since their lives had not been taken in the eighth minute after they passed the confines of Christendom, as would have been the case if mischief had been intended, it was certain that they would be permitted to return in security, even though the Old Man should not see his way to help them against Saracens, enemies of him as of all. So, they masticated their repast at their ease; and, Sir Fulk having predicted it, they lapsed into profound slumber: for their puddings were infected (after the manner of the Assassins) with that magic drug called Health in Sleep, which is the least potent of their Seven Sacred Potions, the seventh and most potent being called Ladder of Eternity and causing a comfortable and smiling decease, after nineteen hours of painless exuberant life with doubled strength of mind and body, the senses being as it were dried up as far as fear or pain are concerned. But Health in Sleep is a sedative after great exertions, producing the pleasing and profound inebriety which causes the repose during which recuperation is effected automatically:[1] it may be detected by an initiate (says Earl Fulk), by its faintly-piquant savour and its odour of bugloss.[2] While they slept, the Assassins washed them in the particular manner of that kingdom, and rubbed their flesh with unguents and the juices of magic herbs, so that though they had fallen weary and travel-stained on sleep, they awoke so clean and so supple in every member that they were much amazed. And slaves brought garments to clothe them after the fashion of the Assassins, such being the custom; and each received a white garment like a shirt without sleeves: it was made of silk, open to the waist in front, the tails twisted up before and behind between the legs and belted round the middle, so that arms and legs and breast were entirely bare. And the garb pleased Sir Arthur, because it facilitated free movements: but, to Sir Fulk, it was not new, he having been there before.

---

[1] The Assassins were rumored to take hashish and potions that caused strange visions or dreams. According to the twelfth-century German chronicler, Arnold of Lübeck, the Old Man of the Mountain gave the Assassins potions that would plunge them into ecstasy and oblivion, and he promised them that they would live in those dreams forever if they died while killing at his command.

[2] "buglossi odore." [Rolfe's note.] Bugloss is a flowering plant.

x. *About the Beauty of Strength*

Lady Johanna was supreme over the household of the Old Man or Grand Assassin; and she was obeyed by all in the castle, saving only the Assassins themselves, who are (in a manner of speaking) military monks such as Templars and Hospitallers are, and they owe obedience to no one but the Old Man whom they venerate as their Grandmaster of their Order of the Kadria. But their obedience bears no comparison at all with the obedience rendered by Templars or Hospitallers to their grandmasters, or by regulars to their abbots, in Christendom: for the Old Man has power of life and death over the Assassins; and he uses it, to the entire satisfaction of all, as usually as he uses his other functions. He, however, maintains a family of wives, with slaves, eunuchs, and so on, for the comfort and health of his monks and the perpetuation of his order, such being the custom of the country and enjoined by his religion. But, what precisely his religion is, God only knows. For my own part, having strictly interrogated Earl Fulk at frequent intervals for more than fifty years, I judge that it is a theocratic tyranny, which the Old Man enforces by means of his amazing audacity, his forceful individuality and his singular proficiency in natural magic. And there are no lepers in his kingdom, all disease being a capital felony. Lady Johanna gained her sway over all, excepting the Assassins initiates, in the following manner. A certain wife, who (at one time) enjoyed the favour of the Old Man, became puffed up and aspired to dominate everybody. But Lady Johanna, as a christian woman who had been the amye of a christian king, would not abide the creature:[1] she, therefore, waited till that misguided upstart presumed to issue commands to her in the presence of credible witnesses; and then she arose with a neat whip[2] and so chastised the slut that (for some time) no posture but a prone one pleased her.[3] And the Old Man viewed this redoubtable gest with deep joy; and he said, "Beauty of form is as naught to beauty of strength." And he gave commandment

---

[1] *"non patiebatur animal istud."* [Rolfe's note.]

[2] *"uirga concinna."* [Rolfe's note.]

[3] *"nullam nisi pronam approbabat scelesta posituram."* [Rolfe's note.]

that all should henceforth owe obedience to Lady Johanna. And, from that day, she ceased from being a wife to the Old Man, for she saw that he went in hideous and ghastly terror of her: but she was faithful to her oath to him, and content to remain as queen in Musse. Bur she ruled his wives and those of the Assassins with most salutary rigour, not permitting them to quarrel or nag, or to stoop or loll, or to paint their flesh or torment slaves, or to poison one another's children or conspire for the Old Man's exclusive attention, as they had been used to do: but rather she kept them as strictly as nuns in a christian monastery, whereby their health was improved and their manners and abilities ameliorated as much as might be. And Lady Johanna lived apart, having the state and amenities and privileges of a regal abbess.

xi. About Sir Arthur fil-Geoffrey his Visit to Lady Johanna

The Assassins in charge of them led Sir Arthur and Sir Fulk with the company into Lady Johanna's presence. And the two great boys paid their respects to her: for Sir Fulk seized his mother by the neck for filial purpose, while she extended to Sir Arthur her right hand, who laid on it the homage of his lips. But, when she had time to look at him, she kissed his brow, as though he were her son and Fulk's twin. She said that he had the real Plantagenet eyes, like the Lionheart his uncle, which is quite true. Then she sobbed a little. Then she smiled, and looked at Fulk, saying that he really was the Lionheart and much more. And she stroked his great bare arms and breast and legs, shivering to herself, with a low sobbing in her throat. Last, holding her son tightly to the side of her most noble heart, she drew my lord the king into her other arm, saying that she pitied his dead mother who could not see so grand a son; and so she gave him welcome. Sir Arthur says that, at first, he hardly understood the noble lady's speech: for she flung out her words as swiftly as possible, having the habit of one in authority with whom it is not safe to tamper, and who may not be withstood. Also, she was agitated in mind by the sight of her son and the Lionheart's in company with the Lionheart's heir. And beside, through long residence in Syria, she had forgotten much of the Frankish tongue, which she interlarded with Syriac words incomprehensible by my lord the king. But, as they talked all day, her mother-tongue came back to her: so that, in the evening, she detained Sir Hugh the priest on the matter of her christian duty, being unwilling that her christian son should have cause for being unhappy about the soul of his mother. The day passed thus, while they sat in the shade of palm-trees, fanned by small slaves lest flies should molest them, and chewing parsley beloved of bees. And, when the prayer-time of the Assassins was past, the hour of audience came when they were to be received by the Old Man. The chief eunuch went before, a guard of mutes followed after, in the midst went Lady Johanna without trumpets and having Sir Arthur and Sir Fulk in hand. And they passed through ante-chambers where were lines of Assassins dozing along the walls, at whom they stared. And they entered the presence.

XII. *About Sir Arthur fil-Geoffrey and the Old Man of the Mountain*

The Old Man (says my lord the king) was extremely white and antique beyond credence. He wore the white habit of the Assassins; and sat on what appeared to be his hams, on white cushions, under a white canopy, having a white cloth twisted round his head, and being without adornment of any kind, excepting a Saint Anthony's cross (called a Tau[1]) within a square bordure[2] of phylphots[3] on a white cord round his neck, which is his badge as Grandmaster of the Order of the Kadria. And there was no colour at all in the presence-chamber, excepting a vermillion device of the said grand-magisterial badge on the canopy of the throne. My lord the king says that the place had the aspect of a nest of unheard-of magic; and even Sir Fulk confessed afterward that it would not have surprised him to see his step-father dissolve and evanesce with a faint odour of brimstone. No one did more than breathe and meditate and stare, for half-an-hour. Then

---

[1] The Tau cross, or St. Anthony's cross, resembles the letter T. It is named after the Hebrew letter "X," which is pronounced "taw." The Antonines wore a habit embellished with this cross.

[2] "Bordure" is a term used in heraldry, meaning a contrasting border around a shield.

[3] Another heraldry term. A fylfot cross resembles a swastika.

Lady Johanna spoke quickly and sharply for a long time, in a low tone and an unknown tongue. The Old Man partly awakened and beckoned Sir Arthur to come near: whom Lady Johanna caused to hold out his glorious gloveless right hand, which the Old Man turned palm uppermost; and he gazed upon it so long that he seemed to be sleeping like a child, so full of sweet innocence was his aspect. Anon, he signed to my lord the king to display the nape of his neck under the yellow-silver hair. The Old Man pored over this feature also; and Sir Arthur felt his breath like a trickle of something dry and deliciously odorous. Then, he let my lord the king stand up again. And, for more than half an hour, the Old Man did nothing but sit breathless without any movement; and his eyes were fixed wide open in a marvellous sightless stare seeing nothing at all. Nor was there any sound, but that of silk shirts rustled by breathing breasts, in the intolerable white stillness. Anon, the Old Man made a sudden sharp sound, like the slamming of a mouse's door,[1] which was caused by his eyes shutting, and he began to breathe again. By this time, the place was nearly dark; and the Old Man looked like a wan phantasma under his canopy: but he moved with a jerk, and clapped his hands. Whereat Sir Arthur started to lick his lips which he found to be rather dry. Entered an Assassin: to whom the Old Man said after this manner: "Shut your mouth. Afdhal, Djerbal, Saad, Mulai, with their mouths shut." He departed; and four half-naked young Assassins crawled in, and lay prostrate and still on the white carpet before the canopy. Whom the Old Man addressed, saying something of this sort, in monotone, very slow, without any pauses at all even for taking breath: "Afdhal shut your mouth Jaffa a city of the accursed Saphadin[2] upon whom be confusion the bazar of the leather-sellers behind the south gate Ali Ibnyussuf of the tribe of Benizeeb in the stall by the waterpipe who is accursed his nephew from Elkuds of the leather-sellers take money for the funeral for his nephew loves him give coffee to the soldiers at the gate from the day of the funeral onward who shall pass by the door of sleep then open the gate to those who attend without a life is a life

---

[1] "*murio portae.*" [Rolfe's note.]
[2] Saladin's younger brother.

wherefore go by the way of ingenious sound Djerbal shut your mouth Ascalon a fortress of Emad the emir holding it in the name of the same Saphadin upon whose name be shame take gold for buying Elmuadham captain of his guard when Emad shall die on the morn of the sixteenth day whom his fellows shall slay as a traitor when the fate of the Emir is known while he finishes his dying let fall a rope in the shade of the battlement by the north side of the tower of the patriarch then go to the wall and two men embracing in death is a signal to those who attend without for life ends in death and paradise begins in death Mulai shut your mouth Safed a city of the accursed set upon a hill many men may be bought for a raid send them to the city of Ascalon to wait for a purchaser cause the truce to be broken on the night of the fourteenth day that the unemployed may have tasks befitting their station for life is a very dangerous thing and few there be who get through it alive Saad shut your mouth look on the face of this great king and on his right hand smell him well for a life is a life and his life is our life both among Franks and among Saracens who are accursed waking and sleeping for a hundred days life is life and obedience is the salt of it."

Then, the Old Man gulped and clapped his hands; and the four kneeled up before him; and two thrust out their right hands; and he laid his left hand on each in turn; and the Assassin called Afdhal repeated the commandment concerning Jaffa, and Djerbal did likewise concerning Ascalon, and Mulai did likewise concerning Safed; and Saad did likewise concerning King Arthur Lefthand. Then, the Old Man slapped their faces;[1] and they crawled out through the gloom. Entered one unseen, whom the Old Man addressed in the same astounding manner, saying "Afdhal fifteen days with authority and he returns Mulai fourteen days with authority and he returns Djerbal sixteen days with authority and

---

[1] "*deinde alapauit Senex facies eorum.*" (Your bishop (catholic) slaps your face (ceremonially, of course) when administering to you the Sacrament of Chrisom, to advise you of what you have to expect if you faithfully carry out the mandates of Authority. Perhaps there is an affinity of symbolism between this episcopal act and the otherwise comic and gratuitous assault described in the text.—P. and C.) [Rolfe's note.] "Chrismation," or confirmation, was conferred with a slap from the bishop in order to emphasize the fortitude associated with the sacrament.

he remains Saad a hundred days or more with full authority and he may remain all with wings and keep hold of the ends of their strings and there is no more to be said." And the invisible Assassin answered, "Hearkening and Obedience;" and retired.

Immediately, there came a tiny rustling pop out of the dark place where the Old Man squatted on his white throne. And a procession of slaves bearing blazing torches entered from the door behind Sir Arthur and the company; and they passed up, through the chamber, and out of it, by a new door, where the Old Man had been on his throne and now was not any more, nor throne, nor canopy, nor anything, but only a white door in a white wall with a few crumbs near.

Then, Sir Hugh the priest began to pray in a high thin voice to Messire Saint Gattwg, a saint of his vicinity, against demons of all sorts, with pointed reference to wizards that peep and that mutter.[1] But Lady Johanna took the hands of Sir Arthur and of Sir Fulk, and led them out of the presence-chamber to her lodging, attended as before, but now with torches and her trumpets also; and she said by the way that the affair had gone magnificently. That night, many things were done. For Lady Johanna explained mysteries, and gave admirable information and advice. And she sent for Saad the Assassin, who had been named the King's bodyguard, and she caused him to instruct the boys in certain new and useful tricks of warfare, such as were likely to be most offensive, specially a certain chop with the hardened hand-edge on the nape, or on the throat-apple, and a certain jabbing or spiking with the hand-point rigid as iron just under the breast-bone where the diaphragm is, all three tricks producing prompt and very painful death in the manner of that part of Syria. She sobbed a little over Sir Arthur and much over her dear son, all night, till the day dawned. And, having obtained leave, she adored the glorious scars of my lord the king. But then a most notable thing occurred, which I may by no means omit to narrate. For when Lady Johanna rose from her knees after she had kissed his beautiful white boyish foot, my lord the king kneeled in turn to her, baring his breast; and

---

[1] Esaias viii. 19. [Rolfe's note.] From the Book of Isaiah: "When men tell you to consult mediums and spiritists, who whisper and mutter, should not a people inquire of their God? Why consult the dead on behalf of the living?"

"Madame," says he, "wounds in the foot and wounds in the hand may be healed, and I was not found worthy to be pierced here in the home of my soul; wherefore I kneel in homage to her whose heart is for ever transfixed and a bleeding wound." At which, says Fulk, "my mother gave a great cry of love and joy, and 'Son,' says she, 'if ever I thought to see you sit on your father the Lionheart's throne, I adjure you now to keep faith with your father's will: for here is his worthy heir, and your king.'" "And," says Fulk, "I who had known Arthur and his regal virtue well and long, nor in any way surprized by manifestations of his supreme splendour, was of the same advice, and content that Lady Johanna should speak so of her own free will." O great souls, generous, and leal.[1] In the morning, then, after Sir Hugh had said mass, by command of my lord the king he gave to Lady Johanna that very holy relic of the True Cross,[2] which his Regal Majesty wore on his young breast since childhood to keep him white and clean, so that it might be her ghostly ease against the time when she should ascend to the superiors. And, having parted from her, Sir Arthur fil-Geoffrey and his company were conducted, by select Assassins, to the confines of Christendom, with all the pomp and ceremonies which had been celebrated at their coming.

XIII. About Sir Arthur fil-Geoffrey his Emprize

On the evening of the eighth day from his outgoing, my lord the king with his company returned to Margat, having held very grave converse with Sir Fulk the Flame and Sir Hugh the priest all the way since they regained sight and freedom on leaving the kingdom of the Assassins. And, being satisfied with the comportment of his Roman squires and pages, while they were in Musse, he commended their courage and obedience, and laid plans for their employment in the emprize which he had in hand. The Marshal of the Hospital, excessively abashed by their flourishing return (for he never expected to see them any more) convinced himself that he had indeed to do with personages of the very highest consequence, and not with mere bombastic boys or false pretenders.

---

[1] Loyal (*OED* OL).
[2] Remnants of the cross upon which Jesus was crucified.

He, therefore, flurried himself to win their kind consideration.
And, when he delivered up the treasure which he had in charge,
my lord the king promised a great gift to the Order of Saint John
in acknowledgment of his obligation to the Marshal of Margat.
For Sir Arthur had resolved to capture the great castle of Ascalon,[1]
and to grant it to the Hospitallers, from honesty of design as well
as for political purposes. And, entering his fishing-boat with his
train and his treasure, he set sail for Acre, going as speedily as
possible, nor even stopping at night; and, being favoured with a
north wind, he reached that seaport on the evening of the third
day. In the morning, Sir Arthur and Sir Fulk went into the city
with well-filled burses; and found no difficulty in buying an apt
army, and also an anachoret[2] to preach a crusade in the church of
Saint Nicholas, the last by advice of Sir Hugh. They gave out that
they had a vow instantly to crusade in Egypt for the liberation
of christian captives from Damietta.[3] And, because they had the
sinews of war (thanks to King Richard Lionheart and Sir Hubert
de Burgh), they were able at once to select a hundred-and-twenty
trained mercenary cotterels, English, Frankish, Pullans, and even
Turkopoles,[4] but no Teutons, from a singularly large number
who seemed feverishly to be seeking situations, owing (they said)
to the increased cost of living during peace-time. And the Seneschal of the kingdom of Hierusalem was so pleased at being thus
relieved of so many unemployed rapscallions, that he gave leave
to buy horses, and let drive among the lepers, so that Sir Arthur
might mount his men and exercise them on the plain beyond the
gate of Saint Michael. Also, my lord the king treated with certain
Venetian agents for the hire of two dromonds[5] for the conveyance
of his power to Egypt; and he bought outright a small swift gali-

---

[1] Ascalon was an important site during the crusades because of its proximity to
Jerusalem. During the Third Crusade, Saladin decided to demolish the city, so
the Christians would not be able to use it as a base of operations for an attack on
Jerusalem. Richard, however, refortified Ascalon.

[2] *"et aptum emebat exercitumatque anachoretum."* [Rolfe's note.] An anchorite or
hermit.

[3] The port of Damietta was a highly contested site during the Crusades.

[4] Mounted archers who fought during the Crusades. Turcopoles were often
mixed race Christians or converts to Christianity.

[5] Large medieval ships.

ass[1] for himself and his treasure and his company, to which vessel he transferred Nicholas and Hasdrubale his Sicilians with Bobo Kemp to govern the steering-paddle. He had to pay the Venetians in full before moving, it being the custom of subjects of their serene republic to set filthy lucre first and foremost. Indeed, says Fulk, though they pretend most excitedly and with paroxysms of fury and indignation that they worship The Trinity, as we do, I nourish an extremely grave doubt as to whether the Venetians are christians or some sort of sib[2] to the filthy fanatics of the Albigeois. For the names of The Trinity which they exclusively adore are not those to which we christians are accustomed, being as follows, namely, first, Pajancha or Money, second, Pojenta which signifies Eating and Drinking Enormously, third, Amor which signifies Lechery, as anyone (unafflicted by deafness) may know who has walked for a single half-hour among articulate Venetians.

My lord the king set sail in his new galiass, with one dromond, alleging (as reason for haste) that he wished to come to Egypt before the news of his coming and so to take the Saracens unawares. And the archbishop of Acre was fetched to bless the emprize from the harbour. The second dromond was not ready, as its cargo still awaited removal: wherefore Sir Arthur placed four knights of the Order of Saint Thomas Beket of Acre in charge of this ship, of whom he named one Sir John Fess, *argent, a fess gules*, as the captain, giving him sealed letters to be opened as soon as he had sailed out of sight of Acre containing commandments to be implicitly obeyed. And the first dromond, led by my lord the king in his galiass, passed southward.

XIIII. *About a Parcel of Kings who demised hurriedly in Turn*

On a certain day, a cry went up on the walls of Acre that the Saracens were coming. So, the gates were shut, and the ramparts manned; and one ran to warn King Amaury and the Seneschal of the kingdom. And, anon, a great power of Saracens appeared before the city shrieking "Din, Din," which (in their tongue)

---

[1] About thirty tons burden.—P. and C. [Rolfe's note.] A large oared warship that is also propelled by sail.
[2] Kin (*OED* OL).

signifies "The Faith, The Faith," for their demons delude these misguided infidels, and they believe that their infidelity is a faith. King Amaury panted up a tower, and directed a sally, wherein the Seneschal led the knights of the household so successfully that fifty Saracens were slain. But, as it was with the Emperor Achab,[1] that very sinful Cæsar of antiquity, so here. For a certain Saracen drew a bow at a venture; and the arrow went into the eye of King Amaury, so that his wisdom and his life and his soul rushed headlong thereout; and he died complaining, on the Wednesday in Holy Week, to the great dolour of his children. And his son Hugh, the firstborn of his first wife Lady Eschive, became king over Cyprus in his stead, who buried his father the same night on account of the hot weather, and departed for that island on the morrow. But, first, he held session of the council. For his half-brother, King Baldwin the Boy, had died of displeasure three hours after the death of King Amaury, being both rickety and imbecile.[2] And Queen Ysabel was left once more Queen-Regnant of Hierusalem in her own right. And Lady Mariol was heritrix of the kingdom.

xv. About Queen Ysabel her shocking Persecution by Ravishers

No sooner had King Baldwin the Boy intempestively[3] ascended to the superiors and King Hugh of Cyprus flitted to his new kingdom, than a certain ill-mannered Frankish knight, by name Sir Gilles Blanchemaison, *vert, a tower argent*, took with him a highly reprehensible archbishop[4] by name Nicholas, whose see (he said) was Bostia, whither he had never been (nor do I know where the place is), the scandal of whose life both I and Fulk believe to have never been surpassed or even equalled; and these two infamous creatures ran into the chamber where Queen Ysabel was bemoaning her dead husband and step-son, and would have committed matrimony on the spot,[5] so that Sir Gilles might become king of

---

[1] King Achab was killed by an arrow. See 1 Kings 22:34.
[2] *"stultus."* [Rolfe's note.]
[3] Unseasonably (*OED* OL).
[4] *"archiepiscopum uituperabilissimum."* [Rolfe's note.]
[5] *"et matrimonium ibidem admississet."*

Hierusalem in right of his wife.[1] Now Queen Ysabel had already
tolerated this sort of treatment three several times: first, when
the wicked Marquess reft her from the arms of Lord Henfrid of
Toron, the husband of her choice:[2] second, when King Henry of
Champagne took her, while the Marquess Konrad's blood still lay
in hot gouts on the stones from the knife of the Assassin:[3] third,
when King Amaury himself (entering the lattice of her chamber
in Acre, where she was dressing the corpse of King Henry for
burial),[4] held the door, till his tame priest[5] (though portentously
obese) followed him through the said lattice and did the business. Which having been successfully accomplished, the Queen
being panic-stricken, King Amaury opened the door, crying,
"Behold your king"; and he laughed sardonically in the faces of
nine lords who were scuffling together there, having come with
their own tame clergymen and similar blameworthy intentions.
And, indeed, the whole court joined in King Amaury's jocosities,
when it was discovered that at least two of the said nine lords had
(that very morning) drowned their own wives, heiresses, in order
to remove such impediments to their projected nuptials with the
queen, by which rash act they had reduced themselves to penury
and rendered themselves liable to the capital charge. After three
such experiences, however, it was hardly to be expected that
Queen Ysabel could be caught unawares a fourth time. And,
when Sir Gilles and his domestic prelate ran in, she drew (from
under her cushions) a huge scymetar of Damascus there previously secreted, wherewith she contrived to keep the pair at bay
while she screamed for her trumpeters. But, when the base archbishop actually began to intone the prayers ore rotundo[6] in spite

---

[1] "iure uxoris." [Rolfe's note.]
[2] Isabella was abducted by her mother and stepfather and forced to annul her
marriage to Humphrey IV of Toron. Her parents believed that she should have a
more important husband in order to strengthen her claim to the crown.
[3] After Conrad's death, Isabella locked herself up in the castle and refused to hand
over the keys of the city to the Duke of Burgundy. Richard's nephew, Henry of
Champagne, hurried to Jerusalem when he heard of Conrad's death and married
Isabella days after Conrad's assassination.
[4] In 1197, Henry accidentally stepped backwards out of a window and was killed.
[5] "presbyter domesticus." [Rolfe's note.]
[6] With elegant speech (OED OL).

of her, she (fearfully flurried at being made the wife of a perfect stranger), waved her weapon so wildly that she slashed off the tip of the archiepiscopal nose, which same particle dropped into his mouth largely and fully open as he intoned the word *Domine*. Whereat, he was much displeased; and withdrew from the Presence, coughing and capering: while Sir Gilles, seeing that marriage was impossible till he could catch another flagitious clergyman, took leave of the Queen, and retired with humble reverences.[1] O manners. But Queen Ysabel instantly required the Council straitly to imprison her and Lady Mariol in the nearest impregnable fortress, until such time as a husband should be selected who was suitable to the kingdom's needs and not repugnant to either of them. And the Council caused Sir Gilles Blanchemaison to marry a German queen[2] the same day, and put the great ban on him. And the Patriarch of Hierusalem, a councillor, having severely censured the Archbishop of Bostia, unfrocked the fellow, on a charge of irregularity as being an imperfect man devoid of a prominent feature and patently hideous, and then he imprisoned him in one of the stricter convents to lie at the Queen's pleasure.

xvi. *About the Bloody Warrior his first Conquest: Jaffa*

Sir Arthur fil-Geoffrey and his power sailed their course till they were a little to the northward of Jaffa;[3] and it was evening. And he bade the shipmaster of the dromond to put in a little below that city where a landing might best be effected: but the Venetian, Tron by cognomen, was prepotent, saying that he would put in at Damietta according to agreement, and not elsewhere. So, he was ironed, and tossed into the hold, as an upstart. Sir Arthur Lefthand put the Sicilian fisher Hasdrubale in his room; and, because this one was entirely trustworthy though by no means as expert in governing large ships as the pert shipmaster, the dromond became totally wrecked in the surf: but no great harm was done, except-

---

[1] *"inclinato corpore discessit a Reginâ et humiliter abiuit."* [Rolfe's note.]

[2] *"scortum Germanicum."* [Rolfe's note.]

[3] Jaffa is a port city south of Acre. This city was a contested site during the Crusades. It was part of the Kingdom of Jerusalem, seized by Saladin, taken by Richard, and then reclaimed by Arab forces.

ing that a few horses went mad and drowned themselves with the said shipmaster, who, by reason of his fetters, could not swim any way but down, which was esteemed a judgment on account of his captiousness. Sir Arthur left his galiass in charge of Hasdrubale and Nicholas the Fish, when he landed also to array his power. This done, he, with Sir Fulk and eight picked men, hooded in striped cloths of camel-hair like Messire Saint John, Forerunner, Baptizator, Martyr, crept stealthily to the south gate of Jaffa, and lay down in a ditch shrouded with deep shadow. The rest of the power, under Sir Hugh the priest, lay in a ravine about a mile away: but the Roman squire Julius Cesarini was perched upon a sand-dune above them, whence he could see the said south gate: for Sir Arthur ordained that a lanthorn waved four times in the gate's shadow should be the signal for Sir Hugh to bring up his power as swiftly and as noiselessly as possible. Dawn began to whiten very far away. The gate was silently opened from within; and Afdhal the Assassin put out his face, saying (as one who talks in his dreams), "A life is a life and I come by the way of ingenious sound." Immediately, Sir Arthur and his nine entered, and took possession of the gate, as Afdhal issued forth, beginning his journey back to the mountain of Musse: for the Old Man had said distinctly, "And he returns." Meanwhile, Sir Fulk gave the signal with the lanthorn, and went back to the captors of the gate, all very uncomfortable, shivering with the cold of dawn, yet (nevertheless) praying to Messire Saint Joshua, Jurisconsult and Confessor,[1] that he would stop the sun again till Sir Hugh had brought up his power. And, when that priest came, Sir Arthur led the way into the city and took possession of it, guarding all the gates very strictly that none might go out excepting lepers. And there was no fuss to speak of, save in the palace of the governor, where the mutes and the captain of the guard behaved unnecessarily: but they died, and ten christians also. Then, Sir Arthur laid a graduated poll-tax on all the inhabitants of Jaffa; and collected it, to defray the expenses of his action; and he liberated eighty-one christian captives, of whom thirty-five were capable of bearing arms. About noon, Sir

---

[1] Joshua caused the sun to stand still during a battle in Gibeon, so he could finish the fight in daylight. See Josh. 10:12-13.

John Fess brought the second dromond from Acre, having obeyed
the sealed letters wherein Sir Arthur had written commandments:
so the christian power was increased by the four knights of Saint
Thomas and the rest of the mercenaries. But Sir Arthur permitted no sack of Jaffa: he paid his cotterels their just wage, and gave
them a gift beside, out of the tax which he levied: for he intended
to make his wars pay for themselves (he being a most sagacious
leader both by nature and by grace), so that he might keep his
treasure intact in case he should meet with some misfortune. And
he did one other thing, the wisdom of which I have never ceased
to admire. He caused his whole power to cover itself with clothes
of infidel fashion after the Syriac manner, which he procured
in Jaffa, whereby his power might be taken for Saracens, which
was extremely desirable, because no christians were suspected of
being at liberty in those regions just then. And Sir Arthur and Sir
Fulk went half-naked in the habit of the Assassins, to the crouching moaning terror of all beholders.

xvii. *About the Bloody Warrior his second Conquest: Ascalon*

Sir Arthur fil-Geoffrey rode southward to Ascalon,[1] arriving
before dawn. He had left Sir Hugh the priest as Baily of Jaffa:
though that converted pirate and devoted clergyman begged
hard, on his knees, on the gravel, with tears coursing down his
face, for leave to accompany my lord the king. But Sir Arthur led
his power alone with Sir Fulk the Flame. And, when they came to
Ascalon before the dawn was white, he made hide all his cavalry
in a quarry: but the rest lay among low bushes near the castle, not
daring to move, but (from time to time) some groaned quietly
by reason of the growing heat. At noon, they were very weary
indeed of watching for the signal of which the Old Man of the
Mountain had spoken. Anon, a cry arose in the great castle; and
two were seen struggling together on the battlement of the tower
of the patriarch, clear and sharp as Panhormitan marionettes[2]

---

[1] Ascalon was another contested city on the coast south of Jaffa. Like Jaffa, it
changed hands several times during the crusades.

[2] *"neuropastae Panhormitanae."* [Rolfe's note.] Palermo, once known as Panormo,
has a rich tradition of "puppet opera" and marionette theatre.

against the hot grey sky. And, together, the two fell. When Sir
Arthur and his power ran from their ambuscade to see the falls,
they perceived that one was an unknown Saracen, and the other
Djerbal the Assassin. The last, having fallen on the first, was not
dead, though all his bones were splintered and their jagged ends
sticking out of him like the quills of a querulous porpentine;[1] and
he spouted blood from his ear-holes. And, when Sir Arthur was
for having him comforted, he said, "Life ends in death and paradise begins": on which words, he relinquished breath, in accordance with the commandment of the Old Man, which said, "And
he remains." My lord the king led his power forward; and found
the ladder of knots, which the excellent Assassin had fixed to the
top of the tower, whereby they all ascended to the number of
sixty. And, when they were securely hidden on the summit, Sir
Arthur conceded to the squire Valerio Poplicola of Holy Cross
the honour of spying out (at the risk of his face) what was toward
below on the other side of the wall: who, peering over into the
castle-ward beneath him, said that the Saracens of the garrison
were engaged in slaying each other. So, Sir Arthur led his power
down the stair; and began to kill infidels indiscriminatingly.
And, after three hours of carnage, he had the castle in possession,
thirty-two christians having been slain and a hundred-and-nine-
teen Saracens. Sir Arthur let liberate several christian captives
whom he found in the dungeons, ninety-one in number; and, of
these, seven were Knights Hospitallers who had been captured
on a buss,[2] and fourteen beside were capable of bearing arms, but
all the rest had their minds completely unhinged by their sufferings. And my lord the king, mindful of his promise to the marshal
of the Hospital at Margat, made over the great castle of Ascalon
to the senior of these seven knights of Saint John, to be held of
the crown. He was a certain Brother Sir Bermond de Luzancion,
party per pale, ermine and ermines, who afterward became prior of
Saint Gilles in Languedoc. But Sir Arthur took oaths from the
other captives, arming the fourteen, and held the place easily for
four days, till the squire Lothario Conti (whom he sent for a rein-

---

[1] A porcupine (OED OL).
[2] "in naue rotunda," i.e. a transport ship, which Hubert de Burgh's England called
a "buss." [Rolfe's note.]

forcement) came by sea from Jaffa with fifty trained cotterels. This then was Sir Arthur's power. Sir Hugh the priest had collected two-hundred-and-thirty mercenaries at Jaffa. Sir Fulk the Flame got ninety-nine mercenaries together at Ascalon. Beside these, my lord the king had four-hundred-and-five miscellaneous prisoners; and, of those, two-hundred-and-fifty-three elected to serve him as Turkopoles, for wages, against the Saracens: for, among the infidels, (says Earl Fulk), there are innumerable dissenters, sectaries, nonconformists, schismatics, each with a particular heterodoxy, altogether different from the state of things in Christendom. And, also, there is hatred of nation for nation, as with us. O manners.

XVIII. *About the Bloody Warrior his third Conquest: Blanchegarde*

Whether the birds of the air carry news of matters from place to place, as a certain prophet is reported to have asseverated,[1] I am not prepared to say: but, true it is that the infidel governor of Hierusalem learned at once of the breaking of truce in the north and the conquests of Jaffa and Ascalon. He, therefore, opining that the war-season had begun earlier than usual that year, came up on the sixth day to make a demonstration, intending either to recapture Ascalon or to destroy it: for he was abashed and dreadfully worried by Sir Arthur's success, and nourished suspicions of treachery. And he lay at Blanchegarde,[2] with fourteen-hundred men of all arms: against whom Sir Arthur Lefthand brought out two-hundred-and-fifty Turkopoles and one-hundred-and-thirty cotterels from Jaffa, and seven knights with thirteen cotterels from Ascalon. Now it is the custom of Syria for the weaker force not to take the field, but to keep within walls, awaiting siege. And, being aware of this, Sir Arthur bade to wrap cloths about the hooves of his horses, and to take care that no jingling or clashing of metal accoutrements should occur: by which ruse, he led his power by the Saracens about two miles to the north: and, at sunrise on the third day from Ascalon, he lay between the gov-

---

[1] Solomon is said to have used birds as scouts.
[2] One of the seigneuries of the kingdom of Jerusalem. Also known as Tell al-Safiya.

ernor of Hierusalem (who was at Blanchegarde) and the Holy City itself. This governor was the Emir Eladel. Sir Arthur was too wise to attack the Holy City, being ware of the strength of its fortifications and the smallness of his power; and, also, he was for playing another trick. For he ordained the stripping of his horses' hooves and the careful regulation of the Syriac disguises of his men; and then he caused a general advance on Blanchegarde, not from northward but from southward, with all the clash and clangour imaginable. And, when challenged by the Saracen outposts, Sir Fulk the Flame replied Syriacally[1] saying that this was the power of the Emir of Nablous come to serve in the south, it being rumoured that Melek Rik (so the infidels call King Richard Lionheart)[2] had risen from the dead and landed at Ascalon from a thousand red ships with fifty-thousand geniuses, and had entered into an offensive and defensive alliance intended to be sempiternal[3] with the Old Man of the Mountain. Having passed the outposts with this stratagem, Sir Arthur fell horribly upon the Emir Eladel at noon, when all the Saracens who were not lepers were napping; and, for four hours, there ensued much fine fighting. At first, the christians had the advantage of the surprise: but, after, the Saracen numbers told in their favour. Sir Arthur Lefthand and Sir Fulk the Flame raged in the heat of the battle, armed only with enormous long-swords, half-naked in their habits of Assassins, for they disdained knightly mail, preferring to confide rather in their own inconceivable agility. And, if ever a boy did manly and knightly deeds, that did my lord the king in the battle of Blanchegarde, slaying more than seventy most hairy infidels with his own weapon, from which (and his awful whiteness) the Saracens first began to call him *Pallida Saracenorum Mors*.[4] Nor was his army much behind him in prowess. But the Saracens were utterly bewildered by the awful velocity of these two, leaping and twisting here and there and everywhere, sweeping their ter-

---

[1] *"Syriaco respondit."* [Rolfe's note.]
[2] In *Richard Yea-and-Nay*, Hewlett states, "Syrian mothers still quell their children with the name of Melek Richard, a reminiscence of the dreadful time when he was without ruth or rest" (317).
[3] Everlasting (*OED* OL).
[4] Pale death of the Saracens.

rific long-swords in mazy circles, hewing, thrusting, shearing, as with whirling wheels armed with scythes like flashes of lightning. Never was anything so frightful seen in Syria, not even the hard knocks which the Lionheart's battleaxe gave, as the lambent coruscating[1] most pernicious per-pernicity[2] of these two gigantic sinewy boys, whom the seven knights of the Hospital supported, like a wall of strength invulnerably fortified in mail; and nineteen times did they devour the Saracens, charging ferociously through them and through them, so that they could not form a line of battle. And the Roman squires rode in the elastic wedge, singing canorously[3] all through the battle *Let God arise and let His enemies be scattered*,[4] by which pious psalm they rallied the hearts of all christians and redoubled the valour of the knights. And, anon, the flexible wedge arrived at the tree, whereby the Emir Eladel was sitting on a white horse passionately proclaiming his opinions concerning the comportment of his Saracens. Sir Arthur bounded upon him: but his well-trained horse swerved, avoiding the onset; and, in avoiding it, left no space for recovering ground which Sir Arthur unerringly covered in a second spring, swooping up like a lithe panther, and vaulting on the Emir's back. And Sir Fulk and the Hospitallers and the singing squires rallied also at the tree: it was an olive, hollow with antiquity, and much venerated by the Saracens, who adorned its branches with tattered cloths and snippets of brocades after their silly ugly superstitious custom.[5] But Sir Arthur, a-straddle of the Emir's horse, clutched that Saracen by the waist with his strong right arm, arms crushed to ribs, and menaced him with the bloody length of steel in his left, till the infidel swooned in discontented melancholy. Then, my lord the king flung him away as prisoner to Sir Fulk with a roar of exultation; and he rode on the white horse, alone, in the crimson saddle with silver trappings very uncomfortably. But, when the Saracens saw Sir Arthur riding in place of the Emir, like

---

[1] Sparkling (*OED* OL).
[2] Quickness (*OED* OL).
[3] Melodiously (*OED* OL).
[4] Ps. 68:1.
[5] "Inhabited" trees, haunted by spirits, were decorated with rags to pacify the trees' spirits.

Pallid Death, white, gigantic in the splendour of nakedness, and incarnadined[1] from head to foot in Saracen gore, they simplicitly sobbed and scuttered away, which they did the more assiduously when the whole of the christian power began to hunt and to harry them. When that happy afternoon had passed and the shadows became long, Sir Arthur checked the chase of the Saracen remnant, so that he might pillage their deserted camp, and sleep there, after taking tale of the slain. And it was found that sixty-four christians had died, two of them Hospitallers, and Luke the Roman page, and more than seven-score Turkopoles: but, of the Saracens, they counted more than thirty-score severed heads, and they fettered five-hundred-and-forty prisoners. Of these last, Sir Arthur enlisted enough of the ablest to recruit his Turkopoles: but he dismissed the others, as they were in no way suitable for his kind of warfare, excepting as victims. And, by this battle of Blanchegarde, he inserted a freezing jelly of fear into the bosoms of all Saracens, whereby not only were his conquests protected from attack, but seven-and-twenty villages and captured castles came back into christian hands: for the Saracens withdrew up country, having castles and fenced cities there wherein to refuge. And, having washed and slept, Sir Arthur returned to Jaffa, with his power and with the immense spoils of the Saracen camp. And he rode through the city on the Emir's white horse, half-naked in the habit of the Assassins, but on his shoulders he wore a tippet of the ermine of Armorica, small, because of the heat. For, on the night of the battle of Blanchegarde, when Sir Arthur lay in the Emir's bath and slaves elucidated his whiteness, there entered to him Sir Fulk fil-Richard with an ermine mantle, saying: "Be pleased, Lord Duke, to don this mantle of Armorica." And my lord the king, with his rare grave smile (like the outburst of the Easter sun), looked at the red bath from which he was emerging; and he said, "Now that I have made myself a Bloody Warrior, and now that I have taught myself something of the mode of warfare in this kingdom, I suppose that I may honourably wear arms." O my king.

---

[1] Reddened (*OED* OL).

XI

THE BOOK CALLED PER ASPERA AD ASTRA[1]

1. *About Duke Arthur his swift Return to Acre*

At Jaffa, Duke Arthur was struck in the face by news of the intempestive demises of the kings at Acre. The tidings came hot from certain Venetian ships; and it also was told him how that no man might land at Acre now without the council's safe-conduct, and that Sir John Brienne, *or, two serpents unduly paly, purpure on a chief vert an oke argent*, had been hastily summoned from Cyprus to marry the Lady Mariol, such being the decision of the Council. Instanter, Duke Arthur takes his amy apart; and says he with portentous solemnity, "O Fulk, as many of us as may go in the galiass must go now to Acre: for there will be very notable doings with this leper of Brienne. And may God and His Mother and Messire Saint George help us to wits and swiftness, and Lady Mariolanthe to keep up her heart till we come. For we are very likely to be late in this matter." My lord the king held a council with Sir Fulk fil-Richard and Sir Hugh the priest and Brother Sir Bermond of Luzancion; and Duke Arthur proclaimed himself Earl of Jaffa in the name of Queen Ysabel, and appointed a Hospitaller, one Brother Sir Fradulph fil-James, *argent*, as viscount over that city, who did homage for it as to Queen Ysabel. Also, Duke Arthur paid his power, giving every man a great gift beside his wages, christians as well as Turkopoles. And he added to his treasure in his galiass, a chest of jewels of splendour and worth inconceivable, as well as much gold as could be stowed, all from the spoils of his conquests. And the vessel having been trimmed by Nicholas the Fish, my lord the king sailed away from what passes for the port of Jaffa.

With him, went Sir Fulk the Flame, and Sir Hugh the priest,

---

[1] "Through adversity to the stars."

and Brother Sir Bermond of Luzancion and Bobo Kemp, and the three Roman squires, and two Roman pages (for Matthew died of his wounds after the battle of Blanchegarde); and thirty very lusty slaves were stripped to row the galiass, wind or no wind, who were promised their freedom at Acre as well as a gift. But Hasdrubale the Sicilian fisher was left behind, he being tipsy at the moment; and he was no more seen of christian men. All that day and all that night, they went most swiftly northward on a helping wind; and by grace of benignant stars and Sir Hugh's continuous invocation of Messire Saint Gabriel (that speedy archangel) and the manifest favour of Messire Saint Thomas Beket of Acre (perhaps also of Messire Saint Elias of Mount Carmel),[1] they won their way to Acre ere the breeze dropped in the cold of dawn. And they saw that the place was straitly guarded: nor might anyone enter the harbour by reason of the three chains.

II. About the Greasy Sewe[2]

Duke Arthur desired to come within the castle of Acre: for he supposed that Lady Mariolanthe might be there, unless the scorbutic Frankishman had already wedded and bedded her. But the castle was even more straitly guarded than the harbour and the city-gates. So my lord the king anchored his galiass in a suitable place without, and packed certain baggage, and gave explicit commandments to Sir Hugh: and, entering his shallop with Sir Fulk the Flame and Nicholas the Fish, under cover of night, he rowed softly as far as the Tower of Flies, tying the boat there. Then, the three, naked but for belts and knives, took to the water, and swam noiselessly as far as the Tower of Saint John, which abuts on the castle-kitchen. Here, Duke Arthur and Sir Fulk sat on the rocky foundation of the said tower, while Nicholas the Fish swam all about, below, above, smelling for any sort of aperture. And, anon,

---

[1] Because he shut up the heavens and stopped the rain for three years and six months with his prayers, Elijah is often associated with control of the weather.

[2] "Greasy sewe" is a phrase that occurs in medieval cookbooks and refers to the greasy liquid that forms when cooking fish in a pan. Rolfe seems to be punning, as the chapter involves Nicholas the Fish swimming in filthy liquid, with the obvious pun on the word "sewer."

he lighted on a hole, guided thereto by a most remarkable fœtidity of the sea and the rocks in its vicinity, all clotted with grease and offal and nameless abominations dear to rats. And, diving thereinto, he found it to be the kitchen sewer, which (since that castle contained at least seven hundred persons) was ample enough for a very fat man to pass through even after a meal. But, such passage demanded a long dive through pestilentially sour-stinking muck, not at all to be commended to a person bathing for pleasure. Nevertheless, the faithful Fish swam under water through the sewer, till it became a pool in a shaft which rose to the kitchen-court of the castle: which pool was filled with rejected tripes, skins, general refuse, and a mixture of liquids. All this he reported on returning to Duke Arthur. My lord the king at no time ever followed anything but his own high fastidious nose, which nothing guided but his own unconquerable will; and, being on his way to Lady Mariol, it was not a mere greasy sewer which could turn him aside. As for Sir Fulk, he followed his amy, for love, and for lust of adventure. So, with the Fish in front, and Duke Arthur at his heels, the three plunged into that dark dirty drain to swim as they never had swum before. And, when they were about to burst, their heads popped up through the scum of greasy slime which floated on the pool in the shaft; and, says Fulk, they gasped at the air as though it were spicy and odorous instead of the almost solid stench which it was. For some time they tried to climb out of the pool, all being silent above, for it was the dead of the night: but this they might not do, by reason of the excessive fattiness bedaubing the walls of the shaft. Anon, Duke Arthur (standing on his amy's shoulders) so prolonged himself that he touched the top of the well, when Sir Fulk the Flame (melting the ointment in which he was submerged with his body's abnormal heat) oilily gurgled an admonition, saying that it would be better for the Fish first to ascend, because the apparition of that hairless and smudged one would surely lead any chance beholder to believe that some singular devil was escaping from his pit. So, the Fish climbed up the slipperiness of my lord the king standing on Fulk's shoulders; and he drew up Duke Arthur, afterward, to whose ankles clung the Flame. And the only witnesses of their emergence were a kitten, a mouse, and a scullion who had risen in the night to pilfer cates.[1] The last, showing a disposition to have a fit of shrieking, took a toss into the pool for his pains. But the three invaders stood in the kitchen-court, most marvellously discomforted notwithstanding their brave irrepressible laughter, stark naked, unbelievably unclean, a duke a king by right divine, a great king's darling bastard, and a simple fisher, with naught but greasy knives to excuse them. They ravished napkins and towels from near by; and rubbed themselves as clean as might be. Then, they sought water, and garments.

III. *About the Robbery of the Frankishman's Wardrobe*

They came to an antechamber having its door open for coolness. Two armed pages snored on the threshold; and their vests bore the extraordinary blazon of Sir John Brienne, *or, two serpents unduly paly purpure, on a chief vert an oke argent.* They were gagged with the mats, and tossed out of the window into the sea, whence they swam ashore; and at once entered religion with intent to amend their previous naughty lives. The antechamber contained numerous valises overflowing with the most sumptuous apparel imaginable. "So well-provided a knight can afford to clothe the naked:" says Duke Arthur, in a whisper, sampling the garments. "The Frank no doubt sleeps within:" says Sir Fulk, with an eye on the inner chamber. "And alone:" says my lord the king, having glanced through the doorway. Whereat he was greatly comforted: for this signified that Lady Mariol was yet a maid, nor wife of any man. So he entered; and, finding Brienne to be dead drunk and sleeping like a toad, the boys laid him on the floor while they washed themselves, using his sheets for towels, and donning such habits as seemed suitable. Meanwhile they set the Fish to squat before Brienne's face ready to offer hairless and fishy grimaces[2] to distract him on awakening. O times. But he continued in his stupor till the robbery was accomplished, and all his remaining garments cast (with his carpets and curtains and arras) after his pages into the sea.

---

[1] Victuals (*OED OL*).
[2] "*offerre oris deprauationes glabras piscosasque paratus.*" [Rolfe's note.]

IIII. *About a Gibing Pass-word*

Duke Arthur bade Nicholas the Fish to return by the sewer to his shallop, and (in it) to the galiass at anchor in the roads, where he was to give this message to Sir Hugh: "At sun-up, at any gate, the pass-word is, *Snake and Goose speak with the same Tongue.*"[1] For, as he sapiently said to his amy, both those beasts hiss, and a knave and a fool can be equally annoying. Such was his opinion of Brienne and his blazon.[2] But Duke Arthur and Sir Fulk betook themselves to the guard-house. On their breasts were Brienne's fatuous armorials: for the Frank had all his apparel still of occidental fashion, being but newly come to Cyprus out of France. And the guards saluted the blazon rather than its bearers. To whom Sir Fulk told brazen but exciting lies. "There are traitors in the castle:" says he; "and the pass-word is changed by order of the Lords of the Council, which even now is sitting to concert suitable dispositions; and the new pass-word is *Snake and Goose speak with the same tongue.*" This the guards accepted, taking the two to be of the household of Brienne who had given himself great airs on the previous day. Fulk then went on to instruct them further, saying that the Council decreed the instant admission of a company with baggage who would seek entrance to the city and castle at sunrise: which decree was to be carried forthwith to the wardens of all the city-gates, with injunctions as to secrecy and most rigorous vigilance against treachery. And, having seen the matter put in hand, Duke Arthur and Sir Fulk retired with awful dignity, to hide themselves among the storerooms, giggling and dozing alternately till day dawned, that day which changed a duke into a king.

v. *About Duke Arthur his Entrance into the Castle of Acre*

At dawn, came Sir Hugh the priest and Brother Sir Bermond of Luzancion and the three Roman squires and Bobo Kemp and

---

[1] " 'Lord Cardinals, the voice of the snake and the voice of the goose are one and the same. They both hiss,' the Pope added before moving on again." (Frederick Rolfe, *Hadrian the Seventh* [New York: Knopf, 1925], 297).

[2] Brienne's coat of arms includes serpents and a goose.

Mark and John and four monstrous magnificent slaves bearing baggage: whom Duke Arthur and Sir Fulk received at the castle-gate, and conducted to their hiding place among the storerooms. There the two imps indued[1] their own apparel out of the baggage; and tossed Brienne's into the sea. By this time, the new pass-word was circulating among the early risers in the castle; and, having told the company to go and dawdle in an empty court-yard with the aspect of having lost their way, Sir Fulk the Flame audaciously beset a chamberlain blinking from his bed, whom he beat on the back, demanding where might be the lodging of the Celsitude of the Duke of Armorica and Earl of Jaffa, newly arrived with his state, and anxious to sleep, having travelled all night. The wretched creature timorously asked for the pass-word; and was informed that *Snake and Goose speak with the same tongue*: which news he thankfully accepted without ado, for Fulk blazed in red and gold and green, and was extremely fierce of eye. The chamberlain, therefore, provided commodious lodging for the whole company, saying that the new pass-word bewildered him as having to do with the blazon of someone in the castle, or of which he had dreamed, a point which he might be able to settle after his morning beer, which beverage he left to imbibe. But, when within closed doors, Duke Arthur freed his four slaves; he enlisted them as willing Turkopoles, and armed them, and set them as his guard. All the others also armed themselves; and, out of the baggage, was drawn most glorious and proper raiment for my lord the king, wherewith (after more prolonged and luxurious washing) he was invested. And, all dispositions having been accomplished, Duke Arthur and Sir Fulk took cat-naps[2] till the time should come for action.

VI. *About a Figure of Fun in the Council Chamber*

Anon, arose in the castle a most plangent[3] hullabaloo when Brienne began to bellow for clothes and company. For, awak-

---

[1] Put on.
[2] "*breuissimis somniis utebantur.*" [Rolfe's note.]
[3] Loud and plaintive (*OED* OL).

ening from stertorous[1] slumbers, he found himself abandoned, nor with any single rag appertinent to him save sheets of ineffable sliminess, with one of which he covered himself girding it with his sword-belt: for, says Fulk, he was one of those men who think foul shame of their persons, and not without good and valid reason. In this condition, flinging about in search of some leper on whom to wreak his wrath, he found his way to the council-chamber, where were the Patriarch, and the Bishop of Acre, and the Grandmaster of the Hospital, and the Seneschal of the Kingdom, and the Chancellor, with Sir John of Ibelin and Sir Rohart of Kayphas and certain other magnates. For perturbation (tending even to the unhinging of minds) was afflicting all in the castle, because of the pass-word changed by God-knew-whom and the persistent warning which everyone gave to everyone to beware of traitors and treachery. And every layman suspected the Patriarch, and the Patriarch suspected the Bishop of Acre, and the Bishop suspected the Grandmaster; and the Chancellor whispered to Sir John of Ibelin that Sir Rohart of Kayphas was aspiring to the crown-matrimonial, despite his wife Lady Eglantine and his pox-pitted face, and the Seneschal Raoul of Tiberye nourished notions such as cannot be written; and the clergymen looked at the laymen, not loving or trusting them at all. And, into their perturbed deliberations, came a noise of uproarious complainings in the Frankish tongue; and Sir John Brienne burst in, clutching his slimy sheet, bellowing quaint conceits[2] in some such words as these: "Pears, pigs' faces, and fesses," says he: "Thunder and stale fish," says he: "Great dumb gods, sweet virgin sinners, and camel-hair petticoat of the Baptist, my clothes, my company, my clothes," and so on, says he. Then he burst out in a fresh place, but more genteelly; and "Venerable fathers and noble lords," says he, "I crave indulgence, but it seems that I am unsafe in this pit of abomination, since my chamber is sacked and my valises emptied, my trumpets have abandoned me, my company has deserted me, and, moreover, I would have you to know that I go stark naked save for this hideous toga."[3] And the Council (for reasons of policy) thought

---

[1] Characterized by snoring (*OED* OL).

[2] "*Excogitatos lepidos.*" [Rolfe's note.]

[3] "*et enucleatus atque connudatus ego excepto tetram istam togam.*" [Rolfe's note.]

to commiserate the spectacular Frankishman[1] with the capital sentence for someone, he being king-designate and destined to marry Lady Mariol that very day.

VII. *About Duke Arthur and the Figure of Fun and the Council*

The usher at the council-chamber door made loud annunciation at the instant of the coming of the Celsitude of the most puissant prince the lord Arthur Plantagenet, Duke of Armorica, Canon of Tours, Earl of Anjou, Jaffa, Ascalon et cetera. And that said Celsitude entered in his state, youthful and clean and awfully strong and terribly pure, wearing his ermine mantle, with a coronal of great pearls and a cap of silver tissue on his yellow-silver hair, and the vermilion boots of a sovereign-earl, and the green gloves of a sovereign duke. He gravely gave the pass-word on entering the door, saying, *Snake and goose speak with the same tongue*; and the ridiculous blazon of Brienne rushed so violently into everybody's mind that most engaged in tittering. And behind my lord the king came Sir Fulk the Flame in his coat, and Sir Hugh the priest and Brother Sir Bermond Luzancion garbed like clergymen in copes[2] of azure brocade, and the squires and pages in cloth of silver tissue with the ermine blazon of Armorica, and the four monstrous magnificent black Turkopoles in panther-skins for dignity. And all were armed to the teeth, dreadfully. Before the Council had breath, Duke Arthur had kissed the Patriarch's ring, and done obeisance to the Bishop, and was seated with calmest assurance at the head of the great table, with Sir Fulk and Sir Hugh on the right and left behind him, and his Turkopoles closing and guarding the door, and Brother Sir Bermond of the Hospital whispering sharply to the Grandmaster of the Order of Saint John. Says Duke Arthur very affably: "We permit the Council to become seated." Sir Raoul of Tibery the Seneschal, a man of the sheepish obstinate kind which thinks too little and talks too much, began to bleat, saying[3] "Who

---

[1] "*histricum Francicam.*" [Rolfe's note.]
[2] A long mantle worn by ecclesiastics in processions and on other occasions.
[3] "*generis ouini et obstinati quod minime cogitat et plurime loquitur, balare incipiebat, dicens.*" [Rolfe's note.]

bids this Council to sit?" The Grandmaster of the Hospital, with a thin head full of news and a slit of a mouth full of pleasant words, up, and says he, "As Earl of Jaffa, our lord the Lord Duke Arthur represents this kingdom's senior feof here present: wherefore, obeying custom, I concur with his presidency." This, the Grandmaster said, because Brother Sir Bermond had told him of his investiture with the castle of Ascalon on behalf of the Order. And Sir John of Ibelin concurred with the Grandmaster. Duke Arthur also spoke, "With the concurrence of the Sanctity of the Patriarch, that strenuous upholder of the assizes of this kingdom," says he very artfully, "We will preside in this council as Earl of Jaffa, and on no other account at present. And, We opine," he added, terribly, "that this is like to be a Council of Regency, since We hear that the Regal Majesty of Queen Ysabel is tolerating duress." And, breaking off, he turned like lightning on Brienne. And "Ho, this figure of fun!"[1] says he.

Certain councillors began to babble. Duke Arthur smote the table, calling for silence. "Be it well known that We rule here and permit speech. Be it better known that We hold this castle and city with Our power." Lord Robert of Kayphas enquired since when. Sir Fulk says that my lord the king, using his peculiar faculty of elongation, towered above the bewildered council with such regal majesty of mien, that resistance ended then, the councillors supposing that in some unknown but legitimate way, perchance by favour of a secret bull pontifical, he actually was paramount in the kingdom. And a party began to form, definitely favourable to Duke Arthur: it was headed by the Patriarch, who followed the Grandmaster and the laymen supporting his Order, and the Bishop followed the Patriarch. Meanwhile Brienne, choking, was sent to be redressed somehow and not too delicately. Sir Fulk had him in charge, with John the page and a Turkopole. On his return, Duke Arthur required the Chancellor to read the acts of the Council's previous session.

VIII. *About Duke Arthur annoying the Figure of Fun*

The Chancellor read in the acts of the Council, how that the

---

[1]   "*ecce istune typam ridiculum.*" [Rolfe's note.]

marriage of Lady Mariol and the ridiculous Brienne was fixed for that day. "Read on, Sir Chancellor," says Duke Arthur, "read the act of the Council which confirms both Queen Ysabel's approval of this marriage and Lady Mariolanthe's consent to it." But, as nothing of that kind had been written, because it had not been done, therefore the Chancellor could not read it. Duke Arthur took the book in his own hand, with a jerk so forceful that the Chancellor bit his tongue quite unawares; and, says my lord the king, "These acts, concerning the marriage of Lady Mariol, being incomplete, are null and void, or easily nulled and voided; and thus We rescind and abrogate what there is of them."[1] With one of his proper sharp tugs, he tore the vellum page from the book of acts; and gave it to Sir Fulk, who haggled it to slivers with his dagger and tossed them to the Figure of Fun. That Frank, seeing his chances of a crown being crumpled up before his very eyes, shrieked (in the foolish Frankish manner) "I am betrayed."[2] But Duke Arthur gave tongue out of his strong young throat, saying, "The Council shall now humbly pray the Regal Majesty of Queen Ysabel and the Supernity of Lady Mariolanthe to preside at this session, being to that end instantly and honourably enlarged from imprisonment." At that, the Council certainly would have shied: but seeing my lord the king quickly becoming like a cold flash of lightning, and lurid sparks gathering in Sir Fulk's lambent green eyes, and casting also a side-look on the armed Turkopoles who kept the door (for they resembled Gog and Magog[3] and similar giants in ruthless ferocity of aspect), when Duke Arthur bleakly[4] required the Council's confirmation of his words, it was done, not without moans, but it was done. And the Chancellor inscribed an

---

[1] John of Brienne did in fact marry Mary of Montferrat (Lady Mariolanthe) in Acre in 1210. Mary died soon after in 1212.

[2] *"proditus sum."* [Rolfe's note.]

[3] Gog and Magog are two destructive forces or a sinister king and his country mentioned in Ezekiel 38:1-4 and Revelations 20:7-9. Gog and Magog appear frequently in folklore as evil giants. According to British legend, Diocletian's daughters and the demons of Albion gave birth to a race of giants, who were then extirpated by Brutus. The two who survived, Gog and Magog, were brought to Brutus's palace, which stood on the site of the Guildhall, and forced to stand guard.

[4] *"gelide."* [Rolfe's note.]

act of it, which Fulk delivered to the usher at the door to be given immediate effect. O times.

While the Council waited, glowering at Duke Arthur because he had come without trumpets and yet presumed to be most abominably prepotent, that young prince gave a dry official account of his capture of Jaffa and Ascalon and of the battle of Blanchegarde: whereat the Councillors sat up in abashed amazement. He had provision made for comforting the Emir Eladel of Hierusalem, who lay prisoner at Jaffa: he had the homage of his viscount of that city duly recorded. He bade the Council to note his intention of making over the castle of Ascalon to Saint John his Order of the Hospital and the Grandmaster thereof; and he caused the same to be recorded as an act of the Council: but he graciously (to pass the time) permitted discuss as to the tenure of the said castle, as to how many knights the Order should provide therefor, as to how long grace should be granted to the said Order before the service of the said knights should become due. And he artfully governed the discussion of these trivialities, so that the Hospital gained an excellent bargain, and its Grandmaster became more and more desirous of dying for him.

VIIII. *About Duke Arthur and a Snake who was a Goose*

Queen Ysabel came, preceded by her trumpets, with Lady Mariolanthe in her hand; and Duke Arthur, having enthroned them in his room, did homage for the counties of Jaffa and Ascalon which he had made free to confer upon himself (their conquistador) in the Queen's Name. Earl Fulk says that Lady Mariol, sitting at the Queen's left, looked on no one but Duke Arthur; and her bright black eyes swam in a mist; and her flower-like face flushed finely. Queen Mariol says that that was because she was so very thankful, when (for the first time) she saw her man manly, masterful, mastering men, superb in his ermine of Armorica. While Queen Ysabel confirmed the acts of the Council done by direction of Duke Arthur, Sir Fulk took occasion to whisper of certain vital matters with the Grandmaster, whom he found complaisant. And then my lord the king rose in his place on the right of the Queen, all a-twitter (says Fulk, who alone knew what the twitching of

the ducal ears portended); and thus he addressed the Regal Majesty of Hierusalem: "Ho, Lady, Queen, and Cousin, the Council
is concerned as to the condition of the kingdom; and discussion
produces the opinion that the question of succession ought to be
provided for and determined. Wherefore, as president of Your
said Council, and in its name, and as senior here present of Your
Crown's tenants-in-chief, I, Arthur, Earl of Jaffa and Ascalon,
Duke of Armorica, and the rest, do pray You, Lady, Queen, and
Cousin, to cause Lady Mariolanthe to become espoused and married instanter, and to determine the succession in her person
and in the heirs of her body, and to proclaim her and her husband as heritrix and heritor of Your Crown and Kingdom, and
(for the sake of security) to associate the said heritrix and heritor
instanter with Your Regal Majesty in Your throne and canopy of
this kingdom of Hierusalem." All the magnates assented to this,
though the clergymen showed bewilderment as to what was to
come, and the laymen looked anxiously about them, manifesting
a certain discontent when they saw that none of them was armed
while Duke Arthur and his company were armed to the teeth.
The ladies sat pondering the petition, looking one on other, the
mother gravely, the daughter bravely and without a tremor after
one swift side-glance at my lord the king, who sat like a great
sharp frosted icicle. And the Figure of Fun, whom no one even
noticed, writhed like a snake this way, waddled like a goose that
way, and, finally, ejaculated a hiccough of such flatulence[1] that
Queen Ysabel made haste to deliver her mind lest a worse thing
should afflict that poor creature. She said that she accepted the
advice and granted the petition of the president of her Council.
Sir John Brienne hiccoughed four times; and the Queen continued. She said that she, being altogether fatigued, by the burthen
of the crown, by a succession of rapes and miscalled marriages,
not less than by the coughing of lepers, was intending retirement,
for the term of her natural life, in the monastery of Madame Saint
Katharine of Mount Carmel, there to mourn for her dead lord
Sir Henfrid of Toron and to prepare her soul for ascension to
the superiors. Wherefore, she commanded the Council to select

---

[1] *"singultum tam uentosum eiaculabat."* [Rolfe's note.]

a husband for her daughter and a king-consort for her kingdom instanter. Sir John Brienne, now struggling with paroxysmatic hiccoughings, cast an imploring glance at Sir Rohart, who rose; and said "Horumpn" by way of preliminary. But the Grandmaster was articulate earlier. (Says Fulk: Lady Mariol looked at Brienne with a disdain which would have insulted a daddy-longlegs;[1] and that Frankish goose, choking, went blue in patches, very livid; and Duke Arthur had a strong motion under his ermine, like a large young tom-cat who swells, knotting himself to spring.) Thus, then, said the Grandmaster: "May it please the Queen's Regal Majesty and the Supernity of Lady Mariolanthe, the Council selects and recommends in this matter, a knight who is a very bloody warrior, and a very great leader of armies, and a very notorious conquistator of infidels in pitched battle." (Says Fulk: Brienne, who had never even seen an infidel in his beastly life, much less met one and treated him severely in battle, shrivelled so serely,[2] choking so agonizedly, that Sir Hugh took silent leave to thump him on the back and to console him with comfits.[3]) The Grandmaster continued: "The Council," says he, "selects and recommends one who is the tenant of great feofs, of regal birth, possessed of kinships whereby alliances of inestimable worth may be expected, richer by far even than the Sophy himself in the spoils of infidels and a personal treasure, whereby the armies of the kingdom may be nourished and rendered invincible; and he is also a very proper youth, whose bodily grandeur and splendour (such as I have never seen surpassed or even equalled) presage most joyful nuptials and a fecund fountain of heirs for the comfort and consolation of the kingdom. The Council, therefore, selects and recommends to Your Regal Majesty and to the Supernity of Lady Mariolanthe, the Celsitude of Duke Arthur of Armorica, Earl of Jaffa, and of Ascalon, and the rest."

x. *About Duke Arthur and the Goose who was a Snake*

Fulk says that there were three parties in the Council: the

---

[1] *"ita ut ei musca ipsa cui nomen Grui aegerrime tulisset."* [Rolfe's note.]
[2] Particularly (*OED* OL).
[3] *"dorsum eius manu pulsare et eum dulcis consolare."* [Rolfe's note.]

party of Sir John Brienne, a party of some standing, bound to him by blood or policy or promises of pelf and perquisites:[1] the party of indifferents, who only cared to see a game well-played: the party (but that hour born) of Duke Arthur, and the Grandmaster with his Hospitallers and all friends of the Order of Saint John. And, of these three parties, the last two coalesced when Queen Ysabel pronounced her pleasure. She took the mind of Lady Mariol; and said: "We thank Our Council for its dutiful selection and recommendation. And, as an Act of Our Regal Majesty in Council, We stablish the succession of Our crown and canopy and kingdom in the persons of Our well-beloved daughter Lady Mariolanthe and of her heirs for ever born of her marriage with the Celsitude of Duke Arthur of Armorica, Earl of Jaffa and of Ascalon and of Anjou and the rest, whom we hereby designate as her husband-elect." (Says Fulk: At that, Brienne hiccoughed more horribly than any christian man can without the direct assistance of a devil; and all who spoke thereafter were obliged to shout their minds in the short intervals between his spasms. O manners. But Duke Arthur moved round to Lady Mariol. She began to cry. He, nonplussed, not knowing what to do with a weeping maid in presence of a queen and her council of State, took her, and gave her a sounding kiss on the mouth[2] in his largest Plantagenet manner, to the admiration of those standing round.) Queen Ysabel continued: "And We command Our Chancellor to inscribe articles of this betrothal here and now:" says she. "And We require Our venerable father the Patriarch to solemnize the said betrothal also here and now, and to solemnize the sacrament of matrimony for the said betrothed at noon tomorrow. And We command it to be proclaimed that, from and after such betrothal and its proclamation, Our said daughter Lady Mariolanthe and Our said cousin and tenant-in-chief Lord Arthur Earl of Jaffa and Ascalon et cetera, irrevocably united in betrothal, are and shall be eternally and entirely seized of this Our kingdom of Hierusalem, its crown, canopy, and dignity, with all its rights, privileges, prerogatives, powers, and paraphernalia, as Sovereign Queen and King of absolute authority saving the said king-

---

[1] "Pelf" and "perquisites" are obsolete terms for property and spoils (*OED* OL).
[2] "*sonore in ore eam osculans.*" [Rolfe's note.]

dom's assizes and customs. And We, Ysabel the Queen, do, from the moment of such proclamation, utterly divest Ourself of these gewgaws,[1] retiring from the throne, canopy, crown, title, power, and government of this Our kingdom. For it is Our purpose to proceed to Mount Carmel within the hour. The Queen wills this." The Council intoned the "Let it be done" not quite unanimously: for Brienne's party sat as silently as lepers in a sea-fog. And, while the Chancellor gave written effect to the Queen's mandate; and, while the Patriarch blessed the betrothal, and, indeed, until after the proclamation had been made in the Council and at the open door also for all the world to hear, Sir Fulk the Flame faithfully took upon himself and the Turkopoles to guard the said door very straitly, letting none pass out or in. For he says that he became perturbed when the Snake-Goose or Goose-Snake,[2] suddenly, during the solemnity of the betrothal, seemed to unpin the pump of his hiccoughs and to sit silent and breathless and wellnigh withered away, but with so fixed a face, like a pouncing pilgrim,[3] that it was evident that he meditated evils. For no bad man would relinquish a blooming girl, whose dower was a crown and canopy matrimonial, without a desperate struggle. Thus Fulk. O times.

XI. *About Lady Eglantine her Alarum*

Lady Ysabel having departed for Mount Carmel, and Queen

---

[1] A bauble (*OED* OL).

[2] *"Anguinanser aut Anseranguis."* [Rolfe's note.]

[3] *"ceu perigrinator insiliens."* (We do not quite know what else to make of this phrase. Of course the would-be festive (but fixed-eyed) party who pops up unexpectedly in all Swiss hotels, and has had a slight misfortune (or disappointment) and would be awfully thankful if one could see one's way to let him have a fare to some other place, instantly occurs to the modern mind as being something not unlike a "pouncing pilgrim." But the likeness between this type and Sir John Brienne consists solely in the fact of their both being needy adventurers. And as an "adventurer" (strictly speaking) is generally an admirably courageous person, and as "need" is not dishonourable (strictly speaking), but in plain fact very far indeed from "beer and skittles," we do not like to confound the comparatively harmless spunge of the Swiss hotels with a dirty ruffian definitely meditating evils like Sir John Brienne.—P. and C.) [Rolfe's note.] "Beer and skittles" means pleasure, as in "Life is not all beer and skittles." See E. Cobham Brewer, *Dictionary of Phrase and Fable* (Philadelphia: Henry Altemus, 1898), 116.

Mariol being secluded in her queenly chambers, King Arthur and his train returned to their lodging in the Tower of Saint John, to take rest: for it was high noon and very hot in the air. The castle buzzed with preparations for the banquet of state and for the homage at night; and every courtyard hummed with arriving magnates who came to adulate the new sovereigns. And to King Arthur, sitting in his privy chamber conversing with his amy and Sir Hugh the priest, entered a certain Brother of the Hospital, a collector of the revenues of that Order, who, coming to Acre from Kayphas, brought a chaplet of beads from the castle of Kayphas, with a message from Lady Eglantine, saying that this was Sir Fulk fil-Richard's chaplet which he had forgotten. And, at the moment, owing to the great heat, King Arthur chanced to be leaning out of the window over the sea, that he might catch any cool breeze coming in his vicinity; and when, on the Brother's departure, he turned to resume the conversation, he says that he saw all Fulk's fiery freckles, separately, one by one, like brown stars on a milky sky, so sudden was the pallor which had come upon that one. Up, and says Fulk: "This is an alarum: for, during the wooing, I gave it to Lady Eglantine to send to me when she should hear of mischief intended." He bit the beads; and spat their splinters on the floor. In one bead was found a thin sliver of parchment, inscribed, *Rohart reports treachery*: in another, another, inscribed, *Be ware of Brienne*. It was sufficient. O manners.

XII. *About the Hissing of the Snake-Goose-Goose-Snake*

O times. Says Earl Fulk as follows.

Says King Arthur Lefthand: "Sir Rohart of Kayphas sat next to the Snakegoosegoosesnake in the Council, and went so far as to say *Horumpm* for him." Says Sir Hugh: "And he returned to his castle after the proclamation, though it was the heat of the day. I wish to know why." Says Sir Fulk: "Brienne, hopes to regain what he has lost, has bought Rohart with a promise; and Rohart has rushed home to grind knives secretly."

Fulk confesses a weakness, for which I and all men of goodwill hereby excuse him. He says that he trembled for the safety of my

lord the king. For those tremors, let him be excused, on account
of natural fatigue after the ingenious machinations of a night and
a day, the real burthen of which rested heavily on his young shoulders. He implored my lord the king to take Sir Hugh the priest, to
go and marry my lady the queen and to get all aboard the galiass
instanter. See now what it is to be a king and born of a kingly
race. Fulk says that, as soon as King Arthur scented his danger, he
forgot his lassitude, the heat of the afternoon, and all excepting
his regal majesty; and he became cheerful, sagacious, alert, as a
sun which eats up clouds trying to veil his splendour. "Kings,"
says he, "We give you to know, are not to be married in corners,
or covertly. Nor, indeed, is there cause for it. We are indissolubly
bound to the queen by betrothal; and Our task is to guard her and
Our crown. No more." The regal humour infected his lovers; and
the three set to devising counterplots against such plots as might
be toward. Here are the acts of my lord the king's first Council.
Like the great general which he was, King Arthur first prepared
a clear way of retreat, being determined to go through with all
the offices of his regal majesty, as though unaware that danger
menaced him, and being determined also to meet treason and to
quell it (if possible) by fearless audacity, or (if impossible) to retire
so as to deal with it efficaciously and horribly later. Wherefore, he
bade Sir Fulk to inspect the banquet-hall: who deftly caused the
regal thrones and canopy to be set by a door giving access to King
Arthur's lodging; and, to do this, involved a change of the tables,
the said thrones and canopies having been so set that there was
no escape for them. Further, observing none of Brienne's fantastic
followers in that part of the castle, Sir Fulk caused roasted lambs,
loaves, cheeses, comfits, a cask of wine, and a cask of water, to be
placed in the Tower of Saint John, alleging that the king (being
Plantagenet) was at all times famishing with hunger, which the
cooks understood perfectly, having heard of King Richard Lionheart's prowess as a trencherman.[1] But, meanwhile, King Arthur
sent Mark (the Roman page) to Nicholas the Fish on the regal galiass in the roads, with a message, bidding that mariner to bring the
ship as near as possible to the Tower of Saint John, to buy two new

---

[1] One with a large appetite (*OED OL*).

shallops and to man them with lusty and beautiful slaves as well
as the old one, and so to cause these three boats to ply continually
midway between the galiass and the said Tower, from twilight
onward, ready to rescue anyone taking to the water and crying
a certain pass-word. And he made the boy learn the message by
rote. Last, Sir Hugh procured a sufficiency of cordage,[1] whereby
all the company might quit the castle for the sea. And my lord the
king proceeded in state to amuse his bride before the banquet. Sir
Hugh, being minded to take a further part in these manœuvres,
and finding Sir Fulk still somewhat distraught, proposed that
they should go and say such words to the Grandmaster as would
cause all Hospitallers to rally round the king and queen in case
of treason. But, on seeking him in all the castle, they learned that
he had gone to visit the Hospital in the city. Wherefore, deferring
their intention, they returned to the Tower of Saint John.

XIII. *About the Miscarriage of Mark and the Message*

As Sir Fulk and Sir Hugh passed along an open gallery, the
voice of Saad the Assassin behind them softly whispered Syriacally, "A life is a life, and his life is our life." A soft bundle was
placed in Fulk's hand: he unrolled it, standing between a pillar of
the gallery and the open sea, where none could observe him. And
he found a boy's head and hand still warm and flexible: the head
was bloody and distorted as by anguish, so that it might have been
anybody's, but Fulk knew the hand for that of young Mark, the
Roman page, for on it was a silver ring set with a toadstone which
the youngster wore as a charm against the Evil Eye. He looked to
see who had given him the thing. There was no one to be seen
in the whole gallery but himself and Sir Hugh; and the priest was
glaring at him and his mysterious handful as though he suspected
necromancy. Fulk explained. The voice of Saad the Assassin spoke
again, aloud, close by, though the form of the speaker remained
invisible: he said "A life is a life, and his life is our life, and the message is not delivered." Sir Hugh recollected himself; and prayed
for the soul, giving the fragments christian burial in the sea. Sir
Fulk asked the Unseen who had done this thing and why. Saad

---

[1] Cords used in the rigging of a ship (*OED* OL).

answered that Brienne and his cotterels tormented the boy, in a
way not to be said, for an hour, for his message. When, at length,
he died, they threw the pieces of his carcase away, of which the
Assassin collected token and brought them. Sir Fulk seized the
very reins of his mind; and, says he, "Who knows the message?"
The voice answered: "None, now, but the great king who gave
it, and I and ye who heard it: for the boy was faithful and died
dumb." Says Fulk, "A life is a life, and his life is our life. Let the
message now be delivered." The voice of the invisible Assassin,
flying away, said "Hearkening and obedience."

XIIII. *About the Cup of Betrothal*

Sir Fulk and Sir Hugh went on their way somewhat comforted at the thought of the Assassin ready to serve; and they told
the matter to the king. There was no doubt now but that very
dire mischief was afoot; and until the Grandmaster could form
a party for the king against the poxy Snakegoosegoosesnake,
confidence must rest entirely on the four Turkopoles, John the
Roman page, Bobo Kemp, the three Roman squires, Sir Hugh the
priest, Sir Fulk the Flame, the open way from the window of the
Tower of Saint John through the sea to the galiass in the roads,
and (of course) in Divine Providence by Whose Sanction kings
do reign. And King Arthur declared this to be amply sufficient.
Anon, then, the king and the queen, regally robed and crowned
and sceptred and orbed, proceeded with trumpets and torches
to the banquet-hall about two hours after sunset. And Sir Fulk
and Sir Hugh with the king's own train went close behind the
canopy of the sovereigns. As they passed along, one who bore
a blazing torch of scented wax, muttered Syriacally in the voice
of Saad the Assassin in Sir Fulk's ear, "The message is delivered;
and the great king's will is done: but a life is a life, and his life is
our life; and death is in the cup of betrothal." Now Sir Fulk had
caused my lord the king, and (indeed) the whole company, to don
mail under their habits of state: but he had not thought to provide against the danger of poison, for no one would have believed

a recrudescence[1] of Arthur's grandmother's filthy concoctions of sulphur or oxalis, and such like, possible. That sort of horror went out of fashion with that sturdy hag Queen Alianora.[2] But, here it was again; and, at the moment, he might not hope to say a warning word in secret to my lord the king. So, all through the banquet, he stood by the canopy, thinking, inwardly fuming, but with his lion's face clear and open. At midnight, the Seneschal of the kingdom made the great proclamation, crying, "Hear, hear, the King and the Queen deign to drink to each other in the cup of betrothal." Now it seemed that the Great Butler of Hierusalem was unavoidably absent (he was found some months after in a well, being a man of probity and not purchasable); and his office devolved upon Sir Rohart of Kayphas, who came with the Butler's trumpets all along the hall, bearing the gigantic golden hanaper[3] in both hands. And the sight of him set Sir Fulk the Flame on fire and made him dangerous: for the wretched traitor's pitted face was set in a ghastly mask, and he licked his lips, and he handled his burthen far too gingerly. From him, the Flame's glance flashed to the Anguinanseranseranguis.[4] He was trying to sip again and again from an empty goblet. Snake he certainly was, with his unscrupulous proclivity for regicide; and, yet, such a goose that he fell in trepidation at the moment when his tool was doing his dirty trade. O scabby niddering. Then Sir Fulk made up his own mind, knowing how keen and alert was King Arthur; and he whispered, "Drink not till I have spoken." My lord the king stood under his canopy, and my lady the queen beside him (says Sir Hugh); and King Arthur smiled at the Seneschal, that fearless smile of innocence formidable which is omniscience and more than once has been the regal majesty's touchstone of traitors.[5] And Sir Fulk also stood nearer; and he called for a fanfare: which having been trumpeted, he made proclamation as though for the king, using these words: "Hear, hear, hear, be it known to all and

---

[1] A revival or relapse (*OED* OL).
[2] Eleanor was said to have poisoned Henry's mistress Rosamond, a story transmitted in the ballad, "Fair Rosamond," and in Swinburne's play, *Rosamond* (1860).
[3] A case for goblets (*OED* OL).
[4] Snakegoosegoosesnake.
[5] "*proditorum obrussae.*" [Rolfe's note.]

singular that the noble knight, Sir John Brienne, desiring to pro-
test unfeigned friendship, loyal love, and honourable esteem, for
the Regal Majesties of King Arthur and Queen Mariol, lest any
should miscredit his distinct good faith, has demanded the privilege of tasting the cup of betrothal, and also of pledging health
and salvation to both the Regal Majesties before they pledge each
other. And the Regal Majesties have granted the said privileges
to the said Sir John Brienne, as a mark of Their singular favour."
So having said, Sir Fulk bore the hanaper to the Frank, kneeling,
and offering it. Now, King Arthur's smile became scorching, each
moment more scathing. The banqueters sat in a maze, only half
understanding what was toward. Sir Hugh saw to it that the king's
company was prepared to meet an emergency. But Brienne rose
in his place, taking the great cup from Fulk (for he dared not to
refuse it); and Sir Fulk went back to the canopy. Then, Brienne's
mind became unhinged; and he began to make silly but dreadful
little noisy screeches in his nose and throat, like the tat-tat-tat-tat-
tao of a sitting hen whose nest four rats are invading;[1] and the cup
tilted in his trembling hands; and he found no words, nor even a
voice, until, at last, he managed to stammer, "Unfeigned friendship, loyal love, honourable esteem, slight mistake, regret——"
And down came the cup with a crash on the table. And the liquid
(which had filled it) spilled across the table, bubbling with the vir-
ulence of its venom, and a pungent smoke rose from the burning
napery where the lethal liquor flowed.

xv. *About Divine Providence His awful Judgments in Favour of Kings*

That poxy hybrid Brienne, hideously stripped naked of his
gooseskins and openly exposed as snaky in essence and intention, had just enough sense to see that hypocrisy would serve his
treacherous purposes no longer, that no course was possible to
him now but those of abject penitence and an appeal for mercy,
or prompt and violent acts of open rebellion. He chose the latter,

---

[1] "*naribus et gutture fatuis sed ualde horribilibus remoribus screari incipiebat ita ut
omnibus haud secus ac gallina incubans uideretur tat-tat-tat-tat-tao conclamans nido iiii
rattis inuaso.*" [Rolfe's note.]

I imagine, because his shame goaded him to madness: for, in his cooler moments, he had not the courage.

Brienne, therefore, with a great number of other leprous and scorbutic magnates in his vicinity, rushed out of the banquet-hall to get their weapons; and a numerous band of cotterels, whose liveries bore the goose-and-serpent blazon, swarmed in, and made toward the canopy. To this day, neither my lord the king nor Sir Fulk the Flame know how or whence the Frank had gotten so overwhelming a power. The Grandmaster with his knights of Saint John, and the few loyal magnates who were left, did not hesitate a moment in flinging themselves, surprised and unarmed as they were, in defence of the throne. They seized knives, they wielded benches, they hurled heavy goblets and stools into hairy faces, smashing many, making a manly effort to impede the traitors. King Arthur stood for a moment, weighing his chances in this affray. But, when he saw how overwhelming was the power opposing him, then his young voice rang like a clarion, crying, "Do nothing more now, o Grandmaster and loyal knights, until We come again to do this job more thoroughly." And, turning quickly, taking the queen and the regalia, he passed the word to Sir Fulk, "Straight to the open sea and cry 'Maryflower.'"

The armed squires went before, through the door behind the canopy: the Regal Majesties followed after, attended by the two pages: Sir Fulk the Flame and Sir Hugh the priest slammed and barred the door, and set the Turkopoles to guard it with their lives. Up the stair fled all, as the faction of Brienne began to use tables for battering-rams.

In the king's lodging ensued a divesting of mail for safety in swimming; and the Roman squires were sent down their ropes into the sea, where they began crying the pass-word Maryflower, in honour of my lady Queen Mariolanthe, to summon the shallops. The door at the stairfoot crashed in; and murder was done down there with much gasping and squealing. Sir Fulk went on his knees, imploring the king and the queen to take to the sea. King Arthur was coolly tying the five-crossed crowns of Hierusalem to his belt: nor would he consent to be hurried. And he bound up sceptres and orbs in a bundle of ermine mantles, hanging them to the queen's bright neck, she as disdainful of peril as he. When the four Turkopoles had fallen below, the would-be regicides came up the stair like the scum rising on a boiling pot. While they were still in the gallery, Saad the Assassin darted out from invisibility in the very chamber, crying, "A life is a life, and his life is our life, and our life is given for his life." And he hurled his half-naked body to the defence of the door. But, then, Divine Providence, in favour of His Anointed, interposed most terrifically. The Assassin fell, in accordance with the commandment of the Old Man of the Mountain, which said "And he remains." And the whole monstrous bulk of the castle and city of Acre began to roll and rock and rumble to and fro, swung by the Hand of God Almighty, Maker of Stars and Constellations.

Mere men gave themselves pause. Most of the murderers and ravishers fled like dislodged emmets,[1] crazy with terror. Some came on. Five were slain by Sir Fulk and Sir Hugh on the threshold. The horrible rocking and rolling grew more indignant: (says Sir Hugh) as though God willed to shake off the vermin molesting His Anointed. On all sides was heard the thunderous roar of falling towers, the crashing of beams, the awful din of the frightened, the shrieks of the crushed in death. The very floor of the regal chamber tilted so terribly, that no one might stand upright. They kneeled. They lay down, in horrible vertigo. They rolled like logs, from side to side, as the castle rocked with ever-augmenting irresistibly-blasting fury. Then, Queen Mariol cried aloud in the very nick of time. She, born and bred in Syria, where God (in His Wrath at the sins of the infidels) frequently makes the earth to quake, she, the queen, knew where the last hope of safety lay. "To the extern walls, where windows are. And stand close there, clutching the cills. For the outside wall is the strongest wall, and will fall last, when floors and inner walls have fallen: but it may perchance stand, offering a bare foothold in the holes from which floor-beams have fallen, if indeed such shall be God's Holy Will:" cries brave Queen Mariol. So they attained the windows whence the ropes still hung; and they clutched the solid cills for their lives: but the king and the queen used but one arm each for the cills, the other for each other. Then, the whole castle shivered and shook dreadfully, and fell in, landward; and the Tower of Saint John

---

[1] Ants (*OED* OL).

slid, with a frightful rending crash, after it in a torrent of broken masonry, excepting the one wall where the Regal Majesties clung, with Sir Fulk the Flame and Sir Hugh the priest and the pages, high up now in the open air. And God looked upon His Work, and, behold it was very good. And His good earth quaked no more at His Anger. He, and His, being ridded of verminous persons.[1]

"Straight to the refuge of the kindly sea:" says King Arthur, when the dust-cloud had subsided, and he could see how the riven pinnacle tottered on which they perched. Queen Mariol denied that she could swim. "We swim for two:" gaily says King Arthur. He hanged the tender girl about his neck, and went down the rope, plunging into the water, and swimming to the darting shallops. The others followed: very fearful was the Roman page; and Sir Fulk was fain to carry Sir Hugh, that priest having been younger at a previous date. When they all stood safely on the deck of the regal galiass, Queen Mariol spoke again. "Now set sail and pull oar with might and main," says she: "for, on the heels of an earthquake,[2] comes a coast-wise roughness, with a heaving and a swelling of short fierce billows, very periculous to navies:" says the Eastern Queen. They hurried out to sea.

xvi. *About King Arthur his Allocution and his Epistle*

All through the rest of the night, the galiass rocked on the deep sea. At dawn, they were in the open, where the angry waves were not, but on the waters a calm like the Peace of God. There, they lay all day, and all the next night, calming their own emotions: but King Arthur sat apart, on the castle of the lofty poop,

---

[1] *"personas amolite bestiolis molestis persimiles."* [Rolfe's note.]
[2] The great earthquake in Palestine, which annihilated Tyre and wrecked the castle of St. Jean d'Acre, is usually ascribed by other historians to the year A.D. 1203. But, according to the present document, it occurred, as nearly as we can calculate from internal evidence, in A.D. 1216 or certainly not earlier than A.D. 1215. At least, that is our inference. Our author seems to have scrupulously avoided the banal vulgarity of littering a work of art with dates; and we are consequently unable to explain this apparent discrepancy in terms comprehensible by, or acceptable to, pupil teachers, university extension lecturers, or even regius professors and reviewers.—P. and C. [Rolfe's note.] Most sources in fact record a severe earthquake in 1202.

pondering plans. And, at the next dawn, he gave the word to return, seeing that the sea was peaceable. When they came to the roads of Acre, my lord the king sent Sir Fulk ashore to observe the state of that city: who came back with news that more than half the inhabitants had perished in the earthquake, that the city was a rubbish-heap and chiefly on fire, that the pest was raging among the survivors to whom the Grandmaster and his Hospitallers were devoutly ministering, that lepers were breaking bounds everywhere being uproarious with hunger, and that Sir John Brienne was either ground to pulp or in hiding or flight. King Arthur caused the slaves of his galiass to be arrayed before him. Black they were, but all comely, giants all, and terrible of aspect, and some preeminently beautiful. Says he: "We promised you your freedom at Acre. There is Acre before you; and now ye are free: for Our galiass must be manned by free mariners who work for a wage." Then, the headman of the slaves arrayed them by the ship's bulwark, where stood Sir Hugh with a bag of gold; and each slave received a piece of gold as a gift, and instantly leaped into the sea to swim ashore in token that he was free, and immediately returned asking to be given service as a free mariner. Which was done. And my lord the king sent the head-man of these free mariners ashore in one of the shallops, to find the Grandmaster and to deliver certain letters to his hand. This is what my lord the king wrote in his letters:

Arthur the King to His well-beloved trusty Cousin Brother Sir Hermenegildus Grandmaster of the Order of the Hospital of Saint John of Hierusalem now at Acre: Greeting.

Know that, when We were an untried knight, Our Most Blessed Father and Lord Pope Innocent commanded Us to go, and to do some knightly deed, and to come again, promising that, on Our such coming-again, His Blessedness would do Us justice concerning Our kingdom of England, now held by that nefarious usurper Earl John of Mortain, Our wicked uncle, in despite of Our right as King Richard Lionheart his sole heir. Which knightly deed We suppose Ourself to have done more than once, in molesting Saracens at Jaffa and at Ascalon and at Blanchegarde. Further, We have won Queen Mariolanthe of Hierusalem for Our bride,

*and the crown of the King-Consort as a gage of our successes. Know
other things also, trusty Cousin. We hold and are seized of an immense
treasure of jewels, which We took as spoil from the Emir Eladel, and of
an immense treasure of gold, which We inherited from Our said honest
uncle King Richard Lionheart. We also hold and are seized of the regalia of the kingdom of Hierusalem. Now We intend Ourself to give an
example to kings present and to come, by Our honourable comportment
to Our lord the Pope, and by Our unflinching determination to achieve
Our rights. Wherefore, We let you know that We are faring forthwith to
Rome, accompanied only by the few who are Our friends, there to seek
from Our said lord Pope Innocent the confirmation of Our betrothal to
the said Queen Mariolanthe by way of matrimony, and the confirmation to Us of Our crown of Hierusalem which We have won, together
with permission to use Our treasure aforesaid for winning also Our said
crown of England. So, We bid you, trusty Cousin, by remembrance of
the favour in which We already have held you, and in consideration of
greater favours which in the future We are disposed to grant to your
Order, that you shall instantly follow or precede Us to Rome, by any
means, there to corroborate these news which We are bearing to Our lord
the Pope. And now fare well.*

GIVEN ON OUR GALIASS THE MARYFLOWER, AT SEA IN SIGHT OF ACRE,
    AND FAIRLY WRITTEN BY ME HUGH DE TURBERVILLE, KNIGHT, AND
    PRIEST, BY COMMAND OF MY LORD THE KING.

Having then sent the headman of the slaves ashore (his name
was Ibnagabetis) bearing these letters, on his return, King Arthur
sailed by way of Candia and Passavant and Messina, coming after
many days to Ostia.

XII

THE BOOK CALLED THE DOOR-MAT IN USE[1]

I. *About certain querulous Clergymen*

I do not admit that the condition of England was improved
by the release of the Wild Ass from the ban of excommunication. The horrible interdict still blighted the country: clergymen
everywhere were bleating for compensation or competing for
the innumerable vacant benefices. And there was a whole peck of
jealousy among the clergymen themselves. Little Mr. Pandulph's
nose was out of joint. As the nuncio, who had checked the Wild
Ass in his mad career, he fancied that the act of Softsword's restoration should have been his by right. And he envied the Primate
Stephen, for stealing a march on him at Winchester: so he said.
So, he scurried back to Rome, with a bagful of grievous tales to
tell, all unfavourable to our archbishop. (Langthon, he said, had
become more English than Roman.) And his lies were believed.
Cardinal-Bishop Nicholas of Tusculum was sent us, with all the
pompous circumstance of legate, charged to eye our Cardinal-
Primate and to keep him in order. O times. As though we Englishmen were incapable of being quite the most loyal and most
generous and most useful of all the Pope's children, and faithful
Englishmen, at one and the same time. O manners.

II. *About the Pope His Vassal and that one his Magnates*

To stablish himself in Pope Innocent's good opinion was
Softsword's prime duty. He summoned four burgesses and the
reeve from every township to a great council at Saint Alban's,
there to assess the compensation due to clergymen. Geoffrey fil-

---

[1] In this section, Rolfe draws heavily from the *Flores Historiarum*.

Peter the Justiciar and Bishop Peter Roches of Winchester ruled it: for John's own mind was to leave the kingdom now that the Pope was favouring him, and to win back Anjou from Philip the August, beginning with bloody war in Poictou. He pranced Dorsetward on his way thither; and, of course, the magnates of England refused to follow him, affirming, as before (and rightly), that their allegiance did not oblige them to serve him oversea.[1] Changeable beast that he was, he fancied that others also were as changeable: so he passionately plunged on shipboard, with his household and hostages and mercenaries, expecting the magnates to follow him. They did not. He sailed as far as Jersey.[2] Finding himself alone there, he rushed back in three days to Studland Bay, so filthily infuriate that the oil ran down his nose[3] and even lepers avoided him. The magnates had gone from the coast to their castles. Softsword pursued them, vowing hideous revenges, refusing to hear the pleas of the Justiciar. On his heels, glided[4] the Primate Stephen, arguing that to war with his subjects would be to break his coronation-oath. John rebuffed that one: telling him to mind his own business, the spiritualities. And so that Wild Ass went galloping on in a boiling rage as far as Nottingham, with the archbishop, pained, not to say angry, fulminating censures. These, at length, prevailed. It was agreed to settle, by law, this question, once and for all, Did their oath of allegiance oblige English magnates to pay their service oversea, or only in England. John, however, dashed about the realm a bit, as far even as Durham, just to let people see his power, which was great, numerous, well-trained, just as long as he paid its wages and gave it cities to sack, and not a moment longer. I say that he was no fool in preferring the service of magnates, if he could by any means snaffle it. A synod was convened at Westminster; and the Primate Stephen played a most notable trick. So utterly lawless had been the usurpation of John, that England had almost forgotten what good law was. Imagine,

---

[1] The knights of John's kingdom claimed that their overseas service was limited to Normandy and Brittany and that they were not obliged to participate in military activity in, for example, Poitou.

[2] *"Caesarea."* [Rolfe's note.]

[3] *"stillebat oleum naso."* [Rolfe's note.]

[4] *"labebatur."* [Rolfe's note.]

then, the Synod of Westminster's thought, when Langthon displayed to it the Charter of King Henry Beauclerk, as a specimen of good legislation.[1] This was a master-stroke. It dissolved the clouds which veiled the mind of magnates, torn this way and that by the whims of a freakish ruler, and the half-considered opinions of otherwise-occupied amateurs.[2] And, the minds of the magnates being thus illumined (as they thought) with sound reason, they set themselves irrevocably on the said Charter, for which (said they) they were willing to risk their lives.

O foxy clergyman, o dunderheaded magnates, King Henry Beau-clerk's Charter, like all earthly things, was sweet when fresh, but tabid[3] after decades of disuse. Having obtained the magnates' assent to it as an example, Langthon ought to have provided a new charter of similar nature but suited to the occasion. He, however, was not a statesman, but a pious clergyman only, and the fillets of his mitre, like the blinkers of a cart-horse, prevented him from seeing largely, says Hubert de Burgh.

III. *About Softsword between Magnates and Clergymen*

Softsword's attention was turned (for the moment) from the magnates by the new Legate, who loomed very largely indeed (with little Mr. Pandulph in his ear-hole), for no less a purpose than to control England at home and abroad and to settle John's amends to clergymen. This is how largely this Legate Nicholas loomed. He took little notice of the Earl of Mortain, and less of the Council of Saint Albans and the Synod of Westminster: he just went on his own way, filling vacant benefices at will, and not even permitting appeals to Rome.[4] As Mr. Pandulph said, the

---

[1] The Charter of Liberties, issued by Henry I. This proclamation acknowledged the feudal rights of the church and the nobles, and, as Rolfe recounts here, was held up by Archbishop Langton as a model for the Magna Carta in 1213. According to Roger of Wendover, after preaching a sermon at St. Paul's, Langton took aside a group of barons to show them Henry's charter and encouraged them to recover their long-lost liberties.

[2] "*semiconcoctes inexpertorum sententiis aliis in rebus uersantium.*" [Rolfe's note.]

[3] Wasted away or decomposed (*OED* OL).

[4] In fact, Nicholas, who was sent by the pope to settle the dispute between the crown and the clergy, is often said to have acted in John's favor, appointing men who had remained loyal to the king during the interdict.

English generally are very fat. But the Legate's legatisms made our Wild Ass unhappy; and, when the heresiarch Earl Raymond of Toulouse came fugitive to England, and legate Nicholas up and expelled him, then, John's fury became so boundless that he actually plastered Lady Jezebel's hair with butter and beat her with a shoe.[1] Also, he took to hanging boys at random out of his camp of hostages, choosing specially the pretty ones, just to annoy their fathers the magnates. And he hanged them in this new way, despite the Justiciar's protests which he drowned with his trumpets: for he roped four youngsters together throats to feet, drawing the top one by his neck slowly to the height of the battlements of the Tower, where they dangled distortedly like limp knotted tassels in the wind for his beastly diversion. Asked to admire, I said that this was a stupid game. He was for raging at me: but, "If you lack men to serve you," says I, "why slay these lusty striplings, fecund fountains of seed to make men who would serve you in place of their fathers who won't?" It was not a chaste commentary; and the unbridled licence, encouraged and even commanded among the hostages thereafter, gravely affected the discipline of their camp: but how many magnates owe their sons and their innumerable grandsons to me, I need not now say. O affable reader, consider bad John's predicament: across the magnates: not daring to come across clergymen, again, as well: paralyzed without the support of one or the other. He had to choose between them. Of the two, he preferred (like a leper) to squirm for the favours of clergymen, the taste of whose awful power still tingled on his hot and furry tongue. So, he went and did new homage to Legate Nicholas, reiterating his surrender of the kingdom, till we said that such was becoming his beastly habit; and he sealed the charters and concessions of the same with golden bulls.

IIII. *About Softsword incorrigibly vacillating*

The arrears, which the Legate condemned the Pope's vassal to pay, were simply frightful. This was due to the long duration

---

[1] "*ut re uera comam dominae iezebellae butyro illineret et eam soleâ uerberaret.*" [Rolfe's note.]

of his violence to clergymen, whose revenues he had been rapaciously seizing for maintaining the mercenaries necessary to keep him in his usurped throne and canopy. While he was considering how he could possibly contrive to satiate the thirst of clergymen for the said arrears, it occurred to him to try once more to come to terms with magnates, like the inconstant traitor which he was, incapable of keeping faith with anyone at all. The magnates, however, had begun to combine among themselves: they would not trust him, nor even listen to him. So, he revolted; and offered sops[1] to bishops.[2]

v. *About the Opening of a third Door*

Earl Geoffrey fil-Peter of Essex died: the Chief Justiciar. "Now, by God's Teeth," brays the Wild Ass, "am I king of the English at last. And Geoffrey may go to hell, to meet Archbishop Walter."[3] But, by the Justiciar's death, England was left like a ship in a storm and without a rudder. That storm began on the death of Hubert Walter, if not before. After the death of Geoffrey, England could not even breathe. Six bishoprics were screaming for bishops. Magnates were sulking, meditating defiances so that they might honourably wage war against Softsword. And one really would have thought, all things being considered, that that Wild Ass was bitted at last. O times. So inscrutable, however, and past finding out, is Divine Mercy, even to the most abandoned of sinners, that, no sooner were the only two humanly-conceivable doors banged in his hairy face, than a third door opened. Earl Ferrand of Flanders thought it might profit him to defy the king of the Franks again, and to throw in his lot with Softsword. And, instantly, Earl William of Holland resolved to do so too. And, with these two alli-

---

[1] Things of small value.

[2] *"et episcipis objiciebat delenimenta."* [Rolfe's note.] According to Roger of Wendover, because the legate favored the king, the payment of resitution to the clergy was for the most part postponed, and the archbishop and bishops received fifteen marks of silver.

[3] This anecdote is drawn from Matthew Paris. John was rumored to have uttered these words on the death of Archbishop Hubert Walter as well as on the death of Geoffrey Fitz Peter.

ances added to his power of mercenaries, the Wild Ass felt strong enough to break right away from clergymen and magnates both, amusing himself with his wished-for war in France. O manners.

VI. *About England How She Was*

John left England in turmoil. He named, as Chief Justiciar and Regent of the kingdom, that Bishop Peter Roches of Winchester, whom all men detested, because he was a Frankish clergyman and a wrong one. Ensued an epidemic of rebellions. The Primate Stephen also, restive at having Legate Nicholas sitting on his head, surged, and spoke loudly about it at the provincial synod of Dunstable: after which, he sent his own brother Simon with a pungent appeal to Rome. Naturally, the Legate appealed too: his envoy was that little Mr. Pandulph. And, thus, the settlement of the church was shoved upon the shelf for months. O clergymen.

VII. *About Softsword his War in Poictou*

John set out to sea with Lady Jezebel and the Earls of Derby and Chester, and forty-thousand mercenary cotterels in busses under Sir Fulk Breauté: whom storms assailed, signifying God's Opinion of this emprize. Thirteen days, they tossed upon the angry sea, lubricating the same with their contents,[1] arriving at Rochelle exhausted by empty retching, and unable to retain even the merest particle of pudding. Not their leprous aspect, indeed, but their overwhelming numbers, gained them a footing in Poictou. And the Poictevin magnates, oblivious of the past, tired of King Philip the August, and (like all Franks) ever-ready for a change, were not disinclined to call a Wild Ass (with such a power as John's) their nominal suzerain.[2] Twenty-six weather-cocks[3] did homage. Sir Savary Malaleone also came back to John's allegiance. And Softsword found that he had all Poictou in his pocket without having stricken a blow. But the city of Poictiers sneezed emphatically, rejecting him. He played about, between

---

[1] "*idem quocunque in uentribus erat lubricantes.*" [Rolfe's note.]
[2] A feudal overlord (*OED* OL).
[3] Changeable or inconstant individuals (*OED* OL).

Rochelle and Niort and Fontenay. For reasons known to himself (not to me, precisely), he named me Mayor and Seneschal of Niort, and Keeper of Causton Park, I being absent in England, and actually governing my pirates and my V Ports from my castle of Dover. By way of diversion, he stormed Sir Geoffrey Lusignan's castle of Mervent on the Eve of Pentecost. On the Festival, he bombarded Sir Geoffrey and his two sons at Vouvant. And, on Trinity Sunday, he took homage from all the Lusignans, including Earl Hugh le Brun X. of the March, his infant Hugh, and Earl Ralf of Eu. Further, to bind these magnates to him, he went so far as to affiance his daughter Lady Johanna aged four (she was not the Wild Ass's bastard of that name) to the infant Hugh, son of the very earl who had been lucky enough not to marry Lady Jezebel, her mother. O manners.

VIII. *About the Pontiff ill-advised*

Pope Innocent gave judgment concerning appeals and arrears. The first thing to be done was to pay one-hundred-thousand marks to the English clergymen as arrears: then, the horrible interdict would be lifted from England. Forty-thousand marks were to be paid instantly: sums already paid would be put down to Softsword's credit: the remainder might be paid in instalments during the next five years. It was a hard judgment: for, as Softsword would never pay, England had to pay, to satisfy her own clergymen. But Rome spoke; and England began to collect the money. The Wild Ass accepted this judgment at Angers, as he did not want to incommode himself with a fresh quarrel during what promised to be a successful campaign. And all this signifies that little Mr. Pandulph had prevailed, and that Stephen the Primate had been slighted and ignored, which shows that our lord the Pope was ill-advised in the matter.

VIIII. *About Softsword the Toss which he took from Poictevin Magnates*

Sir Aloys, son of the clammy-souled pig King Philip, appeared, leading an army to Chinon in Softsword's despite. Softsword chased him away; and sat down quietly to besiege Les Roches aux Moines. Sir Aloys, goaded by fiery Frankish magnates, came back again, displaying his power in line-of-battle. Lest I choke myself with premature chuckles over my writing, let me be brief in narrating the consequence. For those glorious magnates of Poictou, Marses, Achilleses, Hectors, Sampsons, Maccabeuses, fearless paladins all, who champed their teeth and spiked their whispers and foamed at the mouth, stamping with ardour of war, crawled to the Earl of Mortain, hemming and hawing, nudging each other to speak; and they very abjectly pointed out that they had not come there to fight pitched battles.[1] Oh, no: nice comfortable sieges, showy storming of cities manned by obese and flaccid burgesses, ravishments of heiresses, commodious highway-robberies, plundering of churches or convents, were exercises quite in their line: but not bold fighting in the open against professional soldiers. The Wild Ass fell in such a panic that he bolted to Niort, seventy miles in a couple of days, leaving all his tents, baggage, war-machines as spoil for the Franks. O culvert.[2]

Pray ponder his plight: deserted by his precious Poictevins, disgraced in the eyes of Christendom as refusing the challenge of line-of-battle, and oh so sorry for having quarrelled with the magnates of England. To the last, in his distress, he yelped. If they would only come to his aid now all should be forgiven and forgotten. To their honour be it said that not a single English magnate even moved a little finger. Let us now chuckle.

x. About the Lifting of the Interdict

Now we in England were occupied with really serious matters. In the cathedral of Saint Paul of London, the bishop of Ely (clad in his pontifical robes, ringing his bells, and reading blessed words out of his bull, his candles being lighted), was lifting the horrible interdict which had been weighing England down during so many years. For we had scraped the forty-thousand marks together, price of our rites; and had paid them to the Legate's exchequer. This having been done, and the festivities concluded,

---

[1] *"abiectissime dixerunt se campestre non esse paratos."* [Rolfe's note.] A "pitched battle" is a planned battle fought at an arranged time and place (*OED* OL).
[2] Villainous (*OED* OL).

a very avaricious assemblage of abbots, abbesses, priors, templars, hospitallers, bishops, and clergymen of every colour, besieged the said Legate, beseeching a share of the spoil. And lo, there was not enough to give them a mark apiece. And they felt more afflicted than before. O clergymen.

XI. *About Softsword how he suffered by Bouvines*

Frankish Sir Aloys recovered all Poictevin castles and cities from Softsword. Nothing was left to the Wild Ass but to fly to pasture and kick with his precious allies in the north. He tried to do this by means of his mercenaries: but Sir Aloys (with a fat excited man's singular nimbleness) exercised him even to sweating in the south; and this left King Philip free to march against the northern alliance, commanded, in the unavoidable absence of John, by the uneasy Duke Hottho of Brunswick, a goat who butted-off a crown imperial.[1] Ensued the catastrophe. The king of the Franks advanced to the bridge of Bouvines. Here, was that northern alliance from which so much was expected. Philip the August, seeing how successful the offer of pitched battle had been in sending tails between legs of curs in the south, offered the same in the north. He capered provokingly. The northern alliance ran at him. He retired to Bouvines; and displayed his line-of-battle. The northern leaguers, having more pluck than John's Poictevins, accepted the challenge. There followed a truly enormous struggle, four hours of wrestling body to body. Earl Walter Saint-Pol, Earl Something of Beaumont, Sir Matthew Montmorenci, the Viscount of Melun, the Duke of Burgundy, really did paladins' work for the Frank, charging like shooting stars into the ranks of the Dutchmen. Nothing could equal the impetuosity of Sir William Barres and the knights of his household: twice, indeed, he neck-gripped Duke Hottho and struggled with an excommunicate Cæsar: twice, he was unhorsed, but so valiant was he on foot that he captured the imperial standard of the eagle-ridden dragon, *or*, which the said Duke Hottho had the insolence to display. O times. O manners.

---

[1] *"hirco qui coronam imperatoriam obarietauit."* [Rolfe's note.]

But, if I enumerate all the doughty deeds done by Frankish knights that day, I shall become as prolix as that Mr. Matthew (late of Paris), than whom no more garrulous old puppy ever drove a pen. And this would greatly grieve me. What more then? This. John's northern alliance was smashed to atoms. Duke Hottho of Brunswick was fugitive. And John, pinned in Poictou by Sir Aloys of France, had no way left open to him but the inhospitable sea. To which, he (blaspheming) took, having been forced to forswear war with King Philip for the next six years. And, so, he came to Dartmouth, (still blaspheming), where even the waggoners of his baggage plugged their ear-holes with their thumbs, lest they should be imbued with demoniacal notions.

XII. *About Hubert de Burgh his Doings in These Times*

I, it was, who extracted the Earl of Mortain from his Poictevin predicament. For, finding me to be the only magnate in whom he durst confide, (so he fondly imagined, grace to my exceeding wiliness which, I firmly believe, was divinely inspired, for I am not a deceiver by nature), Softsword, I say, taking me to be his only really trustworthy confidant, named me as his embassador to get terms from the king of the Franks. And, though my dear wife Lady Beatrix was dead, and I was marrying my dear wife Lady Margaretha (she was Sir Robert Arsike's heiress),[1] I went to France and made the terms already specified, namely, that the Wild Ass was not to caper in France for six years. For, it seemed to me that Duke Arthur's interests would best be served by penning the Wild Ass in England, and by helping him to work out his own damnation there, with no scope in France to refuge in when he should have made England too hot to hold him. I confess, though, that, when I had sealed the six years' truce, I doubted the wisdom of it, for my dear wife Lady Margaretha incontinently died; and I wondered whether this betokened Divine Displeasure. I considered the point during many days while I was eating my pud-

---

[1] While many earlier texts claim that Hubert de Burgh's first wife was Margaret, daughter of Robert de Arsike, according to S.H.F. Johnston, Margaret de Arsike is a "completely fictitious person." See "The Lands of Hubert de Burgh," *The English Historical Review*, 50.199 (July 1935): 427.

dings, and, upon the whole, I judge that it did not, her dowry being inconsiderable, and my babies not being fond of her. My babies are Sir John de Burgh, vice-constable of my Kentish castles and subwarden of my V Ports, and Sir Hubert II de Burgh, who will have my earldom of Gloucester.

XIII. About Softsword at Grips with Magnates and Commons and Clergymen

The Earl of Mortain came back to a land appallingly angry with him. The commons detested the legate and the justiciar: the magnates were combining together for themselves: the clergymen were still bawling for money and immunity and perquisites, as usual. The greatest tact was needed to treat this state of things successfully. The Wild Ass, wildly and asininely, instantly resurrected the burning question; and brought the whole wasps' nest about his hairy ears. He demanded scutage-fees from magnates who had refused to follow him to Poictou. They resisted this impertinence, making the very ribaldest gestures at him.[1] Also, they mustered in force at Bury Saint Edmunds under the Primate Stephen, pretending a pilgrimage; and they sent him word that either he must give them their blessed King Henry Beauclerk's old Charter, or they would remit their faith to him and (after such defiance and renunciation) treat him to open war. Softsword, of course, tried once more to deprive the magnates of the support of the clergymen: by pelting the last, he thought to gain the favour of the first. But, in the nick of time, our lord Pope Innocent was inspired (divinely, I do not doubt), to recall both the objectionable legate and that mischievous little Mr. Pandulph. This cleared the field. The clergymen of England (almost to a clergyman) adhered to the magnates, who themselves were governed entirely by the well-meaning Primate Stephen. Softsword entrenched himself at the new Templary in London; and merely shuffled when the magnates reiterated their demands. He tried to sow dissensions among them. And he prepared for war. As for them, they talked too much, and did too little. But John most madly ordained that all men should take a new oath of allegiance to him, which

---

[1] "motus dantes perobscoenos." [Rolfe's note.]

oath contained a new clause disowning King Henry Beauclerk's obsolete Charter. Was there ever such a wild and asinine Wild Ass as this one, who tried to rid Englishmen of one of their silly notions by force? Anyone with gumption would have let the thing expire of its own inanity. To try by force to kill it, gave it fictitious strength, as though it were not strong enough already. For it was undeniably strong. In fact, from the very moment when the Primate Langthon first let men of that generation see King Henry Beauclerk's Charter, all desire and all affection died, save for King Henry Beauclerk's Charter. Never before, since the Conquest, had the magnates and the commons and the clergymen been united in the single idea of extorting a single concession from the holder of the English crown and canopy. O times.

XIIII. *About Softsword without a Friend excepting one Friend*

The Earl of Mortain suddenly became ware that he ran the very gravest risk of losing not only his ill-gotten usurpations but his own life as well. What could he do alone, against the combination? Nothing. To whom could he turn for help? To none, save one. Not a prince in Christendom would ally with him any more, after the stupendously malignant luck which he had plainly brought on all who had hitherto had to do with him. He had lost the whole of the vast Angevin empire in France, and disgracefully. The three estates of England[1] were united against him: their hands were on his hairy gullet. He had none to depend on, save his mercenary cotterels; and he could only count on them as long as he could pay them; and it seemed that he could not pay them much longer, unless out of his treasure at Corfe; and a king (though John was not a king, his unction being void, because of the impediment called Arthur),[2] who cannot levy taxes and get them paid and (consequently) is forced to use his hoard, is not very far from a most cataclysmal downfall. For even such a hoard as that at Corfe can be exhausted. And, when it was exhausted and he could no longer pay his forty-thousand cotterels, then, indeed, his worthless life would lie at the pleasure of anyone who

---

[1] The nobility, the clergy, and the commoners.

[2] *"impedimenti causa dicti Arthuri."* [Rolfe's note.]

liked to take it. How many these would be, he well-knew. Touching the comportment of Hubert de Burgh, at this time, with his multitudinous offices at castles filled with garrisons of picked veterans, and knights my tenants bound to serve me, it may be asked, o most affable reader, why John did not enjoy the help and comfort which I could have given, certainly sufficient to make his lot much easier. The answer is simple. I was not asked. I was not even approached on the subject. I rather fancy that the Wild Ass feared to command me to join him. I opine that he was reserving a cringing appeal to my piety as his ultimate resource. I really judge, indeed, that he did not dare to apply to me, in view of the sternly detached attitude which I used to him through all these turmoils, lest he should precipitate my definite denial and defiance. He had made me too strong. He had a delicacy about seeing me thumb to nose and fingers fanned. He preferred uncertainty to certainty, being a Wild Ass all the time. So, there remained but one whose aid he might invoke; and he set himself to curry favour with our lord Pope Innocent, that he might at least gain immunity for his miserable life. He sent an envoy to Rome, begging apostolic maledictions for his enemies, apostolic benedictions for his cause, promising that (if these were conceded) he would take The Cross, and go crusading against the Saracens of the Holy Land.[1] Observe the cunning of that act.

xv. About our Lord Pope Innocent the Great His apostolic Opinion of His Vassal

"Ho," says our lord the Pope, "here, now, We have this tiresome king of the English (so His Paternity called the Earl of Mortain at that time), who is being dreadfully worried by his very disagreeable magnates. He, though obedient enough to Us, will, We believe, be better by far out of that remote island, where he quarrels so facilely with everyone in turn, clergymen as well as laymen. And, no doubt, God's Mercy intends for him a holy and comfortable and highly respectable demise, in battle against those infidel Saracens, against whom he now desires to wage war. So let it be.

---

[1] Roger of Wendover similarly asserts that John took the cross out of fear rather than devotion.

We admire at his piety and bless him. But, lest peoples should imagine vain things, fondly thinking that they are permitted to cough at will at such kings as are obsequious to Holy Mother Church, it will be well, and We decree, that John should first restore order in his realm, with the assistance of Our apostolic benedictions as requested." Such, I conceive, is something like what our lord the Pope was pleased to think and to say in the matter. And it soon became known in England that His Blessedness was favouring the Wild Ass. So, with perfect reverence for the former, the magnates (under the Primate Langthon) set themselves to deal as faithfully as might be with the latter. There was no notion of defying the Pope, Whose Paternity did not speak of anything save of approval of the Earl of Mortain (being, as I say, ill-advised regarding that beast); and His said Paternity emphatically did not say a word about damning magnates who proposed to lead the said Wild Ass (peradventure by the snout) into paths of righteousness. Which adroitness[1] of our lord the Pope vastly comforted most Englishmen.

xvi. *About Softsword defied by the Magnates*

John added, to the number of his mercenaries, as many as he could bring his meanness to afford. The magnates mustered their knights and tenants at Stamford; and marched to Northampton. Bishop Giles Braose joined them to avenge the fate of his family. Sir Robert fil-Walter came in: so did Sir Geoffrey Mandeville, the new Earl of Essex: they were forty-four great magnates in all, and many eldest sons of magnates who stayed at home to hold their castles. When the Wild Ass was ware that horrors really were intended, he asked the magnates for their terms. Stephen the Primate came, and recited his piece. "By God's Teeth," brays the Wild Ass, "they might as well ask for the kingdom." And he tossed the Primate out. So, the magnates proceeded to defy him with appropriate solemnity, renouncing the homage and allegiance which they had sworn to him, that they might be quite free to break his peace. And they elected Sir Robert fil-Walter as their leader,

---

[1] *"sollertia."* [Rolfe's note.]

naming him Marshal of the Army of God and the Church, which
was a sweet hearing for our lord Pope Innocent.

xvii. *About Hubert de Burgh his Demeanour to Softsword and to the Magnates*

I became very busy indeed, saying nothing nice or nasty to
either party, running round among my castles, confirming the
savage Welshry, noting magnates likely to be faithful to Duke
Arthur, and, in short, making ready to strike a very shrewd blow
on a suitable spot at a proper occasion. For, though I had no word
from my lord the king, I had full confidence in his appearance
at the right time. This reticence of mine (as I say) worried the
Wild Ass dreadfully, so that, not daring to demand my service
in the field, lest I should set the horrible example of an earl of
my magnitude defying him, he continued to add to my dignities,
meaning thereby to retain me (if not on his side) at least neutral.
For he could not but be ware (and, no doubt, sorry) that he had
already given me enough power to make me most valuable to
whoever should secure my service. I have mentioned, I believe,
that he was singularly wild and asinine, even for a Wild Ass. So,
he made me Justiciar of England, deposing that detested bishop
of Winchester: thus currying favour with the commons. And he
sent me, as ambassador, to whine on his behalf before the magnates. I was to plead that he was a crusader and the Church's
vassal and (therefore) sacrosanct as to his person; and he wanted
four arbitrators elected by him, and four elected by the magnates,
to meet in the Pope's Presence as supreme arbitrator, to settle all
disputes. Now, when I had laid these terms before the magnates,
I let my left eyelid droop with great solemnity over my left eye
for at least three minutes, saying nothing: which done, I retired
(in awful silence) to eat my pudding. And, marvellous to relate,
the magnates understood the portent, and refused to agree with
John. But I must say that they refused for another reason beside
my winking: for the city of London, under Mayor Serlo a haber-
dasher, with the secret connivance (I do not say instigation) of one
Hubert de Burgh, who was Chamberlain of London and Warden
of the Exchange and Mint, threw open its gates to welcome the

said magnates, who thus gained possession of the chief city in the kingdom.[1] As for the commons and the clergymen, there were rebellions at Exeter and Northampton and Lincoln: but the major of the people sat still, for the moment, with its tongue in its cheek, and looking down its nose.

XVIII. *About Softsword his Submission to the Magnates*

Not knowing precisely what to do in these puzzling circumstances, and not being anything but what they were as to wits, the magnates played awhile with King Henry Beauclerk's Charter. This suited John. He held the Tower of London and thirteen castles, Norwich, Chester, Bridgenorth, Gloucester, Bristol, Exeter, Marlborough, Winchester, Orford, Oxford, Berkhampstead, Wallingford, Newcastle-under-Lyne: and he only wanted time in which to scratch together another fifty-thousand foreign mercenaries, wherewith he undoubtedly would have been able to make the magnates look extremely silly. So he feigned willingness to do what they wanted. They should have their accursed charter, says he, if they cared to come for it. And, from Merton, he issued safe-conducts for them to meet him at Staines. And they agreed to come; and, with the greatest gaiety, they continued to add to the sum of their demands. Softsword moved to Windsor to meet them: but they, having some small inkling of how wild an ass he was, came fully armed, and lay at Runnymede, with their new and preposterous Great Charter,[2] which by that time was about twice as large as that of King Henry Beauclerk. I called it preposterous, because (while some clauses were most meek and timid) the charter as a whole placed the government of the country actually and absolutely in the hands of the clergymen. I yield to no earl in reverence for religion; I concede (nay, I insist),

---

[1] The mayor of London, Serlo the Mercer, opened London's gates to John's opponents on May 17, 1215, and they entered the city, plundering the houses of those loyal to John.

[2] The Magna Carta. While the Magna Carta is often posited as the origin of democracy in England, it concerns itself primarily with the relationship between the king and his barons rather than the promotion of equal rights for all individuals. While the charter does place some limitations on monarchical privileges, it also works to solidify the power of the upper classes.

that clergymen should have the chief place: but I am not such a Godforsaken fool as to think that they ought to have, or that they wish to have, sole control over secular matters to the exclusion of able and adept seculars. Yet that is precisely the sense and essence of the much-vaunted Great Charter. But the Wild Ass offered no objections. He did not intend to keep faith with the magnates and their idiotic Great Charter, when once he should have assembled sufficient mercenaries to enable him safely to break it. So, he dabbed his seal[1] on their vellum, grinning with his great jaws the while; and the magnates obsequiously renewed their homage, flattering themselves that they had done something excessively intellectual.

XVIIII. *About the Confusion caused by the Great Charter*

The Great Charter mended no evils at all: it, in fact, created new ones. First, it was essentially null and void, because no vassal can grant such concessions (as it granted) without the consent of his overlord. That should suffice to damn it. But more, it effected confusion worse confounded. For example: it devised that twenty-five magnates should work it, and it carefully omitted to state which twenty-five. So, the magnates began to quarrel condignly[2] among themselves, and thoroughly enjoyed themselves at the expense of commons and clergymen, until twenty-five pushed themselves forward, and began to try to govern the country in the terms of their mad bad Great Charter. And, then, our lord Pope Innocent stepped pontifically into the muddle.[3] First, He quashed the Great Charter, as futile, and as compiled and enacted without His apostolic assent or authority. Second, he commanded the clergymen either to quiet the magnates, or to damn them.

The clergymen tried. They convoked another council to meet at Staines. Naturally the Wild Ass refused to attend it: he gibed cacophonously at clergymen and magnates both, bidding them to make what they could of their precious charter. Primate Stephen became haggard of aspect: clergymen fondled their dewlaps in a

---

[1] *"sigillum tetigit."* [Rolfe's note.]

[2] Deservedly.

[3] *"in turbam succedebat pontificaliter."* [Rolfe's note.]

dreadful quandary. No one knew what to do. Not a clergyman, not a magnate, ever came near to grasping the great truth that the slit throat of Softsword would solve their difficulty.[1] At least, none of them attempted such slitting. The clergymen did not dare to disobey the Pope: they were also very averse from behaving unpleasantly to the magnates, who were now capering and snorting like excited bullocks. So, for safety's sake, they mildly anathematized perturbers of king and country, naming by name neither king nor perturbers. And, all the while, Softsword was collecting forces.

xx. About the Magnates malignantly imbecile

I will not disguise any longer that the magnates were wellmeaning but excessively stolid dunderheads.[2] Why, then, did I not lead them into ways of wisdom? Because leading of this kind is never efficacious when offered, but only when asked-for. And the magnates puffed themselves up with a firm opinion of their own singular sapience. Wherefore, I left them alone, till their errors should have wrenched that opinion from them, with howlings.

Obstinate persistence in error produces actions which are malignant as well as imbecile: every earl ought to know that. The magnates resolved to depose the Earl of Mortain, and to offer the crown and canopy of England to Aloys of France.[3] It was the beginning of their self-disintegration. All the bishops coughed at the bare notion. So did the earls of Salisbury, Warwick, Chester, Pembroke, Surrey, Derby. The bishops further expressed their disapproval, by staying (very supererogatorily) at Dover, on their way to an œcumenical council in Rome,[4] merely for the pleasure

---

[1] *"nemo fuit omnino episcoporum magnatorum omnino fuit nemo ueritatem magnam unquam ad cogitatione complectendum appropinquabat guttur Mollensis scissum soluturum difficultates suas."* [Rolfe's note.]

[2] *"barones beneuolossed nimis stolidos."* [Rolfe's note.]

[3] According to Roger of Wendover, the motive of the barons was to deprive John of his foreign soldiers. Most of John's soldiers were subjects of the king of France, so it was assumed that they would desert John when Louis came to England.

[4] Query. The Fourth Council of Lateran?—P. and C. [Rolfe's note.] The Fourth Lateran Council, held in 1215 by Pope Innocent, was a highly significant ecumenical council that established important doctrines concerning transubstantiation and heresy.

of assuring the Wild Ass of their fidelity. And, moreover, the bishop of Winchester and that little Mr. Pandulph actually took upon themselves to suspend the Primate Stephen. O manners.

xxi. *About Softsword his Relapse into Sacrilege*

The main body of magnates seized my castle of Rochester, which I (by chance) had denuded for cleaning; and I did not look in that direction, for reasons. John, elated by the accession of the six earls and the bishops, showed his delight in the wild and asinine manner natural to him, bursting out in paroxysms of new violence, using the cathedral of Rochester for stables, while he besieged the castle during seven weeks till its starving garrison surrendered. Whom (not content with his horrible sacrilege in the cathedral) he was for hanging in bunches instanter: but Sir Savary Malaleone warned him that that was the way to lose mercenaries, whose stake in the game depended on the ransoms of prisoners. And Softsword, ware that he himself depended on his said mercenaries, had to be content with the contortions of a few strangled bankrupts.[1] Then, he pranced on, to harry all England. Being an ass and a rabid one, he used no discretion in his crimes. Not only did he overrun the Midlands and Northumbria and devastate the Lothians, but (befriended, as he was, by clergymen, and with his overlord the Pope damning his magnates for him, and with bishops on all sides bounding to adulate him), he found it quite impossible to keep his hooves out of Church property, and needs must engage in a series of sacrileges, beginning at Rochester as afore-narrated. On Christmas Day, he plundered the abbey of Tilty: the abbey of Coggeshall, on the Festival of The Circumcision; and Saint Audrey's of Ely he utterly ravaged later. Whereat, a whole cluster of grieved and much-pained clergymen packed their valises, and scurried to Rome, to offer news of the manner in which the Pope's vassal, a client of clergymen, was performing his christian obligations. O manners.

---

[1] *"decoctorum paucorum."* [Rolfe's note.]

xxii. *About Pope Innocent supporting Softsword*

Our lord the Pope, ignorant as yet of the Wild Ass's abominable ebulliences, supported him splendidly, forbidding Sir Aloys of France to dare the crossing of the narrow sea. Further, His Paternity sent a cardinal, Walo by name, telling King Philip to keep his fat and fussy son in order. That clammy-souled pig of a Frank, however, bitten with the itch of having his said son a king, and a king of the English too, was less than assiduous in obeying pontifical commands. He did not defy Pope Innocent openly: but he artfully contrived a legal argument, hoping (with such a bait) to distract so eager a canonist as our then lord from the more important matter. His thesis was, that a king cannot alienate his kingdom without the consent of his magnates, that John's feudality to Innocent was such an alienation, that (therefore) the Pope could only blame Himself when John's magnates set themselves to amend John's wrong doing. So, Philip (pretending to consider the Pope as out of the question, and John as deposed by his magnates, and the said magnates as purely prancing with eagerness to have Sir Aloys for their king), calmly went on with his schemes for the conquest of England. Sir Aloys embarked at Calais. Sir Eustace the Monk (that pious and most useful pirate) was induced (I need not say by whom) to command the great Frankish fleet. And, Almighty God having scattered Softsword's navies with a gale, Sir Aloys landed in England, emitting interminable proclamations to the English categorizing the crimes of John.

xxiii. *About Hubert de Burgh*

I have one more little word to say about myself. I thought fit to stick closer than ever to Softsword, while annoying him in every possible manner: for I got great and most admirable news of my lord the king, whose stars at length were benignant, and his hour nigh at hand. And it seemed well to get everything which could be got out of his wicked uncle, while yet the said sinner had anything to give, all for the use and comfort of my lord the king. The first thing, then, which I got at this juncture, was the most excellent Lady Havis fil-Robert the Countess of Gloucester, nefariously put away by the said Earl of Mortain when he married Lady Jezebel, married anon to Earl Geoffrey Mandeville IIII. of Essex, and now three months a widow. Her I cheerfully married, obtaining a perfect wife, with her earldoms of Gloucester and of Essex, her castles, and her treasure.[1] And, also, the Wild Ass heaped other new honours on me, naming me constable of five more castles, and shire-reeve of four more counties, and steward of the Honours of Rayleigh and Peverel. So that I was a person of really excessive importance, and the numbers of my trumpets were well-nigh unmanageable.

---

[1] John's first wife, Isabella of Gloucester (sometimes referred to as Avisa), did marry Hubert de Burgh. She was divorced from John on grounds of consanguinity and then married Geoffrey de Mandeville, earl of Essex, who died a couple years later. The marriage to Hubert de Burgh took place a year after her second husband died, and Isabella died less than a month later. Henry III was Isabella of Angoulême's son.

XIII

THE BOOK CALLED COMING AGAIN WITH JOY
AND BRINGING SHEAVES[1]

1. *About King Arthur his Coming to Rome*

When King Arthur touched Ostia, it was told to him that the
Grandmaster of the Hospital had reached that port several days
before him, in a swift especca belonging to the Order of Saint John,
and that he had gone toward Rome. "So much the better," says my
lord the king, "for that knightly clergyman knows how and when
to be discreet with his tongue, and who it is who can and will give
him jam for his pudding." And he sent a secret messenger to the
said Grandmaster, bidding him to bring a train of knights to attend
the Regal Majesties, and to take charge of their treasure, when
they should land in Rome. But my lord the king remained at Ostia,
collecting a company of fifty well-formed mercenaries to wear his
liveries, and providing suitable apparel for himself and the queen
and for their people. Also he bought slaves, to clean the galiass
from the muck of the voyage, and to row it up River Tiber with
awful pomp and solemnity, bearing the Regal Majesties and their
train all happed in brand-new habits of a quality superior to the
emperor's. Arriving in Rome about mid-morning, the Grandmaster with fifty Hospitallers waited them at the quays. Forty knights
remained on the galiass, in charge of the treasure sealed with the
seal of Saint John, which to break is sacrilege. O second Solomon.
But the Grandmaster with ten Hospitallers led the king's progress
to the court of Lateran, to catch Pope Innocent at His daily business, and to furnish Him with a public opportunity of redeeming
His apostolic promise. O child of man.[2]

---

[1] "He that goeth forth and weepeth, bearing precious seed, shall doubtless come
again with rejoicing, bringing his sheaves with him" (Ps. 126:6).
[2] Christ is referred to as both the Son of God and the Son of Man.

II. *About the Father of Princes and Kings: a great Chapter*

Our lord the Pope was discovered in His court listening to
a cluster of way-worn clergymen, who crouched at His feet on
shabby valises, and poured complaints into His ears. And His
Paternity seemed much vexed by their narrations, biting His
lips and bumping about His throne[1] with annoyance. To Whom
entered the Grandmaster and his Hospitallers, preceding my lord
the king and my lady the queen wearing their coats *quarterly*,
Hierusalem and Armorica; and their five-crossed crowns were carried by Sir Fulk the Flame and Sir Hugh the priest; and their orbs
and sceptres, by the three Roman squires and Bobo Kemp the
page. Their heralds and men-at-arms made them a path through
the mob of petitioners; and they stood in the midst of the court,
magnificent, silent, until the dusty clergymen were out of breath
with complaining. Pope Innocent's eyes blinked and glared in
opposite directions, so that it was useless to enquire which eye He
used for purposes of sight. His brow was corrugated. His hands
were very anxious. His whole aspect was that of an immeasure-
able clergyman[2] seriously upset by news of disaster. He put a
thumb to his chin; and plunged into cogitation so profound that
all looked dumbly at Him, wondering when and what His next
word would be.

King Arthur gave the Pope a quarter-of-an-hour; and then he
bade the Grandmaster to let a trumpet toot and to call attention
to his regal affairs, saying: "Most Blessed Father, here is the poor
unknown youngster, whom Your Paternity sent to do a knightly
deed, who has done it, and brings tokens of it."

Pope Innocent showed a harassed mind, an unseeing face;
and, in the dull drone of a devout despot in a dream, He enquired:
"Who may this youngster be?" Then, awfully blared the heralds' trumpets, and magniloquently responded the Grandmaster. "Blessedness," says he, "he is Sir Arthur fil-Geoffrey Plantagenet, Duke of Armorica, and the rest, and King of Hierusalem,

---

[1] *"toto corpore solium tundens."* [Rolfe's note.]
[2] *"clerici immensurabilis."* [Rolfe's note.]

betrothed to Queen Mariolanthe of the same kingdom here also present; and he comes, with crowns, and Saracen spoils, and an immense treasure, and what not, to be married and crowned and confirmed, and to claim performance of promises." Our lord the Pope leaped out of His reverie all of a sudden, as though blasted by the unexpected trumpets; and His oblique gaze concentrated like pin-points on the company before Him. "Ho," says His Paternity, "be welcome, you tall and very pale youngster. And let Us hear you make good these admirable annunciations. For it appears to Us that you are just the very one piece of concupiscence in all the world Whom We want at this moment." "Testify, o Grand-master:" curtly says my lord the king. So the Grandmaster swore his oath, as a man, and a christian, and a knight of Saint John, and a crowned and anointed sovereign of that Order; and he told the tale of Lord Arthur's three great victories over the Saracens, of his betrothal to Lady Mariol, of Queen Ysabel's abdication in their favour, of the awful earthquake at Acre, and of the coming to Rome. Pope Innocent listened, as though he was listening for His life. And, at the end, He shook Himself; and pounced upon the Queen: and "Young lady,"[1] says He, "does Your Supernity deem it a modest or respectable matter to go gadding about over half the world,[2] alone with a galaxy of youths? For We see no females in Your vicinity." This He said, being a clergyman, by way of diversion while He took time for thinking. Up, then, and answered my brave lady the queen. "Most Blessed Father," says she, "what I have done I have done for lack of ability to do better, and because it pleased me: nor am I any the worse for it, either in body or soul: nor am I sorry, but proud and glad to be with my lord where he is anywhen and anywhere." O superb response. Up, also, and speaks young Lord Valerio. "Most Blessed Father," says he, very boldly, "and may it please the Queen, let now my sister Lady Danae be brought to serve Her Regal Majesty." At that, several magnates tumbled over one another, offering their daughters with shouts: of whom were chosen the said Lady Danae Poplicola of Holy Cross, and Lady Alemena of Velletri, and Lady Mafalda

---

[1] "*Damigella.*" [Rolfe's note.]
[2] "*huc et illuc cursitare per orbis dimidium.*" [Rolfe's note.]

of Sabaudia, to be maids of Queen Mariol. "So far, so good," says our lord the Pope; "and, now, let all follow Us into Our cathedral, where We shall bless these tardy nuptials and settle these well-won crowns." And forthwith, Pope Innocent enthroned Himself in His church of Saint John of the Lateran Palace, to the immense admiration of all standing round. There, with fearful solemnity, He married the Regal Majesties: there, He crowned and sceptred and orbed them with the insignia of Hierusalem: there, He apostolically blessed them; and all the world intoned *Te Deum laudamus*.[1] "And now," says His Paternity, "what more do you want, you tall and very pale young Majesty?"

Says my lord the king, with serene imperscrutable[2] liveliness, "Deign an act of justice, o Most Blessed Father, to me, King Arthur of Hierusalem, Duke of Armorica, Duke or Earl of all sorts of other places, and only rightful heir of King Richard Lionheart: for my wicked uncle Earl John of Mortain nefariously has my inheritances." "Ho," says the Pope, "well and very well: but We seem to have heard something of this kind before. And We observe that the appetite for crowns appears to grow with the gratification thereof." Says the king, very sturdily, "What shall we settle now, Most Blessed Father, concerning my kingdom of England? For, since my Lady Mariol shares her crown of Hierusalem with me, I wish to share with her my crown of England, as becomes her true knight and loving husband." Says the Pope, teasingly, but He was perfectly benignant, "Can that already-crowned young head bear the heavy weight of yet another crown?" Says the king, most artfully, "Aye, indeed: for I will wear the crown of Hierusalem enclosed in the great crown of England, so that it shall be secure from Saracens and similar trash." Says the Pope, "These be good words enough. But, what if We give you this crown? And how will you get it when given?" Says the king, "I will get it by the aid of God, and of my Right, and of Messire Saint George, and of my treasure. And, having gotten it, I will do well with the English. And, having done well with the English, I will do well also with my kingdom of Hierusalem, faring thitherward with

---

[1] A chant beginning, "We praise Thee, O God, we acknowledge Thee to be the Lord."

[2] Inscrutable (*OED* OL).

a mighty power of my English, to drive out the infidel Saracen, and to make the Holy Land secure until the consummation of the world."[1]

Everybody burst into loud sobs of thankfulness for these high noble words, says Sir Hugh; and our lord the Pope pondered them with fearful solemnity, squinting portentously in every direction for half-an-hour. Then, He began to rattle out words like hailstones and coals of fire. "Hear now the judgment of God's Vicegerent,[2] o tall and very pale young Majesty," at length says He: "for We will no longer conceal from you, that that infernal uncle of yours has lapsed yet again into the stinking cesspool of his unutterable iniquities, where he wallows, dirty as a duck amid dunghills, while the stench of his putridity corrupts all the region round about him. But it is for the last time, Our apostolic patience being completely exhausted. We support him with benedictions for himself, with maledictions for his foes. He repays Us by plundering abbeys, defiling cathedrals, desecrating shrines, snaffling the revenues of clergymen and burning their granaries, not once nor twice, but seventy-times-seven times. Our gorge heaves at him. Our stomach molests Us at the bare mention of him. We have had enough of the mere thought of him. We abhor from, and vomit egregiously at, the very sound of his beastly name. Let all this be well-known unto you. Know you, also, that Sir Aloys of France is doing Our work for Us, menacing that Earl of Mortain: but not with Our permission. For We should not give him such permission, if We had had (as We now do seem to have) a better knight in Our society. We are, in fact, by no means fond of the said Frankish Sir Aloys: a light-minded lumpish-bodied young man he is, and much too fat all round. And We dislike his father excessively, though We have no particular motions against King Philip at this present. Wherefore, and for all these causes, Our apostolic judgment is as follows: Inprimis,[3] that Earl John of Mortain, your wicked uncle, is a usurper and an incorrigible traitor

---

[1] Arthur's offer to "drive the infidels from the Holy Land" would have sounded particularly attractive to the Pope around the time of the Fourth Lateran Council, which called for a new crusade.

[2] God's representative (OED OL).

[3] In the first place (OED OL).

deserving deposition; and We despose him:[1] Item, that if you, o
tall and very pale young Majesty, can get the crown and canopy
and kingdom of England, you may have and hold the same as
your lawful right. This, We will. So, We command. Let Our will
be sufficient reason."

"Confirm me that grant, o Most Blessed Father:" sharply says
my lord the king. "We do hereby lovingly confirm it; and now go
you and make it good:" says the Pope. "I go," says King Arthur: "I
go my own way; and I will make it good. But I go my own way;
and damned be all they who stand in it." "Amen. And a blessing be upon you all. Amen. But go quickly. Amen:" says our lord
Pope Innocent the Great. O times. O manners.

III. About King Arthur his Company

In preparation for his new emprize, King Arthur took forty
knights of the Hospital, by treaty with the Grandmaster thereof,
as wardens of his immense treasure, to have it in constant ward
with him in all his journeys, as it were his regal exchequer, of
which he named Sir Hugh the priest as his chancellor. And each
knight was attended by a man-at-arms and a squire and a page,
all of the Hospital, for dignity. This, my lord the king did, so
that anyone (swayed by the devil) who might be moved to steal
all or a part of the said treasure, should instantly incur not only
the military attention of its wardens, but, also, the blighting and
blasting bans[2] which they (as clergymen) were able to inflict on
sacrilegious marauders. My lord the king also named his amy Sir
Fulk the Flame to command his fifty mercenary men-at-arms,
as a regal bodyguard for himself and his three Roman squires,
and for Queen Mariol and her three Roman maids. And he kept
Sir Hugh as his priest as well as his chancellor, to whom he gave
Bobo Kemp the page, for comfort, that youth having manifested
(quite recently) a notable growth in grace, and a liability to hap
himself up in priestskins at the age canonical.

---

[1] Pope Innocent in fact supported John during this period, instructing the barons
to be loyal to the king and referring to the their decision to take arms against him
as criminal.

[2] *"proscriptiones flaminosas atque comburentes."* [Rolfe's note.]

IIII. *About John the Roman Page his nauseous Manners*

But my lord the king dismissed John the Roman page, on account of that one's bestial and indolent habits. So indolent, indeed, and so bestial had he become, contrary to all expectation, that he was a grave cause of scandal, specially to the English page with whom he chiefly companied. For example, he nibbled his fleas, instead of cracking them decently; and several times he was punished for ignorance, contumeliousness, and intermittent intoxication: but he persevered in his disgusting courses. One specially nasty custom of his it is my painful duty to gibbet,[1] that it may serve as a shocking example. At bed-time, instead of prudently extinguishing the candle (stuck on the wall on a candlestick) with the breath of his mouth, or with his fingers, before he clambered into bed, he was used to take off his clothes, and to lay them on the chest, but he invariably retained his shirt; and, having climbed into bed, still wearing the said shirt for warmth, he would wait till his natural heat had heated the bed: which done, he would peel off his shirt, and fling it at the candle, certainly extinguishing the light thereof, but not without soiling his shirt with the candle-snuff, and not without great risk of setting the house, or the ship-cabin, or the tent, on fire. And affectionate reprimands and very severe smackings having failed to produce more genteel manners, the said John was returned to the train of the legate from whom he had been taken. O manners.

v. *About the Fortunes of Sir Fulk the Flame*

Queen Mariol made occasion to say to King Arthur, "Sweetheart and lord, let us do something benignant to our excellent cousin Sir Fulk fil-Richard, giving him some place warmer than his little lordship of Cuigny; and let us marry him to some nice girl[2] as soon as may be. For I think that he, also, deserves to have treasures." So, the Regal Majesties took the lord of Cuigny; and

---

[1] To hold up for contempt (*OED* OL).
[2] "*et cuidam aptae puerae et eleganti eum collocamus in matrimonium.*" [Rolfe's note.]

invested him with my lord the king's own great feof of Jaffa, receiving his homage for that earldom, and naming him grandmaster of the household as well as captain of the bodyguard. Whereat Earl Fulk went out with great glee, and commanded several pairs of vermilion boots,[1] apt to an earl for constant wear. And the king and the queen eyed him thenceforward to discover upon which girl his fancy fell, so that they might make the marriage. And my lord the king says that (for some time) he found Fulk fairly fastidious.

VI. *About the End of Nicholas the Fish and about Emperors and Others*

The company went from Rome by sea to Arles in the regal galiass, with the exchequer and its wardens in a buss. And, at Arles, King Arthur parted from Nicholas the Fish, who feared hugely to leave the sea, and wept all over from every aperture (even out of his ears) at parting, though the king gave him the galiass and five gold marks for his sole use and solace. I am told that this Nicholas afterward came to a bad end: for the emperor[2] caught him, and caused him to dive for a gold cup in the raging whirlpool of Charybdis, which he retrieved once, but (the second time) a marine monster took him for a tid-bit,[3] and he was no more seen of christian men. I may say, also, that this emperor's inquisitive mind caused grave detriment to his righteousness. For, once, wishing to know whether rest was better than action after eating, he fed two robust youths quite full, and sent the one to hunt and the other to sleep for the next four hours thereafter. And, when he had assembled his chirurgeons,[4] they bound both youths securely, and removed their living entrails: from which it seemed that the sleeper had digested his victuals, but with the hunter it was otherwise.[5] And it was this very emperor whom the vile Sir John Brienne called Devil-son-of-a-Butcher. But Sir

---

[1] *"nonnulla minianorum para calceorum fieri iussit."* [Rolfe's note.]

[2] Frederick the Second.—P. and C. [Rolfe's note.]

[3] *"accipiebat eum marina belua pro cuppediis."* [Rolfe's note.]

[4] Surgeons (*OED* OL).

[5] These anecdotes seem to have been drawn from *The Chronicle of Salimbene*.

John himself, after having officiated as Emperor of Romania, became very holy at last, and died in the habit of a friar-minor.[1] O manners.

VII. *About King Arthur advancing on Armorica*

King Arthur went northward from Arles along Rhonebank on the other side, not in regal state, as he desired to go speedily. And, riding plainly through the Virelais, they were beset by the ferocious armed heretics who infest those parts and all the south country of the speech of Oc.[2] These blasphemers were for making idolators of the whole company: but the king and Earl Fulk worried them so dreadfully in the slippery postures of the Assassins, that they slew thirty with hand-chopping on the nape and abdominal or diaphragmatic digs with the hand-point; and the dead they pitched into the River Rhone, lest the stench of excommunicate carcases should afflict a christian country.

At Lyon, Archbishop Renaud of that province entertained them graciously as crusaders of quality and friends of our lord the Pope: but they told him not of how high a quality they were. And he made much of Lothario Conti the squire, bidding that youth to pray for him, giving him jam on his pudding,[3] having him to sit at table, and putting him in a bed by himself although but a squire, for he was own nephew to the Pope's Blessedness, and the archbishop was not yet a cardinal. And, on their departure, that prelate commended them to God and his nephew the earl of Nevers, to whom he gave them letters commendatory.

At Nevers, the said earl (having caused their letters to be read) housed them most handsomely: for he was minded to be his uncle's heir, and he did that clergyman's pleasure in all things. He rode with my lord the king to another of his earldoms at Auxerre, where they lay by night in the castle. Ensued a joyous match of troubadize, wherein Earl Fulk showed that he inher-

---

[1] Sir John Brienne died in the habit of a Franciscan friar.
[2] Languedoc, an area in southern France where the Cathar, or Albigensian, sect flourished in the twelfth and thirteenth centuries.
[3] "*placenta cum baccis conditis.*" [Rolfe's note.]

ited his father's art and was acclaimed as victor.[1] It chanced, also, that some of the mercenaries babbled in their cups that night; and rumour ran through the castle that the king and the queen of Hierusalem were entertained there unawares: whereupon the earl was for treating the Regal Majesties with much worship, and would even have attended them as far as Laon: but they excused him. Earl Fulk the Flame, however, to do him kindness, set out his merits in a chant-regal called *The Generous Host*, which he taught to a bald minstrel to sing to the archbishop of Lyon, who (incontinent) made his will in favour of the earl, though he did not die for many years. And, from Auxerre, they went by Troyes and Rheims to Laon, where King Philip diverted himself on a hill-top for coolth in the warm weather. And King Arthur mused much as to the method of his coming dealings with King Philip, who (as King Richard Lionheart declared) was ever a cold pig and clammy as to nape and pettitoes.[2] O manners.

VIII. *About King Arthur his Musings*

My lord the king says that he mused at this time in this manner following.

He was Duke of Armorica by inheritance, confirmed by King Richard Lionheart. He was King of Hierusalem by right and fact, confirmed by Pope Innocent the Great. He was also, by right, King of the English, Lord of Wales and of Ireland, Duke of Normandy and Gascony and Acquitaine, Earl of Anjou and Maine and Touraine and Poictou, Overlord of Toulouse and Auvergne and Antioch and Armenia, and the rest. But, of these, he was master of none, saving that he was crowned of Hierusalem, which was afar; and usurpers occupied his crowns and canopies in all the others. How, then, to acquire his own? Specially, how to pluck the crown of England from his wicked uncle? He had no place whence to start on such an emprize. No land, no city even, acknowledged him as its lord: no prince was of his alliance: only the Pope approved him. He might wear his ermine of Armorica:

---

[1] Richard the Lionheart composed several songs in French and Provençal.
[2] Pig's feet (*OED* OL).

but his second step-father Thouars ruled that duchy for his half-sister Lady Alys. He might wear his broom-sprig of Anjou: but King Philip the August held that earldom with Normandy and Maine and Touraine. And John Softsword held England and Wales and Ireland and Gascony and Acquitaine. It would be well to oust Philip. It was imperative to oust John. None but a fool would instantly claim the lands which Philip held. Yet, something short of a claim might be attempted. The Pope was his friend, not Philip's. And Philip's title to Normandy and the four earldoms was very fragile: he had but escheated them from John, who usurped them, and had no claim even to lose them. Moreover, in presence of the rightful heir, the judgment of the Frankish court of magnates (transferring them to Philip) would be null, specially if the Pope were to set canonists and civilists of Paris to find flaws in the said judgment. And the Pope might favour a crusading king of Hierusalem, as a friend.[1] Beside, Philip himself might grant investiture of feofs which he neither held nor might hope to hold. It would be quite in that cold pig's best manner to get himself well-paid for giving nothing, or for giving something which was not his to give. But he would never help the purchaser to get what he had bought. O scorbutic.

My lord the king settled that he must have, at the very least, one place, one port, whence he might spring upon England. He must have Armorica, since Philip had Normandy and was most unlikely to part from it. How to get Armorica. Mark the masterly device. My lord the king planned to go to King Philip, and to take that cold pig unawares, and suddenly to renew his homage (before witnesses) for all feofs which he could possibly claim to hold from the Frankish crown. This, done, could not be undone. Then, he would bargain away his rights over Normandy, Maine, Touraine, Anjou, even Poictou if necessary, in return for recognition of his rights in Armorica and Acquitaine and Gascony, with leave to raise armies in King Philip's country for ousting the usurpers of those three poor duchies. That was the first step. The second was far more important, being no less than a coali-

---

[1] "et Pontifex ut amico accommodaret regi Hierosolymitano bellum sanctum estienti." [Rolfe's note.]

tion between the power of the victor of Armorica and the power
which Hubert de Burgh was collecting for that one in England.
But the first step must be taken speedily, speedily, speedily. And
Philip must not suspect that England was in question. That fat
Aloys, prematurely wedded to a Spanish lady,[1] and the mirror of
fashion, whose moppings and mowing and mincings were mim-
icked by all monkey-men of the Frankish court, that said fat Aloys
had just landed in Kent, it was said, and was trying to persuade an
English bishop to anoint him as king of the English as the Franks
already called him. No: King Philip must not be made unhappy
about England. Nor must Sir Guy Thouar learn of one on the way
to upset him, lest he should raise the duchy of Armorica and initiate state-riving civil war. Nor must Softsword become ware of
what was toward, lest he should bray the business out to all the
world, with the foaming of rabies and the kickings and plungings
of wild-assishness.

VIIII. *About King Arthur Lefthand and King Philip the August*

My lord the king rode into Laon, under safe-conduct from
the bishop of Troyes commending the company through the
country; and he lay at the inn of The Golden Lily. And, when he
and Earl Fulk were washed and dressed in clean garments, they
rode to the castle, where the said safe-conduct procured their
admission. But King Arthur left commandment that his power
be ready to ride at dawn, being at the gate and passing out as
soon as it was opened. The two at first entertained themselves at
the end of the hall, listening to the fools and minstrels, or chat-
ting with magnates. They called themselves Angevins, crusaders,
newly arrived from the Holy Land; and they gave no new news
of it, and were deemed dull. But news, new and vital, was given
to them: for one spoke of a report from oversea that Sir Aloys
had been anointed at Westminster by the legate: which another
denied, saying that it must needs be false, seeing that the Pope
had withdrawn the legate from England. A third, however, had
other news, brought hot foot to the king that very evening by way

---

[1] Louis VIII was married to Blanche de Castile at the age of twelve.

of Calais: Sir Roger Baudricourt, *or, three baldrics tranched azure*, brought it at the behest of Sir Aloys, and it was that the magnates had pulled Softsword off the throne, but not before he had desperately caused Henry Lackland, his only legitimate son, to be crowned at York as joint-king. Also, 'twas said that John no longer called himself king: some said that he had gone into religion as a Cistercian, gone to hell said others, or in a dungeon, but at any rate he had retired from business as king, and Henry Lackland, happed up in his kingskins, held all the North Country.[1] Such was the news; and, when the teller affirmed that it was the same as that which Sir Roger had given to the clammy-souled pig under the canopy, then, my lord the king bade his cousin to do what had been determined. Earl Fulk said secretly to the marshal that the Regal Majesty of the King of Hierusalem desired to confer in love and amity with his cousin King Philip the August. Whereat the marshal, dreadfully worried by so high and sudden an annunciation, would have denied him, alleging the lateness of the hour and the absence of adequate trumpets for the reception of majesty. But Earl Fulk became very vermilion and made himself larger than usual,[2] squashing the marshal considerably, and saying that when King Philip was ware of his comportment he would certainly be gravely amerced[3] and perhaps tormented. So, proclamation sent everyone flying from the neighbourhood of the canopy, excepting the Frankish king and his archbishop Roger de Rossy of Rheims.

x. *About King Arthur his Arrangement with the King of the Franks*

King Arthur Lefthand, attended by Earl Fulk the Flame, emerged from the mob, kneeled to King Philip seizing his hands, and he said, without any fuss and as quickly and clearly as possible, "I, Sir Arthur Plantagenet, son of Sir Geoffrey Longcheek and Lady Constance of Armorica, hereby renew my homage, which I did to thee, my lord king Philip, at Gournay, on the Fes-

---

[1] Henry III was not crowned until his father died in October of 1216. He was at the time only nine years old.
[2] *"etiam maiorem quam solitum se faciens."* [Rolfe's note.]
[3] Punished (*OED* OL).

tival of Messire Saint Martin,[1] for my duchies of Armorica and
Acquitaine and Gascony, for my earldoms of Maine and Touraine
and Anjou and Poictou, for all their rights and jurisdictions and
prerogatives and powers, and I am thy true man therefor, I and
my successors after me to thee and thy successors after thee." And
he rose, as swiftly as he had kneeled, and kissed the Frank on both
chops, calling archbishop Roger and Earl Fulk to witness that this
homage, done lawfully, renewed his right to the feofs with which
he had previously been invested.

Earl Fulk says that it is hard to imagine a more portentous
figure of fun than King Philip at that moment. Expecting to see
the King of Hierusalem, the only person (with his cognizance)
liable to appear in that capacity was Sir John Brienne. Instead,
comes the Lord Arthur, several years murdered and (by now) perfectly putrid, as he believed: the sight of whose ghost bourgeoning with the freshness of youth and the vigour of majesty, and
the irremediable act of homage so neatly and poignantly paid to
him, almost unhinged his mind. And, "La-la-la-la," he stuttered:
for he never could say the right thing at the right time to the
right person.[2] But King Arthur, well ware that he would serve his
purpose best by being very affable, pretended not to notice that
cold pig's perturbation; and he went on, talking quickly, telling
the tale of his doings, unravelling mysteries which puzzled King
Philip, till that Frank, freed from fright, seemed able to converse
with some propriety. And my lord the king spoke as much for the
archbishop's ear-hole as for his regal cousin's. King Philip's first
idea, when he had recollected his senses, was to find some pretext wherewith to save his face, if necessary. "But what," says he,
"majesty and cousin, what if the duchies and earldoms (wherefor
you do this abrupt homage) are otherwise occupied?" "In that
case, cousin and majesty," says the regal Lefthand, "they must be
occupied by traitors pestilent to you, my liege, as well as to me;
and I will take your permission to deal horribly with them." King
Philip laughed vacantly, which (perhaps) was the best thing he
could do. The archbishop was gazing very assiduously at my lord

---

[1] November 11.

[2] *"enim iste rex nec cui nec quod nec quando oportebat dicere non poterat."* [Rolfe's
note.]

the king, radiant in his careless youth and beauty: for that prelate had pleasure in seeing a devil-descended[1] Plantagenet and a king of Hierusalem in fleshly form, both breeds being very famous and (in those old days) quite rare. And King Arthur saw that he might count the archbishop as favourably disposed, and like to be useful. "But," says the Frank, "We ourself hold Anjou and Touraine; and Sir Guy Thouars has done homage for Armorica on his girl's behalf; and a certain wicked uncle of yours holds the rest, though We admit that he stands attainted and holds those feofs contumaciously in Our despite. And, majesty and cousin, in comparison with these, who, and what, are you?" "Once a king in fact, by Grace of God and Favour of the Siege Apostolical, once a king in right, by the will of King Richard Lionheart, thrice a duke and four-times an earl, by homage to my liege King Philip, seeing which, all tenures in my despite are feudal malfeasances, and null:" says my lord the king. "But, by our Lady's Lily, what about Maine and Touraine and Anjou and Poictou, sweet boy?" says King Philip. "I confess that I have been absent over-long from my feofs," says King Arthur; and he flashed his glance at the archbishop with awful and admirable significance, continuing, "and perchance," says he, "if the Church, to Whom I hereby appeal, should so adjudicate, I would pay a reasonable fine for neglecting my feudal service." Magnificent stratagem.

XI. *About King Arthur haggling for Armorica*

I have noticed this queer trait in the customs of clergymen: the higher they are in the ecclesiastical hierarchy, the less capable do they become of doing anything at all, voluntarily, spontaneously, of their own unaided force and volition. A poor plain priest puts on his own apparel. A bishop has to be dressed, even to his buskins and galligaskins; and a lighted candle follows him everywhere, to enable him to read things known by rote out of his book in broad daylight. An archbishop is thus, yea and more also, seeming to doze continuously, and having to be goaded by nudges

---

[1] The Plantagenet family legend was "From the devil we sprang, and to the devil we shall go."

and replenished with words put into his very mouth, when it is indispensable that he should recite his little piece. And a cardinal slumbers, sweetly, or stertorously (according to his habit of body and the position of his previous pudding), all the time, uttering what he has to utter, and doing what no smaller clergyman than he can do, as it were in the deep depth of his dreams, when some knowing person excitedly pokes him or pinches him.[1]

Archbishop Roger of Rheims, then, having performed his archiepiscopal yawns, was already snoozing (so it seemed) in the proper archiepiscopal manner. Perceiving which, Earl Fulk placed himself nearer, so that he might jog the prelate into action at a fitting time. This, he did, when my lord the king made his appeal to the Church. And the archbishop lethargically intoned in response, saying, "The Church notes the appeal, withholding judgment till the case be argued." And he sank back in his ritual slumbers. The two kings set to haggling like hucksters. King Philip was eager to grasp a chance of legalizing his own usurpation of the four earldoms: for the judgment of the Frankish court of magnates against Softsword, which had been his pretext for resuming them, was indubitably invalid in presence of the rightful heir of them. And King Arthur, by straining after Armorica (which he called his dear motherland) while appearing quite careless of the earldoms, prevented the Frank from imagining that he really was aiming at England. And the archbishop nodded, napping, emitting satisfactory and stately snores at intervals all the time.[2] At last, making it a great concession, King Arthur agreed to pay a fine to King Philip, consisting of the four earldoms with his rights over Auvergne and the Toulousain and his claims upon

---

[1] "pecularitatem quamdam in clericis moribus notaui. sic fit ut quo magis sit honorabilis gradus eorum in hierarchia ecclesiastica eo minus possint quicquid uoluntate et sponte sua alieno sine impetu efficere, presbyter uir pauper et perhumillis se uestit ipse. episcopo oportet ut alj uestimenta etiam in partibus inferioribus in ducant eumque candela accensa quocumque sequitur scilicet ut librum suum et pleno solis lumine legere possit. archiepiscopo eodem modo fit et iam plura: uidetur enim obdormire et quandocunque libellum suum recitare oporteat molibus assistentium somno diuellitur ut et uerba aliorum dicat in os eius inserantur. et cardinalis continue dormitat seu dulce seu stertorose secundum corporis habitum" etc. [Rolfe's note.]

[2] "et archiepiscopus dormitans nutauit emittens placentes fastuososque sterterationes interuallis omni tempore." [Rolfe's note.]

Normandy: this cost him nothing, for of none of these feofs was
he seized or in joyance. And the fat cold Frank, also as a great
concession, then and there invested my lord the king with the
duchies of Armorica and Acquitaine and Gascony, nearly all of
which were held by his greatest enemy and the rest by a disloyal
stiff-necked vassal. And the archbishop, having dreamed of how
the cat was jumping (as they say),[1] awoke to semi-consciousness
when Earl Fulk administered a shoulder-pinch, and pronounced
the fine to be just, and the payment ample, and the matter settled
in the Name of The Trinity, with the Church's benison[2] freely
imparted to the high contracting parties, names forgotten. Confirmation upon vellum ensued, my lord the king being insistent,
so that he might have proof to give to Thouars of his disseizin[3]
from the duchy of Armorica. And, while the chancellor tediously
affixed the great seal over King Philip's manual, carefully knotting the strings, the said high contracting parties conversed with
Earl Fulk and the archbishop (now awake) in affable love, regarding the recent notable increase of leprosy and the similar scarcity
of herons for sport. Ensued also much talk of the crusade; and my
lord the king let his regal cousin know what was good for him
to know and no more. And he said naught about his visitation
of Musse: for the Frankish king simply crept with frigid terror at
any mention of the Old Man of the Mountain. And King Philip
enquired, as though by sudden inspiration, where Queen Mariol
might be. So Fulk the Flame, fancying that the Frank looked
slightly sly, instantly responded, before his amy's ingenuousness
could betray the fact, saying that Her Regal Majesty had gone
under escort to Bec in Normandy, having a mind to prepare her
soul at that abbey for her coronation as Duchess of Armorica.
This he said, suspecting that the clammy-necked pig intended to
demand her as hostage for King Arthur's leal behaviour, which
would have been both awkward and intolerable for my lord the
king. And, King Arthur having promised an Armorican bishopric
to any red-haired nephew over sixteen years old of archbishop

---

[1] "*et archiepiscopus qui in somniis interim uiderat quomodo saliret felis ut aiunt.*"
[Rolfe's note.]
[2] Blessing (*OED* OL).
[3] Dispossession (*OED* OL).

Roger whom that clergyman might desire to settle in life, the two came away with what they went for. O times. O manners.

xii. *About King Arthur in Armorica*

My lord the king rode from Laon at dawn, and came to Compiègne in the evening by way of Soissons. Next day, he rode to Beaumont through Germont, passing Gisors at noon; and he lay at Les Andelys under Saucy Castle that night, which he spent in cursing Softsword, the lecherous and bestial niddering who lost it and Normandy with it. And, in the morning, King Arthur came by Louvier to the abbey of Bec. Here, he bestowed his Hospitallers with the bulk of his exchequer. Here, also, he left the queen, for safety's sake, though much against her will: but he let her know that damsels of her sort were impediments when the winning of a duchy by the sword was concerned; and he pledged faith to her that he would work hard and late and fast to have her by his side again. The same day, having left the queen praying for his success with a flurried abbess and forty obsequious nuns buzzing in her vicinity, he pushed right on to Argentau over a vile road by way of Bernay, and came on the morrow to Domfront where he bought two-hundred horses and forty mercenaries at a fair, to the amazement of all roundstanders. He and his mercenaries drove a hundred horses, next morning, to Mayence, where he bought sixty new mercenaries: but Earl Fulk took a hundred horses to Alençon with twenty of the king's men-at-arms: and he bought seventy mercenaries there. And the two companies met at Laval, collecting yet forty more mercenaries on the way thither: for the whole country was creeping with cotterels out of work and lusty young farmers ruined by the last war. Having thus in his hand a power of two-hundred mounted men-at-arms and thirty footmen, my lord the king went on as far as Loirou, where he lay for the rest of the day, bidding his company to sleep, it being too hot to ride in the sunlight. And he crossed the march of Armorica by night, pressing by Chastelgiron, and coming into a bosky[1] glade unfrequented by lepers, where he lay through the next day, having captured three peasants whose malignant stars caused them to per-

---

[1] Bushy (*OED* OL).

ceive and to shout about him. King Arthur rode, at dusk, to the gate of Rennes called Mordelaise, coming thither about an hour after sunset; and, for this last journey, he donned his ermine coat and let display his banner of Armorica. When they approached the gate, and cried to open in the Duke's Name, the warder (peeping out) saw ducal ermine and ducal banner silvery white in the twilight, and, thinking of no treachery nor ware of any duke save Thouars, he opened the gate; and King Arthur with his power rode into the city. So soon as all were passed in and the gate occupied, the warder was about to be laid by the heels, when, lo, he recognized the son of Geoffrey Longcheek, and he seized King Arthur's knee, praising God for letting him live to see the instauration[1] of his native Duke, beseeching leave to raise the city for Duke Arthur, seeing that all the duchy groaned (he said) for a legitimate sovereign. And my lord the king gave order accordingly, riding onward swiftly by the cathedral to the castle, having learned at Domfront and Laval that his step-father and half-sister lay there. Now the castle was held by a very small garrison: for the duchy was not rich, and the duke-regent was poor, and no one had the faintest idea that radical changes were at hand. So, King Arthur sent Julius Cesarini, his squire, in a herald's tabard, to proclaim his arrival and to let Sir Guy Thouars know that he was destituted from the duchy in favour of its legitimate duke. Meanwhile, my lord the king detached sixty of his cotterels under Lord Valerio Poplicola of Holy Cross, his squire, to take over all the towers in his name; and yet other thirty cotterels under Lothario Conti his squire (nineteen were Armorican autochthones[2]) were instructed to go with the Warder to raise the city, crying that Duke Arthur fil-Geoffrey had come to his own again. And all this was well-done.

XIII. *About King Arthur his Conquest of Armorica*

In the castle, Sir Guy Thouars by chance was diverting himself with troubadize and minstrelsy, he being a light-minded knight

---

[1] Restoration (*OED* OL).
[2] "Sons of the soil," or original inhabitants (*OED* OL).

addicted to raptures. And, as it seemed good to his chamberlain
to delay King Arthur's herald, the first annunciation of the state
of things came from a howling and screeching population, who
pervaded the streets and the market-place, applauding the accession of Duke Arthur, and demanding the vital organs of Thouars.
Hearing which, and not understanding the purport of the noise,
that Regent gave order to turn out the guard and to scourge the
crowd within doors: but, suddenly becoming ware that the shoutings were treasonable, incontinent he smashed his arch-luth,[1] and
had himself put in armour. Then, only, did the chamberlain (a
most pitiable fellow) think fit to announce King Arthur's herald,
who spoke up boldly, intoning exciting tidings. Sir Guy, in a fuss,
cries, "Where is this posthumous spawn of Longcheek's, if not
long since in hell; and, what may his power be at this time of
day?" "He is here, and he holds this city:" says Cesarini shortly
and sharply. "Then, by The Lord God's Back,[2] I am betrayed,"[3]
shrieks the Frankish-like Regent; and he bellowed for what there
were of men-at-arms. Fourteen stolidly tramped in. Says Sir Guy:
"We are trapped, as in some hole of hell, by a devil from the dead.
Yet, perchance, we may break out of the city, for, may be, he has
not had the wit to keep the gate." Everybody ran downstairs, Sir
Guy planning to escape to Nantes, where was a great castle, and,
moreover, on the road to Thouars, where he might raise a power
of his own tenants. But to go by stealth, as he wished, was impossible: for all Rennes was up in arms against him, and very joyfully,
he being a hard knight, unjust, light-minded, cruel, and detested
by all respectable people. So, his only chance lay in sudden sally,
wherein he would not be incommoded by Lady Alys his daughter, whom he happily left behind, ware that none would harm so
sweet a maid, and thinking to bargain for her (if she was held as
hostage), or to sell her in marriage for Nantes or some other lord-
ships, if his affair should turn out badly. And he paid no attention
to the herald Julius Cesarini admonishing him for God's Sake not
to be a silly fool: but he, and his power of fourteen, mounted in
the castle-court, armed from head to foot and with lances in rest:

---

[1] Archlute, a large lute that plays bass notes.
[2] "*Dozdedompnede.*" [Rolfe's note.]
[3] "*proditus sum.*" [Rolfe's note.]

and they charged, through the suddenly-opened gates, into the thick of King Arthur's power outside, breaking the line by sheer unexpected ferocity. And he would certainly have got clear, but that my lord the king had (by God's Grace) been moved to hold the gate of the city. So, Sir Guy made a stand there. Three times, King Arthur offered him life: three times he refused it, cursing my lord the king for a bastard, who, blazing with Angevin anger and Plantagenet passion, instantly slew him for the honour of Lady Constance, in which pious act he was helped by a rampageous burgess, who dexterously hamstringed Sir Guy's horse from below with a bill,[1] causing him to lose his seat.[2] And the said burgess and his heirs (by cognomen Apxequypec) to this day enjoy coat-armour, *ermine, a bill proper*, and a manor, whereof the feudal tenure is a hamstrung water-beetle on a pewter platter annually on the Festival of the Epiphany. In this manner was conquered the city of Rennes and the duchy of Armorica.

XIIII. *About King Arthur and Lady Alys and Earl Fulk the Flame*

King Arthur rode into the castle, acclaimed as lawful duke; and, when he had entered the hall and was seated beneath his canopy, there was an appearance of trumpets and women-folk wailing and waving their sleeves; and the chamberlain, starting to serve his new master, proclaimed the coming of Lady Alys. Her half-brother and sovereign took her in his arms, all frightful and trembling. She was the daintiest little duck in the world,[3] with a skin like mother-of-pearl, so white it was, so flushed with delicate pinkish fluctuations. Black as night were her hair and the wonderful eyelashes fringing her great grey eyes. A sylph she was, perfect, just marriageable, and shy with her fifteen years. My lord the king said that she was precisely what he would have chosen for a sister; and he embraced her, called her his, kissed her, told her to cheer up for her father had just died fighting very creditably, and that he was her dear brother who would now protect her. At which, says my lord the king, Earl Fulk the Flame improvisedly coughed

---

[1] A military weapon.
[2] Sir Guy Thouars actually died in 1213.
[3] *"exquisitiosima erat mundi deliciola."* [Rolfe's note.]

and choked, perturbing many, who took it for a portent. And King
Arthur kissed his sister again, frowning so awfully at her ladies
the while, that they beckoned her trumpets and led her away.

xv. *About King Arthur Duke of Armorica*

King Arthur, sitting in his hall of Rennes, received the homage
of burgesses with their mayor, ordained the defence of city and
duchy, took in hand the government, issued writs of summons to
the estates, prepared for the funeral of Sir Guy on the morrow and
for his own ducal coronation on the day after, all as to the manner
born. Sir Guy de Thouars had sepulture in awful and sinful pomp,
with my lord the king and Lady Alys following his feretory[1] as
mourners: the order being that he should have a burial becoming
a husband of Lady Constance and step-father of the duke-regnant.
Furthermore, he had a vast tomb with his mailed effigy thereon,
and a blazon of armouries, with his canopy supported by the
twenty-four saints of Armorica, and a chantrey[2] attached in the
same cathedral with a priest to sacrifice daily till the world's end
for his soul's refreshment *in refrigerium*.[3] But so sprightly a funeral
has been seldom seen: for all the folk went wild for Duke Arthur,
kissing the silver boot on his hallowed foot as he rode among
them, and invoking benedictions in their Welsh language which
they speak among themselves, though their wealthier burgesses
use the Frankish tongue as well.

My lord the king got his coronet and unction as Duke of
Armorica from the bishops of Rennes and Dol and Saint-Malo:
but the other Armorican bīps had not yet come up, excepting
him of Saint-Brieux whose goitre choked him. And Earl Fulk
stood by the canopy; and my lord the king perceived that he was
making eyes (of a solemnity and magnitude and greenness hitherto believed impossible) at Lady Alys all the time. And the Duke
proclaimed from the high altar in Welsh and Latin. And he swore
to abide by the franchise of the duchy and the lawful liberties of

---

[1] Bier (*OED* OL).
[2] A chapel endowed with priests to sing daily mass for the founders of the church
or for others specified (*OED* OL).
[3] A "refrigerium" is a respite granted to the souls of the damned (*OED* OL).

the lieges, which oath he faithfully kept all the days of his life, to my certain knowledge. And he received the homage of magnates, whose names are more Welsh than real Welsh names, and far too Welsh for me to write though my lord the king has often spelled them to me every one.

xvi. *About Lady Alys and Earl Fulk fil-Richard*

On the fifth day, Queen Mariol came from Bec with the regal exchequer in charge of Sir Hugh the Chancellor and the Hospitallers; and, when she had gotten her new coronet as Duchess-Consort, there was a solemnity of crown-wearing and a parliament of the estates of the duchy. But, before the crown-wearing, the king and the queen exchanged their news; and the result of this was that Queen Mariol made use of her eyes while she sat enthroned beneath the ducal canopy; and the result of that was a word which she whispered to King Arthur; and the result of the said word I will now proceed abruptly and without tergiversation to narrate.

Duke Arthur made an oration to the council, saying that he wished to have it declared that the duchy was vested in his person for life and for ever, and, that, lest the said duchy should be encumbered by such a person who would covet to aspire to it, whom the subjects of the duchy could not find it in their hearts to love, dread, and obediently serve, as their sovereign lord, the crowns of Hierusalem and Armorica should never again be united after he himself had ascended to the superiors, he having power to limit the crownlet of the said duchy, by letters patent, or by his last will made in writing and sealed over his hand, to such person or persons in possession or remainder and after such order or condition as he should judge expedient. And he said, also, that he confirmed the great earldom of Nantes to his half-sister Lady Alys as heiress of Sir Guy Thouars. And he said, further, that he gave the said Countess Alys of Nantes to his loyal cousin and amy Earl Fulk fil-Richard of Jaffa, in lawful marriage, as a pledge of affection, desiring to have the said earl as a brother-in-law. At this, Earl Fulk the Flame (more flaming than ever) took Lady Alys by the hand in the sight of all (but she was by no means unwilling); and he led her to the nearest bishop (him of Dol), loudly demanding dispensation from any impediment of consanguinity which might be, so that betrothal could be effected then and there. Whom the bishop blandly denied, saying that no dispensations were necessary since bastardy over-rode bloodkinship. But King Arthur, risking no risks, insisted; and was obeyed; and the betrothal was done next.[1]

XVII. *About the King-Duke his Appetite for England*

At the parliament of the estates, all the Duke's will as stated above was confirmed; this, from sheer joy, because the said Duke was young, strong, resplendent, sacrosanct, native-born, and *ducalissimus*. Also, a three-tenths was voted for his comfort, as well as the usual feudal aid; and the clergymen gave him a four-fifteenths and the mayor of Rennes offered two hundred gold marks in a bason in the name of the city.[2] Earl Fulk married Lady Alys, half-sister to the King-Duke's Regal Majesty, in the morning; and, having done homage for her earldom of Nantes, the pair rode away to be seized of it, returning on the fourth day. For, my lord the king yearned to win England, now that he was secure of Armorica; and his regal exchequer was already increased by payment of part of the aid due, as well as his tenths and fifteenths.

END OF THE FIRST TOME, CALLED FAITH

---

[1] Philip actually arranged for Alix of Thouars to marry Pierre Mauclerc of Dreux in 1213.

[2] "Tenths" and "fifteenths" are taxes imposed on property as a form of royal subsidy (*OED* OL).

THE SECOND TOME, CALLED HOPE

XIIII

THE BOOK CALLED THE THIRD CROWN

1. About King Arthur in England

King Arthur brought so many cotterels and hired so many ships, that his port of Saint-Malo seemed to be the starting-point for another Conquest like that of the Great Bastard of old.[1] Departing out of Armorica, he left Queen Mariol as duchess-regent with Countess Alys of Nantes and Jaffa, to console and to be consoled; and with him there went Earl Fulk and his household with a hundred knights, squires, pages, and two-thousand men-at-arms. On the day of embarkation, he sent embassadors to the king of the Franks, advising that liege of his successful coronation and dutiful allegiance as Duke of Armorica. And he gave out to his power that he was making a campaign in Flanders under the Frankish king, so that news of his actual intention should not excite undesirable alertness in England. But, having sailed by Aurigny and northern Normandy, my lord the king kept his ships on their course instead of steering eastward; and he sent signals to each ship saying that he had had a vision of Messire Saint George desiring to see a really good blow struck at the usurper of England. Whereat, those of his power who still possessed themselves (for most were vomiting) contrived wide smiles, or emitted most blissful shoutings. For the weather was foul; and the passage occupied four days; and very grievous melancholy was caused by the instability of the sea. One knight, indeed, by name Sir Theoul Ploubarzlanezque, *paly, vert and or,* leaped incontinent overboard, but whether by reason of excessive displeasure of retching, or of a spasm of mania, or of an irresistible temptation of mermaids, it is impossible to decide. But his companions (as far as circumstances permitted) bewailed

---

[1] William the Conqueror is also referred to as William the Bastard.

him till the fleet reached Yarmouth in Wight, in a sea-fog, being miraculously protected (as no one can doubt) by Messire Saint George, the patron of knights and security in stormy seas. And, on the morn of the fifth day, King Arthur sailed up the Water to Southampton in a chilly calm.

II. *About King Arthur his Artfulness with the Shire-reeve*

My lord the king debarked his power outside the city: for the gates were closed against him, though no one dared to hinder his landing. And, all being on firm earth, and well-supplied with pudding, and arrayed in line, King Arthur also landed with acclamations. He wore a new coat of England and Armorica and Hierusalem in vermilion and gold and ermine and silver; and he wore a boot of silver tissue on his hallowed left foot, and a glove of the same on his hallowed right hand; and he wore a gilded helmet on his head, quite contrary to his custom and for a special reason, which helmet was insigned with his token of the Angevin broom-sprig having two pods and three leaves. When Sir Hugh the chancellor had sung mass, it was seen that a shire-reeve was approaching: twenty archers attended him, desiring to know what was portended. But the peace was kept, for King Arthur instantly sent him a safe-conduct; and he came on, into the midst of the array. And, advancing up the beach to meet him, as far as the place where green grass begins to oust the sand and mud, came the Regal Majesty, alone. Fulk says that this moment was of such solemnity that the whole power gasped for more breath. King Arthur swung his long-sword from his shoulders, brandishing it in his invincible left hand, to north and south and west and east, like the glittering tails of comets trailed across the sky; and he cried clearly "By God and my Right," for all to hear. And, with his long-sword, he cut a turf.

Then, Earl Fulk led up his horse; and he vaulted on the saddle, holding up the turf for all to see, crying clearly for all to hear, "I, Arthur, King of the English, have taken seizin of my kingdom of England." Next, my lord the king removed the broom-sprig from his helmet, dashing the helmet to the ground; and he cried clearly, saying, "I, Arthur, King of the English, make vow to God and to Madame Saint Mary the God-bearer and to Messire Saint George of England that I will no more cover this my head but with my undisputed crown of England." Now there was a golden fillet[1] round his head, confining his yellow-silver hair; and, in this fillet, he twisted the broom-sprig, proclaiming it as his badge and token. And his power most mightily acclaimed him. But, as yet, he had no Englishmen in his array.

King Arthur Lefthand, knowing that it is the first step which counts, rode toward the shire-reeve, demanding whether that one's conscience would serve him so far as to let him give allegiance to the Lionheart's only rightful heir. And, says the said obese person, glumly, in a quandary, "Who may Your Spectability be?" Says my lord the king: "I am Arthur the King." "Then," says the shire-reeve, "you are the fourth of that style now in England. Yet I will give allegiance to you, as to those others: for I perceive that you have a power and a fair face, in which last you have the advantage of your rivals." So he bended over his saddle-bow and recited his piece: which done, he was for babbling garrulously, explaining that, if he seemed half-hearted, it was due to the fact that he was most dreadfully worried, for he truly desired to be leal to a true king of the English, and he had been named reeve of the shire of Southampton by a certain King John (called Softsword), who, seemingly was not now any more a king, even if he had ever been one, on which point there were grave discussions: but, later, letters had come from a certain King Henry (called Lackland), and from a certain King Aloys (called God-only-knew-what, and gravely suspected of being a black man with a long tail like an ape), both declaring themselves to be kings of the English, decrying all others as pretenders, and demanding allegiance. Last of all, confusion worse confounded, came word that he must hold his shire ready to declare for John as king yet once again. Wherefore, he durst not pretend that his mind was not in danger of becoming unhinged, when a fourth arrives, saying "I am King of the English." King Arthur, only a boy, laughed cheerfully; and, "O Shire-reeve," says he, "my mind also would become unhinged, were I not myself one of these same tetrarchs. But, help me a little,

---

[1] A headband or ribbon used to bind the hair (OED OL).

now; and together we will clear your doubts away with those
other three: for one of them is a puddock,[1] and another is a foreign cockerel, and the third is a damned devil severely censured
by our lord the Pope, and not one of them is rightful king of the
English." The shire-reeve (that stolid heavy bladder of pudding)
was not more than half satisfied. "God damn all foreigners:" says
he, and spat hard at the ground. "Amen:" says my lord the king.
"A true Englishman boggles not when he says the *Twister*, the
which no damned foreigner can say without tying fifteen knots
in his damned tongue:" says the shire-reeve, blinking slyly with
a rustic's cunning, but withal somewhat doubtfully. King Arthur
exploded with such a triumphant shout of boyish laughter, that
everyone eyed him intensely. "Hear Me, then, Shire-reeve; and
tell me whether I be a true Englishman, or no:" says my admirable lord the king. And he intoned the old rhyming incantation
against hiccoughs,[2] with which, by God's Infinite Mercy (so he
told me), his mother Duchess Constance had imbued him in his
tenderest infancy, little thinking of what signal service it would
prove to him on the verge of his manhood. And he said, all in a
single breath, crying clearly for all to hear,

> *If a twister (twisting) would twist him a twist,*
> *for twisting a twist four twists he must twist;*
> *but, if one of the twists untwists from the twist,*
> *then the twist (untwisting) untwists the twist.*

And, instantly, the shire-reeve burst into boisterous blubberings,
and fell raging upon his archers. "Acclaim the King of the English, ye lobs:" says he. So they acclaimed King Arthur.

And I narrate this as a specimen of my lord the king's superhuman quickness of wit, to snatch (out of his rich mind's remot-
est chamber) the one and only thing essential at the moment for
gaining him an advantage. Every other man in the world would

---

[1] A bird of prey. When used in reference to a person, this term is meant to indicate
that the person in question is rapacious (*OED* OL).

[2] Most tongue twisters originated as antidotes to hiccups. In order for the charm
to be effective, the whole twister must be said in one breath. See James Orchard
Halliwell, *The Nursery Rhymes of England* (London: 1886), 137-140.

not have understood the test so slightly and so unexpectedly proffered, or would have forgotten, or (at best) would have produced a botch. But, as with his supple limbs and his elastic body, so with his flexible and prudent mind, King Arthur was lord of himself, and (so) of much land beside. Is it any wonder that he, the Hope of England, hoped with good hope of winning England? O most affable reader, is it?

The shire-reeve loyally escorted the Regal Majesty into his city of Southampton. The King sat in his state, with his canopy and fifty trumpets, in the Bargate, receiving homage, which the folk did very willingly at the shire-reeve's bidding: for the whole kingdom was in such a muck of faction, and John and Henry and Aloys were such rotters,[1] that everyone was glad to hail that clean bright boy as king.

III. *About Queen Mariol her Artfulness with the Primate*

No sooner had her lord and lover left her, than the Duchess-regent of Armorica mopped her cheeks, and set her wits to find what service she might do for him on her side of the narrow sea. And she found that the Primate Stephen, in Frankish exile, would be like to jump at a chance of getting out of the Pope's bad books[2] (whereinto a parcel of sneaking aliens had thrust him) by supporting that king of the English who was flourishing in the said Pope's favour. So, she sent a Hospitaller to the Cardinal-Primate Langthon, with a message advising him of King Arthur's progress, and of matters necessary for him to know. And Stephen, well ware of the worth of this opportunity, instantly collected a handful of clergymen, to support his archiepiscopality and to gauffre[3] the embroidery of his cardinalature; and he sailed for England in a fishing-boat, praying hard, and arriving at Southampton at the

---

[1] *"et tam tabidi sunt Johannes et Henricus et Aloysius."* [Rolfe's note.]

[2] When Stephen Langton refused to excommunicate the rebel barons according to the Pope's instructions, Innocent denounced Langton as an accomplice of the disturbers of the kingdom, and the papal commissioners suspended the archbishop.

[3] To "gauffer" or "goffer" is to flute or crimp the edges of lace or trimmings of any kind (*OED* OL).

moment when my lord the king was quitting that city for Winchester. Whom King Arthur received as a king should receive his primate, and as Langthon never yet had been received, namely, with the open arms and the blooming cheek of love and amity and the bent knee of respect. And so it came about that, in Winchester, Arthur King of the English Everywhere was hallowed and anointed and proclaimed from the rood-screen[1] by the Primate of All England, in English and in Latin, after the Bull of Pope Innocent anathematizing and deposing John had been duly intoned. And, from Winchester, my lord the king sent messengers to Sir Hubert de Burgh, and to the mayor and aldermen of London, and to all the bishops of his kingdom, demanding feudal service and announcing his ensuing coronation. O times.

IIII. *About Hubert de Burgh his Apology for careful Writing*

Now, as I have said, England was in a muck of faction; and it needs a clever knight conversant with state-affairs to unravel the tangles: for we lived in webs of treasons and mazes of sudden loyalties and labyrinths of unexpected desertions; and most knights did their deeds for reprehensible motives, some for self-interest, some for salving personal honour, some because a friend had done this, some because an enemy was about to do that. But, speaking generally, it may be said that there were factions four, with four chiefs of them, namely in order, John, Henry, Aloys, Arthur. And I am vowed to set down all history of those times, that future Englishmen may know precisely from what pit of desolate damnation this kingdom was delivered by King Arthur; and, also, that my truth may choke the contemptible lies in the hairy throats of certain grubby monks, specially Mr. Matthew (late of Paris), who stewed in stinking little coops, hot as hens who hatch, imagining fond tales of chimerical emprizes, while I, Earl Hubert de Burgh, was living and serving and seeing and hearing and doing in the very midst of activity, helping not a little (as I may faithfully declare) in the making of the histories here set forth fully and fairly. So, by reason of the late coming of King Arthur, last but

---

[1] A screen that crosses the nave of the church (*OED* OL).

not least on the field, it behoves me to treat first of the powers of
the three pretended kings, before I display the battle-array of the
Regal Majesty of England.

v. About John Softsword, Earl of Mortain, and Wild Ass, the Tale of his Power

I begin with the Earl of Mortain: for he had longest been called
the king, and by me among others, but for good and sufficient
reason. This base stinking fellow, I say, then, lay like a leper at
Corfe with a small power, until he was forced to flit to Gloucester, as I shall narrate anon. At Corfe, he had his treasure; and he
was very fearful of the proximity of King Arthur at Winchester,
because the main body of his cotterels lay in Severn Valley fresh
from a raid in the north. In the west, Wilts, Dorset, Somerset,
Gloucester, Devon, Cornwall, were loyal to him, excepting (of
course) those numerous magnificently-garrisoned and impregnable castles whose constable was Hubert de Burgh. With John's
adherents in Gloucester, living at free quarters upon the abbot,
were the bīps of Winchester and Norwich and Exeter, and the
abbots of Waverley and Beaulieu. So much for his clergymen. His
magnates were the earl of Devon and Wight, the earl of Pembroke and Striguil, Berkeley, Albemarle, and John Marechal. His
captains of cotterels were Sir Walter Buch, the shifty Sir Savary
Maleleone, Sir Fulk Breauté. Sir Hugh Boves would doubtless have
been of this precious crew, but that that dribbling beast was cold
and drowned (or perchance unhappily hot) in hell.[1] The Wild Ass
held the castles of Oxford, Bridgenorth, Newcastle-under-Lyne,
and Barnard, which last was held for him by Sir Hugh Baliol, *gules,
an orle argent*: but these were all more or less besieged by Henry
Lackland's power. In the east, the Wild Ass also held Berkhampstead and this Tower of London, round which sat the power of
Aloys, respectfully and quite helplessly, for it needs more than

---

[1] Hugh of Boves shipwrecked while sailing with an army from Calais. Many who
drowned on the ship were women and children, giving rise to a rumor that John
intended to engage in genocide and repopulate the kingdom with foreigners. In
fact, many mercenary soldiers brought their families to war with them. See Alan
Lloyd, *The Maligned Monarch* (Garden City, N.Y.: Doubleday, 1972), 329-330.

a pap-and-gravy-fed Frank and a handful of traitors to take this Tower. And, finally, Striguil was held for John: which we of King Arthur's power would have set the Welshry to besiege, had not its earl's heir loyally come over to us, neutralizing his father's mistaken adherence to Softsword.

VI. *About Henry fil-John, called Lackland, the Tale of his Power*

Young Henry fil-Wildass, called Lackland, was a stolid oaf, high-shouldered, glum-faced, glowering, like a sulky calf; and he might seem to an ignoramus, or to an oblique-eyed monk like Mr. Matthew (late of Paris), to have a better claim to regality than the others, because he held, or had held for him, not only all England north of Trent but Salop, Stafford, Worcester, Leicester, Northants, Oxon, Bucks, Beds, and Herefordshire as well.[1] But, of the two last, he had not the castles: for I brought Hereford to King Arthur, and that traitor Beauchamp gave Bedford to the Frank. So, Henry besieged these two, as far as he was able, and also his father's castles of Oxford, Newcastle, Bridgenorth, and Barnard. But he held Eye (besieged by Aloys) in the east, and also Nottingham and Newark. As for his clergymen, he had bīp. Walter Grey of Worcester, who had been named by Softsword to the northern primacy, and won over by Lackland who promised to confirm him therein: as though the right of confirmation lay with any man save Christ His Vicar. Also, this glum calf, I say, had bīp. Jocelyn of Wells, who fled from John's exactions leaving his see to be laid desolate, and bīp. Richard le Poer of Salisbury, addicted to fits but he saw to it that the mitre and crook[2] of Salisbury departed not out of his family, and the bīp. of Chester and Durham his kinsman who was also earl-palatine of Sedbergh, and bīp. Geoffrey of Lichfield who sat frightfully still in a castle, and bīp. Eustace of Ely all a-twitter because there were Franks squatting on his temporalities: but bishop Bernard of Carlisle would

---

[1] Though he did at times express criticism of the king's policies, Matthew Paris was on very good terms with Henry III. Henry was only nine at the time of his father's death. Rolfe seems to be representing him as a bit older, so he may serve as an appropriate adversary to Arthur.

[2] A bishop's staff (*OED* OL).

have to do with none of these, being chained to his see by lumbago.[1] And I am told that York, in those days, was simply creeping with abbots, ready (as the abbatial manner is) to play two games, worshipping rising and turning backsides to setting suns. O manners. So much for Lackland's clergymen. His magnates were the earls of Salisbury, Chester, Surrey, Derby, Ferrers, Warenne, and Warwick, and nearly all the northern magnates, Mowbray, Percy, *or, a lyon azure*, Roger Lacy who brought Chester and held it against our Welshry, William Stuteville, Robert Ros, Multon and Malet, Vaux and Gresley, fil-Alan, fil-John, fil-Warine: but Eustace Vesci was dead before Barnard Castle.[2]

VII. *About Aloys, called Cocky, the Tale of his Power*

As for the Frankishman, who looked like a cross between a cockerel and an owl, and strutted like a peewit,[3] with a pigeon's breast, and a chameleon's slobbering tongue, perfused with liquid odours,[4] weak-eyed, soft-handed, we just called the creature Cocky.[5] All the east was held for him, Norfolk, Suffolk, Huntingdon, Lincoln, Cambridge, Hertford, Essex, and even Kent, excepting (of course) my by-no-means-unnotable castles. But he had no clergymen. For bishop William the Foundling held London (he said) for God: also, he said that, when anyone was king of all England, he would attend to him, but, till then, he was for feeding his flock, and he would see to it that no silly sheep of his went a-whoring after false shepherds, he being a very scriptural clergyman, wherefore he collected a college of expert tormentors, and barked bitter bans on all who approached the city in arms, and cut off supplies from the Tower, and bade the mayor to be about his proper business seeing that statecraft befitted not craftsmen but statesmen. Superb opinion.[6] But several magnates were not ashamed to

---

[1] Rheumatism in the lumbar region (*OED* OL).
[2] Eustace de Vesci, one of King John's worst enemies, died attempting to capture the royal banner at Barnard Castle in Yorkshire.
[3] Lapwing (*OED* OL).
[4] *"perfusus liquidis odoribus."* [Rolfe's note.]
[5] *"Gallinulus."* [Rolfe's note.]
[6] *"superba sententia."* [Rolfe's note.]

crouch at the feet of the Frank; and such were the earls Bigod of
Norfolk and Suffolk, Saer Quincy of Winchester, Monthermer of
Hereford, Arundel and Sussex, Huntingdon and Cambridge, with
William and Philip Daubigny, fil-Walter, Montacute, Montfitchet,
William Beauchamp who held Bedford Castle, Roger Cresci, and
Hugh Neville who held the castle of Marlborough. Furthermore,
Sir Aloys the Cocky placed over his power that very earl of Nevers
who but recently had been King Arthur's generous host, as Earl
Fulk said in his chant-regal; and I must say that the English were
extremely vexed about it.

VIII. *About King Arthur, the Tale of his Power*

Having enumerated the legions of the misguided and the various incubi and succubi infesting them, I come to the tale of those
true men who were not led away by flittering fancies of expe-
diency, prudence, vanity, malice, or imbecility, but held leally
to King Richard Lionheart's only rightful heir designated and
approved as such by God's Vicegerent. King Arthur had two clergymen. The first was the Cardinal-Primate Stephen Langthon,
very anxious to recover the grace of our lord the Pope, which he
lost when he played the fool in the matter of that idiotic Charter: he went straight from Winchester to his archiepiscopal see of
Canterbury, but (being pursued by foppish Franks) he was forced
to lie up in the castle of Rochester. And the second clergyman
enjoyed by my lord the king was bishop Giles Braose of Hereford,
who came down to Winchester as fast as his mule might trot
when he heard of the coming of Arthur. And my lord the king,
beside his two clergymen, had but one poor magnate, by name
Earl Hubert de Burgh of Gloucester and Essex. That unpurged
traitor, however, brought with him the little matter of the wild
Welshry, and the V Ports with their navies and pirates, and the
fifteen castles of Hereford, Norwich, Orford, Dover, Canterbury,
Rochester, Lafford, Dunster, Launceston, Wallingford, Windsor, with the quadrilateral of Grosmont and Scenefrith and Candidachester and Monmouth on the March of Wales, the smaller
castles garrisoned by twenty knights with their squires and pages
and sixty men-at-arms apiece, the larger by fifty knights apiece

with their squires and pages and one-hundred-and-fifty men-at-arms, all picked men and all veterans. Also, King Arthur had Hants and Bucks.[1]

These, then, were the four factions, with the chiefs of the same, namely in order, John, Henry, Aloys, Arthur, with the tales of their several powers.

VIIII. *About King Arthur in Council*

My lord the king held his first council in Winchester, as soon as I came there to render account of my stewardship. First of all, he deigned to accept my homage, permitting me to purge my former treason; and he confirmed me in my offices. Next, these things were decided:

that the King should instantly display his banner of the Panthers of England and the Dragon of Wales, summoning all true men to his service on pain of being declared culverts and nidderings:

that an emprize should instantly be initiated against the castle of Corfe, where the earl of Mortain lay with Lady Jezebel and God-only-knows-how-much treasure for we never found a farthing of it—this, upon the instant, lest the said earl should fly to Gloucester or bring his cotterels thence to Corfe:

that a march should be made to Rochester, for relief of the Cardinal-Primate, besieged in the castle together with Sir Reginald of Cornhill my viceconstable:

that Sir Eustace the Monk should instantly be bought from the Franks and retained for my lord the king's service, I having recommended him as a most worth and pious pirate who had given me valuable tokens of his usefulness.

Now, King Arthur had about twenty-one-hundred foreign knights and men-at-arms, and about two-hundred Englishmen; and veterans were coming fast from such of my castles as would bear some depletion of their garrisons, but I dared not to take any from Windsor, where the earl of Nevers was with a power,

---

[1] "Hants" and "Bucks" are abbreviated names for Hamptonshire and Buckinghamshire.

though the main Frankish power was in the east country, sitting down in front of Lincoln Castle, with an appetite whetted by the capture and plunder of that city. But we would have esteemed it an ill-omen if my lord the king had left his regal city of Winchester at that moment: wherefore, he agreed to remain in the ancient capital of his kingdom as a rallying-point for his adherents.

x. *About the Setting of the Flame to the Castle of Corfe*

Earl Fulk of Jaffa and Nantes was bidden (after much begging on his part) to flame away most flagrantly to Corfe, with every man who could be spared. This, in the greatest haste: for rumours came to Winchester, saying that Softsword had summoned his cotterels from Gloucester, to assemble at Salisbury, for a fierce attack upon my lord the king at Winchester. But his cunning wounded his own pate.[1] He had been clever enough never to keep both his treasure and his cotterels in the same place: but he was not ware that (without his treasure) he could not keep his cotterels, who only served for wages, and would desert him for a richer master should such occur to them. And now he was so flurried, that he was obliged to risk the danger of bringing his cotterels to protect his treasure. This Softsword, then, sat in his castle of Corfe, without any trumpeters, chewing his nails, and praying that the reputation of the place (haunted by male and female spectres of all ages and ranks in every stage of starvation)[2] would prevent his awfully resurrected nephew from attacking it. And, with him, there were thirty criminals (not counting Lady Jezebel), of such amazing wickedness that their only hope of continuing to exist in this world lay in cleaving to John, for any other master would have roasted them on sight. And, by aid of these, he wrought his ruse.

xi. *About Burgesses the Bane they Are*

When the burgesses of Winchester heard that more than half

---

[1] Head (*OED OL*).

[2] The aforementioned twenty-two knights who starved to death in the castle at Corfe as well as Maude de Braose and her sons.

of King Arthur's power was to go with Fulk the Flame, leaving them but poorly protected against the Johannines whom they believed to be at Salisbury, and in face of the Franks at Guildford (as they were pleased to think), then they sobbed, lamenting that they were all undone and their city left open to its enemies. And the tumult of their terror was so passionate, that I myself went to my lord the king, and I hummed[1] in his regal ear advice that he should countermand Earl Fulk's emprize for the sake of policy, and that the said earl should be sent secretly by night with no more than fifty knights and a hundred-and-fifty men-at-arms. Which grievously galled the soul of an Angevin Plantagenet, as was but natural; and, though he acted on my recommendation, my lord the king took special order ever after that mobs of sweaty burgesses should not have a chance of swaying either the destinies of kingdoms, or the inclinations of their betters, with their vast and malodorous vociferations. But, on this occasion, he spoke them fair. O second Solomon.

XII. About the Flame at Corfe

Earl Fulk the Flame and his little power sailed down the Water from Southampton, and landed at Poole, where they caused the citizens to arm hurriedly against the Wild Ass by preparing a gallows for the mayor and fire for the town. Thus, more than a hundred-and-seventy men of all kinds were added to his two-hundred, and arrayed behind his men-at-arms, to march and countermarch, whereby the garrison of Corfe opined that an enormous power was menacing them. But, when Earl Fulk's heralds summoned them to surrender, it was seen what a ruse Softsword had played. For a certain scoundrel named Milo of Mons (a bastard, some say, of the bishop of Luttick), peeped over the battlement of the barbacan, demanding terms: which the Flame had not expected: but he said that he would take no lives, nor prisoners, nor even ransoms, but he must have the castle, and the Earl of Mortain, and that beast's treasure. So the gates were opened; and there was

---

[1] "*mussabam.*" (This is Vergil's word for the sound made by bees.—P. and C.) [Rolfe's note.]

no one there but the thirty criminals aforesaid: for Lady Jezebel
had shipped herself to France from Swanage; and the Wild Ass
had pranced by night to Gloucester with only enough cotterels to
carry his treasure and the regalia of England. The Flame, then,
having flamed (frightfully, they say), at the Winchester burgesses
whose howls had delayed him and caused this ill-luck, shipped
the thirty criminals to France from Poole, as a pleasing present
to King Philip the August; and, what happened to them afterward, I do not know: but one (at least), that young Milo of Mons,
renounced his incredible iniquities, and went crusading to Romania, where he married the daughter of one of their emperors with
a considerable feof. And then Earl Fulk flamed after John.

XIII. *About the Flame on the Wild Ass his Heels*

The chase was a long one, though it took but a short time.
Softsword was so fearfully flurried that he dared not to make a
stand anywhere; and Earl Fulk flamed after him with every intent
to devour. At Gloucester, some of his cotterels got to know that
his treasure was in the baggage-waggons; and they promptly
demanded higher wages. He (most inopportunely avaricious)
denied them; and escaped with great difficulty. So that, when
Earl Fulk came up, he found several mercenaries seeking new
situations, which he provided, adding them to his power, and
continuing the pursuit. At Oxford, the Wild Ass was all but hal-
tered: but the manner of his evasion there was so comical that
I will narrate it at length. O times. He camped for the night by
Godstowe, with his baggage-waggons well-guarded; but he, with
four whom he could trust, went, disguised, and secretly, at dusk,
into the city, that he might find out whether the castle (which
was held for him) would serve as a safe refuge. And, while he
was prosecuting his nefarious inquiries, curfew rang, and the
city-gates were shut, closing him in. Meanwhile, Earl Fulk rode
up from the south, and occupied the city, having lost track of the
Wild Ass at Abingdon and not dreaming of his proximity. Now
the pursuers were much fatigued; and vigilance that night was
by no means keen: had it been otherwise, all England would have
been robbed of a subject for perennial laughter. They say that,

when John was ware of his plight, he inside with an enemy, and his treasure outside with persons conceivably unscrupulous and certainly venal, his comportment resembled nothing so much as that of an agitated and sobbing flea. He lay at a low inn at the back of the market, drinking beer all night to hearten himself; and, in the dark silent hours before dawn, he and his four crept round to all the gates looking for God-knows-what chance of escape. And, at the north gate, he found a slight (but the only) one: for the guards were slumbering heavily, and the gate (being in need of repair, the road through it also being hollowed somewhat by traffic), let room for (let us say) a dog to wriggle underneath it. What more. After some stealthy scraping of the roadway with their knives, two of the Wild Ass's cotterels (lean malefactors) crawled through the enlarged crevice into the open country, while the other two remained to follow him. He then, prone on his belly, began to writhe himself through. His head passed: his shoulders and arms passed; but he stuck fast with his beard in a puddle and his fingers scrabbling in the mud outside, and, inside, his base parts bloated horribly with luxury and recent beer. The two cotterels inside tried to pull him back by the legs, that they might enlarge the passage: the two outside tried to deliver him by forward, which of course wedged him more tightly than ever. And he did not dare to scream, or to whimper his blasphemous opinions above a whisper. Time passed. He felt hurt. Dawn was very near. The two cotterels inside could not escape, though they were even leaner than the others, for their master blocked the only orifice. And, at last, they whispered to their comrades outside to haul at the beast's arms again, while they themselves stamped on his prominent portions, compressing his bloated bulk and squeezing the beer out of him, until they had flattened him so that he could be wrenched from his uneasy posture. Which done, they followed; and, having got him to his camp, they put him in a baggage-waggon to recover breath, resuming the flight northward to Northampton. He made for Northampton for very good reasons. His power had seen him looking highly ridiculous and he was the object of incessant derision. He knew that it was but a very short step from this premiss to the next, namely, that nothing but he at whom they gibed stood between his cotterels and his treasure. And the conclusion was obvious, even to him. So, he artfully chose the most faithful of faithless men, and the swiftest horses, to guard and to carry his treasure; and he rode headlong on with these, leaving all stragglers behind, invading Henry Lackland's country with the idea of seeking reconciliation and a dual kingdom with his son. But, what a son! And, what a father! And what a wild and asinine Wild Ass to hope for half from him to whom he had given half and (having half) was for taking the whole! But Henry fled before him; and Earl Fulk flamed on a bee-line in his wash,[1] picking up his cotterels by handfuls behind him. Even in this predicament, he could not relinquish his abominably beastly habits. At Oundle by Peterborough, he had one of his saddle-galled cotterels filed usque ad mortem,[2] and frightened the monks into giving him all their money; and, then, he burned their barns, merely to annoy them with the prospect of starvation for their lepers in the winter. This was his last raid but one. At Lynn, a dysentery diseased him: but he ramped back on his tracks to Wisbech, Earl Fulk hard-pressing him, driving him across the quicksands at the Mouth of River Welland. Here, the Lord God flung an ocean at him, striking him in his tenderest place: for an incoming tide rose roaring, and ingulphed the heavy waggons of his baggage and his treasure.[3] Quite ruined, deserted by all his cotterels but thirteen, hunted by Earl Fulk, and Cocky Aloys, and by the beggarly son whom he had set on horseback to ride to the devil (and these three hunted each other as well as the Wild Ass) he was for taking sanctuary at Swineshead. But the abbot, a prudent man, was not affable, carefully fending him off from the church, and only giving him a drink, telling him that the weather was propitious for riding, and asking where he might have left his trumpeters. Southward, then, straight, he came, stark mad; and Earl Fulk, perceiving his course, was for driving him slap into the

---

[1] "*flagrabat rectam vestigiis ducens.*" [Rolfe's note.]
[2] Condemned to death.
[3] The popular legend of John's loss of his baggage train while crossing a river is drawn largely from Roger of Wendover, though Wendover sets the event at the Nene river. This was, according to most sources, a humiliating loss and a trauma for John that contributed to his declining health. He died soon afterward on October 19, 1216.

arms of King Arthur. But again he missed him, by three hours, this time in the density of the New Forest: which three hours the Wild Ass wisely used in diverging to his abbey of Beaulieu, wrapping his arms round the calves of monk Hugh whom he had made abbot, craving protection of the Church and of the Cistercian Order which he had so bitterly persecuted.[1] O manners.

XIIII. *About Softsword in Sanctuary*

When Earl Fulk came up, inquiring for a body of a certain criminal, Abbot Hugh was very haughty; and he said that he knew of none such infesting the precincts of his abbey, which, indeed, contained no stranger at that time, excepting (what he called) the Regal Majesty of King John deigning to visit his pious foundation and bedesmen[2] of Beaulieu. Fulk says that he would gladly have given a lewd guffaw, but, ware of the stupidity of barging like a bull bottom-upward against a dignified clergyman, and, yet desirous of getting even with this abbot without annoying him (lest that should act to King Arthur's hurt) he said pleasantly that he feared that the latest news had not yet reached Beaulieu, which was that our lord the Pope had been deposing Softsword and setting Lefthand in his room, anathematizing abettors of the former with the singularly severe censures. At this, the abbot looked glum as a gowk[3] with a smacked face: but then, collecting his manners, he smiled, and supposed that Sir John fil-Henry might be admitted to sanctuary as well as any other malefactor or notorious evil liver. Fulk laughed openly at this adroit retort, and told the abbot that he was a white[4] man: which so pleased the monk that he invited him forthwith to taste a monastic pudding. After dinner, the two went together to inspect Sir John, shivering under the high altar where he had crawled, very cold, for the

---

[1] St. Hugh actually died in 1200. According to Adam of Eynsham, Hugh's biographer, the miracles that followed his death inspired John to reconcile with the Cistercians and found the abbey of Beaulieu.
[2] "Bede" is a Middle English term for prayer, so "bedesmen" would be "men of prayer" (*OED* OL).
[3] A fool. Also refers to the cuckoo bird (*OED* OL).
[4] The word "white" can be used to mean honorable or free from malignity or evil intent (*OED* OL).

sweat of his nine days' riding was still wet on him, and the stone whereon he lay was not an oven-top: also, he was starving, and in far too awful a panic terror to quit his recess. Thus, Earl Fulk saw his uncle (a horror) for the first time; and he was very much displeased with him. And the Abbot mentioned to Sir John that he saw his nephew, whereat the contemptible animal moaned and muttered maledictions. So Abbot Hugh ordered him out of the church, to clean himself and learn manners and eat a pudding or two; for he had a little pity for the cringing creature, and, moreover, he was ware that much advantage for himself and his order might be gained by circumspect conduct of the situation. Wherefore, when Earl Fulk charged him solemnly, in the King's name, to hold the Wild Ass in straight ward during the regal Majesty's pleasure, he agreed to do so; and, on the morrow, he blessed Earl Fulk returning to Winchester.

xv. About Accessions to the Power of King Arthur

All the world was agog at my lord the king's good luck, and the amazing collapse of Sir John, fallen (they said) like a rotten medlar[1] flat on to a flag; and it was spread throughout the kingdom that there were now but three kings to count, the fourth having become an earl, who was a prisoner, liable to degradation and capital sentence or (at least) perpetual seclusion with lepers. And King Arthur added to his power the pick of Softsword's cotterels which Earl Fulk brought in: but the rest he shipped to France, thumbless, I having called up the navies of my V Ports, twenty-one ships from Hastings, Dover, Folkestone, Feversham, Margate, ten from Winchelsea, five from Rye, Hithe, Sandwich, Sarre, Reculver, Deal, sixty-seven ships in all, with fourteen-hundred-and-seven mariners to man them and sixty-seven boys to comfort them. The Earl of Devon and Wight came in with his power, that he might save his lands in that island. For, having this navy in hand, to be maintained by the barons of my V Ports for fifteen days from hoist of sail, and, further (as the King willed)

---

[1] The fruit from the medlar tree, which resembles a small, brown apple. This was also a slang term for the female genitals or for a disreputable person (*OED* OL).

to be kept by ordinance of the King, and, seeing that the conveyance of the rejected cotterels could be done in a week and Wight
taken on the return, King Arthur sent word to the said earl that
more than two days' stiff-neckedness would cause those lands of
his to be a wilderness, wherein nothing nice would ever grow
again. The Earl of Pembroke and Striguil also came in with his
power to save his heir who had come in before as hostage for his
father's good behaviour, and also because our wild Welshry were
being extremely fussy in his vicinity. And all Softsword's clergymen came in, excepting the bishop of Winchester, who said that
he had a soul to save and feigned to run away crusading. The
others made (as their manner is) a vast parade of their piety in
floating with the stream (a feat which any dead dog can perform
with ease), and a vast parade of their loyalty in licking the boots
of their master (a complaisance which every live dog is eager to
accomplish), and a vast parade of their virtue civil and canonical
in serving Cæsar as well as Peter, they being much more afraid of
the young Cæsar throned under his canopy at Winchester, than
of the old Peter out of sight and out of mind in Rome: for my lord
the king was fiercely white and cold to those hireling shepherds,
neither courting nor rebuffing them, accepting their belated allegiance as his just due and by no means as a favour deserving gratitude. But he diminished them forever of their trumpets.

xvi. *About King Arthur going forth to War*

Having got the castles of Marlborough and Oxford, the one by
purchase and the other by storm, my lord the king advanced eastward, to deal with the Franks, and to bring the Cardinal-Primate
safely out of Rochester. For we were all clamouring for a real regal
coronation. The earl of Jaffa and Nantes and earl Hubert de Burgh
rode with the Regal Majesty. The earl of Devon and Wight was
trusted with a thousand cotterels under Sir Fulk Breauté to ride
westward, strengthening Gloucester and Hereford, heartening
the Marches: for Henry Lackland's northern rebels were pressing the loyal Welshry very hard, having taken Bridgenorth and
relieved Chester. In fact, there was a plenty of small fighting to be
done all along the west; and the king's right would have suffered,

if the earl of Pembroke and Striguil had not amended his carouses at this time, for his accession set free many loyal knights, who ceased from annoying King Arthur in the south that they might annoy Henry Lackland in the west. O times.

XVII. *About the Chasing of Cocky*

Cocky Aloys in Canterbury had got himself crowned by a certain undesirable alien[1] who said that he was bishop of Elephantopolis[2] in the parts of the infidels. No English bishop would commune with this fatuous Frank. Nor were any Englishmen present at his so-called coronation, excepting the earl of Winchester and a handful of inquisitive burgesses. Moreover, Aloys had been spat upon in the streets, and pelted with crowns made of pumpkin-rind, lewd little ragamuffins knocked their heads against the gutters, crying "O Cocky" as he passed. Wherefore, he had five of them clubbed to death; and the riot which ensued was so fierce, that much of the city was burned and two-hundred Franks slain, while the rest were banned with awful pomp by the abbot of Saint Austins, and (after) expelled by the burgesses and most fearfully vilified. And, after the flight of this Frank, the said burgesses held their city against all of his nation, in the name of Messire Saint Thomas-à-Canterbury, and the mayor and aldermen kneeled the whole night through at the shrine, that they might learn from their patron who ought to be king of the English. And, in the morning, they came out not-at-all-sleepy, proclaiming King Arthur; and they hanged forty-one Franks (found in water-butts[3] and granaries) to invest the occasion with due solemnity. But Cocky fled to his camp before Rochester, that being his nearest power, all his other adherents having gone either to Guildford for a campaign westward or to the Tower of London for which he had an affection. And, at Rochester, he bravely beheaded six charcoal-burners, and he made Sir Gilbert of Gant earl of Lincoln, or so he said. So, all Kent sat up to spue Franks. Mr. William Vaux

---

[1] *"quodam peregrino non expetendo."* [Rolfe's note.]
[2] A town along the Nile where ivory tusks were swapped for spices and other goods. Most sources insist that Louis VIII was never actually crowned King of England.
[3] Casks set up to catch rain-water from a roof (*OED* OL).

of Collingham headed the men of Kent: for which service my lord
the king knighted him later. And the navies of my V Ports com-
bined with that of Sir Eustace the Monk (that cheerful and religious Pirate), and they did such a do at Dover, that the Frankish
siege of it fell to pieces, while, of the Franks who beleaguered my
castle, not one lived to offer an apology.[1]

XVIII. About the Capture of Cocky

Hearing King Arthur's chase of him, Cocky withdrew his
reserve from the Tower and from Rochester, and made for Guildford, where the earl of Nevers was chafing at inaction. The revolt
against Franks spread from Kent into Surrey and Sussex; and
insidious rumour reported that my lord the king had won a great
victory over them, though (in fact) no battle had yet been fought.
But the said rumour so flustered the earl of Arundel (who pettishly sulked in his castle because Cocky had named Nevers to
command his power), that he, believing Cocky crushed, declared
for King Arthur, abominably blasphemed all Franks since Charlemagne, adorned the tops of his tenants with snippets of yellow
samite[2] because he could get no broom-sprigs, and marched his
full power to Guildford to share in the sackage of the Franks.
Moreover, as he went along, he proclaimed King Arthur, mag-
nifying the unwon victory, till all believed it true. And thus it
came about that the Franks were everywhere much vexed and
annoyed; and, when they fled, as they did anon, the fear of them
had been so delightfully dissipated, that young clowns and yokels
took them for mooncalves, and put them out of their misery quite
casually, in hedgerows, with hoes or hedging bills or with any
weapon which might be in hand. But the actual battle took place
at Godalming, the Franks having come out of Guildford, for fear

---

[1] After John died, Louis gradually lost most of his English support. A decisive
battle, known as the "Fair of Lincoln," forced Louis to abandon his siege of Dover
castle. Louis was then defeated again in sea battle off the coast of Sandwich.
(Eustace the Monk in fact fought on the side of Louis in this battle, opposing
Hubert de Burgh.) Following this defeat, Louis signed the Treaty of Kingston (or
Lambeth) and abandoned his claim to the throne.
[2] A rich silk fabric worn in the Middle Ages (*OED* OL).

of miscellaneous domestic missiles usual in the narrow streets of a hostile town. And a fine conflict ensued, with but little of skill or stratagem, and plenty of plain hard hitting. King Arthur led about four thousand: Sir Aloys the Cocky, rather more. But, even when our charges broke the Frankish centre, we should have been denied suitable (or even reasonable) slaughter of the vanquished, but for the arrival of Arundel with his yellow men. And after a two-hours' battle, we captured Cocky, sobbing, with a crown of sorts bashed down over his broken nose, and also the earl of Nevers with seventy knights and about four-hundred men-at-arms: but, as for the rest of the Franks, they were either slain on the field, or they took to the forests, where they were pestered by peasants and never heard of again.

xviiii. *About the Collapse of the Comporters of Cocky*

King Arthur had a pleasant surprize, when he went to catch the Franks who beleaguered the Tower. For the disloyal Earl of Winchester deserted the siege of Rochester (which he left to the Viscount of Melun) and he joined the Frank-made earl of Lincoln: they, then, led their powers to London, and fell upon the Franks besieging the Tower, utterly smashing them, by aid of the Londoners who, tired of their bishop's neutrality, broke out to fight for King Arthur. Then the two earls dealt so righteously with the Johannine constable that he was persuaded to surrender the Tower to them for my lord the King, who, when he came, was met by the trumpeters of two penitent earls in shirts and rope-collars presenting the said Tower as their peace-offering. Meanwhile, the Viscount of Melun, much vexed by my Rochester garrison, the hostility of Kentishmen, not less than by nocturnal visitations of the Holy Baker of Bradstowe[1] whose shrine was hindered of candles by reason of the straitness of the siege, he, I say, had no more heart left in him, when he heard of Cocky's captivity. And, the next time that the Cardinal-Primate, from the wall, offered

---

[1] Saint William of Perth was a pious baker from Scotland who was murdered in Rochester in 1201 as he made his way to the Holy Land. The monks of Rochester established a shrine to the baker meant to rival the shrine of St. Thomas at Canterbury.

him terms of safe-conduct unransomed to France with his power, on his raising the siege and plighting his knightly word to refrain from mischief against my lord the king, he gladly accepted; and England was ridded of him.

xx. *About the Coronation of King Arthur as King of the English*

After the victory of Godalming and the raising of the sieges of Rochester and the Tower, King Arthur met the Primate Stephen at Croydon in the sweetest love and amity. He might not yet proceed to Westminster, for much remained to be done. The earl of Warwick lay at Harrow with a power extending to Pinner. Beauchamp, having deserted Cocky for Lackland, marched a power from Bedford to Islington, that he might try for London, where he broke his nose, for Bishop William held that city for God (so he said). And news came that Lackland's stars were benignant: for his earl of Derby had bitten our Welshry dreadfully at Wrexham, while Cocky's earls of Norfolk and Huntingdon had joined Softsword's son at Banbury. Much remained, I say, to be done, and to be done quickly. For, though anointed, King Arthur delayed to be crowned of England; and the mobile vulgar were cackling that, though Lefthand had frustrated the Franks, nevertheless Lackland was the crowned king. Which is just what the faex[1] would say, being part of the truth, and worse than a down-right lie. O manners. So, we escorted the king and the cardinal-primate to Winchester with simple solemnity, and they lay at Wolvesley Castle near by, against the coronation on the day following. News came in that night, of small disasters in North Wales, of small successes in South Wales, of Henry Lackland offering to Sir Fulk the Flame recognition of his earldoms of Jaffa and Nantes and investiture with the earldom-palatine of Richmond as the price of his abandonment of King Arthur, from which portent we augured that Softsword's glum calf of a son was actuated both by malignance and imbecility. Also, another earl (whose name I have forgotten) came in that night with a hundred knights, and the Abbots of Glastonbury, Waverley, Beaulieu, and Abingdon with their powers.

---

[1] The dregs. From *faex populi*, the dregs of the people.

Then was crowned King Arthur as King of the English, at Winchester, by the cardinal-primate, on the transferred festival of Messire Saint Magnus.[1] But there was found no crown wherewith to crown him: for Sir John fil-Henry had lost the crown of England to the sea of the Fenlands in his fearful flight.[2] The cardinal-primate was for using the antique crown of King Knud,[3] which glowed beneath its canopy on the Great Rood. But, superbly says my lord the king, "Knud gave it to God, to Whom Arthur confirms it." And he took from his regal neck a necklet which he had snatched from the neck of Queen Mariol, when he left her sobbing bravely at Saint-Malo: formed of little square golden plates linked together, it was, each plate carrying a great sardonyx; and he took an ounce of the Lionheart's treasure, redly virgin, hammering it with his own long-sword's hilt into a wire of the shape of a ring, wherewith he stiffened the necklet, while we all kneeled behind him speechless in reverent love. And thus he was crowned of England. We proclaimed him, Arthur, First of the name. This, for two reasons, beside the reason that he certainly was the first of all men then in life. And the first reason was that the wild Welshry took him for their own Arthur of old, come again. I am by no means certain that they erred in this belief: anyhow, it was a noble one, and a simple, explanatory of very many still-insoluble mysteries; and we deemed it unwise to complicate or disturb it. And the second reason was that the Englishmen would not have approved of a Welshman to reign over them. Therefore, my lord the King was King Arthur the First, in one sense, for his Welshry, and King Arthur the First, in another sense, for his Englishry. O times. Then, we all did homage, and had our trumpeters regulated. And, that night, at the crown-wearing, King Arthur suddenly invested Earl Fulk with the palatine earldom of Richmond:

---

[1] While there are three saints named Magnus, Rolfe presumably refers to Saint Magnus of Füssen, whose feast day is September 6.

[2] The king's treasures and the coronation regalia were lost with John's baggage carts.

[3] King Canute the Great (994-1035) had grown tired of his men's flattery. They insisted that it was impossible for anyone or anything to disobey him. To prove them wrong, he commanded the waves to stop rolling. In order to show that the only all-powerful ruler is God, he removed his crown and refused to wear it again, placing it instead upon the crucifix in the cathedral of Winchester.

"For," says he, "it is not meet that a friend should suffer for his friendship; and since Our cousin Lackland has seen fit to offer what he indeed might make good did he not lack land, We take it upon Our Regal Majesty to do what he has said that he would do." And I was told, by one who saw it, that Henry was so vexed, when he knew that Richmond was no longer a bribe, that his stomach rejected his pudding for a day and a half.

XV

THE BOOK CALLED THE CLEANSING OF ENGLAND

I. *About the Powers*

King Arthur rode from Winchester with four-thousand-three-hundred men-at-arms and three-hundred-and-fourteen knights, beside his magnates and bishops and abbots, as though he was going to Gloucester to join the South Welshry; for the earl of Derby, having annihilated many of the North Welsh, had come to Presteigne, where he lay wasting the country and threatening Hereford. But this drew Lackland from Banbury. So, we came and lay all along the ridge of the downs above Burford, where was a bridge with a shrine of our Lady of the Windrush, such being the name of the river. And Lackland's power came through the Wychwood, and lay along the hills over Fullbrook; and the valley was between us. Now Lackland's power was larger than the king's: but he was not ware of the ford over River Windrush, at a mile below the said bridge, just where the mill-stream falls in again.

II. *About the Battle of Burford*

On the sixth day, it seemed good to King Arthur to offer battle, which the rebels joyfully accepted: for I am bound to say that we neither of us had any more puddings to eat. So, we came down, and made to cross the bridge; and Lackland's power went up to stay us. And a very pretty battle was joined, in which were no dodgy devices or careful stratagems, owing to the simplicity of the site: for none might cross the river above the bridge, excepting three miles away, where both powers had companies guarding both sides of the crossing; and, at the bridge, King Arthur's power was the more numerous. Yet, because of the treason of

Sir Fulk Breauté, who had secretly sold himself and his power to Lackland while still taking wages from Lefthand, we suddenly found ourselves in a very parlous[1] plight indeed: for, on reaching the bridge, that monstrous traitor ceased from fighting, and surrendered Burford to the rebels.[2] O manners.

III. About the Battle of Burford at the Bridge

Then, King Arthur could no longer hold his power. Many fled in a panic-terror toward Cirencester. And the peril of our predicament lay in this, that one-third of us were seen to be traitors, and one-third culverts and nidderings. However, my lord the king was the hope of England, and he knew it, nor did his divine gift of hope ever desert him, or waver, even for an instant. He, indeed, was always most radiant of hope when his circumstances seemed most hopeless. Witness the present occasion. His power reduced to a third into two parts: with the one, he passed swiftly through the ford at a mile below the bridge, and made a fierce attack on Lackland's left flank: while Earl Fulk the Flame, with the other, recaptured part of Burford, to which a leal burgess, by name John Search, admitted them by a postern: which burgess now wears *paly, gules and ermine, a postern proper.* Earl Fulk, then, fired the town: for the wind blew toward the bridge, which Lackland's whole power was trying to cross, thickly pressed together like ants, so that advantage might be taken of Breauté's treachery. But the smoke of the burning town seriously displeased their horses, so that they pranced with vexation, causing casualties among the crowd, in which commotion the bridge incontinently collapsed, squashing many, and drowning many more. Thus, Lackland's power was cut clean in two: half lay assaulted by King Arthur:

---

[1] Perilous (*OED* OL).

[2] Falkes de Breauté was one of John's most loyal followers during the baronial uprisings, but he did have "the reputation of a desperate adventurer and a soldier of extreme ruthlessness" (Ellis 51). During Henry's reign, he openly defied the king's justices, so Henry and Hubert decided to lay siege to his headquarters, a castle at Bedford. Falkes de Breauté was exiled and died of fish-poisoning abroad. The trouble he caused Hubert de Burgh may account for his representation as a traitor here.

half had passed with Lackland into Burford, which they found to
be so blazing hot and so dense with smoke that they skipped or
tumbled out again with ludicrous celerity. Upon whom fell Earl
Fulk the Flame, and slew many whom the smoke had blinded:
but, as their numbers grew, he had to retire up hill, having not
more than eight-hundred men still with him. Meanwhile, my lord
the king with a thousand horse came round by Fulbrook, and
fell violently upon Lackland's rear, which he penned between the
broken bridge and his charging array. And they were very gravely
incommoded: for King Arthur fought mercilessly, being annoyed
that treachery should diminish him of victory, and opining that
unmitigated slaughter is the best behaviour in warfare, as indeed
it is, for a knight desirous of peace.

IIII. *About the Battle of Burford after the Change effected at the Bridge*

Now Lackland's rear was led by his earl of Norfolk, rather
foppish and dainty in his manners; and he, bursting through the
press and the smoke-cloud, choking, screamed that he was getting fearfully dirty, and, that, Lackland being dead (which he was
not yet) he, Bigod, for one, was for swearing allegiance to King
Arthur, who, being a clean knight and given to the wearing of
ermine, would doubtless take order that decent magnates were
not rendered unsightly or uncomfortable. With which, he surrendered his power to my lord the king, cheerfully black and bloody,
who thus found a new power in place of that which had betrayed
him.[1] So, I got order to come down with my knights, to lead a general movement on the Burford side, while King Arthur remained
in Fulbrook to be washed, to receive homage, and to see to the
treatment of his wounded. And, thus, I received Earl Fulk and
the Earl of Arundel who were holding their power of eight-hundred, bringing them safely away, and abandoning their camp to
Lackland. And so it came about that, after the battle was ended,
Lackland had our camp and a third of our power, and we had
Lackland's camp and a third of his power; and near upon a thou-

---

[1] Roger Bigod, the 2nd Earl of Norfolk, was one of the leaders of the baronial
uprising.

sand men in all were slain; and near upon two thousand were in flight, Witneywards, Cirencesterwards, Warwickwards, Banburywards; and neither party had lost more than it had gained. And the very air stank with the putor[1] of new treacheries. O scorbutics.

v. About the Hanging of Sir Judas Iskarioth Breauté

The bishop of Durham, ill a-bed, sent his handsomest nephew in palatine state to offer allegiance to King Arthur. But he was not much cheered by it: for the battle of Burford was as a thorn rankling in his eye, specially the matter of Sir Fulk Breauté's treachery: for he had wasted friendship and treasure on that beastly snake, who (in return) had bitten him badly, depriving him of a victory. I must say that my lord the king was always excessively impatient of everything excepting perfection: for, as I am bound to make plain, he was not a holy saint, but only the bravest of boys and the greatest of all men who ever embellished God's Earth, endued at birth with the usual load of original sins and the usual meagre and rudimentary selection of christian virtues: but I, Hubert, aver that I witnessed him purging himself of the former, each in turn, and wrestling with himself and with legions of devils to acquire the latter, one by one, until he had them all, and killed himself in getting the last and the greatest of all, namely, Charity. O my lord, my king.

The same night, then, in spite of his weariness, King Arthur and Earl Fulk the Flame, with a couple of cotterels and a spare horse and a useful-looking bag, saying nothing to anyone, rode secretly, through the darkness, across the ford, into Lackland's camp, which they found in confusion, full of wounded men, dead men, tipsy men, and men searching for quarters. No one noted them: for they wore no coats, nor were attended by their trumpeters. They inquired for Sir Fulk Breauté. They found him. He was returning from supping with his new master, unattended, perhaps slightly inebriated. King Arthur stepped from the shadow of his tent into the moonlight, looked the wretch over with scorn, and gave him a

---

[1] An unpleasant odor (*OED* OL).

chop on the throat-apple with his hardened hand-edge, abolishing
his voice and interfering seriously with his swallowing. Without a
word, they crammed him (dribbling dreadfully) into the bag, filling its interstices with all the treasure in his tent; and, throwing the
bag over the led horse, they smoothly rode away. On the morrow,
before dawn, my lord the king sent for a clergyman, and caused the
highest elm near by to be denuded of its branches save one sixty
feet from the ground; and he hanged Sir Fulk Breauté there, belted,
and spurred, with a bag of his gold tied to his feet, elongating his
broken neck.[1] And it was a marvel to both camps how the Judas
came to be there. And the king was fairly satisfied.

VI. *About the Confederate Earls*

No advantage having been gained by either side in the battle
of Burford, both sides felt somewhat fastidious about fighting
further. True, my lord the king and I and Earl Fulk of Jaffa and
Nantes and Richmond were for carrying on the war at once
with most frightful ferocity: but, because of the insistence of
the magnates, we were obliged to make a truce of seven days.
And, during those seven days, the earls of Arundel and Norfolk
and Warwick and Huntingdon, together with the earls of Derby
and Devon who came up on the third day, formed themselves
into an alliance which they cumbrously called The Confeder-
ate-Earls-Of-Madame-Saint-Bride-For-The-Instauration-Of-Holy-
Peace-To-The-Distressful-Kingdom-Of-England. And the cardinal-primate burst out in a fresh place, and thought fit to get up
and cough, threatening to blight and blast both my lord the king
and Sir Henry Lackland with the bitterest species of ban, in case
of the truce being violated. Insued negociations. The confederate
earls laboured heavily, bringing forth one abortive notion after
another. The truce was extended to Christmas. All the bishops
and all the earls in England (excepting two earls unnecessary to
be named) joined the Confederation. And King Arthur and Sir
Henry fil-John found themselves in the predicament of being but
little better than prisoners. For, my lord the king had exhausted

---

[1] Falkes de Breauté died in exile in 1226.

that part of his regal treasure which he designed for the conquest of England; and Sir Hugh the Chancellor died of dismay when he refused to send for the other part wherewith Queen Mariol was consolidating Armorica. And no one would give worship to a king in poverty when there were rich earls at hand. So, I scurried round and scratched gold out of my nine shires for the king's expenses; and I, with Earl Fulk, attended him to his castle of Windsor, where he lay, chafing bitterly in his mind. Sir Henry fil-Wildass went to wait at Warwick. But bishop William the Foundling still held London for God, saying nothing either to the king or to the Confederation, and scheming (if we can believe rumour) to make himself master of that city, so that he might form it into a patrimony of Messire Saint Paul rivalling that of Messire Saint Peter. O ghastly ghostly manners.

VII. *About the Confederate Earls their Monstrous Parturition*[1]

At Christmas, after awful and windy heaving and groaning, the Confederate Earls became painfully delivered of a monster. Lord Arthur, said they, should enjoy the style of King of the Southern English, and Lord Henry should enjoy the style of King of the Northern English. The two kings, said they, should hold their courts respectively at Winchester and at York. The government of the realm, said they, was to be conducted by the Confederate Earls, who were to serve in turn as members of a Council of Seven, which should rule in the names of both kings: but writs were to run, according to their locality, in the name of the King of the South or of the King of the North. O euphony.[2] And this settlement, said they, was to last for ever, the heir of each king succeeding to half of the kingdom but never to the whole. Such was the fruit of long gestation. I call it a monster. O unnatural parturition.

VIII. *About the Confederate Earls and bawling Bishops*

Need I say that the bishops began to bawl like lepers. They had

---

[1] The act of giving birth or bringing into being (*OED* OL).
[2] The quality of having a pleasant sound (*OED* OL).

no part or lot in this matter; and they naturally damned it as diabolical. Asked for their alternative, they insisted on a reconciliation between Lefthand and Lackland: but, what kind of reconciliation and on what terms, they were quite unable to specify. Insued
quarrels between the Confederate Earls, in a moment when the
bishops were hoarse and speechless, as to where was to be the
line dividing north from south. After a month, they decreed that
King Arthur might have Wales and Hereford and Gloucester and
all England South of Thames, and that Sir Henry might have the
rest.

VIIII. *About King Arthur active*

That was the limit. King Arthur got up in his Regal Majesty,
and did several mind-unhinging things all of a sudden. He sent
me secretly with letters to Lackland: from whom I brought secret
letters in return. He sent Earl Fulk the Flame with letters to
the cardinal-primate: "Be ware, lord archbishop," says he, "that
God's Vicegerent confirmed our kingdom of England, not to Sir
Henry fil-John, not to manœuvering magnates, but to Us:" and
again, "Be well ware, lord archbishop," says he, "that We shall
have no cause for sending Our regal request to Rome for your
Grace's damnation as rebel against Pope and King." Whereat the
cardinal-primate was so dreadfully worried, being most undesir-
ous of incurring the wrath of Rome again, that he instantly rode
to Windsor, said that he was sorry, and made his peace with the
king. Then, the four of us sat in solemn council for two nights and
a day.

The Primate Stephen and Earl Fulk fil-Richard and Earl Hubert
de Burgh bore Letters Patent to the Confederate Earls, who lay
at Oxford, announcing as follows. My lord the king (called for
this occasion Lord Arthur fil-Geoffrey) and Sir Henry Lackland
(called for this occasion Lord Henry fil-John) had performed the
solemnity of appeal to God, the King of kings, to manifest, in
Ordeal of Battle, which of the two was the rightful king of the
English. The Cardinal-Primate, acting for God, had accepted the
appeal, ordaining the festival of Messire Saint George as the day,
and Oxford as the site, for the Ordeal. If the Confederate Earls

(swayed by the devil) should interfere with this divine action, preventing the battle, diminishing the Ordeal of its due solemnity, and refusing its result, then, the said Lord Arthur fil-Geoffrey would defend his unction and his coronation as king of the English, and would abide by his original claim to the kingdom of England as the Lionheart's heir confirmed by our lord the Pope to aid him with the javelins of apostolic censures, bans, anathemas, and maledictions upon all who should oppose him, and, further, he would bring all sorts of undesirable aliens into the said kingdom to enforce his said claim. Lastly, in earnest of these determinations, the Confederate Earls were to know that the said Lord Arthur fil-Geoffrey, eluding the guard set upon him at Windsor, was intrenched in his castle of Dover, prepared for an interminable siege with the navies of his regal pirates and his V Ports under Sir Eustace the Monk holding the narrow sea in his rear.

x. About the Split Confederation

Such deep dismay afflicted the Confederate Earls that their minds became (as it were) unhinged. For, while they held two prisoners, they could act in their names, seemingly by their authority, and so deceive the people: but, with one prisoner at large, capering and gibbering at them, they were helpless, for the English never prefer the tyranny of oligarchs to that of a crowned and anointed king. Aside this also, many magnates (greater and lesser) were coughing and sneezing at the earls. And naturally the clergymen (if offered adequate persuasions) were inclined to harken to the Pope in the matter. But, for a fortnight, the Confederate Earls dillydallied: indeed they only rescinded their act when the counties began arming, for the King in the south, and for Lackland in the north. And by chance or by God's mercy (the latter, as I believe), quite the most ferocious and hectoring letters came, just then, from Rome, demanding why settlement of the kingdom under its lawful king was not yet accomplished, and threatening that, unless all clergymen comported themselves with propriety, instantly, every particular bishop and every singular magnate would be damned individually by name *ipso facto* and *lata sententia*[1] and that the kingdom would be set groaning and screeching under a new and very invidious interdict, and that all Englishmen throughout the world would be declared excommunicate and out of law, excepting such as were actually in the Holy Land and then only when they were actively engaged in the crusade or ministering to lepers. So, the Confederate Earls had to make a virtue of their necessity, and yield: for my lord the king was openly riding abroad with trumpets, acclaimed by the lesser magnates, as well as by the gentry, burgesses, and commons. And the earl of Arundel renewed his homage: after which, King Arthur swooped on Warwick and released Lackland, who could not of himself escape from durance. That glum calf rode to Westminster, and refuged (under the table, some say), in the abbot's parlour near by Sanctuary. And the Confederation split into two factions, as in the beginning.

XI. *About the Preparations for the Ordeal by Battle*

There were lists prepared at Oxford in the meadow under the wall by Cherwell side; and seats were set for persons of quality; and two altars were builded by. Very early on the festival of Messire Saint George, all the world came thither; and students and citizens combatted beyond mailed men-at-arms who kept the barriers; and two heralds simultaneously proclaimed safe-conducts to all men in the name of King Arthur and King Henry. The cardinal-primate held his court in the lists, hearing attorneys who rehearsed the claims and set forth the genealogies of the claimants; and his judgement was that the court could not decide the matter, and that appeal lay to the Ordeal by Battle. Compurgators[2] of ten-thousand marks were sworn, and the compurgation sealed, that the claimants should appear in their proper persons, the claim being of too high moment to bear intrusting to cham-

---

[1] These horrible descriptions of the particular species of damnation to be incurred have, we believe, an ecclesiastically technical meaning, and, as such, are perhaps better left untranslated.—P. and C. [Rolfe's note.] To say that the clergy would be damned *ipso facto* and *lata sententia* is to say that they would be automatically damned by the very fact of their behavior.

[2] One who testifies to another's veracity or accuracy (*OED* OL).

pions: no man under obligation to either claimant was accepted as compurgator.

King Arthur's pavilion was set in the sun; and therein were placed a table, a chair, a bason, six loaves of bread, two gallons of wine, a mess of beef and a plain pudding, a roasted pheasant and a rosemary pudding, nineteen baked eggs and a cheese, a board and a pair of trestles to set his meat on, a broad-cloth, a knife to cut his meat, a cup to drink of, a cask of water to wash him, a dozen tresses of arming-points, a hammer, a pincers, a crowbar, a dozen hob-nails, a long-sword, a short-sword, a dagg, a kerchief to wipe his mouth, a pensel[1] to bear in his hand. King Arthur was armed in his tent by two earls, namely, Sir Fulk fil-Richard earl of Richmond and Jaffa and Nantes, and Sir Hubert de Burgh earl of Gloucester and Essex. We stripped him naked as born, and washed him, venerating his glorious scars; and we put on him (instead of a shirt) a doublet of fustian lined with satin cut full of holes to give air to his skin, and strongly bound with kid-skin, with gussets of mail sewn in the bend of the arm and the armpit. His arming-points were fine twine which is used for cross-bows, trussed small and pointed as points, waxed with cordwainers' wax so that they might not reach or break. We put on him a pair of hose knitted by Stamyn Sengille,[2] with a pair of bulwarks of thin blanket to be about his knees and for chafing of his loins: a pair of shoes of thick cordwaining[3] fretted with small whip-cord, three knots on each end, three cords sewed fast to each heel, and five cords to each sole, with a three-finger space between the frets of heel and sole, fine shoes for gripping the ground, Gabriel Ded made them. We covered him with mail, setting on his mail-shoes over his leathern shoes, tying them with small points which could not break; and then greaves,[4] and then thigh-pieces, and then breeches, all of the

---

[1] A small flag or streamer (*OED* OL).

[2] Hose of worsted cloth specially made in Norfolk. Rolfe's detailed discussion of Arthur's outfitting for battle seems to be drawn from "How a Man Shall be Armed at his Ease When He Shall Fight on Foot," a set of ordinances concerning knights' arms, which was reprinted in H.A. Dillon's "On a MS Collection of Ordinances of Chivalry of the 15th Century belonging to Lord Hastings," *Archaeologia* 57 (1900): 29-70.

[3] Cordovan leather (*OED* OL).

[4] Armor for the shins (*OED* OL).

finest chain-mail. And then his great tunic of chain-mail reaching from throat to wrists and ankles, slit up to the crutch before and behind. And his gloves of mail; and his dagg on his left side, he being Lefthand;[1] and his short sword on his right side, in a round ring, all naked, to pull it out lightly. And we put on him his coat, quarterly, *England and Armorica, Hierusalem in pretence*, girding it with his knightly belt of gold. And, on his head, we put his coif[2] of quilted kidskin, and his coif of mail, and his helmet pinned on two great staples on his coif of mail, with a double buckle behind to make his helmet sit just so. And we put his long sword in his hand, and his banner in his hand, painted of Madame Saint Mary the God-bearer and Messire Saint George, to solace him as he went toward the field and in the field. And my lord the king said: "If I fought for my life, I would rather fight stark-naked with my hands; but as I fight for my kingdom, this gear must serve: but bare my head, I pray, because I have a vow." So we bared his regal head. And a silly old man named Hubert was for choking: but Fulk trembled not at all. And we attended King Arthur with his trumpeters to his altar.

Mass was said at both altars: both claimants saw God made, and received Him, swearing that they used no secret arms, nor art-magic, nor witchcraft, nor necromancy, nor conjurations, nor philtres,[3] nor periapts,[4] nor relics, nor any invocations of demons. The cardinal-primate confirmed the terms: the challengers mounted simultaneously, having satisfied their compurgators of their identity. And the said challengers, preceded by their banners, rode forward, claiming the crown and canopy of England, saying, "I, Arthur fil-Geoffrey, born in wedlock, as next brother's heir to King Richard Lionheart, do claim my crown and canopy of England." And "I, Henry fil-John, as son of my father, do claim my crown and canopy of England." They cast down their gages of battle, and rode round the lists, shewing themselves to the people. The scholars vociferously acclaimed my lord the king,

---

[1] "How a Man Shall be Armed at his Ease When He Shall Fight on Foot" specifies that the dagger should be worn on the right.
[2] Cap (*OED* OL).
[3] Potions (*OED* OL).
[4] Amulets worns as charms (*OED* OL).

because they admired his bare head, and his claim had many nice points about it, being far more subtile than Henry's, who wisely refrained from averring birth in wedlock, on which point I have but one word to say namely, that my dear wife Countess Havis of Gloucester and Essex, who had been Sir John fil-Henry's wife before he married Lady Jezebel, came to me intact, and has often told me that she had never even seen the creature, meaning Lackland. But the commons bellowed for Lackland, just because the scholars shouted for Lefthand. And my lord the king held aloft his hallowed hand as he rode, bearing his broom-sprig of Anjou. All the clergymen then withdrew, because the matter touched blood: but a little priest was kept to assoil[1] and anneal[2] the slain; and the bishop of Durham remained, not as bishop, but as earl-palatine of Sedbergh, and he had himself named marshal of the lists. This chapter is, I believe, particular enough to let all men know precisely how we conducted an Ordeal of this kind fifty years ago. And the battle was joined.

XII. *About the Ordeal by Battle*

They laid their lances in rest, and charged. Lefthand, preferring to fight on his proper legs, lanced Lackland's horse, avoiding the lance with a lizard-like writhing aside. Lackland, being dismounted, Lefthand dismounted too; and they met, brandishing long swords. Henry was short and squat of form, solidly strong, sullenly slow in action like a sulky young steer: wherefore, King Arthur easily avoided his attack, though his guard was such that some time passed without giving either claimant an advantage. Little splinters of steel, rings of their mail, shavings of metal, snippets from their coats, chipped off like sparks, or floated away like snow-flakes, in the sword-play. They fought without weariness: not every day do a couple of boys fight hand to hand for a kingdom. They fought round the lists, and round the lists: but, for Henry's every round, count forty rounds to Arthur: for, as Henry revolved on his heel, Arthur was bounding and leaping round and

---

[1] Absolve (*OED* OL).
[2] To "anele" is to anoint or to give extreme unction to the dying (*OED* OL).

about him at long-sword's length, as the glittering iron of a new bond revolves round the linch-pin of a rolling wheel. And, now and again, they scratched one another's faces.

We began to hear their panting breath, above the clicking and the clashing and the clanging of the long-sword blades. Very terrible was the silence of the multitude. Absolutely awful was the glare of innumerable wide-open earnest eyes. A timid old totterer[1] named Hubert de Burgh, became so fearful that he dared not to look at the fighters: he lowered his gaze to the sunlit green grass at his feet. For my lord the king was bare-headed. Uncountable throats sobbed suddenly. King Arthur had slipped on a bloody plaintain, and slid along the ground with a shattered long-sword. In an instant, he rebounded, like a scintillation from a blacksmith hammering on an anvil, flashing out his short-sword; and I read in his eyes an intention to make an end. They fought with short-swords at close quarters; and my lord the king's flickered so awfully that my eye could not follow it. It was as though flashes of flaming lightning leaped from his hand: but he stood firm on his feet, his body motionless, every nerve and sinew intense and aquiver, like a kitten, crouching, like a panther, the panther of England, collecting its forces for a spring. Icily gleamed his young eyes. And he sprang.

We saw not the springing. He was standing, at sword-play. He was high in the air, kneeling on Lackland's shoulders, grinding a fat head between his thighs. Henry staggered: both came crashing to ground. An unrecognizable blade whirled in the sunlight as they fell, rolling over together, in a great geyser of blood spouting to heaven.

King Arthur stood, superb, alone, lifting dead Henry's head on high, crying clearly and strongly, "Now for the second time, I take seizin of my kingdom of England."[2]

---

[1] *"timidus senior et vacillans."* [Rolfe's note.]
[2] Henry III actually died in 1272.

XIII. *About Arthur, by the Grace of God, and by Favour of the Apostolic See and by Unction and by Coronation, and by Ordeal of Battle of the English, King.*

There was a great hush. Several persons prayed. The staring head swang aloft by its hair. The bishop of Durham proclaimed, "By God His Grace is Arthur King." And the people broke into enormous roarings and vociferations, acknowledging the justice of God's Judgement, acclaiming the King. And all the bishops with their clergymen trooped into the lists, very alert to celebrate suddenly extemporized solemnities. O manners.

But my lord the king lifted up his voice again, and, says he, "Here lies dead Henry who (some say) has been king of the English. Be that as it may: but let all men make due mourning for him, for he was the grandson of the king, and shall have burial befitting a king, tomorrow, in the Abbey of Saint Frideswide. It is the King's will."

We bore King Arthur to his palace of Beaumont, where his dear worthy body was bathed and his limbs suppled in the Syriac mode by pages whom Earl Fulk directed. And, being clean and well-refreshed, he went into his great hall, to receive the keys of his city and castle of Oxford, and to hear odes intoned by doctors. And he supped there, enthroned, served by the two loyal earls, in a state of two-hundred trumpets and a canopy of gold brocade from Damascus, wearing England and his ermine mantle of Armorica. And he commanded forty chaplains, commanding waxen torches for them, commanding forty masses for the soul of Sir Henry fil-John, being ever generous to the memories of former foes. But, to the Confederate Earls who simply crawled at him on their hairy bellies, he would not say a single word, nor would he accept their homage, saying aloud to me (as though these miserable magnates were not there) that His Regal Majesty would attend to the cravings of certain culverts, nidderings, and several other offensive designations, at his pleasure, after the said caitiffs should have properly purged themselves of treason.

XVI

THE BOOK CALLED THE FLOWERS OF THE TREES

I. *About things in general*

When King Arthur had achieved all his rights, and had been crowned again of England, with Queen Mariol, at Westminster, according to all the ancient customs of the kingdom, there remained some persons whom he was bound to dispose, some deeds which he was bound to do. And, of course, there were also several new persons, and several new matters, which sprang to birth about him, to deserve his attention and treatment during his glorious reign. Consequently, it is my duty to write of these. And I will begin with a simple enumeration of certain new persons concerned in the history of my lord the king.

II. *About the Regal Progeny of King Arthur and Queen Mariol*

Earl Richard Plantagenet of Cornwall was heir of England and Hierusalem. He married Lady Ysabel Capet, daughter of King Aloys VIII of the Franks.[1] And he died in the year of The Lord 1249, leaving a regal progeny, which I will name in due order. R.I.P.

Lady Johanna Plantagenet was the eldest daughter of England and Hierusalem, a blue-bell. She married King Alexander II of the Scots.[2] And she died, leaving a regal progeny, which I need not name. R.I.P.

Lady Ysabel Plantagenet was the second daughter of England and Hierusalem, a daffodil. She married the Emperor Frederick

---

[1] Saint Isabel of France, Louis VIII's daughter, never married and founded a convent.

[2] Alexander II of Scotland actually married Henry III's sister, Joan of England.

II, Stupor Mundi Semper Augustus.[1] A.s.d.l.a.r.P.w.I.n.n.n. R.I.P.

Lady Alianora Plantagenet is the third daughter of England and Hierusalem, an azalea of flesh. She was given in marriage to Earl William of Pembroke and Striguil who died, and (sadly) to Earl Simon Montfort of Leicester who died.[2] As abbess, she rules the regal abbey of Syon.

Lord Fulk Plantagenet is the second son of England and Hierusalem, and Prince of Galilee in the latter kingdom with the title Regulus.

Lady Richilda Plantagenet is the fourth daughter of England and Hierusalem, a wall-flower like the Regal Majesty of Queen Mariol her mother. She married Sir John de Burgh, my heir.[3] And I will name their progeny in due order.

I come to the second generation, the regal progeny of King Arthur's eldest son Earl Richard Plantagenet of Cornwall and Lady Ysabel Capet of the Franks.

Lord Edward Plantagenet of England is the eldest grandson and heir of England and Hierusalem. He married, last year, Lady Alianora of Castile, sister of King Alfonso of that kingdom, who is called King of All the Spains on account of his eminence.[4] And King Alfonso knighted Lord Edward, because he was handsome and walked like a gentleman.[5] And King Alfonso gave him a charter of quit-claim[6] of all Gascony in his favour, sealed with a golden seal. And then King Arthur gave to his grandson Gascony, Ireland, Wales, Bristol, Stamford, Grantham so that he is as good as a king.

Earl Edmund Plantagenet of Lancaster, *gules, a tricorporate lyon or*, is the second grandson of England and Hierusalem.[7]

---

[1] Frederick married many women, including King John and Isabella of Angoulême's daughter, Isabella. In this section, Rolfe selectively uses the names of John and Henry's children and inserts Arthur and Mariol's (or Mary of Montferrat's) imaginary progeny in their place.

[2] John and Isabella's youngest daughter, Eleanor of England, married William Marshal, Earl of Pembroke and Simon de Montfort.

[3] John actually married the daughter of William de Lanvaley, Avisa.

[4] *"propter eminentiam."* [Rolfe's note.] Edward is the name of Henry III's son, who married Eleanor of Castile.

[5] *"honeste et lepide et liberaliter incessuit."* [Rolfe's note.]

[6] A renunciation of a claim (*OED* OL).

[7] Henry III had a son named Edmund.

Lady Margaret Plantagenet, an azalea of light, is the eldest granddaughter of England and Hierusalem. She married King Alexander III of the Scots with a dispensation.[1]

Lady Beatrix Plantagenet, an azalea of fire, is the second granddaughter of England and Hierusalem.[2] She married Sir Fulk II fil-Richard, grandson of Earl Fulk fil-Richard of Richmond and Jaffa and Nantes and of Earl Hubert de Burgh of Kent and Gloucester and Essex.

IIII. *About the spectable Progeny of Earl Fulk fil-Richard and Lady Alys fil-Guy*

When King Arthur's half-sister, countess Alys of Nantes, became of an age, and her husband, Earl Fulk, was free to attend to his duty, this spectable progeny enriched them.

Earl Richard fil-Fulk of Penthieve is heir of Earl Fulk and Countess Alys. He married my dear little daughter Lady Douce de Burgh, a primrose. And Sir Fulk II fil-Richard is their son, who married Lady Beatrix Plantagenet, an azalea of fire, second granddaughter of England and Hierusalem.

Sir Arthur fil-Fulk of Holderness is the second son of Earl Fulk and Countess Alys.

Earl Hubert fil-Fulk of Brecon is the third son of Earl Fulk and Countess Alys. He married Lady Auriol, heiress of Earl Reinald Braose of Brecon. And Mr. Arthur their son is page to Queen Mariol in the thirteenth year of his age.

Queen Constance fil-Fulk, queen-mother of Cyprus, a wildrose, is the eldest daughter of Earl Fulk and Countess Alys. She married King Henry I of Cyprus. He died three years ago, leaving a regal progeny, namely, King Henry II of the said Kingdom.

Lady Johanne fil-Fulk, a mayflower of hawthorn, is the second daughter of Earl Fulk and Countess Alys. She married Sir Philip de Montfort, who will have the earldom of Jaffa in right of his wife, when Earl Fulk the Flame shall have ascended to the superiors with Earl Hubert de Burgh, following our dear lord the king.

---

[1] Margaret of England was Henry III's daughter, and she married Alexander III of Scotland.

[2] Henry III also had a daughter named Beatrice.

IIII. *About the spectable Progeny of Earl Hubert de Burgh*

By marriage with Lady Beatrix Warenne of Wirmegay, I got an heir, and a son.

Sir John de Burgh is heir of my palatine earldom of Kent and my earldom of Essex. He is Viceconstable of my Kentish castles and Subwarden of my V ports. He married Lady Richilda Plantagenet, fourth daughter of England and Hierusalem, a wallflower like the Regal Majesty of Queen Mariol her mother. Their children, my grandsons, are Sir Arthur de Burgh of Richborough, heir of my son John, and bishop Hubert III of Llandaff, who ascended to the superiors last year. R.I.P.

Sir Hubert II de Burgh is my second son. He will be heir of my earldom of Gloucester, if he does not take the holy habit of the Friars Minor within the next few weeks.

When Lady Beatrix died (R.I.P.), I married Lady Margaretha, heiress of Sir Robert Arsike: a barren nuptials. When Lady Margaretha died (R.I.P.), I married Countess Havis fil-Robert of Gloucester and Essex: a barren nuptials. When Lady Havis died (R.I.P.), I married Lady Margaret, daughter of King William the Lyon and sister of King Alexander II of the Scots. By her I got twins, a splendid son and a darling daughter.[1]

Archbishop Boniface de Burgh of Canterbury, the Primate of All England, is my third son.

Lady Douce de Burgh, a primrose, is my daughter. She married Earl Fulk fil-Fulk of Penthieve, all as aforesaid.

So much for new persons. I revert to certain old ones.

---

[1] Hubert's daughter by Margaret of Scotland, Margaret (Magota), secretly married Richard de Clare, which angered Henry III. This complaint against Hubert played a large role in his final trial. According to Clarence Ellis, Magota was the only one of Margaret and Hubert's children to survive infancy (110).

XVII

THE BOOK CALLED THE MORALS AND
MANAGEMENT OF MAGNATES

I. *About a Concentration of Effort*

Seeing that I am becoming older every day: seeing also that I find this world extremely tiresome, and so most earnestly yearn to be with my lord the king as usual where he is in the kingdom among the blessed dominations, I will make haste to finish the writing of these histories. Not that I am inclined to scamp my task. By no means. That would be to minish my lord the king of his glory, a most heinous felony, which I am now too old to compass, even if I had the mind to it. Which I have not. But, nevertheless, I will no longer discourse of all and sundry, but solely of those great forces which King Arthur had to handle, and to bend to his sovereign will, during his reign. I mean these, the magnates, and the clergymen, and the kingdom of Hierusalem, and the King's Giwen. And I must not forget to record the decent proper end of Sir John fil-Henry, sometime our Wild-Ass. O times. O manners. This, then, is the book about the magnates.

II. *About eminent Magnates*

I suppose that no one is rash enough to deny to Earl Fulk fil-Richard palatine of Richmond, and to Earl Hubert de Burgh palatine of Kent, the right of considering themselves far and away the most eminent of the magnates of England, on account of their enormous powers, the length and continuity and quality of their service, and the numbers of their trumpets. We knew all about everybody and all about everything; and we never lacked means of doing what it seemed good to us to do. Needless to say, we never once swerved from our allegiance to King Arthur. We loved him. Enough said.

And, looking back upon all these fifty years, I am of opinion that Earl Simon of Montfort was the magnate next in importance after me. He was a man of the most elegant and alluring manners conceivable by the human mind: he had a most pleasing and plausible personality: he gained immense popularity and multitudinous adherents (despite his fickle temper) far more easily than better and solider men can collect contumely and enemies. King Arthur himself, endeavouring to keep this knight righteous, gave him Lady Alianora Plantagenet of England in marriage. More: My lord the king confirmed him in his father's earldom of Leicester, to hold it with his Frankish earldom of Montfort. What beside could an earl desire, even a very vigorous earl who requires very wide scope for his energies? But this Simon was predestined to damn himself. And, damn himself he did, most dreadfully, by abusing his natural gifts and potencies, choosing the broad road whereon traitors spadge[1] to their own destruction. O manners.

III. *About Circumstances*

Owing to the horrible years which preceded the reign of King Arthur, it was necessary at first (as must be plain to everyone) that the Regal Majesty should refrain his natural inclination and earnest desire for leniency, and govern England with more than a small degree of strictness. For England was like a mettlesome charger, who has been ridden long by a weakling unable to rule his beast, or by a rider demented whose madness infects that which he touches. Such a steed, when mounted at last by a man, must be made to feel the master's hand on his bridle; and, only after this lesson is learnt, comes the time for caresses and carrots. Consequently, King Arthur ruled by my advice at first, I being a knight well known to the Regal Majesty, and enjoying a reputation for taking serious matters seriously.[2] We encountered numerous nui-

---

[1] *"exspaciuntur."* [Rolfe's note.]

[2] After the death of William Marshal in 1219, Hubert de Burgh became Henry's most influential advisor. He seems to be playing a similar role in the court of young King Arthur.

sances; and cleared them away. For example: bishop Peter Roches
of Winchester was a nuisance.[1] He had been warden of Sir Henry
fil-John, and was grieved when the glum calf suffered the Judgement of God in the Ordeal at Oxford, whereby he lost a place of
power and profit; and, for two years, he annoyed me in the right
ruling of England, collecting foreign mercenaries, intriguing
with Prince Llywelyn of Wales, and with certain Irish magnates,
all to thwart me. Such was his overweening impudence, that he
actually occupied several of the king's castles before I could take
them over: for multifarious were the matters which fell upon my
shoulders at that time. But the Primate Stephen found it best to
stand by me; and, presently, he with the javelins of censures and
maledictions, and I with more persuasive weapons, forced that
wretched bishop to evacuate the stolen castles and to pluck up
courage to go on his frequently-feinted crusade. Then there was
the affair of Will, brother of that Sir Fulk Breauté who was once a
cotterel of the Wild Ass, and egregiously hanged by King Arthur.
This knight still held his barony of the exchequer and six shire-
reeveries, which he got from Sir John fil-Henry; and I had to dis-
seize him by force; for he was bad, an abductor of heiresses, an
intimidator of justice, and some people in the midlands said that
he was as good as king of those parts. So I hanged him. In revenge,
his lieutenant seized one of my travelling-justices, whose name
(I fancy) was Sir Henry Braibrock, stripped him naked, slit his
nostrils, and flung him in gaol in Bedford. Naturally, I went up
and took Bedford after some resistance; and I hanged the whole
garrison for fruitlessly standing out against me when they knew
that they had no chance of relief.[2] Then there was the affair of Sir
Savary Malaleone, that powerful Frankish magnate, who was the
terror of the narrow sea, slaying and plundering like a chartered
pirate, until I used the properly chartered pirates of my V Ports to
drown him. And, of course, too, I was obliged to levy new and not
small taxes as well for the suitable conduct of King Arthur's government as to let the nation know that good government costs

---

[1] Peter des Roches was displaced by Hubert for the justiciarship, and he never
forgot this indignity, attempting many times to avenge it.
[2] William de Breauté's men abducted a justice, Henry of Baybrook, on his way to
the king's council. Henry III had him hung after the siege of Bedford castle.

good money. And, of course, many fools chose to feel displeased, obliging me to beat them sternly below the armholes as examples. Earl William Fors of Aumale jumped up and put himself at the head of a parcel of displeased magnates, causing me no little trouble before we beheaded him.[1] And, as for the London riots, I only stopped them when I caught their inciter, one Constantine fil-Alulf, and hanged him.[2] Now it is necessary to understand all this, before I can rehearse the histories of how Earl Simon took advantage of the discontent (which circumstances forced us most reluctantly to cause) when he was minded to make mischief against King Arthur.

IIII. *About Earl Simon*

The beginning of this Earl's estrangement from my lord the king was on this wise. Certain noble ladies assembled at the Tower of London, to accompany Queen Mariol to a monastery for her purification after she had given birth to Lady Margaret Plantagenet, an azalea of light, who married my brother-in-law the king of the Scots. And Earl Simon of Montfort and Leicester, swayed by a proper devil, came with his wife to assist at the festive ceremony: which wife, I grieve to say, he had basely and clandestinely treated before marriage. O manners. Whereat King Arthur's stomach was so moved, that he loaded the said earl with reproaches: who withdrew in confusion, hastening by water to his lodgings in the palace of the bishop of Winchester which my lord the king had generously lent to him. King Arthur, however, impatient of his so indecent audacity, pursued him with an order to quit the premises, saying, "You raped my daughter before marriage; and when she complained to me, I gave her to you to keep her honest, though you were as repugnant to me as to her. Don't you know that you ought to walk humbly, not thrusting in among virtuous earls? Nor is this impertinence the worst which I have

---

[1] William de Forz cooperated repeatedly with Falkes de Breauté.
[2] According to Matthew Paris, Constantine fitz Athulf played an integral role in the riots concerning a wrestling match that took place in 1222. Hubert de Burgh did have him hung, and he was accused of causing the unjust death of Constantine during his trial in 1232.

against you. As a crown to your naughtiness, you have (by false witness) been making me your surety, without either my knowledge or consent. Be you ware then, niddering, that I have found out all about those twenty-eight-hundred silver marks which you borrowed from Sir Peter Mauclerk, pretending that I authorized you to do so."[1] At which shocking disclosures, Earl Simon was so fearfully abashed, that he at once went down Thames in a shallop, with his wife and not a single trumpet, nor did he stop till he reached the coast, whence he fled across the narrow sea.

v. About Earl Simon his Spasm of Penance

I am bound to record my opinion, that Earl Simon's guardian-angel would seem presently to have gotten the better of the proper devil who usually goaded him to iniquity: for, after reflection, he became in a great state of alarm about his marriage. I do not allude to the prenuptial indiscretion amounting to felony afore-mentioned. What was done could not be undone; and the best had been made of it. But his conscience was uneasy on another score. For when Lady Alianora's first husband died (he being Earl William of Pembroke and Striguil), she, wishing to lead the rest of her broken young life as a hallowed widow, bound herself by a vow of chastity sworn before the Primate of all England. Then, when, for good cause, the said countess complained to her regal father of seduction, Simon was made to marry her with proper dispensations from her vow from Rome. But there can be no doubt that his conscience was very tender on the point as to whether even our lord the Pope Himself has power to release (as He did) from a vow of chastity. And so, to quiet his ridiculous scruples, and to secure admission to heaven, he took the cross, with his lady-countess and most of his household knights, as soon as he reached his Frankish earldom. This pleased King Arthur, for two reasons: first, because it kept Earl Simon out of his sight, my lord the king never being able to tolerate hairy persons in his proximity: second, because (like the blessed angels inhabiting heaven) it was his habit to rejoice over a repentant sinner.

---

[1] Henry III had a similar series of disagreements with Simon Montfort about money and Simon's marriage to his sister, Eleanor.

vi. About Earl Simon seneschal of Gascony

To encourage the Earl of Montfort and Leicester in his pious dispositions, King Arthur sent him letters patent appointing him to the seneschalty of Gascony for six years.[1] Now, I maintain that, if I had been in Simon's shoes, this job would have suited me precisely. It was not a bed of roses: contrariwise, it was a most difficult and onerous situation; and just for that very reason, it afforded (to any witty earl, who really wished to give tokens of his wit and knighthood), a splendid chance of acquiring credit. For the Gascons were vain devils, utterly obstreperous even toward such great kings as King Henry fil-Empress and King Richard Lionheart; and they only acknowledged King Arthur as their duke, to save themselves from King Aloys of the Franks, his father King Philip the August having gone to glory. Moreover, my lord the king gave Simon (as seneschal) four extra trumpets and a free hand, furnishing him neither with money nor with a power, but leaving him to supply himself, either from his own resources or from taxes upon the Gascons, so that all the credit of a successful seneschalty might be Simon's, and no one but Simon's. O princely benevolence.

vii. About Earl Simon his Incapacity as Seneschal

Simon as a seneschal gave way to such fits as generally afflict a fickle fool. I admit that he captured poor old Sir Gaston de Bearn, as a leader of troublesome Gascons: but my lord the king enlarged that knight because he had been a leal friend to the Regal Majesty's honest good uncle. But Simon took umbrage at this act of clemency; and thought proper to return in inglorious haste from Gascony, attended only by three poor squires, with his horses worn out by hunger and hard riding, boots split in half across the instep by the spur-straps, and a total absence of trumpets. O manners. And, in London, he demanded of King Arthur a pro-

---

[1] In 1248, Henry sent Simon to Gascony, which was at the time beset by feuds and rebellions, to restore order.

vision of money and mercenaries for crushing the insolent Gascons, whom he had cravenly left in open rebellion against him. This is what I call the comportment of a very silly fool. My lord the king, however, treated him with singular lenience. "By God's Eyes, sir earl," says the Regal Majesty; "We will not deny aid to any knight who doughtily serves Us: but, loud cries of complaint reach Us that you very unpleasantly prison and slay knights who come to you peaceably at your own summons."[1] The earl denied it. "Lord king," shrieks he, "they make me sick; and their treachery deprives them of the right to be listened to, even when they swear." The king thought well to forbear a little longer. He gave the earl three-thousand marks wherewith to buy Brabanxon mercenaries for supporting his authority; and packed him back to his duty.

VIII. About Complaints and Complainants

Earl Simon did nothing but muddle; and we soon had him back again in London, complaining. Now complaining I hold to be a practice in which no knight endowed with regal authority ought to engage: for honour demands either that he should fulfil the task which he has undertaken, or that he should perish with great good cheer in a vigorous attempt at such achievement. Simon, however, was a champion whimperer. As is the custom of incompetent persons, he would volubly explain in words instead of doing such deeds as would save him from the trouble of talking. His remarks about the Gascons were more than explanatory: they were inflammatory: they also were extremely tiresome into the bargain. But he was not the only complainant. Several sackfuls of complaints against their seneschal came to my lord the king, from the Gascons themselves. They called Earl Simon an infamous traitor: they affirmed that he was heaping up vast wealth, which he extorted from clergymen and magnates and commons, sparing none, not even lepers, pretending that King Arthur was needing such aid for going on a pilgrimage, but secretly keep-

---

[1] Simon de Montfort was widely criticized for using excessive force during his time in Gascony. He was eventually put on trial for violating the Gascons' rights.

ing it all for himself. And, lastly, they alleged that he used a very disagreeable method with his enemies, whom he peacefully summoned under safe-conducts, to partake of puddings and to counsel him, and then (like Sinon, not Simon)[1] starved them to death in his dungeon, or boiled them.

VIIII. *About Inquisitors and Inquisitions*

This lighted a fire of impatient indignation in my lord the king: his Regal Majesty detested the bare notion of suspecting evil in a knight whom he disliked, who had injured his honour, who had seemed to have repented of iniquity. Such was the clean just mind of King Arthur. So, to learn the truth, he took Sir Henry of Wingham, his clerk, a clever prudent knight with straight hair, exquisite manners, and a perennial pimple, who had been seneschal of Bordeaux and (therefore) knew the place, to whom he joined Sir Rocelin de Ros, the master of the London Temple and a Gascon born; and he sent this pair to Gascony, to make a careful inquisition, and to bring him certain information. Earl Simon chose to go, in fury, expounding his lamb-like innocence to all who would listen, until my lord the king estopped him gravely and not a little sternly, saying, "Simon, if all is clear, what harm can inquisition do, excepting that it may perchance restore your fame?"[2] Whereat Montfort withered away with abashment and melancholy; asking leave to return to his seneschalty, which was instantly granted; and the king gave him another three-thousand marks to be ridded of him. So he crossed the narrow sea with his feelings far from calmed, proposing to take condign vengeance on his accusers. O culvert.

X. *About Foxiners*

Simon brought a new power of Frankish mercenaries, both knights and their followers; and he called on King Thibaut I,

---

[1] The phrase "like Sinon, not Simon" is lifted directly from Matthew Paris's accout of these events. The name of Sinon, the Greek spy who convinced the Trojans to bring the wooden horse into the city, is synonymous with treachery.

[2] According to Matthew Paris, this is how Henry III responded to Simon de Montfort's protests.

Navarre, and Earl Eskivat Chabannais of Bigore, and many other foreigners, to aid in exterminating his subjects. He so strengthened his power, and so afflicted the spirits of the Gascons with his atrocities, that (had not England been their best customer for their Bordeaux wines), they certainly would have defied the king of the English, their duke, transferring their faith to some overlord who would give them a seneschal less savage than Simon. And at this point, that earl began to be foxy: for he very cleverly arranged that Sir Henry of Wingham and Sir Rocelin de Ros should fail to find out anything very particularly in his disfavour. But, seeing that the king's inquisition was likely to fail in its object, certain Gascons set to work to assist it. Archbishop Gerard Malemort of Bordeaux, with several magnates from Lareole and other Gascon cities, hastened by sea to London, and laid laments about the seneschal's tyranny before my lord the king. King Arthur, however, was not inclined to believe these persons, who enjoyed very dubious reputations: but, anxious to get to the facts, and these new complainants seeming to be dreadfully in earnest, the Regal Majesty sent two more Gascons, Sir Nicholas Molis and Sir Drogo Valentin, who each had been seneschal of the duchy aforetime, with orders to make further inquisition. This, of course, deepened Earl Simon's displeasure. No wonder. Nothing exasperates an inveterate offender more than prolonged patience.

xi. *About Accusations*

Archbishop Gerard and the Gascon Magnates remained in England, and continued to cough vehemently against Earl Simon as their would-be annihilator. Troops of other Gascons joined them; and vast were their vociferations in chorus. And then the regal inquisitors reported that Earl Simon was undoubtedly in the habit of treating his subjects with grave inhumanity, in proof of which they submitted five specimens of cauldrons used for boiling opponents.

The seneschal of Gascony was summoned to meet his accusers. Here is a category of the lesser charges which he had to answer. He was accused, first, that he devastated the duchy with the ferocity of a foreign foe: second, that he snubbed magnates whom other seneschals had treated as friends: third, that he very carefully sent magnates (known as friendly to King Arthur) to Frankish prisons, where they instantly died somehow: fourth, that he was guilty of grievous extortion: fifth, that he imprisoned and starved or boiled to death faithful magnates whom he enticed under safe-conducts, on pretence of desiring their peaceable counsel: sixth, that he habitually seized other magnates' castles by the basest species of treachery by means of hired lepers, rummaging the same for plunder from battlement to barbacan so cataclysmally that they became uninhabitable. O manners.

XII. *About a Sermon*

Confronted by these accusations, instead of defending himself as a knight should, first by offering his body in challenge to his accusers to make good on, second by producing evidence rebutting the accusation, Earl Simon gazed upon us all as though he had no hope of encountering any of us above, and proceeded to favour us with a sermon. He, with the air of one actually happed up in bishopskins, exhorted us, in general terms, on the divers but certain manners in which Almighty God rewards virtue and punishes the evil-doer. O trite booby. And my lord the king was much disappointed. As for me, I could not refrain my stomach at so heinous a mockery of religion; and, when I saw many pious fools preparing to believe no evil of so beautiful a preacher, my disgust (at a knight deserting his knightly office of deeds for the clerkly office of words) became so uncontrollable, that to the end of one of his most impressive periods, I appended a grand amen, bellowed nasally with all the wind at my disposal. Whereat everyone gulped thrice and burst out laughing and hiccoughing. At that, Simon completely lost his temper, as I intended: for I knew that we should get at the kernel of his mind by stripping him naked of his piety. And so we did: for, having harangued us in abuse of his accusers, he swore by his chin, and burst into a torrent of blasphemy against my lord the king, charging the Regal Majesty with breaking troth, by secretly trying to void him of his seneschalty before the six years of it had expired. O manners.

xiii. *About the Breach with the Traitor*

King Arthur suddenly blazed with Angevin anger, retorting, "Certainly I will break troth with an unworthy traitor: for it is lawful to withdraw from agreements made with a wretch who breaks them continually, as you do; and it also is lawful to deal unashamedly with the openly malicious, such as you plainly shew yourself to be." Insued a most awful altercation. The earl declared that my lord the king was a manifest liar meanly sheltering beneath his crown and canopy: "Who," he screamed, "could believe you to be a Christian? Even if you ever were shriven, you have never shewn contrition." For, even yet, the humbug kept flapping the tatters of his piety to hide his shame. Then King Arthur, infused with Plantagenet passion, said terribly: "For one thing I am most truly contrite, in that I ever permitted you to enter England, or to hold lands and honours there where you grow fat and kick me." And, so saying, he bade the faithless Frank to be gone, lest dire dooms should blast him.

xiiii. *About a Second Opportunity*

King Arthur kept silence for two nights and a day. Simon thought that he was either weakening or meditating evils: but I knew well that he was struggling to keep control on his by no means unjust ire. When he emerged from seclusion, my lord the king radiated his usual grave and vivid serenity, so that Simon and the Gascon magnates (who came to hear the judgement) marvelled greatly. Says, then, King Arthur to the Earl of Montfort and Leicester (now cooled down and dreadfully worried), "Return yet again to your seneschalty, that you (being fond of war, and a fomenter of it), may have enough of it, and bring back your merited reward, as did your father." Superb sentence, full of meaning as an egg of meat. Simon crawled away to France, where he was well acquainted; and he gathered an immense power of Frankish cotterels, promising them boundless booty. These, more greedy than bloodsuckers, gladly followed him, not to retrieve his honour but to take revenge on his defamers. And, whenever he caught a

Gascon knight alone, he overthrew him, and shamefully sold him for his full worth; and what he thus gained he shared with his cotterels; and no earl in the world could be more beloved than he was. So, the last state of Gascony was far worse than the first. O times.

xv. *About the King's Going*

The magnates and citizens of Bordeaux advised my lord the king that, unless he himself came thither, instantly, with a great power, he would lose his duchy, for they were simply bored to death by the Earl of Montfort and Leicester. Then, indeed, King Arthur arose in regal majesty; and, having redeemed Simon's charter of seneschalty at a cost of three thousand marks for each of the three years which it yet had to run, nine thousand marks in all, he had proclamation made by heralds throughout Gascony, deposing Simon for tyranny and oppression and unknightly malfeasances, ordaining that no man need henceforth heed or obey him. Which act gave great satisfaction to the Gascons. Next, after naming Queen Mariol and Earl Hubert de Burgh as Wardens and Regents of England, my lord the king put to sea, from Portsmouth, with a tolerable wind, accompanied by three-hundred galiasses and more numerous navy of busses and eseccas. The regal galiass was a new *Maryflower*, named after my lady the queen and builded by the shipwrights of my pirates at Sandwich; and it was the most seaworthy and most splendid ship possible to be made by man without the direct intervention of angels. It was a hundred-and-ten-feet long, and forty broad, and eleven-and-a-half-feet deep in the hold, and six-and-a-half-feet deep between decks. And there were two chambers in it, for the king's shelter when he willed, both wainscotted with cedarwood. And there was another chamber to place the king's things in. And the crew consisted of five captains and fifty mariners and five-and-fifty ship-boys, all healthy and of faithful fearless minds, picked by me. And now, that I am remembering so many matters, I will record how that young Lord Edward Plantagenet of England, after his regal grandfather had embraced him many times, stood on the shore, bravely choking his youthful grief, nor would he return with me so long as he could see the swelling sails of the ship. For King Arthur had promised to give the duchy of Gascony to Lord Edward after that he had ordered it conveniently; and the modest imp was overcome at the approach of his first great dignity.

XVI. *About Simon's Secession to the Franks*

Frankish magnates made overtures to Earl Simon, as a Frank. Their king was fighting for God in the Holy Land: Queen Blanche was dead: the best knights of France had fallen in the crusade. So the Frankishmen begged Earl Simon to abide with them as Warden of France, promising to heap wealth and honours upon him as merited reward. They knew (said they) that he, like Simon his father who had fought so very virtuously against the obscene pestilent ferocious heretics of the Albigeois, had, from of old, a genuine affection for the Frankish kingdom, nor was he any stranger to the Franks in blood. What they did not know, was (and very few men knew it then), that Earl Simon was possessed by a discontented devil, who pricked him to fail in plain straight-forward dealing, and to run away on every possible occasion. I do not think that King Arthur would have demurred from his quondam[1] seneschal's retirement to Frankish bosoms: for my lord the king was merciful, not willing the death of the sinner (which I earnestly advised, and prepared both rope with gallows and axe with block for it), but rather that he should convert himself from his wickedness and live comfortably elsewhere than in England or the Angevin feofs. However, Simon's discontented devil prodded him to refuse the excellent situation offered by the Franks, and put a new plan into his mind whereby he might make himself a worse nuisance than ever before.

XVII. *About the Sulphureous Foetor[2] of Earl Simon*

King Arthur, valiantly warring among the rebels of Gascony, demanded fresh supplies of money, which I freely sent him, with news that Earl Simon, taking advantage of his absence, was buzz-

---

[1] Former (*OED* OL).
[2] Stench (*OED* OL).

ing about this country, whispering wickedness in the hairy ears of such magnates as were ill-humoured or unstable (as some always are, with reason or without) thus beginning a new career of mischief against my lord the king. Of these hellish machinations, I vainly warned King Arthur, seeing plainly (as I saw) that the recreant earl, whose memory exhales a sulphureous foeter[1] was gaining a considerable audience among magnates and chiefly among clergymen and commons, clowns being always all a-gape and sweating to admire and to worship a honey-tongued rascal ostentatious of grievances or piety. But my lord the king remained steadfast in his determination not to molest the traitor any further at present, partly because he disdained him, partly out of love and pity for Lady Alianora, and (I believe) partly because the Regal Majesty was ware that a traitor generally destroys himself with his treachery. "Leave the bug alone," said my lord the king, "and let him go to the devil by his own way."

xviii. About the Earl of Leicester his Treason

I have treated all Simon's behaviour as Montfort: now I will deal with his doings as Leicester. When King Arthur returned with peace and honour from his Gascon campaign, a quarrel (by chance) broke out one day in The Presence, between Earl William de Valence of Pembroke and Striguil (who was Lady Alianora's son by her first husband) and Earl Simon de Montfort of Leicester (who was second husband of Lady Alianora). The former, a lusty honest youth with a glaring eye and impatient of pettifoggery, called the latter a damned liar and bloody traitor, and stamped on his toe. Notwithstanding the precision of the terms, there certainly would have insued a mortal combat on the spot, had not the king intervened, using his hallowed hand and a Syriac wrench which separated the would-be combatants, saying that his scorn of Simon was such that he would not have one of his good earls dirtied by contact with such an one. And the dregs of enmity, which this incident generated, never afterward lost their strength.

---

[1] *"cuius memoria sulfureum exhalat foetorem."* [Rolfe's note.]

Simon, then, once again mistaking toleration for timidity, and flattering himself that he was fearful to King Arthur, made no further concealment of his Punic faith,[1] and began to collect a power of magnates apt to treason. These met at Oxford; and drew up certain Provisions which they hoped would be conceded by the Regal Majesty. They asked for the king's castles, his warden-ship of heiresses, his forests: they wished clergymen (specially bishops and abbots) to be prevented from holding feofs: they would limit the king's rights of governing his Giwen and of grant-ing charters: they would have no fortified castles at seaports or on islands.[2] Ridiculous provisions and totally indigestible, such as none but inurbane provincials, clownishly-minded and inex-pert in state-affairs, would dare to produce to daylight. Neverthe-less, they served Earl Simon's purpose, giving him (as it were) a solid grievance against my lord the king: for a claimant without a categorical complaint may be neglected: but, once provided with a definite list of grievances, just, or unjust, he at once becomes certain of some adherents, and therefore dangerous, and must be noticed or dealt with as severely and suddenly as possible. At least, that is my opinion.

XVIIII. *About the Traitor Simon his Traitors his Ditties*

Traitorous magnates, adherents of Simon, were the bishops of Worcester and Winchester (the latter of course), earl Humphrey Bohun of Hereford, Sir Roger Marshal, Sir Roger Mortimer, Sir John fil-Geoffrey, Sir Richard Gray, Sir Wilham Bardulph, Sir Piers de Montfort, to begin with: others joined him later. And London city, I regret to say, was minded to side with these trai-tors. Now there is no denying that they were all very uneasy in their minds, their anxiety being increased by the approach of the month of August with its scorching Dog-star[3] and pestilence-

---

[1] Treachery. The Punic, or Carthaginian, people were thought of as treacherous by the Romans.

[2] Simon de Montfort was instrumental in the drafting of the Provisions of Oxford, a plan for reform that placed the government under the direction of the king and a council composed of fifteen barons. The parliament was to meet three times a year. This document is often referred to as England's first written constitution.

[3] Sirius. When rising with the sun, this star was supposed to cause excessive heat.

breathing Lyon[1]: for they were not quite agreed as to the method or scope of their treason. Angry words passed between Simon and Humphrey: the former in a fit of passion (to which he was subject from a child) accused the latter of wavering. "I care not to converse with so false a knight as my lord earl of Hereford:" shrieks huffy Simon; and forthwith flitted to France: O artful devil. The traitorous magnates, too frightened to stand alone, pressed Sir Humphrey till he weakened, passing over the insult to his honour; and then they all howled for Simon to come back and lead them on his own terms. Thus, the storm was appeased: but though the Earl of Montfort remained abroad, the renegades gathered confidence from hope of his affable return. What was he doing, that arch-traitor? He was scribbling rotten songs in his own favour, for distribution among the communalty: truly a devilish device, seeing how facilely the mobile vulgar are moved by a mind-grieving ditty. Witness the ditty which begins *Earl Simon hight of Montfort, thou powerful man and brave, be not dismayed by menaces nor terror of the grave.*[2]

xx. About King Arthur his Measures and Proclamation

My lord the king made time for taking some measures against Earl Simon's mischief. He was not discommoded, but rather he rejoiced at the prospect of dealing with unsought danger. Not that the danger was insignificant: contrariwise: for the new and hardly-won kingdom of England was rather like a broken reed to lean upon in time of stress, considering the king's long absences in Gascony, Anjou, Armorica, the Holy Land, and other parts of his enormous dominions. It happened that King Arthur was keeping Christmas with my lady the queen in the castle of Windsor, when Earl Fulk the Flame brought the disgusting news of the Londoners wishing to side with the Simoniacs. And then burst

---

[1] Leo. Also supposed to cause summer heat. Matthew Paris similarly makes note of the manner in which the "plague-bearing lion and the furiously-raging dog" disturb "the repose of the air." See Matthew Paris's *English History From the Year 1235 to 1272*, Vol. III, translated by J.A. Giles (London: Henry G. Bohn, 1854), 294.
[2] According to Marion Florence Lansing, this was a popular song of the period. See Lansing's *Patriots and Tyrants* (New York: Ginn and Co., 1911), 108.

out Plantagenet passion. "Never, by God's Eyes, shall sweaty burgesses thwart me again:" cried my lord the king. And we three
rode to London with all the trumpets available. King Arthur fortified himself in the Tower; and broke the locks of the regal treasure
chests which I was storing there, knowing that the time was come
for spending money like water. He collected masons to strengthen
the fortress in suitable places. He let guard the city all round with
bolts and bars. He assembled all the citizens from twelve years old
and upward; and took their oath to keep faith with him. And he
made proclamation by heralds, that all who would fight for him
should come forward at once, and be supported at his expense,
with beer and beef and puddings twice every day.

xxi. *About Rebels*

When they heard that we were not at all terrified and eating
beef and pudding as above quite cheerfully, the rebels' minds
shewed signs of becoming unhinged; and they assembled their
powers outside the walls, lodging in the city being strictly forbidden them. The cause of their quandary was not only the shock of
finding us able and very willing to do a deed on them. The fact
is that they none of them thoroughly trusted their leader. For,
though they were not averse from playing traitor to King Arthur,
not a knight of them was cat enough to consider the aggrandise-
ment of the monkey Montfort (which was what was actually contemplated) a sufficient reason for burning their paws in the fire
of rebellion. As indeed it was not. So, while the beetle-brained
magnates were settling their minds as to whether they should
fight at all, and on what pretext, that is to say, whether to avenge
Earl Simon's grievances against the king, or to keep themselves
warm (it being very cold that winter), or for some more proper
and plausible reason, Montfort himself most awfully put a term
to their hesitancy.

xxii. *About Earl Simon his Hypocrisy*

Simon plainly perceived (foxy hypocrite which he was), that
his particular cause by itself was not sufficient to justify him, or

any other magnate, in open rebellion. Therefore, with a dexterity indubitably diabolical, he retired all his own matters into a decorous background; and, with tremendously trumpeted Tarataran-taras of his virtue, he thrust into the foreground of his conspiracy, the lamentable case of Sir John fil-Henry, sometime our Wild Ass, now, in awful old age a miserable snivelling gibbering maniacal pensioner of the monks of Beaulieu, an object of daily derision (so Simon alleged, and God forgive me for writing it in an urbane tongue), to the upstart usurper, Arthur.[1] O manners.

xxiii. *About Short Memories*

Men's memories are short. The traitorous magnates, carried away by the plausible pleadings of Simon and his audacious ideas, forgot all which their fathers had told them, and all which they themselves knew, of the horrid old times, when the Wild Ass ramped at large, and crouched at the Pope's subdeacon's footstool, before the coming of Arthur to give good laws and righteous government to England. And they acclaimed King John (forsooth) again, riding in haste to Beaulieu to enlarge by force that dreadful dotard and to use him as their figure-head. Which done, they sent their defiance to King Arthur, and took new oaths of allegiance to his wicked uncle. O manners. And thus the rebel magnates began their running. O times.

xxiiii. *About King Arthur his noble offer of Arbitration*

King Arthur took into his counsels King Aloys of the Franks, whom he regarded as a very holy knight and worshipful soldier of King Christ,[2] offering (by letters patent) to submit his case with that of his rebellious magnates, to the judgement of the said King Aloys. Earl Simon agreed, not without reluctance though; and I shall shew the good faith of that perjured traitor very briefly. The first news, which we in England got of it, came in the letters of archdeacon John Chishull and Sir Imbert Montferrand, proctors

---

[1] King John was long dead at this point, having died in 1216.
[2] Louis IX was extremely devout, and he was canonized in 1297.

for my lord the king at the Frankish court. They said that, when King Aloys had heard and understood them, he seriously and succinctly rehearsed their articles and petitions and business in the very terms which they had used for explaining them: this, to make clear his regal perception of the case. Which done, he said that he would hear Earl Simon of Montfort and Leicester. But, lo, that shuffler, after some vulgar abuse of King Arthur, requested the king of the Franks to move no further in the matter. Whereupon, King Aloys, at Amiens, in presence of the bishops and magnates of France, seeing that no defence was offered, solemnly pronounced judgement for King Arthur, condemning Earl Simon and the rebellious magnates, and annulling those precious Provisions of Oxford as our lord the Pope also was annulling them.[1] And Simon, false as ever, broke his agreement, refusing to abide by this judgement. O manners.

xxv. *About the Rebels their Running*

My son Boniface, the primate, nobly used the fervour of his youthful eloquence for King Arthur. Clad in his pontifical paludaments,[2] and with his bells ringing and his candles lighted, he held a fine damning in King William Redhead's great regal hall at Westminster, censuring and excommunicating and anathematizing and banishing from the threshold of Holy Mother Church, all the infidel traitors. At which, Sir Roger Clifford, and Sir Roger Leybourne, and Sir John Vaux, and Sir Hamo Delestrange, and some others whose names I have forgotten (I being a very old man) made haste to desert Earl Simon and the Wild Ass his bestial puppet, returning with sobs to their lawful allegiance. But the rebels captured my city of Gloucester. For Sir John Clifford and Sir John Balun covered themselves with Welsh mantles; and went riding on two wool-packs without trumpets, as though they were chapmen. And, when the gates were opened, down they hopped, and cast away their mantles, and stood armed terribly from head to foot. Whereat, the porters, dreadfully worried, threw them the

---

[1] Louis did annul the Provisions, and this decision was confirmed by the pope.
[2] Cloaks (*OED* OL).

keys and refuged in cupboards, while the rebels held the gate till
Simon's power entered the city led by his son Sir Henry Le Head
whom they called Courteous. Thus, the rebels held my city: but
my castle held for the king; and there was always between them
the wildest bickering.

XXVI. *About the sometime Wild Ass*

I find that I have left unwritten many things necessary to be
recorded concerning Sir John fil-Henry, sometime our Wild Ass,
and later the puppet of Earl Simon. My lord the king, from the
first, treated his wicked uncle with astounding mansuetude,[1]
benignancy, and clemency, though (of course) he estopped him
of trumpets. The miserable old sinner was let live as he pleased,
in monasteries which cared to entertain him, generally at his own
pious foundation of Beaulieu where he had at first taken refuge
and sanctuary. When he escaped from these sacred enclosures,
(as he frequently did, out of merely beastly wild and asinine wan-
tonness), he was quietly chased back again, spitting: but no other
check was put upon his liberty, excepting that he was forbidden
to consort with lepers, because prophetic conversation had an
exciting effect on his temperament. King Arthur used to send his
regal acknowledgments (in the shape of gold ingots) to all such
monasteries, not letting his left hand know what his hallowed
right hand did, but using me as his secret almoner: for he never
could bear to see his wicked uncle, who had kept him out of his
inheritances and thrice had attempted his life. At first, Earl Fulk
the Flame and Earl Hubert de Burgh advised and implored the
Regal Majesty to strike the spurs from the heels of the perjured
infidel John, and to hand him over to the common hangman, not
so much by way of retribution for his innumerable unequalled
crimes, but for the sake of the peace of the kingdom. Never shall
I forget the awful candour of that grave young face which King
Arthur shewed to us both. Brother Adam of Marish,[2] his pet friar,

---

[1] Gentleness (*OED* OL).

[2] Adam Marsh exercised an immense influence over the nobility. He had close
ties to both Henry III and Simon Montfort, and tried to act as a mediator between
the two.

was at his side. "Leave us alone," says the king. We left him. As we went, "If you forgive not—" says the holy friar. "Forgive," roars Lefthand, blazing with Angevin anger, bursting with Plantagenet passion. Thus much we heard before we closed the door. I and Fulk sat on the stair outside, one hour, two hours, to take the king's pleasure. Then, he came out, whiter than ever, wrapped in his ermine, colder than frost; and never another word said he about his wicked uncle. I did what I pleased, just letting the Wild Ass graze on such puddings as they eat in monasteries, and nowhere else. That what I pleased pleased my lord the king, there can be no doubt: for, from time to time, he would say to me, "Hubert, steal four gold ingots" (or six, or nine, or nineteen, as the case might be) "from our privy treasure, and take them to the abbot of such and such a monastery secretly;" and the monastery named was always the monastery which I myself had named to the Regal Majesty, on the previous day, as the monastery where his wicked uncle at the moment was harbouring. Sometimes, too, in after years, when the regal train rode by chance past some sanctuary where the Wild Ass champed his thistles, some thoughtless knight would shoot out the smilingly scornful gesture of thumb which betokens cognizance not unmixed with contempt. But my lord the king never deigned a single sign, save that awful lambent whitening of his whiteness which betokened the fierce struggle raging in his soul. O my king.

XXVII. *About Earl Simon his puppet*

When Simon nefariously set up John against Arthur, my lord the king took great care to make it clear that he was going to wage war solely against the rebel earl, and never against his wicked and still impenitent uncle. For, as soon as the rebels began their running, King Arthur took twelve knights of Saint John from the Grandmaster of the Hospital, for a special service; and he charged them, "Guard with your lives, the Old Horror whom Simon has in his company: capture him; and return him to the Cistercians of Beaulieu when occasion serves." In this way, among many other ways, my lord the king purified his soul against the time when he should ascend to the superiors.

xxviii. *About the Battle of Lewes*

King Arthur brought Earl Simon to battle at Lewes. Now that recreant rebel had caused to be built a cunningly devised waggon, the whole of the outside of which was covered with iron, hung with those flags which are called pennons round and about it. Herein, he secluded his puppet John, a dreadful dribbling toothless blear-eyed rheumy-nosed spindle-shanked palsied old mumbler and screecher of curses, hideous and shocking in senile antiquity, who scrabbled and chewed the trusses of straw which were there to comfort and warm him. And Simon himself rode near the iron carriage, coatless and bannerless, that the king and his power might be deluded. Honour, that traitor knew not; and virtue, he detested. So, when my lord the king went forth to war, those in the van of his array noticed this iron waggon hung about with pennons; and they straightway hurled themselves against it. For Simon's knights, instructed by him in mendacity, said that they were keeping the said Earl of Montfort and Leicester safe in this manner, not being quite sure of him, and fearing lest he should betray them to his father-in-law King Arthur. At which delightful intelligence, the knights in the van of the regal array were much emboldened; and they used all their energies in assaulting this deceptive vehicle: but, because of its iron armour and the power which surrounded it, they lost their ground and their courage at the same time. King Arthur, sitting on his great white stallion near at hand, saw how things were going; and, in a flash he turned, and bade me to summon the knights of the Hospital. With these at his call, he commanded them to keep their charge, so soon as Simon's power about the iron waggon should be broken. "For," says he, "the rebel earl is not within but without the waggon, and unblazoned." And he shewed us a pink knight, who struck no blows, but continually made signals with a long lance in that vicinity. Then, he took the knights of the regal household, and led them in person, charging at full gallop; and so fearful was our onset, that the waggon was overturned, crushing many rebels whose malignant stars prevented them from perishing beneath our horses' hoofs. But phrenzied yells from the bowels of the waggon made known that its inmate was alive; and, having caused it to be righted on its wheels again, my lord the king gave it in charge to the Hospitallers, turning his own attention once more to the general battle. And, when four-thousand-five-hundred men had been slain, both knights and footmen, and the shades of evening prevented him from collecting his widely scattered power, then, my lord the king said that the affair must be finished on some future day after he had obtained certain information. He, therefore, dismissed Lord Edward Plantagenet, his beloved grandson and heir, to take sanctuary with my Friars Minor at Gloucester; and he sent me, with Earl Fulk the Flame to my lady the queen, to take order for the next battle, wherein, having found out all secrets for himself, he was intending to smash Simon finally. Then, King Arthur rode away, yielding to Earl Humphrey Bohun of Hereford, who was the highest of the rebel rout, and the most respectable.

XXVIIII. About England in Prison and out

Now I will tell how England was, during the short time when the rebel Simon held King Arthur as his prisoner.[1] Every magnate instantly jumped up and seized the opportunity of having a smack at his neighbour. As everyone naturally strove to defend his own, the country was ravaged, fields laid waste, and all cattle were carried off for revictualling castles. One would have thought we were Scots. Neither churches nor churchyards were spared. The houses of poor rustics were rummaged and plundered, even to the stinking straw of their beds. And, although Simon made much fuss with plausible promises of decapitation for violators of sacred places and annoyers of clergymen, so vile was his double-facedness and so small his power of keeping his solemn engagements, that no bishops or abbots or religious persons could put a foot out of doors (much less journey from town to town) without being plundered and stripped mother-naked by highwaymen.[2]

---

[1] Henry was similarly taken prisoner at the battle of Lewes in 1264. His son, Edward, was taken prisoner as well.

[2] This account of the disorder following the capture of the king is drawn directly from the continuation of Matthew Paris's chronicle, previously attributed to "Matthew of Westminster."

And these things so shocked Lord Edward Plantagenet, that he ardently left the sanctuary; and went to tell his regal grandfather in captivity all about everything.

xxx. About England out of Prison and in

Simon led my lord the king about with him everywhere; and I am bound to record that he treated the Regal Majesty with reverence, taking order that he should be received with due worship at all times among the rebels. It was, however, a very good job that Lord Edward of England did as he did do. For King Arthur had assured himself that Simon was stinking most grievously in the nostrils of very many rebel magnates: his chief offence being that he arrogated to himself all such revenues of the realm as had fallen into his hands, together with the ransoms of captives and other doubtful profits which (according to their convention) ought to have been equally divided between them. Wherefore, my lord the king wished to let me know how to make certain dispositions, now that thieves were falling out, and the time at hand when honest knights might get back their own. For Simon, maddened by what he fondly imagined to be irreversible success, was refusing to restore to the earl of Hereford the knights which the said Sir Humphrey himself had captured at Lewes; and, more, he forbade the same earl to amuse himself with a tourney which he had prepared at a great expense. O impudent upstart. Wherefore Earl Humphrey and his friends, mindful of Simon's previous prepotence, and incensed at his so tyrannous frustration of their just designs, were uttering bitter reproaches, saying that it was ridiculous for this undesirable alien (for, never let it be forgotten that Simon de Montfort was not English, but merely a fickle fantastic Frank), should presume to thrust the whole realm under his yoke. And their amicity curdled into inimicity. Neither his oath nor any other consideration could pacify the Earl of Hereford, who, making no more ado, came over with loud shouts to join my nobler knights of the Welsh March, namely, Sir Roger Mortimer and Sir Roger Clifford and Sir James Audley, whom Simon (by public edict) had ordered to quit the kingdom. The bishops of Winchester and Worcester babbled, begging (nay badgering), Hereford and Leicester to make peace all without avail. Humphrey would not; and Simon could not. The King's power on my March was joined also by Earl John Warenne of Surrey and Sussex and Earl William de Valence of Pembroke, on their way by sea to the west parts of Wales. In this way I completed my preparations.

xxxi. *About Young England out*

When my lord the king had satisfied himself, Lord Edward of England escaped from Simon,[1] with a message for me, in this delightful manner. Having leave to spur steeds outside the city, and a fair company of knights to attend him, he set them racing till he had tired them: but fresh was his own steed. While they all panted loudly, softly he spurred till he was well in advance of them. Then, he pricked hard and away, wishing them good-day. What need of a long tale. The prince took the road to Wigmore Castle, whence I escorted him in regal state to Queen Mariol in the Tower at London.

xxxii. *About the Powers collected*

Acting on King Arthur's instructions, Earl Hubert de Burgh and Earl Fulk the Flame brought up an immense power, with Lord Edward Plantagenet at its head in place of my lord the king. Because Simon's footmen were chiefly the old mercenaries armed with the cross-bow, as in the days of that Sir Judas Breauté whom King Arthur hanged, we took care to arm our footmen with the new long-bow, a much more deadly weapon, whose two yards' length would drive a clothyard shaft through four good inches of oak-door.[2] And, with this power, we affronted Simon the rebel. He skipped from Worcester before us, through Hempsey to Eve-

---

[1] Edward did in fact escape imprisonment and go on to lead royalist forces to victory at the Battle of Evesham.

[2] John E. Morris argued that the longbow was of Welsh descent and was introduced to England around the turn of the fourteenth century. See Morris's *The Welsh Wars of Edward I* (Oxford: Clarendon Press, 1901). However, other scholars have argued recently that the longbow was introduced earlier by Scandinavians.

sham, where, bethinking himself of his pious professions, he had masses said for himself and his folk, and sat down to listen to sermons preached by bishop Walther of Worcester, *gules, three fleurs de lys or*. Finding, however, that we were not inclined to delay while he humbugged the credulous, and seeing that no course lay open but to fight to a finish, he made his preparations for battle. Having received Sir John fil-Henry from the knights of the Hospital, who had guarded him after King Arthur's strategic surrender at Lewes, Simon placed that senile monster by his own side, wearing *England* over mail and a crown upon his helm, with two knights to prop him in the saddle, he being a puppet of very shaky and vacillating presence. But the rebel Simon disposed my lord the king in the forefront of his array, hidden in plain knightly mail from head to foot, with a monstrous hat of iron concealing his face, nor any coat or blazon of knighthood, nor any insignia of regal majesty by which one might distinguish him. O manners.

xxxiii. *About the Battle of Evesham*

Despite his youth, Lord Edward arrayed his power right well. For he gave me five hundred of my knights, and to Earl Fulk the Flame he gave five hundred more, with the customary footmen, and leave to do precisely as we pleased. Which indeed we did, with sobs of hilarity and thankfulness for that King Arthur was not our commander at that time, a time eminently suitable for causing a regrettable occurrence. So, while Earl Fulk drove his power like a wedge between Simon and the main body of the rebels, I led my power at full gallop charging over the ground (violently) which the said Simon and his household were occupying, with very special reference to the station of Sir John fil-Henry, till nothing remained of that one (nor indeed of his neighbours) to trouble England any more, excepting a dreadfully juicy red jelly spiked with splinters of shattered white bone and grey bits of broken armour. Simon himself was slain then;[1] and Sir William Malthravers, *sable fretty or, on a canton argent three leopards gules*, carved his feet and hands and all his limbs. Every one of his folk were slain also, Sir Henry le Head, his son, Sir Hugh Despencer,

---

[1] Simon de Montfort did die at the Battle of Evesham.

argent and gules quarterly, a fret or, and Sir Piers de Montfort, *gules, a lyon argent,* Sir William Deperons, *vert, three stone steps proper,* Sir Ralph Bassett, *argent, a bassett proper,* Sir John Saintjohn, Sir John Dive, Sir William Frussell, Sir Gilbert Denfield. Never was so much slaughter done in so little time. But, meanwhile, Lord Edward Plantagenet led his power of knights with a serried[1] array of pikemen, all covered with a curtain of long-bow men, against the main body of the rebels, which Earl Fulk had cut off from its head and offered for his attention. Dreadfully worried was the regal imp, because he could not see the Majesty of his grandfather, whom he desired to redeem from the society of traitors as soon as might be. For, as I say, Simon (swayed by his proper devil) had set King Arthur in the forefront of the hottest battle, like Messire Saint Uriah in the Sacred Scripture,[2] having thoroughly disguised him, hoping thus to have the Majesty of England slain by loyal Englishmen. O manners. O scab. But, almost as soon as the battle was joined, Earl Edmund Plantagenet of Lancaster, and Earl Richard fil-Fulk of Penthieve (*ermine, upon a canton gules a lyon and a heart or*), and Sir John Baliol, *gules, an orle argent,* and Sir John Deverdun, and Sir Robert Maleran, and Sir Roger Deleybrun, and Sir Nicholas Deltham, became ware separately and together of a very astonishing portent. They saw an unknown unrecognizable knight, in front of the rebel array, turn right round, at the very moment of onset, and attack his associates with unparalleled and incomparable ferocity. For, gripping his charger between his thighs and knees, goading it to fury with his armed heels and guiding it with the points of his toes, he seriously affected his neighbours with his empty mailed hands, which he used as choppers or as pokers in tender parts, he being strangely deficient of knightly weapons. Curvetting[3] on one side, he chopped knights under the gorget, so that they coughed hardly in great displeasure and tumbled sidewise to be trodden to pulp underfoot. Caracolling[4] on the other side, he dug with the flashing point of

---

[1] Pressed close together (*OED* OL).
[2] David put Uriah in the front of battle so that he might die after impregnating his wife, Bathsheba. See 2 Sam. 11:15.
[3] Causing his horse to leap (*OED* OL).
[4] Causing his horse to half-turn (*OED* OL).

an iron hand through the bars of vizors, doing undoubted detriment to eyeballs, if one may judge from the melancholy shrieks which insued and the number of eyeless knights who survived the battle. And he drove his charger's rump, like a ram, against fat knights, rolling them prone. So, the seven loyal knights (named afore) hovered in his proximity, to find out the meaning of his amazing and amusing behaviour. And they hear the well-known voice of England rumbling, like the billows on the shingle, in the close uncrested helm of iron, roaring: "Let them all come. Thus deals Arthur the King with damned traitors. Let them all come."[1] Whereat they joined themselves to him, shouting, "Hail Sire," and "Hail Lefthand," and "Hail Arthur," and "Hail England," and as many other large divine comfortable words as they could think of at the moment, being half-dazed and more than half-choked with admiration and with adoration. And, moreover, spinged by Sir Robert Leybrun, they assiduously herded selected rebels for the king's hunting, and carefully completed such sketches as the exigencies of his means compelled him to leave but three-parts done. And when Lord Edward came up, having cleared his part of the field, the unblazoned knight became ware that none but his friends were at hand, whom, perceiving, he bade to unlock his helm. Which was done by Crutchback,[2] his son, the crusader. And all the army saw once more the strong white face, the straight-gleaming dauntless eyes, of King Arthur triumphant in battle. No one had the heart to fight any more. There was no more a wicked uncle, no more a rebellious magnate, to annoy my lord the king; and, so, he came back to his crown and canopy, to the great satisfaction of all enemies of Simon and the other killed rebels. I ought to say that King Arthur suitably rewarded those seven knights, saying that they had afforded him a most regal diversion. And, as Sir Roger Deleybrun was a poor knight, with but one suit of mail to wear, and his coat much faded and mended, he was provided-for in this manner. King Arthur granted by tenure the Manor of Little Weldon in Northamptonshire, for the stablishment of the Regal Buckhounds, fifteen in number, to be maintained for

---

[1] "*ut veniant omnes.*" [Rolfe's note.]
[2] Edmund Crouchback was the second son of Henry III.

the King's hunting, attaching the said Manor in grand serjeanty
to the Mastership of the said Regal Buckhounds, which Mastership he declared hereditary, and conferred it with the Manor
on the said Sir Roger Deleybrun, with a salary of sevenpence a
day when he waited on the king at court and twelvepence a day
when absent from the court on the king's service elsewhere. And
I cannot remember anything else to record about King Arthur's
methods with his magnates.

XXXIIII. *About King Arthur his method with one Magnate*

Nevertheless, I have one thing which I must write of King
Arthur's particular method with that particular magnate who
was his most faithful servant and lover, namely Sir Hubert de
Burgh, earl-palatine of Kent and earl of Gloucester and Essex, et
cetera. On the Eve of the Easter next after the battle of Evesham,
I, by chance, was strolling in Queen Mariol's wonderful garden
at Windsor, among the wall-flowers which we call Bloody Warriors and Eastern Queens. I was uncomfortable as all other men,
denied their pudding by reason of the fast: but I was feeling rather
holy and quiet in my mind after my shriving;[1] and, while waiting for the king, I comforted myself by looking forward to the
morrow's festival which ends all human grief or pain. Anon, my
lord the king came to me, there; and his beloved Brother Adam
of Marish was with him. "Are you shriven, Hubert?" says he. I
answered that I was shriven in London that very morning. "The
guilt of murder, then, no longer smirches your fair soul, Hubert?"
says he. "Murder, lord king?" says I, in a maze: for I could not
remember that any man's blood was crying to heaven against me,
murder not being a habit of mine, though very many owe their
deaths to me, in battle, or by my justice as Justiciar of England
and Ireland. "Murder?" says I again. "Murder:" says my lord the
king, looking me straight in the eyes with his regal eyes most
solemn and grave.

Now I do here swear, as a man and a christian and a belted
knight and a crowned earl-palatine, by God and by all the shining

---

[1] The first edition reads "striving."

company of heaven, that King Arthur was and is utterly ignorant
and utterly innocent of the death of his wicked uncle. Mine, and
mine alone, were the mind which planned and the heels which
did the death of Sir John fil-Henry. The deed was all mine, incep-
tion and completion, done for the sake of Arthur and of England,
in Arthur's absence, without his knowledge. When I did it, I
thought it very good. When I had done it, it did not seem to be so
very good. I did not brag about it. I did not want praise for it. But
I never thought of it as murder. And yet, when King Arthur persisted in asking me whether I was shriven of murder, suddenly,
my mind accused me of the murder of Sir John fil-Henry. "No,
lord king," says I, "I am not yet shriven of murder." And I was for
riding forthwith to my palace of Whitehall, where I might send
to Holborn for one of my Black Friars to finish my Easter shriving. "Shrive you here and now with my Grey Friar:" says my lord
the king. So I knew that a plan was toward, which I might not
withstand; and I kneeled to Brother Adam instantly there, among
the fragrant wall-flowers. King Arthur walked away; and I told
my tale with all contrition, to be clean against Easter. "Kneel you
here, my son, and beg your penance from our dear lord the king:"
says the Grey Friar, when he had heard and assoiled me. King
Arthur returned. I did as I was bidden. The Regal Majesty bent
down, whispering in my ear, "What holy thing will you make me
an oath by, Hubert?" I took his hallowed hand, and bared it of the
glove, and let my lips lie on his splendid scar. The hand shook suddenly, but it remained on mine: a sudden hot tear, not from my
eyes, fell on it. There was silence. Then, in my ear, "Bind yourself
by what oath you will, Hubert, most faithful loving friend, that
you never will bear arms for me again:" says King Arthur. I swore
it on that pierced hand. And I begged God to let me die. But I did
not die. I have always served my lord the king: but never in arms
since the Easter after Evesham. That is all about King Arthur and
his magnates.

XVIII

THE BOOK CALLED THE CONFUSIONS OF CLERGYMEN[1]

I. *About Briars*

Wait patiently, o most affable reader, whoever you are, till I
have cleared away some briars, roses as well as thorns (as I may
call them) and so become free to whet the axe of my justice for
the felling of the noxious tree. For the tree which annoys me is
the task which I have set myself, namely, the writing of the true
histories of my lord the king, against the untrue fables which that
Mr. Matthew (formerly of Paris) writes when he is not prancing about in Norway. And the briars, roses and thorns, are the
little people and the little things, nice, and nasty, which must be
cleared before I can expound the whole truth. For, as the adage
says, *Every Crab has his own Moon;*[2] and, though I certainly shall
reach the truth, I cannot approach it directly, but must go side-
ways at it, as it were.

II. *About Pontiffs*

Pope Innocent the Great ascended to the superiors with a quartan fever.[3] Our lord Pope Honorius the Third (Who succeeded
Him) most unnecessarily sent that old Cardinal Walo to govern

---

[1] The following section concerns itself primarily with the building tension
during the thirteenth century between England and the papacy. During Henry
III's reign, the English became increasingly exasperated by the appointment of
foreign clergy to English benefices and the constant demands placed upon the
English church by a papacy that was at the time in conflict with Frederick II.
Frederick engaged in war with the Papal States during this period, and Frederick
was excommunicated twice.

[2] *"Sua cuique Canceri Luna."* [Rolfe's note.] The moon is the planetary ruler of
Cancer. As mentioned above, Rolfe identified himself with the crab, and his
literary alter-ego was named Nicholas Crabbe.

[3] A fever that causes a paroxysm on every fourth day (*OED* OL).

England as His legate. I say unnecessarily: because England was no longer infested by a Wild Ass given to furnishing us with didactic spectacles of reverend gentlemen swinging by scores to be eaten of crows in their sacred habits; and, also, because Stephen our Cardinal-primate, having learned salutary lessons, was perfectly capable of governing the Church in England with due decorum, and (for the rest) there was King Arthur Lefthand, not forgetting Earl Hubert de Burgh, the Justiciar and Admiral and Warden and Regent of England. Therefore, I say that Cardinal Walo was unnecessary.[1]

III. About an ill-advised Pontiff and the first Legate

Pope Honorius was very ill-advised; and this caused him to plunge headlong, and to stick, in the pitchy pit of blunders most terrible. Imbecilities are to be expected from imbeciles;[2] and His idiotic informers kept Him in ignorance of the very things most necessary for Him to know. For example, they neither hummed nor hammered into the apostolic head these most important considerations, namely, that though Sir John fil-Henry the Wild Ass had given England, which was not his to give, to Pope Innocent the Great, receiving it again as a feof and swearing the feudal oath to His Blessedness on behalf of himself and his heirs, all the same, King Arthur Lefthand was not reigning in England as John, or as John's heir, but as heir of King Richard Lionheart, confirmed by Pope Innocent, and by right of conquest and the Judgement of God in the Ordeal of Battle, a unique impregnable title. Therefore, Arthur was not bound by any acts of John. Contrariwise. Not that we English wished to be pert to the Holy See. Contrariwise also. But we did intend to make ourselves understood, even though we had to shout our meaning in the Pope's ear-hole; and we were determined not to submit to undue interference from anybody alien, no matter how pompous. These ideas, then, we manifested in the usual manner, very politely: but the legate, a weak man with a predilection for woodcock before his pudding, strutted back to Rome in a stout and sulky silence. That was one.

---

[1] Guala Bicchieri was sent to England as a papal legate during the baronial uprising of John's reign and remained in England until 1218.
[2] *"Imbecillis imbecillia exspectantur."* [Rolfe's note.]

iiii. *About the second Legate*

Persisting in the mistaken notion that He was King Arthur's overlord, Pope Honorius sent us another legate, that little Mr. Pandulph,[1] who so pluckily had bitted and bridled the Wild Ass; and was supposed to know all the proper artful ways of dealing efficaciously with us English. But it was not a Wild Ass who wore the crown of the English this time; and, apart from that, our lord the Pope piled a second blunder on the first one: for, thinking to give His little Mr. Pandulph a footing among us, He preconized[2] him as bĭp. of Norwich.[3] My lord the king, and the Primate Stephen, and Earl Hubert de Burgh accordingly put their heads together, and we found that nothing could possibly have suited us better. Lord Pandulph arrived, swelled with unutterable pomp and inclined to be affable to all and singular. We received him honorably, and looked intensely down our noses. He began to hector in the usual manner. We continued to be complaisant and encouragingly obsequious. Stephen the Primate obliged him so far as to lend him a footstool of fur to keep his feet warm. Then, he presented his breve[4] of preconization. And, instantly, Cardinal Stephen happed himself up in all his best primate-skins on the summit of the throne of Messire Saint Austin, requiring from Lord Pandulph the oath of canonical obedience as bĭp. of Norwich, a mere suffragan of the province of Canterbury. Whereat the little legate hiccoughed horribly, and hurried back to Rome. That was two.

v. *About Lord Stephen Langton our own Cardinal and Primate and Legate*

To give an egregious token that we English were not to be

---

[1] Pandulph was reappointed as legate on Guala's departure, but Hubert de Burgh and Stephen Langton were able to convince the pope to recall him in 1221.

[2] Proclaimed (*OED* OL).

[3] The pope actually postponed the consecration of Pandulph as Bishop of Norwich, so that he would not come under the archbishop's jurisdiction. Pandulph was consecrated on his return to Rome in 1222.

[4] Brief (*OED* OL).

taken as wantonly naughty tumelious sons of Holy Mother
Church, my lord the king began to build a new Lady-chapel,[1]
with a crown of apsidal chapels surrounding it, about the shrine
of Messire Saint Edward the King in the abbey of Westminster.
Meanwhile, Cardinal Stephen proceeded in primatial pomp to
Rome, there to explain the case of England (in quite simple words
of three letters at most, such as a child could understand) to our
lord Pope Honorius. Which he indubitably did; and there was no
gainsaying him: for he came back with the legateship apostolically attached to the archiepiscopal see of Canterbury as long as
the world should endure: so that no foreign prelates henceforward
would be able to sit on the faces of the primates of England. So,
we fondly imagined: for we had yet to learn the length of pontifical memories, the worth of pontifical promises, and to fear the
Greeks who came to us with gifts.

VI. About the Friars

At this time came to England the Friars, Pope Innocent the
Great's new species of clergymen: first the Dominicans in white
and black, like magpies, given to preaching: then the Franciscans
in grey, like sparrows, given to loving and laughing.[2] I must say
much about the Friars: not because I love my Black Friars who have
shewed me how to live godly: not because a Grey Friar so loved my
lord the king that he sent him straight and most gloriously to glory
eternal,[3] but just because the Friars were the Godsend (I am too old
to mince words) who kept England christian in these years, when
the secular clergymen were either ousted or rotten to the core and
the regulars lived in their abbeys, chiselling stones, or writing fairy-
tales. O Mr. Matthew. I wish, then, to say that the friars differed
from the monks who lived in pleasant places, in that they settled in
the slums of cities: and they differed from the secular clergymen,
in that they strove for humility. Their rule was simplicity itself: to
observe the Holy Evangel in life, with obedience, and chastity, and

---

[1] A chapel dedicated to the virgin.
[2] The Domincan and the Franciscan orders were established in the thirteenth
century.
[3] Adam Marsh was a Franciscan.

the poverty which has no possessions and so is the lord and sovereign of all things. They wore vile raiment, amended with sackcloth
when necessary. They never owned anything, much less valuables,
and money they would not even touch. They lived with the dregs
of the people to whom they ministered: where were the lowest
of the low, there were the friars. They even trained their novices
in lazar-houses,[1] and habitually consorted with lepers. And they
begged their daily pudding. At first, they were mocked. Then, they
were shunned. Lewd fellows of the baser sort, and jealous clergymen, made songs against them: witness *The Owl and the Nightingale*, wherein the elegant songster inveighs against the plain coat
of the useful destroyer of vermin.[2] But the friars were so cheerful,
and so clean, and so assiduous and pre-eminent in learning, and so
very good, that they soon became (as is well-known) more beloved
and honoured than any other kind of clergyman. From the Friars
Minor of Oxford, sprang these two great Englishmen who, more
than the whole bench of bishops and abbots, have helped me and
my lord the king to rule this realm rightly: I mean bishop Robert
Greathead of Lincoln,[3] who died two years ago, and Brother Adam
of Marish, who stood by King Arthur at last, opening the very door
whereby the Regal Majesty of England ascended to the superiors.
O me. I end this chapter. I was absent.

VII. *About a Beginning of Religious Revivals*

Everybody everywhere began to excite themselves about religion. The excitement of some took weird and awful forms. Mr.
Matthew (late of Paris) admired a mad and vociferous She, who
went about preaching in defiance of Messire Saint Paul Apostle his
explicit injunctions. O monk. And the Benedictines were solemnly
forbidden to wear overalls.[4] Our lord Pope Honorius died: Whom a

---

[1] Houses for the diseased (*OED* OL).

[2] *The Owl and the Nightingale* is a debate poem written in the twelfth or thirteenth
century. The nightingale mocks the owl's plain appearance. Some critics have
argued that the owl is a figure for monks.

[3] Robert Grosseteste (1175-1253), bishop of Lincoln and renowned scholar.
Grosseteste actively resisted the perceived tyranny of the papacy.

[4] "*supertotos*" [Rolfe's note.]

nephew of Pope Innocent the Great succeeded, by name Pope Gregory the Ninth, heir to His apostolic uncle's dominating temper, not to His greatness, not to His justice, a raspberry-faced long-nosed sourmouthed apostle addicted to malevolence. Died, also, Cardinal Stephen Langthon, Primate of All England. Instantly, our lord Pope Gregory set aside the right of the Canterbury monks to elect the new arch-bishop; and Himself gave us Lord Richard Legrand, the chancellor of Lincoln, for primate, at the same time demanding a tithe for some nonsense or other. Here, therefore, we began disagreeable relations with Rome. O times.

VIII. About a second ill-advised Pontiff

Owing to the ill-advice which their Romans afforded, both Pope Honorius and Pope Gregory treated us English unfairly. Chagrined, I imagine, by the loss of so profitable a vassal as the king of the English, Their Blessednesses seemed to have formed a plan for milking the patient English cow of her golden stream in another and even less legitimate way. O hedgehogs. Roman clergymen were forthwith foisted upon the English benefices, with (and without) the consent of the patrons of the same; and these undesirable aliens, when they condescended to come and perform the duties for which England paid them (which was seldom) paid taxes on their English stipends to the Roman exchequer. O manners. These intrusions were all effected without any fuss; and, for some years even I myself did not know how enormous was the sum of English money which these foreign clergymen annually sucked out of the kingdom. And, when I did begin to know, I did not know everything, nor indeed did anyone, till very much later, so insiduously were these high facinorous[1] actions conceived, carried out, completed. O horse-leeches. O vampires.

VIIII. About the secular Clergymen

These, whose rottenness was the chief cause of the evil, being dreadfully worried when they saw the very pudding snatched out of their mouths, instead of trying (by amendment of life and strict

---

[1] Very wicked (*OED* OL).

attention to duty) to recover their lost position, banded themselves together in a secret society, with one Sir Robert Twenge as
their leader; and they indicted threatening letters to all patrons
of benefices, promising them progressive and graduated mutilation of person till death ensued, if English money was permitted
to be soaked up by unshaven aliens any longer. They were very
serious about the matter, as (indeed) all men are (specially clergymen) when they get pinched in the pocket. And I, believing
their grievance a just one, wrote several commendatory letters
in their favour: emboldened by which, they went further than I
had intended, and began to rob and outrage foreign clergymen on
sight.[1] Consequently, it became my painful duty to place a period
to their riotous behaviour, making examples of the most violent,
for the sake of decency and order. So I took Sir Robert Twenge;
and made him fill himself with excellent pudding, and deliver his
mind in the Presence of my lord the king. "Tush," says the Regal
Majesty, after ten minutes: "stop these tumults in my kingdom;
and take these twenty marks as a sweet gift; and get you gone
suddenly to Rome, where you shall tell your horrid tale to our
lord Pope Gregory, saying who sent you to tell it."

x. About Primates

In those days occurred the Great Alleluia, when all Italy
caught the popular infection and went stark mad about religion:[2]
in which pudder,[3] I believe, Sir Robert Twenge either lost himself
or found congenial occupation, for I never heard of him again.
Then, Richard the Primate died, having done nothing; and Lord

---

[1] Rolfe refers to a secret society, *Universitas*, which consisted of "the whole body
of those who prefer to die rather than be ruined by the Romans" (Ellis 127).
Led by Robert Tweng, a knight from Yorkshire, they assaulted papal couriers,
and, when arrested, produced warrants that were supposedly granted with the
compliance of Hubert de Burgh. According to Clarence Ellis, while these letters
may have been forged, Hubert's hatred of aliens may have led him to turn a blind
eye to the violence.
[2] The Great Devotion, a religious revival that occurred in Italy in 1233.
[3] Puddle. The term "puddle" can be used to refer to a state of confusion, a
muddle, or a mess (*OED* OL).

Edmund Rich[1] canonically succeeded him, a very holy man, a doctor of logic at Oxford, and married to Madame Saint Mary the God-bearer of Abingdon. And I began to think that, with a saint for our primate and the friars in our cities and the monks snug on all the sweetest sights in the country, something really might be done to improve the order of clergymen. But the time was not ripe yet. We had not yet enough of high good men on The Lord's Side. There was a preponderance of black sheep in the fold; and, as the adage says, One tainted wether suffices to infect a flock. Consider Archbishop Walther Gray of York, who kept four harvests stored in his granaries at Ripon when his archdiocese was smitten with famine. O hireling shepherd.

XI. About the great-headed Bishop of Lincoln

The chapter of Lincoln turned the scale in favour of God and His Righteousness, when they elected Lord Robert Greathead, the rector of the Oxford Friars Minor, as their bishop. With that strong simple unflinching son of thunder on the throne of Saint Hugh, it became possible to begin to order the clergymen of England rightly. Read, o most affable reader, how Bishop Greathead at once began to reprove the clergymen of Lincoln: *Perform the Divine Office: shunt your concubines: lead your people to hear sermons of the friars of both orders, and to be shriven of them: suppress stageplays: prevent christians from dwelling with Giwen*; and, o most affable reader, kindly try to imagine the state of the secular clergymen to whom their new bishop had to say such words as these.[2] O times. O manners.

XII. About the Third Legate and the Four Things Necessary For A Good Christian

News went to Rome of the way in which King Arthur was

---

[1] Edmund Rich, the archbishop of Canterbury, played an instrumental role in the reconciliation between King Henry and Hubert in 1234. He worked hard attempting to secure the rights of the national Church, but eventually became exhausted by the demands of Rome. He then retired to the abbey of Pontigny, where he died.
[2] Bishop Robert Grosseteste worked extensively to reform monastic and clerical abuses.

trying to improve the clergymen of England, but I do not think that our example was very much admired there: though I am bound to record that our lord Pope Gregory issued a bull, damning the canons of the Holy Sepulchre at Hierusalem, for forgery of a fire at Easter, which (they falsely affirmed) came down from heaven. That, at least, must be said to His apostolic credit. But, contrariwise, His Blessedness behaved abominably in England: for He went back on the engagement made by Pope Honorius with our Primate Stephen, and sent us another legate (for reasons not to be inquired for), namely Cardinal-deacon Hottho of Saint Nicholas in the Tullian Gaol. Now, when Pope Gregory fussily proclaimed that He would not be bound by the decrees of His predecessor in the matter of the legateship, it was to me like a smack across the face; and Primate Edmund did not help me to bear it easily, he being so meek a clergyman that he witnessed the intrusion on his own legatine office without even whimpering. But, when I was for jumping up with howls to resent the Pope's behaviour, my wise young lord the king soothed and comforted me, saying, "Be you ware, Hubert, of the four things necessary for whoever will live and die a good christian, namely, as follows: First, we must have a faith which will move mountains: Second, we must be ware that we have our treasure in very earthen vessels: Third, we must be ware that there was a Judas among the apostles: Fourth, we must cultivate to keenness our sense of the ridiculous." O second Solomon. Now, see, o most affable reader, with how sharp a needle these sage aphorisms touch every point. What but faith could move the mountains of iniquity which bid fair to crush England? The treasure, the awful sole power of binding and loosing, where was it deposited but in Pope Gregory, of vessels the most earthy? Judas, false: false Gregory. And, what cheerfully-minded knight could restrain his laughter, when he observed the legate? O wise King Arthur.

XIII. *About the Third and laughable Legate*

Cardinal Hottho at first went modestly and prudently. Contrary to Roman custom, he wriggled his wrists and waggled his head, when we offered him the usual presents. When we offered them a second time, he gently closed two fat holy eyes, and talked of other matters. When we offered them a third time, he even spat quietly, totally rejecting them, though (as presents) they were worth anyone's acceptance. Thus, falling short of the general expectation by his well-ordered demeanour, he allayed the anger and antipathy which the clergymen and magnates of the kingdom had prepared for him. But, anon, he must needs proceed to Oxford, where he was received most honourably and lodged in the abbey of Osney. And, there, ensued amusing but fatal actions. For, having had good reports of the legate, and being anxious to exhibit correspondence in urbane manners, the scholar-clergymen instantly sent him an honourable present of meat-puddings and beer for his breakfast; and, afterward, they themselves came to the abbey to pay their respects. But the legate's porter, a Roman, jesting improperly and inopportunely, opened the gate a little and bawled, "What do you want here?" "To pay our respects to the lord legate," said the scholar-clergymen very genteelly, feeling sure of receiving honour for honour. But the porter, wanton in prepotence, taunted them and abused them and refused them admittance. They made a rush; and got in. The legate's apparitors beat them badly with sticks. They used their fists. Ensued a very noble shindy.[1] Now, by chance there was a poor clergyman from my March of Wales standing at the kitchen-door, to beg a pittance of pudding, as poor Welsh clergymen are wont to do. [And the master of the legate's own brother, the said lord legate always being dreadfully worried lest some one should envenom him.] And this master-cook, desirous of joining the affray, paid no attention to this poor Welsh clergyman, until the latter came quite close to him, screaming most horribly into his very earhole, demanding at least a little scrap of bread and cheese. At which, the chief-cook went furious, and seriously affected the features of the poor Welsh clergyman with a ladle-ful of hot gravy from a cauldron where puddings and rich meats were being stewed. Whereupon a certain Irish clergyman roared, "Shame, that we

---

[1] Rolfe is referring here to a student riot that occurred at Osney abbey in 1238. The riot was motivated by nationalist feeling, as the clerks attacked the legate's Italian servants.

clergymen should tolerate wrongs from a mere Nabuzaradan."[1] And, drawing a bow which he carried (for the clergymen had snatched up all weapons near at hand), he offended the chief cook with a dart in the eye-ball, and slew him outright. Immense was the tumult then: so that the legate, overcome with amazement and excessive melancholy (such as may befal even the most stead-fast), snatched his canonical hood, and nested in the church tower among jays and magpies for security, having caused the door to be shut very gently behind him. All day long the riot raged: but when night put peace to it, Cardinal Hottho doffed his legateskins, and mounted his best horse in haste, crossing the river at the nearest least-known ford, flying as quickly as possible to the wings of my lord the king for protection. Meanwhile, the clergymen (phrenetic with fury) hunted for him in all the most recondite recesses of the abbey, shouting, "Where is that usurer, that simoniac,[2] that plunderer of revenues, that thirster for money, who would enrich aliens with the spoils of our benefices." And when the fugitive legate heard them as he fled, he said within himself *cum furor in cursu est, currenti cede furori.*[3] And, patiently enduring shame, for lack of spirit to resist it, he became as a deaf man in whose mouth are no reproofs. Thus, palpitating and breathless, he came to King Arthur at Abingdon, absolutely buttonless, totally devoid of strings, snuffling with deep sobs that he was indeed undone. And I ask, o most affable reader, what cheerfully or churlishly-minded knight can restrain his laughter when considering this laughable legate?

XIIII. *About the extortionate Legate and the meek Primate*

King Arthur despatched Earl John Warenne of Surrey and Sussex with a power to Oxford, to rescue the Romans who nested

---

[1] "Chief of Cooks," *Hieremias*, xxxviiii, 9. [Rolfe's note.] The captain of the guard, a trusted official of Nebuchadnezzar.
[2] One who buys and sells benefices and ecclesiastical preferments (*OED* OL).
[3] Ovid, *Remed. Amor.* i. 119. A sweet work for a legate's impromptu citation in the agitation of a panic-flight.—P. and C. [Rolfe's note.] "When madness is on the run, give way to madness as it runs." This quotation is drawn directly from Matthew Paris, but the original source for this phrase is Ovid's *Remedia Amoris.*

in the pews of Osney Abbey, and to arrest any obstreperous clergymen who might (by chance) be identified. But the legate (his snare being broken and he delivered), preened his plumage and assembled a parcel of bīps., aided by whom he laid an interdict on Oxford city, excommunicating abettors of the offence committed against him. And, much encouraged by the thought that he had been wronged and very commodiously avenged (it being the nature of clergymen to give themselves inflated airs in such circumstances), Cardinal Hottho seized the occasion to throw off his prudent and moderate mask. For our lord Pope Gregory had been damning no less a personage than the Emperor Wonder of the World; and was wanting money wherewith to wage war against that censured Cæsar.[1] The legate, therefore, presumptuously demanded moneys from English clergymen; and, when the bishops slid spirally away from him, he had recourse to the low estate of the monks, from whom he extorted no small sums which he called procurations. O Mr. Matthew (late of Paris).[2] And, swelling himself still more, he summoned archbishops, bishops, and abbots, to the abbey of Reading where he harboured; and, there, happed up in legateskins and awful pomp and solemnity, he unfolded urgent pontifical commands for a fifth of all their goods for discomforting the said Emperor Frederick. At first, the clergymen hotly and tartly declared that they were tired, and would in no wise undertake so insupportable a burden. But Edmund the primate, meekest of meek men, did yield a fifth of his archiepiscopal revenues; and, when the other clergymen saw that their head was tottering, they tottered also, and gave way. Through this crack gushed the flood. Our lord the Pope naturally lost no time in snaffling an ell from the totterers who yielded His inch.[3] He afflicted the Primate Edmund and bishop Robert Greathead of Lincoln and bishop Robert Bingham of Sarum with a new warrant, commanding them to reserve the next three-hundred Eng-

---

[1] Emperor Frederick II (*Stupor mundi*, or "the wonder of the world").
[2] Matthew Paris was quite critical of Otto, accusing him of extorting money from the English.
[3] To "snaffle" means to seize or steal, and an "ell" is a unit of measurement, so the Pope has essentially taken a yard from those "totterers" who have given him an inch.

lish benefices which should fall vacant, for three-hundred Roman
clergymen who happened by chance to be in want of well-sala-
ried situations: intimating further that all English bishops were
absolutely inhibited from appointing English clergymen to English benefices, till after the said three-hundred hungry clients of
His Blessedness had been suitably provided for. Amazement and
horror seized on every heart. Many fell into the gulph of despair.[1]
The Primate Edmund, too meek to rebel, too true to obey, too
weak to carry his crozier, collapsed with the weight of it, shunted
responsibility, went into exile in France with a meagre retinue
and no trumpets, fasting and praying to his heart's content at
Pontigny, whence, once, Messire Saint Thomas,[2] another Primate
of All England, issued triumphantly to die for the rights of the
Church. O times. O manners.

xv. About the Absence of a Pontiff and the Vanishing of a third Legate

Strange to say, none of the clergymen directly affected by the
legate's extortions coughed at all wildly, excepting certain insignificant rectors of Berks. I myself was wholly in favour of making
a fuss; and I would gladly have supported any bishops or abbots
inclined to show themselves fussy. But our lord Pope Gregory
ascended to the superiors and Cardinal Hottho dashed back to
Rome, on the chance of snaffling the popedom; and my lord the
king wished to defer action, till the new pope should have given
us specimens of His notions of pontifical propriety. That was the
last we heard of Cardinal Hottho: he was the third. The new pope
was our lord Celestine the Fourth; and he made haste to ascend
to the superiors after a mere fifteen days' taste of the paparchy:[3]
whereat the cardinals, gravely convulsed and disconcerted, scattered helter-skelter, scampering quadrivious.[4] This pleased the
Emperor hugely; and, when the Sacred College regained its sense

---

[1] During this period, English clergymen complained frequently about the
appointment of foreign clergy to English benefices.
[2] Thomas Becket spent two years at the Cistercian abbey of Pontigny.
[3] Pope Celestine's papacy began on October 25, 1241, and he died on November
10, 1241.
[4] In four directions (*OED* OL).

of decency and duty, and desired to convene in Rome for the election of a pontiff, it was found that Cæsar Wonder of the World had set guards on all the roads, capturing every clean decent-looking traveller, lest any such one should succeed to the throne of Peter. By these means, Christendom was bereaved of its father for two years, or thereabouts.[1]

xvi. *About a small Pontiff*

Then, for our sins, The Lord God afflicted us with our lord Pope Innocent the Fourth, or the Small, a dwarf-souled avaricious cunning vindictive little apostle and an ill-advised scold, who instantly happed up His cardinals in red hats instead of comely mitres, continued the pontifical war against the Emperor, and squeezed gold out of all Christian countries, especially England. Of course His Blessedness sent us a new extortioner, not a legate this time, but a nuncio with legatine authority and legatine trumpets, one Mr. Martin by name, a dromedary-faced clergyman who could snarl, with pendulous lip, disdainful regard for inferior persons, and a vicious capacity for biting. He had breves empowering him to excommunicate and inhibit and punish in many other ingenious ways any misguided clergyman who should dare to oppose him. And he began by suspending all our bishops from appointing to English benefices, till revenues for certain clergymen, aliens (of course), kinsmen of our lord the Pope (who seemed to have thousands) should have been provided. This was an addition to the three-hundred English benefices sequestrated for the three-hundred pets of Pope Gregory. O bad manners.[2]

xvii. *About the rapacious Nuncio*

Mr. Martin was far worse than a legate. He would not demean

---

[1] During this period of intense antagonism between Frederick and the papacy, the Holy See remained vacant for two years, from 1241 to 1243.

[2] According to F. M. Powicke, "No papal nuncio ever had a worse reception in England than Master Martin had." See Powicke's *King Henry III and the Lord Edward* (Oxford: Clarendon Press, 1966), 356. He was eventually driven out of England. In this account of Master Martin's "rapacity," Rolfe again draws heavily from Matthew Paris.

himself by accepting less than thirty marks from anyone, lest so great a clergyman as he should be regarded as an ordinary snapper-up of unconsidered trifles. He demanded presents (specially palfreys) from prelates (specially abbots). He proposed, even to priors, that they should provide horses suitable for a very particular clergyman of our lord the Pope. Some refused: and were suspended: for example, take the abbot of Malmesbury and the prior of Merton. He seized the best canonry with the precentorship of Sarum; and conferred them on a snivelling little male infant who was the Pope's nephew. So, the English clergymen bit their thumbnails instead of puddings, in the bitterness of their hearts. Is it astonishing that they called Mr. Martin *Mr. Mastin*[1] on account of his sleepless rapacity? Every day, he displayed new charters from the Pope, all adapted to his own wishes or to any sudden emergency; and infuriated clergymen slapped clenched fists into open palms at arm's length, asseverating (not without some show of reason) that he had a sackful of blank parchments ready sealed with the Fisherman's Ring,[2] so that he could write on them whatever he pleased.

XVIII. *About the Rapacious Nuncio his Knavery*

When this sophistical nuncio came to my lord the king, the Regal Majesty deigned him a sweet smile and a stony silence, nor would comfort him with any promises of countenance or of assistance. Mr. Martin, therefore, retired, with humble reverences, mewing, his mien being somewhat dejected. To console himself, he convened the dignified clergymen, and discoursed to them very prepotently. They chose Sir John Mansel, dean of Saint Paul's, a discreet eloquent speaker, to give him a decidedly disappointing answer. But he continued to scratch up revenues wherever he could stick his claws into them. I, however, must refrain my indignation: for it will be more honourable (out of respect for the Holy Apostolic See) to keep silence about a very great deal of this knave's wanton and noxious voracity, than to offend the sus-

---

[1] "Martinus—Mastinus," cf. Fr. Mastin—Mastiff." [Rolfe's note.] The nickname, "Mastiff," was meant to indicate the rapacity of Master Martin.

[2] A ring used to seal documents by the pope.

ceptible heart of you, o most affable reader, as well as the minds of the faithful, with every minute particular.

XVIIII. *About the Nuncio Nonsuited*

Seeing several things, namely, that the emperor had chased our lord the Pope and the cardinals from Rome to Geneva, and thence to Lyon; and that King Arthur's forbearance was becoming frayed out at the edges; and that the clergymen of England were minded (for once) to cease from biting one another's necks, in order that regulars might combine with seculars against the wolf of Rome who preyed upon them, lambkins, Earl Hubert de Burgh thought well to set the magnates and pirates of the V ports on watch, secretly, to prevent any fresh powers from reaching Mr. Martin. And, at Dover, I myself arrested a pontifical courier with four large valises entirely filled with new pretexts (divers and all devilish) for extorting money. Mr. Martin flew savagely to my lord the king for vengeance; and butted up against a grave strong smile and free leave to take any vengeance pleasing him. Moreover, Earl Fulk the Flame (who had taken care to be by chance in the Presence at the moment) was requested to escort the chagrined nuncio, with an imposing power, to Dover, and to do what could be done to enlarge the pontifical courier and to recover the alleged pontifical bulls. But, strange as it seemed, both these objects defied Mr. Martin's search: the bulls having been burned to ashes by me, and their bearer (placed by me in the ship of one of my best pirates) was taking tosses on the narrow sea between England and France.

XX. *About the Profession of Piracy its Rules Regulations and Charter*

I may as well mention that it had seemed good to me, some time before this, to avail my lord the king of the services of persons incorrigibly addicted to piracy, seeing how much signal virtue and piety was running to waste in that direction. Very many bloody young men inebriated with the fever for bloody adventures, fell into criminal courses solely for lack of legitimate opportunities of exercising their singular faculties. To escape my justice, they revolted to piracy. Such was dear Brother Adam's own uncle, Sir William of Marish, a fat sinner, bald, long past beauty, somewhat melancholy to behold, and a proscribed murderer, who seized Lundy Island and made it a fortified piratical stronghold, over which he ruled as kinglet.[1] Dartmouth and Lynn and all the Norfolk ports also were nests of pirates. Nor may I forget to mention my V Ports and Sir Eustace the Monk, that truly pious and patriotic primate and pattern of pirates, the splendour of whose deeds is a sempiternal diadem about his name. So, having advised my lord the king in the matter, something very simple in the way of charter by letters-patent was devised and issued to Sir Adam Derobemolt and Sir William Lesauvage and Company, as follows, *Arthur by the Grace of God and the Favour of the Apostolic See, King, et cetera. Know all men that We have granted and given this Charter to N.N. to annoy Our enemies by sea or land where they can take them so as they share with Us half their gains.* O admirable statecraft. For by these means, masterless men were furnished with an acceptable master and useful service, and considerable sums accrued to the regal exchequer; and, also, I always had ready to hand a power composed of inveterate daredevils, who were always agog for, and asked for nothing better than, jobs which were (so to speak) extraordinary. Wherefore, when I was warned of Mr. Martin's desire for my head on a plate, I finished my pudding and burned the bulls, and procured the pirate on duty to put the pontifical courier over the narrow sea politely and in the strictest privacy.

xxi. *About an epistolary Correspondence with the Pontiff*

The affair of the bulls caused me and King Arthur to think that an elegant epistle in an urbane tongue, to the Reverend Father in Christ Innocent by the Grace of God Supreme Pontiff, from the magnates and commons of England, containing commendation and kisses to his holy feet, could do no harm, and might

---

[1] *"regulus."* [Rolfe's note.] William de Marisco was implicated in the murder of Henry Clement, a clerk and messenger of the justiciar of Ireland. He fled to Lundy Island, off the coast of England, and built a stronghold there. In 1238, an assassin who made an attempt on King Henry's life confessed that he had been sent by William de Marisco.

be productive of good. Accordingly, such a letter was written: it rehearsed our grievances, categorically, at portentous length, and in the most urbane of tongues; and I and King Arthur sent it, by the hands of Sir William Deperois and Sir Henry Delamare, to our lord the Pope where He lay at a council in Lyon for deposing the emperor. And we also sent letters to the Pope, from the king, from the suffragans of Canterbury, from the English abbots and priors, and, also, a letter from King Arthur to their worships the cardinals, chiding them for not keeping our lord the Pope in a gracious state of better-advisedness.

xxii. *About the Pontiff His Immoderation*

Those knights, our messengers, came back with news the most nauseous, declaring that they saw no sign, either in the Pope's demeanour or in His apostolic allocutions, of any moderation in the matter of our oppression. "The King of the English," says His Blessedness, "who is now following the example of the emperor and kicking against our apostolic pricks, knows (no doubt) what he is doing: We, also, know what We are doing; and We are not to be wheedled from doing it." And, forthwith, our Most Blessed Father announced His claim to the property of clergymen dying intestate;[1] and he also demanded sudden subsidies. O manners.

xxiii. *About an English Cardinal who could not help talking pertinently*

Being an Englishman not quite devoid of sensibility, Lord John Tolet,[2] cardinal-presbyter of the Title of Saint Lawrence in Lucina, got up and withstood Pope Innocent the Small to the face, as Messire Saint Paul did to the Blessedness of Messire Saint Peter because He also was a Supreme Pontiff much to be blamed. "Spare your indiscreet ire," says Cardinal John, "put the curb of moderation upon the impulse of your will, considering how very evil

---

[1] Not having made a will (*OED* OL).

[2] John of Toledo cautioned the pope against angering the English further and perhaps inspiring a revolt at a time when the papacy was in exile and ill feeling against the Church was manifesting in Hungary, Germany, Spain, and France.

are these days. *Hora novissima tempora pessima sunt vigilemus.*[1] The
Holy Land lies in peril from the Charismians: the Greeks have
seceded: Cæsar Frederick, who has neither superior nor equal
among princes (excepting King Arthur of the English, that splendid martyr and paladin facile princeps[2]), is opposing You: You,
Who are the Head of the Church, and, we, who are Your counsellors, are expelled from the Holy See, from the Holy City, from
Italy itself, yea, and we dwell in exile: Hungary expects nothing
but ruin from the Tatars: Germany is sliced in two by Konrad, the
emperor's son, warring against that Henry of Thuringia whom
You so fatuously have protruded as emperor: Spain has gone stark
mad: and King James of Aragon tears out bishops' tongues: France,
You have reduced to pauperism: God only knows what You have
done with Portugal. And, now, England, whom You have injured
many times, talks, like Balaam's ass, with the voice of an angel, in
the most exquisite Roman, rebuking You, being tried beyond its
strength. I ask You, therefore, Most Blessed Father, do You intend
to make Yourself another Ishmael (or is it Cain), with Your hand
against every man and every man's hand against You?"[3]

XXIIII. *About King Arthur his Method with Mr. Martin*

Pope Innocent's small mind was not moved to remorse by
these spirited expressions. He yearned, indeed, for vengeance
as well as for our money. Even the news, that my lord the king
would rebuild the whole of the old abbey of Westminster and
its chapter-house, in the most sumptuous manner imaginable,
with windows of painted glass, and all the diapering gilded and
coloured, and the walls within and without covered with pictures
in mosaic work of colours and gold, gave no satisfaction to Our
Most Blessed Father, nor abated his horrid ire by one jot or tittle.

---

[1] "It is the last hour, the time of adversity, let us watch!" From Bernard de
Morlaix's *De Contemptu Mundi* (12th century).
[2] The term "facile princeps" is used to refer to one who is easily first or is the
acknowledged leader (*OED* OL).
[3] This quote refers to Ishmael, the son of Abraham: "And he will be a wild man;
his hand will be against every man, and every man's hand against him; and he
shall dwell in the presence of all his brethren" (Gen. 16:12).

So, King Arthur said, wearily, "Oh, very well then. Be pleased to chase me hence that abominable Mr. Martin."

xxv. *About Mr. Martin his objection to King Arthur*

I had bestowed the dromedary-faced nuncio with my friends the knights at the New Temple, he having gotten himself so disliked that he needed protection. And, to him, there came Sir Fulk fil-Warenne scowling horribly, saying, "Leave England immediately." "By whose order?" screams Mr. Martin. "I," says Sir Fulk, "order you in the name of England in arms, who, after nine hours, will carve you in thin slices with saws, you, and all your people." And he withdrew in great wrath, heaping hideous threats upon terrible blasphemies, frightening the cat up the chimney. Mr. Martin, breathless with horror, flew to my lord the king. "I," says King Arthur, "am the author of this proceeding: for, so far, I have tolerated your depredations, which exceed all manner of justice; and, now, I will no longer restrain my English from attacking you and from mincing you with your Romans into little shreds." Mr. Martin trembled so fearfully, that his pendulous lip dangled down demonstrating that he was afflicted with great gumboils; and he abjectly whispered, "I humbly beg of Your Regal Majesty, for love of and reverence for our lord the Pope, a free exeat and safe-conduct from your realm." The king, very angry because the awkward beast whimpered so meanly, said "Go to the devil, and ask him for a safe-conduct through hell."

xxvi. *About Mr. Martin his marvellous but merited Misfortunes*

When my lord the king had eaten his dinner of cold mutton and a rosemary and marjoram pudding, and was thereby somewhat appeased, I advised him; and Sir Fulk fil-Warenne and Sir Robert Norris the marshal of the palace were ordained to conduct Mr. Martin safely as far as the narrow sea. But I took upon myself to charge these two knights, privately, to see to it that the said Mr. Martin should be so suitably instructed by the way as that he should not carry with him any erroneous notions as to the docile character of the English, which charge the two hilariously per-

formed in the following exquisite manner. They carefully selected
(for their retinue) knights and mercenaries, fifty of each, all distinguished by unparalleled personal ugliness, most truculent carriage, most raucous voices, and conversation entirely composed
of bloodcurdling imprecations. These, they armed heavily, with
spikes bolted on to all joints: so that Mr. Martin's terror might
be augmented to panic, by their ultra-ferocious aspect, as well as
by the exaggeration of their customary violent language caused
by the clumsiness of their spiky protuberances. Thus, then, they
set forth, calling the nuncio after them as one calls a hound to
heel. But, though he quaked like custard for fear of them, yet he
snuggled up against them lest he should happen on worse devils
by the way; and, though he begged them not to be so rough, yet,
when he saw riders passing by, he was so palsied with fear (but
for being goaded posteriorly) he would have taken the nearest
two turves[1] for a hiding-place. Whereat, Sir Fulk, or Sir Robert,
or both, used to jar his back, or his belly, or both, heavily, bidding
him to pluck up his courage. When they came to Saints Cosmas
and Damian in the Blean by Canterbury, it happened that one of
the archiepiscopal woods was being offered for sale; and a mob
of yeomen had assembled to purchase the lot of timber. Whom
espying, Mr. Martin squeals, "Alack and alack, what I feared has
now occurred. See there the posse ready to ravish and undo me.
O my dear sweet friends, Sir Fulk, and Sir Robert, have ye nor son
nor nephew nor kinsman nor friend for whom ye desire an ecclesiastical benefice? For I will grant you all your demands, gratis,
if you protect me in the lovely shadow of your wings from these
who lie in ambush for my life." And, he fumbled with his blank
parchments and his ink-horn and his pen-case, ready to make a
grant embellished with the sigill[2] pontifical upon demand. Says
then Sir Robert Norris, "God forbid that any man of mine should
get an ecclesiastical benefice in that way: but wait you here, you
great slinking beast, while I ride onward; and, if these fellows are
ill-disposed, I will check their rashness by displaying the king's
warrant." So the retinue and the nuncio drew up at the roadside

---

[1] Sods of grass (*OED* OL).
[2] Seal (*OED* OL).

to wait; and Mr. Martin slid under his horse's belly to hide beneath its caparisons,[1] while the whole company hoarsely began to narrate dreadful stories of the diabolically ingenious torments usually administered by Kentishmen to persons whom they deemed displeasing. At which, Mr. Martin's sweat gushed out of him in such incredible volumes, that the puddles of it streamed from beneath his horsecloth and coursed across the road, affecting many. O manners. Sir Robert, knowing the truth, but desiring to tickle the nuncio's terror as near to phrenzy as might be, quickly returned, saying, "With much difficulty, I have refrained from fury for the moment, preventing them from tearing off your toes, fingers and points generally with the cords of their faggots, such having been their pious purpose. Now, therefore, let us proceed stealthily and cautelously: for I am credibly informed that four-hundred atrocious caitiffs, led by four bald swarthy youths (who play well, in their leisure, with chessmen) are lying, not more than a mile hence, waiting for your passage, having sworn on the Four Evangels[2] to put their four knives fairly deep in your breast, just where your heart is not, but near it, and to light four times four little slow fires of sulphur on your belly below your diaphragm, and to let four-times-four-times-four large black rats eat what is left of you four hours later, so that none may come after you." At which horrid intelligence Mr. Martin made no more ado: but he just belched a curse and a little prayer, and lapsed to the ditch in a swoon. In which condition, they looped him over his horse and brought him to Dover, where I gave him to one of my pirates, to be tempted with very fat pork fried in his proximity, and to be set across the narrow sea on the festival of Messire Saint Swythun.[3] He was the fourth, and the last.

XXVII. *About young Boniface Primate of All England*

When the Primate Edmund died in exile (self-imposed) at Pontigny, my lord the king found it necessary to say to me that a different quality of clergyman (if possible a little less saintly)

---

[1] Coverings for the saddle of a horse (*OED* OL).
[2] The Four Gospels (*OED* OL).
[3] Saint Swithun's Day, July 15.

ought to succeed him. I assented, such being my duty and my
overwhelming pleasure. And I and my lord the King sat looking at each other's eyes for a quarter of an hour without speaking. Then, says he, "Give good advice, Hubert, from your mind's
store of cruel kindness and bloody benignity and knowledge
unequalled of how men and affairs ought to be handled." Thus,
indeed, did King Arthur of his sweet grace designate me. Says
I, "The monks of Canterbury must elect; and our lord the Pope
must confirm. Remains to settle who shall select the primate so
to be elected and confirmed." "I, by God's Dear Eyes, will choose
him, this time; and I will choose one not given to running away
from cows and bogeys:" says King Arthur. And again we used
fixed regard in silence for a space. Then, says the Regal Majesty,
"Whom have you in your mind, Hubert?" "Lord King," says I,
"whom have You in Yours?" King Arthur took a sliver of vellum,
and threw me another. "Write your primate's name, Hubert,"
says he, "while I write the name of mine." We wrote. I prayed
God to put my primate into the king's mind. We read. On both
slivers was the same name: Robert Greathead. So, the bishop of
Lincoln was summoned, and informed of the king's pleasure.
"I am unwilling to be archiepiscopated," instantly says he: nor
could arguments nor entreaties nor vituperations alter his sturdy
determination. Thus, we were as we were at the beginning, with
this difference, that there were now three persons in the king's
counsel. And we pondered; and the good bishop led us in prayer;
and again we pondered the matter. "See You here, lord king," at
length says Greathead, "and since you wish to save Your blooming
soul by saving the Church in England, I will name You a better
clergyman than old Robert of Lincoln for Your Primate, and one
who will not hasten to ascend to heaven almost immediately, not
being world-worn as I am." "Name him, lord bishop," says the
king, "and he shall be Primate of all England." "Vow it to God,
lord king:" says the bishop. "I vow it to God:" says King Arthur.
"I have had him in my family," says Greathead, "since he reached
the age of reason. Noble of birth he is, noble also of soul and parts
and person; and I myself did the breeding of him, if it please You.
Judge how I esteem him when You know that at twenty years I
priested him; and never have I let him leave me, because what

wisdom and what strength I have has come to me through the
lively limpid lovely soul of him." At this, I began to be very excited:
for I had not even dreamed of so audacious an idea, my son not
having attained anything like the age archiepiscopal and being
quite unknown, though of course his lofty stature and monstrous
beauty (not less than his morals and his wisdom) rendered him
desirable in any capacity. "Name your clergyman, lord bishop,"
says the king, impatient; "name the Primate of All England, will
you." "He," says Greathead, "is my secretary, by name Mr. Boniface de Burgh, son of the Earl-palatine of Kent here present; and
he waits without in the antechamber at the king's pleasure." "He
shall be Primate of All England:" affirms my lord the king. Thus
was my son Boniface selected for the vacant archiebishopric of
Canterbury.[1]

xxviii. *About Greathead Boanerges Hammer of Pontiffs*

The Canterbury monks, just then, were anxious to be obsequious to King Arthur, so that they might have his Regal protection against Archdeacon Simon Langthon, their ancient persecutor, who, having had a primate for his own brother, was inclined
to give himself presumptuous airs. They, therefore, faithfully
promised to elect my son Boniface; and promptly did so with
every possible solemnity. His confirmation by our lord the Pope
was a more uncertain undertaking: because we English were not
being very affable to Mr. Dromedary Martin, though we had not
yet finally dismissed him; and his reports, about our manners
and customs, were not making Pope Innocent the Small entirely
pleased with us. It therefore behoved us to walk with much circumspection; and we walked in this way. The bishop of Lincoln,
though very aged, was active and singularly able, in persuasion,
or in bending to his will those with whom he had to do, specially

---

[1] Boniface of Savoy, the son of Thomas, Count of Savoy, was elected archbishop
of Canterbury in 1241. He was extremely disliked by the English, in part because
he was foreign-born, a crisis Rolfe averts by replacing him with Hubert de Burgh's
son, a native Englishman. Boniface was also a member of the Council of Fifteen,
so it is vital for the narrative's movement toward aristocracy and away from
democracy that Boniface disappear.

monks, his volume of voice being simply enormous; and a clergyman who can manage monks, is capable of managing any kind
of clergyman, even the Immeasurable Clergyman. So, Greathead
took my son Boniface elect of Canterbury with him, and went
his way to Perugia where our lord the Pope was lodging; and, by
King Arthur's will, they travelled attended by so many trumpets
and such awful and indescribable pomp as had never been seen
before. In the midst of their splendid retinue, the two clergymen
carried themselves with almost majestic serenity, the old one solid
and firm, the young one bourgeoning with strength and beauty,
both monsters, pre-eminent above clergymen who act on earth.
Even our lord the Pope (that shabby exile) although His apostolic
displeasure against us English sometimes nearly choked Him,
deigned an immediate audience, and suffered Lincoln to speak
to him pretty plainly. For Greathead's method was a very sage
one. He would not speak, nor would he give Our Most Blessed
Father a chance of speaking, about filthy lucre: but he confined
his discourse entirely to the question of the primacy. That was
his way of beginning. Pope Innocent, hankering (as ever) after
English gold, having some idea of calmly conferring our primacy
on someone of His numberless unemployed nephews, and being
aggrieved because no new news of Mr. Martin's mission was being
laid before Him, chose to comfort Himself pettishly, turning to
His cardinals and saying: "Hear this old dotard, who would teach
Us how to do Our deeds. By Messires Saints Peter and Paul, if it
were not for Our natural generosity, We would deject him into
such profound perplexity that he should be a fable and an example and a warning and a wonder to the whole world." O manners. Greathead was not a bit dismayed by this harangue, having
prepared himself for similar ebulliences; and, having made for
himself an illustrious name in England for ever, as the indefatigable fatiguer and hammer of bumptious monks, who deemed him
tyrannous and severe and austere as well as inhuman (according
to Mr. Matthew, late of Paris),[1] he was both able and very willing to fatigue and to hammer our lord the Pope, if necessary.

---

[1] Matthew Paris represented Grosseteste as excessively severe in his treatment of
the monks and reformation of the monasteries.

Beside, before he began to speak again, some of the cardinals themselves got up to cough remonstrances at the Pope, saying: "It is not expedient to deal harshly with this bishop, for he speaks the truth which cannot be condemned. Is he not catholic, nay, most saintly, of more excellent life than we? Do not all men agree that he has no superior in the body of bishops, nor even a peer? So say the clergymen of France and of England; and our contradiction would be useless. Also, he is a great philosopher, deeply learned in Greek and Latin letters, zealous for justice, a trader in theology, a lover of friars, a prince among preachers, a master of chastity, a ferocious persecutor of simoniacs, and what more can Your Blessedness want?" (My son Boniface the Primate reported to me these sensible sayings of the cardinals.) When, therefore, our lord the Pope had been thoroughly well advised by all parties in Presence, in the manner afore-stated, Bishop Greathead (booming like a second Boanerges[1]) took up his parable again, labouring to inspire His Blessedness with a right judgement in regard to the Primacy of All England. "Most Blessed Father," he began, "I have also to say as follows, not particularly, but parenthetically, and by the way. My august sovereign lord the king of the English is vastly scandalized by the swinish situation of Your Blessedness, chased about from place to place like a greedy vicious ignorant slobbering wild-hog such as we keep for our diversion in the forests of England, exiled from Your city and from Your siege apostolical. Wherefore, my said lord the king of the English is minded (should it seem good to Your Blessedness) to speak very paternally to Frederick the Emperor, saying that it is quite stupid for a christian prince to molest Christ's vicar in the mode imperial. For, when a decent godly righteous sober knight desires to estop a noxious cock from crowing, he purely wrings his neck, it being outrageous as well as fatuous merely to chivy[2] the noisy lecherous fowl from one dunghill to another. And, seeing that my said august sovereign lord the king of the English has given his daughter Lady Ysabel Plantagenet[3] (a daffodil) in marriage to the

---

[1] "And James the son of Zebedee, and John the brother of James; and he surnamed them Boanerges, which is, The sons of thunder" (Mark 3:17).

[2] Chase (OED OL).

[3] Frederick was married to Isabella of England, the second daughter of King John.

said Cæsar, it is plain that he may speak to him with a freedom
and an authority which no other prince can use. For, whatever
else may be alleged against King Arthur Lefthand (mistakenly
and most mendaciously) I know that he would defend, with his
knightly and regal and hallowed body, the personal sacrosanctity
of the Roman Pontiff. But, meanwhile, it is essential to avoid the
detestable sin of simony and to provide England with a primate,
namely, Lord Boniface here in presence, canonically elected, and
a person pleasing to our lord the king, in order that the said king
of the English may not labour for God in his kingdom single-
handed." In this delicious way, Bishop Greathead obtained the
archiepiscopal pall for my son Boniface, with his confirmation by
the Pope as Primate of All England.

xxviiii. *About a new Pontiff*

Our lord Pope Innocent the Small was forced to continue bel-
ligerence against the emperor alone; and my lord the king was
not drawn into this quarrel, for a very simple reason. It pleased
divine Providence to retire Cæsar Frederick to Abraham's bosom;[1]
and King Arthur had no ground for commenting on the comportment of Cæsar Konrad who succeeded him. So the Pope, in turn,
died of His spleen at Naples. And instantly another member of the
same noble house of Conti was elected to the throne of the Fisherman, imposing upon Himself the name of Alexander the Fourth,
a good-enough clergyman, and moderate in His counsels: but
addicted to the practices of His predecessors whenever possible.
In the case of England, however, the ruin of the Church by extortion was no longer possible: For King Arthur, assisted by his right
trusty and well-beloved counsellors the Primate Boniface, Bishop
Robert Greathead of Lincoln, Earl Hubert de Burgh, Earl Fulk
fil-Richard called the Flame, had thoroughly settled that matter,
precisely defining the position of England, just before the demise
of our Lord Pope Innocent the Small, in the manner which I will
now narrate.

---

[1] Frederick died in 1250.

xxx. *About Pope Innocent the Small His Apology by Hubert de Burgh*

I earnestly hope that I have written clearly, as well as truly, about our Lord Pope Innocent the Fourth or the Small, for I have no wish to write history in the manner of Mr. Matthew (late of Paris), who writes of matter which he never touched and (therefore) never knew. But I did touch these matters, and I assert as plainly as possible that Pope Innocent was as susceptible to the influence of good advice as any clergyman alive. I also assert, with equal lucidity, that, in the absence of such good advice, He lapsed into undesirable behaviour as easily as the proverbial bason.[1] The foisting of foreigners into English benefices was His fixed idea. The very moment when he found himself temporarily free from his actual job as apostle, then did He disport Himself in the art and mystery of money-grubbing to the chagrin of people who wished to respect Him. He bitterly reproached us English as Ghibellines, a most bestial epithet; for if ever a nation on earth was Guelph[2] to a man, in loyalty to and veneration of Peter's successor, Christ's Vicar, God's Vicegerent, in the shape of the Roman Pontiff, I say that that nation is England. I restrain my anger, as I have one thing more to say about Pope Innocent.

xxxi. *About a Specimen Impontificality*

It was the holy penitential season of Lent. Bishop Robert Greathead incurred pontifical displeasure, for refusing to admit a pontifical nephew, Mr. Frederick of Lavania, to a canony in Lincoln Cathedral, and another Roman clergyman (ignorant of the English tongue) to a rich benefice in his diocese. The condemnation of our great bishop was bad enough; and my lord the king was about to express both a purely personal and also a regal opinion, when, suddenly, came the last straw which actually did break the back of the willing patient useful over-worked English jackass. This last straw was a pontifical breve. I transcribe it here, that

---

[1] Badger (*OED OL*).
[2] A medieval Italian political party that supported the popes as opposed to the emperors (*OED OL*).

you, o most affable reader, may see how we used to be worried by
the Roman Apostle, and (pondering well the purport of it) may
perceive the manifold contempt and injury and oppression which
eradicated our forbearance. Here is the said breve: *Innocent bishop
of bishops to His well-beloved sons the abbot and convent of Saint Alban
in the diocese of Lincoln Greeting and Apostolic Benediction. Whereas
Our well-beloved son Mr. John de Camezana Our nephew and chaplain
unknown to you holds the benefice of Wengrave worth forty marks a
year and more the right of patronage wherein as We understand belongs
to you with fatherly affection We beg you to exchange the said benefice
for the first other benefice in your patronage which shall fall vacant and
be acceptable to the said Mr. John or his proctor none the less reserving
the said benefice of Wengrave for Our Own gift and this notwithstanding any reservation or inhibition or even that indulgence which is said
to have been granted to the English namely that the benefices of Ytalian
clergymen who die or who cede their benefices shall not be immediately
bestowed on another Ytalian clergyman.*[1]

XXXII. About the Primate and the Impontificality

Apart from the impudent incorrigible injustice of this breve,
the fact (that Lincoln and her magnificent bishop should be sin-
gled out for pontifical aggression) chiefly aroused the fury of us
Englishmen. For my son, the Primate Boniface, had hardly had
time to give us a specimen of something really distinct in the way
of archiepiscopality; and bishop Robert Greathead was certainly
the most honoured clergyman in the kingdom, not even excepting our dear Brother Adam of Marish. But my son, the Primate
Boniface, had shewn what manner of clergyman he was, on the
very first day after he was seized of the plenitude of archiepiscopality, by making ready for expected pontifical aggression in this
way: he sent his mandate to all bishops and abbots and priors in
the kingdom, requiring them to advise him instantly of any fresh
attempts which might be made upon the liberties and privileges

---

[1] The privilege granted by the Council of Lyon was *Ne scilicet Ytalicus immediate
succedat.*—P. and C. [Rolfe's note.] At the Council of Lyon, English clergymen
complained about the practice of appointing French and Italian clergy to English
benefices, but it was declared that Italian would succeed Italian.

of the Church in England. Good boy. And King Arthur at once became ware that Primate Boniface quite merited the encomiums of Bishop Greathead, and set himself majestically to support the primate as only a king can. Blissful collaboration. Therefore, the abbot of Saint Alban's brought Pope Innocent's breve to the Primate Boniface, who (in turn) shewed it to my lord the king. And, four days later, when King Arthur had prayed and composed his mind and was shriven of dear Brother Adam, there were summoned to the Presence, the Lord Boniface of Canterbury, the Lord Robert of Lincoln, the Earl-palatine of Kent and Gloucester and Essex, and the Earl of Richmond and Jaffa and Nantes.

XXXIII. *About the King and the Primate and the Finish of Impontificalities*

We assembled in privy council before the king and the queen throned and canopied in the palace of Westminster; and my dear lord's strong white face had so awful a rigour of kingliness as to tell me that we were not summoned to counsel but to hear him. Brother Adam stood by the king's hallowed right hand; and we four sat on our stools in face of the Regal Majesties. Then, says King Arthur: "Reverend fathers, and trusty earls, the time has passed when Englishmen might respectfully ask our lord the Pope to do them justice, honestly and faithfully; and the time has come when We, Arthur, King of the English, must warn Our said lord the Pope that His Blessedness will no longer be permitted to pursue our Englishmen with injustice, dishonestly and faithlessly. Hear therefore, these letters, which We, with Our Own left hand, have written to our lord the Pope Innocent the Fourth, that ye may testify to Our Regal sealing and delivering of the same." He took a pergamen[1] from Brother Adam; and began to read from it, as follows:

To the Reverend Father in Christ, and Lord, Innocent, by the Grace of God, Supreme Pontiff, ARTHUR *and* MARIOL, *by the same Grace and the Sanction of the Apostolic See, king and queen of the English, king and*

---

[1] Parchment.

queen of Hierusalem, lord and lady of Ireland, prince and princess of the Welsh, duke and duchess of Armorica, Acquitaine, Gascony, Normandy, earl and countess of Anjou, Poictou, Maine, Touraine, et cetera, Greeting, and kisses to His holy feet. The more that the son submits himself to the pleasure of the Father, and the more ready and devoted that he shews himself to His commands, the more does he merit the reward due for his devotion and service. Since, then, o Father, We, during the whole of Our reign, have shewn Ourselves and Our dominions obedient to You in everything, We are displeased that You do not reward Us, but burthen and oppress Us. For, not satiated with the buss-loads of Pennies which the English pay annually to Peter,[1] as ordained by Our Predecessor the Venerable Servant of God King Alfred the Great, You extort heavy contributions from all English clergymen, and You try to extort yet heavier, by means most dishonest and nefarious. And You with insatiate greed, continually demand collections, procurations, tallages, tithes, thirds, fifths, subsidies, and assizes. And You are never faithful to Your solemn promises. And You forbid English patrons to present English clergymen to English benefices: but You fill them with aliens ignorant of the English language, who carry English money out of England, impoverishing Our said kingdom beyond endurance: for You shall know, that Your said aliens, who live not in England, who leave their spiritual flocks without spiritual pastors or fodder and let their churches in England fall in wrack and ruin, take, out of Our kingdom of England, annually, revenues amounting in total to sixty-thousand marks, that is to say, a sum which is three times greater than Our Own regal revenue of Our said kingdom of England. Now, then, We are moved, to write thus particularly to Your Blessedness, by the apostolic breves lately addressed to our lord bishop Robert of Lincoln and to our lord abbot Squinter of the convent of Saint Alban, which breves (now in Our archives) are not consonant with apostolic holiness, but are alien and discordant therefrom. And We believe that it is impossible for the Holy Apostolic See to do anything which is not for edification: for that would contravene Divine Promises, be a falling-away from and a corruption and a misuse of holy plenary powers, and a complete departure from the Glorious Throne of Jesus Christ, and a very close sitting-side-by-side with the double principle of darkness

---

[1] Peter's pence, a tax of one penny per household paid to the Papal See in the middle ages.

in the seat of the pestilence of hellish penalties. Wherefore, seeing that the said apostolic breves, to Our said bishop and to Our said abbot, are manifestly very far from being for edification, and are indubitably for destruction, it is plainly evident that the Holy Apostolic See cannot issue them. And, since the said Holy Apostolic See cannot issue them, it is needless for Us (or for anyone) to notice them, excepting for the purpose of damning and defying them. But, on the ground of the debt of obedience and fidelity in which We are bound to the Holy Apostolic See, and, from strong of unity with It in the Body of Christ, We are (however) willing to gratify Your Blessedness, by making and conceding the following provisions: First: all benefices in Our kingdom of England, which are held by alien clergymen, are now void, and the patrons of them are to fill them as soon as may be with such clergymen of English birth as Our English bishops may deem suitable: Second: all Our subjects of Our Kingdom of England are to offer Pennies to Peter, once a year, voluntarily and liberally according to the English custom, as ordained by Our Predecessor the Venerable servant of God, King Alfred the Great: Third: We Ourselves are willing and do faithfully promise to pay to the Roman Pontiff the sum of one thousand marks annually, which sum our wicked uncle Sir John fil-Henry agreed to pay for himself and his heirs to Pope Innocent the Great and His successors in the Holy Apostolic See, not because We acknowledge that the said Roman Pontiff has any right to require the said sum of Us, for We are not John's heir but King Richard Lionheart's, and We do not hold Our kingdom of England as a feof from the said Roman Pontiff, but by God and by Our right, namely, by Our right in accordance with the will of King Richard Lionheart confirmed to Us by Pope Innocent the Great, and by Our right of conquest, and by the Judgement of God manifested in the ordeal of battle; and, therefore, We concede the said sum of one thousand marks annually as a free grace and a sweet regal gift, solely because We desire to dwell in love and amicity: Fourth: beside the said Peter's Pennies and Our said sweet regal gift, it is Our will that no other payments shall be made to the Holy Apostolic See from Our kingdom of England. And, finally, with regard to apostolic breves similar to those which are not to be noticed by anybody, as afore ordained, and with regard to those of like tenour which may come hereafter, We decline to obey, or to let be obeyed, the demands contained in the said breves, or any demands paragonable to them, because such demands tend to the sin of disedification, which We condemn as most abominable to the Lord

Jesus Christ, most pernicious to the human race, altogether opposed to the Holiness of the Apostolic See, contrary to the Catholic Unity. And the discretion of Your Blessedness cannot ordain any censure or severe thing against Us on account of these letters and these Our edicts and decrees, for all Our saying and doing in the matter is neither opposition nor rebellion, but it is the filial reverence due to the Father in accordance with the Divine Mandate. Filially and reverently, therefore, We decline to permit Your Blessedness to disedify the Church in England by draining it of its revenues, We oppose, We rebel, asking for Your holy prayers and a share in Apostolic Benedictions.

ARTHUR THE KING. MARIOL THE QUEEN.

In this manner dealt my lord the king with the clergymen, and with the Immeasurable Clergyman their head, delivering us from attempted pontifical aggression, so that my son Boniface the Primate might order the Church in England decently and godly and righteously and soberly, is seen and known of all men. I say no more, therefore, of pontiffs, or of impontificabilities. There is no more to be said.

XVIIII

THE BOOK CALLED THE WAY OF THE CROSS

1. *About King Arthur taking the Cross*

On the morn of Marymass[1] in August, in the year when one of
our lords the Popes ascended to the superiors, we were by chance
hearing the mass sung by the bishop of Ardpert in the cathedral
of Winchester, very devout of mind for good reasons, I, and Fulk
the Flame, and the earl of Pembroke and Striguil who was about
to depart for Antwerp in the Low Country on an embassage, and
the slim young earl of Salisbury, and Sir Roger Dequincy next to
him in a rather glowing new coat *gules, semee of mascles or,* whose
mother had just returned to her post among the queen's ladies.
In front of us, was my lord the king, pure and white as mother-
of-pearl in his regal raiment of ermine and tissue of silver, with
my lady the queen beside him as ever. And bishop John, in his
sky-coloured vestment, was illumined by the shining sun, rubi-
cund and cherubic of visage. When we were fed of God, King
Arthur moved not, nor did any of us. And the bishop was flurried when we did not rise, he being ready to make his reverence
before departing. But the Regal Majesty went on praying; and we
were agog with wonder, for it was not his usual custom, he being
always quick for his pudding, nor could the queen abide prolongation of the fast. But, anon, he rose from his knees; and "Ho, lord
bishop:" cries King Arthur. Lord John of Ardpert began to totter,
the words not being in the liturgy: for he was an ordinary clergyman, Irish, and a suffragan; and he sat suddenly on his faldstool,[2]
jouncing with his hands upon his lap, all a-twitter at being called
out of his mass-book before so large and influential a congrega-

---

[1] The Feast of the Assumption, August 15.
[2] Stools at which worshippers kneel during acts of devotion (*OED* OL).

tion. Then, cries the king again, cold and white of visage as of habit, "Ho, lord bishop, bring me here a rosy cross, and therewith insign me for a new crusade: for, by God's Dear Eyes, I vow to keep this festival next year at Nazareth."

II. *About King Arthur his Call to the Cross*

Uprose then such a buzz as I cannot describe. Every magnate assailed his neighbour's ear with words, not waiting to listen for an answer. But I understood that an inspiration had come suddenly to the king, it being his sacred and regal privilege to be celestially visited in all great and wide affairs. And the bishop began to be busy; and clergymen fluttered to and fro all over the floor, being unable to find any but tonsuring scissors, nor any red stuff in the vestry which might with reverence be cut. And the aspect of my lord the king was becoming bleaker than frost, because of his impatience. But the Cardinal-Primate Stephen, seeing how things were, proffered his doctor's habit of scarlet cloth furred with sables, which (by God's Providence) he had donned that day, being too old and feeble to sing mass at breakfast time. So, the clergymen cut up this gown, making a potent cross of the scarlet cloth, which the bishop blessed and fixed upon the regal breast and back, splendid as blood on snowy ermine. Then, King Arthur took my lady the queen by the hand, and turned round upon us, fearful and still: and he cried in our faces, "Who goes with Us to Nazareth?"

III. *About Earl Hubert refused the Cross*

Instantly, we all leaped forward, tumbling over our faldstools, each knight being fearful of being sneered at as the last to follow the king. Nor was the cardinal primate's gown sufficient for ensigning so great an array: wherefore we fell upon other doctors present, snatching their rednesses will-he nill-he to cut into crosses for that occasion. But, when Sir Hubert de Burgh shoved forward first with Sir Fulk the Flame, cross in hand and feverish to get at the bishop, my lord the king let me with his hallowed dexter,[1] not suffering me to press on, and saying, "Stay back, Hubert, for We have other jobs for you." Which indeed, he had: for, the same day, he issued to me new letters-patent, naming me admiral and warden and justiciar and regent of England and earl-palatine of Kent. So I rode quickly through London to Dover, having no time to be sad, nor indeed for eating my pudding, being burthened with all the realm's affairs, and overborne with business night and day, collecting navies from my V Ports and from my pirates. And thus I stayed behind, while King Arthur and Queen Mariol and Earl Fulk the Flame and Countess Alys went crusading, with half the magnates, and seven bishops, and abbots and knights enough to frighten Salahadin himself, had not that infidel been dead and sufficiently frightened already.[2] And a great host sailed from Southampton on the festival of Messire Saint Giles,[3] in a most mighty fleet led by my lord the king and his train in a new buss called *Mount Carmel*. Now all these histories here following, of King Arthur's voyage and his crusade in the Holy Land, I record in the words which I had from Earl Fulk when he returned, as nearly as I remember them. So this is not my tale, but his; and I tell it as he told it to me.

IIII. *About King Arthur his Voyage to Terrasancta*[4]

Says Earl Fulk: Nothing of great import befel the crusaders on the voyage. Earl Fulk's little maid, Lady Constance (a wild-rose) flung her parrot in a pet into the sea, and herself after it when it sobbed; and must needs be rescued by two-score ship-boys and eleven knights and her father and two very large bishops, to say nothing of my lord the king, all plunging incontinent, she having come with her mother Countess Alys who had her train with the queen's. Nor did any other parlous thing occur, excepting the sickness of many, who (at first) besought their saints not to let them die empty, and (then) prayed angrily for death to ease them

---

[1] Right hand (*OED* OL).
[2] Saladin, the Muslim leader who recaptured Jerusalem from the Crusaders, died in 1193.
[3] September 1.
[4] Holy Land.

of their pangs. But it is generally thus with knights on shipboard, though I myself (as befits an islander) am greatly comforted when I am on the sea. And, when they touched harbour near Agrigent in Sicily, four abbots manifested a sudden disposition to take the road to Rome, one alleging a vision, another imperative business of his convent, a third a vocation for the eremitical life, a fourth a reserved case: wherefore Earl Fulk, suspecting that their real reason was an aversion from sea-water, secreted all their clothes by night, excepting their crooks and mitres, and offered (with perfect gentility) to set them ashore and to speed them on their way thus. At which they said that their business in Rome could be postponed to a more convenient season; and accepted their rations of pudding with ordinary urbanity. And the fleet, being revictualled, departed, making as though to put in at Acre, where was Sir John of Ibelin and Baruth, the king's baily: but, warned in the night by the mariners that the wind favoured his secret desire, King Arthur let change the course; and, by noon on the morrow of the festival of Messire Saint Martin, the power had landed at Ascalon, and had heard mass sung by the abbot of Glastonbury, one of the four afore-mentioned.

v. *About the Grandmasters*

The young earl of Salisbury went northward with letters from my lord the king, for the Baily in Acre, and for Sir Peter the Grandmaster of the Temple of Tortosa,[1] and for his brother Sir Guerin, *gules, a tower argent quarterly with the cross of Saint John*, the Grandmaster of the Hospital at Irak, bidding them in the names of the king and the queen to collect their full powers, and to hold them ready to act at a word. Now, it chanced that both Grandmasters were with the Baily in Acre at the time, and quite ignorant of King Arthur's great crusade: for my lord the king had come more swiftly than news, which (says earl Fulk) travels with greater velocity than a bird in those infidel parts which are swayed by the devil. Thus, the young earl, instead of having to make three journeys, accomplished his errand in one; and, when

---

[1] A stronghold of the Knights Templar.

the Grandmasters (in the manner of knightly monks) said "Hum" and "Haah" and began to discourse of their privileges, the boy plainly spat in their faces certain mind-unhinging information, saying that King Arthur Lefthand loved not disobedience, and habitually deprived of their trumpets and burst with his hand-point the spleens of persons who dared to think half of what the said Grandmasters misguidedly were saying. Whereat Sir Peter and Sir Guerin mused, nibbling on their chin-pieces; and having bethought themselves that King Richard Lionheart's nephew and heir was excessively Plantagenet in his passions, they ceased from thinking about their privileges and made ready to obey.

VI. *About the Archangelic Order of the Candid Girdle*

Meanwhile, a strange thing happened. My lord the king, in the castle of Ascalon where the Hospitallers welcomed him as their most signal benefactor, suddenly was visited by nine extremely old knights, who rode in, hot-foot, imploring an immediate audience. Which being granted, the ancient of them cast down at the regal feet a goodly wallet of parchments; and, says he, "Grace and favour, lord king;" and set himself to pant like forty windmills. "Grace and favour be with you all," says King Arthur; and he commanded wine and puddings and stools to be brought for the old men's comfort, for he saw that they were highly respectable though no trumpets attended them. "And speak your minds without fear," says he, when they were comforted. So, the ancient took up his parable; and, "While the Grandmasters and the Temple and the Hospital are bickering, as we hear, at Acre," says he, "here is the whole Archangelic Order of the Candid Girdle of Saint Thomas of Acre ready to serve Your Regal Majesty;" and, being horribly old, and fetching his breath with difficulty, he could say no more. And, seeing that my lord the king had forgotten him and the humble hospice where the Regal Majesty first harboured in Syria, the ancient waggled blue and yellow hands at another old knight signifying that the word lay with him. And each of the eight tried, in turn: but they mouthed and gibbered so toothlessly and wheezed so anxiously, almost like lepers, that no one could understand them; and, in the end, they could do no more than fall over one another like ninepins and wag their wallet of parchments. So, my lord the king commanded the abbot of Reading to examine the same; and it was seen that the nine knights were the sole survivors of two-hundred, whom King Henry fil-Empress sent to the Holy Land, compounding his vow to go crusading in person on account of his regal share in Messire Saint Thomas's martyrdom,[1] which two hundred knights King Richard had chartered, as the Archangelical Order of the Candid Girdle of Saint Thomas of Acre, after he had besieged and taken that city under the invocation of the said Messire Saint Thomas. All this and many other things, were plainly declared by the charters; and the badge of the order was named as a white cord knotted with fifteen knots to bind on the naked loins, and a white cord to bind over mail and coat, similarly knotted, in memory of the white cord which fifteen archangels bound on the naked loins of Messire Saint Thomas, when he was chancellor, to preserve him in pristine purity.[2] And, when the nine old knights saw that King Arthur understood the thing, they up and made disclosure of their Candid Girdles. "Well done, good and faithful servants," says my lord the king; and he offered to the Grandmaster, the ancient, the kiss of peace as between one sovereign and another, whereat everybody was commoved to sobs of admiration. Then,

---

[1] Henry II swore to go on a crusade to atone for his part in the assassination of Thomas Becket.

[2] These historic facts are frantically interesting, when pondered in connection with others, namely, (a) that Richard's order of Saint Thomas Beket of Acre subsequently became absorbed by the Temple: (b) that one of the charges against the Templars, at the time of their atrocious persecution, was that they wore a white girdle next to their skin: (c) that the Order of Friars Preachers (Dominican) actually *has* a "Confraternity of the Angelic Girdle" (white, and knotted as described) which they say originated with their Dominican Saint Thomas of Aquino, on whom it was conferred in the manner and for the purpose described in the text. We cannot help asking (with considerable excitement) why the Angelic Girdle of modern Dominicans (chiefly worn by clergymen and seminarists) is not the lineal descendant through the Order of Knights Templars of King Richard Lionheart's very respectable knightly Order of the Archangelic Candid Girdle of Saint Thomas Beket of Canterbury and Acre? We should like to hear the point discussed by Father Hugh Pope, O.P., the Bishop of Nottingham, Mr. Gilbert Chesterton, Mr. A. C. Benson, Mr. G. B. Shaw and other competent and unbiassed historians.—P. and C. [Rolfe's note.]

says King Arthur again, "We have here, the Archangelic Order of the Candid Girdle of Saint Thomas of Acre, sitting in chapter to fill the one-hundred-and-ninety-one vacancies in the said order. Now, therefore, let one-hundred-and-ninety knights of Ours, who wish to bind themselves with this girdle of purity, freely come forward, led by Us, Sir Arthur Lefthand, King of England and Hierusalem, to ask for admission by our lord the Grandmaster here in Presence." Insued much cutting and knotting of new tent-cordage; and the king's will was obeyed. This done, the nine old knights were armed with a new charter confirming all their rights and privileges and endowing their hospice in Acre with four feofs; and they themselves were conveyed there in litters, with a charge to prepare beds for the wounded in the coming battles. But, to the hundred-and-ninety new knights of that Order, who remained under arms, was entrusted the policing of camps with power to purge them of lewd and naughty fellows and their followers, by beatings, mutilation of noses, and death by impalement for the first, second, and third offences respectively.

VII. About King Arthur Crusader

Melekamel, soldan of Babylon, held the Holy Places: but he was no friend of his cousin Gathadin, soldan of Aleppo, grandson of Salahadin, who ruled in the north and saw to it that no mere prince of Antioch should preen the plumage of over-weening prepotence. Nor was the said Melekamel friendly disposed to his nephew Melekennasser, son of soldan Conradin of Damascus, whom he falsely alleged to be a painted and padded leper, a futile and ridiculous statement, as anyone who has wrested with Melekennasser can testify, he not even having the smell of one of those unfortunates. My lord the king, therefore, designed to bring a power upon Hierusalem from the north, by way of Napolis, while he attacked from Blanchegarde; and he took order that no reliefs should come up from Egypt through Darum: for he said, "We have but eight months wherein to wend our way to Nazareth, which way lies through Hierusalem." This, he said for a purpose: for he might have ridden to Nazareth in three days and with all his trumpets, at any time, nor would any man have dared to incommode him. And he could have done this, in this security, because neither Melekennasser nor Gathadin would so much as spit to save Melekamel from dying of thirst. Yet, lest some fanatic Saracen should jump up, coughing, and preaching a Jehad, which would bring all the infidels from everywhere buzzing about the christian power, my lord the king ordained the Hospitallers to throw out fifty knights with a thousand mercenary cotterels under the Turkopolier,[1] to pass over toward Banias, heeding that none should go by them, either to spy out behind them, or to bear news before them. This was promptly done; and all the christians were vastly amazed to see the Hospitallers obeying anyone. O manners.

VIII. *About the Grandmaster of the Temple*

Earl Fulk told me this, believing it comical. It appears that Sir Guerin de Montacute, Grandmaster of the Hospital, obeyed my lord the king out of love and amicity, not only because of their former relations, but because he had been sovereignly entertained by the Regal Majesty in London when he came to visit the Clerkenwell Priory: but his brother, the Grandmaster of the Temple, only obeyed for fear of major force. For, when my lord the king wrote to him fairly, *Arthur the King and Mariol the Queen to their Reverend Father and dear Cousin Peter Grandmaster of King Solomon his Temple and Order of the Poor Fellow-soldiers of Christ, Greeting,* the said Sir Peter saw fit to stiffen his neck, and to discourse of his experience in eastern warfare, the privileges of his Order, his sovereign dignity, and such-like festered and fly-blown and wind-inflated toys. He was not for doing the king's will; he would not bring his power from Tortosa by sea, but he made as though to attack Melekennasser and to raise Damascus as a hornets' nest about our ears, because (forsooth) three villages of the Templars had lately been spoiled by that soldan, and he desired to teach him a lesson, forgetting that such teaching would be far more efficacious if administered by King Arthur. Had the Temple, indeed, indulged in a little war of its own, King Arthur's plan of the cru-

---

[1] The commander of turcopoles or the light-armed soldiers of the order of St. John of Jerusalem (*OED* OL).

sade would be nulled: for my lord the king knew that no one might eat the myriads of three soldans in a single mouthful, and was most wisely intending to bite them one by one. And, lo, this clergyman, this knight would teach the conquistator (before the age of twenty) of the two kingdoms of England and Hierusalem, as though it were a case of grandams and the eggs of pullets.[1] O manners. So King Arthur, blazing, sent for Earl Fulk, where he was eating his pudding, and, says he, "Flame, to Baruth, where the Templars have come from Tortosa, and say, 'Arthur the king to Peter the monk, unless you keep your Christmas before Hieru-salem, We will inter the right side of you in Ascalon and the left side of you in Tyre, both sides broiled, on the festival of the Epiph-any.'" And Earl Fulk with a heart full of glee and a face like glow-ing iron, brought the message forthwith to Baruth. The Grand-master said, "How dare you?" Earl Fulk lifted his eyebrows. The Grandmaster said, "Is it really serious?" Earl Fulk answered, "He is Angevin, he is Plantagenet, he is England." The Grandmaster bit large bits out of his beard, and writhed upon his saddle, for he was sovereign, and a proper knight, although he was a monk as well; and he looked upon his Templars, the Damascus road, the sky above his head, the earth beneath his horse's hooves, at Earl Fulk the Flame. Then, he munched the iron hoop of his basnet,[2] and swore some select oaths by Noe's ark and other ancient edifices constructed by Templars, heartening himself thus two or three times; and again he eyed Earl Fulk. (It was as good as any mys-tery to see Earl Fulk imitating him. He did it once in my palace of Whitehall before five bishops; and they laughed till they sobbed.) Sir Peter, then, eyed Earl Fulk. That Flame made a sign with his flat pointed hand, as though to spike himself in the diaphragm, the mere sight of which gesture conduces to horrible nausea; and, then, he made as though to chop himself in two neat halves from crutch to crown. Whereat the Grandmaster suddenly jumped, as one who (through inadventure) sits plump heavily on a tenpenny nail; and ordered his knights to ship forthwith to Acre. This was the first time when he had obeyed any other sovereign since he

---

[1] A young hen (*OED* OL).
[2] A steel headpiece (*OED* OL).

was made Grandmaster: but it was not the last; and his soul's health was much ameliorated by these salutary humiliations, his brother said.

viiii. *About Soldan Melekamel*

The Templars marched from Acre to Napolis to reach the Holy City from the north. Earl Fulk returned to Ascalon, where he found that a power under Sir John Delacy of Halton, *quarterly, or and gules, a bend sable and a label argent*, had gone to watch Darum, a castle of the Saracens full of sparrows and a key of the way up from Egypt. King Arthur went by Gelady to Blanchegarde, which he refortified; and there he lay till his plans should mature. Now the soldan Melekamel, with a handful of emirs and about five hundred horsemen, had come up from Egypt by the periculose way of Montreal, for he was loath to lose Hierusalem; and he lay at Saint Abraham, his nearest stronghold to Blanchegarde, striving to collect a proper power. But there was not much heart in the Saracens; and his emirs counselled him to make the best peace possible, and to wait till he had secured the friendship of the soldans of Aleppo and Damascus, before undertaking war. Which good rede,[1] Melekamel rejected: for he was leaning on the counsel of Emir Abdulla of Zuzz in the south country, a very fierce black man, whom (afterward) Earl Fulk spiked.

x. *About Lord Richard Plantagenet*

Young Lord Richard Plantagenet, the king's son, and the young earl of Salisbury, and old earl Ralf de Blondeville IIII of Chester (he who had wanted to be King Arthur's step-father and Duke of Armorica) rode toward Bethlehem on the day before the vigil of the Nativity. It was the king's own wish that Sir Ralf should accompany the youngsters: for, after Brother Adam converted him, he was a most holy earl, and his age and weight made him a model of prudence and as good a mentor as any young knight could wish to company with: though I myself never went mad about him.[2] They

---

[1] Advice (*OED* OL).

[2] Hubert de Burgh and Ranulph de Blondeville were often in conflict with one

took with them some five-hundred mercenary cotterels, of which half were archers: for a Giwe had brought news that Melekamel was passing mutton-puddings into Hierusalem from the south, sheep from Edom, and corn from the rich feof of Oultre-jourdain; and they were to find out whether Mr. Giwe spoke the truth. This, indeed, was so: for a great caravan of mules, donkeys, sheep, and goats, was discovered coming northward.

XI. *About the Capture of the Caravan*

Fearing the spate of River Barsheim, they rode all night by Gibilin; and at next noon, they overtook the caravan near Phagor. The Emir of Zuzz (not yet spiked) was commanding the power which escorted the caravan; and he held Saint George over River Barsheim, where he confidently expected attack, for the spate had run away before he arrived there. Lord Richard's power, therefore, fell upon the caravan, and drove it at a sheep's fastest, intending to gain the course of the river, and thereby to pass to Blanchegarde. But some of the slaves attending the beasts escaped, and warned Emir Abdulla in Saint George: else the caravan certainly would have evaded, for it raised no dust by reason of recent rain. He, having a great power, swiftly pursued down the high land above the valley, with intent to come between the said caravan and Blanchegarde before my lord the king could be advised. But Lord Richard, a born man-of-war (despite his blooming youth) perceived the infidels' plan; and he dispatched a knight, Sir Nicolas of Eltham, well-mounted and riding lightly to swoop with the news round by Elgedide. And the marshal of the camp at Blanchegarde instantly admitted Lord Richard's courier to the Presence, for the matter was serious, in that king Arthur's power also was running short of puddings. So, a power was flung out under Sir Richard Dalbiney, *gules, a lyon or, an escallop for difference*, uncle of the young earl of Arundel, but it advanced no further than Bothune, before it heard the buzz of battle blending with the bleating of sheep. For the Emir of Zuzz, having overtaken the caravan, stopped it by slaughtering

another. In 1223, Ranulph was part of a group of castellans that demanded the removal of Hubert de Burgh from Henry III's administration, "for he was the despoiler of the king's treasure and the oppressor of the people" (Ellis 75-76).

the front flock of sheep, which butcher's work was done by a few, while the many fell upon Lord Richard in the ravine, where the christians were at a disadvantage: for the Saracens rained arrows and rolled rocks down from the summits above. But, when our archers were dismounted (it was the Earl of Chester's forethought which had brought them), they contrived such a shower of good clothyard shafts[1] that the Saracens were abashed till our men-at-arms had climbed up and occupied the heights.

XII. *About the Bethlehem Battle-cry*

Thus, they were, when Sir Richard Dalbiney came up with them. Also, Earl Fulk came with his power, being but newly returned from scouting in the vicinity of Saint Job, for he hastened up when he heard of the king's son's imbroilment. And, so, when the Emir of Zuzz perceived cheerful christians advancing in crowds from all parts of the world, he had an attack of fastidiousness, despairing of recapturing the caravan; and he retired toward the Holy City by way of Betharhatap, not being at that time prepared for a proper battle. The christians, therefore, partook of a slight refection; and proceeded in the direction of Phagor: for, when King Arthur was ware that the Saracens were retreating, and that he had all their mutton puddings, he commanded a general advance. And, by dawn on the Festival of the Nativity, the King's power lay between Naline and Phagor, while Melekamel and his infidels held the highlands between Artais and Saint George. And Bethlehem was behind them both. Mass was sung before the christian power by the bishop of Chichester and the bishop of Durham and the patriarch of Hierusalem himself (my lord the king sent to Acre to bring him); and King Arthur proclaimed, as his battle-cry, *Hail Holy Stall*. And they set on.

XIII. *About the Battle of Bethlehem*

Melekamel had a power of twenty-thousand infidels: his right was led by the Emir Abdulla of Zuzz: his left by his son Emir Adel. King Arthur had a power of not more than fourteen-thou-

---

[1] Longbow arrows (*OED* OL).

sand: for the Hospitallers had not come up, Apollyon[1] (or perhaps Beelzebub) holding them off with a very abominable sea from Ascalon, where they had been bidden to land. The Saracens impiously began to shout *Allah is God and Mahomet is the Prophet of Allah*; and they waved green banners, crying: *The Faith*. Whereat, Bishop Richard of Durham, having required a pullan to tell him the meaning of these obstreperous or reprehensible babblings, became frightfully exasperated at being expected to listen to such public performance of blasphemy; and he set himself to wave his banner of Saint Cuthbert,[2] intoning in a mighty voice, *The Lord He is the God*. Which edifying example was followed by the knights in his vicinity, and anon by the whole power, whereby the pagan utterances of the Saracens were overborne and no more heard. And so, the battle was joined. For a long time, neither power gained any advantage: but, if it had not been for singular valour on the part of some christians (my lord the king, for one, and Earl Fulk, of course, though he denies it, and the bishops of Durham and Chichester, and the young earls of Salisbury and Winchester and Arundel, all paladins), the christians would have taken horrid tosses from the numbers of the Saracens. But, about four hours before noon, there was a lull in the battle, both powers being out of breath. The English washed their wounds and ate their puddings without sadness, seeing that they had advanced about two miles since dawn: but the Saracens retired to their lines, and lighted fires of thorns, in accordance with their bestial custom.

XIIII. *About Belligerent Bishops*

The bishop of Durham, drenched with blood and brains, and very messy, through fighting all the morning with a monstrous mace most dear to him, would take no rest. He, says Earl Fulk, came running out of the broken mellay,[3] sobbing to himself, as

---

[1] "They have as king over them, the angel of the Abyss; his name in Hebrew is Abaddon, and in the Greek he has the name Apollyon" (Rev. 9:11).

[2] During the Middle Ages, Saint Cuthbert, an Anglo-Saxon monk and a favorite saint of the English, was particularly important to the people of Durham, where his remains had been interred after being transferred repeatedly.

[3] Battle (*OED* OL).

though he was alone, saying, "Sweet God, forgive me, Thy bishop, for being so bloody as I seem to be, fitter indeed in hue for the morrow's mass of Thy martyr Messire Saint Stephen,[1] than for this festival of Thy Candid Nativity": whereat some knights were diverted and guffawed: but the priors took great edification from the delicate piety of the bishop. And my lord of Durham washed his hands, and took a stole, and ran away to assoil the dying; and other bishops and abbots did likewise. But the bishop of Chichester lay groaning under a mulberry bush: for some infidel (swayed by the devil) had been stamping on his shoulder, which was badly bruised. But, when they had bound his arm to his ribs, so that he might not hurt his shoulder any more by moving it, he mounted a fresh horse (his own having been killed under him), and rode about to encourage the christians, bearing the banner of his see, which is a picture of The Lord inthroned on His Altar with a sword issuing from His Mouth. And the queen's own fingers wrought the banner in rich silk, for the bishop who was confessor to Her Regal Majesty.

xv. *About Ghuzzards*

When it was time to make the second onset, the christians saw with amazement that the Saracens were flying toward the Holy City; and the thing was a mystery. My lord the king surmized that they had news of the Templars' advance from Napolis, and that the soldan trembled for Hierusalem. So, indeed, it was. Messengers came, a Templar and two mounted pullans with his Trumpets arrived by way of Belmont and Bether, bringing word that Grandmaster Peter with two hundred knights and ten thousand Turkopoles had left the great Mahomery at sunrise after hearing the masses sung by the archbishop of Cæsarea. Therefore, King Arthur ordered a cautious advance: for he did not believe that the Saracens intended to avoid him thus entirely. And he did well. There are certain fanatical monks of the muslim infidels, very devout in their diabolical species of devotion, who from time to

---

[1] Saint Stephen was the first Christian martyr, and his feast is the day after Christmas.

time become swayed by their proper devils into such a rictus[1] of phrenzy, that they rush madly straight ahead, with glaring and protruded eyeballs and mouths frothy and foamy, to exterminate any christians whom they may encounter, nor may anything hinder them, excepting death, which they gladly welcome. And these monks are called Ghuzzards, and are accounted of inconceivable sanctity. Threescore, then, of these Ghuzzards did Melekamel set running back at the christians, to cover his flight, armed with awful long knives and clubs; and they wrought rather grievously, slaying many and wounding more, before they themselves were dismissed to hell.

xvi. *About the Emir Abdulla of Zuzz*

When the advance was begun again, Emir Abdulla of Zuzz rode out alone from the Saracen array, a very prepotent person, challenging a christian champion to fight in single combat for his faith. But King Arthur perceived that the infidel's ruse was to delay the advance, so as to secure a retreat for the soldan: wherefore my lord the king desired Earl Fulk to go and spike the emir as soon as possible. Which that Flame did, with joy: not that the Zuzz man was a mean fighter, and, as regards blind unreasoning courage, he might have been an instructor of Ghuzzards. But he prepared to meet a champion in mail; and he was gravely disconcerted when Earl Fulk flashed at him in a buckskin suit and green-silk coat charged with his golden heart and lyonceux[2] instead of chain and plate and steel. And Earl Fulk's hands finished him in an instant: the left, with its hardened hand-edge, chopping his nape: the right, jabbing with fingers rigid as iron just below his hairy breast-bone, both producing separate and dismally painful deaths. And, when the Saracens saw it, they screamed with one voice, "Assassin, Assassin," which, says the Earl palatine of Richmond and Jaffa and Nantes, was one of the proudest moments of his life, for it showed that he still remembered lessons learned in boyhood, and was able to enact them well enough to be mistaken for one of the very doctors who had instructed him. So the christians passed on: for my

---

[1] A gaping grin.
[2] Young lions that tend to appear on heralds.

lord the king was very desirous of arriving at Hierusalem before
the Templars. And, everywhere, the Saracens fled screaming and
bleeding before them, until they reached the wide hill northward
of the Holy City, and pitched camp there, having heard the clang
of David's Gate as they galloped up above the valley of Hinnon.

XVII. *About the Siege set to Hierusalem*

At sunset, the christian power was encamped, with proper
scouts and watches, along the west side of the city beyond the
valley; and the king lay on the north. And when the Templars
came, King Arthur gravely saluted them, asking courteously after
their health and the kind of weather God had deigned to them at
Napolis. And they kept their Christmas by Hierusalem, as had
been the king's word to the Grandmaster which Earl Fulk bore.
On the morrow, being the festival of Messire Saint Stephen, the
Turkopolier of the Hospital arrived from Jericho, having come
down the gorges of Jordan with six great cats[1] from Banias, by
way of Tabary (a city of flagitious fleas) and by way of Bessan,
where they had done battle with an emir, the morsels of whose
body they flung into the river as their manner was. And they had
occupied Banias with a power, sufficient to hold it for the king
and queen, having found no infidels there. And they did the same
at Bessan after the sudden demise of the emir. On the morrow,
being the festival of Messire Saint John, the Grandmaster of the
Hospital with a hundred knights and five-thousand men-at-arms
arrived from Ascalon where he had landed in a changed wind.
They brought eight perfectly new cats; and my lord the king disposed them on the Mount of Olives, away from the Templars,
lest disputes should affect their strength. So now, King Arthur
had a power of some seven-and-twenty-thousand before Hierusalem, most meek and obedient everyone, the like of which had
never been seen or heard of before, seeing that both grandmasters
were in the array and the patriarch also with not a few knights of
the Sword in his train, he being greatly addicted to germans and

---

[1] Medieval siege weapons, screens that could be wheeled up to walls to protect
siegers while attacking.

other buffoons: but never any one of all these durst think of crossing the will or the way of King Arthur Lefthand.

On the morrow, being the festival of Holy Innocents,[1] about
noon, news came from Sir John Delacy of Halton (by the young
earl of Salisbury) that he and his power had watched Darum so
straitly that they were now inside that fortress, having perceived
(by dint of much staring) a ruinous postern in one of the out-
works, whereby they secretly entered, and captured the place,
slaying quite a parcel of Saracens. And he craved order to garrison Darum and to bring up his power to the siege of Hierusalem:
which order King Arthur graciously issued. On the morrow, being
the festival of Messire Saint Thomas Beket of Canterbury and
Acre, the hundred-and-ninety knights of the Archangelic Order
of the Candid Girdle in camp feasted with my lord the king, the
hundred-and-ninety-first knight, in the regal pavilion. And King
Arthur accorded accolade of knighthood to his son, Lord Richard
Plantagenet, with the earldom of Cornwall, and to the young earls
of Arundel and Salisbury and Winchester, to celebrate the solemnity. And, on the festival of Messire Saint Silvester,[2] the bishop of
Durham in a most sumptuous cope of the prides of white peacocks
sewn on silver samite, led the whole christian power in procession
round the Holy City, intoning canticles, and offering incense at all
the gates great and small, not forgetting even the posterns. And so
the siege was laid. But, (says Earl Fulk) my lord the king spent the
rest of the day in his tent, not willing to be seen in paroxysms of
Angevin anger and Plantagenet passion caused by pure chagrin.
For he had news that the soldan had fled away secretly by night
after the battle of Bethlehem, and had escaped to Engeddi, and,
so, toward Montreal and Egypt, leaving his cousin Emir Ishmael
to hold Hierusalem in his name. O times.

xviii. *About the still Siege*

When the siege had been kept very straitly for upward of
seven weeks, it being after Ash Wednesday, my lord the king sent

---

[1] December 28, a festival commemorating Herod's slaughter of the children of
Bethlehem.
[2] December 31.

the Grandmaster of the Hospital and Sir John of Halton, with
suitable powers, to assault Saint Abraham, which the new Emir
of Zuzz (brother of the deceased Abdulla) was holding for the
soldan. With whom were certain Ghuzzards. In this way King
Arthur barred the south: for rumours were coming up out of
Egypt that the soldan was preparing a great power to come by
sea and land for the relief of the Holy City, which is holy to Saracens as well as to christians, but for a different reason.[1] And King
Arthur would not assault: because the soldan Salahadin and his
successors, after they had taken Hierusalem in the reign of King
Guy,[2] had strengthened the walls and the towers, cutting away
the scarps and digging a great ditch along the foot of the north
wall. Moreover, Emir Ishmael was a gallant commander, plagu-
ing the christians with night attacks and improvised sorties. And,
also, the christians' artillery was small and of no great strength
though the cats and mangonels[3] of the Hospital and Temple were
all that could be desired. Nor were there enough men to be risked
in assault. For which reasons my lord the king wisely pursued
his emprize by sitting quite still, feeding select lepers outside
the walls, nothing being more weakening and unnerving to a
city besieged than the prolonged spectacle of an immutable and
apparently noncurant[4] besieger supplied with (and wasteful of)
interminable and most appetizing puddings.

XVIIII. *About King Arthur and the Dead Sea*

While the siege was set, after the capture of Saint Abraham
and the opening of that rich region to the purveyors of victuals,
King Arthur himself rode down to Engeddi with the Grandmasters, but without any trumpets, or any of their knights, that there
might be no duels; and Sir John of Ibelin and Baruth the baily of
the kingdom was left in command before the Holy City. They

---

[1] Muslims believe that Muhammad was transported from Mecca to the Temple
Mount in Jerusalem, where he ascended into heaven.
[2] Guy of Lusignan lost Jerusalem to Saladin in 1187.
[3] Another medieval siege weapon, used for hurling stones against an enemy's
position.
[4] Indifferent (*OED* OL).

occupied Engeddi, having voided it of infidels; and my lord the king bathed in the Dead Sea, and expressed the opinion that it was damned, seeing that he could not summerge himself therein, and that all his sacred person was covered with a pox for two days thereafter, though no fever molested him.

xx. *About a diabolical Swaying of Soldans*

When King Arthur returned on the tenth day, great news awaited him. Sir James of Tournay, the marshal of the kingdom, had turned traitor, and had tried to betray Bessan, where the king had placed him after the Turkopoles of the Hospital captured it. And Sir Hugh of Mompelgard, *or three hostlers sable, a crescent for difference*, had estopped the treachery; and was holding Bessan against Soldan Melekennasser, having sent the traitor in chains to the camp before Hierusalem. The import of this news was grave: for, if Damascus moved from the north and Egypt from the south, then Hierusalem stood in a fair way of being relieved from christians. Moreover, it shewed that a newer and bolder kind of devil was swaying Melekennasser to attack, for his proper devil did not infect him with any love for the Soldan of Babylon his beastly uncle.

xxi. *About King Arthur his Fame and his Alliances*

The traitor having been shriven and hanged, King Arthur made the knight of Mompelgard marshal of the kingdom in his room, sending the letters-patent by the Grandmaster of the Hospital with five-thousand men: so many might now be spared, for Sir Adam of Antioch, the marshal of Cyprus, *or, a pile gules*, had come with a power from King Henry Lusignan; and Sir Thomas Deham, the constable of Tripoli, *argent, three martels, sable*, had come with the levies of that country; and Sir Robert Mansel, the constable of Antioch, *sable, a chevron between three mollets or*, had come with a power from Prince Bohemond. And, when Melekennasser found that Bessan must be fought for (if his lust for it was quite incorrigible), and being unable to snaffle it either by gold or guile, he (having sobbed) ceased from committing a nuisance against my lord the king. Wherefore, the Hospitallers returned.

And, forasmuch as King Arthur's name and fame (*Pallida Sarace-norum Mors*)[1] were the subject of songs everywhere, not merely because he was King Richard Lionheart's nephew and heir, but because of his own deeds of arms, and because he was the first prince who had ever made both the Grandmasters simultaneously and intelligently ware of their limitations, and excessively obsequious, all the great sovereigns of the East began to strive in his favours. And even King Ayton and Queen Ysabel of Armenia (she was Philip of Antioch's widow) sent a power under their constable, one Sir Constantine of Pardzerpert, who bore very strange armorials, namely, *sable, a cockatrice gessant of flames reguardant a Saint John Baptist in a bath, all proper.*

xxii. *About Abbot Fradulph of the Temple*

King Arthur's power increased to two-and-thirty thousand by the middle of March, being yet a matter of ten days before Easter, which fell next after the festival of the Annunciation;[2] and he desired to end the siege, for the weather was growing warm, and his power could hardly abide the sun in the open, and it might become necessary to raise the siege and to refuge in some cool city during the summer, and to do all the work over again later. Which was most disappointing. And so things were till the Wednesday before Easter, when there suddenly arrived from Acre (where he had a job as hermit) a very holy Abbot named Fradulph, mitred and of the Temple. He came to pay his respects to my lord the king, hoping to make a Pilgrimage to the Holy Places after the capture of the city. From whom King Arthur learned of a certain secret entrance, known only to the said Abbot Fradulph.

xxiii. *About Abbot Fradulph his Aperture*

For, long ago, when the said Abbot Fradulph was a young monk in the Temple, he (by chance) prayed, one night, in a holy cave, wherein was said to be a side-entrance to hell. And, emboldened by prayer, he was moved to lift up a stone slab which closed

---

[1] "Pale Death of the Saracens," a name originally used to refer to Nicephorus II.
[2] March 25.

the hole, in order that he might examine the consciences of some of the damned, for whom he had a certain pity. This he did with difficulty, no man being ware of it; and, finding that no foetor (which he could recognize as essentially hellish) offended him, he went down, through five great holes and four caverns, into a passage. There, however, a windgust extinguished his lamp; and he was forced to return to rekindle it. He also took with him the tinder-box, and further armed himself against the powers of darkness with a small relic, snaffled from one of the altars. Thus, again descending, he passed through a long tunnel in the rock to the apparent end of it: but a strong wind blew his light about, coming from certain crevices, into which he hastened to insert inquisitive fingers; and, lo, he dislodged a stone, which forthwith fell outward, splashing into unseen water. When he had finished praying violently, he peered through the aperture: and he saw that he was actually outside the city, above the face of the rock over the Pool of Siloam,[1] into which the stone had fallen, for (being winter-time) there chanced to be a little water in the Pool. And, being now convinced that the passage did not lead to hell (at least in the theological sense of the word, for monks regard both hell and this world as being much of a muchness, both residences of the damned, speaking generally), he returned, closing the slab, and reverently replacing the relic in its shrine. Vehemently inter-rogated by my lord the king, he said moreover that he had never spoken of the matter, lest he should be penanced for the affair of the relic, for which indiscretion he preferred to penance himself.

XXIIII. *About King Arthur his new Emprize*

My lord the king questioned Fradulph exhaustively: but the holy man's toes being crumpled up by the straitness of his hermit-age, and he unable to walk far, he was obliged to explain in words, as far as his memory permitted, the exact situation of the hole above the Pool of Siloam. And, having eaten their puddings, my lord the king and Earl Fulk secretly sought the said hole all night long: but they might not find it, by reason of the rubbish which

---

[1] A pool where Jesus cured a man of blindness. See John 9.

had fallen when the old walls were overthrown by Salahadin in order to rebuild them impregnably (as he fondly imagined) from the very foundation. Nor might they move much of the said rubbish at one time, lest the noise of such movement should alarm the Saracens, and cause stricter measure of vigilance. They, therefore, could only crawl about silently, shrouded in long brown cloaks of the hue of rocks by night, probing with staves and shifting stones as quietly as possible; and they found naught that night of Wednesday. On Thursday, after they had seen God's Body inshrined till the morrow on an altar in the regal pavilion, they prayed till nightfall in the garden called Gethsemane; and, when it was dark, they resumed their quest; and they instantly found the hole. Its situation was manifested to them by a certain faint but very holy luminosity, of the form of a rosy cross-potent-elongate in a white primrose, which undoubtedly was sent by the king's special patron Messire Saint George, to whom my lord the king builded a chapel on the spot or near it after the capture of Hierusalem. That was King Arthur's opinion; and he deemed himself rightly the recipient of very signal and friendly favour from Messire Saint George, in return for having rededicated the Kingdom of England to that celestial knight after the Ordeal of Oxford a few years before. In the morning, after the Creeping to the Cross[1] and other proper rites had been celebrated, my lord the king executed documents which would be useful to his son Earl Richard of Cornwall in the event of the Regal Majesty's improvised ascension to the superiors; and he prayed for the three hours with Queen Mariol. And, after dark, he set out quietly and secretly, attended only by Earl Fulk the Flame and the earls of Winchester and Salisbury and Arundel, all very slim young men, strong and limber as kittens, for the hole was not large, according to Abbot Fradulph's description; and with their bundles, they took torches and much cordage and pudding enough for a night or two.

xxv. *About King Arthur in the Holy City*

For a weary while they wriggled upward over broken rock, till

---

[1] An English Good Friday ceremony that involved crawling to the cross and kissing it.

they passed the tunnel and found the place where was the slab, as the abbot had predicted, which (at first) they failed to move, because the cavern into which they had climbed was of the shape of a chimney, and not less than nineteen feet high; and though my lord the king and Earl Fulk were the tallest youths in England and Armorica and Hierusalem, they were not as tall as that chimney. But King Arthur used his faculty of prolongation; and Earl Fulk, standing on the regal shoulders, levered up the slab with his sword; and anon the five ascended into the holy cavern where the relic had been. And, having covered themselves from head to foot with clean white mantles in the manner of the Saracens, with hoods like those of monks covering their heads, they passed unobserved to the gate called Oire, which they captured, slaying the guards with silent sudden dabs and chops, taking them unawares.

XXVI. *About the Capture of the Holy City*

King Arthur gave a predetermined signal, with his remaining puddings, from the said Gate Oire; and the bishop of Durham came up with a power of five-hundred, all softly shod and hooded in white mantles, very calmly entering the city, and proceeding straightway to the ramparts along Mount Moriah;[1] and, after him, came the Grandmasters with their full powers of knights, all similarly shodden and disguised. Thus, by reason of the silence, the miraculous darkness of the night, and the protection of Messire Saint George and other saints venerated by the English, my lord the king had a power of seven-thousand in his hand inside the city when day dawned. Insued but little fighting, owing to consternation and panic-terror which seized upon the Saracens; and King Arthur captured the Tower of David[2] by merely walking into it, no visitors being expected at that early hour. There was fighting, however, after breakfast, when my lord the king split the spleen of Emir Ishmael for him; and some ten-score infidels perished in scrimmages in the alleys of the Giwerie, among them many half-awakened Ghuzzards. Also, not a few christians met a blessed

---

[1] The location of the Temple Mount, the site where Abraham nearly sacrificed Isaac.
[2] An ancient citadel in the Old City of Jerusalem.

death. But for the major part, the Saracens fought (with violent
panting among themselves) for the privilege of rendering themselves prisoners, believing that the City had been captured by art-
magic: for, said they, what else could be expected from a power
led by him who was Pallida Saracenorum Mors, own nephew to
the Melekrik (as those beasts call King Richard Lionheart), and
by another who was not only the Melekrik's love-child and living
image, but also a master among the Assassins and a special pet of
the Old Man of the Mountain himself. And, of these prisoners,
the rich were permitted to ransom themselves at prices which
reduced them to impotence (as foes) for life, which ransoms were
divided proportionately among the christians, while the poor
were exchanged for christian captives in Alexandria and other
parts of the infidels, after King Arthur had beaten Melekamel in
battle at Darum, when the Great Peace (which still endures) was
sealed in the tent of the captured soldan by the sounding sea. O
great times.

xxvii. *About King Arthur his Justice his Mercy*

When Hierusalem was in the hands of the christians,[1] the Saracen prisoners were safely bestowed, and a strong guard placed
over them lest the populace should massacre them to celebrate
the festivity. King Arthur was fastidiously strict; and sentenced to
be hanged twenty-eight pullans for raping and rieving[2] in the very
first hour of his mastery of the capital of his and Queen Mariolanthe's kingdom. But, seeing how great a number of minds were
becoming unhinged with terror at his awful severity, he did not
give the signal for the hangman to drag at the eight-and-twenty
ropes, but he cried, as by inspiration, "Let them go free for this
single occasion." Whereat all the people did most extraordinary
reverence, admiring greatly. But the Patriarch of Hierusalem
coughed discontentedly, remonstrating with my lord the king for
preventing so excellent and so moral an example. To whom, King

---

[1] Jerusalem was under the control of Emperor Frederick II from 1228 to 1244, but
it fell to the Khawarizimi Turks in 1244. It was not "in the hands of the Christians"
again until 1917.
[2] Robbing (*OED* OL).

Arthur, frostily-visaged pallidly-glowing, says finely: "Lord Patriarch, how shall Our Salvator rise in Our heart with the morrow's
morn, if We shall have weighed Him down today with the corpses
of christian sinners for whom He yesterday deigned Himself to
die." Superb sentence.

XXVIII. *About the Easter Procession*

My lord the king ordered that a pompous procession should be
celebrated, the most solemn and mighty ever seen in that vicinity
since the day when Messire Saint Joshua, Jurisconsult and Confessor, with all his archbishops, proceeded seven times round Jericho,
and the whole city fell flat at a cadence of hautboys superadded to
their awful trampling.[1] So, on the morrow, being Easter Day, and
the Lord having risen indeed, as testified by the dancing of the
sunbeams, King Arthur ordered everybody's trumpets to sound
for the space of an hour after mass; and, as soon as the sun was
calm again, the procession moved on its way. First, went nine-
and-ninety singing-boys chanting very sweetly. Second, went
twelve gigantic knights bearing a scaffold, whereon was reared
a cross, wherefrom The World's Salvator ruled all men in His
Immortal Splendour. Third, went monks and clergymen wearing
copes and bearing tapers and singing most canorously. Fourth,
went thirteen bishops very gloriously wearing mitres of the latest
fashion, with their copes displayed by deacons, and the banners of
their sees borne by boys, as follows: bishop Rainer of Bethlehem,
azure, The Nativity with a star in chief, all proper: bishop Walkran of
Baruth, *sable, a cross or charged with a dolphin azure*: bishop Peter
of Tortosa, confessor to the Grandmaster of the Temple, *per pale
sable and argent, an Agnus Dei proper*: bishop James Major of Sidon,

---

[1] "On the seventh day, they got up at daybreak and marched around the city seven
times in the same manner, except that on that day they circled the city seven
times. The seventh time around, when the priests sounded the trumpet blast,
Joshua commanded the people, 'Shout! For the LORD has given you the city! The
city and all that is in it are to be devoted to the LORD.' . . . When the trumpets
sounded, the people shouted, and at the sound of the trumpet, when the people
gave a loud shout, the wall collapsed; so every man charged straight in, and they
took the city" (Josh. 6:15-20).

vert, *a camel proper bearing a cross argent*: bishop James Minor of Sebaste, *gules a fess argent between the Three Holy Children proper*: bishop James the Magpie of Acre, *or, the Twelve Apostles all proper excepting Judas Iskarioth sable for difference*: bishop Eustace of Valarie, confessor to the Grandmaster of the Hospital, *gules, a cross argent between four chalices or*: bishop Richard of Durham, earlpalatine of Sedbergh, carrying the naked sword of his earldom as well as the crook of his bishopric, *azure, a cross or between four lyons argent*: bishop William of Exeter (*arms blazoned elsewhere*): bishop Peter of Winchester (*a.b.e.*): bishop Alexander of Lichfield (*a.b.e.*): bishop Ralph of Chichester, the chancellor of England, *azure, The Lord inthroned in glory proper*: bishop Hugh Foliot of Hereford, *per pale gules and argent a cross quadrate counterchanged between four crosses likewise counterchanged.* Seventh, went two mitred abbots, Fradulph of the Temple and Henry of Valjosaphat, without banners. Eighth, went archbishop Nicholas of Nazareth with his banner, *gules, a carpenter's plane and hammer or, in chief an Agnus Dei.* Ninth, went archbishop Peter of Cassarea with his banner, *azure, an eagle displayed or insigned with the Divine Monogram upon the breast gules.* Tenth, went a canopy of gold tissue, surrounded by four-and-twenty thurifers[1] and borne by twelve magnates, namely, Sir Robert Mansel constable of Antioch, Sir Thomas Deham constable of Tripoli, Sir Constantine constable of Armenia, Sir Adam constable of Cyprus, Sir Renard of Kayphas chamberlain of the kingdom, Sir Raymond seneschal of the kingdom, Sir Hugh of Mompelgard marshal of the kingdom (he arrived that morning), Sir John of Ibelin and Baruth baily of the kingdom, Sir Thomas marshal of Antioch, Sir Stephen Boutier viscount of Acre, Sir Henry Delembriac viscount of Giblet and kin to Sir Raymond the seneschal, and Sir Simon the Turkopolier of the Hospital. And, under the golden canopy went the Patriarch Gerard bearing the Lord God in a crystal custodial guarded with silver and pearls. And, after The Lord God went Arthur the King and Mariol the Queen, wearing *Hierusalem*, carrying their crowns in their hands; and their son earl Richard of Cornwall held their mantles of ermine. And, after the Regal Majesties went earl Fulk

---

[1] Individuals carrying burning incense (*OED* OL).

of Jaffa bearing the banner of the kingdom, and the earl of Winchester bearing the banner of England. All these went under the
golden canopy with The Lord God. Eleventh, went the ladies
and the maids of my lady Queen Mariol. Twelfth, went Countess Alys of Jaffa and Nantes and Richmond with her children and
her ladies. Thirteenth, went the Grandmasters bickering about
the impropriety of walking behind ladies even of blood-regal.
Fourteenth, went the two-hundred trumpets of the Regal Majesties. Fifteenth, went all the knights with their squires, pages,
banners, trumpets, according to their order, with companies of
trumpets between each order. And they sang the psalm *Magnus
Dominus*. And they sang a new psalm at each gate, namely, at the
first *Laudate Dominum*, at the second *Non Nobis Dñe*, at the third *In
exitu Israel*, at the fourth *Exultate Deo*, at the fifth *Exurgat Deus*, at
the sixth *Benedicite omnia opera Dñe Dñe*, at the seventh *Benedictus
Dominus*. And, when the canopy was halted before the Gate of
David, they sang, *Lift up your heads, o ye gates; and be ye lifted up
o ye everlasting doors; and the King of Glory shall come in.*[1] And the
canons of the Holy Sepulchre sang from within, *Who is the King
of Glory?*[2] And those without responded, continuing the psalm.
Then the gates were flung wide open; and The Lord God passed
into His Holy City, borne by the Patriarch and all men prostrated
themselves when the Lord God went once more into the Dove
suspended over the altar of the church of the Sepulchre. And all
day long the bells were rung; and the trumpets sounded till the
sun had set. Thus, my lord the king kept Easter in Hierusalem. O
triumph.

xxviiii. *About the Government of Hierusalem by King Arthur*

My lord the king gave good government to the Holy City. He
divided it into regions, after the Roman mode, assigning one to
the infidels (for his mercy did not drive them from their homes so
long as they should not behave themselves excessively), and one
to the Greeks (but he would not suffer their schismatic patriarch

---

[1] Ps. 24:7.
[2] Ps. 24:8.

to reside in the City)[1], and one to the Pullans (as they called christians of mixed or native birth), and one to the Giwen, and one to
the Latins, and one to the English and Armoricans and Gascons
which he called the Regal Region. Also he provided suitable residences for lepers.

The accursed Giwen besought my lord the king to enlarge the
region which he had assigned to them, desiring to include in it
certain streets of the region of the Greeks and of the Latins. And
he curtly denied them. But they besought him the more, saying
that their proper ancestor and pater patriæ, Messire Saint David,
King and Confessor, had indeed builded the Holy City: wherefore
they prayed for a more prominent share of the place which their
own king had made. A scabrous[2] argument.

xxx. About King Arthur and the Giwen of Hierusalem

The elders of the Giwen were summoned to the Presence
in the Town of David, where King Arthur sat arrayed in white
silk, crowned with the five-crossed crown of Hierusalem; and his
ermine mantle was cast about the throne, for the weather was
very hot. By his side, were the bishops in copes of silver tissue,
and the Templars in their snowy habits; and the armorials of the
kingdom were displayed on the cloth of estate about the throne
and on the canopy above. And there was a great silence till the
Giwen were put in, most of them hairy gabblers, and all of noisy
demeanour. They kneeled; and presented their petition; and, as
though that was not enough, they all began to talk at once, like
lepers, emboldened by the silence of the christians present and
the rigid attitude of the Regal Majesty. From mere cackling, they
passed to blustering, and something very much of the nature of
riot appeared to be about to occur. And the eyes of the Templars
rolled in the direction of King Arthur, ready to catch the expected
signal for clearing the Presence-chamber with battle-axes. And

---

[1] The Greek Orthodox Patriarch of Jerusalem. The "schism" to which Rolfe refers
occurred in the eleventh century, when the Eastern Orthodox Church separated
from the Roman Catholic Church.

[2] "Scabrous" can mean difficult and thorny, harsh and unpolished, or abusive and
disgusting (*OED* OL).

Earl Fulk says that my lord the king barely breathed, but sat as still as stone lest his regal aversion and indignation should make him seem to tremble. And at length King Arthur beckoned his herald to approach to the throne, to whom he said certain few words under the excited babble of the Giwen (the herald was Sir William Deredham, *gules an escutcheon within an orle of martlets argent*). My lord the king drew off the glove of white silk veiling his hallowed right hand, which he displayed bare, palm outward, to his Giwen; and all the christians kneeled, venerating the so dear solemnity. Then, the herald blew his trumpet, and proclaimed to the accursed Giwen: *Ye are now to look on one whom ye have pierced.* And they, blinded by the radiant splendour of the cicatrix,[1] whiter than whatever is whitest, where the nail went through the palm, were struck with terror, becoming beside themselves with dread lest they should instantly be cut in pieces: they writhed backwards on their knees away from the king; and all their faces were wan, but not so white as the king's, so cold, so hard; and his eyes glittered ruthlessly like icicles in the flare of a frosty moon. So all remained, till the bishop of Chichester laid his cross on the king's hand with the sceptre. Whereat King Arthur mastered his fury; and anon he set himself to speak gently to his Giwen. He said that inquisition should be made, and, if their numbers demanded it, and the rights of the Greeks and Latins permitted it, he would take order to enlarge the Giwerie so that the prosperity of the city might be augmented. And the Giwen retired very obsequiously, being turned from their stiffneckedness by the regal gentlehood as well as by a certain terror.

xxxi. *About King Arthur his Revenge on his Giwen*

When the Giwen were gone and the place had been perfumed with frankincense, King Arthur said to the Earl of Jaffa, "O Fulk, he was there who held the very nail which pierced my hand: he knew me and I knew him, for he was a boy of my age then. Therefore were they so terrified when I showed my hand, for they had not imagined that I should recognize that one after

---

[1] Scar.

these many years." From which it may be seen that a certain miscreant (Serfden of Oxford, he was), had escaped my long sword in
Bristol, fleeing the country, and secreting himself in the Giwerie
of Hierusalem, till he had become secure that his hideous sacrilege and treason were long forgotten. Earl Fulk naturally was
for having him sought out and minced alive at once: but my lord
the king forbade it, saying that he left the matter of his personal
wrongs to the Lord God, and would only take vengeance on his
Giwen for wrongs which they did to the weak and unprotected,
or to widows, maids of both sexes, and orphans. O my king.

XXXII. About King Arthur and the Peace-offering of his Giwen

The Giwen, however, had been most mightily commoved:[1] for
it seems that they crept, that very night, into the Presence of my
lord the king, humbly praying his acceptance of a voluntary aid,
spontaneously offered, of thirty-thousand silver marks. Which
having been the price paid to his wicked uncle for his dear sacred
regal body when Sir John fil-Henry sold him for crucifixion to the
Giwen of Bristol, King Arthur graciously accepted; and he forthwith assigned half of it to the Order of Hospitallers of Saint John,
for the maintenance of the great hospital of Ascalon, and the utter
extermination of Ghuzzards: and a part to the clergymen of the
kingdom for the reparation of churches and shrines: and a part
to the viscount of the Holy City for purifying the ways and for
erecting suitable crucifixes and images of Madame Saint Mary the
God-Bearer, and of Messires the Apostles, and of other eminently
holy persons, at all street-corners: and a part for the afforestation
of the road up from Jaffa, that poor pilgrims might recuperate in
shady groves, and a part for erecting lazar-houses outside all the
chief cities in the kingdom. But my lord the king himself would
not keep the money, nor touch it, nor even suffer it to be brought
near him, lest any of it should be the price of blood.

---

[1] Disturbed (*OED* OL).

xxxiii. *About the Knights Companions of the Valiant Order of Saint George*

On the festival of Messire Saint George,[1] my lord the king (mindful of the aid which that holy and glorious patron of knights had rendered during the siege of Hierusalem, manifesting his rose and cross luminously at the aperture in the rock), was pleased to dedicate a chapel and to appoint nine canons to sing daily till the world's end in that saint's honour.[2] And, after mass, King Arthur standing on the steps of the altar, called up to him Earl Fulk the Flame of Jaffa and Richmond and Nantes, on whose neck he placed a gold collar with a carven image of Messire Saint George slaying the pterodactyl,[3] and he kissed the earl on both cheeks, holding him by both hands, and intoning these words, "Welcome brother, valiant knight, and dear companion of Saint George." And King Arthur did in like manner with Earl Richard of Cornwall his son, and the earls of Arundel and Winchester and Salisbury, saying the same words, and placing the same collars in their necks, having first invested himself similarly. My lord the king also, on the same day, sat in council with these five knights of Saint George. And they made a rule that day, together with such other knights as should be named by the regal majesty of England from time to time, should meet each year on his festival at some shrine of Messire Saint George, to venerate him on account of his heroic gests,[4] specially the service which he deigned to do on the dark night before the capture of Hierusalem. And they stablished a rule that no new knights of Saint George should be named excepting such as had done some signal service for the king who is England, nor any who was not already knighted for some knightly deed, clergymen being excepted. And

---

[1] April 23.

[2] The cult of Saint George grew during the crusades, and the Council of Oxford in 1222 ordered Saint George's festival to be observed as a holiday of lesser rank in England. Edward III founded the Order of the Garter in the fourteenth century, and Saint George is the patron saint of the Order.

[3] While the first pterosaur fossil was not found until the late eighteenth century, the term "pterodactyl" comes from the Greek *pterodaktulos*, meaning "winged finger."

[4] Notable actions (*OED* OL).

they confirmed a rule constituting the king who is England their grandmaster and autocrat to whom they owe absolute obedience. And they bound themselves by a rule to go always clad in white, with their proper coats, and with a dark-blue mantle, of the colour of heaven above Gethsemane,[1] where King Arthur prayed before he saw the vision of the shining-white primrose[2] insigned with the rosy cross; and they placed on the mantle the said shining-white primrose with the shield of Messire Saint George bearing *argent, a cross-potent-elongate gules*. And the first new knight named by the Regal Majesty of England was a sentimental old imbecile called Sir Hubert de Burgh who had been left at home to govern England when my lord the king went away crusading. And King Arthur Lefthand (who was England) sent me letters-patent saying that, on account of matters too tedious (and much too well known) to be recapitulated here, I was named Brother of the King, and Seventh Valiant-Knight-Founder and Dear Companion of Saint George, conferring on me also the golden collar of primroses with its pendant as aforesaid, and bidding me to get my habits made and to wear them as a knight of the new order. These letters-patent came by the hand of that bishop of Winchester, who (having purged his naughty life by true penitence) was named chancellor of the said order and sent home to govern his diocese decently. I, therefore, (blubbering like a baby) caused the said bishop (on pains not fit to be specified) to invest me with my new insignia in a most splendid solemnity after mass on the anniversary of the very day when King Arthur took the cross to go to Nazareth. And, I will say that, in all my deeds hereafter, I never have forgotten for one instant that England himself had chosen and named me Brother of the King, nor have I ever acted excepting as such. O king, O brother, thou knowest it.

XXXIIII. *About the Homage at Lebanon and the hot Patriarch*[3]

As the summer advanced, King Arthur went northward to the

---

[1] A garden on the Mount of Olives, the scene of Christ's agony. Christ's agony occurred at night, and when representing this moment, painters tend to paint the sky a dark blue.

[2] *"primae rosae candidae."* [Rolfe's note.]

[3] The patriarch referred to in this section is the archbishop of Jerusalem.

Lebanon for the sake of coolness. And while Earl Fulk went on to salute Lady Johanna in Musse, and to give her his news which her mother's heart yearned for, and also to bear letters of fraternal amity from my lord the king to the Old Man of the Mountain, King Arthur held a great assize of the kingdom at Napolis, where he appointed Mr. Robert Demauley, *or, on a bend sable three eaglets argent*, a Yorkshire squire of Earl Fulk's train, to be viscount of that city for him and for Queen Mariol. And he let Earl Fulk give the accolade of knighthood to the viscount, on his return from Musse. But my lord the king kept the festival of Marymass in August at Nazareth, where the patriarch released him from his vow, declaring the same to be well and duly performed. And the same night there was a crown-wearing after the banquet; and King Arthur and Queen Mariol held a crown-wearing; and they granted feofs and investitures, as follows: to Earl Fulk the Flame of Jaffa and Richmond and Nantes the constabulate of the kingdom and the principality of Tyre: to Sir Hugh of Mompelgard, the principality of Tabary with leave to marry the heiress thereof: to Sir John of Halton the barony of Saint Abraham: to the earl of Winchester, the castle of Saint George: to bishop Maregnan, *vert, an orle or*, the cancellariate of the kingdom with the judgeship for his bastard Mr. Maurice: and other feofs to the church and the Great Orders. My lord the king also made all do homage to him and to my lady Mariol the queen, as King William Conqueror, the Great Bastard, did on that day long ago at Winchester, when he made every magnate and every clergyman swear to hold his feofs of him the king as well as of and above his proper overlord: whereby the powers of overlords were regulated and the fountain of authority was unified. And even the Grandmasters did homage for the feofs of their Orders, swearing to the king's men; and so likewise did the bishops for the feofs of their sees. But the patriarch, got hot, and sat up, and said "Tush!" O manners. Whereat my lord the king, blazing with Angevin anger, swore that he would not be bullied by any bīp. alive; and he sent for the tormentors and the headsman. And, when the hot patriarch babbled of sacrilege, censures, and maledictions, then says King Arthur, "Hands, perhaps, We may not lay upon Your Reverency, but We are not interdicted from water." And he bade the headsman to pour many bucketsful of cold water upon the patriarch, beginning with the cavity between the horns of his mitre. Which was done, to the admiration and great joy of all round-standers; and the heated bile of the clergyman was so cooled, and his haughty spirit so purified and washed away by the volumes of water, that he became sweetly reasonable; and when he had got his breath back, and the tormentors had mopped him sufficiently, he did homage not only for the feofs of his patriarch-ate but for those of the Sepulchre and also for all feofs held by the Church in the Kingdom over again, in order that no disputes might arise to distract the good government stablished by King Arthur and Queen Mariol in their kingdom of Hierusalem.

xxxv. *About the Place of this Book*

These are all the tales, given to me by Earl Fulk, which I can remember, concerning King Arthur's crusade. And it has seemed good to me to place this book of the said crusade here, after the book about magnates and the book about clergymen, and before the book about the Giwen, so that you, o most affable reader (whoever you are) reading these histories, may have before the eye of your mind an accurate diagram, illustrating my dear lord and brother the king's great (though gradual) growth in grace. For, you have seen him, from the beginning, pre-eminent in the virtues of Faith and of Hope, pre-eminent in possession of the gifts of intellect and fortitude and godly fear. And you have seen him (in his dealings with unstable inconstant peoples, with naughty magnates, with tiresome clergymen, with most noxious infidels), gathering unto himself the further gifts of wisdom and counsel and knowledge, with equanimity and longanimity and magnanimity. And now I will show you how, at the cost of his majestic and regal life, King Arthur attained to, and captured, and added to his crowns, that transcendent gem which is the gift and virtue of Charity. O my lord, my king. O me.

END OF THE SECOND TOME, CALLED HOPE

THE THIRD TOME, CALLED CHARITY

XX

THE BOOK CALLED THE GALLIMAUFRY[1] OF
THE GIWEN

1. About the Justiciar and the Giwen

What perturbed me most, at the beginning of King Arthur's resplendent reign, was the innate incorrigible depravity of the King's Giwen, and the manner which my said lord the king would use to them. On account of their notorious unpurged crimes, and of their detestable principles, and of the incessant terrible menace to the king's peace which their hairy existence constituted, I, for my part, would have donated to them their lives and their goods and their valuables intact, and also their liberty of person, ordaining the capital penalty against all and singular of their accursed race found in the kingdom on and after the festival of The Lord's Circumcision[2] next insuing. However, on consulting my honour as a knight and my conscience as a christian earl, I deemed myself incompetent to act in the foresaid manner, for the simple reason that the affair was not mine but the king's. Furthermore, I, as Brother of the King, had to consider my dear lord and brother the king's eternal salvation: for I have always been his truest lover, loving his regal soul as I loved his sacred person. And, so, it seemed to me that, for his soul's sake, King Arthur ought not to be molested, or even moved (unless he commanded me to move him), in his treatment of his Giwen. For, on the one hand, while King Arthur was a christian knight in every thought and word and deed, wise, brave, gentle, very strong, awfully pure, more merciful than ruthless even to evil doers, on the other hand it is impossible for me to express, in urbane Latin, the towering and

---

[1] A medley or a hodge-podge (*OED* OL).
[2] Dwelling on Christ's circumcision could be associated with anti-Semitic feelings. The Festival of the Circumcision was often observed as a fast.

devouring disgust and fury and revulsion and repugnance and abhorrence and fastidious abomination which, at all times and in all places raged in his regal mind against his Giwen. The reason of this is not far to seek. Need I name more than the wrongs which his over-pampered Giwen put upon his comparatively unprotected christians, their mockery and malignance against our Holy Faith, their habitual incorrigible dishonesty, their irrepressible quibblings among themselves, and (above all) their loathesome outrage against his sacred and regal person? Wherefore, I say that I left King Arthur unmoved (as far as he permitted me), and (at all times) unmolested, in the matter of his Giwen, so that he might gain, by himself, all merit possible to be gained by him for his high soul's salvation. Very bitter, very long, was the conflict in that white soul, where perfect knowledge of right and the will to do it contended, single-handed (excepting for the Grace of God and the grace of inherent and anointed kingship), during fifty interminable years, against the natural desire of a man to satiate the vengeance due to a monstrous and intolerable wrong. And most magnificent was the victory.

II. *About the Charters of the Giwen*

When my lord the king became seized of his crown and canopy of England, he graciously forced himself to compose the following Charters wherewith to comfort and assure his Giwen:

ARTHUR AND MARIOL BY THE GRACE OF GOD AND THE SANCTION OF THE APOSTOLIC SEE KING AND QUEEN OF THE ENGLISH, ET CETERA:

i. *Know all men that We have granted to Our Giwen to have free and honourable residence in Our kingdom of England and to hold from Us all which they do now reasonably hold in lands and fees and mortgages and goods and that they have all their liberties and customs and exemptions ordained by Our good uncle and predecessor King Richard Lionheart just as they hitherto have held them but better and more quietly and more honourably:*

ii. *If any dispute arise between a Christian and a Giwe (which God forgive) he who summons the other must have two witnesses, namely, a lawful Christian and a lawful Giwe:*

iii. *If a Giwe be summoned by anyone without valid testimony he shall be quit of that summons on his sole oath on his Book. On a summons of things belonging to Our Crown a Giwe shall be quit on his sole oath on his Roll. If there be a dispute between a Christian and a Giwe about accommodation of some money (which God forbid) the Christian shall prove the interest and the Giwe the capital:*

iiii. *Wherever the Giwen are let it be lawful for them to go when they will with all their chattels and let none estop or prevent them in this they being Our Own property:*

v. *Let the Giwen be free from all Our new customs and tolls and modiation[1] of wine as they already are exempt from all dues exacted from Our subjects by Our predecessors according to Article I of this present Charter they being Our Own chattels. And We ordain all men to guard and defend Our Giwen. And We prohibit any man from summoning Our Giwen against this Charter on the foresaid points on Our forfeit:*

vi. *When a Giwe dies his carcase shall not be retained above earth but his heirs shall have it with his money and his debts. And it shall be lawful for Our Giwen to receive and to buy without difficulty all things which may be brought to them excepting things of the Church and Our treasure-trove and things stained with Christian blood.[2]*

Given at Marlborough the tenth day of April the second year of Our reign in presence of

✠ *Me, Hubert de Burgh, Earl of Gloucester and Essex:*
✠ *Me, Fulk fil-Richard, Earl of Richmond and Nantes and Jaffa.*

On the same day, at the same place, in presence of the same witnesses, my lord the king comforted and assured his Giwen with the following additional Charter:

---

[1] A tax assessed by volume (*OED* OL).
[2] This charter echoes the charter Richard I gave to the Jews, which confirmed the liberties granted by Henry II's charter. John confirmed this charter again in 1201. Jacobs reprinted the charter in *The Jews of Angevin England* (134-136, 212-214).

*ARTHUR AND MARIOL BY THE GRACE OF GOD AND THE
SANCTION OF THE APOSTOLIC SEE KING AND QUEEN OF
THE ENGLISH, ETC.:*

i. *Know all men that We have conceded and by this present Charter do confirm to Our Giwen in England that excesses which may arise
among them (excepting those which belong to Our crown and justice as
homicide or mayhem or premeditated assault or burglary or rape or arson
or treasure-trove) shall be brought before judges of their own according to
their own law and they shall do justice thereon among themselves.*

ii. *And We also grant to Our Giwen that if any Giwe summon another
Giwe on a charge which pertains to Us We will not compel any of them
to witness against his fellow but if the summoner has a reasonable and
lawful witness let him bring him with him.*

iii. *And if some criminal and overt deed occurs among Our Giwen
which pertains to Our crown and justice as in the foresaid pleas of
Our crown even though none of Our Giwen shall have become accus-
ers thereon We will cause that charge to be investigated by Our lawful
Giwen in England as the Charter of Our grandfather King Henry fil-
Empress reasonably testifies.*[1]

These two Charters were sealed by King Arthur, and delivered
by him to the said Earl Hubert and Earl Fulk, to read them in the
presence of the b͞ips. of London and Norwich, and in the presence
of Sir Pernass (or Pernicious) one of the b͞ips. of the king's Giwen.
And, when Earl Hubert and Earl Fulk had received security for
the payment of the paltry sum of four thousand marks for the
regal exchequer (namely, one-thousand immediately, one-thousand at midsummer, one-thousand at Michaelmas, one-thousand
at Christmas), then, they delivered the said Charters to the said
Sir Pernass (or Pernicious) for the king's Giwen, in the presence
of the said lord b͞ips. And I wish to inquire, o most affable reader,
whether any human crucified king ever behaved, or ever could
behave, more nobly in regard to his crucifiers?

---

[1] The rights discussed in this additional charter were also confirmed by John in
1201 (Jacobs 214-215).

III. *About the Gratitude of the Giwen*

Now I will narrate how the Giwen repaid the mansuetude and benignancy and clemency of King Arthur. O times. O manners.

The Giwen instantly began ill practices against my lord the king, in this way. They clipped slivers, and sometimes slices, with scissors, from the edges of the clumsily-minted silver pennies coined by Sir John fil-Henry, whereon was no device which would betray the mutilation: so that they profited by the scraps of silver thus stolen, and our money became gravely debased in value. I hanged many Giwen convicted of this crime of coin-clipping, but not enough to estop its perpetual commission, the crime being easy and profitable, while the risk was slight because detection was difficult and desultory. For, though we were obliged to use money more by weight than by tale, in those old days, the Giwen as money-lenders were able to force any coins they pleased upon their needy clients. Vainly, I ordered to be proclaimed in all baili-wicks, fairs & markets, and church porches, that all who carried clipped money should lie at the king's mercy, giving safe pledges, and their chattels being attached for obtaining the said money. Vainly, I ordered to be proclaimed (in like manner, only more so), that clipped money, found with Giwe or Giwess, should be taken and perforated and placed in a strong box for the king's need, and that the body and goods of such Giwe or Giwess should be taken and treated and retained according to the king's pleasure. Vainly, I ordered that old money, lacking two shillings and sixpence in the pound at most, might be current among goldsmiths and for-eign merchants, for buying their victuals and clothing, but not for offerings to my lord the king, for which, and for merchan-dize, I ordered that strong and great money of lawful weight only should be used.[1] All in vain. All in vain. O manners. O lepers. O scabs. Consequently, I proceeded more severely through the whole kingdom, taking four waggon-loads of gallows with me. And, after hanging twoscore and seventeen professional coin-

---

[1] This passage paraphrases the entry on "Clipping Money" in Jacobs's *The Jews of Angevin England*. Jacobs notes that complaints against the Jews for clipping money were very frequent in the thirteenth century.

clippers, all Giwen, all caught in flagrant fault, anon I hanged
Mrs. Belaset the Giwess of Wallingford, a notorious practisant
long successful in evading justice. And this hanging strangely
caused a certain squeamishness of stomach to molest me, so that
I could not eat my pudding for four days, by reason of her flapping petticoats as she kicked in dangling violently. So I begged
my lord the king to let me not hang any more women. "Tie them
tightly, and drown them suddenly in a sufficient pit, when necessary:" says King Arthur most mercifully. Moreover, in order to
diminish the number of these hangings, if possible, my lord the
king determined to mint new pennies bearing his own image and
superscription. Wherefore, he devised a new device, as follows:
On one side was his said image, canopied, crowned, sceptred,
orbed, in regal majesty: but the cross on the other side, instead
of being small and in the centre as on the old pennies, was large
and prolonged to the edge of the coin, with the English primroses
of King William Conquistator in the four angles of it, so that no
one could clip these new pennies without mutilating the cross,
which shocking sacrilege would be instantly and quite easily visible. And the device was so pleasing, the primrose being also the
flower of England and of Messire Saint George, that my lord the
king caused gold pennies to be struck from the same dies, of the
value of twenty silver pennies each, and of the purest gold. But his
grateful Giwen did not even try to clip these: they merely stole
them whole, and melted them for the value of the metal, which
was worth about one-and-a-half silver pennies more than the
face-value of coin. So the mayor and alderman of London brought
the citizens' humble petition imploring my lord the king to recall
his issue of gold pennies and to let use silver pennies of the new
coinage exclusively, for the sake of simplicity. Which was done;
and I hanged no more women and not more than four men a year,
for the crime of coin-clipping including sacrilegious mutilation of
The Cross.[1]

---

[1] The learned Mr. Joseph Jacobs's treatise, called *The Jews in Angevin England*,
contains very many indeed of the facts narrated here, and onward, though
there they are naturally criticized from the Israelite point-of-view, as here (not
unnaturally) from the opposite. P. & C. [Rolfe's note.]

IIII. *About the Duplicity of the Giwen*

The Giwen also practised evil against my lord the king in this manner. That it may be seen how great was their malignance, how great their obduracy and obstinate teaching, even against their own weal, I will record what they did in spite of one of their own historiographers, a certain ancient Joseph, whose histories of the Giwen they preserve, fairly written in the Hebrew tongue, and esteemed authentic: and yet they will not accept his testimony about Christ. O manners. Now, Mr. Robert, the prior of Saint Frideswide's at Oxford, an old clergyman but quite trustworthy, was also a man of letters skilled in the Scriptures and not at all ignorant of the Hebrew tongue. He, moved by innate virtue, sent to divers cities of England where there were Giweries, to borrow many histories of the Giwen written in Hebrew by this Giwe Joseph, that he might study them. And he gained them with great difficulty, the Giwen being ware that he understood their language. And, in two of these histories by Joseph (which he got from lepers) he found the testimony about Christ written fully and at length, but it was scratched out as it were quite recently: while, from all the rest it had been removed earlier. And, when he had shewn this to the Giwen of Oxford summoned for the purpose, they were abashed and convicted and confused at this manifestation of their fraudulent malignance and bad faith against Christ.[1]

v. *About the Devilry of the Giwen*

The Giwen also practised ill against my lord the king in this manner; and, that there may be no doubt as to their mockery of our Holy Faith, deeply paining us in the heart's core, I will narrate the following.

Mosse of Wallingford was a Giwe a little less detestable than

---

[1] Josephus was a first-century Jewish historian. In his *Jewish Antiquities*, he refers to a man named Jesus who performed surprising deeds. The authenticity of this passage has been debated extensively, and many critics argue that this was a later Christian addition to the text.

the rest of them. He had a son named Deulecress, which means *May God increase him*:[1] for the Giwen use prayers instead of Christian names. This Deulecress, inflamed by diabolical purulence, was wont to insult the devotion of Christians and to deride divine miracles with blasphemous words. On account of which depravity, it would seem that The Lord God Himself decided to punish him, so that the justice of my lord the king should not be troubled on his account. For the said Deulecress came to Oxford; and (swayed by his devil) derisively threw down his hands and stretched them out, and likewise halted on his feet, in imitation of cripples and paralytics, and (afterward) he walked upright, gaily boasting that he could do miracles as well as Madame Saint Frideswide,[2] and saying that gifts ought to be made to him as well as to her. O manners. Whereat, a faithful christian beldam[3] who frequented the shrine, unable to restrain her virtuous indignation, sat up and bade him out for a pig of a Giwe, and cursed the whole left side of him severely and particularly. He however, nothing abashed, and swayed yet more violently by his devil, redoubled his blasphemies, till, at last, he was rebuked by his aged and somewhat respectable father, who (with much difficulty) persuaded him to come home and to have his mouth filled with some sort of tasty pudding for supper. But, even then, he ceased not from foaming out the most foul abuse of our Holy Faith, so much so, indeed, that Mosse (his said father) could stand it no longer, and threatened to curse him himself in the forms prescribed by the Giwen. But, at that moment, the scab's left side was struck palsied from toes to crown: so that eye, nostril, half the mouth, ear, arm, hand, leg, foot, and also the exact half of his head, neck and body, became (as though by a lightning flash) as stiff as stone and much worse than useless to him. Whereby he was gravely displeased, and declined in a panic-terror. And, the same night, when the quiet of darkness had replaced the labours of the day, the semi-wretch contrived to leave his bed, and to roll into his father's kitchen all alone; and, lest his gloomy infatuation should be frustrated, he

---

[1] "*Deus eum crescat*," cf. Heb. Gedalyah. [Rolfe's note.]
[2] Saint Frideswide, the patron saint of Oxford, cured a leper by kissing him. Her shrine became known as a site of miraculous cures.
[3] An aged woman (*OED* OL).

closed the door with wax from the inside. Then, his belt served for rope; and, joining together his neck and the beam, he (like the traitor Judas) in verisimilar manner ended his life. And when his purulent carcase was being carted to London for burial, as the custom was (before my lord the king permitted his Giwen to buy cemeteries for themselves outside the walls of cities which they had leave to infect), then, a large congregation of dogs followed the said cart with vociferous barkings, as is the custom of dogs, performing suitable obsequies for the blasphemer.

VI. *About the Depravity of the Giwen*

Beside the blasphemer of Wallingford, several other Giwen continually made themselves obnoxious, by excessive contempt of our Faith. One Simon Chasid particularly went about complaining of sacred images and pictures. Insolently these Giwen swelled themselves against us christians: they were, indeed, far more troublesome than lepers. Their pertinacity in disputing with anyone foolish enough to argue with them was unspeakably exasperating. Worse remains. I was constantly called to do justice upon Giwen for assaulting christians, even sacrilegiously, as when Cresselin Deulesalt knocked off the clergyman's cap at Bosington on the very altar itself, which outrage cost him and his family twenty marks for amercement.[1]

Very hard indeed, it was to restrain good christian men from visiting their just resentment on these irritating Giwen. No one ought to be amazed because, every now and then, a Giwe got himself hurt. See, now, how inveterately untrustworthy they were. Potelin, a Giwe of London, chanced to be beaten so badly that he feared that he was dying. To save himself from further beatings, he requested Prior William of Saint Mary's to baptize him: which that excellent clergyman did, in the church of Holy Innocents, giving him his own name William, and delivering him from persecution. And, furthermore, the said prior took him in and healed him of his wounds. And, when King Arthur passed by, the new William (late Potelin) who from Giwe had been made

---

[1] A penalty left to the mercy of the inflicter (*OED* OL).

christian, was presented (not without proper pride on the part of the prior) to the Regal Majesty. "Who are you?" says my lord the king, admiring at his nasal configuration. "I am Potelin, Your Majesty's Giwe of London, obsequiating Your Majesty:" says the bestial apostate. King Arthur, blazing with Plantagenet passion, says to the Primate Edmund who rode near, "Did you not say that he was a christian?" Edmund answers, "Yes, lord king." Says the Regal Majesty again, "What now?" The archbishop of Canterbury, in a very holy fury, answers less prudently than he ought, saying, "Since he does not wish to be Christ's man, let him return to be the devil's man." Now, if my son Boniface the primate had been primate (and present) then, he would have made one of his dove-like and serpentine answers, for instance, "Lord king, he cannot help being a Giwe because he was born of that nation: but he lies at your mercy, and the church demands a judgment on him, seeing that he willingly became a christian and now seems to have forgotten all about it." For of course the miserable animal, his mind having become slightly unhinged by the proximity of the king's majesty, had only forgotten for the moment what his new name was. But, as no one prevented him from lapsing, the Giwe slid back into the Giwish depravity, and died at Northampton shortly after, when the Giwen rejected him from their cemetery because he was baptized, and the christians refused to admit him into theirs, not because he was circumcized, but because (like an obscene dog to his vomit) he had returned to that rite. O manners.

VII. *About the Dishonesty of the Giwen*

Nothing could keep the Giwen honest. I maintain that the surveillance of lazar-houses was a sweet sinecure compared with the control of the Giweries. The infinitely superior treatment secured to them, by their enviable position as the king's own chattels (which to touch is treason), failed to earn from them anything of the nature of honesty in return. They were only too ready to invoke the king's protection against christians whom they goaded to madness by their licentious superiority and excessive malfeasances; and they were not one whit less ready to invoke the same protection against their fellow-Giwen, when such suited their base and reprehensible purposes. They did not even know how to keep honour among themselves, as the vilest thieves are wont to do. Witness the case of Benedict fil-Jacob of Lincoln: he had a question against Deudon fil-Aaron and Jacob Oldman of Lincoln, both also Giwen; and rather than have the said question settled by the Giwish justiciars according to his own law, he willingly paid two gold ounces to have his matter heard in the king's court.

VIII. *About the Deceits of the Giwen*

If Giwe could not trust Giwe, certainly no Giwe could be trusted by a christian. You, o most affable reader, may perhaps imagine that gratitude to my lord the king at least would have protected the Regal Majesty from these plunderers. In that case you would be deceiving yourself, and the truth would not be in you, o said most affable reader. In case you are not convinced by what I have written already, ask yourself this: when a chance occurred of plundering my lord the king, who so prompt to pounce upon it as the king's own Giwen? Pray consider that Josce fil-Benjamin of Oxford who dared to buy a treasure-trove of gold with permission of justice. For which felony, I had the pleasure of punishing him, recovering the said treasure-trove for the regal exchequer, and amercing the said Giwe of a fine of ten marks as well for feloniously daring to buy a thing which was the king's by right. And consider contrariwise, o most affable reader, how heavily the king's justice scourged the king's christians, whenever there was the slightest ground for suspecting them of indifference to the interests or idiosyncracies of the king's Giwen. Remember the town of Ospringe and its awful calamity.[1] Remember the nameless (but accursed) Giwe who was found there, apparently murdered near the house of that Mephibosheth[2] whence (for-

---

[1] There was an outbreak of anti-Semitic riots and massacres in the late-twelfth century, and a riot did occur in Ospringe. According to Jacobs, "The immediate cause of the riots was the fever heat to which the crusading spirit had risen. To the rough logic of the people, it seemed absurd to go many thousands of miles to fight the 'enemies of Christ' and yet to allow some of them to live at peace at their own doors" (130).

[2] The son of Jonathan, "crippled in two feet," whose name means "One who destroys shame." See 2 Sam. 9:3-5.

merly) the devil took the soul of the coin-clipper. Who was the
said Giwe? Was he indeed a Giwe? God only knows. So long dead
was the piece of dead man which was found, no more than a left
leg and hip, and a little bit of belly, that to make a fuss was purely
foolish. Yet, when a hairy parcel of Giwen came howling to the
Justiciar, I was only doing my bounden duty when I made that
poor little town starve through the winter, by fining it twenty
marks, because it had not thought it worth while to raise the Hue
and Cry as the law directs for the imaginary murderer of that perfectly putrid piece of purely putative Giwe. O times. O manners.

vIIII. *About the Personation of the Bearded Lady Giwess*

I will tell a true (but merry) story about the abominable dishonesty of the Giwen. Henna, a Giwess, daughter of one Sir Vives
Levesq who had been one of their bishops, was afflicted with a
huge black beard, of far more immoderate dimensions than the
hairy insect-nests and coverts usually appended to the jaws of
males of the Giwish depravity. She, finding herself unmarried at
the age of thirty-four, was moved (by God's Inexplicable Grace) to
submit to baptism and the christian name of Anna; and the nuns
of Syon cheerfully let her harbour in their community. The said
Henna, or rather the Lady Anna (as I ought to call her) being rich
in this world's goods, which she inherited from her deceased
father the Giwish bīp., sent a humble petition to my lord the king,
praying for a remission of some small part of her fortune, which
(as the law directs) had been escheated to the regal exchequer on
her conversion: for she piously desired to make a small thank-
offering to the hospitable abbey of Syon. Which petition, King
Arthur graciously granted; and, further, he rescinded that part of
the law of escheatment which confiscated the goods of the king's
Giwen who ceased from being his chattels by denouncing their
depravity: for, he said that he wished to encourage all his Giwen
to embrace a state of grace without fear of incurring temporal
disability by such blissful action. But when, one year later, Lady
Anna still found herself without her fortune, the abbess of Syon
took occasion to make certain very severe and biting remarks to
my lady Queen Mariol on a visit to the said abbey. Which Regal

Majesty was forthwith moved to share her bites with others; and she graciously bit in various directions so efficiently, that immense perturbation unhinged the minds of the clergymen of the regal exchequer. For they, bitten badly (as it were) all over their necks, dismally shrieked to the stars, affirming (truly, on this occasion, as it happened), that no such escheatment had ever taken place. Where, then, was Lady Anna's fortune? A month later, we found that it was being enjoyed by a tranquil individual, passing under the name of Henna, and practising the Giwish depravity in the same place where, and just as, Lady Anna had practised it before her gracious conversion to Christianity. And the case seemed to be of such insuperable mystery, both the depositions of the abbess and nuns of Syon in favour of Lady Anna, and the compurgations of a parcel of the king's Giwen in favour of an individual called Henna, being (at one and the same time) of such apparently irre-fragible[1] validity and also so stringently contradictory, that the whole matter was transferred to the Chief Justiciar. And I must frankly confess that, having summoned Lady Anna and the indi-vidual called Henna to my court, I had never before found myself involved in so appalling a quandary. For, on the one side of me, was a bevy of the sweet nuns of Syon, verdantly blooming in modest holiness, and fearfully terrified, with a tendency toward anger; and they encompassed an animated lump, happed up in ladyskins and apparently female, white robed, veiled from crown to toes, which replied to my interrogations in the curious little thin throaty unbroken unmistakable voice of a spinster or a nun. And, on the other side of me, surrounded by a hairy parcel of Giwen (bīps., I believe, chiefly), was another animated lump, also apparently female and happed up in ladyskins, black-robed (for the late lamented Sir Vives, it was explained) and veiled from crown to toes, who answered me in rather bronchitic whispers. The white claimant affirmed that she was a christian named Anna, having formerly been a Giwess named Henna, daughter of Sir Vives Levesq deceased; and she claimed the fortune devised to her by her said father and restored to her by my lord the king's clemency after her conversion to christianity. And the abbess and

---

[1] Incontrovertible (*OED* OL).

nuns of Syon swore by God that her oath was clean. That ought
to have been enough. It was not so. The black claimant then
affirmed that she was a Giwess named Henna, and proud of it,
daughter of Sir Vives Levesq deceased, whose fortune she was at
present enjoying. And the hairy Giwen, her compurgators, made
compurgation in the mode of the accursed Giwen. As for the Justiciar, having prayed silently to Messire Saint Solomon, King &
Confessor, that he would inform me of his artful devices for
extracting truth, I was moved to ordain that both claimants
should unveil, so that I might mark the mobility of their blooming features while proceeding with my inquisition. And, instantly,
was confusion worse confounded. For the black claimant brazenly unveiled at once; and showed a smooth sallow face, slightly
haggard, flickering black eyes, two chin-moles, the ham-shaped
nose common to that sect, the whole not by any means alluring.
But the white claimant sobbed passionately under her ladyskins,
declaring that she was undone (which she was not) and she had to
be coaxed and comforted by nuns, for forty minutes by my glass,
before her veil could be lifted: when, lo, a pink fattish pudding-
face almost hidden under an enormous black and curly beard,
with whiskers and moustaches all complete, which rolled and
tumbled in magnificent cascades down as far as below her waist-
band. At which portent, to prevent my mind from becoming
unhinged, I freely tore my own hair, telling my trumpets to proclaim that the case was reserved for the Regal Majesty. All was
then gone over again before my lord the king in the palace of
Westminster, my lady the queen also sitting by him: for Queen
Mariol had been much piqued by the commentaries provided by
the bitter little abbess of Syon; and her honour provoked her to
see justice done in the matter, more specially because the Justiciar, Earl Hubert de Burgh, plainly averred that the thing was
very much too high, even for him. And Miss White whimpered in
the voice of an old maid, and was bashful beyond belief. And Miss
Black persisted rather brazenly in raucous whispers, not (however) without a certain degree of timidity. Both appeared to be in
good faith, and female Miss Beard poggy and flaccid, Miss Bald
undeniably scraggy. And the said Miss Bald's Giwish compurgators were certainly as convincing as the said Miss Beard's nuns,

being (at the same time) infinitely more vociferous. And there we were: not a christian stirred, not a Giwe stirred, no one stirred. Then, Queen Mariol, that strong wise lady, suddenly leaned from her throne, and whispered with King Arthur, proffering an opinion and an advice and a request, obtaining the last. And, forthwith, my lady the queen dismissed her maids: but she summoned her ladies more closely about her, namely, the countesses of Hereford, Suffolk, Brecon, Norfolk, Oxford, Pembroke and Striguil, Salisbury, Surrey, Winchester, Warwick, Chester, and "Here we have a jury of twelve matrons," says my lady the queen. I and King Arthur guffawed, perceiving the ruse intended. Queen Mariol eyed us austerely. "Be pleased, lord king, to retire with your earls and so forth," says she (bleak), "while we use our simple woman's wit in this affair." So King Arthur led us away, sniggering scandalously; and the doors were shut upon the queen, and her ladies, and the abbess and nuns of Syon, and the white claimant, and the black. For two minutes we thought about our puddings and twiddled our thumbs, in the antechamber. And, then, such terrific shrieks arose within the throne-room, that we all burst the door open and fell pell-mell in. O what a portent met our gaze. The abbess and nuns of Syon were heaped up, face to floor, on top of the bearded lady, all squealing. The queen and her jury of matrons clutched each other on the throne, scarlet, eyes all flaming. And the smooth-faced claimant in black was widely pattering hither and thither, in search of a commodious rat-hole. At whom Queen Mariol darted a furious finger. And, "Arrest me that caitiff," cries my lady the queen. So we snatched at Miss Bald and tore off her ladyskins. And, lo, she was a bony young man of the Giwish persuasion, Geremia by name, who bellowed with terror when the tormentors pawed him about in hammering his fetters on him. And he hastened to confess the conspiracy of the Giwen of London to keep Lady Anna's fortune in their own beastly dirty hands. O manners. My lord the king was compelled to refrain himself in silence for a quarter of an hour, lest he should do injustice in the fury of his just anger; and we all sat, and trembled, anticipating terrible judgments. At length, in a clean tone of disgust but no more, King Arthur said as follows: "Let the bishops of our Giwen see to it that Lady Anna's fortune be restored to her in full, with arrears, before noon on Friday next insuing: or We Ourself will take three such fortunes out of our Giwerie in London, before sunset that same day. And let the compurgators of this our Giwe Geremia be at the charges of it. And let all our Giwen now in Presence be washed and shaved and well whipped in Our Giweries to which they pertain, at noon on every Friday for four lunar months, beginning with Friday next insuing. And let this Our Giwe Geremia also pay to Our regal exchequer one mark every Friday for four lunar months after his whipping as aforesaid, for his felony of Impersonating Lady Anna. The King wills it." O righteous judge.

x. *About the Dreadful Deeds of the Giwen*

After laughter, tears. The Giwen also practised evil against King Arthur in this manner; and I loudly thanked God that this shocking affair (which I am about to narrate), occurred at a time when my lord the king was absent from his kingdom of England, because I was ware how awfully his regal indignation would afflict us his lovers, and (indeed) all persons concerned. I myself have never been scourged, crowned with thorn, and cruci-fied, all naked: had I had that experience, I know precisely how I should have felt against my outragers and all their miscreant race. It would have blinded me so that I could never see to do jus-tice any more. How, then, in the case of my lord the king, whose sacred regal body in boyhood's bloom was violated by so fearful an indignity? So, I say that I was thankful that King Arthur was absent from England, when the commotion occurred which I am about to narrate. Fool of an earl, not to have known that such forebodings were fatuous, not to have known how nobly the can-dour of King Arthur's left hand would raise him, at a fit occasion, far above such natural human infirmity. O my king. O me.

I do not believe much more than half of the present story. I am convinced that some horrible thing happened: but what, or how, or why, I have no means of knowing precisely. For, in all the testi-mony, which was collected for me or made before me, I could not find one clear point on which I might do the king justice. But it is my duty to set down all the said testimony, lest I incur reproach by slurring even the smallest part of the history of King Arthur's reign. On Lammas Day, then, that year, they found a boy's body unburied, in the graveyard of Saint Bennet in the city of London. His legs and arms and bosom bore a regular inscription in Hebrew letters, scratched in the smooth young flesh. Many people assembled to see the sight; and, being unable to read the inscription (though they knew the letters of it to be Hebrew) they sent for some converted Giwen inhabiting the hospice which my lord the king founded for such in London. These, they adjured, for honour and fear and love and dread of my said lord the king, to interpret the said inscription without any quibbling. For it was thought (without reason) that Giwen had crucified the boy as a taunt and insult against Jesus Christ (which would be nothing new) and, also, it was thought (with reason) that they had tormented him in various diabolical ways before crucifying him, and (when he died of his anguish) had cast him out as not being strong enough to bear the honour of the cross. For the body was marked with livid weals, such as are caused by scourges; and there were clear traces of other unutterable outrages: but the hands and feet and heart were not pierced. And the regal bailies were present to conserve the peace: for several agitated lepers were leaping about, prophesying; and the mob did not like them. The converted Giwen (brought to decypher the inscription) did their best: but, through the extension and contraction of the wounded flesh, the letters were much twisted and distorted, and some were quite illegible. Nevertheless, christian names (conjectured to be those of the victim's father and mother) namely, Edward and Eliza, were decypherable, but not their cognomen; and, also, there was a statement that the Giwen had taken the boy from a Frankish Giwe for a purpose, which last was blurred and illegible. While this was going on, a whole clot of the Giwen of London fled into the provinces, a circumstance which I regarded with suspicion; and I instantly sent my mandate to the city-fathers that they should raise the Hue and Cry for the murderers. Meanwhile, it became bruited[1] abroad that the dead boy was a martyr, on whose behalf The Lord God was deigning to work miracles. And, when folk

---

[1] Reported or rumored (*OED* OL).

remembered former deeds of similar nature which the Giwen had undoubtedly done, and how the holy crucified bodies (after reception into a church) had been illustrated by astounding miracles, then, the Canons of Saint Paul's took the body of this unknown martyr (though, as I say, the five wounds were not marked in the hands and feet and side), and they buried it with ornate pomp in the cathedral near the high altar. And, of the miracles which insued, I prefer to be silent.[1] But the fourth day of the Hue and Cry brought fearful things to pass. Another boy, apparently Frankish, was found making a hullabaloo at the house of a well-known one of the King's Giwen (whose name I omit for clear and sufficient reason), with a shrill voice and an admirable flux of words abusing the said Giwe, accusing the same with strident yells of the murder of his friend. "You spawn of a foul strumpet, you thief, you traitor, you demon, you have crucified my friend:" says he. And, "Woe is me:" says he. And, "If I had the strength of a man, I would tear you to pieces with my hands:" says he. His shouts brought christians and Giwen from all parts to hear him. Rendered more fearless in the presence of so great an assemblage, he redoubled his accusations. The bailies arrested both him and the Giwe, as well as a woman who also began to make herself conspicuous; and brought them all before me, in my court at White Hall. I, then, in accordance with my office, made the accuser speak first. "Lord earl," says he, "see if there be any sorrow like to my sorrow: for this Giwe here is a devil, who has torn my heart from my breast, who has butchered my friend, and (I believe) actually began to eat him. For a certain devilson, a Frankish Giwe, gave my friend letters of death to this Giwe here, and seduced him to this city." And so saying, the youngster gasped for breath and swooned out of pure melancholy. While he was being recovered, it seemed good to my sagacity to cause a posse of my tormentors with some of their apparatus to occupy a prominent position in my court: it being plain that there was going to be great difficulty in finding out the truth in this matter. For, though I am not fond of tormenting, I know that truth arises earlier out

---

[1] In the case of William of Norwich, most of the miracles and visions related to this saint occurred when his body was transferred from a chapter-house to a cathedral.

of error than out of confusion, and (consequently) may be extorted
by torment, or by fearful anticipation of the same, as adjuncts to
very sagacious interrogation, in which last (together with the
aspect and carriage of the interrogator) I place my chief confidence. Wherefore, when the boy had recollected the use of his
mind, I spoke as kindly as possible, bidding him to have no fear of
fierce-looking persons or hideous things which might be in his
vicinity but were not intended for him, promising him the king's
protection, and requiring him to tell me quite calmly all which
was in his heart and mind from the very beginning. He, then,
said: "I am Amys, and my martyred friend was Amyl, both Frankish by birth and named after the saints in the romance,[1] both bastards, of low condition, orphans, of extreme poverty. In Paris, we
pursued the art and mystery of cobbling; and we lived in the
house of a Frankish Giwe named Léon Depunteise, to whom we
gave our earnings from our cobbling, receiving puddings and
lodgings in return. He, pretending to pity our misery, frequently
persuaded us to come to England, as to a land flowing with milk
and honey, assuring us that the English were well-fed and liberal,
and that no one who wished to live honestly need die poor among
them. We, ready (like all Franks) to do what you will, girded ourselves for foreign travel, having naught in our hands but our awls,
naught in our wallets but crusts: thus, we came to make farewell
to our Giwe. 'Quit yourselves like men and be strong,' says he,
'and may the God of my fathers lead you as I desire for you.' Then
he placed his hands on the head of my friend; and I must say that
Amyl was of a most beautiful shape, and of a mien so brave and
ardent that people stopped in the street to look at him, whereas I
(though strong) am by no means as comely. The Giwe, therefore,
laid his hands on the head of Amyl, as though he were a scapegoat;[2] and, after some clearances of his gullet and some muttered
imprecations, he said, being (as I think) secure of his prey: 'Be ye
of brave mind: forget your nation and your country, for every

---

[1] *Amys and Amylion*, a medieval poem about the friendship between two knights.
[2] In the Mosaic ritual of the Day of Atonement, a goat, the scapegoat, is sent
alive into the wilderness, symbolically carrying the sins of the people. During the
ritual, the priest lays his hands on the scapegoat to symbolize the transferral of
the sins of the people to the animal.

country is a fatherland to the brave, like the sea to the fish and any clear space to the vacant bird.[1] And, when you come to England, pass quickly through Winchester, for I greatly dislike that city. All kinds of men flow into it from every country under heaven, and each celebrates his own vices there. No one lives in Winchester who is free from crime: every citizen abounds in deplorable obscenities; and even the infants boast of their flagrant delictuousnesses.[2] And the man is the more highly esteemed there, the more profoundly he is immersed in atrocities. I know to whom I speak. I am ware that you have warm minds and cold memories, which qualities are so balanced in you, that you possess a well-tempered reason. So I do not fear for you, unless you live with habitual criminals: for evil communications corrupt good manners. Well: well. You go to Winchester. So, I give you this warning, that whatsoever things evil or malignant or depraved are in all or every part of the world, the same you shall find collected and celebrated in the city of Winchester, like filth in a cess-pool. You will meet more bullies there than there are in the whole of France. Avoid the society of pimps. Do not mingle in the mob of gamblers. Keep from dice and mysteries and taverns. Innumerable is the company of parasites. Actors, buffoons, eunuchs, garamanters, flatterers, pages, sluts, poltroons, lovers, dancing-girls, apothecaries, favourites, witches, fortune-tellers, vultures, owls, magicians, egyptians, mimes, lawyers, mendicants, and many more, fill every house. Consequently, unless you want to live with naughty persons, you will not stay in Winchester. Mind you, I am not speaking about learned men, whether they be Giwen or clergymen, although I imagine that such persons are less perfect there, seeing that they choose to harbour in Wicked Winchester. Nor am I talking in this way to prevent you from dwelling in a city. Contrariwise: I am advising you not to dwell anywhere but in a city. And which city? If you go to Canterbury it will be a fruitless journey: for, there, is the complete congregation of lost souls adoring a man recently deified, I forget his name, but he used to

---

[1] cf. Ouid. *Fast.* i. 493. [Rolfe's note.] From Ovid's *Fasti* (*The Festivals*): "To the brave every land is their country, as the sea / To fish, or every empty space on earth to the birds."

[2] A "delict" is a crime or delinquency.

be the arch-clergyman of Canterbury, where, for want of work
and bread, men die in the open air and streets. Rochester and
Chatham are mere villages: and there is no reason why they
should be called cities, excepting that bishops have seats therein.
Oxford does not sustain her own inhabitants: much less does she
satisfy them. Exeter feeds the same corn to both man and beast.
Bath is clearly the very gate of hell, placed (or misplaced) at the
bottom of a valley filled with dense air and sulphureous exhala-
tions. Worcester and Chester and Hereford spend life cheaply on
account of their proximity to the savage Welshry. York is infested
by Scots, foul and fickle apologies for men, all pimply, vain, libidinous, prepotent, and traitors born. The village of Ely is always
putrid, because of the swamps which surround it. In Durham and
Lincoln and Norwich, there are few people like yourselves, and
none who speak the Romance language. At Bristol there is no one
who is not a soap-boiler, or who wants to be one; and every Frank
hates a soap-boiler as he hates a scavenger: beside, they sell you
for slaves there. Every other town and village and manor has rude
rustic inhabitants; and the Cornishmen are what we Frankishmen consider the Flemings to be. Nevertheless, the land is very
rich in the dew of the sky and the fatness of the soil: in every place
these are good: but in one city alone they are very good, namely,
in London. There, alone, they enjoy perpetual peace. There, is
the school for those who wish to live and thrive. There, real men
are made. There, they have bread and wine for everyone. There,
are monks of such piety and courtesy, clergymen of such wisdom
and generosity, citizens of such civility and good faith, women of
such beauty and modesty, that I know not what keeps me from
going there and becoming christian among such christians. So, I
direct you to London, the city of cities, the mother and mistress
of all. It has, however, one fault (but only one) in which it com-
monly indulges. I say it with submission to Giwen and other men
of learning, but the Londoners tell worse lies even than clergymen do when they narrate their experiences. Therefore, I give
you these letters to a friend of mine, a Giwe in London, a most
holy trustworthy elegant man, who will put you in the way of
earning a really honest living; and you will be rewarded by having
to do with him.'" At these words the lad panted hard, interrupting

his lively harangue[1] simply for want of breath. Says my young
brother Bobo of the Preaching Friars, who sat by me for ecclesiastical reasons, "Whether his tale be true or false, a boy with such
fluent facile fecundity of speech is wasted in the gutter, where he
withers, living on his awl when he could far better use his hon-
eyed tongue." Good idea. I asked the boy whether he knew the
content of the letters, which the Frankish Giwe had sent by him
and his friend to this Giwe of London. "Lord earl," says he, "I
know it as well as I know my prayers: for he read it to us when he
had written it: and these were his words: *'Hail to thee (name omitted) that thou hast shewn thyself worthy of partaking in the holy work
and the price of the lambs is four marks English apiece and the lads bearing this letter desire to rise in this world being able and I believe perfect
and for love of me use them treating them suitably so that one at least
may be lifted up and both if need be. From thy friend Leon Depunteise.'"*
I asked "What lambs?" having heard muck of this kind before.
The lad replied that the Giwe Leon had said that he was selling a
couple of Frankish lambs to this Giwe (name omitted) of London,
in the course of business, for the monks called Cistercians who
desired to improve the English breed of sheep. I bade the lad to
continue his story. "Lord earl," says he, "we came to London. Our
awls sufficed us for a living; and, unfortunately, the hospitality of
the Giwe here served us for solace by means of those letters. We
worked, and we ate, by turns each day. Each night we slept in one
cot in a cow's manger. Day followed day, night followed night,
and month month; and the time hastened to approach when my

---

[1] There is more than a very strong flavour of Richard of Devizes about this "lively
harangue." In fact, throughout the whole of these documents, one is continually
being rendered liable to suspect scores of subsequent writers, including even
such extremely prosaic scribes as the compilers of the *Pipe Rolls*, of a certain
unmistakable conversation with the writer of this history: or vice versa, of
course. Perhaps the decision is better left to the "affable reader," or to the erudite
and invariably just Mr. Vernon Rendall.—P. and C. [Rolfe's note.] This story of
the cobbler and the discussion of the vices of Winchester and the wonders of
London are drawn almost word for word from *The Chronicle of Richard of Devizes*.
However, Hubert de Burgh, or Rolfe, has inverted Richard's "harangue," for
Richard argues that London is the locus of evil in England, while Winchester is
"a school for those who want to live and fare well." See *The Chronicle of Richard of
Devizes of the Time of King Richard the First*, edited by John T. Appleby (New York:
Thomas Nelson & Sons, 1963), 64-69.

beloved friend Amyl had to depart, on an errand, as I thought. And I, wondering at his absence when he did not come to bed for two nights, became frightened, and dreadful dreams alarmed me. Then, when I did not find him, though I searched several days through the whole city, I returned to this Giwe here, to enquire whether he would give me the week's provision for myself and my friend. But he, instead of receiving me kindly as usual, was both bitter and brutal, telling me to go to hell as he had no further use for me. And I, noticing this marked change of word and of aspect, began to cry shame upon him, speaking my mind freely and with all my might, till the bailie took me and brought me for a judgement." Thus, the boy Amys, whom I set by himself in a chamber with a pitcher of milk and a basket of buns for his comfort. Interrogation of the Giwe (name omitted) produced nothing to the point. He said that he had taken the two boys in charity, because they were recommended to him by a Frankish Giwe with whom he sometimes did business. They worked at their cobbling; and, for the money which they earned thereby, he gave them his protection, with a weekly provision, and a good cow-house for their lodging, with something in their wallets beside, suited to the diversions of their age. Thus they had been with him for seven months; and then Amyl (a very handsome lad) had disappeared: but, whether he had gone after a gipsy-girl, or whether he had run away to the wars, the Giwe (speaking) neither knew nor cared. As for the lad Amys, he had done no work for a week; and then came yelling as one yells at an obstreperous leper; for which cause the Giwe (speaking) had retorted bitterly, but not for any other reason. And I am bound to say that the said Giwe spoke fairly, with frankness and moderation, nor was he noticeably incommoded or perturbed by the proximity of my tormentors with their apparatus. Next, interrogation of the christian woman produced as follows: She was called Adeliza; and was employed by the Giwe (name omitted) to nurse the little Giwen in the same house. She swore that she knew both Amys and Amyl by sight, having seen them frequently. And she swore further that, a few days after the festival of Madame Saint Magdalen,[1] she

---

[1] July 22.

had seen Amyl (a fine pretty upstanding lad, with a leg of his own) descend into the Giwe's cellar, toward evening, by invitation of the said Giwe: but she had never seen him return; and the cellar-door was kept constantly padlocked. This seemed something like a scent; and I promptly laid the Lord's hound on it,[1] my young Brother Bobo Kemp of the Preaching Friars, who took a posse, and went to examine the Giwe's cellar while I proceeded with my inquisition. I demanded of the boy Amys, whether he knew well the body of his friend, if any birthmarks or other distinct features might be there. He said that he knew it as well as his own: but it was without spot or blemish of any kind. Required to describe the person of his friend, he said that it was of a ruddy colour all over, having plenty of rich blood, with black hair very thick and wavy, eyes very blue and piercing, body and limbs sinewy and supple, and very smooth-skinned but beginning to be hairy about the shins. Also he spoke of callosities on the little fingers, caused by pulling on waxed threads in the exercise of his art and mystery. Anon, I removed my court to the cathedral of Saint Paul within the neighbouring city of London; and I induced the mayor to cause the canons to produce the corpse of their new martyr, wherewith I confronted the boy Amys. He was most dreadfully squeamish: indeed, it was only after many gentle pitiful words of mine that he was able to do what I required. But then, though he would gladly have recognized his friend, for the sake of the aversion which he entertained against the Giwe, he equally gladly would not have recognized that poor cadaver as Amyl for the sake of the love which he most certainly bore for the friend whose society he desired so very ardently. Moreover, I believe that I should not have attached importance to any recognition, had such taken place: because the corpse (which the canons proudly displayed for me) was in so advanced a stage of putrefaction, hairless, black, blue, green, yellow, absolutely lacking great gobbets, and of so revolting a stench and tabidity (the weather being sultry) that no one could have said (with certainty) whose soul had formerly inhabited it. So, I transferred my court to my palace of White Hall near Westminster where the new abbey is. There, my

---

[1] *"Domini canem."* [Rolfe's note.]

young Brother Bobo of the Preaching Friars reported that, having broken open the door of the cellar in the Giwe's house, he had found the interior very clean and tidy, but not suspiciously so, and mainly occupied by faggots prepared (perhaps somewhat early) against the winter: which faggots he had had cleared away, and restacked, without discovering marks of the commission of crime or felony. I adjourned the case till after noon. While I unlaced a rabbit for my dinner, I picked the brains of my dear young Friar, who said two things which I bore well in mind. First, he cited a decree of some Lateran Council, ordaining that Giwen and Saracens were not permitted (any more than damned or censured Germans are) to have christian servants living in their houses, for the purpose of tending their children, or for any other cause, and, that christians (swayed by the devil) who accepted such service, became damned and excommunicated (and, consequently, infamous) by the very fact.[1] Secondly, he said that, if the boy Amys wished it, he would undertake to persuade the prior of my convent by Ludgate to receive him as a novice, and to give him such christian comfort and education as his singular misfortunes, parts, and aptitudes, deserved. O good friar. Now, when I had considered all things, namely, that no undeniably irrefragible link, connecting the accused accursed Giwe with the mutilated body of the boy found in the graveyard of Saint Bennet, actually was forthcoming: that neither the tale of the boy Amys, nor the tale of the christian woman Adeliza, could be legally used as accusations against the said Giwe so as to force him to compurge himself, the said boy Amys being under age, and the said woman Adeliza being infamous because excommunicate as a willing christian servant of a Giwe, then, I warned the said Giwe as severely as possible, having caused him to swear on his Book that he was innocent; and I dismissed him at liberty (there being no legal ground for detaining him), as quit of the summons. But I did this with profound regret: because I was, and am, convinced in my mind, though not in my reason, that the ceremony of murder

---

[1] "The provisions of the Lateran council about the Jews" are quoted in Jacobs's *The Jews of Angevin England*. Jacobs argues that these rules reflect the growing "tendency to restrict intercourse" between Jews and Christians at the end of the twelfth century due to an increase in "the fear of conversion to Judaism" (185-186).

had been celebrated (with unusual solemnity) upon that festering body of a christian boy, and I had, and have, strong intuitions that that Giwe (name omitted) was guilty of, or at least a participator in, that felony. But I could not (as justiciar) give lawful credence to more than half of the testimony presented for my judgement; and that half, most annoying, emanated from persons incompetent of and disqualified from testifying.[1] O times. O manners.

xi. *About a Case of Usury*

Enough of horrors. Let me now shew how excessive in quibbling were the Giwen. Judas (apt name) a Giwe of Bristol, paid two gold ounces to my lord the king, to have inquisition made in the Chapter of the Giwen[2] which they called Bethdin,[3] as to whether one of the king's Giwen might lend money on usury to another of the king's Giwen. The three bishops of the Giwen called Dayanim, who sit on that tribunal, examined the roll of their law; and gave judgement in the negative.[4] Now, o most affable reader, be pleased to mark with what loyal fidelity this Judas, Giwe of Bristol, observed his own accursed law, for whose judgement he was willing to pay his two gold ounces, so that he could design his premeditated sin in legal security. The fact was that he lusted to lend four hundred marks to Ysaak Furmager, another Giwe of Bristol, for a purpose not to be named. How, then, to do it, in face of the prohibition of Giwish law ascertained as aforesaid? But, so facile in quibbles are these Giwen, that (when once they make up their minds to do it) not even their own law can keep them from felony: for they (swayed by the devil their lord) know well how to evade the said law. Here, then, is the method of Judas. Some Franks from Cahors (or some say from Lombardy) swayed likewise by their devil, were settling in England to practise the sin of usury in common with the king's Giwen, a most shock-

---

[1] In Richard of Devizes's account, "the accusers failed: the boy because he was under age; the woman because her being employed by Jews made her infamous" (69).

[2] "*in capitulo Giudaeorum.*" [Rolfe's note.]

[3] A rabbinical court.

[4] cf. *Deut.* xxiii. 20. [Rolfe's note.] "Thou shalt not lend at interest to thy brothers." Cited by Jacobs in *The Jews of Angevin England.*

ing degeneration on the part of putative christians. So, Judas betook himself to one Ubaldo, a Cahorsin and a person of no repute, introducing his friend Ysaak Furmager as a would-be borrower of four hundred marks. The Cahorsin, not having so much money by him, sobbed as passionately as any leper at the notion of losing so sweet a slice of business. What then could the said genial Judas do but offer to lend to the said Ubaldo the said sum of four hundred marks (which, by chance, said he, he happened to have in a bag beneath his gabardine[1] at that identical moment) for a little less than his usual sixty per cent of usury, say for fifty per cent of usury, it being Giwishly lawful to lend to a Christian and Giwishly meritorious to do good to any man. And Ysaak Furmager, that sanctified innocent, was willing to borrow a similar sum of four-hundred marks from Ubaldo the Cahorsin, also for a little less than his usual per cent of usury, say for fifty-five per cent of usury, it being Giwishly lawful for a Giwe to borrow of a Christian when he could benefit himself and his brother-Giwe at one and the same time. O generation of vipers.

XII. *About certain of the Imbecillities of Clergymen and Giwen*

O clergymen. I wish to state, as one of my most pondered opinions, that, if clergymen were possessed, not of that common sense which every morose peevish puffed-up fatwit claims as his property by right divine, but of that uncommon sense which friars and earls and archers and mariners generally use when they adapt their ordinary methods for dealing with extraordinary cases—I say that, if clergymen had had the uncommon sense not to sit down and sob like silly God-forsaken fools in regard to the Giwen, the task of treating the said Giwen would have been very much easier. I mean that, if clergymen could manage to make themselves voluntarily admired and respected and loved, the Giwen would be deprived of a proximate occasion of mockery, and so would become at least more tractable to us of the King's justice who had the treating of them. But, apart from tussling and scuff-

---

[1] A loose garment often associated with Jews. See Shakespeare's *The Merchant of Venice* I. iii. 113: "You . . . spit upon my Jewish gabardine" (*OED* OL).

ing in mundane competition and rivalry (of which I say nothing, such being scandalous), the clergymen, with that damnable superiority and ridiculous cock-certainty about matters outside their province, which they fancy is alluring and habitually practise, and, also, with that fatal facility which they have for mixing grace with nature and human knowledge (poor thing) with divine mystery, prate (I say) at large, unreservedly, most indiscreetly, quite dedecorously; and, so, they make themselves (first) a laughing-stock, (second) a plainly accented nuisance, (third) an object to be scorned, to be smacked back into its ministerial place, or to be neglected as a mere nothing. And, as a shocking example, I will narrate the following. A phrenetic archdeacon of Wales, one Sir Gerald, told fatuous tales, which, if not slightly thin, would have made a cat grin and staggered the reason of snails. He[1] declared that he had seen thousands of atoms on a single log of driftwood on the seashore, unnaturally produced there, looking like bits of gum, which anon changed into minute shells, each containing a tiny wild goose attached to the log by its beak, which portentous fowls (in process of time) became covered with feathers, and (growing to a suitable and eatable size without ever having assimilated visible nourishment) dived into the sea and flew in the free air, till they were caught to be eaten of bishops and other dignified clergymen of Ireland on fast-days in place of beef-puddings.[2] From which incredible (but most agreeable portent) Sir Gerald gaily deduced a deep spiritual and moral argument, in the manner of talkative clergymen, namely, that the accursed Giwen ought not to cough so horribly at such articles of our holy faith as the Virginal Parturition of Madame Saint Mary Deipara.[3] Here is his gay and festive process of reasoning: "The first man was generated of dust without either male or female, namely, Mes-

---

[1] This undoubtedly is the individual known as *"Geraldus Cambrensis."*—P. and C. [Rolfe's note.] Gerald of Wales, or Giraldus Cambrensis, was a medieval chronicler and clergyman.

[2] This passage reproduces the discussion of "barnacle geese" in Giraldus Cambrensis's *Topographia Hiberniæ*. According to Giraldus Cambrensis, Irish clergymen ate these fowl at times of fasting, believing this was allowed because of the birds' marine origin.

[3] Mary's virgin birth. "Deipara" is a title of the Virgin Mary.

sire Saint Adam, Patriarch and Confessor: the second was generated from the male without the female, namely, Madame Saint Eve, Matron. These you may not deny, if you venerate your own law, o miserable Giwe:" gratuitously says the highly superior Sir Gerald. And he airily continues: "The third generation, namely, generation from male and female, alone you (with your hard beard) approve because it is so very usual. But the fourth generation (by which alone comes our salvation) namely, from female without the male, that (with obstinate malignance) you detest to your own destruction. Blush, you rascal, blush, and turn at least to Nature, who provides an argument for our faith, seeing that she procreates (without either male or female) and produces these barnacle-geese,[1] every day for our conviction." O dangerous dolt of an archdeacon.

Jurnet, son of the Giwe of Norwich, came to my court, citing the foregoing so-called christian doctrine, and saying that his teacher Leo (a Giwe of Paris) told him that his father Ysaak (of the same city) said that another Frankish Giwe named Tam (who was a bishop of their accursed depravity) had directed that the foresaid barnacle-geese might be eaten also of Giwen, providing that they were canonically slaughtered according to the rites and solemnities of the said Giwen.[2] And the said Jurnet demanded a judgement. Him, then, I addressed thus: "You bring me here four credible christians, friars or earls or archers or mariners for choice, who will swear on the Four Evangels that they, with their own eyes, have seen, more than four times, at least four of these gummy atoms on logs producing themselves as limpets or as mussels, which, as everyone knows, taste like goose-livers, though they do not produce themselves in the form of geese: but you bring me here four live geese so produced, with the said four credible christians who have seen such production; and then I will give you a most blooming judgement."

Whereat the said Jurnet paid his fees, and went out with his mind unhinged and looking rather foolishly: nor have I ever heard any more of him.

---

[1] "*bernacoe.*" [Rolfe's note.]

[2] Drawn from the responsa of R. Meir of Rothenburg. Cited in Jacobs's *The Jews of Angevin England.*

XIII. *About the Mauleverers and the Giwen*

Here is another example of the difficulty of dealing with Giwen, due (of course) solely to the peculiar depravity and privileges of the said Giwen. The affairs of the Mauleverers, *gules, a chief, or*, became frightfully complicated. Now there were three of them who bore the name of Reinald, that is to say, Sir Reinald Mauleverer of Chalion Gunter, and Sir Reinald Mauleverer, his son, and Sir Reinald Mauleverer of Castro Gunter who was warden of his sister Lady Emma. Let so much be clear. Sir Reinald Mauleverer of Chalion Gunter and his son Sir Reinald Mauleverer, having followed the king through his crusade, whereby they profited nothing (excepting in regard to their souls) owing to King Arthur's austere righteousness in the matter of plunder and ransoms, came back to find themselves dreadfully worried, their castle infested by Giwen in possession, all on account of a paltry fifteen hundred marks, which they had borrowed from those usurers, for their outfits and expenses in the Holy Land. Nor could their relation, the said Sir Reinald Mauleverer of Castro Gunter, afford them any help, he being afflicted with five bad harvests and a quartan fever, and unable to have meat with the puddings at both ends of his table. Very sad it was to see magnates of such ancient lineage eating fish every other day on the dais, so that every day their families and servants might eat meat below the saltcellar. O times. And my difficulty was that (as Justiciar) I could not do the king's justice to Mauleverer without doing injustice to the king's Giwen, and to the king by not doing justice to his Giwen. So it seemed. Indeed it really seemed so. But, at last, one who loved my lord the king was moved to go suddenly and ask my lord the king, as it were a riddle, "Can a man do as he pleases with his own?" King Arthur conceded an affirmative answer. Then, the same lover of my lord the king very wilily pointed out that, apart from the Apostolic Mandate,[1] the Mauleverers undoubtedly deserved well of my lord the king; and, that to reward the Mauleverers, would in any case cost the king something: but, that,

---

[1] *i.e.* of Eugenius P.M. III, that all crusaders should be free from exaction of usury. [Rolfe's note.]

to reward the Mauleverers by cancelling their debt to the king's Giwen, would be to give them what was not possessed by the king, though it might be possessed by the king at his will, his Giwen and all their goods and ill-gotten gains being the king's. Admirable subtilety. Whereupon the four Mauleverers were summoned to the Presence, that King Arthur might take note of them and reward them openly as good and faithful servants. But, when he observed Lady Emma and the young Sir Reinald, he ordained instant issue of letters patent as follows:

ARTHUR BY THE GRACE OF GOD AND THE SANCTION OF THE APOSTOLIC SEE KING, ET CETERA

Know all men that We have quit-claimed and given and caused to have quit-claimed by Our Giwen the debts of Sir Reinald Mauleverer of Chalion Gunter and of Sir Reinald his son which We and Our Giwen have on the castle and land of the said knights, on condition that the said Sir Reinald Mauleverer son of the said Sir Reinald Mauleverer of Chalion Gunter shall marry Lady Emma Mauleverer youngest sister of Sir Reinald Mauleverer of Castro Gunter before the festival of Messire Saint Blaise next insuing:

And this charter shall be in the hands of Sir Hubert de Burgh earl-palatine of Kent and Our justiciar et cetera till the said marriage and after the said marriage has been duly consummated Our said justiciar shall hand this charter to the said Sir Reinald Mauleverer of Chalion Gunter in token that he and his son Sir Reinald are quit of all debts to Our Giwen but if the said marriage is not so consummated then this said charter is void and the foresaid debt returns to Us through Our Giwen.[1]

XIIII. *About a Case of an Eye for an Eye*

Here is an instance of the difference between christians and Giwen. Hakelin fil-Josce Quatrebuches the Giwe of London spat on the right eye of Sir Adam Decolebrooke, *onduly, argent, and azure, a chief sable,* being displeased because the said knight would not give place to him in a crowd. O manners. Whereupon, Sir

---

[1] This order to marry was in fact issued by King John in 1200. The letter patent is quoted in Jacobs's *The Jews of Angevin England*, and Rolfe reproduces the original document almost word for word.

Adam simply took him, and held him at the king's mercy, being prevented by his conscience from murder, and by his fealty from damaging seriously one of the king's Giwen. This Hakelin was a lively prepotent young Giwe of twenty-two years, a firebrand, a ne'er-do-well, and a great grief to his apparently respectable father. Being more or less a bully, and so able to snaffle money, he would not labour honestly, but delivered himself to rioting and lechery though never (so far) to really red iniquity. For which causes the said Josce Quatrebuches would much rather not have begotten such a son; and he jumped at the opportunity of getting rid of him, offering forty marks for the cost of judgement on his said son Hakelin according to the king's justice in the plea between him and Sir Adam de Colebrooke. Hearing this, the brazen Hakelin went one better; and offered four-and-forty marks to the said Sir Adam, by way of compensation, in order to disappoint and chagrin Josce his father. And thus the case stood when it was brought to me. And I made short work of it, that the integrity of the king's justice might be maintained. Sir Adam very rightly scorned the bare notion of compensation in money, believing that the aggressor's right eye was his just due. Conceded. When the said eye had been taken out and duly delivered, I apprenticed the Giwe Hakelin to a very strict one of my pirates at Romney, in which situation he would have scope for his natural violence; and I bade him to keep on shipboard, unless he wished to learn to dance convulsively on nothing, an art which my hangman would teach him if he set foot in England for three years. And the marks of him and of his father, I escheated to the regal exchequer.

xv. *About a Rite of the Giwen*

See how these accursed Giwen, also, bite each others' necks, and expected not their own law but the king's to allay their uneasiness. A parcel of these depraved ones came and worried me dreadfully, for a judgment as to what they ought to do with male babies born marked as the Giwen mark their males after birth. But I discovered that one of their own bīps., a certain Sampson fil-Abraham, had already written a judgement on this point, in a most florid and ridiculous manner, for the comfort of one Ysaak

fil-Yomtob of Joigny, ordaining that blood must be drawn for the
blood of the covenant, whatever that may mean.[1] And, disdaining to be let from my pudding while I attempted to understand
their abominable scrupulosity, I bade them to bide by the doctrine and judgement of their foresaid Sampson, and be damned
accordingly.

XVI. *About the Complex Betrothals of Ysaak fil-Hosea*

A blooming young Giwe of Hull named Ysaak fil-Hosea, with
his father Hosea fil-Menacham, and his grandfather Menacham
fil-Somebodyelse, with a christian yeoman's son named Jocelyn
Tup, and another Giwe named Morel, all five frantic, with their
minds completely unhinged, and capering all over the place in
sheer perplexity, invaded my court, demanding a judgement.
Silence having been enforced, young Ysaak unfolded his grievance.
His father Hosea and his grandfather Menacham had betrothed
him (at the age of reason and according to the rites of the Giwish
depravity) to the daughter of Morel. So far, so good. I required the
youth to continue his recitation. But his father and his aged grandfather began to gibber and to shake their aprons so very tumultu-
ously, that it was necessary to gag and to fetter them. Ysaak then
accused Morel of having not one daughter but three daughters,
to all of whom he was betrothed by the abominably unlimited
terms of his betrothal. And he demanded a judgement. Hosea,
released from his gag and his mouth oiled, asserted that his son's
tender youthful conscience made him a liar, seeing that no male
in christendom is permitted to be betrothed to three females at
once. Menacham, also freed to speak, screeched that his grandson
was wronged and all undone, in that (although betrothed to one)
he could not possibly marry till he knew to which one he was
betrothed. And the ancient simply squealed, wailing, bemoaning
himself in that no legitimate great-grandchildren could accrue to
him to pray for the repose of his soul in default of a judgement.
And all three cried together for a judgement on that rank deceiver

---

[1] Circumcision was enjoined upon Abraham and his descendants as a token of
the covenant made with him by God. When a child was born circumcised, a drop
of blood was to be shed as a sign of the covenant.

Morel, alleging that he had singularly and particularly wronged all three of them.

Up, then, and spoke the said Morel, proudly beboasting himself of his enormous prudence and sagacity, in that (when betrothing his daughter to the said Ysaak) he had carefully omitted the furnishing (to that youth's silly parents) a specification as to which one of his three daughters he thus disposed, so that (in case of the demise of one, or even of two), he would be secure of a husband for the third. But, seeing that all three survived, and were now nubile, he, also, bawled for a judgement as to which of his said three daughters he could enforce in marriage upon the said Ysaak. Last, the christian Jocelyn Tup, a lusty, hobbedehoy of eighteen years, bellowed that he burned most awfully with love for the middle daughter of Morel the Giwe, by name Avigay, and that the said Avigay burned most awfully with love for him; and he demanded a judgement as to whether he was free to wed her openly in a church. O manners. Whereat the four Giwen pranced, foaming at the mouth and coughing so violently, that I had them gagged again, while I ate my pudding and pondered these complexities. And, although they were of a most maddening nature, I finally effected their disentanglement, giving judgement as follows: "Ysaak is betrothed to the daughter of Morel, who is three persons. Trigamy being illegal, and sinful, the said betrothal must not be confirmed by marriage. The said betrothal, therefore, is annulled. And Ysaak is free to select one of the three daughters of Morel for a new betrothal. Which selection and betrothal must be made and the marriage consummated within one hour from this present, to make an end of the matter. And the christian Jocelyn Tup is to be well-whipped here and now for lusting after a Giwess." What more, o most affable reader, whoever you are?

XVII. About the Complex Divorce of Rubigotsce alias Sabecock

I remember yet one more example of the bestial depravity of the Giwen; and I will record it and be done with them. Rubigotsce, alias Sabecock, a Giwe of Hereford, came to my court demanding a judgement. And this is another proof of the truth of what I have said before, namely, that the Giwen generally preferred the king's justice to their own, much as they complained about it when complaining suited their base and questionable purposes. The said Rubigotsce averred that he wanted to divorce his wife Duzelina (widow of Moss-with-the-nose),[1] because she gave him no sons to pray for his soul; and, having divorced the said Duzelina, he wanted to marry Cinora, a Giwess of Cambridge, as the detestable law of the Giwen ordains. I asked him then why he did not do so and be damned. He answered that, having been at the point of death with a quinsy[2] a little while ago, he had changed his name of Rubigotsce into Sabecock, so that the angel of death (who, perchance, had received instructions to collect Rubigotsce) might not recognize him under another name. And now he was in a quandary, not knowing whether he need divorce his wife seeing that he was Rubigotsce when he married her and now was Sabecock, or, whether he need not divorce her at all seeing that he was Sabecock who had not married her excepting as Rubigotsce. Wherefore he demanded a judgement. Sickness, sufficient to extinguish a fire, twisted me at this specimen of the superstitious depravity of the Giwen; but, when I had curbed the spasm, it seemed good to me to take the mind of a clergyman before proceeding further; and, my young Brother Bobo Kemp of the Preaching Friars being at hand, I set the question before him. He affirmed that the wretched Giwe was the husband of Duzelina, widow of Moss-with-the-Nose, whether he called himself Rubigotsce or Sabecock; and that no power on earth could separate them, such being the Divine Law. He said, also, that the change of name made no difference in the man's individuality; and the notion of deceiving Messire Saint Azrael Angel of Death was simply silly, first because the blessed angels are not born imbeciles, second, because the blessed angels are God's ministers and (so) experts, third, because the Lord God Omniscient is ware of all and every, and specially of the unspeakable depravity of the Giwen. I, being greatly comforted, then said, "Seeing that this wretched Rubigotsce otherwise Sabecock is one of the king's Giwen, and seeing that these have free liberty of their own law

---

[1] *"Duzelinam Mossis cum Naso viduam."* [Rolfe's note.]
[2] An inflammation of the throat (*OED* OL).

secured to them, and seeing that their said law permits them to divorce their so-called wives, and seeing that my judgement is not asked as to the validity of the proposed divorce but merely as to the name in which the said divorce is to be given, I wish to be advised on this point." Brother Bobo pondered it, while I went on giving judgements on less fantastic matters; and the double-named Giwe bit his finger-nails anxiously in an angle, attending my pleasure. Anon, says Brother Bobo, whispering in my good ear, "It is written in the Sacred Scriptures, of Messire Saint Jacob Patriarch and Confessor, 'Thy name shall no more be called Jacob, but Israel';[1] and yet we find him called variously Jacob or Israel several times afterward." "Enough," says I. And I instantly delivered a blooming judgement, bidding the accursed Giwe to write two bills of divorce, the one with the name of Rubigotsce, the other with the name of Sabecock, and to give the two bills simultaneously to Duzelina (widow of Moss-with-the-Nose) not that it was possible to divorce her, if they had been christians christianly wedded, but, they being Giwen, such was my judgement of their detestable depravity.

And that is all which I have to say about the Giwen. All? It is not half. But the rest I will narrate in a book by itself, as it deserves.

---

[1] Gen. 32:28.

XXI

THE BOOK CALLED ARTHURUS CONQUISTADOR

I. *About a Near End of All*

Now I put all records and even all memories of the past behind me; and I come to the event of this dying year, which has seen my dear lord and brother the king die, and will see my death too when I have finished my task. For I am very old, and my strength has left me, and no one wants me, so that I care not for anything, excepting the weariful finishing of these histories, for the glory of my lord the king, in despite of Mr. Matthew (late of Paris) and for that monk's complete confusion. Indeed I have no wish to live beyond that near day when I shall have written all which I have in mind, and when I shall have read these my writings to Earl Fulk the Flame for his sanction. That done, I pray The Lord God, of His Infinite Justice and Mercy, to put me instantly in my place by my said dear lord and brother the king.

II. *About the Report current after Marymas*

This year, then, two days after the festival of Marymas in August, news became rumoured in London of a most horrible felony committed by the Giwen of Lincoln, which crime was being illustrated in every particular by a unique and continuous and perfectly incontrovertible miracle. It was said that the said Giwen of Lincoln had been crucifying a christian boy: which most blissful martyr, though more than a fortnight dead in the height of summer, the sun being in Leo, was miraculously preserved in pristine beauty from corruption, and continued singing aloud a hymn in honour of Madame Saint Mary the Godbearer.[1]

---

[1] This is "Little Saint Hugh of Lincoln." The Jews of Lincoln were said to have crucified him in 1255. According to Jacobs, "the (French) ballad of the Jew-boy

It was said also that men of Lincoln city and shire, not only Giwen but christians also, had died of sheer affright at so astounding a portent.

III. *About the Relighting of the Fire*

I instantly sent Sir John of Lexington, a man of learning, wise as well as prudent, to Lincoln, with a power of fifty knights and five-hundred well-mounted footmen with the usual trumpets, to examine the matter and to bring me a report of it. And then I went fast, with ten horses to my litter, to the castle of Windsor, to take the mind of the king. As I feared (though I knew it to be my bounden duty as Brother of the King), this was to lay the spark to all the fuel collected in King Arthur's lifetime in the furnace of his regal fury against his Giwen. But I did relight that fierce devouring flame, deliberately and without compunction, knowing (as I well knew) that the time had come when King Arthur's wrath, like a consuming fire, must be allowed to rage, nay, must be urged to rage, till it was quite burned out. I thought (old fool which I am) that it would consume the king's Giwen, and rid the kingdom of their pestilential depravity. I never imagined that it would burn up the only cord which tethered my lord and brother the king to an earthly kingdom, that it would purge the only earthly dross which weighed that pure gold regal soul down from attaining his kingdom celestial.

IIII. *About the Fire Relighted*

King Arthur heard my news, in the queen's wonderful garden, the paradise, where he chanced to be taking the air in the cool of the evening. And, because of my legs, he would not have me rise from the litter to kneel to him: but he came and stood by me, holding my hand, and helping me to deliver myself of my dreadful burthen. As I spoke, I looked straight into his kingly eyes: he, into mine; and I saw the little sparks of his irrefrainable fury flash

---

who was converted and murdered by his father, and sang hymns to the Virgin after death, occurs in many English MSS" (342). Matthew Paris recounts the story of the boy's execution in detail.

out, and flicker, floating to and fro. As I spoke, I declare that I saw the last threads of colour leave the yellow-silver hair of his grand head and of his fine clipped beard, and the last sunny honey-hued tinge fade from his ever-young unwrinkled skin. And, when I had spoken, he still stood, lithe as a great boy, but rigid with the instant rigour of one who has just taken a whole lance-head in his groin, white in summer raiment of silk, white as new ivory touched with hoar-frost, as clear, as smooth, as hard, as cold; and in his adamantine eyes were scintillating flames of fire.

"This must be the end, Brother Hubert:" at length says he.

"This must be the end, Brother and Lord King:" says I.

v. *About the Issue of the Mandates of Summons*

Having spoken together of the way whereby the end might be best attained, I and King Arthur devised a new mandate for Sir John of Lexington, instructing him to take the Giwen of Lincoln (every male of them above the age of reason) with all and every other Giwen found and inculpated in the same city, with the bailies and other credible witnesses, and to bring these at the king's cost to the Tower of London, without delay.[1] And a second mandate was sent to the chapter of Lincoln, ordaining that the canons should instantly repair to London, translating thither the blissful body of the martyr with suitable pomp and reverence: for my lord the King was minded to let all England see and know the inveterate depravity of the Giwen, and the marvellous manifestation of Divine Justice, before His Regal Majesty did justice on the criminals. Lastly, that this signal doing of justice might have primary and perdurable importance, my lord the king ordained that the trial of his Giwen should take place at a great crown-wearing, in King William Redhair's hall in the palace of Westminster, before the bishops and magnates and knights and commons of England: on which account, he indited a third mandate of summons to the Shire-reeve of Lincoln, a certain earl Hubert de Burgh, in form following: *We Arthur the King do order you that you cause to come before*

---

[1] In response to the accusations concerning the murder of Little Saint Hugh, Henry III imprisoned ninety-two of the Jews of Lincoln in the Tower of London and executed eighteen.

Us and Our justiciars at Westminster on the morrow of the festival of Messire Saint Oswald King and Martyr[1] next insuing twenty-four legal and discreet knights of your shire and neighbourhood of Lincoln and twenty-four legal and discreet burgesses of the city of Lincoln to certify Us and Our foresaid justiciars concerning the death of Hugh son of Beatrix whom as is said Our Giwen have crucified and slain seeing that Our said Giwen accused thereof and detained in Our prison at Our Tower of London are put upon the verdict of the foresaid knights and burgesses.

vi. *About the forced Defection of Earl Hubert de Burgh*

But, on the festival of Messire Saint John Baptist his Decollation,[2] my leeches on their part also issued a mandate, forbidding me from appearing in my proper person, at Westminster, as Shire-reeve of Lincoln and Chief Justiciar of England and Ireland, on the day appointed for the trial of the Giwen, alleging that the pangs of being moved thither, and the commotion of mind certain to be provoked by so portentous a solemnity, would procure my death. And, having said this to the king, they instantly took sanctuary to avoid the *peine fort et dure*[3] which I ordained my tormentors to administer to them. And, when king Arthur had heard them, and also a report of my weakness from some little tattling busybody here, whom my said tormentors have never been able to discover for me, he sent me word that he himself would sit as Chief-Justiciar, with the other six as his assessors; and he bade me to name earl Fulk the Flame as my proxy for my shire-reevery of Lincoln, for the occasion of the great crown-wearing, while I stayed here at my ease, quietly taking care of my health. Consequently, o most affable reader, you shall understand that what I shall narrate hereafter is what earl Fulk the Flame told me. And it is truth, he being my brother and both of us being brothers of the king.

vii. *About King Arthur preparing his Regal Majesty*

King Arthur went into the abbey of Westminster from the

---

[1] August 5.

[2] The beheading of St. John the Baptist, which is celebrated on August 29.

[3] A type of torture typically applied to those who refuse to speak.

palace, with his canopy and trumpets, soon after sunrise, to pray alone; and he was shriven of Brother Adam at his regal faldstool, before the mass which the Primate Boniface sang for the Regal Majesties by sanction of the abbot of Westminster. And Queen Mariol kneeled in her place by the king. And King Arthur received his rites with great gravity; and his kingly eyes brimmed with tears when The Body of The Lord came to him. After, he prayed again till nine of the dial, when he went to dinner. He ate sparingly, refusing all the spits presented, and only consenting to let the sewer[1] mince a plover for him when earl Fulk fil-Richard affirmed that the occasion was not one for either fasting or abstinence.

VIII. *About the Court prepared*

The great hall in the palace of Westminster was set after this manner. Very high above the three-and-thirty steps at the end, were set the thrones of great silver panthers of the king and queen, with a cloth of estate, and a reredos,[2] and a canopy, of England and Hierusalem, upheld by the two-and-thirty magnates of my Cinq Ports. Round and about the thrones, were heralds, trumpets, knights of Saint George, knights of Saint Thomas of the Candid Girdle, great officers of the regal household, all with their proper coats, banners, and insignia. On each side, and a little lower, were set three small thrones: these for the six justiciars. Below again, were set twenty-four seats for the legal and discreet knights, on the one hand, and twenty-four seats for the legal and discreet burgesses, all of Lincoln, shire or city, who were to give their verdict. Along the sides of the hall, reaching half-way, were let the seats for the magnates of England: each earl being attended by a knight with his banner and a squire with his shield and a page with his gloves. Half-way down the hall, in the middle, was set a great octagonal scaffold as high as a tall man's eyes, covered with damask of scarlet with great golden primroses. On the edge of this scaffold, stood eight acolyths wearing albs[3] and amycts[4] with

---

[1] An attendant at meals who oversaw the table and the serving of dishes (*OED* OL).
[2] An ornamental screen or wall-hanging (*OED* OL).
[3] Long, white tunics (*OED* OL).
[4] Pieces of white linen wrapped around the head and neck.

scarlet apparels, guarding eight monstrous torches of pure wax; and there were also eight thurifers,[1] similarly arrayed, offering frankincense in golden thuribles,[2] one thurifer between each pair of acolyths, one acolyth between each pair of thurifers, sixteen boys in all and sons of earls. And, high on the middle of this scaffold, was set another smaller scaffold, like a bier, elevated as high as a boy's waist, covered with damask of scarlet with great golden primroses, and a canopy over it of the same, whose poles were borne by four canons of Lincoln during the trial. On the floor of the hall, on that side of the scarlet octagonal scaffold which faced the regal thrones, was set an archiepiscopal throne for the primate of all England raised on five steps, with thrones about it for the episcopal officers of the primacy raised on three steps; and, there, were set thrones for the bishops and mitred abbots of England. And round and about the said scaffold, were set seats for friars and monks and clergymen of low degrees.

Thus, was the court set for the trial of the Giwen, namely, foursquare, with the Regal Majesties and their officers and the six justiciars and the eight-and-forty jurors on the first side, and the scarlet octagonal scaffold with the bishops and abbots and clergymen of the third side, and the magnates and knights enclosing the vast empty square of the middle space on the second and fourth sides. And the lower half of the hall, below the scarlet octagonal scaffold, was filled to the great door by the commons of England. But the Chief Justiciar and the Shire-reeve of Lincoln were absent, the earl-palatine of Kent being infirm and bidden to stay at home with the Constable of the Tower. Oh me.

VIIII. *About the Great Entrance*

At the high end of the hall, from the palace, entered the Regal Majesties with their trumpets: they wore habits of white silk, with coats of *England* and *Hierusalem*, and mantles of silver tissue reversed with the ermine of *Armorica*, and garlands of rose-rubies confined their hair. Before them, went my grandson Sir Arthur

---

[1] People carrying incense (*OED* OL).
[2] Censers (*OED* OL).

de Burgh of Richborough, carrying the banners of England and Hierusalem: and my son Sir Hubert II de Burgh who will soon have my earldom of Gloucester, carrying the orbs of Hierusalem: and my son Sir John de Burgh the vice-constable of my Kentish castles and subwarden of my Cinq Ports who will soon have my palatine-earldom of Kent and my earldom of Essex, carrying the orbs of England: and earl Hubert fil-Fulk of Brecon, carrying the sceptres of Hierusalem: and Sir Arthur fil-Fulk of Holderness, carrying the sceptres of England: and earl Richard fil-Fulk of Penthieve, carrying the caps of Acquitaine, Maine, Touraine, Poictou, Anjou: and earl Edmund Plantagenet called Crutchback of Lancaster (that perpetual crusader), carrying the caps of Normandy: and prince Fulk Plantagenet of Galilee, carrying the coronets of Armorica, Ireland, Wales: and Lord Edward Plantagenet of England (wearing *Gascony*) carrying the five-crossed crowns of Hierusalem: and earl Fulk fil-Richard called The Flame of Richmond and Jaffa and Nantes and prince of Tyre, carrying the great crowns of England, with his thirteen-year-old grandson, Mr Arthur fil-Hubert of Brecon, a page of the Majesty, as his page to carry his coronets. But the earl-palatine of Kent and the earl of Gloucester and Essex had to be absent on account of infirmity. Oh me.

x. *About the first Silence*

When the Regal Majesties were inthroned upon their silver panthers, then the great doors far away at the other end of the hall were opened; and the morning-sunlight streamed in, laying a pathway of gold. And an immense silence fell on all the multitude of magnates and commons waiting within: nor was there any movement, not even of the straight flames of the eight tall torches on the scaffold, but only the movement of light shimmering on the mystical candour of the silk and silver and ermine of majesty, in the shade of the canopy, high over all.

xi. *About the first Sound*

Through that silence, came the gentle gentle sound of reverent footsteps, footsteps, drawing nearer, nearer, nearer. And, weaving and woven among the gentle gentle sound of footsteps, footsteps, footsteps, drawing nearer, nearer, nearer, nearer, through the silence came—oh, marvel—came a thin sweet fresh little thread of a voice, ebbing, flowing, leaping exultantly high, sinking fully and low, a young boy's limpid unearthly voice, singing, singing, as though to her and himself alone, a song in honour of God's Mother. And every breath was stilled to listen. And every eye was strained to see.

XII. About the Procession of the Marvellous Songster

Entered, out of the sunlight, a solemn procession from my convent of Black Friars by Ludgate, a procession of the friars and monks and clergymen of England, of bishops and abbots in scarlet capes carrying their crooks and precious mitres, surrounding a cluster of canons of Lincoln, who bore aloft a golden ark or feretory,[1] wherein lay at length the blissful martyr, singing alone and incessantly, as a quirister sings in his dreams:

> O Virgo prudentissima
> quam caelo missus Gabriel
> Supremi Regis nuntius
> plenam testatur gratiâ.[2]

And, after the marvellous songster, came my son Boniface the Primate of All England, preciously mitred, carrying his archiepiscopal crozier, attended by the bishops of his primatial court; and in his left hand, he led a woman darkly veiled in blue.

Through the silence silently they passed along, silent, save

---

[1] A shrine that contains a saint's relics. (OED OL)

[2] This hymn appears to be quite in the best manner of Canon Angelo Ambrogini, tutor of Leo P.M. X. and Clement P.M. VII: but it is difficult to prove that the MSS. of Hubert de Burgh ever came under the notice of "Poliziano," though it is pretty plain (from some of his Greek verses alone) that that writer was not a bit above lifting from prior writers.—P. and C. [Rolfe's note.] Poliziano, a Renaissance poet, wrote a poem, "O Virgo prudentissima," in praise of the Virgin Mary. The lines sung by Saint Hugh reproduce Poliziano's verse word for word. The first stanza in English: "Oh most prudent virgin / to whom Gabriel, sent from heaven, / messenger of heaven's king, / bears witness, (woman) full of grace."

for the dead boy's miraculous singing: a miracle undeniable, for
who ever heard of a dead boy singing, without ceasing, daily and
nightly, for more than a month from his martyrdom, not in the
ears of fools, or of liars, or of ecstatics, not in the ears of nine or of
nineteen, but in the ears of a nation, a hard-headed nation? And,
when they came to the scaffold of scarlet damasked with golden
primroses, there they lifted and set the golden ark high on the
bier beneath the canopy, spacing the acolyths with waxen torches
and the thurifers with golden thuribles round it, so that all might
see the dreadful deed of the Giwen and the wonderful works of
God.

XIII. *About the Crown-wearing for the Marvellous Songster*

My son the Primate Boniface left the blue-veiled woman
weeping quietly on the steps of his archiepiscopal throne, by the
martyr's feretory: but he passed on with his pomp, ascending
the three-and-thirty steps to the canopy of the Regal Majesties.
There, to the sound of trumpets, he crowned Arthur the King and
Mariol the Queen with the crowns of England, delivering also the
sceptres and orbs of regal insignia, while bishops and abbots and
magnates did on their precious mitres and their coronets. Then,
he returned to his own primatial throne by the scaffold. And the
marvellous voice of the martyr went on singing:

> *Cuius deuota humilitas*
> *gemmis ornata fulgidis*
> *fidentis conscientiae*
> *amore deum rapiat.*

XIIII. *About the Martyr the Marvellous Songster*

The king and the queen, robed and crowned and sceptred and
orbed in regal majesty, came down with their court, through the
vast void square space in the hall, and ascended the scarlet octagonal scaffold damasked with great gold primroses, to venerate the
blissful martyr.

Earl Fulk says that that one was a slim little healthy boy of the people, strongly and finely formed, thirteen years old, lying quite straight and still, stark, in the gilded ark, wherein the canons had laid him on scarlet samite for greater reverence, leaving open the arches of its sides and ends so that all might see and hear. Earl Fulk says also: his small round head was clustered with red-shining hair: his flesh was as white as cream, and faintly flushed where the scarlet samite kissed it; and he lay at length, on his back, with his light feet pointed together, and his hands palms-downward by his thighs, as a child stretched out in sleep. Earl Fulk says further: the pretty eyes were closed, the eyes of the innocent perfectly-satisfied happy face of the little red-gleaming head which reposed on the pillow of scarlet samite: but the smiling mouth was a little open, the rosy lips rhythmically moving, letting glimpses of little white teeth be seen; and the slender throat which sprang from the firm white motionless breast throbbed and swelled with melody, soft and slow and true, thrilling at times, piercing the heart like the note of a dreaming bird in a wonderful night of starlight far from men, singing:

Te sponsam Factor omnium
te matrem Dei Filius
te vocat habitaculum
Suum Beatus Spiritus.

And the pure young brow was marked with the wounds of thorns. And the little right hand and the little left foot were marked with the prints of nails. And the little left wrist and the little right ankle were abraded with light-drawn cords. And over the heart was the wound of a spear. And, below it, was the gash, of the length of a man's hand, whereby . . . (*Horroris causâ deest tralatio*)[1]. . . . But earl Fulk the Flame says that none of these cruel mutilations was molesting to the mind: for the canons of Lincoln had washed and purified them, and Almighty God was deigning, to these tokens of passion, a similar glory, a similar starlike white-

---

[1] Literally, "Because of horror, the translation is missing." In other words, "There's no translation, because it would be too horrible." According to Matthew Paris, the Jews of Lincoln pierced Hugh's heart with a lance and disemboweled him.

ness, a similar fascination of radiance, to the splendid scar in the
hallowed hand of our lord and brother King Arthur.

xv. *About the Majesty and the Martyr the Marvellous Songster*

When the Regal Majesties had ascended to the golden feretory, they stood awhile, gazing, dumb with wonder at its content,
the melodious marvel. For the dead boy sang, with a smile of ineffable happiness, in the low clear voice of one who knows more
than men:

> *Per te de tetro carcere*
> *antiqui patres exeunt*
> *per te nobis astriferae*
> *panduntur aulae limina.*

And my lord the king and my lady the queen, having kneeled
to thank God for so signal and comprehensible an exposition of
His Omnipotence, rose; and, bending down, they kissed those
glorious scars one by one and the singing mouth of the martyr.
And, receiving again their sceptres and orbs, they turned, descending, from the reliquary, to cross the empty space and to ascend to
their thrones and canopy.

xvi. *About Majesty and the Mother of the Martyr the Marvellous Songster*

But, when they came down into the hall, and were passing the
primatial throne of my son Boniface, the woman darkly veiled
in blue (who stood there) suddenly sank upon her knee, lifting a
face smirched with unspeakable agony to worship the Regal Majesties; and, "Justice, lord king:" cries she, with the shriek of one
bereaved of all and demanding dreadful dooms.

King Arthur stayed in his progress. "Lord king," says my son,
the Primate Boniface, "you see Beatrix of Lincoln, mother of
this blissful martyr here inshrined, crying to heaven and to Your
Regal Majesty for justice." "Hail, Beatrix, blessed among mothers, and be very sure that exact justice shall be done:" says King

Arthur. And, when she made to kiss that hallowed hand of his, which earls and archbishops—and, now, archangels—joy to see, he did not forbid her: but, crowned king as he was, he stooped to let her have her will, baring his hand of the glove. But Queen Mariol relinquished her sceptre and orb to Sir Arthur fil-Fulk of Holderness; and she took the desolate Beatrix in her lovely regal arms. And, "Go on alone, my lord and king, and do your justice," says she: "But my part is to stay here for the comfort of this most honourable afflicted mother:" says she. And Queen Mariol kissed Beatrix on the lips; and she sat down, crowned, and robed in tissue of silver and ermine, on the scaffold by the feretory, cherishing the wan mother of the martyr.

My lord the king ascended high to his lonely throne; and let sound the trumpets summoning the prisoners for trial. Earl Fulk says: at that moment, every fibre of every limb of our dear lord and brother the king began to quiver with the shocking vehement access of his anger: he sat alone, and very high, on the great silver panthers of his throne, refraining himself, wrestling with himself, stiffening in rigour, beneath his canopy of England and Hierusalem; and awfully his eyes like adamant began to glitter in the mystic obscurity. He was very stark.

XVII. *About the Murderers of the Martyr the Marvellous Songster*

Excepting the gasps or hiccoughs of some moved magnates, and the low sobs of the martyr's mother, and the gentle soothing murmurs of Queen Mariol there was no other sound in that vast hall, but the rhythmical sweet melody which welled from the dead in the golden ark. That still went on, at its regular intervals, now crooning quietly, like a lullaby for invoking long-sighing sleep:

> *Tu stellis comam cingeris*
> *te lunam premis pedibus*
> *te sole amictam candido*
> *chori stupent angelici.*

Entered, then, a procession of pikemen, escorting my lord the king's Grey Friars of Newgate, with nine-hundred-and-ninety-four of my lord the king's Giwen, from the dungeons of this Tower of London. A terrible growl arose from the commons of England, as these passed up the hall through the crowd, a terrible snarling growl menacing instant death. And, but for the squadron of friars who went in front, and the pikemen who walked at the flanks and in rear of the prisoners, no whole Giwe would have got as far as the scaffold of the feretory: they would have been torn to pieces alive by furious boys. As for the mien of those accursed and doomed ones, they huddled and cowered together, every movement a mere paralytic gesture of terror; and their hanging heads, and their downcast shifty eyes, and the awful clack of their dry tongues on their fevered palates, bespoke their shame and most hideous anxiety. And, above the sound of their slipshod staggering, of their clanking chains, of the rubbing of their greasy gaberdines, and, above the terrific minacious[1] snarling of the commons, and the grinding teeth of magnates, high above all shrilled the soaring light-resounding singing of the martyr:

Audi virgo puerpera
et sola mater integra
audi precantes quaesumus
tuos Maria Seruulos.

Yet, as the Giwen passed the golden feretory, wherein lay the bright example of their crime, they cringed almost to the earth, dragging, themselves fearfully by the thrones of bishops and abbots, till they were shot out into the empty space prepared for them, between the blissful martyr, and the king with his justiciars and jurors, where grey friars clustered on the throne-steps; and pikemen hemmed them squarely in.

XVIII. *About the Testimony of Sir John of Lexington*

Sir John of Lexington read my mandate directing him to inquire concerning the accusation against the king's Giwen; and he testified, saying as follows: "I came to Lincoln on the festi-

---

[1] Menacing (*OED* OL).

val of Messire Saint Bartholomew Apostle;[1] and I summoned
fifty respectable burgesses to declare their minds to me in this
matter. They said, that the King's Giwen living in their city had
been stealing a christian boy named Hugh, of the age of thirteen years, son of Beatrix, a widow; and, shutting him in a secret
chamber, where they fed him on milk and other childish food to
strengthen him, they sent to all the cities of England inhabited
by Giwen, summoning the chiefs of that sect from every city, to
be present at a sacrifice at Lincoln, in contumely and insult of
Jesus Christ; for they had a perfect boy concealed there for the
purpose of crucifying him. A great number of Giwen forthwith
assembled at Lincoln; and they elected a Giwe of Lincoln to act
the part of Pontius Pilate; by whose sentence, and with the concurrence of all concerned, the boy was subjected to various torments. They scourged every inch of him from shoulders to heel
till blood flowed: they crowned him with barberry-thorns: they
mocked at and spat upon him: they gave him gall to drink: they
scoffed at him with blasphemous insults; gnashing their teeth and
calling him Jesus the false prophet: they crucified him: and they
thrust a spear into the depth of his heart. When he was dead, they
took the body down from the cross, and (for some reason, it was
said for the purpose of their magic arts) they eviscerated it, filling
the cavity with goose-feathers. And the sacred body was found,
and the crime discovered, in a miraculous manner, by the martyr's own mother. Thus much, the gossip which I collected from
the burgesses. And, on it, I proceeded with my inquisition. But,
when the regal mandate reached me, then, I altered my method
in these particulars following. First, I caused the city-gates to
be shut and guarded, and the walls manned, forbidding egress
on pain of death at sight. Eight of the king's Giwen, attempting
escape, met painful ends in this manner. Second, the body of the
martyr Hugh, had been given by the bailies to the canons of Lincoln who had asked for it, displaying it honourably in their cathedral, openly, to an immense number of people as the precious
body of a martyr. This I permitted, till the time when the feretory for its reverent transport to London, which I commanded at

---

[1] August 24.

the king's cost, should be completed, all for the greater glory of God. Third, I took Beatrix, and the two bailies of the city, with seven-and-forty credible christian witnesses, who were present at the miracle of the finding of the body; and I secluded them comfortably in the castle. Fourth, I used my power of knights and men-at-arms to sweep every living thing out of every house in the city, simultaneously and unexpectedly, and to cause every male of seven years old and upward to pass before me where I was holding my inquest in the chancery; and, to each such male, I proffered the Holy Cross for reverent adoration. By this simple means, I sifted Giwen from Christians; and I found them to be nine-hundred-and-ninety-four persons, whom I have conveyed hither, with the said Beatrix, and the said two bailies, and the said seven-and-forty christian witnesses, that my lord the king may do justice in the matter." Thus, Sir John of Lexington. And the fresh young voice of the incorrupt dead sang clearly, clearly, carelessly, as a sweet boy sings in spring-time's moonbeams:

> *Repelle mentis tenebras*
> *disrumpe cordis glaciem*
> *nos sub tuum praesidium*
> *confugientes protege.*

XVIIII. *About the Testimony of Beatrix of Lincoln*

King Arthur said, "Let Us hear Beatrix, the mother of the boy Hugh." And he spoke so appallingly, in a harsh dead voice devoid of vibrance so utterly unlike his own, that the six justiciars and the forty-eight jurors below him, turned, looking upward to see who had spoken. And King Arthur said again, in words which cut and stung like the wounds made by jagged icicles, "Let Us hear Beatrix, the mother of the boy Hugh." Queen Mariol brought the shuddering woman darkly veiled in blue, right through the mob of Giwen clotted in black swathes on the floor, up the steps of the throne, a little above the grey friars, a little below the jurors, Beatrix said, and my lady the queen (crowned and robed in regal

majesty) held her, comforting her while she was speaking thus:[1]
"I waited all night for my little boy: but he did not return. As soon
as daylight came, I, with dreadful busy thought, sought him at
the school. Some neighbours said that they had last seen him in
the Giwerie, playing with some children of his own age. But the
Giwerie is a street through which men ride, open at both ends;
and, at the farther end, is the christian school, where very many
children of christian blood learn to sing and read their doctrine,
as small children do in childhood. I, half out of my mind, and
with a mother's piety in my breast, went first to every other place
where I supposed that I by likelihood might find my boy; and
only afterward did I seek him in the Giwerie. And most piteously
I begged of every Giwe who dwelled there, to tell me whether my
child had passed them by; and they denied it. Then, Jesus of His
Grace put this thought in me that, in that very place where I cried
for my son, there he was hidden secretly." Here the voice of the
dead trilled limpidly, ever so softly:

> *Da nobis in proposito*
> *sancto perseverantiam*
> *ne noster adversarius*
> *in te sperantes saperet.*

Beatrix, shaken with sobbing, flung up her hands to the radiant
feretory, when the young voice flowed through the fragrant cloud
of frankincense; and she surely would have swooned: but Queen
Mariol supported her, comforting her, urging her to continue her
testimony. And Beatrix, waning, said, "Oh, lord king, thus then he
sang when he was alive; and thus he sang when dead, so that I found

---

[1] Query: whether this is not the original of the Canterbury Tale of Chaucer's
Prioress?—P. and C. [Rolfe's note.] The following passage reproduces sections
of Chaucer's "The Prioress's Tale," which similarly deals with a boy martyr
murdered by the Jews:

  This povre wydwe awaiteth al that nyght
  After hir litel child, but he cam noght;
  For which, as soone as it was dayes light,
  With face pale of drede and bisy thoght,
  She hath at scole and elles-where hym soght,
  Til finally she gan so fer espie,
  That he last seyn was in the Jewerie.

him." King Arthur asked her, "Beatrix, why does he so sing?" Beatrix responded, saying: "Lord king, I know not: but he always has sung so since he was nine years old. For, when he sat reading in his little primer at school, he used to hear the quiristers learning their antiphonary[1] and singing this same song. And, when he dared, he drew near to hear the words and the notes, till he had gotten the first strophe of this sweet song by rote. He knew not what the Latin was to signify, being of an age so young and tender: wherefore he asked his comrade to expound this song in his language, or to tell him why it was in usage. Often, on his little bare knees he begged this knowledge. His fellow was older than my child; and, thus, he answered: 'This song, as I have heard say, is about Madame Saint Mary the Virgin God-bearer, to salute her, and to pray that she will succour us when we die. But, more, I know not: for I learn song-singing, and I know but little grammar.' Then says my innocent child: 'And is this song made in reverence of God's Mother? Then I will do my diligence to learn it all by Christmas, though I neglect my primer and be shaken, or beaten, three times in each hour, yet, for our Lady's honour, I will learn it all.' Thus, my little son. And, thereafter, as they wended homeward, his fellow taught him privily from day to day, till he had it all in mind, and sang it well and boldly word by word according to the note. Twice in each day this song passed through his sweet throat, when he went schoolward, when he came homeward: so, on God's Mother, did he meditate, that, in her honour, as he went to and fro, full merrily he used to sing *O virgo prudentissima*: nor could he ever stint of his clear singing." Then, shrilled the boy, who, in his golden feretory, lay stark and dead, high above the multitudinous murmuring of England congregated there, like a little lark upspringing, singing blithely, over an army passing across a moor:

> *Sed et cunctis fidelibus*
> *qui tuum templum uisitant*
> *benigna mater dexteram*
> *da caelestis auxilii.*

Beatrix sobbed bitterly for some time; and continued, saying:

---

[1] A book containing the verses sung alternately by two choirs.

"When my heart told me that I should find my little son in Giwe-rie, there I set myself to search all night. And, when dawn-light had come, and children were wending their way to school, sud-denly, somewhere, I knew not where, I heard the sweet voice of my little son, at a great distance, singing his accustomed song." And the dead boy, from the bier of scarlet samite damasked with golden primroses, sang very lowly:

> Ecce virgo concipiens
> intacta Dei genitrix
> ecce Iessea uirgula
> de qua flos pulchra emicat.

Beatrix, aided by my lady the queen, continued, saying: "I intently listened, to hear whether the voice of my child came nearer to me. But since it remained, singing unceasingly at regular intervals, but very far away (as it seemed) I put myself quietly to follow. Seven days and nights did I follow it; and many christians, my friends, joined themselves to me: for the Giwen were increasing in number about me, and I could go but slowly alone. And, on the eighth day, which was the day after Lammas, because I had many christian friends with me, and because of another reason, no obstacle impeded me, no door was shut upon me demanding my little son. For it seemed that the Giwen, whom we met, were struck mad, or dumb, or pal-sied by some immense fear. So, I went more freely through the Giwerie, entering every chamber of every house, coming always nearer to the song and singing-voice of my sweet child till I came to the house of the Giwe called Little Jacob, here present as I believe; and, there, I found my lovely boy." At which word, Beatrix swooned away: whom my lady Queen Mariol hastened to bear, in her regal arms, to the lofty golden feretory, where her son lay, stark, slain by atrocious Giwen, but pouring out a sweeter greater strain of his flowerlike song, blithely and bravely singing:

> Huc huc omnes occurite
> Immanuelem visere
> Que in iacentem praesepio
> vos adorant et asinus.

And my lady the queen let the dolorous mother rest her brow on the little cold feet of her blissful boy, so admirably illustrated by his marvellous singing. Then, strongly cried Queen Mariol, across the great square of the hall, where the Giwen crouched in agonies of most fearful and most appalling conviction. "That, lord king," says she, "is the testimony of Beatrix; and the rest you must hear from the bailies and the christians of Lincoln."

xx. *About King Arthur his Rising Rage because of the Martyr the Marvellous Songster*

King Arthur sat immutable, to all seeming on the panthers of his silver throne, his adamantine eyes fixed wide-open ominously glaring, in the shadows of the canopy, high and distant, over and away from all, like a white god chiselled hardly out of the flawless inflexible impenetrable light of the brightness of sharpened steel. And sweat poured down from the frost-white waves of hair which his great crown encircled, so that the neck of his coat was wetted and the ermine of his mantle. Moreover, the glove on his hallowed hand split across the back, loosening the ornament of rose-rubies there: such was the inconceivable violence of his grip on the golden sceptre. Fulk the Flame, no less frantic with wrath, sent Mr. Arthur his page running to the palace for a pitcher of fresh water: But my lord the king would not even notice it. And the clear little voice of the long dead boy carolled gloriously:

> *Cuius Natali iubilant*
> *celsi reges exercitus*
> *et magnum nocte gaudium*
> *adnuntiant pastoribus.*

Still my lord the king remained rapt in the ecstasy of his ever-increasing anger. And, anon the rippling voice of the dead flowed on noncurantly again, like a stream exultantly dancing with sunbeams:

> *Videte stellam praeviam*
> *Sanctis Eois regibus*
> *qui vagiente Domino*
> *aurum myrrhum tus offerunt.*

XXI. *About the Testimony of the Bailies of Lincoln*

"Let Us hear the bailies of Lincoln:" at length says King Arthur, in a voice which boomed like a sudden passing-bell. So, the bailies of Lincoln stood up together; and the senior began to testify, saying: "Lord king, we confess our fault and humbly sue for mercy. For, when the widow Beatrix came to us, crying that her holy son was lost, we spoke roughly, saying that it was the habit of well-grown lads to play truant now and again, and that we were not to be bothered in the matter. Wherefore, she went away, grievously weeping, and for good cause, as it now seems, though then we were ignorant of it. But, anon, hearing that there were dreadful doings in the Giwerie of our city, thither we flitted, thinking to protect the king's Giwen according to law; and, in the house called Dunestall, occupied by the Giwe called Little Jacob, we indeed came upon most dreadful doings, namely, these, in manner following. In the middle of this house, we saw a courtyard, foursquare, but rather longer on the north and south sides than on the east and west sides: which courtyard contained numerous christians, chiefly women, all making noise, and not a Giwe to be seen, excepting at certain windows looking over, and most fearfully frightened. And we heard the voice of a young child singing a holy song, as sing the quiristers in the cathedral; but, at first, we saw not the singer. And, on looking closer, in a corner of the said courtyard, we saw a pit or wardrope,[1] wherein the Giwen purge their entrails. And, on the verge of this pit, we saw the widow Beatrix, sobbing bitterly, waving her hands, and crying, 'O cursed folk, o new Herods, what will your ill intent avail you, murder will out, it surely cannot fail,' and words like those. Further, lord king, when we looked where she looked in the wardrope, there, this gem of chastity, this emerald, this bright ruby of martyrdom, lay upright among the ordure;[2] and, though slain, he sang so loudly, that all the place rang, echoing his holy song. We therefore, hastily sent for the provost: he came without tarrying; and, praising Christ the King and heaven, and Christ

---

[1] A privy (*OED* OL).
[2] Excrement (*OED* OL).

His Mother the honour of mankind, he let bind the Giwen found there lest any should escape from justice. But we took up the dead boy out of the wardrope, with most piteous lamentation, he singing his song alway; and, having washed him, we carried him to the cathedral that he might there be honoured with proper solemnities. But his mother would not leave him: nor could any bring this new Rachel[1] from that bier. And so we pray mercy, lord king, from your Regal Majesty and this most blissful martyr." Thus, the bailies of Lincoln. And the sweet little voice of the dead sang again, solemn, and slow:

> *Heu iam tenellum sanguinem*
> *fundit ex lege veteri*
> *dum simeonis gremis*
> *Desideratus incubat.*

XXII. *About the Testimony of Sir John of Lexington most horridly continued*

Sir John Lexington stood up; and he said, "Lord king, I have more to say now." King Arthur answered not a word. Shadows deepened about him, there, aloft; and the awful whiteness of his frown glowed like lightning in snow-time, freezingly pallid with the perfervid pallor of devouring fire. Even his strong white teeth were seen, bare, gleaming. And the gentle dulcet voice rippling from the golden feretory, sang:

> *Uidete matrem uirginem*
> *Herodis metu pauidam*
> *latentem cum Filiolo*
> *Aegypti regionibus.*

Seeing how silence held King Arthur then, Sir John made bold to continue his testimony. "Lord king," says he, "be it known to Your Regal Majesty that, obeying Your mandate, as I believe, I took aside Your Giwe, by name Little Jacob, in the wardrope of whose house

---

[1] "Thus says the LORD: In Ramah is heard the sound of moaning, of bitter weeping! Rachel mourns her children, she refuses to be consoled because her children are no more" (Jer. 31:15).

was found the body of this most blissful martyr marked by indu-
bitable wounds, he being (for that reason) a very great object of
suspicion. To whom I said: 'Wretched man, do you not know that
a speedy end awaits you? All the gold in England would not suffice
to ransom or to save you. Yet, unworthy as you are, I will tell you
how you can save your life and limb from destruction; and both of
these I will save you, if (without fear or falsehood) you will expose
to me all which has been done in this matter.' And this Giwe, this
Little Jacob, thinking that he had found a way of escape, answered
me, saying, 'Sir, if you will repay my words with deeds, I will
shew wondrous things to you.' And, when I zealously urged and
encouraged him, he said: 'What the christians allege of us, is true.
For, almost every year, we crucify one boy at least in injury and
insult to Jesus Christ. But a perfect boy is not found every year: for
we must work privately and in secret places. And this boy Hugh,
we Giwen indeed crucified mercilessly; and, after he was dead, we
eviscerated him, for the body of a virginal boy is considered useful
for augury,[1] as to when we Giwen may hope to possess again our
city of Hierusalem; and, then, we wished to hide his corpse: but
we could neither bury it nor conceal it. For, in the morning, when
we thought that we had hidden it away safely under the flags of
the courtyard, lo, the very earth vomited and cast it forth, singing
aloud most awfully, as indeed it had sung incessantly, four times in
each hour or oftener, from the very first moment when we began
to torment it when alive. And it lay unburied, a constant menace
by its irrefrainable sweet singing, and a maddening distraction for
us Giwen. At last, thinking to stifle that terrible adorable voice,
we thrust the corpse into the ordure of the wardrope. But still we
could not hide it: for, even the insensate ordure shrank from defiling that marvellous head with its nimbus as of red gold, but rather
supported it, floating it up to continue its admirable singing.'"

XXIII. *About King Arthur the Flame of his Ire*

King Arthur suddenly thundered in direful anger, crying to
Sir John of Lexington, "How can you have promised life and limb
to so wicked a being as this? How can you have promised what

---

[1] Divination (*OED* OL).

you have no right to promise? For a murderer and blasphemer, such as this Our Giwe, has deserved to die many times over."[1] At which rebuke, Sir John stood back, and was silent; and a wave of ultimate fear washed over all hearts, at this manifestation of the flaming ire of King Arthur. But, from the golden feretory, the pure little voice welted more limpidly than ever:

> *Cernite mox sollicitam*
> *cum Puer templo disputat*
> *cernite rursus hilarem*
> *dum sacras replet hydrias.*

XXIIII. *About the Confession of the Giwe concerning the Martyr the Marvellous Songster*

The accursed Giwe, Little Jacob, seeing his case desperate, and (therefore) being unafraid of further fulminations, up and said: "My death is imminent, nor can Sir John give me any aid. So, I will now tell all the truth. For, nearly all the Giwen in England agreed to the death of this marvellous songster; and, from nearly every English city, where we have our Giweries, some Giwen were chosen by lot to be present at this sacrifice, as it were at a Paschal sacrifice." And, at that, a most tremendous tumult burst out in the vast immensity of the hall: for all the bishops and magnates and knights and commons of England leaped to their feet, writhing in contortions of fury irresistible, spitting and groaning and yelling against the Giwen; and all the Giwen (or nearly all) fell flat, screaming most frightfully for mercy. But, high above the horrible din, the sweet and inerrable canorous voice of the dead, soared, strongly singing:

> *Spectate miserabilem*
> *de cruce Nati pendulam*
> *commendatam discipulo*
> *cor saeuo fixum gladio.*

---

[1] John of Lexington did pardon a Jew named "Jopin" or "Joscefin" in return for his testimony against the other Jews of Lincoln. Henry III, however, revoked this pardon and had him dragged around the city tied to the tail of a horse and hanged.

xxv. *About Honour for the Mother of the Martyr the Marvellous Songster*

"Lord king," cries Queen Mariol, suddenly, "care for this mother here, when you do your justice." Beatrix kneeled at the foot of the bier, rigid, her arms spread forward to embrace the tender body of her child; and my lady the queen regarded her intensely.

"Let Lady Beatrix be noble: let her have the manors of Belton and Corby by Grantham for her maintenance; and let all men bend the knee to her henceforward. The King wills it:" came in one stupendous breath from the Regal Majesty. And, quickly King Arthur came down from his throne of silver panthers, passing over the necks of his prostrate Giwen, so violently that his mantle of ermine and silver flocked behind him, streaming, fluttering out of the snatching hands of his pages, so irresistibly swift was his going, so very stark was he. And, still more strongly, the voice of the long-dead boy rang out, with a weird and wonderful resonance like to the music of strings and cymbals, singing:

> *Uidete tandem radiis*
> *magna uicentem sidera*
> *undantem plena gratia*
> *splendentem clara gloria.*

Swiftly then King Arthur ascended the octagonal scaffold of scarlet damasked with great gold primroses, where my lady the queen and Beatrix of Lincoln were, by the bier, in the midst of the acolyth's waxen torches and the fragrance of frankincense offered by thurifers. And, first of England, King Arthur bended his regal knee to the mother of the martyr.

xxvi. *About the Marvellous Martyr and the Marvellous Majesty*

There was silence for a great while; and the marvellous voice of the dead sang, in thrilling cadence:

Regina caeli maxima
sanctissima purissima
sustenta tuos seruulos
defende tuum populum.

Then, King Arthur, looking on the innocent dead, spoke again in a full low tone, a tone which seemed to twang the heartstrings of all England, there, with unimagined vibrations of pity and of love: for the live white king, robed and crowned and sceptred and orbed in regal majesty, was speaking face to face with the dead white child, naked and cruelly wounded and outraged atrociously, even as he himself had been in part in the days of his childhood. And, "O dear child," says he, "I ask you, by virtue of the Holy Trinity, to tell me what your cause is for this most piercing-sweet singing, since you are dead, or so it seems to me." And then, o monstrous miracle, the dead lips gently moved, but the dead eyes were shut as in sleep, and the dead boy answered my lord the king: he said, "My heart is speared right through to my backbone; and, by way of my kind, I should have died long time ago, but that Jesus Christ has willed His Glory to endure: wherefore, for the honour of His Mother, I still may sing my song *O Virgo prudentissima*. For I always loved Christ's Mother, that well of mercy, both before that I conned[1] her song and after; and, when I was to lose life, she came to me, bidding me to sing her antiphon in my dying; and methought she laid a grain upon my tongue. And so I sing; for I must sing, in honour of that blissful Mother-Maid, until the grain be taken from my tongue: for she said to me, 'Sing, little child, sing, and fear not that I will forsake you, and I will fetch you when the grain is taken from your tongue.'"[2]

xxvii. *About the Stilling of the marvellous Singing*

King Arthur beckoned my son the Primate Boniface and the bishop of Lincoln. They mounted to him, trembling, for every man in that great hall was quivering in the very marrow of his bones, at so splendid and so awful a manifestation. And, "Lord

---

[1] Learned (*OED* OL).
[2] This detail is also drawn from "The Prioress's Tale."

Primate take away the grain, for we can bear no more of this most piercing-sweet singing:" says King Arthur. "Nay, lord king," promptly says my excellent son Boniface, "for this anointed hand of mine is not worthy, when a regally anointed hand hallowed by the mark of Christ's Passion is toward." King Arthur turned to Lincoln, "Take away the grain, lord bishop, for the blissful martyr is a lamb of your flock:" says he. "Nay, lord king," says that bishop, "for, though I am of the northern province, I follow the southern primate on this special occasion." So, King Arthur drew off the torn glove from his own hallowed hand; and, stooping a little, he caught out the tongue of the martyr, and took away the grain. And the fair boy gave up his spirit to God's Mother. And the pulsing of his singing throat was stilled.

xxviii. *About the Acclamation of the Saint*

King Arthur wrapped the miraculous grain in his glove, and gave it to the bishop of Lincoln: "Keep it as a precious relic:" says he. "And now, what more?" says he. "This much more, lord king," says the bishop, speaking up very boldly: "we have one saint already, called Hugh of Lincoln,[1] and we are greedy for another. Illumined by Great Saint Hugh, sometime our Pastor, we claim this Little Saint Hugh our Martyr. A boon, lord king, we demand this boon!" cries the importunate bishop, betaking himself to his knees, and holding high the glove which contained the miraculous grain.

King Arthur accepted his sceptre; and he stood, crowned and sceptred and orbed, in his robes of regal majesty, by the bier, with the martyr's mother and my lady the queen by his hallowed hand, where the white scar glistened openly, whiter than whatever is whitest, whiter than any star, and the primate and the bishop at his mighty left hand, hand of war, hand of victory, all there aloft on the scaffold of scarlet damasked with golden primroses. And King Arthur raised his hallowed hand, waving the golden sceptre with tremendous gestures of invocation, turning himself in turn to the four quarters of the hall; and mightily he spoke in the tone of archangelic clarions, spoke to the bishops and the magnates

---

[1] Saint Hugh, bishop of Lincoln (c. 1140-1200).

and the knights and the commons: "Speak, England:" says he. And, then, England spoke, in resonant acclamation: "Hail, Little Saint Hugh:" says England. And, says the king of the English, to the dead boy of the golden feretory, "Sing, in heaven, for England, now, o Little Saint Hugh." And he turned to salute Lady Beatrix of Belton and Corby. But Queen Mariol suddenly rose from her regal knees, saying, "Lord king, this mother hears her son singing forever for England before the Son of the Mother of heaven." For Lady Beatrix was dead with Little Saint Hugh. "Now shall justice be done:" says King Arthur.

xxvIIII. *About the Verdict of the Jury*

In swift solemnity the Regal Majesties ascended to the silver thrones high at the shadowy canopy. And, as my lord the king passed, the violent heat of his anger, seven times heated, seared like the scorching blast from a comet. And, on the great silver panthers of his throne, he sat him down, a very panther in power, a panther of panthers in fury; and no magnate dared even to let a breath betray his proximity, so terribly pregnant with awful doom were the rigour of aspect, the lightning-blazing eyes, the tense overwhelming immovable paramount majesty of my lord the king. And, to the legal and discreet knights and burgesses of Lincoln (moving no more than his pitiless inflexible lips), he cried, in a voice like a thunder-clap, "Ye have heard. Ye have seen. And now what verdict will ye give, whereon He may do Our justice?" And the eight-and-forty jurors answered as one man, "We say that the Giwen are guilty of parricide done in contempt of the christian faith."[1] And all England present shouted, "Evil shall he have who evil will deserve." And the six justiciars nodded assent.

---

[1] Parricide is not patricide, as everyone knows.—P. and C. [Rolfe's note.] In the Middle Ages, "parricide" referred not just to murder of the father but to murder of close relations, and the punishment for this crime involved being placed in a sack with a "malfeasant" animal, such as a dog or a viper, and thrown into the river. This penalty was also applied by Charlemagne to "Jews who have committed some evil against the Christian law or against a Christian." See *The Encyclopedia of the Middle Ages*, edited by André Vauchez, Richard Dobson, and Michael Lapdidge (New York: Routledge, 2001), 1091.

xxx. *About the Starkness of King Arthur*

King Arthur sat, as one who devises dooms of unheard-of atrocity, so intense with indignation, so ecstatically raging with boundless fury, that his grand eyes ceased from glittering, and luridly burned, unwinking, unquenchable, like blazing cressets of coal: he was so stark. Now and then, Queen Mariol looked at him: once, indeed, she touched him. But, in his awful white rigour, he saw her not, nor felt her hand. He was so very stark. Now and then, from the mob of his Giwen, clotted in black swathes far below his footstool, came a faint whimper of mortal terror, a faint whine for mercy. But he saw neither Giwe nor christian at that time: nor even heard them. He was so very stark. There was no idea of mercy in his mind. He was quite without ruth.[1] He was inflamed, and consuming, with the loathing and detestation and hatred, secretly flagrant in him, but restrained for fifty years, and now blazing unrestrainedly, with the anger of all the Angevins, and the passion of all the Plantagenets, and his own outrageous wrong, and this new capital felony, so foul, so enormous, that it was rightly called parricide, fuel for the conflagration of his vengeance: so, very stark was my lord the king.

xxxi. *About the Defender of the King's Giwen*

But, like a pure snowflake, tender and refreshing, emerging as a portent on a sunbeam, from a boiling cauldron of offal, dear Brother Adam stood up among the friars minor, and quietly says he, "Brother king, who speaks on behalf of Your Giwen." And, like a great rock hurled from a mangonel, crashed the reply from the throne, "He speaks who dares." "That dare I, brother king," says the grey friar.

xxxii. *About the Daring Defence*

All England gasped with horror, lest a regal fulguration[2] should blast Brother Adam where he stood. None came.

---

[1] Compassion (*OED* OL).
[2] Flash of lightning (*OED* OL).

Now I ought to make it clear that this friar minor was the friend of all England, a man out of the ordinary, never hot, never cold, never precipitate, never tardy, always strong, cool, gentle, irresistible, ready, always loving all and loved by all from the king in his castle to the leper in the lazar-house. And (says Earl Fulk) at that moment he faced an incensed king and an infuriate nation with perfect serenity. "That dare I, brother king," says the grey friar: "and, first, I will dare to inquire why You are agonizing to devise dooms of daedalian[1] and diuturnal[2] dolour, for these nine-hundred-and-ninety-and-four Your Giwen, when as yet You know not, even now, which of them actually enriched us with this glorious young saint and martyr." "Stand not between the Panther of England and his lawful prey, brother friar:" hissed my lord the king, with a sob like the fearsome whistling of an arrow sped from a long-bow. "Nay, brother king," says the grey friar, "but I will stand, not between a panther and his prey, for I see no such vermin here, but only between a christian king and nearly a thousand other sinners, all shrewdly in need of mercy." "Mercy for these?" roars the king, with mantling ire. "Yes: mercy for these, that You may find mercy at Your need:" says the friar minor.

XXXIII. About the Confession of the Giwen

The regal adamantine eyes relentlessly glared, from the summit of the shadowed throne, down, into the strong gentle fearless eyes of Brother Adam. In the silence which insued, the mob of Giwen (clotted in black swathes on the floor of the hall) drew a little together; and there was some small hasty muttering among them. Then, eighteen of them stood up in a group, and five-and-thirty of them stood up in another group; and "Hear us, lord king:" they cried out, most excruciatingly. "Choose you one of you to speak to brother king, and he will surely hear you:" instantly says Brother Adam. For King Arthur was far beyond power of answering. So, the Giwen chose that Judas Levesq of Lincoln, a bishop of their depravity: who said, "Lord King, we

---

[1] Ingenious, like the labyrinth of Dædalus (*OED* OL).
[2] Lasting (*OED* OL).

eighteen and we five-and-thirty of Your Giwen do now confess
that the death of this christian child is due to us. For, moved by
our tradition and custom, we eighteen and we five-and-thirty,
fifty-three of us in all, we, and we alone, devised the deed, and
chose the victim, and took him by allurement, and did dire deeds
on him. But his blood is not on the hands of the five-and-thirty:
for only we eighteen tormented and slew him. And we believe
that we afflicted him with no pains: for, at the moment when
we stripped him, he was fearful, but, from that moment, he sang
aloud and incessantly four times in each hour and oftener, nor
did any incisions or piercings make surcease his radiant happy-
smiling serenity." The strong white teeth of King Arthur gnashed
together, gritting most hideously: bared, they remained bare, and
menacing, like the teeth of a death's head disposed malignantly.

"Who, then, brother Giwe, are these thirty-five?" says the grey
friar. "Rabbi," says Judas Levesq (for the Giwen denominate their
own clergymen Rabbi), "we may not deny that these five-and-thirty
of our faith came to assist at the sacrifice, many of them from the
other Giweries of England, for we freely confess that Little Jacob
has testified truly: but we eighteen alone were the sacrificers."
"Swear all this by the Book and the Roll of your law:" says the
friar minor. Instantly, all the King's Giwen leaped up and shouted,
"By the Book of our Law, and by the Roll of our Law, we swear it."
Again, says the grey friar, "Tell me now, brother Giwe, are you not
all of you affrighted with any amazement, because of what you
have done?" "Rabbi," says the Giwe, "that, indeed, we are." And,
all incontinent, he, and very many others of the King's Giwen, fell
to quiet hopeless weeping, most bitter, almost piteous. Earl Fulk
the Flame told me that there were several fine robust lads of the
Giwish depravity, in that immense black clot on the floor, who
were quite beside themselves with sheer terror, aching with nerve-
rigour beyond all ordinary, stiff, staring, as though impaled upright
on two spears transfixing their armpits. Brother Adam looked up
to the lofty canopy where was inthroned incarnate inclemency.

XXXIIII. About the Argument for the Defence

"See, now, brother king," says the friar minor, "how that here

You have not nine-hundred-and-ninety-four ferocious impenitent wolves, bloody to the hackles, whom You ought to exterminate, but just eighteen confessed murderers and five-and-thirty confessed accomplices before the fact and nine-hundred-and-forty-and-one consenters to the same, all penitent (as I believe) and all suing for mercy, upon whom You shall do justice." King Arthur spoke: he was so suffocated with unassuagable wrath that it was hard to hear him: "Enough, Brother Adam: make an end; and let justice be done:" says the Regal Majesty. "Is extermination justice, brother king?" says the grey friar: "Is it?"

xxxv. *About the Argument for the Defence continued*

None answered Brother Adam; and he went serenely on. "Brother king," says he, "Come, let us reason together as to what justice is, in this matter of Your Giwen. And, first, I will lovingly advise You, or rather not I, but the apostle of God through me, that You ought not to believe in every impulse. We hear, and we rejoice, that the zeal of God burns in You: but it should not altogether fail to be tempered with knowledge. What knowledge? Brother king, this knowledge. And it is vital. Hear me, then. For I say that You ought not to persecute Your Giwen, nor to slay them, nor even to put them under Your ban."

Frightful roars from all the bishops and magnates and knights and commons interrupted him. Earl Fulk says that the thirty-two magnates of my V Ports shook the poles of the canopy, and even the six justiciars beat their tables, while one of the scribes threw his pounce-box[1] at the audacious friar. "If brother king will silence me, silent I will be:" says Brother Adam, quite clearly. And the tumult stayed, at least as to the imprecations and the howling: but everyone was on his feet, shaking something or other, and capering angrily. As for my lord and brother the king, that Regal Majesty was as a longbow, a longbow strung, the notch of the shaft well-fitted to the cord, gripped between ruthless unreasoning fingers, and drawn behind the ear. The friar continued. "I say that brother king must not persecute, or slay, or even banish His

---

[1] A box containing the powder spread on paper or parchment before writing to prevent the spreading of ink.

Giwen," says he. "Consult the Divine Pages," says he. " 'The Lord will shew unto me about mine enemies: slay them not: never will my people be forgotten:' are the words of the Psalmist.[1] 'At last, when all the heathen shall have entered, then all Israel shall be saved:' are the words of the Apostle.[2] And, I ask, if the King's Giwen be altogether ground to powder, how, at that last day, shall their promised conversion and salvation prosper?"

"Ha:" says my lord the king, choking.

XXXVI. *About the Interrogation of the Defender*

My son the Primate Boniface interpolated a word. "Tell me, then, Brother Adam," says he, "what justice our dear dread lord the king may do. It is true that these Giwen have given us a distinct and glorious martyr. So much the better for us. So much the worse for them. For, in enriching us, they have done most heinous murder. And, if our lord the king may not punish these parricides as they deserve (for again another scripture says 'Whoso sheddeth man's blood, by man shall his blood be shed[3]) how, then, are the King's Giwen to be prevented from adding yet other atrocities to the already overwhelming brother of their crimes?" And the dear friar minor, not a whit abashed, answered the primate, saying: "No one denies that the King's Giwen deserve to die for their sins, as do all christians also, if we are to believe apostles and evangelists and other possessors of the Vision Beatific. But, you tell me this, brother primate: when brother king has slowly and ingeniously and meticulously slaughtered these nine-hundred-and-ninety-four His Giwen, will He then have frightened the others so that they will refrain from offering us any more martyrs, or, will He have merely cured these same nine-hundred-and-ninety-four of a very evil and reprehensible habit? Will brother king have embellished His kingdom with nine-hundred-and-ninety-four putrefying scarecrows? Or will He have made of his Giwen a people prepared for the Lord. Tell me, please, brother primate?"

---

[1] cf. *Ps.* lviii. 12, A.v. [Rolfe's note.]
[2] cf. *Rom.* xi. 26, A.v. [Rolfe's note.]
[3] Gen. 9:6.

xxxvii. *About the Argument*

Boniface told me that he then betook himself to learning lessons. From the very first, that boy of mine was always eager to learn from anyone who plainly knew more than he knew. "What then?" says he.

"Here," says Brother Adam of Marish, "is a company of the King's Giwen. They, face to face with fearful death, freely confess that they most cruelly have crucified and slain a little innocent boy. We all have heard that sweet child's marvellous piercing-sweet singing, and the simple holy words which he, dead, spoke to brother king. But I, for one, did not hear him demanding vengeance of carnage and hecatombs."[1] "He did not:" says the Primate Boniface. "Also," the friar minor continued, "we all know of certain other of the King's Giwen, who, more than fifty years ago, crucified another innocent christian boy in the full bloom of his boyhood. And we know that this one, being by God's Goodness saved from death, and doubly anointed and invested with the plenitude of regal majesty, has, for more than fifty years, sought no vengeance, but has ruled His Giwen, as their king, with a merciful justice as fine and as free and as noble and as generous and as magnificent as God's Very Own."

xxxviii. *About the Great Conclusion of the Argument for the Defence*

All England, in the great hall of Westminster, buzzed and hummed like a hive in summer-time. The lambent flames in the grand eyes of King Arthur suddenly went out, as though extinguished by a gust of the winds of heaven. But the awful rigour of his fury kept him stone still. The grey friar turned away from my son Boniface the Primate; and addressed himself directly to my lord and brother the king. "Brother king," says he, "once upon a time, other of the King's Giwen also crucified and slew another king, The King of Heaven: nor did That King seek vengeance, when He, dying, said, 'Father, forgive them, for they know not what they do.'"

---

[1] A tremendous sacrifice of many victims (*OED* OL).

XXXVIIII. *About the Silence called for the Judgement*

The friar minor said not another word. He came down, from the steps of the throne whereon he had made his oration; and he put himself to walk about, among the miserable Giwen, stooping to them, as though to comfort them. "Oh, what more?" says my son, the Primate Boniface, with a great lump in his throat, as he told me, but feeling (for our dear lord the king's sake) that the word lay with him. The grey friar looked up; and said serenely, "Hush, brother primate: for brother king is about to do justice."

XL. *About the King his Justice and the Just Man made Perfect*

This is what Earl Fulk the Flame says. He says that King Arthur stood up, towering high above all men on earth, robed and crowned and sceptred and orbed in regal majesty, with his mantle of ermine and tissue of silver flowing over and down and round the great silver panthers of his throne, with all the caps and coronets and crowns and sceptres and orbs of his vast dominion by him, with the canopy of empire overshadowing him; and, on the summit of his greatness, he stood, still, stiller than whatever is stillest, stiller than Death: white, whiter than whatever is whitest, whiter than Dawn: strong, stronger than whatever is strongest, stronger than Hate: perfect, more perfect than whatever is most perfect, more perfect even than Love: conquering himself, himself the conqueror.

There was silence. My lady Queen Mariol sat on her own throne, covering her eyes. Near her, kneeled Lord Edward Plantagenet of England, rapt in love and worship of the king.

Then, King Arthur took firm hold of his regal voice, a firmer hold than he had ever held before. He said: "Let all Our Giwen wear a yellow cross of a cubit's length and breadth, on the breast and on the back of their cloaks and of their gaberdines, at all times, and in all places, now, and evermore that they may be known of men. The King wills it."[1]

---

[1] The Pope declared that Jews were to wear a distinguishing mark in 1215. This decree was renewed by Henry III in 1253. The Jews were expelled from England by Edward I in 1290.

The voice of the grey friar came up from below, in a luminous undertone, " 'They know not what they do.'"

The voice of the white king came down from the lofty altitude of England's throne, "'Father, forgive them.' God, forgive Me, as I forgive."

The orb and the sceptre fell crashing to the ground. King Arthur staggered, but stood, spreading his Majestic arms like the Crucified. "Go in peace: and sin no more:" he said to his Giwen, with his last breath on earth.

Faith, he had. Hope, he always had. And, having won Charity (the greatest of the three) in mortal and most furious conflict with himself, King Arthur Lefthand took the kingdom of Hierusalem, by violence. And, so, he ascended to the superiors.

O my lord, my king. O God, restore me to my place near him, now, very soon.

EXPLICITUR

ARTHURI REGIS

HISTORIA[1]

---

[1] Ends the story of King Arthur.